CW01642549

Doomdark's Revenge

Doomdark's Revenge

Drew Wagar

Book two of the Midnight Chronicles

based upon the original Doomdark's Revenge strategy game by Mike Singleton and the remakes by Chris Wild.

First Published 2021 by Fantastic Books Publishing

Cover design by Jurij Rogelj

ISBN (eBook): 978-1-914060-20-5

ISBN (paperback): 978-1-914060-19-9

Imiriel
Fororn
The Frozen Empire
Imgaril
Kahangrorn
Lorelorn
Kingdom of the Giants
Varangrim
Zarashand
Thudrane
Obigrorn
Mormarg
Glormarg
Lorigriel
Kahudrun
Arvulane
Arvormane
Carangrane
Ulformane
Theleon
Fangrorn
Ingenarg
Imgorarg
Anvildrak
Carorthay
Ganigrorn
Carormarg
Glormane
Kingdom of the Dwarves
Thortheon
Outlands of the Barbarians
Thormand
Fansrim
Sirium
Imgorad
Imorthorn
Morildrane
Kingdom of the Fey
Zarorthane
Carorthane
Careneon
Lorangriel
Varenorn
Torinarg
ICEMARK

Thanks To:

Once again, my immediate family deserves huge praise; my lovely wife Anita, my sons Mark and Joshua. Over the last two years of putting this book together much has changed for us, but allowing me to write has been kept as a family priority. If they weren't as supportive as they are, my stories would not exist. Anita has also been a huge help in proofreading and making many helpful suggestions – I even know what a "fronted adverbial" is now!

To Chris Wild, the lore-master of all of these magical realms. Chris has been working with me on this book throughout and, though we've had less face to face meetings than we would like due to Covid-19, we have been able to stay in touch via video conferencing, I suppose that can be considered a type of magic! We've continued to work hard on the overall lore, attempting at all times to keep true to the vision of Mike Singleton. Chris always has the final say on such matters of course. He was also able to provide me with an especially modified version of the game so I could navigate around without peril, a privilege the characters in the story do not enjoy!

To Richard Harris, for getting in contact with me only to reveal that he was the original winner of Doomdark's Revenge! He provided me with photos of his winner's award; miniatures of the Doomdark's Revenge characters arranged in a diorama.

To Stewart Beatt for forwarding me a copy of the letter he received from Beyond software after he entered the Lords of Midnight competition.

To Prentice McHoan for the name of Tarithel's horse. Álainn is the Irish for 'beauty' and the horse is black. A little nod to you know who.

To Dan Grubb, my publisher, for producing the finished work once more. There's magic in taking a word document and turning it into a novel you know.

To Mae, my editor, for more magic. She has the ability to cast a dramatic 'improvement' spell over my prose, making it sharper and stronger throughout.

All the folks on the Multi-User Midnight forum who enjoyed the first book and encouraged me onwards into the Icemark for the second. I hope and trust I will do you proud again.

To all the fans of Doomdark's Revenge from all those years ago. I've met many more fans over the last few years since the publication of the first book and all have that certain knowing gleam in their eyes when we talk about Mike Singleton's creations. There's a sense of shared knowledge and adventure … a certain camaraderie that emerges when the stories of great battles of long ago are told.

Of course, to Mike Singleton. Doomdark's Revenge was bigger in all ways than the Lords of Midnight, something I've had to wrestle with during the writing. That he was able to cram so much into 48k of ZX Spectrum memory is still a magical thing to me.

We can't mention that wonderful Sinclair computer without acknowledging the man who created it. Sadly taken from us this year, my final thanks goes to Sir Clive Sinclair, creator of the seminal ZX Spectrum computer upon which these games were built, in my opinion the greatest 8-bit computer ever made. Eccentric and eclectic, Clive was one of the most memorable and visionary of English entrepreneurs and inventors, making a huge impact on the computing industry and responsible for many careers in IT, my own included. Thank you, sir.

Author's Note

Many moons have passed since I wrote the Lords of Midnight. Many of you rode alongside me, taking up the challenge of defeating the cruel Witchking of Ushgarak. You'll need no reminding of that epic struggle. As a novel, The Lords of Midnight had many false starts long before I was involved, and it took me a further two years to pull it all together. The story of Doomdark's defeat has now been told decades after the game that inspired it was created.

I was very wary of what the fan response to the book was going to be. It was something of a departure for me, I'm more acquainted with writing the SF genre than the fantasy one and the transition was tricky in places. I hadn't written a pure fantasy novel before, and yet here I was, writing something that was not only based on a game that so many people held very close to their hearts, but also had to work in a standalone fashion and not be dismissed as some 'half-hearted' Tolkien knock off. On the positive side I did know the game very well, I felt confident that I could genuinely tell this story and I had the greatest of sage counsellors alongside me managing the lore and background – Lords of Midnight would not have been possible without Chris Wild's vast and knowledgeable input.

Yet the response has been overwhelmingly positive. I hoped to capture the essence of the game, the feel of it, the essential "Mike Singletoness" of the experience of playing. From the reviews I've received it seems that I did manage that. I am proud that I've been able to provide so many of you with a story that satisfied the youngster in you that so fondly remembered this game and, at the same time, the adult that required a healthy shot of nostalgia and a tale worthy of a grown up perspective in the 21st century.

We always intended to continue of course. We hoped Lords of Midnight would be a success and deliberately left the ending at the finish point of the first game and the introduction to the second. Doomdark's Revenge (which, curiously, has almost nothing to do with Doomdark at all!) continues the tale without a pause and will segue straight on from the events you're already acquainted with.

With Lords of Midnight we had to make certain choices. Should we concentrate on Morkin's quest for the Ice Crown, Luxor's military conquest of Doomdark, or both? We decided that the latter was correct, for both played a big role in the original game and a complete victory felt that it needed the two components. We also introduced characters into the Lords of Midnight novel, such as Tarithel and Shareth, who weren't present in the original game, because they need to be there for this sequel. However Lords of Midnight had the advantage that the story was pretty straightforward. Luxor vs Doomdark; Morkin and his quest to destroy the Ice Crown.

When we came to look hard at Doomdark's Revenge, the first question that Chris and I asked ourselves was … what is the story? A look in the manual for the original game shows that there are many different ways to win and different levels of victory. What should be the definitive telling of these adventures? Should Luxor simply seek to rescue Morkin and return home? Should he attempt to defeat Shareth by military means? What part is there to play for Tarithel and for Rorthron in all this? What of all the other races of the Icemark?

In Lords of Midnight the antagonists were the, rather faceless, Doomguard. The forces of the Free and Fey are the protagonists, a fairly black and white affair with not too much complexity. In Doomdark's Revenge we have a different situation, with five unique races all vying for their own aims and objectives. This often led to quite a confusing gaming experience. Sometimes you'd make the most unusual of allies in your travels, sometimes Shareth would die upon some unknown warrior's sword without you even meeting her!

A few things are set in the canon. Tarithel has a special role in the rescue of Morkin that no other can replace. Mike Singleton's novels set out Shareth's ambitions and her plans. There is lore beyond the tales of Doomdark's Revenge that we have to honour. Such things are sacrosanct and cannot be changed, but the detail of the Fey, the Barbarians, the Giants, the Dwarves and the Iceguard in the original material is sparse and needed expanding. So expand we have.

There are also the additional details of the game itself. Doomdark's Revenge is bigger than Lords of Midnight in all respects. The map is larger. There are 128 characters in the canon, an unfeasibly large number for a single novel to manage. Due to the computerised generation of most of the names, each made up of three syllables woven together from a predetermined list, some of them end up sounding very similar, another difficulty for us to cope with. We've had to make hard choices here, and some will be disappointed that their favourite character doesn't have a major role. The game also added other features, underground tunnels, mists and magic Talismans to name a few, these have to be woven into the story in a sensible and sensitive way, so that they feel right, but don't look contrived. Such is the art of paying homage and writing something new.

Sadly, Mike Singleton was taken from us in 2012 and never knew of the existence of this novel or the previous one. Many fans have let me know that they considered my previous book to be a worthy memorial to the man who gave us such a rich world and remarkable game-play all those years ago. I hope that Doomdark's Revenge will be as well received. It's been more of a challenge to write for the reasons outlined above and not least the massive inconvenience of the Covid-19 pandemic. With the fabulous assistance of Chris Wild holding court over the lore of the series I have tried to embody this story with all the essential essence of the game. We have spent long hours agonising over motivations, characters, background lore and aspects of the game which are hard to represent in a story, always going back to what 'feels' correct, with Chris always having the final say as the loremaster of the realms of Midnight and Icemark. This has taken us quite some time to get right and I hope our efforts have been worth it.

The end of night is close at hand. I hope that you are not at all despondent and not at all tired, because today we ride forth into the Icemark.

Dawn breaks.

Drew Wagar (October 2021)

Dramatis Personae

Of the Free of Midnight

- **Luxor** – Moonprince of Midnight and slayer of the Witchking of Midnight. Luxor is the leader of the Free folk of Midnight and led them to a military victory over the Witchking's forces.
- **Morkin** – Young son of Luxor and betrothed of Tarithel. Morkin destroyed the Ice Crown, the source of the Witchking's devastating weapon, the Ice Fear.

Of the Fey of Midnight

- **Tarithel** – Newly appointed Lady of the Forest, young daughter of Araleth, the Lord of Dreams and betrothed of Morkin.
- **Corleth** – Friend of Luxor who helped rally the Fey in the battles of Midnight.
- **Araleth, the Lord of Dreams** – Father of Tarithel and leader of the Fey of Midnight who stood beside Luxor and the Free at the battle of Ushgarak where the Witchking was slain.

Of the Wise of Midnight

- **Rorthron** – The only member of the Wise who is determined to aid Luxor in his quests. Rorthron is young as the Wise reckon things, but has seen many centuries pass.
- **Lorgrim** – One time tutor of the Witchking, Lorgrim knows many dark secrets. Lorgrim is one of the eldest of the Wise of Midnight having lived longer than any of its other inhabitants.

Of the Fey of Icemark

- **Imorthorn** – Leader of the Fey of Icemark and head of the Council of the Fey. Imorthorn's city lies in the heart of the great Forest of Fangrim.
- **Carorthane** – Member of the Council of the Fey. His city lies to the far west of Fangrim. Brother to Carorthand.
- **Carorthand** – Member of the council of the Fey. His fortress lies in the centre of Fangrim. Brother to Carorthane.
- **Imgorthand** – Member of the council of the Fey. His city lies in the far east of Fangrim.
- **Morildrane** – Vassal of Imgorthand. His fortress lies in the south of Fangrim.
- **Thormand** – Vassal of Imorthorn and ward of the northern reaches of the Forest of Fangrim.

Of the Barbarians

- **Imgorad** – Leader of the Barbarians of Icemark. His city lies in the far west of the Barbarian's realm.
- **Careneon** – Barbarian chieftain, given to guarding the Barbarians' territory in the far south.
- **Torinarg** – Vassal of Careneon, given to guarding the Gate of Varenorn.
- **Kahudrarg** – A noted chieftain amongst the Barbarians. His fortress lies in the heart of the Barbarian's domain. Brother of Kahudrak.
- **Kahudrak** – A noted chieftain amongst the Barbarians. His fortress lies on the border with the Fey. Brother of Kahudrarg.
- **Thortheon** – Barbarian chieftain, his fortress guards a strategic point on the border with both the Giants and the Dwarves.

Of the Dwarves

- **Glormane** – Leader of the Dwarves of Icemark. Glormane's city is the capital of the Dwarven realm, in the centre of their territory.
- **Imgorarg** – Chief Dwarf of the northern regions and rival to Glormane.
- **Imulorn** – Young Dwarf Lord of the southern territories, typically given to great consideration. Brother of Imelorn and vassal of Thigrak.
- **Imelorn** – Young Dwarf Lord of the south-eastern territories, fond of his axe. Brother of Imulorn and vassal of Thigrak.
- **Carorthay** – Wise and elderly Dwarf of the eastern regions.
- **Hagudril** – Vassal of Carorthay, with territories in the east of the dwarven realm.

Of the Giants

- **Carangrane** – Leader of the Giants of Icemark. His city lies behind the Mountains of Anvormane in the heart of their territory.
- **Varangrim** – Vassal of Carangrane, and appointed heir of Carangrane's leadership.
- **Anvildrak** – Giant of the Icemark. His city guards the southern passage into the Giants' realm.
- **Fenorn** – Giant of the Icemark. Vassal of Obigrorn.
- **Obigrorn** – Giant of the Icemark. His fortress guards the northern passage into the Giants' realm.
- **Ulformane** – Giant of the Icemark. His city guards the eastern flank of the Giants' realm.
- **Imgenarg** – Giant of the Icemark. His city guards the heartlands of the Giants' realm.
- **Ganigrorn** – Giant of the Icemark. His fortress guards the southern flank of the Giants' domain.

Of the Frozen Empire and the Icelords

- **Shareth the Heartstealer** – Daughter of the Witchking of Midnight, her father was slain by Luxor. Shareth calls herself the Empress of the Frozen Empire. She rules her Icelords from the Fortress of Kahangrorn.
- **Imgaril** – One of the six warlords of the Frozen Empire, vassal of Shareth. His city lies in the far east of the Frozen Empire.
- **Zarashand** – One of the six warlords of the Frozen Empire, vassal of Shareth. His city lies in the heartlands of the Frozen Empire.
- **Glormarg** – One of the six warlords of the Frozen Empire, vassal of Shareth. His city lies in the southern end of the Frozen Empire.
- **Fangrorn** – One of the six warlords of the Frozen Empire, vassal of Shareth. His city lies in the far south-east of the Frozen Empire.
- **Lorelorn** – One of the six warlords of the Frozen Empire, vassal of Shareth. His city guards the dark and mysterious Forest of Farorn.
- **Anvireon** – One of the six warlords of the Frozen Empire, guarding the prized and ancient City of Imiriel in the remote north of the Frozen Empire.
- **Talorthane** – Icelord holding territories in the east of the Frozen Empire, vassal of Lorelorn.
- **Imgasharg** – Icelord holding territories in the west of the Frozen Empire, vassal of Fangrorn.

Prologue

Shareth the Heartstealer stands at the Fortress of Kahangrorn, looking south in the mist.

Kahangrorn rang to her cries. The fortress echoed to her screams, an unearthly howling interspersed with an animal-like screech of fury. The very rocks that formed the foundations rang and shook with her passing. Stone burst asunder, cracked and fragmented, as her elegant fingers slashed and ripped at the walls surrounding her. Darkness swirled about her like an ephemeral cloak, lit from within by an evil cyan glow.

Before her a guard stood, rooted to the spot in fear and awe. As he watched she spun around, her tormented gaze falling upon him.

'Such tidings! How dare he? How dare he usurp me!'

Before he could think to move aside, the guard found her fingers at his throat. He was hoist bodily into the air, struggling to free himself.

Yet, to be the bearer of ill tidings before the Heartstealer …

Her fingers, now claw like and possessed of some fell strength beyond the limits of humanity, crushed his neck. Her other hand swept across his torso. Blood splattered as she ripped his body to shreds with her bare hands, luxuriating in the strangled screams that, all too briefly, echoed around the chamber.

Moments later, careless of the blood and gore, she threw his body aside, her bloodstained dark robes somehow cleansing themselves as she strode forward, her eyes glittering with hatred and thoughts of revenge.

'I will bathe in his blood! I will feast on his very flesh! How … dare he!'

The words were a scream of fury and rage.

The heavy oak doors of the hall flew back with an echoing clang as she gestured to them, crashing back on their hinges and ringing with the impact. Her form moved through the darkened fortress faster than any could see, a darkness almost without shape, until she came to a halt on the battlements.

There, on the southern walls of the Fortress of Kahangrorn, Shareth screamed out her hatred and frustration, summoning to her all the shattered remnants of the power her father had commanded. Cloud and wind shrieked about her as she gathered her inheritance.

Below, vast armies stood awaiting her commands, standing motionless in the lashing rain and sleet. There would be time enough for their application in the days and moons to come. For now a greater wrath consumed her.

She trembled with apoplexy.

Luxor has slain my father, freed the lands of Midnight from his grasp. My father's death was to be mine and mine alone!

She caught her breath, staring down at the forces gathered below her.

Shareth had long watched the arts of her father, the Witchking of Midnight, from afar. She was the offspring of his brief union with a cold queen of the Icemark. Shareth possessed the body and mind of a beautiful temptress, but was imbued with a heart and soul of ice, colder, if possible, than her own father's frozen and emaciated corpse.

He had loved her too, but Shareth herself had no time for such frailties.

There was no grief, no remorse at the Witchking's passing. Her heart channelled only darker emotions and lusts.

Luxor has stolen my right to subdue Midnight, taking it from my father as I had long planned. Very well, moon-princeling! Steal from me and you earn all my wrath ...

She had heard the Witchking's dying words, if death was the right word for his end. A cry, cold and penetrating, that shocked northwards through the Frozen Wastes, across the Kingdom of the Giants and onwards to the Frozen Empire in which her fortress lay.

AVENGE ME, SHARETH, AVENGE ME!

The words had echoed around Shareth, but she had not answered him. He died alone, her indifference cold and calculated. She laughed, knowing that in his final moments he must have realised the contempt she held him in.

My wrath will be my own ... dear father ... but it will be no less terrible!

The battlements of Kahangrorn darkened further as the storm clouds gathered, summoned from the ice-barriers of the north by Shareth's incantations. Dark clouds swirled above, torn asunder by sharp crackles of cyan-hued lightning and the echoing booms of thunder as she raised her arms to focus her powers on the subject of her thoughts.

She cried into the wind, uttering words of power none could understand. The storm leapt and swirled as her strident voice pierced the air, far louder and potent than any call a mortal throat could utter. Across the Frozen Empire, from Fangrorn to Imiriel, the tortured sky erupted into boiling turmoil. Ferocious storms, twisting billows of cloud and angry squalls focussed their fury at her beck and call.

It took but a single gesture. Shareth had learnt her father's fell arts well.

She stretched out her arm and pointed south.

A violent wind arose and the clouds moved, swifter and mightier than any army of Free, Fey, Dwarf, Barbarian or Giant. The storm flung itself across the sky, rolling and boiling, lashing down with snow, sleet and rain, pounding all before it in a howling gale.

Trees fell, boulders were strewn and even the ancient mountainsides cracked before the fury as the maelstrom moved away, leaving only storm damaged wreckage in its wake.

Night fell upon the Icemark far to the north-east of the realm of Midnight. Within the great city of Varangrim, the Giants of that realm gathered and watched as the storm broke across them. Likewise from Carudrium to Carorthay, the Dwarves redoubled the watch upon their lands, fearing trouble from Shareth's own loyal Iceguard.

To the south of the Frozen Empire, the great forests of the Fey bent under the onslaught. In the city of Imorthorn, deep within the Forest of Fangrim, the Fey of Icemark met in council to discuss the import of the great tumult in the sky. Some claimed the Dwarves had betrayed them to the Heartstealer, others counselled patience and observation, reasoning that even if that were so, it would be better to fight the Iceguard in the midst of their forests rather than march forth upon the open plains.

Lord Imorthorn though brought the council to order. Three Lords they were grave and stern; Carorthane, Carorthand and Imgorthand.

'You will have heard by now, surely my Lords,' Imorthorn said, looking at his fellow council members, 'rumours of the war that has been raging in the lost land of Midnight, far to the south-west of Icemark. If it be true, a revealed Moonprince of that realm has won victory over the Heartstealer's very own father, the Witchking. His name? They call him Luxor.'

The Lords of the Fey of Fangrim hung on his words, waiting for further revelations, muttering together in consternation.

Imorthorn continued. 'Rumours of secret traffic between the Heartstealer and the Witchking have often come to our ears. She supplied armies to him on many occasions, defying both us and the Barbarians of the west. On the eve of the Solstice mere moons ago, did we not waylay a band of dark and foul warriors riding north from the Gate of Varenorn? I know it is many, many moons since any of our number have dared its terrors, but that is the only passage we know of that still leads to Midnight, doubtless Shareth and the Witchking knew of it too.'

Muted mumbles of agreement greeted this statement.

'I am sure,' Imorthorn said, raising his voice. 'The Heartstealer sends the storm not against us, but against this Luxor, this legendary Moonprince of Midnight. Even now, the storm turns south-west!'

The assembled council could attest to his words. The dark, flying clouds were indeed headed in that direction. They argued back and forth about what to do about the matter. At length, they agreed that their brothers in the land of Midnight, the Fey of the Forest of Dreams and other realms long sundered from them, must be warned of the peril of the Heartstealer.

'We Fey cannot cross the Frozen Wastes,' Imorthorn said. 'Nor can we take the ancient road through the Gate of Varenorn; it now lies in the territories of the Barbarians. Thus I will send one of our most prized white falcons with a missive. They are the swiftest of any kind of messenger, and the only creature that could brave the wastes with a chance of survival.'

The assembled Fey nodded, knowing that they too should make ready for war, for there was no doubt that Shareth's plans would threaten their own safety too. If she desired to take revenge upon the Moonprince and attack Midnight, her passage across the Icemark would not be peaceable.

Far to the south, in the realm of Midnight, Luxor's high council, summoned to decide the fate of the Witchking's old dominions, put aside its purpose and fell to reminiscing. The mead flowed, brave deeds grew braver, terrors waxed more terrible and the day drew on. Morkin, son of Luxor himself, exhausted though he was, had taken a bath and returned, clean and dressed the part, but those about could tell he only had eyes for Tarithel.

They had met amidst the wreckage of war. Morkin had been exhausted following the destruction of the Ice Crown, thinking that his part in frustrating the will of the Witchking had come too late and none of the Free or Fey had survived the relentless onslaught of the Doomguard. Tarithel had found him as he stumbled his weary way into the Forest of Dreams, tending him and easing his tortured mind. Somehow, whether by magic or some other force, they had seen visions of each other in their struggles to free Midnight and rouse their people. Whatever the reason, their love had blossomed once they found themselves in each other's presence.

Hours passed. Luxor held court with his friends and Lords. Here at the Citadel of Dreams he celebrated with his son, Morkin, with Tarithel beside him. Corleth the Fey stood nearby, a friendship recently renewed. Tarithel's father, Araleth the Lords of Dreams, provided the feast, with the Lords of the Free enjoying themselves with gusto.

Twilight fell upon the grounds. The lights of candles illuminated the grand arches of the pavilion. As the company was thinking of retiring there came a fluttering of wings.

A white falcon flew in through the open doorway of the pavilion, circled three times above the high table, then came to rest on the shoulder of the Lord of Dreams. As the company stared in amazement at the bird, Tarithel reached a gentle hand towards it and nimbly untied its jesses. The bird seemed exhausted from its long flight, yet, at a soft word from her, it took flight again and disappeared beyond.

'It is a message …' she exclaimed, unwrapping a leather thong and presenting it to her father.

He took it, puzzling over the seal for a moment, then broke it apart to unravel the parchment with grim care before turning to Luxor. His expression was a mixture of astonishment and concern.

'My Lord Moonprince,' he began. 'This message hails from lands beyond our ken, from the distant lands of the Icemark, far to the north-east beyond the Frozen Wastes.'

'From beyond the Frozen Wastes?' Morkin asked. 'How is it possible? Nothing can cross the wastes … can it?'

'Falcons are swift,' Dreams said. 'We Fey oft use them to carry messages. I have not heard of them crossing the wastes but …'

'And those lands have been sundered from Midnight for a thousand moons and more,' Luxor replied. 'A jest, surely …'

'It is written by a Lord who calls himself Imorthorn,' Dreams continued. 'Addressing himself to his brothers Fey of the Forest of Dreams. It warns of a great storm flying from the north towards Midnight and of the evil designs of one he calls the Empress of the Frozen Empire. He hints that she may have made some pact with the Witchking before his demise.'

Luxor frowned. 'An Empress? I've heard tales and rumours, but … know you of this … Imorthorn, did you say his name was?'

'I know him not,' Dreams replied. 'Yet one thing is certain – it was indeed written by the hand of a Fey. The ancient runes are known to few of us and by no others.'

Corleth nodded, taking a look at the parchment. 'This could not be faked by one not of the Fey, that is for sure.'

The Moonprince shook his head, as if lost for anything to say. A heavy burden seemed to have fallen on his shoulders. He looked around at the faces about him. Once again, all waited, hanging on his next utterance.

'If this message bears the truth,' Luxor said. 'Then it seems our long struggle is not over yet, but surely this Imorthorn cannot be right. As you say, the Frozen Wastes lie between us and the lost land of Icemark. Why else was a falcon sent to bear the ill-tidings to us? I cannot see how any Empress of the North, however evil her intent, can threaten the peace that now befalls Midnight …

'The ice melts all around us,' Tarithel said. 'Perhaps the wastes are no longer the impassable barrier they once were?'

Corleth rubbed his chin. 'Those to the north do not fail; some fell magic sustains them still. Where they remain, none can cross the Frozen Wastes.'

Luxor nodded. 'As for warning of a storm, should we sharpen our swords, wax our bow strings and prepare to do battle against the wind and snow? This message makes no sense. What does this Imorthorn ask of us?'

'We can at least tighten the guy-ropes of our tents and wear thicker cloaks,' shouted the Lord of Ithrorn, already somewhat the worse for wear from the mead. 'Perhaps this Lord Imorthorn is a dealer in furs and cannot find a market for his wares!'

The company of assembled Lords of the Free broke into laughter at this. More ribald suggestions followed and the portent of the strange message was forgotten in the general merriment. Yet Luxor remained troubled. He drew Corleth and the Lord of Dreams aside and spoke to them. Only Morkin and Tarithel could see the concern etched on their faces.

'My friends,' Luxor said. 'See what more you can discover of this matter. Though I cannot see how, I fear this message is more timely than we imagine.'

'The Fey do not use such messages unless in dire need of

secrecy,' Corleth replied. 'This Imorthorn must have serious concerns.'

'What know you of this Empress?' Dreams asked.

Luxor rubbed his chin. 'Little enough. I have heard dark stories of a powerful witch beyond the Frozen Wastes, but always dismissed them as childish fantasies, we had enough woe to deal with in facing the Witchking! Perhaps there is more truth in them than I suspected.'

'And why should she turn her wrath upon us here?' Corleth replied. 'A pact with the Witchking?'

'Might she be in league with him?' Dreams asked.

'Read the message once again,' Luxor said. 'Leave out no detail.'

Dreams did as he was bid, but there was little new to be discerned. 'He calls her the Empress of the Icemark … but there is also another name here … Heartstealer.'

A gasp from beside them turned both heads towards the source of the sound.

Tarithel's face was white. 'What did you say?'

'It is written here,' Dreams said. 'Heartstealer …'

Tarithel grabbed the parchment and scanned it carefully, her mouth dropping open in horror.

'What know you of this?' Morkin asked, clasping her hand.

Tarithel's gaze grew distant.

'In the forest,' she whispered. 'Before the Doomguard attacked our city. The Lith spoke to me … showed me a distant land far to the north … strange names … Anvulane … Kahangrorn… Heartstealer was one of them!'

She was trembling. Morkin pulled her close, seeking to comfort her.

'It spoke to me of this being only the beginning,' she said, her voice ashen. 'That we must prepare …'

'Prepare for what?' Luxor demanded. 'War once more? Say this cannot be!'

Tarithel's eyes were wide with fear and her cheeks were streaked with tears.

'War and worse. The Heartstealer cometh!'

Shareth had returned to her private sanctuary, a room set high in the central Tower of her fortress, her fury spent for now. Few had seen the inside and none had lived to tell the tale. It was told that men she took a fancy to were invited within, but none had ever emerged after she had her way with them.

There were no ceilings or walls, yet the room had a strange substance to it. Everywhere was mirrored, leaving her abode a shifting collection of images all focussed on her. It was how she saw herself, and how she intended the world to see her.

She lay, lithe and voluptuous, upon the silken sheets of the bed in the very centre of her boudoir. Men would see her as she wished when the mood took her. A young, beautiful woman, yet mature in her desires and lusts, ready and willing to share the delights her body advertised with little concealment.

Her cheeks were flushed; her sculpted face a perfect and irresistible glory. The strongest wills crumpled at the sight of her when she so wished it. No man had ever been able to turn her down. Her curves strained against the satin of her gown.

'I am so beautiful,' she smiled, appraising herself in the mirror above. 'The whole world will love me, or they will perish … perhaps both.'

She laughed at her own conceit, knowing it to be true nonetheless.

Her father had loved only one thing. Shareth followed his example. As he had loved her, she loved herself too. She fell asleep each night marvelling in her own perfection and beauty, waking each morning more irresistible than ever.

She stepped to the window, looking out over the darkened landscape.

Clutching her staff, she strained her thoughts out in the lee of the storm, reaching out with her vision as her father had taught her, seeking knowledge of the adversary that had stolen away her inheritance. Pain smote across her forehead and she winced, such was the cost of power. The staff began to glow, first a dull red, then a burning amber, yet still she held it firm. She cried out from the pain of it. She would not be able to maintain the spell for long.

In her mind's eye, she could see the lofty spires of a great Citadel. Her father had spoken of the cursed Fey often enough for her to know it as the Citadel of Dreams. She looked closer, seeing Fey and Free dancing in the clearings and the courtyards as snow and ice melted from the trees about them. The garish sun was bright and strong, the green of a long delayed spring already sprouting about them.

She spied the hated Moonprince himself, standing shoulder to shoulder with the Lords of Free and Fey, drinking in celebration at her father's demise. Rage took her again and her screams of fury rang out once more.

Smoke was rising from her clenched hand, the smell of burning flesh filling the air about her, still she did not relent.

She spied two others. A young man and a pretty Fey-girl, arm in arm. There was a touch of ice about the young man, something had speared him to the heart, the unmistakable mark of one who had held the Ice Crown itself. Shareth caught her breath, her rage cooling to a lustful desire.

The boy, the one who destroyed the Ice Crown ... that must be him ...

She admired his tall stance, his blonde hair and youthful features. Not a boy, a young man on the cusp of adulthood, possessed of virility, vigour and youth. She saw him embrace the young woman, a red-haired Fey-girl, and then smile at Luxor. The family bond was clear. A grimace grew on her face and she licked her lips.

A name came to her, summoned from the memory of ice.

Morkin ...

The pain was too much. With a cry she let go of the staff, gasping with agony. It clattered to the floor, cooling in moments to a solid ebony. Her vision spell failed. She nursed her injured hand, wincing with the pain, crying out for long moments until she recovered enough strength to dull the pain a little. Such magic was dark and unpleasant, demanding much of those who conjured it. Even with her powers it would be days before she could recover.

But I have seen enough!

Night was falling now, casting a deeper pall over the fortress. She cradled her scarred hand and then grasped the icicles that hung about the window, crushing the ice into her seared flesh. The pain eased further as a thought became a scheme and the scheme became a plan.

So, Luxor has a son? Betrothed to some tawdry Fey maiden? We shall see what mischief temptation will afford!

With a brief tug, her satin gown fell from her, revealing a sheer and naked beauty. Shareth stood upright, the pale light silhouetting her curves. A new spell formed upon her lips, the pain brushed aside by desire.

Come to me Morkin, son of Luxor. I will teach you things no Fey maiden could even dare to dream!

Chapter One

Tarithel the Fey stands at the Citadel of Dreams, looking west to the Forest of Dreams.

Night fell, the stars bright and diamond sharp in the firmament above. The snow, save for where it lay across the mountains, was in full retreat under the warmth of a long anticipated spring. Water flowed, blossom and the scent of wild flowers was in the air around the Citadel of Dreams. The great forests that surrounded it were already playing host to more wildlife than had been seen in countless moons.

The curse of the Witchking was broken.

The Ice Crown was no more.

Within and without the walls of the Citadel, folk were turning in as the hours lengthened. The celebrations had taken their toll on many. There would be more than one servant who would arrive late to do his master's bidding on the morrow.

The next dawn would herald yet more celebrations. Not only was the evil that had kept the lands locked in winter for time immemorial broken, but the Citadel was playing host to an unexpected wedding between the daughter of the Lord of Dreams and the son of the Moonprince.

Such a union between Fey and Free had not been heard of in living memory and none of the gossips nor soothsayers had seen it coming.

Tarithel herself had taken on the mantle of 'Lady of the

Forest' from her mother, yet already many were talking about her gifts and wisdom. It was she who had roused Lord Dreams himself to resist the Witchking, and perhaps some said, all the Fey with him. Amidst the terror of the Doomguard attack on the citadel she had stood firm. The forest itself had responded to her, turning upon and destroying the invaders. None amongst the Fey had been able to wield such power before; her abilities seemed lifted straight from the pages of myth from long ago.

Yet, to other eyes, she remained Tarithel, the only daughter of the Lord of Dreams, a slight, red-haired Fey-girl with bright green eyes, in the first full glow of womanhood.

Morkin was new to the court of Dreams too. He had made quite the entry, staggering in supported by Tarithel, his clothing rent and stained, his visage smeared with mud, his face unshaven. His role in all that had transpired was soon told; by his hand had the Ice Crown been destroyed, assisted by the heroic valour of a skulkrin called Fawkrin and a mighty dragon called Farflame. Aided by them, Morkin had flung the Crown into the water of Lake Mirrow and there its evil had been consumed. He was the living embodiment of the ancient Lay of Yanathel, a prophetic song that claimed that one born of Fey and Free would break the bane of Midnight.

And so it had happened.

Their immediate betrothal to one another was the talk of the citadel. They had only just met, surely? Yet it seemed to those that watched that a great bond had already formed between them and that it was a wholesome one, like a flower blooming in the first warmth of a renewed spring.

The couple stood together on the ramparts of the western tower, looking out across the forest. The hour was late; even as they spoke, midnight passed and the early hours began.

'It is held amongst my people that it is bad luck for the groom to see the bride upon the wedding day,' Morkin said, taking her hand. 'But I would risk it to glance upon your face all the same.'

Tarithel smiled and leant into his embrace. She spoke no words.

'You're still troubled,' Morkin said. 'This message from the far north. The Empress?'

He felt her shiver. He saw her free hand clasp the jewel that lay on a chain about her neck, turning it back and forth in her fingers. A faint green light shone against her skin. Morkin knew it was a family heirloom, given to her when she had been given her title, Lady of the Forest.

'Surely she can be of little real threat to us here,' Morkin said, hoping to reassure her. 'We have defeated the Witchking, the Ice Crown is no more and, even if she's real, she lies far beyond the Frozen Wastes.'

'She is real enough. I saw her,' Tarithel answered. 'Even as the Witchking's fate was being sealed, the Lith of the forest revealed her to me.'

'The Lith?'

'A vision given to me by that ancient rock,' she explained. 'I saw a gate, forests peopled by Fey I did not recognise, austere mountains and a dread fortress, and her. She is powerful, she means us ill …'

Morkin took her by the shoulders, turning her around and then lifting her chin towards him.

'Think no more of her,' he scolded. 'A new day is begun and it will be our day. Let it not be tainted by some warning of woe from far away. We have won a great victory. You and I have played our parts, our service complete. Do we not deserve rest and happiness after all our toils?'

'I …' She sighed. 'I wish we could take that dragon you spoke of, fly north and burn her to ash!'

Morkin smiled. 'I'm sure that Farflame has taken himself away for a well-earned rest. He was sorely wounded by the

Iceguard … besides, he told me that not even a dragon can pass the Frozen Wastes.'

'Well …'

He rested his forehead against hers.

'We are surrounded by mighty warriors. Your father and mine together command all the hosts of Midnight and everyone amongst them would lay down their lives for us. None can assail us here. Cast your worries aside. There will be no more war or hardship for us now, I promise.'

Tarithel swallowed.

'The message told of a storm,' Morkin said, looking up and gesturing about him. 'Yet have you seen a more beautiful night? The sky is clear and the air fragrant with spring. Do not let the fears of tomorrow snatch away the joys of today.'

At that she smiled and nodded.

'You are right,' she said. 'It does not do to dwell in dark thoughts.'

He kissed her.

'Perhaps we should tempt fate no longer,' he said. 'There is much to do. But I will have your hand today, my love. Nothing shall prevent that.'

'Nothing,' Tarithel returned, with a smile. 'Always together.'

'Then sleep now,' Morkin said. 'For soon we will be joined forever.'

He kissed her on the forehead. She departed, turning back to look at him with a smile, before retreating to her chambers.

'That's it?' Luxor exclaimed, stifling a yawn. The hour was late and it had been a long day. It was not only the Lords of the Free that had consumed much mead.

The Moonprince of Midnight stood alongside the two Fey, looking at the scroll on the table before him in abject surprise.

'It is ancient,' Corleth replied, his voice sounding apologetic.

'And all we have,' Dreams added. 'The scholars tell me there is nothing else of note. There has been no trade, no communication with those lands, since before the time of King Ushgarak. The Frozen Wastes saw to that. This land of Icemark is virtually unknown to us.'

Luxor looked at the scroll again. It was a map, though it barely met the description. It was crudely drawn, with little detail. To the southern end, a forest was marked out sweeping from the centre to the right side. The text was unintelligible to him.

'Here,' Dreams said. 'It is written in the old tongue of the Fey. This is the City of Imorthorn, and here Lorangrim.'

'And what of this,' Luxor asked, pointing at larger inscriptions running the length of the map.

'They indicate realms,' Dreams said, indicating the forest. 'This is the realm of the Fey, for instance. But there are others.'

Corleth peered at the map. 'Outlands … and the kingdoms of Dwarves and Giants.'

'Dwarves and Giants?' Luxor asked. 'More child's bedtime tales? This seems fanciful …'

'That is what it says,' Corleth said.

Dreams pointed to the top of the map, in what would be the far north of the land it represented.

'But this lends credence,' he said. 'These glyphs spell out Frozen Empire and this one the Fortress of Kahangrorn.'

'Kahangrorn. Just as your daughter spoke,' Luxor said. 'And as this Lord Imorthorn inscribed; the Frozen Empire. You think this map can be relied upon?'

'The Fey do not make such things in jest,' Corleth said. 'I agree it is crude and lacking in detail, but of what it shows I believe it shows honestly.'

'If this then is the realm of this Empress,' Luxor said. 'Then she hails from the far north of Icemark. If I judge these mountains as to those of Ithril in Midnight, then this land is as big, if not bigger than our own.'

'I believe that to be true enough,' Dreams said.

'Then we have little to fear in the near future,' Luxor said. 'She cannot strike us from such a distance, nor can she penetrate the Frozen Wastes themselves. Why, the Wastes would destroy armies a thousand times stronger than the Witchking's before they ever reached our borders. There is no route from the Icemark to Midnight.'

'None we know of,' Corleth whispered, looking apprehensive.

'And what is this mark?' Luxor said, tapping his finger on the lower left edge of the map.

Dreams examined it. 'It is written as the Gate of Varenorn,' he said. 'Not a name I recognise.'

'It must be of some importance to have been marked on the map,' Corleth added.

'A gate implies a gateway,' Luxor said. 'And it is nearest to Midnight if I read this right. I will ask Rorthron when next we meet, he may have knowledge of such things.'

'Imorthorn's message speaks of a pact between the Witchking and this Empress,' Dreams said. 'That implies they could communicate in some fashion. Perhaps she has more than armies at her disposal?'

'You speak of fell crafts, magic and the like?' Luxor shuddered. 'I have seen enough of those for one lifetime. Say not that the ice-fear will return!'

'There is no hint of that,' Dream answered.

'This Imorthorn, if he be the same one that bears the name of this city,' Corleth said. 'He would not send such a message without good reason.'

Luxor nodded. 'And yet, there is no storm. The weather is fair. What is the worst a storm can do? We batten down our shutters and wait for it to pass.'

The two Fey exchanged a look before turning back to Luxor with a shrug.

'I see in your eyes the same foreboding I feel in my heart,' Luxor said. 'But what can we do? Let us turn our minds to happier things. A wedding awaits. Let us sleep upon this mystery and return to it after our celebrations are concluded.'

Morkin was troubled by dreams. He woke in a cold sweat, for a moment unable to remember where, or even who, he was. He sat up, his heart pounding, the bed covers falling from him as he gazed around his darkened chambers.

The walls of the room seemed strange to him, ephemeral. He blinked, seeing starlight through the windows … and through the stone walls.

This can't be … is it some magic of the Fey?

He blinked and the room came back into focus around him, solid and reassuring once more. He shook his head.

Just a dream …

Sleep eluded him. He got to his feet and dressed before stepping outside his chambers. The Citadel was quiet about him. He descended the great stone stairs and wandered restless around the encampment, pausing at the dying campfires to gaze into the embers and wonder what the future held for him and his beloved Tarithel.

In the distance, he heard a vague rumble of thunder.

He looked up, drawing his cloak tighter about him.

A storm? Surely not …

He peered into the sky. Just visible between the tall pines of the forest, far in the distance, soft-flickering flames of lightning lit heavy clouds. Almost a minute passed before another faint rumble reached him.

He watched for a while, seeing the clouds roll towards him

and boil above. One by one the stars were extinguished. A shiver ran through him; there was something otherworldly about the clouds, something unnatural in the way they moved. In the far distance they churned southwards, yet overhead they were almost motionless.

An urge took him to see the glade where Tarithel had found him after his long ride from Lake Mirrow. Almost without conscious thought he saddled his horse and found himself riding through the blackness of the forest, his way lit only by the memory of that first meeting.

Perhaps it was his horse that remembered the route, but he found himself at last in the glade, the remaining snow glowing on the ground like a phosphorescent pool. The horse trotted forward into the heart of the glade and waited while Morkin looked around, remembering the sweetness of beholding Tarithel for the first time.

The air was calmer here, the clouds gathered above seemed of no concern to him. The glade was peaceful, enchanted, the scent of wildflowers triggering his memories.

He closed his eyes and breathed in, somehow sensing a feminine presence.

Tarithel woke with a scream.

Her heart was pounding in fear. She looked across her room with eyes wide with fright. The windows had blown in, they were rattling back and forth in their frames. Through the window she could see storm clouds billowing and circling over the Citadel of Dreams, almost as if they were looking for something.

Around her neck, the jewel was pulsing with a sharp green light. She remembered how it had done that before, as the Forest of Dreams came to her against the armies of the Witchking.

It is a warning!

She ran to the windows, heedless of only being dressed in her nightgown, leaning out of the windows to see.

She gasped in shock.

Thunder cracked and lightning raked the steep walls of the great fortress, scouring the stone with its blinding fire. The light seemed foul in some strange way, not the bright white of lightning she had often seen before, but with an unhealthy cyan tinge. Sheets of hail hammered at the roofs and windows of the huddled houses and the taut canvas of the encampment beyond. The wind wailed and raged through the empty streets, tearing at slates and shutters, rending proud banners, flinging itself at the tall wooden gates until they groaned and shrieked at the onslaught.

Despair clawed at her heart. She knew, with no shadow of doubt, from whence the storm came. She had already uttered the truth herself.

The Heartstealer cometh!

Tears blinded her eyes.

'Morkin!'

The gale rushed outwards from the citadel, whirling through the ancient trees of the forest, stripping them bare of their leaves and snapping their stout limbs.

A flurry of debris and flying leaves rushed into the clearing where Morkin now sat astride his horse. Yet, at the very centre of the glade, the air remained unruffled. Everything grew still. Beyond Morkin, a torrent of sharp and icy hail lashed down. His horse, not waiting for a command, started for the shelter of the trees but before they reached the edge of the clearing a single bright tongue of cyan fire crashed down from the tormented sky and seared into the ground before them. The horse reared, throwing Morkin to the ground, then galloped away into the darkness.

Stunned and half-blinded, Morkin clambered to his feet to go in search of his terrified steed. Once again, lightning struck down ahead of him, so close that he could feel its heat upon his face.

Morkin felt his skin tingle and tremble as its power crackled about him, but somehow there was no pain, no hurt or any form of injury. Bolt after bolt cascaded down about him until Morkin was caught in a circle of raging, incandescent fire. So fierce was it that his very muscles seized and locked. He was helpless, frozen by the lightning; he could only stare into its blinding cyan flame.

His legs crumpled under him and he sank to his knees.

He blinked, his eyes seeming to be the only part of him that would obey any instruction from his mind.

The storm relented, the lightning stopped and the towering clouds melted away in moments. The bright stars gleamed in the sky above once more. The calm that followed was beyond tranquil; Arcadian, hushed and still.

A vision formed. A woman.

Tarithel?

Her face came closer, beautiful, perfect, tight and flawless skin and deep eyes. He felt his heart quicken at the sight.

But it was not his beloved Fey maiden. Another woman stood before him, taller and darker, draped in a deep maroon gown. It seemed woven in a strange manner; thick and obscuring one moment, yet transparent and revealing the next.

He jolted upright.

'Who are you?'

She waved a hand gently towards him with a knowing look upon her face, mouthing strange soft words as she approached. All urgency left him. She was supposed to be here, was she not? Clearly she was. Panic and alarm were replaced by a growing curiosity and interest.

She stood before him, beckoning. Her gown floated around her in an alluring way.

He gaped as enticing curves were revealed, before being hidden once again. The woman's gaze was mischievous, tempting and coy all at once.

The vision cleared still further. The gown, now unnecessary and an encumbrance, faded away, forgotten and no longer needed.

The woman stepped forth into the brightness. She uttered soft words of enchantment all the while. Morkin tried to remember, but all thoughts of some half-remembered Fey-girl were banished from his mind as if they never were.

Lust, of a strength and passion he had never known, suffused his body. This woman, this creature, whatever she might be … he must possess her, take her, bend her to his will. Passion subsumed him, burning through his limbs and into his very core, lighting his heart with a burning, primitive ardour.

She stood there, every delicious aspect of her revealed to his leering eyes, every promise her body could offer on display, if only he would reach out and take her. She beckoned with an outstretched finger, licking her lips as she did so. She stood there smiling, radiant in her beauty, her deep crystal eyes mocking him.

You must run to catch me, my love, you must run swiftly!

Morkin found his arms and legs responded to his commands and he scrambled forward, his mind lost in thoughts of desire and yearning.

His hand was grasped. There was a strange twist and he let himself be pulled through an elusive barrier. There was a sense of moving at some astonishing pace. Scenes both familiar and not so flashed around him; cities, forests, frozen wastes and great mountain ranges soared past in bare instants of time at a dizzying speed.

A fortress swirled into view, enormous, forbidding and wreathed in mist. He was drawn to one of its towers and then, somehow, though its very walls to the chamber within. All about him were mirrors, reflecting images of the landscape about.

But then, there she was, lying naked upon a silk-strewn bed, her skin lit only by starlight.

His mind was blank and numb, but her beauty was more ravishing and voluptuous than ever.

Come to me, Morkin son of Luxor!

Around the Citadel of Dreams, the storm raged. The trees creaked in the gusts, leaves blowing around the courtyard. Rain, whipped into whirls by fierce yet fickle squalls, slashed at the windows, rattling them in their frames. Soon everything was sodden, Fey and Free alike had retreated within the solid walls.

A lone figure ran down the empty hallways, her eyes streaked with tears, her hair flying about her as she ran.

Tarithel was sobbing, whimpering with a grief she could not articulate. She staggered, clutching at her midriff as pain lanced through her. She gasped for breath, pushing herself onwards, running upwards to the northernmost tower of the citadel.

She pushed open the wooden door that barred her way and stumbled out into the parapet, heedless of the drop below. Wind and rain slashed at her face and her night gown was soaked in moments, whipped tight against her as she crept forwards, looking up at the tormented sky.

She screamed out into the rolling darkness.

'Morkin!'

Above her, the sinister lightning flashed, sharp and evil shadows flickering around the stonework of the tower. Thunder crackled down out of the boiling clouds.

Wind rose about her, roaring and spinning her about; almost tossing her over the edge of the crenellations. She clawed her way back, her hair streaming out behind her.

'Please, no!'

The storm was already receding, the clouds retreating from whence they had come, fleeing northwards, as if they were a carpet of darkness being rolled up and tidied away. Lightning crackled again, but the thunder was faint now.

Tarithel caught the faint sound of a woman's laughter, cruel and mocking.

Misery washed through her, crushing her spirit. She sank to her knees, trying to conjure up her fortitude, but she was bereft. An aching anguish filled her soul.

Her eyes rolled up in her head and she collapsed to the sodden stones below her as the last of the rain and hail cascaded down.

The stars returned, but their light was cold and harsh.

Luxor and the Lord of Dreams ventured out into the early morning light, looking about them. The streets were littered with leaves, twigs and branches torn from the nearby forest and swept into untidy piles. Here and there tiles had been ripped away from roofs, windows broken and shutters cracked from their hinges. In the encampment some of the sturdy tents had been blown down or torn, their occupants fleeing either into the citadel or to the safety of other tents, huddled against the unexpected storm.

'It seems to have blown itself out,' Dreams said. 'But for a storm to come in the night hours and be gone by morning in this fashion is most unusual …'

'The warning of Imorthorn seems far less of a matter for jest now,' Luxor agreed. 'But if the storm was sent by this Empress of the North, what was her purpose? A minor inconvenience at worst. Everything will be tidied up within hours and we will resume our lives. What did she hope to achieve?'

'Intimidation?' Dreams asked. 'A show of strength, perhaps? That she has the means to reach us despite the Frozen Wastes?'

'It will take more than a storm to make us cower,' Luxor replied. 'Yet your Imorthorn spoke of evil designs. What form can they take? I feel a sense of woe in my very bones.'

Dreams grabbed his arm. 'Come my Lord, we have a wedding today. I will get my folk to clear this mess. We will have a great celebration and see our daughter and son start on a life of happiness. Perhaps tomorrow we can look further into matters of lore and history, see if there is more we can determine. But, for now, do not spare it another thought.'

Luxor smiled. 'You are right. Today belongs to the young folk. Let us see Tarithel and Morkin blessed and on their way.'

'I will summon them both to break the morning fast. A hearty meal will improve spirits all around.'

Luxor nodded. Dreams withdrew into the citadel. Luxor took to walking around the walls for a few minutes. The sky was clear again, but a mischievous breeze flapped the banners this way and that. Some had been torn down in the storm, their bright colours muddied and tarnished. The sun seemed weaker than it had been, despite the spring, the air felt chill once more.

Luxor shivered despite himself.

His thoughts kept churning.

The Icemark, a land far northwards of here. Locked off from Midnight since the time of King Ushgarak and the rise of

Gryfallon himself. An Empress of the north who has doubtless heard of our victory and decides to set herself against us. Why? What possible business can she have with Midnight?

He toyed with the idea of donning the Moon Ring one more time, using its far-reaching vision to see what he could discover. He shuddered at the thought. The Moon Ring was a great boon in times of war, but he well remembered the effect it had on him. It seemed to consume his own energy to drive its own, somehow leaving him weakened as the ring put forth its power.

Yet if this Empress can summon a storm, what other powers might she possess? Tarithel called her Heartstealer, claims she had a vision … of war and worse …

Already Luxor could see the Fey people below beginning to clear away the debris from the storm. The sun would grow stronger. It would be a good day. A day to celebrate his son's wedding, unexpected as it was.

I cannot blame him! Tarithel is as beautiful and charming a maid as any man could hope to find. Morkin is half-Fey himself, it seems only right that such a union is made. Young love is a force to be reckoned with. They have both lived through great calamity, who I am to say they should wait? Who can tell what tomorrow might bring? Dreams is right, now is not the time to fear the future, let us seize the day.

There was some kind of commotion behind him, he heard raised voices. Luxor turned to see a servant walking towards him, his face troubled.

'My Lord,' the servant said. 'Lord Dreams requests your presence urgently.'

'What has happened?' Luxor replied.

'The Lady Tarithel sire,' the servant answered.

'What of her?'

'She is not well, sire.'

Luxor nodded. 'Take me to her. Summon Morkin as well.'

Luxor was led to Tarithel's bedchambers. The young woman was asleep under the covers of her bed. Luxor could see her face was pale, her eyes closed, her red hair was dark and sodden. Maids were tending to her, under the watchful eye of the Lord of Dreams and his wife. A fire was roaring in the room, the heat palpable.

'What has happened?' Luxor asked, striding forwards, alarmed at how weak the young woman looked.

Dreams turned.

'She was found minutes ago in the north tower,' Dreams said. 'Outside on the parapet, dressed only in her nightgown. Soaked through and in a faint upon the ground.'

'What was she doing up there?' Luxor demanded.

'A good question,' Dreams replied.

'Is she sick?' Luxor asked.

'She was stone cold when found; it seems she was outside most of the night.'

Luxor leant in closer. Tarithel's breathing was slight, but a little colour was returning to her cheeks. A necklace hung about her neck, but the jewel attached to it was dark.

'I would ask Morkin if he knows more,' Dreams said, his voice lower.

'I have summoned him,' Luxor said. 'He will doubtless … you don't think he had something to do with this? I saw him retire early to his rooms.'

'I would hear his words,' Dreams said. 'Perhaps a lovers' quarrel?'

'Husband!' Lady Dreams said, speaking for the first time.

'Morkin would never have left Tarithel in such a state,' Luxor growled. 'My son is a gentleman, brought up to …'

'My apologies my friend,' Dreams said, holding up a hand.

'It's just … this day has not started as it should, this does not auger well for the future …'

'Let us see what Morkin has to say for himself,' Luxor said. A servant appeared at the door. 'Ah … some news … Morkin … ?'

'Sire,' the servant replied. 'Squire Morkin's room is empty, the bedsheets folded and neat. His horse is gone.'

Luxor stopped and stared.

'Gone?'

'Yes sire,' the servant replied. 'A stable hand reports seeing someone saddle a horse an hour after midnight and ride out of the citadel.'

Luxor turned to look at Dreams.

'It seems my son has some explaining to do,' Luxor muttered. 'It is I who must apologise.'

'Let us find out the truth before we cast blame,' Lady Dreams said. 'Tarithel will …'

A moan from the bed turned all heads to Tarithel.

She stirred, shaking her head back and forth for a moment before opening her eyes.

'Morkin!'

She sat bolt upright, her arms out in front of her, reaching out. 'Morkin, no! Please!'

'Tarithel!' Lady Dreams said, grabbing at her daughter's arms. 'What happened?'

Tarithel didn't seem to notice her for a moment, her expression drawn into a tormented sadness as she stared forwards.

'Tarithel!'

Tarithel looked about her, blinking.

'Mother?' Tears dripped down her cheeks. 'Oh Mother!'

Tarithel fell forward into her embrace, hugging her close.

'Say it isn't so,' Tarithel cried. 'Say it was only a dream!'

'What, my daughter?'

'Say not that he has been spirited away,' Tarithel wailed.

'Spirited away …' Dreams echoed.

'Morkin?' Luxor asked. 'Do you know where he went?'

Tarithel's expression dropped at Luxor's words. She released her mother, still looking about her in fear and anguish.

'He is here?' Tarithel asked. 'He is, isn't he? It was a dream, yes? Please tell me it is so!'

Dreams and Luxor exchanged a look.

'Morkin has taken a horse and ridden beyond the citadel,' Luxor said. 'Doubtless he will return soon enough. Did you argue? Where there words? All can be mended I'm sure … Tarithel …'

Tarithel collapsed inwards, sobbing. For long moments there was nothing but the sound of her shrieking wails. Her mother tried in vain to comfort her.

'He is gone,' Tarithel choked out, her voice crackled with hysteria. 'She has taken him away …'

'She?' Dreams asked.

'The Heartstealer,' Tarithel whispered and then fainted.

The jewel about her necklace flickered with green light and then faded to black.

Scouts were sent out, riding in all directions at the orders of the Lord of Dreams. Many of Luxor's men joined in the hunt as well, half the day passed but there was no news. Morkin was nowhere to be found.

Tarithel slept for long hours before she roused again, but her story remained unchanged.

'I do not understand this,' Luxor said. 'My son is not given to such recklessness and irresponsibility.'

'And Tarithel casts no blame upon him,' Dreams said. 'According to her they said their goodbyes late in the evening and both went their separate ways. It was the last she saw of him. Then her account grows strange …'

'This dream of hers?'

Dreams nodded. 'She claims she was roused from sleep, fearful that Morkin was being stolen away somehow. That this Empress, this Heartstealer, was somehow behind it. Tarithel remembers running to the tower, crying into the storm and hearing cruel laughter above the wind. And that is all.'

'I would give little credence to all this had we not had a warning of a fell storm and an Empress from afar who wished woe upon us,' Luxor said. 'And Morkin going missing at the same time? Yet, how can a storm have spirited him away? It is nonsense.'

'I am sure he will be found,' Dreams said. 'Pre-wedding jitters of the young is most likely. Perhaps he feels the wedding is premature, and does not know how to say so and has ridden out to find his thoughts.'

Luxor nodded, but both knew they didn't believe the words. 'Perhaps, but that is not my son's way. He would tackle a problem head on, brashly, perhaps even clumsily, but he would not willingly treat Tarithel like this on her wedding day. Something has happened.'

A servant ran up to them, breathless and gasping.

'Sires, news!'

'What is it?' Dreams demanded.

'Squire Morkin's horse has been found,' the servant wheezed.

'Where?' Luxor asked.

'In the vales to the north and east,' the servant answered. 'On the borders of the forest. It was saddled but not prepared for a long journey.'

'And Morkin?' Luxor pressed.

The servant shook his head.

'Alas, my Lord. There is no sign.'

Hundreds of the Fey and Free joined in the search for the missing squire, focussing in the long tracts of forest, radiating outwards from the Lith in the direction his horse had been found. Some were despatched west towards the plains of Kor, other north-east towards the plains of Ithril. Luxor himself rode out to the Lith, searching for any sign of his son.

Afternoon was well advanced when Luxor drew up his horse near the Lith having ridden a long circuit up to the Lake of Dreams and back down.

He paused, considering his next move, hoping to spot some clue, or perhaps see his son riding out of the green of the forest.

Such a scolding I will give him when I find him!

Even as he thought it, something moved in the forest nearby. Luxor drew his sword as a rider and horse emerged.

It was not Morkin, but Luxor lowered his sword when he recognised a much older face.

'Rorthron!'

Luxor recalled his first meeting with the mercurial and elusive member of the Wise. They were a race for the most part unknown, hidden in their towers which dotted the landscape of Midnight. Long ago they had failed to prevent the rise of the Witchking and retreated, never to be heard from again. Rorthron was the only one known who had deigned to speak to the Free or the Fey in living memory. The Wise had their own agendas and Rorthron was no different, though he seemed well disposed towards the Free and the Fey, having assisted them in their struggle against the Witchking. In form he seemed to be an ancient bearded man, dressed in dark magenta robes, always carrying a staff with him, upon which he leaned when walking.

'Aye, my Lord Moonprince,' Rorthron replied. 'I have ridden hard to find you. I was on an errand at the Tower of Kor and saw the storm break over the Forest of Dreams. Straightaway I knew it to be no natural affair.'

'My son, Morkin, is missing.' Luxor said. 'Spirited away by some means!'

'This is evil news,' Rorthron replied, a frown creasing his features. 'A mystery I will attempt to unravel. This has to be bound up with the demise of the Witchking and the Ice Crown …'

'Have you heard anything?' Luxor caught something in Rorthron's tone. 'You suspect something? Tell me! My son is missing, perhaps hurt …'

Rorthron returned his gaze. 'I always have suspicions,' he replied. 'What I must determine is whether they have any merit.'

Luxor knew well enough that he would get little out of Rorthron until he was prepared to speak. The Wise always kept their secrets close.

'Can you tell me anything?' Luxor asked. 'We received a warning, an Empress to the north, this storm …'

Rorthron's frowned deepened. 'I have heard rumours of an evil beyond the Frozen Wastes, but know little more. As yet I have nothing I can add, I ride now to find answers. I will return as soon as I am able.'

Rorthron turned his horse about and spurred it on.

'Wait for me at the Citadel of Dreams,' he called. 'I will not be long delayed.'

And with that the only member of the Wise that Luxor had ever met rode away into the forest, heading north-west, disappearing into the trees. With a sigh of frustration, Luxor turned his horse about and headed back towards the citadel.

Tarithel was not to be comforted. No words of reassurance could reach her.

They search in vain, I know it is so. They will not find him … she has taken him far away. Morkin is lost to me, lost to me forever!

She could not eat, she could barely drink. She lapsed into a faint once more, dreams swirling around her troubled mind.

Once more her vision was directed across the Frozen Wastes, untold leagues of sharp icy wilderness that none could pass and live. It swept below her, travelling past at a dizzying rate before coming to an end, revealing a land wreathed in mists.

She spied the ruined gate she had seen before, some sort of passage beneath the ground. She only just recognised it before her vision was wrested away. Now she flew over a dark forest of pines, seeing a city before her, proud banners fluttering in the wind. She could see the emblem of the city, a white falcon.

The City of Imorthorn!

She could make out Fey standing along its walls, looking up at a turbulent sky, the remnants of the storm that had assailed her home. She could see armies standing proud in the plains around the city; some great assemblage of the Fey of that realm.

Her vision now moved north, interrupted here and there by thick mists which blocked her sight. Strange buildings erupted from the mist, their structures gaunt and austere in the gloom. Strange pyramids, temples and palaces caught her view, their architecture so far removed from those familiar to her.

The terrain became rougher, mountains rising up all around as far as she could see, their peaks sharp and pointed as if trying to mimic the razor sharp edges of the Frozen Wastes themselves.

Anvulane …

Her vision swept ever onwards, another forest came into

view before sparkling shards of the Frozen Wastes again could be seen.

But this time, there was something else. She spied a fortress, a palace, in an ice-locked valley, somehow within the Frozen Wastes yet not subsumed by them. A glittering city of ice …

Words came to her, names she did not recognise uttered by a voice she did not know, yet somehow seemed familiar.

Berangria, Imiriel, Anvireon! You must make haste!

She descended, looking closer, her vision drawn to them. The building flashed towards her and she was helpless to resist her headlong descent. Rock and stone flashed past.

And then.

Naked, chained by manacles in a dark and fetid dungeon.

Her heart lurched in horror and sympathy.

Morkin!

Even as she reached out, she sensed another presence; powerful, indomitable, controlling. Tarithel flinched as she perceived a woman's face, beautiful but cruel.

You!

There was a smug sense of superiority about her. A grown woman, voluptuous, dressed in a dark flowing gown, her skin pale and her head topped by a bright silver tiara.

Ah … the sad little Fey maiden cometh! Well, little girl, I have your beloved in my clutches, he is mad with love for me and lies at this very moment locked in one of my less pleasant dungeons, pining piteously for my embraces!

No!

Give him up, little girl. He is mine and I will have my way with him!

Tarithel woke with a cry, her eyes wide, blinking in the dim light. The afternoon had swept on, it was evening already. She had slept an entire day.

My Wedding day … stolen from me by her! But I know where he is, I can find him. I will find him!

Her sobs were gone, the tears dried. She sat up, looking around her. Food, untouched, was placed on her bedside table, along with a glass of water. She devoured the food, washing it down with the water in great gulps.

She got to her feet, dressing herself.

She walked down to the hall where many of the Fey and Free of the realm were gathered. Luxor and her father, Lord Dreams, were also returned from their respective searches. She could see their faces were glum.

'No news?' she asked, matter of fact.

The Lords turned to regard her. Dreams gestured to her and she came close and gave him a hug.

'No sign,' Dreams said. 'The search continues. His horse was found near the Lith, but even our best trackers have failed to find a trace of him.'

'It is good to see you better, my Lady,' Luxor said.

Tarithel bowed.

'Your search is in vain,' she said, her voice sure and steady. 'Morkin will not be found in Midnight.'

Conversation around them faded away, all eyes were on her now.

'Tarithel?' Dreams asked.

'She has taken him,' Tarithel said. 'The Empress we were warned of, the Heartstealer. She has him. I have seen it.'

'How do you know this?' Luxor demanded.

'I dreamt it,' Tarithel answered, already seeing the doubt in the eyes of those around her. 'I saw the lands beyond the Frozen Wastes. A gate, a forest. The City of Imorthorn, mountains higher than any here in Midnight. Beyond all that lies the realm of the Heartstealer. She has taken him, she holds him prisoner.'

Dreams shook his head. 'But it is not yet a day since Morkin disappeared, how could he be so far away? The realm of this Empress is far …'

'She has him,' Tarithel insisted. 'That storm, I've told you, he was spirited away. She is no mere Empress, she is a sorceress!'

'A sorceress,' Luxor said, his expression dour. 'And what business does she have with us? Why has she taken Morkin?'

Tarithel shook her head. 'I know not, but she has him. I have no doubt.'

'Our scouts have found nothing,' Dreams said. 'Our best trackers can determine no path that Morkin took. I fear Tarithel's explanation is the only one that makes any sense.'

Luxor sighed. 'So, a warning from the sundered Fey, a freak storm, a missing son and a sorceress.' He looked at Tarithel. 'And you spoke of war and worse.'

Tarithel nodded. 'She bears us no good will.'

'And the warning from Imorthorn spoke of a pact with the Witchking,' Dreams added.

Luxor nodded. 'Rorthron the Wise has gone to find out more. Of us all, he alone may uncover the truth about this Heartstealer's intentions and what we may do about them.'

'What we may do about them?' Tarithel cried in response. 'Why, we must make ready to depart. Morkin lies captive, we must rescue him.'

'I hear you, Lady of the Forest,' Luxor said. 'And I would ride out this very day, if I knew but where to go. Yet we know not where he is, nor how to reach him, or even how to cross the Frozen Wastes …'

'I can lead you,' Tarithel said. 'I have seen the way. My dream is clear. There is a path beneath the ice …'

'Daughter,' Dreams said. 'The way is perilous! Worse, it is closed. The Frozen Wastes permit no one to cross them, this you know.'

'There is a way, I have seen it,' Tarithel argued. 'We must save Morkin!'

'And a way we will find,' Luxor assured her. 'But if we are to travel to this realm of Icemark we must be prepared. Rorthron himself has promised to seek out answers and bade me wait upon him here this very day.'

'But there is no time,' Tarithel cried. 'Morkin is in peril. I can feel it, sense it ... we must go now. We cannot tarry!'

'We must,' Luxor said. 'To attempt to forge a path into the unknown without counsel ...'

Tarithel was shaking her head.

'Tarithel,' Dreams said. 'We cannot truly know the depth of your pain and loss, but we all feel Morkin's absence mostly keenly. He is dear to all. We will find him, but we must know what we are up against before we embark ...'

'True enough, a rash strike oft goes astray,' Luxor said, standing alongside her father. 'But once the path is clear, have no doubt young Tarithel. I have only known Morkin as my son for but a handful of moons and he is my only heir. I will pursue this Empress, find my son and take him back, and woe to her when I find her!'

Tears dripped on Tarithel's cheeks.

'Come,' Dreams said, gesturing to her once again, opening his arms for an embrace.

But she turned and fled, her sobs echoing around the hall.

Dreams sighed. Luxor grabbed him by the shoulder.

'Let us hope that Rorthron is not long delayed,' Luxor grunted.

Far to the north, past the forest and mountains of the Icemark, lay the desolate plains of Anvoril. The plains were locked, by magic of great potency, behind a curving wall of ice brought down from the very wastes themselves.

Within this impenetrable defence lay a city, wrought of ice, its walls as strong as the stone and rock from which its foundations had been built long ago. None lived there anymore, its streets empty and swept by cold and brutish winds.

Imiriel.

Within its many courts and halls, the Heartstealer maintained her most private dwellings. Safe from invasion, safe from spies. Kahangrorn served well as a base of operations for her campaigns across the Icemark, but Imiriel was her retreat from the chaos of the world.

There was no escape from Imiriel unless she wished it. Only she, versed in the arts her father had taught her and then honed through many moons of practice, had a route back out from this hidden valley into the wilds of the Icemark.

As the westering sun set upon her realm, she looked forward to a diversion. Stratagems and plans could wait until the morrow. Tonight she had a prize to enjoy once more, her latest conquest.

At the briefest of gestures from her outstretched fingers, flames ignited from oil burners within her private chambers. Her chambers were lit with candles and incense burners, creating a heady perfume of intoxicating scents, mingling with the spells she had wrought upon the place.

She stood amidst the trappings of finery, dressed in a shimmering white gown that revealed more than it concealed. Her form exquisite, her hair dark and sultry, her lips enticing.

None have ever been able to resist me ...

The door creaked from behind her. She turned to see him walk in. She gestured and the door closed behind him with a resounding clang.

With a curl of single figure she beckoned him forward.

Then he stood before her.

She walked around him, admiring his figure. He was young, strong and doubtless virile. She would test all his capabilities in time. Blonde hair swept back from a strong and handsome face. She returned to face him.

'You have come to me,' she said. 'Morkin, son of Luxor.'

Morkin's voice was dreamy.

'You have brought me here,' he replied.

Shareth's voice rose a notch. 'You came because you wanted me, you sought me, chased me.'

Morkin didn't reply.

'Whom do you desire?' Shareth insisted.

'I desire ...' A confused expression crossed Morkin's face. He looked around him, before looking back to Shareth.

'You desire me,' Shareth insisted. 'It is I who you crave, I alone who can satisfy your desires. You will come to love me in time ...'

'Love you,' Morkin repeated, his head nodding.

'Yes,' Shareth said. 'Swear your allegiance to me, Morkin. Proclaim your devotion, your service.'

Morkin swallowed.

'To Shareth, my queen,' he said, his voice thick and ponderous. 'I give myself to you, forsaking all others. I will be faithful, be yours alone as long as we both shall live. You may do with me whatever you will. I am yours forever. This I pledge to thee.'

'You bear no loyalty to your father, that despised Moonprince?'

'I would slay him should he seek me out.'

'And to Midnight, your homeland?'

'Let me lay it waste in service to you.'

Shareth smiled, licking her lips.

'And what of that pathetic Fey-girl who once fawned upon you?'

'She is nothing, I despise her. Her beauty cannot compare with yours. It is for you my heart sings, you alone I have eyes for.'

Shareth smiled.

'As it should be.'

Chapter Two

Rorthron the Wise stands in the Forest of Doom, looking north to the Tower of Doom.

Dawn broke. Rorthron had ridden hard and, in the manner of the Wise, augmented his travel in ways known only to his folk. Long before sundown he had reached a keep on the edge of the Forest of Dreams.

The keep overlooked the barren plains of Kor which stretched out as far as the eye could see to the west. To the south stood the mysterious line of Liths that had somehow allowed the armies of the Moonprince to venture north to assail the Witchking's realm. To the north, the mountains of Ugrorn and the Citadel of Kor could just be seen on the horizon.

Rorthron sighed. It was beyond those mountains that his destination lay; the ruined realm of the Witchking.

He could not delay, no matter how wearisome the journey.

On the next day, the Plains of Kor fell behind him as he rode his horse hard to the north-west. His passage was swift and soon the deserted walls of the Citadel of Kor rose above him. He did not stop, but kept on riding, now turning north.

Ahead lay another Citadel, once mighty and proud, but now a crumbling ruin of darkened rocks. The ice and snow was receding even here, washing away a tumult of broken masonry and ironworks, once the domain of the Witchking himself. Before this very place, scant days prior, had the final battle for the freedom of Midnight been fought. Luxor had slain the Witchking, even as his power was decimated by the destruction of the Ice Crown, the frightful Talisman which had enslaved the hearts of Free and Fey.

But the Witchking was vanquished, his power at an end. Midnight continued to wrest itself free from the icy grip of a winter that had lasted a thousand moons.

The third day saw him reach the Plains of Despair. They were empty now, dank and abandoned. The going became slower as the ground, now freed from the ice, had become a fetid swamp in many places. Some of the keeps had collapsed as their foundations had given way. Rorthron could see the land in turmoil; rocks twisted, rent by landslides and, in all directions, a great morass of churned mud.

Dusk was upon him as he drew close to his goal. Before him a maze of twisted and dried timbers blocked his path, the remains of a forest. He had seen it long ago, before the Witchking's power waxed to its full extent. Back then it was tended by the Fey themselves, but they had been banished when the Witchking came into his own. The lands hereabouts were abandoned; even their names had been forgotten.

This dried and desiccated forest was known for the fear and loathing that had accompanied the Witchking's reign. A single word.

Doom.

Here Morkin had ventured to snatch away the Ice Crown. Against all odds he had succeeded, his unique ancestry, of both Free and Fey, keeping him immune from the devastating Ice Fear that would otherwise have crushed his mind. Not even the Wise, with all their powers, could have approached while that fearful Talisman remained potent.

And it had been housed in the building ahead of him. Once known as the Tower of Gryfallon the Stargazer, it now shared the same name as the forest.

Doom.

Rorthron left his horse at the boundary of the forest, muttering soft words of instruction to it. It tossed its head in acknowledgement. He picked his way within the twisted branches, mindful to avoid the sharp and brittle thorns that would otherwise rip at his clothes and tear his skin.

A faint mist hung above the ground. The air was still.

About him Rorthron could see the remains of the trees were bent, all shocked outwards and blasted away from the same focal point.

The Tower rose above him, a vast edifice of rock and stone. It was unharmed by the ravages that had struck the other buildings in the domain. It would take far more than just a mere rending of the earth to unseat the Towers of the Wise.

Long moons ago it was, that these were crafted!

Still nothing moved. The land was bereft. Even with the thaw, there was no life here. Whilst the evil that had long inhabited it was gone, it would be many moons before the taint would be washed from the lands hereabouts. Perhaps it might never heal, so long and heavy had been the curses and spells of the Witchking.

Rorthron pressed onwards.

The tower gates were just ahead, rusting metal standing stark against the rubble all around its base. Around him were scattered fragments of wood and debris. He stepped around it, careful not to disturb anything.

Before him, a darkened archway provided access within the tower. Rorthron climbed the gloomy central staircase, noting the runes curved into the stone work as he climbed. They had been runes of power, but they were impotent now, their purpose to notify the Witchking of any intruder within his domain.

He reached the top-most stair and looked within.

In common with many of the towers of Midnight, the room

was eight-sided, with views out to all eight compass points. Fragments of broken glass lay on the floor, but there was little else. Not so long ago, the Witchking himself would have stood in this very place.

At the centre stood a carved stone pedestal engraved with yet more runes. Rorthron knew it to once have been the resting place of the Ice Crown. Now it was empty, standing mute and solitary, its purpose served.

There were no books, no tomes, no tapestries, no inscriptions, no charts or maps. The room was bare. Rorthron paced about, but found nothing more.

He held out his staff before him, closing his eyes and concentrating. Brief words came from his lips and a faint pulse of white light flickered from the tip of the staff. It flickered around the room, outlining the edges of masonry, arches and pillars, cascading this way and that as if looking for something.

The light swept around and then stopped. A bright crimson spark flashed against one wall, angry and defiant. The whiteness faded, but the red glow remained.

Rorthron moved across, watching the red spark for long minutes as it hovered in the air before the wall. It did nothing but flicker and burn, as if it waited for some signal.

He rubbed his beard.

An invitation of sorts. Such magic is not to be trusted ... but I have come this far and cannot go away empty handed ...

He inclined his staff towards the red spark, mumbling an incantation under his breath.

The crimson glow crackled, growing and splitting into more sparks. These danced and swirled in patterns, drawing a shape in the air. The outline of a woman's face appeared. Rorthron watched, his staff poised before him, gripped by both hands in readiness.

The woman's face was striking, perhaps it would even be

considered beautiful to the eyes of men. Her cheekbones were high and distinct, eyes wide, lips full and pouting. Rorthron could sense her enticements; the woman's visage was laced with enchantments and snares for the unwary, radiant with cold and piercing beauty.

The woman turned and Rorthron found himself face to face with her.

Then she spoke.

'Ah … Child of the Wise,' she said, her voice filled with scorn. 'Come to seek answers have you?'

'You are the sorceress of the Icemark?' Rorthron asked.

'I am Empress of Icemark!' The woman's rejoinder was sharp and angry.

'Then I would ask you of your intentions,' Rorthron replied, his voice guarded.

'Would you indeed?' The woman laughed. 'Earn your answers. Wrest them from me, if you can. Try your strength against me. I dare you.'

'I do not seek conflict,' Rorthron replied.

'But I do.' The woman's voice turned colder. 'I seek to rid the world of an upstart Moonprince, know you of him?'

'And what quarrel do you have with the Moonprince of Midnight?' Rorthron asked.

The woman scoffed. 'Quarrel? Oh, it is but a little affair. Is it not right that a daughter seeks to avenge the murder of her father?'

'The Witchking was your …?'

'Gryfallon was his name,' the woman hissed. 'Slain by your precious Moonprince! Well, he will rue the day he took up arms against my father. Midnight was my inheritance, it was promised to me long ago and I will have it yet.'

'Midnight belongs to its people,' Rorthron said. 'We will not suffer another evil power to rule over us. You will find us well prepared for any conflict.'

She laughed.

'Is that what you think?' the woman replied. 'Yet have I not already snatched your precious Moonprince's son from within his own court? You heard of his loss? Yes, it is true indeed. Morkin is his name and I have him enslaved already. How he pines for my embraces. See how his betrothed Fey-girl wails and cries. But it is all in vain, for she will never see him again. He is my servant now.'

'Return him to us,' Rorthron demanded. 'Surely we can negotiate a peace …'

'I do not want a peace!'

'A war will not serve anyone …'

'It will serve me,' the woman replied. 'You are all so puny and pathetic! Know this, most infant of the so-called Wise. I will have my vengeance upon your precious Moonprince and the lands of Midnight. I will set his very own son at the head of my armies and send him back to Midnight to shatter such peace as you think you have already attained. I will ride forth to avenge Gryfallon, my beloved father. The Frozen Gates I will tear down. Midnight will be laid waste and through the portals of Xajorkith I will pass in glory. A queen for all to love and fear. Know me, for I am Shareth, the Heartstealer!'

'The Moonprince will not stand for this,' Rorthron replied. 'I warn you …'

Shareth laughed, her scorn drowning out his words.

Her eyes were cold and her gaze piercing when next she spoke.

'Then let your Moonprince ride forth to hammer at my door. He will find defeat more swiftly.'

Her image disappeared and Rorthron was left in the dank and dark emptiness of the Tower of Doom.

The scouts and messengers returned to the Citadel of Dreams over the following days without news. Morkin was indeed gone, no trace of him could be found. Luxor and Dreams poured over ancient manuscripts, seeking any further information about the land of Icemark, but there was precious little new to be discovered. With the wedding cancelled and the celebrations of victory over the Witchking at an end, the armies of the Free and the Fey camped beneath the battlements were dispersing, winding their way southwards to home and hearth and kin. A garrison of Moonguard warriors, fiercely loyal to Luxor after his victory, remained.

Tarithel watched the grim faces of her father and the Moonprince, but they would not be swayed from their choice, they waited for Rorthron to return with news and guidance.

But how long will that be? Days, weeks, even whole moons? It is time Morkin cannot afford, I know he can't …

As another day drew to an unhappy close, she bid them goodnight and went to her room. Night fell once more, clear and starlit, but she did not go to sleep. Once the halls of the Citadel were quiet, she rose, dressed in travelling gear and shouldered a pack she had prepared during the day. Within were provisions for a long journey, cloths, knives, a sleeping mat and blankets.

Tarithel had never been on a long traipse in the wilderness, but she had camped out on trips with her father in all weathers and was well versed in forest lore. She twirled the green and delicate jewel that hung around her neck. It glowed under her caress.

And I am Lady of the Forest. Such powers as I can command I will use.

She left no note for fear of it being found and riders sent to overtake her. The Lord of Dreams would be furious and Lord Luxor would doubtless try to stop her.

But I cannot tarry. Not while Morkin is held in her clutches. There is no time. I am sure of it.

She made her way down to the stables, slipping between the shadows without a sound. She was adept at it now, having often evaded the guards of the citadel, knowing their routes, patrols and times. She took her own horse Álainn, a mare which she had ridden since childhood, saddled her and led her out into the courtyard.

The stars twinkled in the firmament above.

I set out to find you, my love.

She guided Álainn about, turning her towards the gates. They were set open, as was custom during times of peace, but two guards stood facing outwards. She had no wish to announce her departure.

She smiled and gestured with her hand. The jewel around her neck glowed bright.

Unnoticed, at the feet of the guards, plants grew out of the cracks in the cobbled stones. Flowers blossomed despite the darkness.

Tarithel watched as the guards sniffed, looking around in surprise at the sweet smell that filled the air around them. A single sniff was all it took. They keeled over, slumping against the walls of the great archway of the outer wall.

It would not last long, but long enough.

Tarithel guided Álainn forwards and through the arch and then urged her on to a gallop. They were lost in the eaves of the forest in a moment, the flowers she had summoned browning and wilting behind her.

Tarithel had no plan but to follow the dreams and visions she had received. They had served her well in the past and, somehow, she knew they would again. She made her way first north-east, riding hard until she reached the Lith of Dreams. She knew it to be unique in all of Midnight, the only Lith deep within the forest. The Fey of her realm had always accorded it much reverence and care.

She reached it in an hour, the route familiar. It stood, shining in the starlight, somehow seeming to glow before her eyes. She rode up, dismounted and ran her fingers across the stones. They were warm to the touch, heated by some power deep within. In the long moons of winter, the Liths had always been free of snow despite the cold.

The warmth grew, almost hot under her fingertips.

Visions flickered in her mind again. The Forest of Dreams, north and west, the far mountains of Droon and the Frozen Wastes … a gap in their sharp icy walls, a tower, a dark cavern reaching beneath the ice …

She gasped as the darkness swallowed her.

Your route, Lady of the Forest. Be swift!

She pulled her hand back as if burnt by a fire, but it was whole and unmarked. The glade around the Lith was silent and still.

Tarithel turned back to Álainn. In a moment she was astride her once more, galloping onwards through the forest.

Dawn broke, cold and miserable above the Citadel of Dreams. A week had now passed since Morkin had disappeared.

'Gone?' Luxor said, seeing the greyness and worry etched upon Lord Dreams' face.

'Last night,' Dreams said, wringing his hands. 'I should have expected her to do something like this; I should have set a special watch upon her, the guards saw nothing…'

Luxor grabbed his shoulder. 'From what I have seen you'd never have been able to stop her, I assume she wasn't spirited away?'

'She took her own horse, a sturdy and swift mare,' Dreams replied. 'Doubtless she used the gifts she so ably demonstrated in the defence of the citadel to hide her departure.'

'She is brave and courageous,' Luxor said. 'And imbued

with a power fearsome to behold. Perhaps love can find a way when the knowledge and strength of warriors falls short?'

'It seems short moons ago that she was just a child, arguing with me about going to bed on time,' Dreams said.

'Our children may surpass our deeds sooner than we might expect or desire,' Luxor replied. 'The moment we have news from Rorthron I will seek her out. You have my word.'

Rorthron had ridden onwards from the Tower of Doom, forging his way eastwards across the Plains of Rathroon and onwards through the Downs of Lorgrim. The weather was grim, dank and overcast for three days as he journeyed on.

He had been this way once before.

Here, not far from the Frozen Wastes that bound the northern edge of Midnight, the snow and ice had yet to retreat. Whilst the weather was fairer than it had been in many a moon, the cold still ruled. The wastes jutted into Midnight a number of leagues, creating a small realm locked off from the outside, but accessible to those who knew their way.

Ahead, Rorthron could see a fissure in the ice, a narrow passage that led through the otherwise impenetrable cold. A track ran up to it.

Rorthron paused in surprise and dismay. Astonished at what he saw.

Horse's hooves ...

Someone had been this way recently; the prints in the snow would have otherwise been covered or swept away.

But who? And how could they have found their way here?

The path was not known to the Free, and even the Fey with all their cunning would not have seen the entrance. It was a secret of the Wise, known only to them, or so he had believed.

The one who lay beyond this barrier had cut himself off from the realm of Midnight, and did not receive visitors gladly.

But this is not of the Wise, no others have stirred and they couldn't have hidden their presence from me ...

There were no answers to be found here.

The fissure opened into a narrow path between the jagged shards of the wastes which in turn led into a canyon. This he followed for a league before it also widened into a gentle valley, sloping down and revealing a plain ahead.

There, in the distance, was his destination.

A Tower of the Wise.

The Tower of Lorgrim.

The pathway to the tower was cleared of snow; Rorthron could see the paved walkway that led to its gates. He urged his horse on and soon approached the base of the tower.

The gates were open and a figure stood between them, awaiting his arrival. Rorthron had expected nothing less. The Wise could scarce disguise their locations one from another, their power marked them out too plainly.

The figure ahead was slight, his robes a purple just short of being black. He appeared to be an old man, leaning upon a staff. Such was the fleshy garb in which the Wise cloaked themselves.

'Fresh from your victory over the Witchking?' Lorgrim rasped. 'And here you come already with more of your questions. What can such as I offer to such a mighty warlord such as yourself? Perhaps I should prostrate myself at your feet? Is that what you seek? Might I gather all the staffs and sceptres of the Wise and offer them to you?'

'I seek only knowledge,' Rorthron replied, with a frown. 'And it was your clues that led to the end of the Witchking, or do you not recall?'

'I stood aside,' Lorgrim said. 'As the Wise are well advised to do. It was your Moonprince who slew him and his son who unmade the Ice Crown.'

'After you revealed …'

Lorgrim signalled for him to be silent. Rorthron's frown deepened.

'He is dead, Lorgrim,' Rorthron said. 'Your apprentice has no hold over you now … unless perhaps … you fear another?'

'And wise I am to do so,' Lorgrim replied. 'For there is one, but I will not utter …'

'Shall I name her for you?' Rorthron prompted, raising his voice. 'Empress of the Frozen Empire? Shareth the Heartstealer?'

'Do not speak her name!' Lorgrim hissed, looking about him with fear in his eyes. 'Come within before we discuss such evil further …'

Lorgrim led Rorthron inside the Tower and up the winding staircase to the chamber at its peak.

'She threatens Midnight,' Rorthron said, as Lorgrim closed the door behind them. 'I have faced her and she is mighty indeed. I dared not test myself against her strength. Tell me what you know of her.'

'She is the Witchking's daughter,' Lorgrim replied, with a dismissive wave. 'Is that not enough for you to know that you should leave her well enough alone?'

'She claims to have stolen the Moonprince's son,' Rorthron countered. 'It seems she is poised to unleash her revenge upon us for her father's death. I need to know if this is an idle boast …'

'An idle boast?' Lorgrim laughed. 'Who do you think it was who sent armies to bolster the Witchking's forces prior to the invasion of the Plains of Blood? Who other than his loyal daughter could send troops? Oh, she is prepared for war, do not doubt it!'

Rorthron frowned.

'Then … there is a way from the Icemark to Midnight, sizable enough for an army?'

Lorgrim looked uncomfortable. Rorthron's eyes narrowed.

'And you knew of it and the movements of armies that came that way in the service of the Witchking,' Rorthron said, anger rising in his voice. 'And you failed to tell us?'

Lorgrim backed away. 'He swore me to silence! Threatened me! A bond with the Witchking is not easily broken. You know this! That passage is no easy route, particularly for an army.'

'Then you had better tell me all you know, and swiftly,' Rorthron demanded. Lorgrim shook his head. Rorthron stepped forward, gesturing with his staff. 'Where is this passage? Show me.'

Lorgrim relented and then pointed north through the windows of the Tower. Rorthron could see the sharp peaks of the Frozen Wastes upon the horizon not more than a few leagues away.

'It lies yonder,' Lorgrim said. 'A frozen gateway in the wastes themselves, buried within the ice. It can only be held open by Word of Power and then for just minutes at a time. It leads to a dark cavern that runs under the ice. A dank and malodorous road it is, broken, slithery and pitted. But it leads into the Icemark, to a gate, the Gate of Varenorn in the south-west of that realm. Once you reach the surface again, then you stand upon the soils of the Icemark.'

'And she knows of this route,' Rorthron said.

'Aye …'

'Then Midnight is not safe when there is free passage. She will mass her armies and attack. I must warn the Moonprince!'

'Armies can make the passage,' Lorgrim said, holding up a hand. 'But not quickly. The route is single file for many leagues. Any invasion could easily be thwarted by an army stationed here.'

'Then preparations must be made,' Rorthron answered. 'Luxor will need to know. What can you tell me of the Icemark itself? Did you journey there in the past?'

Lorgrim sighed and turned away, looking out of the windows of the Tower, his gaze directed northwards.

'I had friends there many moons ago,' he said. 'Long ago, before the Frozen Wastes, before … well, I have told that tale before. Firorn, Thildrak, Varudriel and Thirand … they were true colleagues of mine. We spoke often in the long summer, their towers were but two days ride from here then. But they have been long sundered from me, I can barely recall their faces now. Oh … and Zarorthane himself …'

Lorgrim chuckled.

'He fancied himself the master of us all did Zarorthane,' Lorgrim continued. 'All hail his might in lore and knowledge! I wonder what became of them all …'

'And yet …' Rorthron began.

'I do not know any more of the Wise of Icemark,' Lorgrim snapped. 'If they have any sense they will have adopted the habits of most of us here in Midnight, not getting involved and waiting for better times to come.'

'If we do nothing, evil prospers,' Rorthron replied. 'We have seen that often enough … it is our responsibility.'

Lorgrim shook his head.

'If you wish to take it upon yourself then do,' he said, turning and fixing Rorthron with a stare. 'I am content to remain here, but expect no help from the Wise of Icemark, Rorthron the Wise. They will heed you not.'

Rorthron straightened.

'Then I will take my leave of you now.'

Rorthron turned, strode to the doorway, opened it and walked down the stairs. He was already about to mount his horse when Lorgrim caught up with him.

'One more thing you need to know,' Lorgrim said.

'And what is that?' Rorthron asked.

'You were not the only one to seek this route.'

Rorthron recalled the hoof prints he had seen in the snow.

'I saw the trail myself,' he said. 'Did you see them pass? To whom did they belong?'

Lorgrim frowned.

'Their true nature was hidden from me,' he said, his expression puzzled. 'In a manner I have not seen before. But I spied a lone figure on horseback, cloaked and secretive. They plunged beneath the barrier into the tunnels before I could assail them. Whoever they were, they had sufficient power to breach the gates. Yet, it was not one of us.'

'Someone from Midnight has travelled into the Icemark?' Rorthron mused, but said no more.

Tarithel! But how?

It could only be her. None of the Lords of Free and Fey would have the power to hide from the gaze of the Wise, nor command a Word of Power. Rorthron had already seen how the power of the Forest had grown in the girl in the last few moons, unleashed, fiery and strong.

But for her to have such power already, how can that be? And she is barely grown and inexperienced, prone to the rashness of youth, for her to command a power that can turn aside the direct gaze of the Wise heralds great danger ...

He had sensed her destiny lay beyond just becoming the Lady of Dreams when her parents surrendered their positions in the distant future. Some other fate awaited Tarithel. But for now, doubtless she intended to pursue Morkin and had taken matters into her own hands.

'You know them?' Lorgrim asked. 'Who was it? Who has such a power if not the Wise? Some upstart sorcerer?'

Rorthron turned back to his horse, vaulting up and turning it about.

'You do know!' Lorgrim fumed. 'Tell me!'

'I cannot divulge such information to one who cannot be trusted to keep it,' he said, regarding Lorgrim with a stern look. 'One moon soon you have may to pick a side and hold to it. I hope you make a wise choice.'

Corleth had led many of the search parties that had hunted for Morkin after his disappearance. He had ridden out again and again once it had been reported that Tarithel was also missing. He had found the barest of tracks, leading north-west out of the Forest of Dreams before they were lost on the plain beyond.

Tarithel had outpaced any that tried to follow, disappearing into the bleak and remotest parts of Midnight.

After several days of fruitless searching, Corleth had turned about and headed back to the Citadel of Dreams, his heart sunk within him.

To lose both is the illest of ill omens …

The Citadel was rising above him as his weary horse plodded into the courtyard. As he dismounted and handed his horse to a stable boy, another rider galloped in. Corleth looked up to see Rorthron leap down from his saddle in a manner that belied his aged appearance.

'Rorthron!'

'Ah … Corleth,' Rorthron said. 'It is good to see you, but pleasantries must wait. I have news for the Moonprince, better for you both to hear it together. Join me.'

Rorthron's arrival must have already been reported within as Luxor and Lord Dreams strode out of the Citadel even as Rorthron and Corleth walked towards it. Dreams led the way, and the four walked into the citadel. Dreams led them to the main hall and signalled for the doors to be bolted behind them.

All eyes turned to Rorthron. He straightened, holding his staff before him.

'Tell us,' Luxor demanded. 'What have you found? Nearly two weeks have passed! Is there news of my son? News of Tarithel? This foul Empress?'

Rorthron nodded. 'I have news of all of them, yes.'

'Is Morkin alive?' Luxor fairly shouted the words.

'He is …'

'And Tarithel too?' Dreams demanded.

'She is,' Rorthron answered.

'And?' Luxor demanded. 'What reason does this Empress have to vent her fury on us? To steal away my son? Who is she?'

Rorthron took a deep breath. 'Who her mother was I do not know … but her father … he was slain by your sword, Moonprince.'

Luxor, Dreams and Corleth stared at Rorthron for a long moment.

'The Witchking had a daughter?' Luxor gaped.

'Her name is Shareth,' Rorthron replied. 'Those of Icemark call her the Heartstealer.'

Luxor straightened, thinking over Rorthron's words.

'Then I understand her wrath well enough,' Luxor said, after a moment. 'She seeks revenge for her father's demise.'

Rorthron nodded. 'And her plans are already long in the making. In the moons prior to the Witchking's strike upon us she sent armies to him to bolster his forces.'

Dreams frowned. 'Sent armies? But how? The Frozen Wastes …'

'Are not quite the barrier we thought they were,' Rorthron replied. 'They can and have been breached. They might be again. Even as we talk she threatens Midnight.'

'How do you know this?' Corleth asked.

'I rode in all haste to the Tower of Doom,' Rorthron replied. 'There I found how the Witchking and his daughter communicated at such distance. Such magic as they used was still potent. We spoke and she challenged me to test myself against her. When I refused she scorned me. Then she boasted of her aims and her successes.'

'Successes?' Dreams demanded.

Rorthron looked at Luxor. 'She has your son, Moonprince. She has turned him against us by sorcery unknown. She states she will send him back to us, but at the head of her armies, his loyalty twisted and his intent evil.'

'No,' Luxor said, staggering back. 'This cannot be.'

'She says she will invade,' Rorthron continued. 'That she intends to lay waste to Midnight from Dreams to Xajorkith and pass on even to lands further south. This she has sworn and it is no idle threat. I deem she has both the means and the power.'

Luxor looked at Rorthron and then turned to Dreams.

'It is all clear now,' he said. 'The white falcon, the storm, Morkin's disappearance. The Witchking's perfidy is far from extinguished, it lives on, in his very daughter!'

Dream's nodded. 'And Tarithel's sudden absence is also explained. She surely guessed Morkin's fate, just as she divined the ways of the forest. She has followed him, listening to her bewitched and troubled dreams leading her on, just as she said.'

Rorthron nodded. 'Indeed. Leaving Doom I rode swiftly eastwards. There I spoke to Lorgrim, he who once tutored the Witchking himself in the distant past. I am convinced that Tarithel has already found her way into the Icemark, she rides onwards in quest of Morkin's fate, even now.'

Luxor took a deep breath.

'Your words are not welcome, Rorthron of the Wise,' he said. 'But I thank you for them regardless, for now we know what manner of foe is ranged against us. This sorceress, Shareth, has my son. Morkin must be rescued. I must venture forth into the Icemark …'

Corleth nodded. 'It would be unthinkable to leave him in such foul hands, even if it were not that this Heartstealer has the power to twist him and use him against the lands of his birth.'

'Perhaps,' Rorthron said. 'But Shareth is as wily as the Witchking, likely more so. She may have simply left open the door of the coop in order to entice a fox within. This threat of invasion, despite her claims, may be just a feint. It was your hand that slew Doomdark, Moonprince; it is your death she desires most of all, even though she lusts after all Midnight. That is why she holds your son.'

'And that is why I must go,' Luxor replied. 'Or do you advise me against this?'

'I merely state the risk,' Rorthron said. 'If you fall, Moonprince, you may seal the fate of Midnight too. Creatures such as Shareth feed on their own success and quaff the power of the slain. If her vengeance is assuaged …'

'Then?'

'I fear she would become unstoppable,' Rorthron replied.

'What are you saying?' Luxor demanded. 'That I leave Morkin in her grasp?'

Rorthron shook his head. 'No, but you must not follow the obvious course. Shareth has set the trap. She will expect you to attempt no more than a rescue before fleeing from the Icemark.'

'You mean,' Dreams said, a frown creasing his features. 'Assault her? Strike at her?'

'She is sure in her arrogance,' Rorthron said. 'That could be used against her. And you have already said that the Witchking's evil resides with her. While she lives …'

Luxor rested his head in his hands, thinking hard for long moments.

'No,' Luxor said, shaking his head. 'We cannot hope to assail her so far away, without proper support. I have no doubt that the Lords of Midnight would once again rally to my banner and assault Shareth's realm if I called upon them. But if the moons go ill for us, Midnight would lie undefended. We do not know where her stronghold lies, nor what might she has at her disposal. Supply lines and reconnaissance for a major campaign in an unknown land would be difficult to organise and easy to disrupt … Midnight we are familiar with through long moons of warfare, but we know almost nothing of the Icemark … it is poor strategy and does not augur well for a victory.'

'And many were slain,' Corleth said. 'We are weakened and tired from our exertions against the Witchking, our strength reduced, much is in ruin across the whole of Midnight …'

Rorthron said nothing, but waited whilst the others fell silent.

'Perhaps there is another way,' Dreams said after a long moment.

All eyes turned to him.

'There are the Fey of that realm,' Dreams said. 'They are long sundered from us, but I have no reason to doubt that they oppose this Shareth. Did they not warn us of the danger first? Perhaps there are others that would take up arms against her given the chance. At the very least the Fey of Icemark would have counsel more accurate than any we can gain from here.'

Luxor nodded. 'To find this Imorthorn of the Fey. That might be a quest we could undertake, we sorely need more knowledge of Shareth's might and power in order to conduct an orderly defence of Midnight.'

'And you have the Moon Ring,' Rorthron said.

Luxor shuddered.

'I hoped never to wear that foul Talisman again,' he muttered. 'To have that invasive presence in my mind once more …'

'If allies are to be found,' Rorthron said. 'It will aid you in securing their loyalty and learning more of the Icemark. You will need all the advantages you can find. You cannot discount it.'

Luxor nodded.

'I like it not, but my task is set. I will venture into the Icemark and seek out the Fey who sent this message.' He looked to Dreams. 'The Moon Ring will also allow me to speak to Tarithel if she is willing.'

Dreams nodded. 'My daughter is stubborn, but I daresay she will welcome your presence and she might take your counsel when the words of a father are less than welcome.'

'I know exactly what you mean,' Luxor said, with a grim smile. 'And … why did I not think of this before? Morkin! I can speak to him via the Ring!'

Luxor pulled the Moon Ring from his tunic where it hung on a golden chain.

'Do not use the ring,' Rorthron called, his voice penetrating. All trembled in the wake of his words. His next words were gentler. 'Not yet …'

'But …' Luxor began. Something in Rorthron's voice quelled his question.

'I will explain,' Rorthron said. 'But not now.'

'Very well,' Luxor said, his eyes narrowed. 'But we must make haste, regardless.'

'And I will accompany you, Moonprince,' Rorthron said. 'The Wise have still much to atone for. Midnight might be freed from the foulness of the Witchking, but the Icemark remains.'

'I care little for the Icemark,' Luxor replied. 'I do not go to wage a war. I will seek out Imorthorn, learn what I can … but retrieving my son will be victory enough.'

Rorthron nodded, but said nothing more.

Luxor looked at Dreams. 'If I can … I will find Tarithel and bring her back to you.'

Dreams nodded.

'And I will come with you,' Corleth said.

Luxor shook his head. 'I have sore need of you to remain here, Corleth,' he said as the young Fey protested. 'Dreams can co-ordinate the Fey, but I need another close to me to carry my instructions to the Free. Midnight must be prepared for an invasion, you must be my eyes and ears here. We have already lost two people to the Icemark, I will chance no more, not at the risk of losing Midnight itself.'

'But, Moonprince …'

'And if Shareth has turned my son against me,' Luxor continued. 'She must already know too much about the disposition of our forces and our strength. Morkin knew much of what we were about and we must consider that I might be captured too. All our plans must be changed, new strategies defined that Morkin and I would not know. Shareth also knows of this strange route between the Icemark and Midnight, it must be guarded fiercely in case of invasion. I will need you to secure the passage. You know the Lords, Corleth …'

Corleth clenched his teeth hard, his expression grim, but he nodded.

'I will do as you bid,' he said. 'Though I am loathe to do so. Midnight will be secure and ready ere you return, never fear!'

'I will instruct Shimeril, Blood and Xajorkith to support you in this,' Luxor said, clasping Corleth's shoulder. 'I have great faith in you as you know.'

'It will not be misplaced,' Corleth answered.

'I will depart immediately,' Luxor declared. 'I will take a garrison of Moonguard riders with me. I cannot risk more in an unknown land without knowledge of what awaits us. Too many armies have been defeated by terrain and starvation before they even had a chance to draw swords on an enemy.' He looked at Rorthron. 'I assume you will guide us to the Icemark. If Shareth was able to send armies to Midnight from the Icemark, the reverse must also be true.'

'You speak truly,' Rorthron said. 'The way is perilous, obscure even. The passage is narrow and difficult. But yes, I will guide you and more besides.'

Luxor strode to the door, knocked and summoned one of the Captains of the Moonguard stationed nearby. A man entered. He was tall, with clean shaven skin, a firm stare and inquisitive eyes. Luxor had known him through several campaigns. He came across, bowing before Luxor.

'My Liege,' he said.

'I have need of a garrison of the best men of the Moonguard,' Luxor said. 'You've served me in many campaigns by now. I need only the doughtiest to ride with me. See to it.'

'It will be done, my Liege.'

Luxor nodded and the man turned away.

'Swiftness will be our watchword,' Luxor said, looking back at Rorthron. 'And a measure of stealth besides. Let us hope that the Fey of Icemark have counsel that will illuminate our path. Let us now make haste.'

Luxor watched as the others made their way out of the hall. Rorthron remained behind.

'You have other words for me,' Luxor muttered. 'Speak them. This Moon Ring?'

Rorthron nodded.

'Words for you alone, Moonprince,' he replied.

'I do not always welcome your words, Rorthron of the Wise,' Luxor replied. 'But experience teaches me I am best not to ignore them.'

Rorthron chuckled.

'Wisdom indeed,' he said. 'It does indeed concern the Moon Ring itself. I must counsel you to use it as little as you can.'

'Why so?' Luxor asked, looking at Rorthron. 'Is it not an heirloom of my house and am I not the rightful bearer of it?'

'You are,' Rorthron replied.

'And yet?'

'Firstly,' Rorthron said. 'Use of the Moon Ring will betray your presence to the Heartstealer. I do not think this is wise. We understand Morkin's loyalties have been poisoned. If you try to contact him ...'

Luxor nodded. 'I see what you mean.'

'Secondly, the Moon Ring is not whole,' Rorthron said.

'Not whole?' Luxor asked, with a frown.

'From Lorgrim I learnt that it once contained the most precious of jewels, set in the midst of it. A gem known as the Eye of the Moon.'

Luxor opened the neck of his tunic and pulled the Moon Ring out to inspect it.

'It does seem fashioned to hold a gem,' he said, 'But I have never seen nor heard of such a thing before.'

'Few have,' Rorthron replied. 'Even amongst the Wise … and it will be best to keep it that way. Perhaps you do recall the story of Rarnor the Unlucky?'

Luxor nodded. 'Corleth related it to me on our journey across Midnight, but I had heard the tale before. The ancient Moonprince who lost the Moon Ring trying to impress a young maiden as I recall.'

'Not quite,' Rorthron replied. 'Rarnor did indeed to try to enchant a pretty maiden and, I dare say, he was successful. But in the morning, when he woke, the maiden was gone and so was the Eye of the Moon, plucked from the ring on his finger as he slept. Neither maiden nor jewel were ever seen again. The ring itself was lost to him much later.'

'Still foolishness then,' Luxor said. 'But why should this trouble me now?'

'The Moon Ring is very potent as you know,' Rorthron replied. 'When the Eye was separated from the Ring … well, the two were never supposed to be apart. The Moon Ring's purpose is sullied without the Eye.'

'This is still riddles!' Luxor grimaced.

'Then I will speak plainly,' Rorthron said. 'Use the Moon Ring as sparingly as you can and certainly not before we enter the Icemark. Guard your thoughts and your intentions closely. Tell no one else of this. As I learn more, I will tell you.'

'Very well,' Luxor answered. 'Using it little will suit my purposes well enough!'

Chapter Three

Luxor the Moonprince stands at the Tower of Lorgrim, looking north to the Frozen Wastes.

Luxor had assembled the Moonguard without delay. Before an hour had passed, the riders of the Houseguard of the Moon thundered north towards Lorgrim, with Luxor and Rorthron at their head. Banners swirled, helm and spears glinted in the clear noon sun. They swept through the Forest of Dreams like a torrent.

They rode on without pause, passing Droonhenge at Midnight, stopping to rest in the shadow of the ancient monument. Another day saw them reach the Plains of Fadrath. By dusk of the third day, the Tower of Lorgrim rose before them, flanked by the grim wilderness of the Frozen Wastes. Only at the foot of the Tower did Luxor bring his riders to a halt, there giving instructions for a camp to be established and rest provided for both rider and horse.

Beyond the tower, the jagged ridge of ice gleamed blood-red as the westering sun cast its fading brilliance on the cold snow and barren pinnacles. The gate itself was hidden within the ice, blocked by mountainous shards that had toppled from the ridge above.

Luxor gazed at the great shards towering before him.

To forge a path through the Frozen Wastes. Just a few short moons ago I would have held such a thing impossible.

'Do not fear,' Rorthron said from beside him. 'We will find

a path. Come, we are expected, though I cannot vouch for the quality of the hospitality we will receive, nor the warmth of the reception.'

Rorthron led Luxor to the base of the Tower. As they approached, Luxor saw a figure emerge. With a brief glance, Luxor would have said that Rorthron had a double, but as the figure drew closer Luxor could tell them apart.

'Moonprince, might I introduce Lorgrim of the Wise,' Rorthron said, with a wry smile.

Luxor appraised Lorgrim. He was ancient to gaze upon, older even than Rorthron, thinner with a narrow face and an aquiline nose. His robes were akin to Rorthron's but much darker in hue, a purple a few shades removed from black.

Lorgrim inclined his head. 'Moonprince. An honour long awaited. To be in the presence of he who slew the Witchking …'

'I understand,' Luxor began, 'that you provided counsel to Rorthron in that matter. Your assistance was valuable to us.'

'The least I could do,' Lorgrim replied.

'Indeed it was,' Rorthron replied. Lorgrim glared at him.

'You are knowledgeable in many matters,' Luxor said. 'I would have the benefit of your wisdom before we embark on our journey.'

'Into the Icemark,' Lorgrim said with a nod, before looking about him. 'Come within, and I will tell you what I can.'

Lorgrim's tower was akin to the Tower of the Moon with which Luxor was familiar. Eight large windows looked around across the compass points and the room was filled with books, scrolls and maps. Lorgrim gestured to the fireplace and flames burst forth, warming the room.

'Let me show you something first, Moonprince,' Lorgrim said. 'Step closer.'

Luxor joined him at the northern facing window, with Rorthron a step behind.

'The Frozen Wastes stretch for many leagues,' Lorgrim said,

'But you can discern their edge. Look carefully and you will see distant mountains.'

Luxor squinted, just able to make out the faraway peaks. 'I see them.'

'The Mountains of Anvulay,' Lorgrim said. 'They lie at the southern border of the Icemark, ten leagues away as the crow flies. Before the ice came, this was a fertile plain crossed with rivers between both lands …

'And what can you tell me of the Icemark?' Luxor interrupted. 'Do you have a map, perhaps?'

'I do not,' Lorgrim replied. 'But I know something of that realm and she who dwells within it.'

'Shareth,' Luxor muttered. 'Spawn of the Witchking, whom you tutored, as I understand it.' Luxor gave Lorgrim a dark look.

Lorgrim swallowed. 'Gryfallon was my student long moons ago, but he was not evil when under my keeping, that came later and it was of his own doing, not mine.'

Luxor nodded. 'A time of ancient legend to all of us but the two of you,' he said, sparing Rorthron a quick glance. 'It seems impossible to me that such a creature was once flesh and blood. But enough of that, tell me of the Icemark.'

'Gryfallon ventured into many lands before he caused the Frozen Wastes to form,' Lorgrim said. 'He travelled far in the days before the forging of the Ice Crown. In the moons that followed he kept watch on those lands, even as he wreaked his evil upon Midnight. The Icemark is both like and unlike Midnight, Moonprince. You will find much there that is familiar, but much that is strange.'

'Such as?' Luxor asked.

'The people of those lands are wild, less alike than those of Midnight,' Lorgrim said. 'There are the Fey of course, they settled there long before the coming of evil, inhabiting the forests as is their habit. Of the Free there are none that you would recognise, in the Icemark the men are Barbarians, rough and uncouth, but no less mighty for that.'

'Barbarians,' Luxor muttered. 'Akin to the Utarg perhaps?'

'Perhaps,' Rorthron said. 'I am not well versed in the lore of the Targ, but it seems likely they could be kin, estranged and cut off by the ice at some point in the past.'

'Further north you would encounter stranger folk,' Lorgrim continued. 'Dwarves and Giants.'

Luxor frowned. 'Dreams told me a similar tale,' he said. 'I fancied these were children's stories grown large in the telling …'

Lorgrim shook his head. 'They are real enough,' he said. 'At least they were, all those moons ago. The Dwarves, though short in stature to the eyes of men, are doughty, fierce and indomitable. The Giants are likewise as you might expect, powerful individuals, ten to twelve feet in height, with strength to match.'

'Hard to believe,' Luxor said. 'But stranger things have proven to be true.'

'Beyond them,' Lorgrim continued. 'You will find the kingdom of the Frozen Empire, the Iceguard, men in the service of the Heartstealer herself akin to the Doomguard of the Witchking. All of these kingdoms vie with each other. There is no tacit peace between them as Midnight enjoyed for many a moon, rather the Icemark is beset by petty feuds and border raids as these factions are intermittently at war with one another. All is chaos and confusion.'

'It sounds more dangerous than I feared,' Luxor muttered.

'Yes,' Rorthron said. 'But there is a glimmer of hope here. Shareth does not hold sway over all the people of the Icemark, they have their own agendas and guard their homelands fiercely. We might turn that to our advantage.'

Luxor nodded.

'Or we might stumble into a battleground not of our choosing,' he said. 'And so, this Shareth, this Heartstealer, what of her?'

'The offspring of a union between Gryfallon and a forgotten queen of the north,' Lorgrim said. 'Quite when she was conceived I know not, but it was hundreds of moons ago. She is not aged as the Witchking was, but in appearance young and in her prime. She is a great beauty if accounts are to be believed, yet none of the people of Midnight, to my knowledge, have laid eyes upon her and lived. Gryfallon left her in the Icemark to keep her away from Midnight and she grew under his distant tutelage. With his guidance she secured her own empire, she is well versed in the arts of sorcery and war. She has gathered about herself the trappings of power. Her rule is, if anything, more foul than his.'

Luxor saw Lorgrim shudder.

'You fear her,' Luxor said. 'More than you feared the Witchking? Why?'

Lorgrim paced around for a moment.

'I knew Gryfallon well, he did not start out by seeking evil,' Lorgrim said. 'Power and knowledge were his vices, and he delved too deep and lost himself to them. While Gryfallon's malice grew deep and abiding, it was understandable, predictable even. Shareth though, she has mixed that same power and evil with her own passions, anger and lust. Where Gryfallon had a reason, even if dark and twisted, for his subjugation of Midnight, Shareth may not need one. Passion, youth and vengeance whip her powers into a fearsome turmoil. She is a wayward rebellious daughter, with the twisted power of the Wise, magnified over and again.'

Luxor rubbed his chin.

'And this is the hagspawn that holds my son captive.'

'Do not give up hope for him,' Rorthron said. 'She seeks you, Moonprince, thus she will keep Morkin alive as bait, a tasty morsel to entice you into her clutches.'

'And thus enticed I must go,' Luxor said. 'This road to the Icemark, show it to me!'

Weariness overtook Tarithel and she reined in her mare; Álainn seemed tired too. The day was not over, but she could carry on no further. She slipped down, staggering to one side as she dropped to the ground. Álainn whinnied, nuzzling her. She patted her gently in return.

'I know,' she said. 'We have come a sore and weary way. We will rest now.'

She led Álainn forward through the forest. It was quiet all about her, few creatures stirred in the wilderness. Before her the trees were thinning out, a line of hills visible between their trunks.

The trail is lost, where now can I seek it?

Ice and snow lay thick across the Icemark; the magic that had once held Midnight in its grip still had potency here. She shivered, but it wasn't from the cold.

Despair had worked its way within her. She felt it clasp at her, cruel and twisting. Her stomach felt knotted.

How brave I was, riding out to rescue my betrothed, to set him free from the power of the sorceress. So bold, so confident …

She wrapped her cloak tighter about herself to ward off the chill. A tear glistened on her cheek.

I was foolish. I should have waited for the Moonprince. I am lost in a strange land, with no friends or shelter.

Her dreams had led her on, their urgency pummelling at her mind, giving her no respite. Morkin is in peril they beseeched her. She could not be free of them and so gave in, sure in the knowledge that she alone could defy the danger.

She had ridden north-east, following those visions, finding

her way into a secret valley nestled in the Frozen Wastes themselves, skirting a tower from which she sensed curiosity and fear.

She had found the dark road that led from Midnight to the Icemark. She could not recall how she had forced a way through a crevice in the hard and brutal ice that guarded the way but she had managed it. Then she had traipsed through the tunnel beyond, at last staggering out into the chill air of the Icemark at the Gate of Varenorn.

There she had paused, sensing the cold, implacable power of the Heartstealer's presence. She dared not use her own powers for fear of revealing herself.

About the gate, the Icemark seemed deserted. She saw no evidence of habitation, save for a tower and the remnants of a broken down hut. She gave both a wide birth, but drove on north-east regardless, feeling the draw of the forest before her.

That forest was dark and forbidding, she felt nothing of the presence of the Fey, and her fears were confirmed when she saw troops of helmeted men marching through with little care for the plants and creatures of the wild. She hid from them, yet making her way onwards.

Then … her dreams had failed her.

No longer could she divine a path, the certainty she had known in following Morkin's trail evaporated as if it had never been. A crushing loneliness descended.

Lost.

That night, with great fear, she had crept to the outskirts of the village she had come across. She hid in the shadows, listening for any clues as to her whereabouts, or anything that might serve her. She understood little, the language coarse and uncouth to her ears, but she learnt something to her advantage. One of the villagers had spoken of the Fey and a city of those folk.

Imorthorn. The city from whence the warning came!

They did not say how far away it was; only that it lay to the north-east. The villagers did not talk well of the Fey either, conversing in dark tones with many a profanity. She had continued on with all haste, hoping to come across the Fey of Icemark. Thus far, she had not.

The forest she was in was called Thisiel, according to the words spoken by the villagers. She had learned that the city of Imorthorn lay in the Forest of Fangrim, some distance beyond.

She took a drink of water from a leather flask, as she did so a faint scent of blossom drifted past. She recognised it straight away.

The tending of the Fey …!

It was an essence that the work of the Fey left about the woods and forests they inhabited. It was subtle, the men of the Free would not have noticed anything, but to her attuned senses, the mark of her people was obvious.

They cannot be far away.

She looked across the hills again. It was hard to see, but it seemed that the forest resumed on the far side, perhaps there lay Fangrim.

I can go on, or I can turn back. I have enough food for the return journey, just … but going back means I have failed.

The image of Morkin, chained and bound in a cell still haunted her.

I will not abandon you. I will find you, my love! No ice, no storm, no sword will keep me from your side, no Heartstealer's twisted dreams shall come between us. Let her fling a thousand foul armies in my path, still I will find you and set you free …

She wiped tears from her eyes.

Despite despondency and tiredness, she would not go back … not without him.

CHAPTER THREE

'Do you trust him?' Luxor asked Rorthron, as they followed Lorgrim across the plains towards the Frozen Wastes. The Moonguard had been roused and they were heading north from the tower, riding towards the frozen immensity before them. Lorgrim was leading the way on foot, with Rorthron and Luxor on horseback a little way behind.

'Do *you* trust him?' Rorthron replied.

'You oft answer my questions with questions of your own,' Luxor said, his face twisting in a frown. 'I have little reason to trust him. He was the Witchking's tutor and my dealings with the Wise, present company excluded, lead me to be suspicious of their motives.'

'I would not necessarily exclude myself from your suspicions, Moonprince,' Rorthron replied with a chuckle. 'But you have answered well. No, he is not to be trusted. He was long under the dominion of the Witchking and may never recover from that shadow. He has seen many more moons than I, and his knowledge is vast. It is a resource we must use, but with great caution.'

Luxor nodded.

The ride from the Tower did not take long. It was not quite a league from its base to the edge of the Frozen Wastes. Lorgrim signalled for a halt.

'Now young one,' Lorgrim said, beckoning to Rorthron. 'I will require your strength for this, and given my advancing years, it is a secret you should probably know and keep as your own.'

Rorthron glanced over at Luxor who shrugged. Rorthron dismounted and stepped up alongside Lorgrim. They stood side by side on a small hillock, facing the wall of ice before them.

The riders of the Moonguard formed up behind Luxor and waited. He could hear muttering of discontent amongst them. He felt the intimidation himself. The ice rose, mountainous, before them. The barrier looked impassable.

Yet Tarithel found a way through ... alone!

Wind blustered around them, the ice creaked in the gale.

Luxor watched as Lorgrim and Rorthron raised their staffs. He heard their voices rise, deep and booming, echoing back from the wall of ice before them. The words held no meaning to him or his riders, but all could sense they were words imbued with potency.

He expected some blaze of light to blast from their upheld staffs, but their words continued for a minute without any pause. Only then did he perceive a change.

The wall of ice was moving.

It was slow, almost imperceptible, but after watching for a few moments longer, Luxor had convinced himself that what he thought he saw was real. The ice was flowing backwards, almost as if it had turned to molten glass. It was retreating all about them, revealing a dark cavern in the ice wall, whose vaulted ceiling rose majestically far above. The ice was withdrawing, parting like a curtain before them, crackling and snapping as it did so.

Then the staffs of the Wise did burst forth with a bright glow. A fiery arc blazed overhead, seeming to prevent the curtains of ice reforming.

Lorgrim's voice bellowed out.

'Ride swiftly!' he called. 'The spell will not hold for long. If you tarry, the gates will come crashing down upon you!'

Rorthron led the way, climbing back astride his horse and launching himself into the black depths, his staff blazing a glowing trail like a comet in the night sky. Luxor and his riders galloped after the fleeing light with as much speed as they could muster.

The darkness swallowed them and there, in the mouth of a broad tunnel, Rorthron signalled for them to halt and the company drew up their ranks and turned about to look back the way they had come.

Now far behind them they could see Lorgrim standing in the snows of Midnight just beyond the entrance, his staff still aloft. As they watched the blazing fire faltered and died. As it did so the ice returned in force, with a crack of thunder it cascading down, echoing about them, rumbling back and forth before it ebbed. The light was cut off and the way was shut behind them.

The only light came from Rorthron's staff, now blazing with a cool white light.

'You can reverse this spell upon our return, I assume?' Luxor asked.

Rorthron regarded him from under bristling eyebrows. 'So it is to be hoped.'

Luxor shook his head.

'Break out the torches!' he cried. 'Onwards now, to the Icemark!'

Dawn broke. Tarithel rose with the sun. As was the habit for the Fey, she had slept in the trees, Álainn tethered below. She leapt down to see to the animal, happy to find it well rested.

'Today let us hope to find our way into forests that know the touch of my people,' she said.

She rode at a good pace, but without pushing Álainn too hard. The hills rolled out before her, rising and falling under Álainn's hooves as she travelled onwards. It seemed the land was deserted. She saw no travellers and there were no signs of habitation either. The hills were unmarked by paths of folk or beasts, desolate and wind swept.

She stopped at mid-day, the sun a cold circle in a washed out sky, giving no warmth that she could discern.

Before her, a forest was coming into view. She could see it on the horizon. Dark and foreboding it appeared from her vantage point, yet she had sensed the mark of the Fey upon it.

Two more hours of riding brought her to its edge. The tangled borders looked unkempt and uncared for, though here and there she spied small scatterings of stunted wild flowers. She climbed down and walked across, seeing brambles and thorns about her. The ground was hard, cracked from the snow and ice.

She reached down to look at the flowers, stretching out her hand. As she did so a bramble slashed across, catching her fingers.

She yelped in surprise and drew back, seeing a small rivulet of blood drip down her palm. It stung like an insect bite. She sucked at it, spitting out the blood and putting pressure on it until the blood stopped.

Before her the flowers had been smothered, torn and pulled apart by the brambles which had somehow snaked around them, twisted and sharp.

All is not right with this land.

Some instinct within her took over and she stretched out her thoughts and feelings.

Eyes, sharp and narrow, a face etched with cruelty and cunning, beautiful yet cold. The vision flickered in her mind for a brief moment, pulsing and painful.

BEGONE TRESPASSER! YOU ARE NOT WELCOME HERE!

Tarithel screamed in surprise and staggered back. The brambles and thorns were thicker still, snagging her clothing, coiling around her. For a moment she panicked, thrashing through the thicket.

Her …

She concentrated again, the jewel around her neck glowing green against her skin. She saw the face once more, now wreathed in smoke and fire but she steeled herself for the pain and resisted it. She thought of spring, of warmth, new growth, buds on the trees and flowers sprouting from well-tended earth.

WHO ARE YOU? DO NOT DARE TO …

She struggled and the vision crackled and died in her mind. She caught her breath, her eyes seeing what lay before her.

The brambles lay, blacked and twisted. As she watched they crackled and broke into dust around her. Flowers bloomed in their wake, a patch of green growing beneath her feet as she walked forward, Álainn following close behind. The brambles retreated, flapping and snapping in their hurry to get out of her way. As she walked forwards, buds popped on the branches of the trees about her. She touched the trunks at the edge of the forest, feeling the faint tingle that came from the ancient ministrations of the Fey.

Much has been lost, much could be regained.

A faint sense of anticipation reached her. She could almost hear the slow, slumberous songs of the dreaming trees.

Fangrim welcomes you, Lady of the Forest!

The passage beneath the Frozen Wastes was dank and malodorous. The tunnel air was fetid and foul, the ground underneath muddy and treacherous. Rorthron's brightly glowing staff cast a faint reflection of vast, curving, blackened walls slick with slime and damp.

Luxor's horse stumbled in the mire and he patted its neck to comfort it as it snorted in frustration.

'What manner of tunnel is this?' he asked. 'It was not hewn by men I wager.'

Rorthron shook his head. 'No it was not. Some long lost creature of the deep burrowed through here long ago, then the passage was found and used in the days before the ice and winter came.'

Luxor shuddered, looking around at the immense walls and trying not to imagine what manner of creature could undertake such a feat.

Rats and other unseen scavengers, revealed only by pairs of eyes reflecting in the darkness, could be heard scurrying away from their passage. The sound of dripping water reached their ears, echoing off the walls.

After hours of weary travel the ground beneath them began to rise, drying out and becoming firmer underfoot. The horses, relieved at the easier going, picked up their pace.

'Not long now,' Rorthron said, appraising the path ahead.

The passageway twisted and turned, growing narrower as they ascended, the dank, stale air gave way to a fresher scent as the foul mud gave way to rock. Soon they were travelling single file through a crevasse between steep rocky walls.

Having wound through twists and turns, the passageway opened into a wide space. Evidence of ancient workings could be seen, pillars carved out of the stone, a smooth floor and two huge stands which Luxor took to be oil burners. Rorthron raised his staff a little and the light from it blazed brighter. Luxor and the Moonguard looked about themselves in wonder.

It was no natural cavern, but a chamber cut from the rocky insides of a mountain. The vaulted ceiling lay far above, perhaps a hundred feet or more, supported by a series of pillars carved with intricate care and craftsmanship. Luxor could spy murals and artistry depicting scenes from ancient histories, perhaps stories of the Icemark long forgotten.

A ramp led downwards to the centre, where a ring of pillars marked out a wide expanse of flat floor space. Maybe it had once been a gathering place, perhaps a market or a forum. It was impossible to tell. When Luxor looked down he could make out more decoration on the floor, patterns and spirals, symbols he had never seen before.

Yet everything was ancient, covered in a hundred moons of dust or more. The place was abandoned, silent. Its pillars standing in mute testimony to happier days long since departed.

'Look,' Rorthron said.

A faint trail of horse hoof prints could be seen in the dust, leading across the empty space.

'Tarithel,' Luxor said, with a nod.

They followed the prints, across to the other side of the chamber, where another ramp led upwards to a raised area. There they could see a pair of mighty gates, perhaps thirty feet tall and wrought of iron, just ajar. A small pile of snow had accumulated in the gap, enough space for a single rider to make their way through.

With the aid of the Moonguard, Luxor pushed the great gates open. They swung back with a great cracking and groaning of unlubricated metal upon metal, rust shattering in dust that floated about them in the pale light. Beyond, the first faint glimmers of dawn lit the sky.

As the Moonguard filed out of the gates and assembled, the sun flickered above the eastern horizon, bathing the plains ahead in a fiery orange and red glow. To the north, in the far distance, a mountain range stood, flanked by a forest on either side. Turning to look south, more mountains rose, with the Frozen Wastes glittering cold and sharp on the horizon.

Only then was the true size of the Gate of Varenorn revealed, the assembled Moonguard stared upwards in awe as they emerged from the iron gates. Built into the very sides of the mountains it stretched for hundreds of feet above them, its walls sheer and stark, rising to a crenelated stone walkway far above them. The stonework, lit a lurid orange by the dawn, was engraved with runes of many languages, here and there decorated with carven images of great beasts and long forgotten kings and queens. Above them all the word Varenorn was inscribed in bright metalwork, untarnished by the untold years since the construction of the gate, standing proud as a testimony to the art of its builders.

As the last of the Moonguard marched out from the darkened interior, the great metal gates closed of their own accord, with a dull, echoing clang that reverberated around them for long moments, before fading away into the morning air.

'So,' Luxor muttered to himself. 'It is the day that the Moonprince rides forth into the Icemark. Almost a moon has passed since Morkin was taken from me.'

'Dawn breaks,' Rorthron replied.

'It seems we have beaten the Heartstealer,' Luxor said. 'I almost expected an army to be lying in wait for us.'

'Mark my words from before,' Rorthron replied. 'Shareth is no fool, she wants you to come to her.'

'Morkin is my concern,' Luxor said. 'We cannot conduct a campaign against the Heartstealer in her own lands without allies and, for now at least, we have none. Let us learn what we can of the Icemark whilst we are here. We must seek out this Imorthorn first, he who first sent us the warning. His counsel will determine what we do next, if anything can be done.'

'Tarithel might be close to him,' Rorthron said. 'Perhaps she may have even reached his city. She had quite the head start on us. She knew of his message and it seems likely that she would seek out her distant kin.'

Luxor nodded.

'The Moon Ring?' Luxor asked.

'It would allow you to speak to her,' Rorthron said. 'But it will confirm your presence in the Icemark. Shareth will read such a sign as clear as day.'

'She will know I am coming,' Luxor said. 'Announcing my presence might speak of a confidence I do not have, perhaps it might sow a seed of doubt in her mind.'

'It will force her to put into play whatever plans she has,' Rorthron said.

'Then this fox will step into the coop with its head held high,' Luxor said, with a chuckle. 'I am feeling bold, let us see what this Shareth has in store.'

From under his tunic he pulled a chain. Dangling from it was a ring, plain save for an ornate circular bezel on top. It had a curious glow about it, as if it were aflame somehow, though its lustre was of gold. It was one of Midnight's great rings of war, the very last of them.

Luxor pulled it from the chain and then placed it upon his finger. The glow from the ring brightened as he did so.

Voices, ancient and unknown, cried in his mind. Visions of battles from times long past flickered across his consciousness. Images of landscapes smote across him in a dizzying rush and then came the surge of power he remembered and the unsettling sense that the Moon Ring had, once again, begun to feast upon his own strength.

Yet, the Moon Ring emboldened him. He was the Moonprince. Midnight looked to him. He had slain the Witchking after all and freed his land from evil. The Heartstealer was another foe set against him. Should the chance come, he might vanquish her too. Here in the Icemark, soon all would know of the coming of the Moonprince.

'For Midnight!' Luxor cried out in a loud voice, unsure if the words were even his own. 'For Midnight and the Free! Hear me, Shareth Heartstealer; we ride to tear your Frozen Empire asunder!'

Rorthron whirled his staff about his head, flinging a storm of golden fire into the chill air; the trumpets of the heralds blew a proud fanfare, and the cohorts of the Moonprince rode forth from the Gate of Varenorn.

Luxor concentrated further, sending the warmth of his mind out across the unfamiliar landscape. He could sense much activity, Icemark was indeed a bigger realm than Midnight. But it was not the people of the Icemark he sought, not yet.

Morkin! My son, I ride to free you. Speak to me!

Luxor spied mountains and valleys, forests and glades, great cities and strong fortresses. His gaze roved ever further northwards through mists and fogs.

Morkin! Answer me!

But there was no answer, no hint of recognition, not even the faintest echo of his son. Either he was held beyond the power of the Moon Ring to find him, or …

Luxor grimaced, not want to admit that possibility even to himself.

Morkin is no longer loyal to us … to me … to Tarithel. Could he truly have been turned as the Heartstealer claimed?

Far away, Tarithel reined in Álainn and paused. The deep and dreaming forest lay all about her. It had eased her passing, the twisted boughs of the trees doing what they could to move out of her way. She listened with her mind as a faint whisper of expectation rippled through the thin mists about her.

She held felt something similar, many moons ago, standing atop her father's Citadel, now far away to the south. A glimmer of sunlight penetrated the gloom, causing her to look up with delight. Hope blossomed within her heart. She smiled, gladness suffusing her soul.

'The Moonprince rides,' she whispered. Then her voice rose

and she shouted out to the silent forest. 'The Moonprince rides. He has donned the Moon Ring!'

Sunlight continued to brighten about her, the last traceries of mist boiling away into nothing.

A voice sounded in her mind.

Tarithel?

'Moonprince?'

She could see him in her mind's eye, proud upon his steed, riding at the head of an army, the gate of Varenorn behind, receding into the distance.

Aye! Are you safe?

'I am,' Tarithel replied, wondering at the strange sense of the communication at such a distance.

I am sore glad to hear it. Your father …

She shivered as she thought of her father's wrath. 'I am sorry I left in the manner I did, but …'

It may be as well you did. Your dreams have been confirmed by the testimony of the Wise. This Heartstealer, Shareth is her name, she has Morkin as you surmised. He must be rescued. I have tried to speak to him via the Moon Ring, but I cannot reach him. Have you any indication of where he might be?

Sadness crept across her.

'I am not sure,' she replied. 'The dreams that led me on so clearly when in Midnight abandoned me the moment I set foot in the Icemark. I have but the names I was given and a sense he is imprisoned far to the north, but no way to find him. I am seeking the City of Imorthorn. I stand within its forests now after many days of weary travel. I do not think I am far. Perhaps Lord Imorthorn will know?'

Seek shelter there then. We have arrived in the Icemark and will ride to you as swiftly as we may. Wait for us there, we will not be long delayed. Your father has tasked me with your safety, I would not wish to disappoint him.

Tears sprang into Tarithel's eyes as she thought of her father and mother, and the worry she would have put them to. She swallowed, but then bit down upon her resolve.

'I will find the Fey of this realm Moonprince,' she called. 'Whence you arrive, a mighty host will be ready to heed your call!'

I do not seek battle, at least, not yet. The safe return of you, Morkin, Rorthron and my kin to the Gate of Varenorn and hence to Midnight will satisfy me entirely. Once that is accomplished we can turn our thoughts to strategy and how to dealing with the downfall of this foul Heartstealer.

'Yes, Moonprince.'

Travel far and travel safe. We will meet soon. I would see you crowned in flowers at the Citadel of Dreams as my daughter-in-law, Tarithel. Be careful!

The communication faded along with the bright beams of sunlight. Courage was kindled in her heart, but alongside it was a premonition of worse to come. Tarithel could not shake off the feeling that Luxor would have no choice but to battle the Heartstealer for the freedom of his son, her beloved Morkin.

She shuddered. Around her the forest seemed to do likewise, almost as if a shiver trembled across the land of Icemark. She rode on fearful that many tears were about to be shed and much blood to be spilt.

The wind howled.

Far to the north, the mist swirled about the Fortress of Kahangrorn. Within its shadowy halls, a woman stood before a mirror, admiring her reflection.

Shareth was tall, her stance firm and authoritative. She was dressed in a long flowing gown of black velvet, a maroon cloak about her shoulders, secured by a brooch fashioned in the shape of a skull. Her hands were gloved in grey and her dark hair secured by a tiara that seemed fashioned out of ice itself. A black staff was held in her right hand.

Her face was beautiful, yet cold and drawn. A smile would have caused the heart of any man to swoon in admiration, yet there was none here to witness it. The lips were pursed, held tight.

The mist swirled like a live thing, drifting around her. She raised her head, her eyes narrowing as if she was listening to a whisper in her ear.

So, the Moonprince dares greatly. He has taken the road beneath the ice and ventured into the Icemark on account of his son. Just as I have planned it. Ride to me Moonprince, ride to your death!

She preened before the mirror, knowing that there was no other as beautiful as her in the whole of the realm. She had made sure it was so. None could challenge her. Spells she had woven about herself for untold moons, enchantments that altered both how she was and how she was seen. Few could bear to gaze upon her perfection, and none were unchanged by the experience.

Unblemished, untarnished, unparalled … none can measure …

She staggered, a pain crackling across her skin, sharp, as if she'd been scratched by thorns. She doubled over for a moment, unable to believe that anything could assail her.

A vision flickered before her, a forest wreathed in green. There was a warmth, a distasteful sense of purity and cleanliness.

Who dares!

She straightened, grimacing against the pain, gesturing with an outstretched hand and pulling the image towards herself.

She frowned.

She could see a girl, dressed in simple travellers' garb standing before a forest, her own hands outstretched. She was stepping forward cautiously.

An interloper! On the edge of Fangrim! Someone who knows the ways of the forest and seeks to …

Shareth's fury blazed.

BEGONE TRESPASSER! YOU ARE NOT WELCOME HERE!

She stared at the image of the girl, recognising her.

The Fey-girl! But she is just a child! She too has entered the Icemark and already stands at the borders of Fangrim?

Shareth knew the Fey of old. They were an ancient people, in tune with the lands about them, learning their ways after long association. Through their tending they could sway flora and fauna to their whim within their realms. In the Icemark most of them resided within the vast Forest of Fangrim and it was seldom that they ventured beyond. Shareth watched their comings and goings, they were few and far between, the spells she had woven into the mists around the edge of their realm advised her when they moved outside.

But this girl seeks to break my spell.

WHO DO YOU THINK ARE YOU? DO NOT DARE TO …

Shareth could see her now. The girl was concentrating, her eyes closed, her arms outstretched.

There was a crack. Shareth clasped at her head as pain smote across it. Her spell was broken, she could no longer tell what was happening.

Shareth shook her head to clear it.

The Fey-girl has a power … the Fey have not wielded such strength in uncounted moons …

She staggered, grasping hold of a pillar to steady herself, hardly able to credit that anyone had the strength to even attempt to defy her. Rage shook her for long moments, but then melted into mirth.

Shareth laughed.

She seeks the boy, her beloved. She will come to me, pining for him, as surely as the Moonprince himself. I will defile the boy for her and once she realises all she hopes for can never come to pass, then will she will be slain too and her people subjugated! A Fey-Girl, A Moonprince and a representative of the Wise, none of them will prevail ... My victory will be all the greater, yet I must be swift ... now is the time to extend my power to its fullest extent!

Chapter Four

Careneon the Barbarian stands at the Fortress of Careneon looking west into the mist.

Fires were burning along the walls of the fortress, but they did little to pierce the gloom, their brands marked by orange halos, receding in the distance. Only the nearest of the four roughhewn walls and turrets could be seen, the thick mists of the Icemark had drifted through the Forest of Fenun, smothering everything in their thick pall.

Careneon the Barbarian pulled his cloak tighter about him, warding off the chill. The mists had a taint about them which had grown stronger in recent moons. Something about them was unwholesome, as if they sapped the strength and courage out of your very soul.

Careneon grunted. The mists would languish for days, the sun powerless to dispel them. It would make managing his domain difficult for a week or so.

'Doubtless the Heartstealer's doing,' he said to himself. 'Her evil seeps into everything like a foul, rotten damp.'

Careneon's fortress lay at the heart of the forest and his domain stretched many leagues about him, he had dominion over all lands south and west of the forest, managed by his two subjects, Torinarg and Anvortheon. The Barbarians ruled these regions, the Outlands as they were called, all the way east until the Mountains of Talenim rose up, beyond that lay the lands of the Fey.

The Barbarians did not venture there without good reason.

Out of the mist to the west came the sound of horses' hooves at a gallop. Careneon looked over the wall. At first he could see nothing on account of the fog, but then discerned the glare of torches and a dozen armed men on horseback. Careneon could just make out the banner held at the fore of the group and recognised the standard of Torinarg.

'Open the gate!' Careneon called. A drawbridge was lowered, and the gates swung outward. He walked down to the courtyard as the riders rode in.

'Torinarg?'

'My Liege.'

Something in his tone gave away his intent; Torinarg wouldn't have ridden in without reason and Careneon could see the horses had been pushed hard.

'Inside,' Careneon said. 'We'll not speak with this mist about, I do not trust it.'

Careneon called for meat and ale to be made ready, before he and Torinarg stepped within the halls of the fortress.

Torinarg was a loyal subject. A strong man and a capable warrior, he had taken part in many campaigns throughout the Outlands under Careneon's banner. He lacked imagination and had little head for strategy. He was best when given an objective, something he would hold to doggedly until it was done.

Servants brought in the repast and Careneon gestured to it. Torinarg nodded his thanks and began to eat and drink.

'You didn't ride here just for my ale,' Careneon prompted.

'Indeed not, my Liege,' Torinarg said. 'News. An army has issued from the Gate of Varenorn.'

Careneon frowned.

'An army? Whose army?'

'We couldn't see the banners clear in the mist, but a garrison nonetheless, riders, bearing north. We were on patrol at the forest boundaries when we spotted them on the Plains of Anviniel and have ridden here ahead of them.'

'Iceguard,' Careneon spat. 'Returning after their ignominious defeat in the south no doubt, creeping back to the foul bosom of she who sent them. She still thinks she can traverse our lands …'

'She is impudent,' Torinarg agreed.

'We have waylaid enough of them in the last few moons,' Careneon said. 'At least that gives us some information about what happens beyond our borders.'

'If they tell the truth,' Torinarg replied. 'Rumours of wars in the lands to the south, great battles, some upset so it seems.'

Careneon grunted in reply.

'Imgorad granted the Heartstealer's minions safe passage through the gate for a time,' he said. 'We did well out of that treaty so he said, but that agreement came to an end several moons ago. Now our borders are closed to them again.'

'And a good thing I venture,' Torinarg said. 'I never much liked having the Iceguard moving through our realm without challenge.'

Careneon nodded and then frowned.

'They're riding through with just one garrison?' he asked. 'Seems strange they would travel with so few given we no longer have a treaty.'

Torinarg nodded. 'It is said that her father was dispatched by a legendary warrior of those southern realms. Perhaps these few are all that remains to her of the forces she sent south.'

Careneon laughed. 'Then let us deprive of her of that too and put her back in her place. They'll be weary after travelling through the tunnels. A slap to her pretty face if so!'

Torinarg nodded, but didn't say anything.

'You don't think it's wise? Speak man.'

'The Heartstealer's wrath is fierce. Would it not be more prudent to let her vent it on the Giants or the Dwarves?'

'Prudent perhaps,' Careneon muttered. 'But I'll not suffer her lackeys to ride through my realm unchallenged. I'll muster my men. Eat up! We'll ride out to meet them.'

Luxor looked up as he and Rorthron rode past the base of the tower. They had seen it from the gate, some four leagues distant, standing tall in the manner of those of the Wise.

'The Wise live in the Icemark too?' Luxor asked. 'I was under the impression they were inhabitants of Midnight alone.'

Rorthron shook his head.

'No Moonprince. All these lands were traversed by the Wise before the Frozen Wastes sealed them off from each other, but I fear you will find no more help from them here than you did in Midnight. They are likely just as moribund as their companions to the south, if not more so, lost in a dreamless sleep, waiting for the world to change about them.'

The tower was still and quiet, with no hint of life about it. The garrison rode on. The plain undulated about them, before a line of trees could be seen ahead. A well-worn track led northwards along the flanks of the forest, heading towards the mountains they had seen from the gate.

Luxor held up his hand and the army came to a stop.

'Tarithel would have likely ridden through the forest,' Rorthron said. 'With her forest lore it would have been the quicker and easier path.'

Luxor nodded. 'We have no such powers and our riders will be slowed down. This is an unfamiliar land, we should take the obvious route.'

Rorthron nodded, but said nothing. He was peering east into the trees.

'You see something?' Luxor asked.

'A mist creeps through the trees,' Rorthron replied. 'I fear it is not just driven by the new warmth of spring.'

Luxor squinted into the distance. He could see the mist rolling over the trees, their tops sometimes visible and at other times not as the mist flowed between their trunks. The mist seemed almost hesitant, sometimes hardly moving at all, but then surging forward to engulf more trees in its damp gloom.

'It's almost alive,' Luxor said. 'You suspect some fell magic of the Heartstealer?'

'Perhaps.'

'If she can command a storm, then a mist would be a trifle for her.'

'We would be best to avoid it if we can I feel,' Rorthron said. 'Whatever its purpose might be.'

They turned their horses around and followed the path northwards. The mountains grew closer ahead of them. The forest reached almost to their flanks, but thinned out before them. To the east the forest stretched out of sight, silent and draped in the mist, which had moved no closer towards them. It swirled around the trees as if unwilling to venture out into the plains.

Ahead Luxor could see a building towering out of the trees. The land was rising as they continued north. As they topped a rise they could see it before them. Luxor once more pulled his horse to a stop.

'What manner of building is that?'

It was old, its sides worn and scarred from long exposure to the elements. It was sharp and austere, a vast pyramid set upon a rocky outcrop jutting from the mountainside. It towered into the heavens, reaching far above the tallest trees, seeming to almost stretch as high as the mountains themselves.

'I am not certain,' Rorthron replied. 'I believe such structures to be related to the henges of our homeland. Temples of a sort.'

'To construct such a thing,' Luxor said. 'Why it would take thousands of men working for uncounted moons ...'

'Or other means,' Rorthron said. We should be cautious; it is clearly ancient and may harbour dark and mysterious forces.'

'Reason enough to give it a wide berth,' Luxor agreed. 'These lands are truly strange. I see no villages, no towns, scarce evidence of any habitation.'

'That may ease our passage,' Rorthron said. 'A blessing.'

'If it be that I will gladly take it,' Luxor said with a grin. 'But where now? The road leads to the right now, through the forest.'

'The trees seem to be thinning out and the mist lies behind us,' Rorthron said. 'Imorthorn's realm lies to the north-east if Tarithel's directions were correct. We should stay on the path, it is taking us the way we wish to go. With luck we can clear this forest by nightfall.'

They rode on, turning to follow the path to the right, passing the vast Temple to their left side. The path wound down into the forests. Thin traceries of the mists hovered between the trunks, blocking any view eastwards.

Tarithel rode onwards through the Forest of Fangrim. The trees were of a different type to those of her home in the Forest of Dreams, taller, of a harder wood and with narrow leaves. Some bore needles, the ground beneath them carpeted in a thick mat of brown where they had fallen.

The forest was still about her, she heard few animals and no birds. Álainn plodded on through the trees.

She sensed the faint tending of the Fey about her, but it seemed stale and old, as if it had been many moons since her people had come this way. She recalled the strange barrier at the edge, the hostile thorns and brambles at the perimeter of the wood. Was it a defence against those outside, or a cage for those within?

That face. Shareth, she who has taken Morkin. She already knows I am here.

Tarithel knew she had announced her presence to the sorceress. What Shareth might do as a result she did not know. There was nothing for it but to press on. Imorthorn's city couldn't be far ahead.

She was climbing, Álainn having to canter to gain a rise in the land. As they came to the top Tarithel could see a small clearing. Below, stretching about before her was a valley and there, nestled between two low hills was a city.

She gasped. It was grand, with minarets and parapets rising high above a circular stone wall, itself many dozens of feet high. She could see flags and banners waving in the breeze. About it lay a succession of concentric gardens, well-tended, their flowers and trees visible even from miles away. A wide road ran to it, and Tarithel could see carts, horses and people walking to and fro. She could spy men upon the walls, their helms glinting in the sunlight.

Amidst the fields were a series of villages, neatly ordered about the city. Smoke rose from chimneys. The vale seemed at peace.

'Imorthorn,' she said. 'It has to be.'

She turned Álainn and spurred her onwards down towards the city.

The men of Midnight travelled for another league without incident before Rorthron signalled for a halt.

The Moonriders came to halt behind Luxor, their horses snorting and pawing.

Rorthron dismounted and walked forward, his staff before

him. The mist swirled around, retreating as he walked forwards. Light glimmered from the tip of his staff. He paused for a moment, before whirling about and striding back.

'What is it?' Luxor demanded.

'We are not alone in this forest,' Rorthron said.

It was only then that Luxor noticed the silence all around. The mist seemed to have drained the sounds from the very air. He could hear nothing, no breath of wind, no birds, no animals. Everything was still and serene, as if the forest held its breath.

The horses were nervous, pacing sideways as their riders tried to hold them in line. Luxor watched as the mist swirled up behind them and to either of the flanks.

It encircles us, as if it were a trap.

Instinctively, he pulled his sword. His men did likewise and the sounds of unsheathing metal pierced the damp air.

No sooner had he done so than he heard a cry. It came from before them, answered by another on their right and left side. The cries of men; the cries of battle.

'Form up!' Luxor yelled.

The Moonguard were well-trained, their horses disciplined. Within seconds the garrison had arranged itself in a protective formation guarding forwards, its flanks and its rear. Halberds were ready and lowered between each horse, forming a formidable defence; swords were raised, with each warrior braced for battle.

Out of the mist figures came running, screaming at the top of the lungs.

They brandished spears and short swords, carrying circular shields daubed with paint. But none of them were the same. In the brief moments he had available to him Luxor could make out tall men, short men, men with beards, youngsters, all charging towards the massed ranks of the Moonguard, heedless of any formation.

A yell came from one.

'Death to the Iceguard!'

Luxor raised his sword and prepared to meet the foe, clipping his visor into place on his helm.

'Hold!' he yelled. 'Hold the line!'

Rorthron broke from the ranks. Luxor watched in stunned dismay as the old man rode forth, alone and unprotected towards the onrushing attackers.

'Rorthron ...!'

Luxor saw him hold his staff aloft, a blaze of light glowing from the top. Then, with a thump of energy, a pulse of power shocked outwards, throwing the attackers to the ground. The horses of the Moonguard reared and whinnied in surprise and fear. Luxor wrestled with his own steed as it bucked beneath him.

Rorthron's voice sounded out, somehow amplified, rising above the tumult.

'Cease this battle! We are not your foes!'

The attackers were back on their feet, grabbing the weapons they had lost as they had fallen, forming loose ranks around the Moonguard, hemming them in on every side. For a moment, all was chaos as men shouted in alarm and fear.

Then a man stepped forward, dressed in a mix of armour and animal fur, a horned helmet atop his head, another stepped up behind him. More shouts, but they were authoritative. The men about them grew silent.

The pair could be seen to be scrutinising the men of the Moonguard.

'You are trespassers in the Outlands,' the first man called. 'We will not suffer you to pass.'

Rorthron turned his horse and rode across towards him. The men raised their swords and spears in readiness. Luxor spurred his horse forward and joined him.

'We have no quarrel with you,' Luxor said. 'We are strangers in this land, we seek guidance, not battle.'

'An Iceguard trick,' the first man said. 'Sorcery and evil arts I deem. We will rid the Icemark of the foul servants of the Heartstealer!'

'Heartstealer?' Luxor cried. 'She is my sworn foe, I have travelled weary leagues from the south to right the wrongs she has inflicted on me and mine.'

The man stopped, looking from Luxor to Rorthron and back, with a wary expression on his face.

'The south?' the man queried. 'Then who are you? From whence do you hail?'

Luxor sheathed his sword and climbed down from his horse, striding toward the other man. They stood face to face. Luxor pulled the helm from his head.

'I am Lord Luxor, Moonprince of Midnight.'

A gasp rumbled through the ranks of men. The leader looked at his companion who nodded.

'Then, the rumours are true,' he said. 'You slew the Heartstealer's father, the Witchking of the southern lands?'

'With this very sword,' Luxor replied, drawing his sword once more and holding it aloft. 'Though not alone, I might add. Many valiant warriors played their part, many at the cost of their lives.'

The man looked Luxor up and down once more before signalling for his men to lower their weapons. Luxor turned aside and gestured to his own men to do the same.

'I am Careneon of the Outlands,' the man said. 'This is Torinarg, a worthy vassal. This is my territory you stand upon.'

'It was not our intention to trespass,' Luxor said. 'We come to the Icemark with not even a map to guide our path.'

'And you?' Careneon said, looking up to where Rorthron was still seated upon his horse.

'I am Rorthron,' Rorthron replied.

'Of the Wise,' Luxor added.

Careneon's eyes widened. 'The Wise! They travel amongst us once more?'

Rorthron nodded.

'Who else but you could wield such a power,' Careneon said, awestruck. 'Such a thing has not been heard of in many lives of men.'

'Well ... we have just the one,' Luxor said, with a grin. 'But, as you saw, potent indeed.'

Careneon turned back to Luxor. 'And what is your business in the Icemark, Moonprince?'

'I seek the City of Imorthorn,' Luxor said.

'The Fey?' Careneon asked. There was a tone of disgust in his voice. A rumble of distaste echoed around Careneon's men.

'Do you know the way?' Luxor asked.

'We do not venture in the realm of the Fey,' Careneon replied. 'They are tricksy folk, treacherous and unpredictable. They do not suffer us to pass into their woodland realms and we guard our borders against their traps and spells. They are of the faerie and not to be trusted.'

'It is there I must go,' Luxor replied.

'They will not let you pass,' Careneon said. 'If you try to pass the borders of their land they will set upon you.'

'Nevertheless ...'

Careneon paused, seeing the determination on Luxor's face.

'I would speak to you at length, Moonprince,' he said, looking about him. 'These are my lands. Only by my permission can you cross them. But it is not wise to talk in the open. The mists overhear our words ... we must be wary. You will come with me to my fortress. It is but two leagues away in the forest. You will be welcome. Any foe of the Heartstealer is a friend of those who dwell in the south.'

Luxor looked at Rorthron, who nodded.

'Then we are in your debt,' Luxor replied. 'A rest would be welcomed by all of us.'

'You are brave indeed to ride into the Icemark unaware of its cares,' Careneon said. 'These lands are deeply troubled. But perhaps your arrival may change things. Come, let us make haste.'

The men of the Outlands and the riders of the Moonguard turned and headed south-east into the depths of the forest.

Chapter Five

Imorthorn the Fey stands in the City of Imorthorn looking south-west to the Forest of Fangrim.

The road into the valley widened, becoming better tended as Tarithel progressed. Before long she could see other travellers making their way towards and away from the city ahead. The valley widened out into fields and farmlands. It seemed the ways of the Fey kept the land fertile and productive, unlike the cold desolation she had encountered on her way from Varenorn.

There was a faint warmth in the spring air, the sun stronger as it rose higher above the city. The traffic along the road increased until she was following in a long line of carts, riders and folks on foot. All were Fey, she saw no men at all.

No one paid her the slightest attention, her travelling gear giving her a cloak of anonymity. It allowed her to listen in to the chatter all about her.

She learned that many of the great Lords of the Fey of this realm were in residence within the city. Lord Imorthorn himself had called a council it seemed and many of his vassals were here. Tarithel could see the banners flying and armies camped around the walls.

This could be to my advantage. If they will give me an audience, perhaps the Fey can be roused to Luxor's service as one!

Thus encouraged, she rode on, patting Álainn to reassure her. The gates were open, with folk going in and out. It seemed the realm was at peace. Tarithel looked about her in delight, the city was fair and bright, decorated with plants, trees and flowers amidst the banners. The buildings were constructed of proud white stones, unblemished and clean. The people about her seemed happy for the most part, shopping and bartering with the traders within the city walls. Tarithel could see meats, fruits, grain and bread being sold. The crowds were thick; these Fey prospered.

She swung down from Álainn, leading her to the stables. A stable boy took the reins from her, giving her a decorated ribbon in return, so she could find her later on. She walked back out into the sunlight and headed towards the second gate which led towards the main city buildings within a second protective wall. Towers rose high above her as she approached.

This gate was guarded. Two armour-clad warriors stood either side of the entrance, scrutinising anyone who drew close. She saw them straighten as she walked up. Her progress was barred as they crossed their spears in front of her.

'The inner city is closed this day,' one guard said. 'Lord Imorthorn is in council and will brook no interruption.'

Tarithel dropped her cowl, revealing her features. She pulled out the jewel hung about her neck that marked her as Lady of the Forest. It was a clear signal of rank.

'Not even to a lady from beyond his realm?' she said, her voice high and authoritative. 'I have travelled far and through many perils to reach him.'

The guards exchanged a look before bowing before her.

'My apologies, my Lady,' the guard replied, straightening once more. 'We were not informed of your arrival. Lord Imorthorn left no–'

'He will not be expecting me,' Tarithel said. 'But I hope he will receive me.'

'Might I enquire as to your name and from whence you come?' the guard said.

'You may,' Tarithel said. 'I am Tarithel, Lady of the Forest, daughter of Araleth, Lord of the Citadel of Dreams in the land of Midnight.'

The guards stared at her, before exchanging an astonished glance.

'Announce me,' Tarithel said. 'For I am in much haste.'

The first guard nodded. 'I will take your request to Lord Imorthorn, my Lady. Please wait here.'

'My Lord, we have heard nothing from the Heartstealer in many moons. She is prone to wrath of many sorts, but she does not see fit to turn it upon us. I counsel to leave well alone. She has no quarrel with us.'

Imgorthand the Fey was a tall fellow, even for a Fey. His eyes were grey and he sported short cut black hair and trimmed beard to match. He stood within the inner halls of Imorthorn's city. About them the walls of the room were decorated by both intricately carved wood and ornately manicured plants, both sturdy and strong, yet alive and vibrant.

'She hems us in, league by league,' another Fey Lord argued. 'We have seen her enchantments at our borders, stealing away the very lifeblood of our forests. She will not engage us directly whilst she can sap our strength bit by bit from afar.'

Sitting across from Imgorthand was Carorthane, a sturdier Fey and older, with flecks of grey marring his long hair. He sat next to his brother, Carorthand. The resemblance between the two was obvious, though Carorthane was the elder.

'We see it all the time,' Carorthand agreed. 'She is wily, pitching the Dwarves against our northern realms, sowing seeds of discontent amongst them.'

'The Dwarves are always discontented,' Imgorthand replied. 'Their lands are riven by factions following first one leader and then another. It's easy for them to blame us for their own failings.'

'Which the Heartstealer supports,' Carorthane said. 'She inflames their insecurities and offers a seeming hand of friendship to them, all the while blaming us for their problems. She does not need to go to war with us; the Dwarves will act on her behalf!'

'And what of the Barbarians?' Imgorthand said. 'A greater threat, I'd wager. They prowl the lands west of here. Have we forgotten how they usurped the Forest of Fenun? Perhaps they draw up plans for Fangrim too.'

'That is an ancient feud,' Carorthane replied. 'And not one we should be proud of, we were as much as fault as they ...'

A fourth figure raised a hand. Conversation ceased. Lord Imorthorn looked around at them. He too was old, even as the Fey measured time. His face was kind, but lined with care, a full beard of grey with matching hair sweeping back from a broad forehead.

The four Fey leaders sat around an old oak table. It was pitted and scarred with evidence of long use. Upon its surface was engraved a map of the Icemark. Despite heavy use, the map was still clear to gaze upon, the various realms marked out. The homelands of the Fey to the south and east. Barbarians in the outlands to the south-west. The Giants to the north-west and the Iceguard to the north-east, with the realm of the Dwarves in the centre.

'The Barbarians do not trust us and we do not trust them,' Imorthorn said. 'That serves both of us well enough for now. The Barbarians have even less love for the Heartstealer than we do. They have set upon the Iceguard when they have the temerity to cross their realms. In that they do us a service. Yes, they are a proud and arrogant people, but that accusation can be levelled at us with equal weight.'

Carorthane and Carorthand nodded, Imgorthand did not.

'The Dwarves do concern me,' Imorthorn continued. 'Thormand tells me he has countered many small incidents in his lands, petty skirmishes along our borders. Their internal wars continue and sides are being drawn up.'

'The Dwarves always fight amongst themselves,' Imgorthand said. 'It has always been that way.'

'Yes,' Imorthorn said. 'But it seems we have two major camps consolidating in their realm. One sets themselves against the will of the Heartstealer by all accounts, the other seems willing to accommodate her wishes. Thormand believes the latter is in the ascendancy. This does not bode well for us. The Dwarves have always been a buffer between our realm and that of the Heartstealer. We have worked long to keep it that way.'

'The Dwarves would never attack us directly,' Imgorthand replied.

'But bolstered by the Heartstealer's own forces?' Carorthane answered, looking at Imorthorn. 'I believe they might. They have always been in a precarious position, caught between all the other races of Icemark.'

'They must know they too would fall foul of the Heartstealer's plans in time,' Imgorthand said. 'She has always desired dominion over all of the Icemark.'

'Our people count many more moons than do the other races,' Imorthorn said. 'What seems to us the recent past is myth and legend to the Dwarves and Barbarians. Not even the giants match us for longevity. The Heartstealer can afford to wait a generation and then spin her lies in new and enticing ways to those that will listen. And now, with the demise of her father …'

'Has there been news from the south?' Imgorthand asked, looking around.

Imorthorn shook his head. 'We received no response to the message we sent, nor can we be certain that it was even received, my falcon did not return. The storm swung back north within days. A moon has passed with no news.'

'We feared the Heartstealer might march hard and swift upon Midnight,' Carorthane said. 'But no, all seems quiet as far north as our scouts dare go. We hear no rumours from the Giants or the Dwarves of anything untoward.'

'She does not need to send her own armies if she can foment the Dwarves to do her work for her,' Imorthorn said. 'Let them weaken both themselves and us and it will be all the easier for her to ravage what remains. Doubtless she plays such a game with the Giants and the Barbarians. She schemes anew. I fear the relative peace we have had for the last hundred moons is at an end.'

'Then what is to be done?' Imgorthand asked. 'Prepare for war with the Dwarves? One such enemy we might face, but we cannot stand against all the Iceguard. If we rise against the Dwarves, the Barbarians will sweep in from the west to take advantage. One false move …'

'Plays into the Heartstealer's hands,' Imorthorn said. 'Indeed.'

There was a knock at the door.

'Come!' Imorthorn called out.

A servant entered, bowing low before striding towards the table at which the Lords were seated.

'Speak.'

'My Lord, apologies for the intrusion, but you have a visitor.'

Imorthorn frowned. 'A visitor? All my guests are present, there are no more to come. Who is it?'

'A lady, my lord. She says you will receive her.'

Imorthorn looked around at the other Lords, all of them looked bewildered too.

'Does she now,' Imorthorn said, with a trace of mirth. 'Her name?'

'She calls herself the Lady Tarithel,' the servant said.

A rumble of conversation flowed between the Lords accompanied by frowns and shaking heads, it was clear the name was known to none of them.

'And from whence does this Lady Tarithel claim to come?' Imorthorn demanded.

The servant swallowed.

'She says she has travelled alone from the land of Midnight, sire. She says she is the daughter of a Lord of Dreams.'

Imorthorn stared at him for a long moment, before looking around at his council. They were muttering, glancing at each other in surprise.

'From Midnight? It cannot be!'

'A woman, travelling such a perilous road alone?'

'How did she pass the borders of the forest unseen?'

'She must be bringing news of the wars to the south …'

Imorthorn held up his hand and the hubbub subsided.

'Well then, it would seem the message we sent was received after all,' he said. He turned to the servant. 'Her arrival is more than timely. Most interesting. Bring her to us forthwith!'

Luxor and Rorthron were seated on huge wooden benches, piled high with animal skins. Across from them Careneon and Torinarg also sat, between them an enormous boar, spit-roasted, turned over a fire that crackled and roared. The room within Careneon's fortress was stone built and bare, save for a wide variety of fierce-looking weapons, helms, armour and other implements of war that were hung upon the walls.

Careneon produced a knife, stabbed the boar and ripped out of a chunk of meat from it. Torinarg followed his example. Careneon gestured to Luxor and Rorthron. Luxor copied the move with his own knife and Rorthron followed.

'So,' Careneon began, 'Your business in the Icemark. You ride against the Heartstealer?'

'I seek my son,' Luxor replied. 'Taken by her foul sorcery.'

'Your son?' Careneon said. 'How so?'

'A storm,' Luxor said. 'Sent from her to our lands. When it cleared, he was missing, spirited away.'

'A storm did indeed blow through these lands perhaps two moons ago,' Careneon mused. 'And it felt like her sorcery. You believe the Heartstealer has taken your son?'

Luxor nodded.

'How do you know this?' Torinarg asked.

Luxor looked over to Rorthron.

'I spoke to her,' Rorthron said. 'She has him in her clutches, brandishing him as a tempting morsel to entice us into her trap.'

'And trap it is,' Careneon said. 'You bring but a garrison, Moonprince. I do not doubt they are mighty men of war and seasoned warriors, but the Heartstealer can summon a hundred times your strength with ease. You have not the might to take her on and she is a sorceress besides. She will crush you should you try to face her.'

'As I mentioned before,' Luxor said. 'I seek only the return of my son.'

'She will not give him up,' Careneon replied, offhand. 'And you cannot forge a path to him without great strength of arms. I see no way you can succeed. Your son is lost.'

'I cannot accept that,' Luxor answered.

Careneon shrugged. 'Then ride on by all means, but it will be your death. Shareth is both evil and powerful.'

'Do not the people of the Icemark wish to see an end to her evil?' Luxor asked. 'We rose up against the Witchking in Midnight and threw him down. It was a hard won battle, but victory went to the Free! You said a foe of the Heartstealer was a friend to those in the south. Can the same not happen here?'

Torinarg laughed, but Careneon gestured for silence.

'We would see her ended sure enough, Moonprince,' Careneon said. 'I would slay her myself if I could, but there is no might in Icemark that can assail her. My folk do not have the means and we must defend our borders against the Giants, the Dwarves and the Fey.'

'The Fey of Midnight are an honourable folk,' Luxor said. 'They stood with us against the Witchking and lost many of their own in the struggle. I do not see why they would not also stand against the Heartstealer.'

'I would not stand next to any Fey,' Torinarg said, his voice cool.

'Nor I,' Careneon said. 'Moonprince, you know little of these lands, so I will explain it for you. Icemark is riven with conflict. We have grievances against the Fey. They poisoned our lands and sent our folk into starvation during harsh winters, evil memories that remain lodged deep in the hearts of my folk. Doubtless they will claim some story of woe against us in return.'

Luxor frowned.

'But even if some treaty could be brokered, that would not be enough,' Careneon continued. 'We fear the Heartstealer, but respect her. The others we hate. The Giants oppress us from the north and oft side with the Heartstealer against us. There are also the Dwarves …'

'And what of them?' Rorthron asked, venturing into the conversation.

'Only a Dwarf's axe is honest,' Torinarg said. 'A phrase taught from childhood in these parts.'

Luxor sighed.

'And beyond them the Heartstealer has her own forces,' Careneon said. 'The Iceguard are men akin to us, but harsh, cold and brutal, well versed in the arts and stratagems of war. They swear fealty to her and they number as many as all the other people of the Icemark combined. They are mighty indeed! Venture northwards and you will be set upon by any number of hostile forces, long before you even reach the realm of the Heartstealer. Many would likely want to capture you themselves and hand you over to her to curry her favour. You will find few friends here, fewer that you could utterly trust and none that would take on the Heartstealer in open conflict. That is folly of the utmost degree.'

'So what do you advise?' Luxor demanded.

'Turn back,' Careneon said. 'Look to your homeland. The Heartstealer knows you killed her father. She will seek your death first and then the subjugation of your lands. She has sent armies through the Gate of Varenorn in the past; her might is such that we cannot prevent it here. She will try to take her father's throne back, mark my words.'

Luxor looked at Rorthron.

'This she has already sworn to do,' Rorthron said. 'We seek to prevent that fate.'

'Then retreat now,' Careneon said. 'Whilst you still can. Guard your own lands and make what preparations you can against her attack. Only death awaits you in the Icemark.'

'You ask me to abandon my son and heir,' Luxor said, glaring at Careneon. 'Is that what you would do?'

'Consider him already dead,' Careneon said. 'Likely that is so. She has slain many. We of the Icemark know her wrath all too well. None ever escape from the clutches of the Heartstealer once she takes them.'

Tarithel was escorted along dark, wooden-panelled corridors within the grand buildings of Imorthorn's city. She could smell polish in the air, the city had a sense of age and preservation about it, reminding her of the halls of her own home in the Citadel of Dreams far to the south. The walls of the corridor were decorated with the heraldry of many different families of the Fey, though none were familiar to her.

She had paid little heed to the long annals of history that her father often enjoyed poring over in the libraries of his citadel.

Sometime long in the past these people and mine would have been kin, but we have long been sundered from each other. Here I am, the lone representative of the Fey of Midnight.

She swallowed, her stomach clenching within her, her breath short.

I am Lady of the Forest. I have seen and done much. I can stand proud!

Her footsteps echoed on the smooth floor. Before her, the servant who was leading her stopped at a pair of huge, wooden-panelled doors. Their handles were wrought in metal, ornate and ancient.

'Come!' called a voice from within.

The servant opened the door and gestured for her to walk in.

Tarithel did so.

'Lady Tarithel, daughter of the Lords of Dreams, from the realm of Midnight, sire.'

Tarithel could see four Fey lords sitting around a table at the far end of the hall. The room was tall and airy, lit by windows high up along both sides, from which sunlight streamed in. Finely carved wooden decorations covered the walls. She was pleased to see many plants and greenery complimented the overall ambiance. The room smelt fresh, like the first breath of air in a forest or woodland. She could see the table before her was carved, bearing the details of a map.

As she entered they all stood. The tallest, grey haired and stern looking, beckoned to her. She walked forward and curtseyed, in the custom of the Fey of Midnight.

The tall Fey bowed.

'You are welcome in my halls, Tarithel of Dreams and of Midnight,' he said. 'I am Imorthorn, Lord of this city.' He gestured to his right. 'Here are Lords Carorthane and Carorthand.' Then he swept his arm to the right. 'And Lord Imgorthand.'

All three of them bowed to her again. She curtseyed in response.

'I thank you,' she said. 'It has been a long road.'

'You have travelled to us alone?' Imorthorn asked. 'With no escort? No companions?'

Tarithel swallowed.

'I was in much haste, my Lord,' she said. 'Your message caused my people much consternation and then ...'

'Is it true?' Carorthane asked. 'There is a Moonprince and he has slain the Witchking who long held the realm of Midnight in his grasp?'

'It is as you say,' Tarithel answered. 'Lord Luxor was victorious more than two moons ago ...'

'And the Heartstealer was sore angered by that news!' Carorthane said, laughing.

'Her anger has been provoked,' Imgorthand said. 'Her fury is at a height not seen before, all because of this Moonprince. I deem this does not bode well for us.'

'Lords,' Imorthorn said, holding up a hand. 'Let the Lady Tarithel speak and let us listen first. There will be time enough for our questions.' He turned to Tarithel. 'I will not forget my hospitality. You have come a long and weary way, would you not rest and eat before we bombard you further with our questions?'

'Your words are a sweetness to my ears, Lord Imorthorn,' she replied. 'And I would gladly avail myself of your kindness. But there is an urgency to my arrival which you do not know. I would have you know it before I rest.'

Imorthorn nodded.

'Then take a seat and speak,' he said. He looked around at the other Fey, gesturing at them. 'And no questions until she is done.'

The other Lords subsided. All took their seats. Tarithel looked at each one in turn.

'We received your message on the very day we were gathered to celebrate the Witchking's demise,' Tarithel began. 'Some doubted its provenance, but my father assured us it was genuine and it was much discussed. The storm you warned us of arrived soon after, crashing upon my home with fury. At first it seemed that little damage was done, but then ...'

Tarithel saw Imorthorn lean forward.

'... then we found Luxor's ... the Moonprince's ... son, my betrothed, he who destroyed the Ice Crown of the Witchking ... Morkin ... he was gone.'

'Gone?' Imorthorn echoed.

Tarithel nodded, tears coming to her eyes. 'Lord Luxor sent scouts everywhere, but no trace could be found. He had been spirited away.'

'By the Heartstealer herself?' Carorthane asked, before subsiding at a look from Imorthorn.

Tarithel nodded, trying to steady her voice. 'She has him in her grasp this very moment. I ride to rescue him.'

Imgorthand coughed, stifling a laugh. There was a long moment of silence.

'You would pitch yourself against the Heartstealer?' Imgorthand asked. 'Alone? My lady, she is a fell and mighty sorceress and you are but a ...'

Tarithel narrowed her eyes and was about to respond.

Imorthorn raised his voice. 'Peace.' He turned to Tarithel. 'Again I say ... you are weary after your long journey. I have many questions, but may I suggest you would be best served now by good food and rest. My city is your city. Would you join me for luncheon, Lady Tarithel?'

'I cannot tarry,' Tarithel said. 'There is little time.'

'You will need my permission to cross my lands,' Imorthorn said, looking up, his voice a touch sterner. 'I am likely to give it to you, but I would know more of what has transpired. There is time enough. If you truly seek the Heartstealer she lies hundreds of leagues away through many domains, mostly hostile to the people of the Fey. Would you not learn more from us before you embark upon such a quest?'

Tarithel sighed.

'I am sorry, Lord Imorthorn,' she said, with a nod. 'My words were impertinent. I meant not to cause offense.'

'And you have not done so,' Imorthorn replied, his voice softer once more. 'I would see you welcomed in a proper manner. You are the first of your people to visit us in more moons than many of us remember. I would see that marked at least.'

Tarithel bowed her head.

Imorthorn reached out and pulled a nearby bell-cord. A tinkle of bells sounded from somewhere above.

The servant returned within moments.

'Have chambers prepared for the Lady Tarithel,' he instructed. 'With hot water and such clothes as she would like. She will join me for luncheon at the midday hour.'

The servant bowed.

'If you will follow me, my Lady?' he said.

Tarithel got to her feet, curtseying once more to the Fey Lords.

'Lords.'

They also rose and bowed, watching as she departed with the servant. The door closed behind her.

Luxor stared back at Careneon across the fire, his appetite lost.

'You say the Heartstealer has sworn,' Careneon said, 'to take Midnight and to venture even further south. This she will do, there is nothing you can do about it. She has might beyond any other in Icemark … she is a sorceress herself. None dare defy her openly. We oppose her indirectly, harrying her troops when they trespass in our lands, hoping others face her greater wrath. You must see to the defence of your own lands.'

'The people of Midnight are reeling from the fight for freedom,' Luxor replied. 'Our armies weakened and tired. They are not ready to face another foe so soon. If the people of Icemark could rally together, why, she might be stopped here. Why could this not be?'

'Stopped!' Torinarg laughed. 'It is much as we can do to defend our borders from those around us. There is no stopping the Heartstealer.'

'I slew her father,' Luxor said. 'I bear a war ring of Midnight, I have allies, Rorthron here …'

'And potent they are no doubt,' Careneon said. 'But to rescue your son you would need to forge a path through to her heartlands, the Frozen Empire itself. It lies dozens of leagues to the far north, through inhospitable terrain peopled with folks who have no love for strangers. By talking to us you have likely made an enemy of others! None will trust you. You would be waylaid along the road and die in battle long before you even reached her domain. Even if you did, by some strange chance, find a way … then Shareth would not give up her prize without a fight. You would have to defeat the Heartstealer herself!'

'And that would need all the might of all the races to rally to your banner,' Torinarg added with a snide chuckle. 'Such a thing is …'

'Unlikely?' Rorthron asked, with a raised eyebrow.

'Impossible,' Torinarg said.

The conversation lapsed into silence, broken only by the crackling of the fire.

'You say you have a grievance with the Fey,' Rorthron continued.

'We have many,' Careneon said.

'And with the Giants and the Dwarves?'

'Those too,' Careneon said.

'Yet you do not perceive that you have a greater foe in the Heartstealer?' Rorthron asked.

'Yes and no,' Careneon answered. 'She could decide to extinguish us should she wish, certainly she has the might to do so, but she has always been content to reside within her own realm … until now.' He cast a dark gaze at Luxor. 'Our neighbours have more oft been at war with us than has she.'

'Surely you can see that working together would free you from her tyranny?' Luxor argued back.

Careneon shrugged. 'She is evil and cruel,' he said. 'But I could claim the same of all the others around us, Moonprince. We fight skirmishes and battles here and there, but outright war? No. She is one of many enemies and not always uppermost in our minds. We are not under her tyranny. Take her away and we would still have many foes.'

'She plays each race against each other,' Luxor said, leaning back.

'You understand our problem well, Moonprince,' Careneon said. 'Shareth is cunning. She never fights a sustained battle, nor does she approach empty handed. In the past she has paid us well for our troubles. She supports some leaders and frustrates others. We play a delicate game, vying for her favour or hoping for her lack of attention. None will risk outright war with her. The other races would be sure to take advantage of any weakened position.'

'Then she controls your destiny,' Rorthron said. 'A stalemate. She keeps you all subservient to her whim.'

Torinarg bristled.

'The Barbarians are subservient to no one.'

'Prove it,' Luxor said, matching Torinarg's glare with one of his own, just as fierce. 'You could help us defeat the Heartstealer.'

Careneon chuckled.

'Clever words,' Torinarg said from alongside his liege. 'But words alone. Will you go to the Giants and convince them too? Will you turn the fickle Fey to your ways?'

'I will talk to the Fey,' Luxor said. 'Surely I will.'

'And I will talk to the Giants,' Rorthron said.

'Words are cheap and easy,' Careneon said. 'It is deeds and actions that have meaning.'

'And what actions will you take then?' Luxor asked. 'I have no choice but to defy the Heartstealer, I cannot … will not abandon my son! If between Rorthron and myself we can bring the Fey and the Giants to my banner, what will be written of the deeds of your people when this all this is done?'

Careneon looked at Luxor and then at Rorthron. He whispered to Torinarg, who looked surprised at whatever it was Careneon had said.

Careneon looked at Luxor.

'I cannot speak on behalf of the people of the Outlands,' he said. 'It is not within my gift. Only my liege, Imgorad himself, can do that.'

'Will you take us to this Imgorad?' Luxor asked.

'I will,' Careneon said. 'You can present yourselves to him. I will vouch for your conduct and give you permission to traverse our lands. Imgorad will be interested in your tale, particularly on the demise of the Heartstealer's father. He will know more of the wider disposition of the Fey and the Giants too. Perhaps he might have some other avenues for you to pursue. Regardless, convince him and perhaps you have a start.'

'And where is he?' Luxor asked.

'His city lies some two days ride north-west,' Careneon said. 'It is not a hard journey.'

'Then we will depart upon the morrow,' Luxor declared.

'Do not expect to achieve your lofty goal of some great alliance,' Careneon added. 'Imgorad may help you on your way … and perhaps the Giants will give you leave to pass through their realm as well, but that is fully the most you can expect. If you do find a way to reach the Heartstealer, remember those of us here who warned you against such folly. It will be the death of you, Luxor of Midnight.'

Imorthorn returned to the meeting hall.

'She is resting now,' Imorthorn reported. 'She was indeed tired after a long ride.'

The Fey Lords looked at each other for long moments.

'She has ridden here alone?' Imgorthand asked. 'She is but a child.'

'To have forged a path from Midnight to the Icemark is no mean feat,' Imorthorn said. 'Few of our folk would dare such a journey, and none unaided. The way via the Gate of Varenorn is dark and evil by all accounts. I have heard tell of it, but I have never ventured into its depths.'

'And she has travelled through the Outland territories unremarked upon by the Barbarians,' Carorthand added. 'And freely walked within our forests without us knowing of it. That is not mere stealth. Some power aides her progress.'

'Then she does not tell us the whole truth,' Imgorthand said. 'There is much more to this girl than meets the eye. I do not like it. Her speech is fair and her appearance beguiling, but she acts more like a spy than anything else.'

Imorthorn rubbed his chin.

'She has much to explain,' he said. 'That's for sure.'

Carorthane nodded. 'And does she not bear a message from Lord Dreams, or this Moonprince? Or has she come upon her own initiative in pursuit of her missing betrothed? We cannot let her wander amidst the Icemark alone and unprotected, certain death awaits her. What are we to do with her?'

'All good questions my friends,' Imorthorn said. 'Questions to which I intend to find answers. I will set a watch upon her movements. Let us observe and listen carefully to what she has to say when she is rested and revived. She will not leave here until I am satisfied we understand what has transpired.'

Careneon was as good as his word. Luxor's Moonriders were well catered for and they, along with Luxor and Rorthron, Careneon, Torinarg and five hundred of his own men, rode out of the fortress as dawn broke across the Forest of Fenun.

The mist still hung close around them, swirling back and forth in the air. Most of the time it seemed to flow with the wind, but sometimes it seemed to defy it, moving with a will of its own.

'Do not speak anything of import until we are well clear of it,' Careneon said, turning his horse to lead them onwards. 'Some say it is the devilry of the Heartstealer and words spoken within it find their way back to her. I do not say that is true, but her reach is long already and there is reason enough to be cautious.'

Luxor looked over at Rorthron, who nodded.

'I would not say such things were impossible,' Rorthron replied. 'The Frozen Wastes themselves were formed out of the mists long ago. There is arcane potency involved, for sure.'

'Then let us ride out of this dankness into the clear sun,' Luxor said.

The riders retraced their path of the previous day, clearing the forest not far from the temple they had spied before. The enigmatic building rose clear of the mists and the forests, rivalling the mountains beyond for grandeur.

'Do you know who built it?' Luxor asked. 'And what it was for?'

'No,' Careneon said, in response Luxor's question. 'We do not frequent such places. Some are home to unsavoury creatures with an appetite for flesh, others harbour entrances to dark underground passages from which few are foolhardy enough to enter and even fewer return. Some of our people hold that there are curses and other evils to be found within. As for what the temples are for, none know nor care. They are scattered through the Icemark and their builders are long dead. The same goes for strange stones, towers, palaces and the like. They are best avoided.'

Their route turned northwards now. The sun brightened and the mist thinned until the last wisps disappeared. Ahead, a low line of hills could be seen. The combined armies rode on through the widening landscape. The sun rose higher, shedding a little warmth on the folk below.

'We have made good progress,' Careneon said, as they topped a rise. 'We now stand upon the Plains of Thulil. Firak's fortress is within our reach today, we will rest there tonight – he is another vassal of Imgorad, of similar rank to myself. The following day we will reach Imgorad. Then you can make your case.'

As they rode northwards Luxor spied a fortress on their right, across the plains, just visible against glare on the eastern horizon.

'Another stronghold?' Luxor asked.

Careneon nodded. 'Yonder lies the fortress of Kahudrarg. He is likewise a vassal of Imgorad and holds sway over the lands to the east nigh to the border with the Fey.'

Luxor caught the warning note in Careneon's tone.

'We will not be stopping there then,' Luxor said.

Careneon's expression was stern. 'Kahudrarg has more reason to distrust the Fey than most of my kin,' he said. 'He would not show much favour to those who count the Fey amongst their friends.'

'I see,' Luxor said. 'I am glad of your counsel, Careneon.'

'Imgorad is wiser than I,' Careneon said. 'He will listen to you, of that I am sure. Whether he will give you the answer you desire, that remains to be seen.'

'For now, an audience is all I seek,' Luxor replied.

Lord Imorthorn was standing within one of the colonnaded courtyards, enjoying the sunlight and the flowers within. Footsteps sounded nearby and he turned to see Tarithel walking towards him.

She looked refreshed, her red hair brushed and braided, her complexion bright and clear. Even from across the courtyard Imorthorn could see her bright green eyes, now matched by a gown of similar colour.

She was a striking young woman, turning heads as she strode towards him. He appraised her for a moment. She was beautiful and elegant in the manner of a high family line of the Fey, a true sense of strength was evident, yet there was a vulnerability about her too. Around her neck hung a bright jewel, also green, sparkling against her skin. The necklace marked her out as a lady, but the jewel was something even more unusual.

News of her arrival had swept around the city like wildfire, a lofty maiden from the far south, unannounced and unexpected. Already the rumours were flying, the stories growing in the telling.

Yet, is she trustworthy? And what is her true purpose? I must divine it.

Imorthorn smiled in greeting, extending a hand to her. She clasped it.

'Lady Tarithel,' he said. 'I trust you are refreshed.'

'Your hospitality is more than I could have hoped for after such a long journey,' she returned. 'I thank you.'

'I thought we might take the air a little before luncheon,' he said. 'A tour of the city if that takes your fancy?'

Tarithel nodded. 'I would love to see it.'

Imorthorn held out his arm for her and she took it. He led her along the walls for a time, pointing out the various spires, minarets, halls and houses of his city all the while telling her a little of the history of the place.

'I am gratified that you have arrived safely,' he said, leading her back towards the colonnade. 'I have no children of my own, but, if I did, I am not sure that I would have let my daughter embark on such a perilous quest alone. Your father must place great trust in you.'

He saw her smile, but it was clear there were other feelings behind her expression.

'You have already divined one of my secrets I see,' she said. 'Alas, I left without permission.'

'I can send word to your father should you wish it,' Imorthorn said. 'To let him know you have arrived here safe, at least. I daresay one of our white falcons can make the trip anew.'

'Thank you my Lord,' she answered. 'But it is not necessary; he knows of my whereabouts well enough.'

'Then you must anticipate my next question,' Imorthorn said, with a raised eyebrow.

Tarithel sighed and nodded.

'I will explain as best I can,' she replied. 'After the storm that beset my home, the one you warned us of, I received a dream, a vision if you like. I saw this fair city of yours, mountains and all manner of strange places. Then I perceived my beloved Morkin, the Moonprince's son, languishing in a dungeon, caught by the Heartstealer.'

Imorthorn listened without interruption.

'Somehow she perceived me,' Tarithel said. 'She mocked me, insulted me.'

'You spoke to her?' Imorthorn asked, the surprise evident on his face. 'The Heartstealer? In your dream?'

Tarithel nodded. 'Yes. Words came to me, strange and unknown. Your name was also given, thus I was compelled to seek you out, to find answers.'

'What other words were given?'

'Berangria,' Tarithel said. 'Imiriel and Anvireon.'

She was looking at him as she spoke, watching his face for a reaction.

'I have heard of them,' Imorthorn replied. 'Berengria was a palace in the remote north. I know little of it I'm afraid. Imiriel was, long ago, the capital of the northlands. It is rumoured to be the home of the Heartstealer herself, but no Fey have ventured that way in untold moons. It is deep within the territory of the Iceguard, they are cold men, loyal only to the Heartstealer herself. I can furnish you with a map that may provide some direction.'

'Thank you. And Anvireon?'

'A powerful Lord of the Iceguard,' Imorthorn said. 'In service to her. A loyal vassal, of which she has six. Warlords of the Iceguard they are, and greatly to be feared.'

'Imiriel is where Morkin is,' Tarithel said, her voice certain. 'I am sure of it. That is where I must go.'

Imorthorn nodded.

'I do not doubt your courage or conviction,' he said. 'To have come this far already proves your worth, but this journey is more perilous than you know. As you have heard, the distance alone is many dozens of leagues. Yet, between here and Imiriel lies more than just a weary traipse. The mountains of Anvulane are said to be impassable without a guide, and dangerous even with one. The kingdom of the Dwarves lies that way and they have little friendship with the Fey. Beyond them is the realm of the Heartstealer herself. She is known as the Empress of the Frozen Empire. Her realm is large and her powers …'

'I am not scared of her,' Tarithel interrupted.

Imorthorn paused for a moment, taking a deep breath.

'You should be,' he said.

Imorthorn saw Tarithel purse her lips. He continued.

'Every other inhabitant of the Icemark is,' he said. 'Even those who serve her. If you are captured, and I can see no way that you could avoid it, she will not be merciful. She is as cold as ice, colder even than the Wastes themselves, but subject to wrathful outbursts of temper too. She has been known to rip her foes apart with her bare hands, or to destroy them by sorcerous means. She may be more powerful, perhaps, than her father, slain at the hand of your Moonprince. Much as it pains me to do so, I must counsel you against your quest. Your betrothed … you must consider him lost. He lies beyond your grasp, beyond the grasp of any in the Icemark.'

'I will not give him up so long as he lives,' Tarithel said, her expression cold.

Imorthorn nodded, a faint smile growing on his features.

'Which is what I thought you would say,' he replied, with a faint smile. 'I can see you are determined to pursue him and little I can say will stop you. You will have need of such fortitude in the moons ahead. Come, let us take some food and we will continue.'

He led her indoors, where a buffet of different foods had been prepared upon ornate, decorated silver serving dishes and china plates. They helped themselves and continued their conversation.

'You say your father knows where you are,' Imorthorn said. 'How can this be?'

'The Moonprince,' Tarithel answered. 'He bears the last of the war rings of Midnight. It gives him the power to see and hear those loyal to him. A deep and ancient magic. It was given to him by Rorthron of the Wise.'

'The Wise,' Imorthorn said, his eyebrows raised. 'Your Moonprince has interesting allies indeed. And I know a little of these war rings. The power of far-seeing and command as I recall. So many legends out of the past seem to have come to life with your arrival.'

'He has set foot in the Icemark too,' Tarithel added. 'He rides to meet with you himself. He bids you welcome and seeks to retrieve his son as well.'

'He brings an army?'

'A garrison of the Moonguard,' Tarithel answered.

'Little enough against the hordes of the Heartstealer,' Imorthorn said. 'And he too rides from the Gate of Varenorn?'

Tarithel nodded.

'The Barbarians will intercept him long before he reaches our lands,' Imorthorn said. 'He will need all his skill with diplomacy to make his way onwards.'

'Luxor is no stranger to such things,' Tarithel answered.

'Which is all to the good,' Imorthorn replied. 'But you also came that way yourself, but alone. You must be stealthy indeed since you have crossed the lands of the Barbarians without challenge. Even to move within our forests without being noticed is an uncommon skill. I must chastise my scouts and guards.'

Tarithel looked alarmed.

'Do not punish them on my behalf …'

Imorthorn allowed his smile to show once more.

'I jest,' he said. 'But there is more you haven't told me about yourself.'

Tarithel nodded. 'I have … my parents granted me a title

on the Solstice just gone,' she said. 'It is ancient, given to the firstborn daughter of my line since time immemorial; the Lady of the Forest. This jewel I wear …'

She held the jewel up for his inspection. Imorthorn could see the faint green glow emanating from it.

'No ordinary stone I surmise,' he said.

'No,' Tarithel replied. 'It is called the Heart of the Forest. It is imbued with the light of summer from hundreds of moons ago, so the legends of my folk tell. It is a wholesome light however it came to be. The title gives me responsibility to tend for the forests of my home. I thought that was all it was, but I soon found out it was much more.'

'How so?' Imorthorn asked.

'The forests … they … speak to me,' Tarithel said, her expression puzzled as she struggled to explain it. 'The words I heard, the guidance I received … the forest of Dreams itself spoke to me … and in our travails against the Witchking, the forest came to my aid.'

'To your aid?' Imorthorn echoed. 'What do you mean?'

'I will show you,' Tarithel said. She gestured to the table, where flowers were arranged in a vase. Some were unfurled, but many were still within their buds, waiting to bloom. Gently, she ran her fingers up their stems.

As Imorthorn watched, the flowers unfurled before his eyes, their petals rolling back, blooming beneath the girl's touch until the bouquet was complete. He gasped. He looked at her, seeing the green jewel glowing for a moment before fading once more.

'The forest set upon and destroyed an army of the Doomguard,' Tarithel whispered. 'At my bidding they were slain and my home Citadel saved.'

'Such a power has never been seen amongst my folk,' Imorthorn whispered. 'Is this something that the Fey of Midnight can do? It is a wondrous thing …'

'No,' Tarithel answered. 'It seems to be mine alone to command.'

'Most interesting,' Imorthorn mused.

'When I came to your forests I could sense the care and tending of your folk,' Tarithel said. 'It was upon the air, in the scents of the flowers and in the life of the trees. There were brambles and thorns that barred my way; the work of the Heartstealer I suspect. I broke them, and the forest welcomed me within.'

Imorthorn rubbed his chin.

'We have cared for the forests in the ways passed down by our forefathers across the generations,' he said. 'But the forests have never spoken to us in the manner you describe. We have none who can do what you have just shown me. Yet these forests are ancient, perhaps even older than those of Midnight. Perhaps they will have a message for you, and for all of us?'

Tarithel nodded. 'I hope so … in fact, I count upon their guidance!'

Imorthorn placed his plate back on the table.

'Let's hope your Lord Luxor is able to find a safe path here. As I said before, your Moonprince will have trouble long before he reaches our borders.'

'Trouble?' Tarithel echoed in dismay.

'Let me tell you a little about this land,' Imorthorn said, pouring himself a glass of wine. 'The Icemark has always been a fractured realm. The Heartstealer claims dominion over it, and her empire commands the most territory and power, but set against her plans are those of other peoples. I have already mentioned the Dwarves to the north of our realm; a hardy folk who have little enough in common with us. The Barbarians lie to the west, the Gate you came through is in their domain. North-west of here is the realm of the Giants. All peoples vie for land and influence. Allegiances change with the moon. Our borders are fluid, moving this way and that, our folk never quite at outright war, but never fully at peace. The Icemark is a troubled land.'

Tarithel listened, but said nothing.

'So,' Imorthorn finished. 'I can see no way for you, or your Moonprince, to reach your goal. For you would need to journey deep within the Heartstealer's realm undetected and that is impossible unless your sorcery matches hers ...'

'I am no sorceress,' Tarithel said.

'Yet you have a power about you that none here can claim,' Imorthorn countered. 'If you can make the very forest rise up in battle at your command ...'

'I do not think that is my purpose,' Tarithel said. 'That was a desperate moment. The forest came to save me, I did not command it.'

Imorthorn nodded.

'Lord Luxor has defeated the Witchking by force of arms,' Tarithel said. 'Might he not do so again with the Heartstealer?'

'Can this Luxor rally all the forces of the Icemark to his banner?' Imorthorn asked. 'Truthfully, it is most unlikely. Each race has deep grudges, feuds and quarrels with the others, buried in hundreds of moons of animosity and mistrust. Such a thing cannot be achieved I fear. Many have tried and all have failed. The Heartstealer herself fans the flames of distrust; it has never been in her interest for there to be lasting and abiding peace.'

'Luxor will not give up Morkin,' Tarithel said. 'And neither will I.'

'Then you are surely playing into the Heartstealer's scheme,' Imorthorn said, his voice sterner. 'Luxor slew her father, perhaps the only person for whom she ever had a care. I imagine she wants vengeance for that loss. She has taken Morkin to that effect, to lure you and he into the Icemark. If you approach her, she will end you both. That is what she wants! The Icemark will be unchanged and Midnight will have lost its fabled

Moonprince and a beautiful, gifted daughter of the Fey. I would not see that happen.'

Tarithel's express was downcast, her shoulders slumped.

'Then what can I do?' she cried. 'I cannot … I will not leave him to her! Will the Fey of this realm not resist her? Fight her? She intends to ravage Midnight, her passing through Icemark will not be peaceable. Would you not see her will thwarted?'

'You ask much,' Imorthorn answered. 'And even if every Fey of this realm were roused to Luxor's banner it would not be enough to wage war upon the Heartstealer. We are sore outnumbered by her ranks of Iceguard and that is before you count the hordes of the Barbarians, Giants and the Dwarves whose allegiance could not be guaranteed.'

'Then it seems I must find my own path, however dangerous you say it is,' Tarithel replied.

Imorthorn thought for a moment.

'Do not make a hasty decision,' he said, after a moment. 'By luck or fate, the council of the Fey is here this moon and your arrival is well timed. Make your case to us, consult with Luxor on what he would ask. We will hear what you both have to say.'

Tarithel nodded. 'I do thank you, Lord Imorthorn. Forgive me if my words sound ungrateful.'

'I sense a depth of care and passion I fear many of us have lost,' Imorthorn replied. 'Do not apologise for love, bravery and determination. You will need all of these on the road ahead, wherever it shall take you.'

Tarithel smiled.

'But for now,' Imorthorn said. 'If you are rested enough, go to the forest here. I will give you an escort to guard you on the way. See if the forest here will speak to you. Tell me of what you learn. Perhaps that will inform our counsel too.'

The girl nodded.

'With your leave.'

Imorthorn bowed. 'It has been an honour, Lady of the Forest of Dreams.'

Tarithel curtseyed to him. 'The honour is mine, Lord Imorthorn.'

Chapter Six

Carangrane the Giant stands in the City of Carangrane looking east to the Mountains of Anvormane.

The Mountains of Anvormane were stark and brutal in appearance, an unforgiving series of peaks that stretched forty leagues north and south down the length of the Icemark. They were second only in majesty to the vast bleakness of the greatest mountain range in the land, those of Anvulane themselves, some days travel to the east.

The mountains formed the backbone of the realm of the Giants, a bulwark which any invading force would have to overcome. Only two choices presented themselves to a potential attacker. There was a narrow valley to the north, the pass of Thudrane, or a wider track through hills of Malorthad to the south.

The Giants shared the natural protection of the mountains with the Barbarians, whose territory covered the southern end of the range.

Further east the lands were more contested. The Giants claimed everything up to the edges of the Forest of Farorn and the borders of the great Anvulane mountain range, yet the Icelords often moved with impunity across the plains of Morormarg. There were often skirmishes between the armies camped at the fortresses of Ulformane and Kahudrun, Giant and Icelord owned respectively.

Further south, the pass of Carormarg led through the ridges

of Anvulane into the realm of the Dwarves. Those smaller folk often issued forth, laying claim to the plains beyond, though they had been quiet of late, more consumed with their own internal troubles.

Beyond them to the south the lands belonged to the Barbarians. They had taken the southern end of the Mountains of Anvormane long ago. Some of the Giants could still remember when the entire mountain range was within the control of the Giants. The memory lingered and festered, though relations with the Barbarians were, perhaps, the least fraught of all.

Here, on the north-west side of the mountains, the peaks were tallest. It was the heart of the Giant's domain, the most ancient dwelling of their people. The City of Carangrane himself.

The city was built out of the very rock of the mountainside and, at first glance, crudely constructed and part ruinous. Untold generations of the Giant folk had lived, worked and died within the old city, and it had been rebuilt, altered and changed many times. What could be seen on the outside was only the smallest part of the whole. Huge halls and caverns had been carved out of the interior of the mountains, and the city was vast within, on many levels, some reaching far below ground. It was reached by a long but narrow road that wound up through the mountains, only widening into a plain at the very foot of the city walls, presenting a formidable challenge to any hostile army.

There was none of the elegance and harmony with the forests that would have characterised the residence of a Fey, nor the practicality and beweaponed efficiency of the Barbarians. Here all was rock and stone. The aesthetics of the Giants concentrated on edges, sharp lines and sheer overwhelming size. Homes were hewn from great blocks of stone, every corner cut sharp and square. There was not a curve to be seen in their architecture. Indomitable strength was their first, and often, only consideration in their buildings. A Giant's fortress might be starved out, burnt, pillaged and despoiled, but it would always remain, as strong as the mountains from which it was built.

There were few titles amongst the Giants, and none that would have translated to King, but in any meaningful way, that was how Carangrane was viewed by his folk. He was the eldest and thus the wisest. Longevity and experience were treasured by his people.

He stood, twelve feet tall and half as wide, looking out from his high vantage point near the peak of the mountain, gazing out across the realm. His childhood home in the Forests of Thenarg could be seen on the western horizon, a low line of trees beyond the hills. The Plains of Glareon stretched as far southwards as he could see, the horizon lost in the mist.

I have kept this realm as my father kept it and his father before him, back to the beginnings of our people.

Carangrane was old, old even as the Fey might measure things. He well remembered the Icemark before the coming of the Barbarians from the south and the Dwarves from the east, long before the lands were sealed off by the evil curse of the Frozen Wastes. The races were confined, hemmed in, forced upon each other as winter's icy grip took hold. Afterwards there was war, then famine, then more war, fierce and brutal. It had been like that ever since as the resources of the Icemark dwindled with the cold.

And the rise of the Heartstealer.

Few of his people had lived before the dark shadow of her reign, but he had. Much of Icemark had once been fair and wholesome, but there had always been a taint upon the distant Forest of Farorn. His father had warned him of it, but had never explained why it was forbidden to go there. Some ancient evil had lurked there, and, with the rising power of the Witchking to the south it had grown and strengthened.

The woman had come to power swiftly, ruling the Iceguard by fear and terror, slaying any who opposed her. Tutored by her father from afar she soon dominated them, fanning their latent resentment into aggression. Much of the Giants' land had been lost in the wars that followed. Only a brief and fractured alliance of the rest of the races of the Icemark had held her at bay.

And she learnt from that too ...

Shareth had surmised that assaulting them all would not serve her purposes. She had retreated, setting a guard upon the borders she defined for herself and disappeared for a generation of the smaller folk. Without the strength to assail her, the Giants had let her be.

Many moons passed before any heard from her again, and when they did, her talk was of alliances and trade, not of war.

And too many fell for her lies, believing her promises. Now she wiles her way into the hearts of all, slowly poisoning them from within, turning them against their own folk. Such evil cannot be marched upon, cannot be slain ...

He sighed, his huge hands gripping the wall before him. The stone was firm in his vast grip, reassuring and solid.

Footsteps sounded alongside him. He turned his head to see Varangrim. He nodded in greeting.

'Woes from the east once more?' Carangrane asked.

'Ulformane's scouts told us yesterday that the armies of the Heartstealer march upon our eastern borders once again.'

'I have already sent word to Torelak, Imgenarg and Obigrorn to bolster the armies at Ulformane's fortress. We will stand off as we always do.'

'This news from the south,' Varangrim said. 'Brought to us by our trained wyverns ...'

'The demise of the Witchking,' Carangrane said. 'Yes, so I hear. Her anger has been aroused once more. The evil intent of the Witchking, whatever it was, rests solely with her now. Long she was his understudy, now the mantle passes to her.'

'What must we do?'

'What we have always done,' Carangrane said. 'We defend our lands, and our lands will defend us. She must be contained and reminded that these lands are ours.'

Varangrim nodded and went to say more, but thought better of it.

'You can say what is on your mind,' Carangrane said.

Varangrim cleared his throat.

'There are many who say we should push against the Heartstealer, not just hold our line.'

'Fenorn and Anvildrak you mean,' Carangrane said, with a chuckle.

Varangrim looked surprised. 'You knew?'

'Of course I knew,' Carangrane replied. 'They are young, they wish to make their mark. They see only glory and conquest in war, not the devastation it wreaks upon our people and our way of life. You must temper them over time.'

'I?' Varangrim replied.

Carangrane glared at him. 'You know very well I see you as my successor. Do not play innocent, stand up in the position I have placed you. I have no sons left … nor will I have any more. That gives me leave to dispense power where I see fit. To you I entrust our people. I consider you worthy of that mantle. Or do I make a mistake in my choice?'

Varangrim swallowed and stood taller.

'You do not.'

'I am gratified to hear it.'

Carangrane's stern face broke into a grin.

'Young folk need quests and diversions; a way to prove their mettle. They are not natural diplomats. Use them for what they are good at.'

Varangrim nodded.

A trumpet sounded nearby. Both giants turned to see a runner approaching.

He ran to them, bowing low.

'Rise,' Carangrane said.

'Mighty ones,' the runner said. 'I bring urgent missives from Ulformane. A great host of Iceguard has assembled at the Fortress of Kahudrun. They have retreated back from marching on the plains, but they continue to arm.'

Carangrane frowned.

'So, the Heartstealer sees fit to flex her muscles once more,' he said, nodding. 'Very well. We must do the same.'

Varangrim looked at him.

'We must travel east to meet them?'

Carangrane nodded.

'We must impress upon her that changes in the south do not mean changes in the north.' Carangrane turned to the runner. 'Have a message returned to Ulformane. He is to assemble the armies I have sent and stand ready, but he is not to attack, only defend should it become necessary. He is safe enough in his fortress. We will ride to him and show the Icelords the folly of underestimating our strength.'

The runner bowed and ran off.

'She tests us,' Varangrim said.

Carangrane nodded. 'Always.'

'But why now?' Varangrim asked.

'She has long coveted our lands,' Carangrane said. 'My sires told me stories of how she would come and go at will in our northern territories in moons long ago. She tried the hand of friendship in those days … seeking something that she never found.'

'What was she after?'

Carangrane shrugged. 'There are ancient jewels, tomes, artefacts and knowledge acquired by our race over the centuries. Some are very old indeed and date from times before our race claimed these lands, remnants of powers now long forgotten, kept here in the vaults below the city. Who knows what would be useful for a sorceress?'

'That she values them would seem reason enough to keep them from her clutches,' Varangrim said.

Carangrane chuckled. 'Wisely said. Doubtless she would steal what she could in the same way she steals the hearts of those who follow her. Our forefathers grew wary of her intentions, fearing that she would become yet more powerful. They drew the line at letting her enter our homelands and searching our cities. She has been cold and hostile to us ever since.'

'And now she wants a conflict?'

'Perhaps not an all-out war, but a reason to invade us might suit her purposes,' Carangrane replied. 'If she perceives a hint of weakness then she will strike. If not, she will goad us, tempt us into a premature attack, hoping to make us overextend our reach. Resisting that will be our greatest challenge. We must give her no opportunity either way.'

'A fine line between the two.'

'Such is the role of leader of the Giants,' Carangrane said. 'Thus it has always been. I see no reason it should change. Assemble our armies.'

'Yes, mighty one. As you wish.'

'Not what I wish, but what must be done.' Carangrane sighed. 'Still, I suppose it will give Anvildrak and Fenorn something to do.'

Varangrim bowed and left.

Lorelorn, Warlord of Shareth and Icelord of the Forest of Farorn, wrapped his dark cloak about him as he dismounted his horse. The summons had been as imperative as ever, and he knew the tone well enough. Delay would not only be unacceptable, it would be dangerous. Lorelorn had seen how messengers with bad news were treated by his mistress. A similar fate awaited any captain of the Iceguard who failed in their task. Occasionally, some unlucky soul might fall foul of her temper. All were dispatched in gruesome ways.

Shareth's lust for violence was strong.

Lorelorn had grown adept at reading her moods, knowing when to speak and when to be silent. Perhaps that skill had allowed him to rise to his pre-eminent position within the ranks of the Icelords. He was one of the six, the dread warlords of the Frozen Empire, Shareth's most trustworthy lieutenants.

The walls of her favoured fortress, Kahangrorn, rose out of the ground like a cliff of deepest shadow. Darkness wrapped them. It was no mere colouration, no oily pitch or deep hued paint. The darkness was something she had wrought herself. She had the means to extinguish not only light itself, but its effects. Shadows obeyed her whims. The very night was at her beck and call.

The others had arrived at the same moment.

There was little acknowledgement, perhaps the faintest of nods in each other's direction. As one they turned and marched within the fortress, their feet in lockstep, marching inwards, her summons ringing loud, yet silent, in their minds.

IMGARIL, ZARASHAND, GLORMARG, FANGRORN, LORELORN, ANVIREON.

She stood, awaiting them at the far end of the grand hall. She stood at the far end, watching them as they marched within, coming to a halt together, facing her in a line.

As one they bowed the knee.

As they stood up, there she was before them, a pace away. There had been no footsteps, no indication of her movement. Her skills stretched far beyond any that others possessed; elemental, ethereal.

As usual, she was in the form of a woman in the prime of her life, of sharp but beguiling beauty. She had always been thus as far as they knew. None of them had ever seen her otherwise. In all their lifetimes she had not aged, she seemed constant, unchanging. Yet they all knew their fathers had seen her thus, and their fathers before them…

RISE.

Her voice echoed in their minds. As they stood she paced back and forth before them, looking into each of their faces in turn, studying them for … what? Weakness? Treachery? It was impossible to tell.

Lorelorn stood stock still. There was nothing unusual about her behaviour; it was a common overture to her meetings.

Satisfied, she stood back.

She spoke, her voice soft and mellow, rich and melodious.

'It is time, my Lords,' she said. 'Long rounds of work come to fruition.'

None of the six spoke. It was unwise to utter anything unless required to.

'The Icemark ripens ready to be plucked,' she said. 'Harvest time approaches, but we are not yet ready to wield the scythe … not just yet. It must be sharpened first. You will ensure our armies are ready for invasion. Weapons, provisions, supply trains, all must be prepared.'

Shareth watched as they all nodded.

'You wish to subdue the Icemark at last?' Imgaril asked, his voice a crackling whisper.

Shareth nodded. 'Indeed I do. The demise of my wretched father leaves an emptiness which must be swiftly filled. To the south the land of Midnight retreats from my grasp further each day. That was to be my inheritance, and he has squandered it in his foolishness. I intend to take it back.'

'And this Moonprince?' Zarashand asked. 'He who slew your father. What of him?'

Shareth stepped forward. The fires that illuminated the room flickered brighter for a moment.

'Luxor is his name,' Shareth said, her voice little more than a hiss. 'And Moonprince he is, descendant of a house my father, in another oversight, counted as vanquished. He missed that little detail. A mistake I will not make.'

'Your plan?' Glormarg asked.

'I have his son in my grasp,' Shareth said. 'A tasty morsel and a bait.'

'And he is well guarded,' Anvireon said.

Shareth nodded. 'Through his pet, one Rorthron of the Wise, Luxor knows this and rides to rescue him. Thus I want him put beyond his reach. Take my prize to Imiriel and guard him there. I will visit him in time.'

'It will be done,' Anvireon said.

'What strength does he bring with him?' Fangrorn asked. 'A mighty host if he seeks to bring battle to your realm.'

Shareth laughed. 'Not so. He knows he needs to guard Midnight should he fail. He leaves the bulk of his armies there to stand against our future attack. He brings but a handful of warriors, a mere garrison.'

'He cannot hope to succeed with so few,' Imgaril said. 'Thus, a direct attack is not his plan.'

'No,' Shareth said. 'It is a feint and a clumsy one at that. I have already divined his intent.'

'Which is?' Zarashand asked.

'Luxor knows little of the Icemark,' Shareth said. 'But he will learn quickly. He is a leader of men, and he will doubtless try to form alliances with the other races. He undertook this trick across Midnight, gaining the loyalty of the people of that realm to overthrow my father. He is not to be underestimated.'

'But he will not attack?' Fangrorn queried.

Shareth smiled and shook her head.

'Luxor is a Lord of Midnight, not of Icemark,' she said. 'He does not care for these lands. He would be quite content to retreat back to Midnight and cower there. But I want him to suffer for what he did, and what he stole from me. Yet, Luxor is no fool, he will not try to confront me directly, not yet anyway.'

'He sends another?' Lorelorn asked, joining the conversation.

Shareth looked at him, her gaze sharp and keen.

'Yes,' she said. 'Exactly. Another …'

She turned and stepped away, raising her hands and waving them through the air. A sparkle of light crackled between her fingers and an image took form.

The six Icelords watched as the comely form of a young woman appeared, floating before them. She was Fey, dressed in the manner of that people, slim, green-eyed and red-haired.

'Behold Luxor's spy,' Shareth said, with a chuckle. 'Luxor's son was to be married on the day he fled to be with me – to this pathetic little soul. She comes to set him free from my charms.'

'A Fey-girl?' Imgaril scoffed. 'What can she do? She is no threat to you. Let her come, capture her, torture her. Set her body on a spit and use it as a trophy.'

Shareth smiled for a moment. 'I may well do that in time.' Her smile disappeared to be replaced by a fierce glare. 'She may look like a child, but she is no mere Fey-girl, or Luxor would not have sent her alone.'

Imgaril rocked back at her glare.

'I don't understand.'

'Then listen,' Shareth snapped. 'This Fey-girl is more than she appears, perhaps given a measure of power by the Wise, or by Luxor himself. She sets herself against me. Her goal is surely to rescue the boy by stealth, whilst Luxor prances before us. If she succeeds, Luxor will retreat to Midnight, there to await our attack and such a fight will be hard for us to win. This is not how events will transpire. I want them both dead, but the girl must be stopped first.'

'A lone traveller is not easily to track …' Fangrorn said.

'No indeed,' Shareth answered him. 'And this girl will be well versed in the lore of her people. She will sneak towards us as Luxor tries to drive our gaze elsewhere. Send out spies, discreetly inform our servants amongst the other races. I want her found and caught. Fangrorn, it is likely she will attempt to make her way through the realm of the Dwarves, so she will approach your lands first.'

Fangrorn bowed in acknowledgement.

'And when she is caught?' Lorelorn asked.

Shareth turned to face him. 'I will take no risks. She is to be killed. Make whatever promises and payment you deem necessary to those in your sway. Once she is dead Luxor will be forced to rescue his son himself. That will lead him to his death and with his death the strength that would resist us in Midnight fails.'

The six Icelords bowed in acknowledgement.

'And how to apprehend this Luxor?' Zarashand asked.

'I intend to entice him further into Icemark, close off his return route,' Shareth said. 'He may seek allies to his cause. Very well. He will find his would-be allies have other concerns and by the time he decides to give up and return to Midnight, it will be too late. Fan the flames of discontent amongst the races. Make them fight each other. Support their battles, just not their victories! Then, when they are at their weakest … that … that is our time to go to war. You know what to do.'

The six bowed once more.

Shareth's plan had been long in the making.

She smiled.

'It starts with the Giants,' she said.

Laughter took her for a moment before her face grew stern.

'You are dismissed,' she said.

The doors behind them swung back with a heavy thump at her imperious gesture. The Icelords turned as one and marched away.

They said no words to each other, but mounted their horses and rode hard away from the fortress, their respective guards falling into position behind them.

Lorelorn rode to the west, into the glare of the afternoon sun, crossing the Plains of Caratrorn and then turning into the Forest of Farorn. It was dark within, the sunlight unwelcome amidst the ancient branches. This Forest was as old as the Icemark itself, grown under the tending of the ancient Fey long ago, still holding its secrets.

The shadows were long on the ground by the time he reached his home, deep within the forest. He had left it to the keeping of one of his vassals, Lord Talorthane, who led a City to the east, on the very edge of the Frozen Wastes. Talorthane himself had taken over the administration of his brother's realm in recent moons. Talormane had met an untimely death in a skirmish with a pack of Ice Trolls. Talorthane mourned him little; they had not been close.

'Let us speak,' Lorelorn said, dismissing the guards. Lorelorn led Talorthane within his chambers, gesturing for the younger Icelord to sit. Lorelorn closed the doors behind them.

'The time has arrived,' Lorelorn said.

'Shareth wishes to attack?' Talorthane asked.

'Soon,' Lorelorn acknowledged. 'It will not be long. The arrival of this Moonprince has tipped the balance away from peace.'

'He should have stayed in Midnight, content with his own victory,' Talorthane said. 'Was that not enough for him?'

Lorelorn smiled. 'I think it would have been, had our leader not goaded him further.'

Talorthane frowned. 'What do you mean?'

'Shareth is ever ruled by her emotions,' Lorelorn said, with a sigh. 'Oft she uses them to her advantage … but this time? I fear she has made a grave mistake.'

'A mistake?'

'Shareth has taken the son of the Moonprince,' Lorelorn said. 'He is to be locked away within the walls of Imiriel so it seems and guarded by that fool Anvireon. In so doing she has sought to force the Moonprince to engage with us here in the Icemark.'

'Few men would not be stirred by the capture of their son,' Talorthane said with nod.

'Quite right,' Lorelorn replied. 'The Moonprince's motivations are easy to understand.'

'And Shareth seeks revenge upon this Moonprince?'

'That and more,' Lorelorn said. 'The Moonprince is a step in her plan. She entices him in, and he has already set foot in her trap. Icemark, Midnight and the lands beyond are what she really desires. It seems the ancient Witchking promised the realm of Midnight to her, she is not at all content that her father died at the hand of this Moonprince before he bequeathed the land to her. She will corner this Moonprince and force him to fight, war will spread across the Icemark and plunge the entire land into conflict again. The Moonprince will fall and that will weaken Midnight. War will spread there too.'

'But why?' Talorthane asked. 'For what purpose does she desire all this territory? We have had relative peace for many a moon. Many will die on all sides to achieve a domination that will be hard indeed to manage and govern.'

Lorelorn sighed and then turned to Talorthane, looking at him with a hard gaze for a long moment.

'Good questions,' he said. 'But questions you should keep to yourself.' He sighed. 'She says she has been denied her inheritance. Could it be mere greed? I do not think so. Shareth cares little for territory itself, the administration of such an expanse would be difficult and beneath her, even if she did desire it. No, she seeks something else.'

'You know what it is?'

'I do not,' Lorelorn said.

'Then …'

'Her military ire is turned against the Giants,' Lorelorn said. 'The first step in subduing the Icemark once and for all.'

Talorthane waited a moment, but no further information was forthcoming from his liege.

'Our orders?' Talorthane said.

'Fan the flames of war,' Lorelorn said, with a grunt. 'Shareth grows impatient. She fears the Moonprince might unite the other races against her. It seems unlikely to me, but by what few accounts we have he is quite the orator. His victory over the Witchking was swift and sure. Shareth is wise to be wary of him.'

'You think he has a chance?'

'To unite all the races against Shareth after hundreds of moons of internecine conflict?' Lorelorn asked. 'No, I do not. But his arrival has changed the status quo. We have balanced the needs of peace for many moons. None truly want a war, it is a game with no winner once all moves have been played. Shareth's war strategy has been sound, to let them all fight each other and weaken themselves in so doing, but their leaders are not fools … at least I hope they are not. Perhaps if the death of the Moonprince comes swiftly, our watchful peace will have a chance once more. Time will tell.'

'Our orders?'

'Firstly to prepare for war with the Giants,' Lorelorn said with a heavy sigh. 'Beyond that, to precipitate conflict between the other races. Where there are factions, support the underdog. Where there are disputes, arm those with a wish to fight.'

'You disapprove of this?' Talorthane asked.

Lorelorn shot him a look.

'They are my orders. Shareth is my liege. I will do what any loyal Icelord would do. Obey.'

Talorthane nodded.

'We are to make ready,' Lorelorn said, raising his voice. 'Send messengers to Imgasharg, Sortharg, Malorthand and Morangrim. Provisions to be stockpiled, weapons to be made ready. When Shareth calls, we will be ready … oh … and there is one more thing.'

Talorthane looked up.

'Yes, sire?'

'We are to keep our eyes open for a young red-haired woman. A lone Fey-girl who may trespass in our realm. Shareth has a particular interest in her.'

'A Fey-girl?' Talorthane asked in surprise. 'What business would a Fey-girl have venturing this far north?'

'Another very good question,' Lorelorn replied. 'It seems she is a vassal or servant of the Moonprince. She seeks to rescue his son.'

'On her own?'

'Apparently so,' Lorelorn replied. 'A feint by the Moonprince perhaps, whilst he puts his own plans in motion.'

'There is more to this than meets the eye,' Talorthane said. 'Much that we do not know …'

'I agree,' Lorelorn said. 'But such questions are not safe to be voiced, do you understand? Whatever business this Fey-girl has in our realm … it is none of our business.'

Talorthane subsided.

'So what are we to do if we find her?' he asked, after a long moment of silence.

Lorelorn looked Talorthane in the eye.

'Kill her,' he said. 'Immediately.'

'You seem troubled, my Liege.'

Imgorthand the Fey turned to see Morildrane, a vassal who had accompanied him to the council of Imorthorn. Morildrane was dressed in the deeper colours of the forest, deep hued greens and blues. He held a fortress on the southern borders of Fangrim and had long been loyal to Imgorthand.

He was not a popular figure amongst the Fey. Many had spoken ill of his family line and his father had been a disreputable fellow, coming to grief having precipitated a dispute with the Barbarians many moons before. The fortress had almost been taken away and given to another house, but Imgorthand had intervened on behalf of Morildrane whilst he had still been a bitter young man, acting as steward until the boy came of age and then petitioning for his house to be restored.

Imorthorn had been persuaded and Morildrane became the fortress' lord. He remained aloof from the Fey, but had a shrewd mind and an insight that Imgorthand often found valuable.

'News from afar,' Imgorthand replied. 'Imorthorn's message to the southern lands was received and we have had a visitor.'

'The young lady from Midnight,' Morildrane replied. 'Quite the talk of the city she is. The rumours fly already.'

'I thought you might have heard,' Imgorthand said with a chuckle. 'Tell me, what has reached your keen ears?'

Morildrane shrugged. 'Only that she crept past the Barbarians and into our realm without asking permission, eluding our guards and our defences. Had she been any other than the daughter of the Lord of Dreams one might have suspected she was a spy. I assume her story has been checked?'

'Imorthorn seems to trust her.'

Morildrane nodded. 'She is pretty, is she not? Many have spoken of her beauty, enough to turn the hearts of even the most stalwart, so I've heard.'

'Imorthorn will not be swayed by a dash of ankle and twirl of a dress,' Imgorthand replied. 'But she does have something more about her …'

'More, my Liege?' Morildrane asked.

'A sense … of power,' Imgorthand said. 'Difficult to put into words. She carries herself with enormous presence for one so young.'

'And she talks to Imorthorn alone?' Morildrane asked. 'Is this wise? We do not know much of the southern Fey, nor the travails of that land. I understand she is sent by this legendary Moonprince. Her arrival is no accident, she comes with an agenda.'

Imgorthand nodded. 'Yes … I fear you're right.'

'Moreover,' Morildrane said. 'This Moonprince has struck and killed the Witchking. The Heartstealer is no doubt angered, her wrath turned against him. Our lands lie between the pair of them.'

'What do you mean?'

'It could be,' Morildrane said. 'That this Lady is here to charm our leaders, recruit them to stand against the Heartstealer.'

'Many would not be adverse to such a stance,' Imgorthand said.

'True enough, but to what benefit for the Fey of Fangrim?' Morildrane asked. 'Our folk would fight and die here in the Icemark whilst Midnight is protected from her wrath. The Moonprince has not brought a mighty host with him, just a token force.'

Imgorthand's eyes narrowed.

'I sense there is more behind your words. You may speak plainly to me.'

Morildrane stepped forward, his voice low.

'For all her fair words, I believe this girl seeks to use the Fey of Fangrim as a shield on behalf of this Moonprince,' Morildrane said. 'The Heartstealer would then have to expend her wrath against us first before she attempts to reach Midnight. This girl will council us to stand against the Heartstealer, when, in these troubled times, we should be seeking all possible routes towards maintaining a peace.'

Imgorthand nodded and sighed.

'And we do not have the strength to stand against the Heartstealer.'

'No indeed, my lord. This we know for certain.'

'Imorthorn has invited this girl to state her case,' Imgorthand said. 'Your words are timely. I will consider them carefully.'

Morildrane bowed. 'Your service, my Liege. As always.'

'It is good to have those you can trust,' Imgorthand said, clapping him on the shoulder. 'Your wisdom grows, Morildrane.'

'If it does, it is under your tutelage, my Liege.'

Morildrane watched Imgorthand depart, watching him until he was out of sight. Then he turned and paced down the corridor.

The axe spun through the air, slamming into the bark of the tree with a heavy thud to cheers from those who watched it. Moments later another one slammed in alongside, dislodging it to even greater cheers.

Imulorn the Dwarf turned to his companion and glared at him.

'Show off.'

His companion chuckled.

'Just keeping you honest, brother.'

Imulorn said something under his breath. His brother, Imelorn, laughed out loud.

The truth was that Imelorn had always been better at sticking axes in things. It was Imulorn who'd always had to deal with the aftermath.

The two Dwarves were on their way to the City of Glormane in the west of the Dwarf kingdom, there to play their part in settling a dispute that had arisen. Their servants were breaking camp within the Forest of Glortheon, two more days travel across the Plains of Thelay were ahead of them before they reached the city.

His brother's fortress was far to the east, and it had taken him almost a week to march to Imulorn's abode. Both had received a summons from their liege Thigrak. He was now too old for a long march, and had instructed them to go in his stead.

His instructions had been very plain.

You are to lend all support to Glormane, he is our leader and I would not see any other take his place. He has the best interests of our people at heart. He will unify the Dwarves and keep the peace with the outsiders. Imgorarg must be stopped before he can do any more damage!

'Still musing on those words?' Imelorn said. 'Or just sore about the axe work?'

Imulorn smiled out from under grizzled eyebrows. 'I would have preferred Thigrak to answer this summons.'

'He trusts us,' Imelorn said. 'And we go with his weight behind us. Which makes it quite a considerable weight all told.'

Now it was Imulorn's turn to laugh. Thigrak had always enjoyed his food.

'I'm more worried about the reception. We're just a pair of rough, country boys measured up against the lords in their fancy cities.'

'Glormane will receive us. Sounds like he needs the backing.'

Imulorn nodded.

'What do you think is going to happen?'

Imelorn clicked his tongue.

'Going to be an interesting one this,' he said, after a moment. 'Glormane hasn't stamped hard enough on the infighting in recent years I'd say. Too many folks with too many petty grievances. That's given Imgorarg the lever he needed.'

'He wants to wipe out the Fey and the Barbarians. He's dangerous.'

'That's just bluster,' Imelorn replied. 'Fires up the young and gets them all excited. He doesn't mean it, but it does get him support with those who are fed up and ready for change. Glormane's father was too introspective. I think Imgorarg makes some good points, we aren't defending our borders as aggressively as we should. We compromise too readily. Glormane is going to have to show he is tougher than his father was.'

'We're supposed to vote against Imgorarg, remember?'

'Yes, and we will,' Imelorn said. 'But Glormane needs to understand the frustrations that have brought Imgorarg to the fore. Unless he does something about that, it'll just fester and grow. The last thing we need is a civil war.'

Imulorn shuddered. Such a thing had happened before between the northern and southern factions of the Dwarves. It was long ago, but there were still those from the northern lands who distrusted those of the south, and vice versa.

Glormane's city stood in the middle of the dwarven realm and it was there that peace had been forged and written down on the hardened clay tablets that Dwarves used for matters of importance.

'No, we don't want that.'

'Anyway,' Imelorn continued. 'It's Carorthay everyone will

end up listening to. If he lends his support to Glormane, everyone will subside and we can all go back to normal. If he lends it to Imgorarg …'

'Thigrak will have a heart attack,' Imulorn mused.

'And your axe had better be sharp and your aim improved,' Imelorn said, his voice low. 'You may need it.'

Luxor, Rorthron, Careneon and Torinarg had left Firak's fortress on the morning of the second day as planned. Firak's hospitality had been similar to that enjoyed at Careneon's abode. Red meats a plenty, but little else, but to the saddle sore riders of the Moonguard and Careneon's own folks, it was warmly welcomed and soon consumed.

The hills fell away behind them as they turned to the north-west.

Luxor noted that Rorthron was gazing at the tower that stood before them, little more than a league away.

'Something troubles you?' he asked.

Rorthron stroked his beard. 'I am not sure,' he replied. 'I heard nothing from the Wise of Icemark, yet this tower draws my eye.'

Luxor looked at it for a moment and then turned his gaze back to Rorthron. 'It seems little different to any others I have seen thus far. The Wise of Icemark lock themselves away just as your countrymen have done in Midnight, they seem even less willing to involve themselves in our affairs.'

'That may be so,' Rorthron agreed.

'Know you of this tower?' Luxor asked Careneon, gesturing to their right as the army continued on.

'That is the Tower of Zarorthane,' Careneon said, with a shrug. 'You speak of the Wise as if they still inhabit such places. None of their kind have been seen in the Icemark for generations uncounted. Most folk hold they are long dead. The Towers themselves are either locked by mechanisms too cunning to unpick, or unapproachable. They hold dark secrets and are best avoided, just like the temples and the palaces, ruins of a time long since gone.'

'The Wise of Midnight still remain,' Luxor replied. 'Though they remain in a stupor, far removed from the cares of the world. I'd wager they are the same here.'

'Perhaps,' Careneon said. 'We count them not amongst friend or foe.'

'Zarorthane,' Rorthron said, almost as if to himself. 'Zarorthane.'

'Come Rorthron,' Luxor said. 'I already have assistance from the Wise, your good self. What more do I need?'

Rorthron smiled, but said nothing more. Luxor noted that he turned his head to look back on occasion as they continued their ride across the plains.

Two leagues and several hours later they stopped to rest both men and horses. The sun was westering now, sunset would not be long delayed.

'You are deep in the heart of the outlands now,' Careneon said. 'Few outsiders venture this far and none unescorted.'

'We remain in your debt,' Luxor said.

'There is no debt, Moonprince,' Careneon said with a chuckle. 'I am interested in the outcome of all of this. There are those amongst us who say that the shambolic and fragile peace we enjoy cannot last. Your arrival and the death of the Witchking in the south might be the very thing that tips the balance. Either way I am intrigued to see what Imgorad will do based on what you say. A change is as good as a rest!'

'What can you tell me of Imgorad himself?' Luxor asked.

Careneon thought for a moment.

'He is much respected by our folk,' he said. 'He deals firmly but fairly with matters of state and justice. Once he has made up his mind there is little chance to change it. He is a warrior of some renown, having fought the Fey and the Giants on many occasions, even the Lords of the Iceguard are wary of him. He does not suffer fools, that much I have seen.'

'He will listen to reason?'

'Yes, if your argument is sound,' Careneon replied. 'If there is a flaw in your plan, he will soon discover it.'

Luxor looked at Rorthron, 'He sounds like Lord Gard.'

Rorthron smiled. Careneon looked blank.

'Gard?'

'A Lord of Midnight,' Luxor said. 'A great warrior too, a veteran one could say. Gard is a man of few words, but when he speaks, it is usually wise to listen.'

Careneon nodded. 'They do sound alike. Is Gard fiercely loyal too?'

'That he is,' Luxor said. 'He would not waver from a path set before him, however difficult the way might be. He sore tested me at times, but he stood alongside me when the Witchking fell.'

'Imgorad is similar,' Careneon said. 'A loyal friend once made; a foe to be feared otherwise.'

Before them, a forest was visible over the rolling plains.

'We are entering his lands,' Careneon said, gesturing. 'That is the forest of Thangrun, in which his city lies. We will be expected. Unfurl the banners!'

Careneon's call was soon answered. Heralds rode to the front of the army. Luxor instructed his men to do likewise. The banners of Careneon, Torinarg and the Moonprince were unfurled, fluttering in the breeze as the armies of Moonguard and Barbarian rode across the plains into the setting sun.

Chapter Seven

Tarithel the Fey stands in the Forest of Fangrim looking west to the Stones of Sirium.

The Fey guards that Imorthorn had sent along with Tarithel remained nearby as she ventured into the Forest of Fangrim. She noticed them keeping a discrete distance as she made her way between the trees.

Are they sent to protect me, or to report on what I do? Perhaps both!

She wandered through the trails between the trees, leading Álainn behind her, a league or two north of the city. The paths were well tended and obvious, many people came this way. Imorthorn had spoken of the nearby fortresses of Carorthand and Tororthane, and she had seen them as she'd ridden across the vale. Further north, on the other side of the forest, lay a border post where another Fey she had not yet met, one Thormand the Fey, guarded the Fey's realm from the Dwarves to the north.

The forest seemed still to her, as if it were holding its breath. There was wildlife about her, but it was subdued. She ran her hands across the bark of the nearest tree, straining her senses, listening for the life within.

There was a faint rustle of leaves above her, but the tree did not respond in any other way.

Something is missing here, the life of the forest seems so distant, buried under years of neglect perhaps? Almost as if it slumbers and has forgotten how to wake ...

Tarithel had ridden out of the city on Imorthorn's invitation, but it had been something of a relief to get away from the crowds of people that gathered when she appeared. It seemed that the novelty of having a visitor from a distant land had piqued the interest of the populace. Her red hair was unusual too, making her stand out whenever she strayed from the halls and corridors.

Imorthorn had asked for her to return at dusk for another meeting of his council, but had been keen to hear her report of her experiences in the forest. She recalled what he had said to her before she left.

'Ah … Fangrim, it is very ancient. It has always been here as long as the Fey, that's for certain. Fangrim is not a Fey word, and I know not how the Forest came by its name. It is far older than we are, so I believe …'

Tarithel looked about her. Álainn looked back at her and whinnied.

So far I have nothing to report! It is past noon already, before long I will have to return to the city.

She took Álainn by the reins and led her onwards down the path, pausing at intervals to reach out to the trees alongside. She sensed little from them at all.

Has the forest been left alone too long? It took little to rouse the forests of my home, yet here …

She stretched out her senses harder, her hand clenching on the bark of the tree she leant against. Again there was a faint rustle of leaves.

She felt a shudder and then a soft groaning noise. She looked down to see roots had pulled out of the ground, the earth turned amidst the frost and snow that lay thin beneath her boots. She bent down to touch the roots, but there was nothing else to see, hear or feel.

She looked up, only then noticing that roots had pulled themselves up from many of the trees before her, bare earth had been left behind, a thin trail snaking away from the well-trodden path.

Tying Álainn to a tree near the path she ventured a few steps into the forest. As she did so, more roots pulled themselves aside further away.

An invitation ... but from whom?

There was one way to find out. She stepped between the roots, making her way along the freshly turned earth, glancing behind her as she did so. She could just see the guards through the trees, but they weren't following. They seemed relaxed and unconcerned, chatting amongst themselves. She half expected the pathway to disappear behind her, but nothing changed. Only ahead of her did the trees pull their roots out of her way.

The path twisted and turned before her. Sometimes she would have to stop and wait as some of the trees seemed reluctant to move. They creaked and groaned as if being coerced by some implacable will, resisting as long as they could, but then succumbing to its desires.

The path led her downhill. She could make out a small valley ahead of her, the sound of a stream gurgling nearby. Two final trees blocked her way, which were wrenched apart as she approached. Twigs and branches cracked and snapped as they did so.

She walked between them, seeing sunlight filtering down from above.

Ahead of her she could see the stream, much wider, filling the floor of the valley. Around it was a carpet of green, a lush meadow that stretched to the rocky edges that formed the valley. To the rear she could see a waterfall, splashing down from an overhang and crashing into a pebbled water course. A warm breeze caressed her cheeks and the smell of spring was all about her.

Amidst all this, three large stones were standing, the centre one taller than the others, all casting short shadows in the afternoon sun. A fine spray drifted past, delicious and cooling, a rainbow glistening in the air.

She paused at the threshold of the vale for long moments, watching and listening. There were no animals, nor birds. Other than the waterfall, the only sound was of the tall grasses rustling back and forth.

It reminded her of the Lith in her homeland, though the stones were much smaller, perhaps twice her height. This place seemed sacred somehow, though it was untouched and hidden.

Yet something drew me here, something wanted me to find it …

She stepped forward, moving away from the tall trees. The sunlight was warm, with no sign of the frost and snow she had ridden through earlier in the day. She was reminded of a time when she had met a strange lord in the Forest of Dreams.

Lord Midwinter …?

There was something of the same sense about the place, but there was no sign of anyone. She looked around, daintily stepping on rocks to avoid crushing any plants, making her way forward towards the stones. She could no longer hear the guards.

The sound of the waterfall was louder here, roaring in her ears, the spray now wetting her face. She reached out a hand, her fingertips brushing against the sandy texture of the rock.

She gasped.

Before her the waterfall had stopped in mid-flow. She could see the sparkling droplets of water splashing up from it suspended in the air. Silence fell about her, the roar gone. She turned to look around her, everything was hushed and still, though she fancied she heard the faintest tingle of sound, as if a sweet melody was being played just out of earshot.

Tarithel.

She gasped, turning about. A voice had called her name.

'Who are you?'

Do not seek to find me, you will not. It is too late for me to be found regardless, I lie deep within rock and stone and tree.

The voice was all around her. She spun around, but try as she might she could not locate it.

'What do you want from me?' she asked.

At this time I seek nothing from you, save your presence in my forest.

'Your forest?' Tarithel exclaimed. 'These woods are the realm of the Fey, if any can lay claim to ownership, it is Lord Imorthorn himself.'

There was a faint sense of amusement, as if a kindly uncle was indulging the childish and petulant words of a favoured niece.

Lord Imorthorn knows little of me. You have learnt more in brief days than all the Fey of this realm have learnt in all of the moons of your life.

'I don't understand,' Tarithel said.

No, you do not. And understanding will only come with time, and time is precious.

'What is this place?'

These are the Stones of Sirium. I have bought you here to aid you on your quest.

'You know of my quest?' Tarithel asked. 'How can that be?'

The trees talk, dear Tarithel. They talk and they listen. News of your presence is known far and wide throughout the Icemark to those who can hear.

Tarithel swallowed. 'I do not like the sound of that.'

Do not fear. For now, most of those who are aware of you bear you no malice. But that will not last long.

'You say you know of my quest,' Tarithel said. 'Then tell me, what do I seek?'

There was the faint sense of amusement again.

You test me? Wisdom in one so young, always encouraging.

'Flattery will not avail you in building trust,' Tarithel replied. 'If you wish to aid me, prove yourself.'

Very well. You seek your betrothed in the Frozen Empire far to the north. He who was stolen away from you. Morkin son of Luxor, Moonprince of Midnight.

Tarithel took a deep breath.

'You speak truly,' she said.

Yet a great power stands between you and your beloved. This you know.

Tarithel watched in dismay as an image of a woman formed before her. Until now she had glimpsed her only in fevered dreams and cloudy visions, but now her image was clear and sharp, standing before her as if she were real. She was motionless, an arm extended, her body wrapped in dark robes, her dark hair sweeping back in seductive curves, flowing down from a bright crystal tiara on her head. She was taller than Tarithel, her stature erect and proud, her body voluptuous and alluring. Despite that, it was her face and eyes that captured the gaze and drew the attention. Her face was beautiful, yet sharp and cruel, her eyes like steely points of darkness.

Behold your foe. Shareth the Heartstealer, sorceress of Icemark, queen of the Frozen Empire.

Tarithel studied the image, her shoulders slumping. Shareth looked like a queen – proud, arrogant and powerful.

Who am I to defy her? Imorthorn is right. I will be caught and captured. This woman will spare me no pain. She will torture me for her amusement, or just kill me outright without a second thought.

Many have tried to defy her, all have failed. Their corpses have rotted and their names are forgotten. Shareth is powerful indeed. Unchecked she will claim all of Icemark, then Midnight and then the lands beyond. Already she makes her move, she plans the undoing of all.

'Then, do you counsel me to turn back?' Tarithel said, tears coming to her eyes. 'As everyone else has done? How can I live knowing that I left Morkin to her without even trying?'

On the contrary, I counsel you to continue.

'But how?' Tarithel asked. 'To defy her is death. Morkin lies in her clutches and she will not let him go. I might find him, but she will be there ...'

So ... Shareth must be overcome if you are to succeed.

'But such a thing is not possible,' Tarithel cried.

There is one who can overcome her.

Tarithel wiped her eyes. 'You speak of Luxor the Moonprince,' she said. 'He would see her slain. But she has turned Morkin against us, and he will fight for her at the head of her armies. Such a fight would see Morkin killed. Even in defeat Shareth would have her vengeance. Morkin is lost to me ...'

She sank to her knees, sobbing.

The Moonprince is a mighty warrior, but it is not he of whom I speak.

'Rorthron commands much power,' Tarithel managed, looking back up. 'But measured against the Heartstealer? Already he has declined that match ...'

The Wise may give guidance, but you cannot look to them for salvation.

'Then who?' Tarithel asked. 'Imorthorn tells me the Fey cannot hope to stand against her. Is there some other power? Some other ally I might find and persuade to rid me of this evil woman?'

The voice didn't answer. Tarithel looked up to see another image taking form between her and the image of Shareth.

It was another woman, arrayed in a golden light, and a gown woven of green and silver, her hair drifting on some invisible wind. She was facing away from Tarithel, gesturing to Shareth. As Tarithel watched Shareth's form dissolved, the glow around the woman brightening enough to make her squint.

Another sorceress. A match for Shareth's evil.

'Who is she?' Tarithel asked, stumbling to her feet, staring at the woman before her. 'Where can I find her?'

Tarithel saw the woman lower her arm and turn her head. The silent wind blew her hair away from her features. Tarithel saw her hair was red, and her eyes green.

Her face!

There was sadness, loss, struggle, hardship and pain written across it. But that wasn't what shocked her.

She stared, her breath caught in her throat.

You have found her.

'No …'

It was her own face.

But yet, it was not. The woman who looked back at her seemed older, careworn and saddened.

What did she see … what did I see?

It is you who must defeat the Heartstealer. No force of arms can prevail, not the Moonprince, not the Wise, not the Fey or the other races.

'I am no sorceress!' Tarithel wailed. 'I'm just a girl, barely a woman.'

A rush of sound buffeted her. The waterfall came to life, water surging around her in a flood, soaking her in moments. The trees shook, their branches swaying back and forth. Leaves were caught and whipped around in a tempest. She stood in the midst of the maelstrom, flinching away from the fury.

The images of Shareth and herself faded.

Just a girl? Barely a woman?

Tarithel shivered at the angry tones of the voice, backing away.

'I meant no offence …'

You are Lady of the Forest. By your hand were the Fey of Midnight roused, you alone have forged a path from Midnight to the Icemark and found your way here to me. Just a girl, barely a woman? If such as you can achieve all this, what deeds might you yet undertake? You know a power resides within you ...

Tarithel trembled before the fury in the voice, but it subsided in moments. Tarithel looked forlorn.

'But how will I find my way?'

The forests of Icemark will guide you ...

The visions returned, landscape upon rolling landscape. Mountains, vales, forests and rivers. Her path laid out before her, always to the north.

'I do not want to be a sorceress.'

Tarithel looked down. Around her outstretched hands flowers had grown; lilies, tulips, roses. She could smell their scents, rising up to meet her.

Dearest Tarithel ... it is much too late for that.

The world slipped away from her and she fell back, lying prone on the soft carpet of grass within the leafy glade, bright blooms of colour all around her.

Three days march had seen the combined army of the giants under Carangrane march to the fortress of Ulformane on the eastern boundary of their lands. Across the plains of Morormarg another fortress could be seen, nestled against a deep forest, guarding a steep sided valley that led north-east into Iceguard territory, the Frozen Empire itself.

About it, just visible on the edge of sight, banners could be seen aloft, a breeze fluttering their devices.

Ulformane greeted Carangrane and Varangrim as they stomped up the stony causeway that led to the gates of the fortress.

'Mighty ones,' he said with a bow. 'It is well that you are here.'

'The Iceguard are up to their tricks once more,' Carangrane said.

Ulformane tugged at his beard.

'Something has changed,' he said. 'The Iceguard oft amuse themselves by traipsing up and down the plains hereabouts as if they own them, but always retreat from any confrontation. Now they assemble in some force at Kahudrun …' Ulformane indicated the distant fortress, some three leagues away. 'I deem they plan some additional mischief.'

'They will back down as they always do once they see we are ready for them,' Carangrane replied. 'Come. It has been a march of many steps. Inwards for meat and wine!'

Ulformane bowed again and led them inside the fortress.

Carangrane caught sight of two other giants within. They were tall and strong, muscled and powerfully built. One was topped with a great mane of red, the other wore his dark hair cropped short.

'Fenorn! Anvildrak!' Carangrane called. 'I thought you might beat us here. You march swiftly.'

The two giants walked across, bowing before Carangrane and giving a nod of acknowledgement to Varangrim.

'Swiftness is necessary when the Iceguard prowl our borders,' Fenorn replied.

'The foul scum,' Anvildrak spat. 'A lesson needs teaching.'

'It is but a little ruse of the Heartstealer,' Carangrane said, waving a hand. 'She pokes us, to see if we will react. Like a trapper will goad a wolf in a cage.'

'I'd bite her hand off given half a chance,' Anvildrak said.

'And have you ever seen that work out well for the wolf?' Varangrim replied. 'His muzzle is bludgeoned by a club to teach him a lesson.'

'Then the wolf must bite faster,' Anvildrak answered. 'And without hesitation.'

'Peace,' Carangrane said, stepping between them. 'We will

have our chance to cave in the skulls of the Iceguard, but I do not think they will want a fight this day. The Heartstealer has some new trouble a-brewing. Fear not, we will find out what it is soon enough.'

Anvildrak bowed, but not before he cast a withering glance at Varangrim.

The sun was already westering, casting long shadows across the plain. Anvildrak and Fenorn followed Carangrane as he walked within the fortress. Varangrim and Ulformane remained outside. Varangrim leaned on the stone wall, gazing out to the east. A heavy sigh escaped him.

'Youngsters,' Ulformane said from beside him.

Varangrim nodded. 'Aye.'

'Give them their first spear and they think they can rule the world,' Ulformane replied.

'Were we any different at their age?'

Ulformane chuckled. 'No, I don't suppose we were, but at least we had a proper taste of battle before this fragile peace was forged. Everything is now just a parade, a show of strength without any real blood-letting.'

'What do think the Heartstealer is planning?'

Ulformane tugged at his beard.

'I think this news from the south has rattled her,' he said, after a moment. 'The death of her father at the hands of the Free of Midnight? Long was that her inheritance. Perhaps her wrath has been kindled anew. That storm she sent south two moons past for instance. She moves once more. This feels like more than just her usual testing of our defences.'

'Then we must be cautious,' Varangrim said.

'We will post a watch,' Ulformane said. 'They have been massing for the last few days and they have a fondness for moving at night. Somehow I don't think her plans will stay hidden for long.'

Imulorn and Imelorn stood side by side on the Plains of Thelay. The plains were windswept and bleak, the snow and frost thin across their flat expanse. A stiff breeze was blowing from the north-east as it had for the last few days. The wind was cold and sharp, promising worsening weather. Clouds were boiling up in the distance.

'Storms are coming down from Anvulane,' Imulorn said, peering into the distance. The mountains were visible as a pale line of peaks on the far northern horizon, overshadowed by heavy clouds. 'We should make sure we're there by sundown.'

Imelorn nodded, still trudging onwards.

The path they were following was well travelled. They had already passed Torelorn's fortress to the east, but the flags were not flying, implying Torelorn had already left and was ahead of them. All the Dwarves had been summoned for the leadership vote.

The city of Glormane was visible now, getting clearer with every step. As with most dwarven cities it appeared as just a high wall from the outside. Dwarven buildings were low and cut deep, with many preferring to live underground. The threat of war required certain practicalities though, and the city boundary was one of them. The walls were given over to the defence of everything within, with many ingenious traps, weapons and devices concealed within and without. Storming a dwarven fortress was a difficult and dangerous undertaking.

Imulorn and Imelorn could see flags along the walls. Each visiting Dwarf lord would erect his own banner in sequence around the rim of the city. Already many were flying in the wind.

'Quite the assembly,' Imulorn muttered.

'There'd better be enough food for us all after this long march,' Imelorn grunted. 'Otherwise we'll have a civil war regardless of who's in charge or what gets said.'

They continued on their way, a low range of hills rising behind the city as they drew close.

An army was camped a league or so before the gates. Its banners were unfurled, but they were different to any flying from the city.

Imelorn frowned.

'That's Imgorarg's banner,' he said.

'I wonder why he is outside?' Imulorn asked.

'Perhaps Glormane has decided he's full and there's no more room,' Imelorn said with a chuckle.

'I doubt it's Glormane,' Imulorn said. 'I suspect Imgorarg has a care for seeing who approaches and what they're about … look, here he comes!'

A pair of banners were moving away from the mass of the army, with a party of stout Dwarves marching beneath them. The newcomers would reach the path long before Imulorn and Imelorn could reach the city.

'He must have recognised our banners,' Imelorn said.

'And it seems he would like to talk to us.'

They marched onwards, coming to halt as the other party approached. Imulorn and Imelorn recognised Imgorarg at their fore.

He was big, big even for a Dwarf, almost as tall as the Barbarians to the south and west. He stood tall, leaning back a little, gazing down upon whomever he deigned to converse with.

'Well met, Imulorn and Imelorn,' Imgorarg began, bowing from the hip. Imulorn and Imelorn did likewise, a little lower, as their lesser rank required.

'Greetings Imgorarg of the northern plains,' both said in unison.

'Thigrak is not able to make the journey I see,' Imgorarg said. 'How is the old fellow?'

'Well enough,' Imulorn replied. 'But, as you say, a journey of this length is beyond his means now.'

'A pity,' Imgorarg said. 'I always found him an admirable sparring partner. I considered him often wrong of course, but he spoke well and made his case in thorough Dwarf fashion. You have come to represent him I assume?'

'We have,' Imulorn said.

'Both of you?' Imgorarg asked, looking at them.

'Imulorn carries Thigrak's instruction,' Imelorn said, leaning on his axe. 'Though we both have a vote. I'm just here to make sure he makes it there and back in one piece.'

Imgorarg looked at him for a moment.

'And will you wield your axe for whosoever is chosen in this vote?' Imgorarg asked.

'I am a Dwarf,' Imelorn answered. 'Our traditions are sacred. Loyalty to our leader is unquestionable.'

'Indeed it is,' Imgorarg said. 'And the safety of our borders the next priority, no?'

'Certainly,' Imelorn said, nodding.

'I'm sure both you and Glormane will uphold both our traditions and the security of our borders,' Imulorn said.

'I would hope so,' Imgorarg said, turning to look at Imulorn. 'I would truly hope so, but the last few moons give me much reason for cause and concern. The Giants test us upon the west, the Fey lurk within their forests to the south, and the Barbarians … why they prowl, waiting for a chance to strike at us. All of them vie for our lands and our defence has not been robust enough. I would see the other races know their place once more.'

Imelorn was nodding, but Imulorn frowned.

'You haven't mentioned the Iceguard,' he said. 'Do they not threaten us from the north in similar fashion?'

'Still the lingering hatred of the north for those who dwell in the south?' Imgorarg replied with a chuckle. 'Are those Thigrak's words, or yours?'

Imulorn's eyes narrowed. 'They are mine.'

'Then consider this,' Imgorarg said. 'The Iceguard trade with us, they have not threatened our borders in more than a generation, unlike the Fey, the Barbarians or the Giants. They are far more numerous than we are, a mighty force it would be better to align with than stand against.'

'Align with the Heartstealer?' Imulorn asked, 'Are we to take sides with evil?'

'Evil!' Imgorarg laughed. 'She is strong and knows her mind, I'll say that. She even has plans to conquer and subdue, but it is not by mere whim. The Icemark would be better served by firmer control, less bickering on the borders. All these petty disputes would be at an end.'

Imelorn was still nodding. Imulorn looked at his brother in disgust.

'She seeks to enslave those bound to her,' Imulorn replied. 'Do you really believe the Iceguard serve her out of loyalty?'

'I do,' Imgorarg said. 'I have spoken to them, face to face. I do not peddle rumours and misinformation like others are wont to do. The Iceguard would value a treaty with us. They recognise our strength and our dependability. We could safeguard our lands forever … if our leadership took the opportunity to do so.'

He and Imulorn stared at each other for a long moment.

'The vote will tell,' Imelorn interjected.

'It will,' Imgorarg said. 'And in the greatest tradition of our people, loyalty will be rewarded and treachery punished.'

'As it should be,' Imelorn said, before stepping back a pace. 'We must make our way to the city. Thigrak's banner must be stood up for all to see.'

'Of course,' Imgorarg said, with a bow.

Imulorn and Imelorn bowed in return and moved off. As they left Imgorarg called out from behind them,

'Loyalty will be rewarded!'

Imorthorn took a long pull from the tankard of mead set before him. He swallowed and set the tankard bank down on the table.

Tarithel sat across from him. She had not touched the glass of wine set before her. She had been most pensive since returning from her ride out into Fangrim.

'The forest did speak to you then,' he said, his eyebrows raised in a question.

She nodded. Imorthorn watched her for a moment. She looked pale, her expression grim. His guards had informed him that Tarithel had stepped off the path, venturing a little way into the forest. At her request that they had kept their distance, but stayed within earshot. They had heard a cry and found her, in a faint in a strange glade none could recall seeing before. They had brought her back to the city before night had fallen.

Tarithel went to speak and then stopped.

'You can tell me, Lady Tarithel,' Imorthorn said, keeping his voice soft. 'I would hear the ancient wisdom of Fangrim, if that is what you heard.'

'The forest did indeed speak,' Tarithel said, hesitating. 'A voice both aged and youthful, far more potent than anything I have heard before.'

'They say Fangrim is the oldest of all forests,' Imorthorn said. 'I have no reason to doubt it.'

'It fears Shareth,' Tarithel said, swallowing and looking up. 'It told me she is coming for all the Icemark, for all of Midnight. It is no idle boast. Her plans are already unfolding and she means to subjugate us all.'

'As we have long feared,' Imorthorn said.

'And it said none can stand against her,' Tarithel said. 'Save one.'

Imorthorn's eyes narrowed. 'One?'

Tarithel nodded. 'I wondered if it were Luxor, or Rorthron the Wise … perhaps yourself Lord Imorthorn …'

'I would stand and fight,' Imorthorn said. 'I have no love for the Heartstealer, but I would not claim to be her equal, that would be a fool's deceit.'

'No,' Tarithel said. 'And the forest told me none of you can hope to prevail against her.'

'And yet, there is one who can?' Imorthorn said, a faint smile upon his features.

Tarithel didn't answer.

'Lady Tarithel,' Imorthorn said. 'Fangrim has appointed you, has it not?'

Tarithel's voice fell to a whisper. 'It called me a sorceress.'

'I have already seen much of your determination,' Imorthorn replied. 'As I said before, the powers you possess are unheard of in my recall, or in the history of our folk. I would not necessarily disagree with that assessment.'

'I am not evil, twisted and cruel!' Tarithel snapped.

'Who said sorcery had to be evil?' Imorthorn countered. 'I see a power, a power that might be used for good or ill. She who wields it decides to what use it is to be put. You have come to us, bravely … perhaps even a touch recklessly, but you have come. The forest speaks the truth when it says that none can defeat her by force of arms. It has been tried in the past … and those who tried, failed. If the Heartstealer is to be defeated, it must be by other means.'

'I do not wish to wield such power,' Tarithel said.

'And you are wise to be cautious,' Imorthorn replied. 'But I have long feared that Shareth seeks to assemble just enough strength, and to weaken those who stand against her just so much, so that she can sweep all before her. The death of her father has fanned her wrath. I do not doubt the words of the forest. It warns us she is ready to strike now. If I believe the forest in that, I must then accept what it says about your destiny.'

Tarithel nodded.

Imorthorn looked at her. 'What did it ask of you?'

'That I alone must confront the Heartstealer,' Tarithel said. 'She stands between me and my beloved Morkin.'

Imorthorn nodded and thought for a moment.

'Then you are resolved to travel northwards to seek him,' he said.

'I have no choice in the matter,' Tarithel answered.

'You know my thoughts,' Imorthorn said. 'By any rational mode of thought it would seem to be the height of folly, such a traipse through lands you do not know, through people hostile to the Fey, to defy a creature so powerful and evil that none have ever withstood her. And by supporting your quest, I set myself and my folk against her in a manner we have shied away from for many long moons. It would be, in effect, a declaration of war upon the Frozen Empire …'

Tarithel stiffened, about to retort. Imorthorn held up a hand.

'But I see your resolve,' he continued. 'And I place much faith in the forest that sustains my folk. You could have eluded my guards and fled northwards, disobeying my command. You did not. You have returned to me as I requested. I believe in you, Tarithel, Lady of the Forest and daughter of the Lord of Dreams. Yet, how will you find your way?'

'The forest will guide me … it told me so.'

'Shareth must be stopped and if Fangrim itself says that may be done by your hand, who am I to argue? I give you leave to go.'

He could see her tremble for a moment, then she reached out to grab his hand.

'Thank you, Lord Imorthorn.'

He drew in his breath. 'You should not thank me. I fear for what you must do, your road will not be easy. Sending a young woman alone into what terrors must surely await you goes against every instinct in my being.' He stopped, considering. 'But I will do everything I can. You must head north through Fangrim. My guards will escort you to the fortress of Thormand. That is the edge of our realm, bordering that of the Dwarves. Thormand knows those lands as well as any. I will instruct him to speed you on your way.'

'I thank you, again,' Tarithel said.

'From there you are beyond my help,' Imorthorn said. 'Rest now, and depart at dawn. Speak of this to no one. In matters of such import I would normally consult my Lords, but …' He smiled at her. 'Sometimes a leader must press on, regardless. There will be much useless talk before I convince them all, you are better away from all that. All it would mean is delay.'

'I will do as you say,' she said. 'I must ask one more thing.'

'Still more?' Imorthorn replied, with a chuckle.

'Luxor,' Tarithel said. 'And I dare say my father too, will not be pleased. If you would stand against the Heartstealer …'

'Yes. Luxor must know of what has passed between us,' Imorthorn said. 'I can send riders to take news to him. It will be perilous for them to traverse the lands of the Barbarians but …'

Tarithel shook her head.

'There is a better way,' she answered. 'The Lord Luxor bears a Moon Ring, remember? Pledge your allegiance to him and he will be able to speak to you directly.'

'More magic out of the stories of legend,' Imorthorn mused. 'How must I perform such a pledge?'

'It is very simple,' she answered with a shrug and smile. 'You say … I pledge myself to Lord Luxor.'

Imorthorn blinked. 'And that is it?'

'It is,' she said. 'I have seen it before. My own father took such an oath not so long ago. I imagine the Moon Ring knows the true intentions of those who make the pledge.'

'Then such a pledge I will make,' Imorthorn said. 'I will put the Fey of Icemark at his disposal. You have proven yourself, Tarithel, you have convinced me. Consider that your first success.'

'I am in your debt, Lord Imorthorn,' Tarithel said.

Varangrim was roused by horns long before dawn. He lumbered to his feet and stomped down to the ramparts of the fortress. He could see the other giants were standing on the eastern side, looking out over the plains. Dawn had yet to break, but he could see fires burning in the dim light.

'Ah, Varangrim,' Carangrane said. 'It seems the Iceguard are bolder than we expected.'

'They've camped on the plains?' Varangrim asked.

'Not yet,' Carangrane said. 'But they are on the move.'

'We saw the lights of their torches an hour ago,' Ulformane said, gesturing out to the east. 'They were clustered around their fortress for a while, but they are marching towards us. They will be here at daybreak.'

'In what numbers?'

'No way to tell,' Fenorn said. 'Only the foremost ranks are marching with torches aloft. Five thousands perhaps, maybe more.'

'You think they mean to assault us here?' Varangrim said. 'They have allowed us to counter their strength unopposed. This is no sneak attack. What do they hope to gain?'

Carangrane rubbed his beard. 'These are not the Heartstealer's normal tactics. Perhaps the news from the south has given her new found arrogance.'

'We should ride out and meet them, teach them the errors of their ways,' Anvildrak said.

Fenorn nodded. 'They already trespass on our territory, are we to let them get away with this?'

Carangrane raised a hand.

'And give up the security of our fortress to stand in the open?' he asked. 'Nay. Let them march, we have strength enough to make them quail should they strike at us. Finish the preparations for a siege and set a watch.'

'And if they strike?' Anvildrak demanded.

'They won't! No ... there will just be more arrogance, more demands,' Carangrane muttered. 'Demands that we will refuse. Insults will be thrown, not spears or rocks. We will not rise to their provocation and it will be them who have a demeaning trudge back across the plains with nothing to show for their efforts but worn soles and sore blisters!'

Anvildrak and Fenorn looked disappointed. Varangrim saw them mutter to each other as they walked a few feet away, peering eastwards into the gloom.

'I wonder if our own people desire a war more than the Iceguard,' Varangrim said, under his breath.

Carangrane nodded. 'If a child crawls towards a fire and is pulled back time and again, sometimes harder discipline is required.'

'And if that doesn't work?'

'They burn their fingers and learn the hard way,' Carangrane replied. 'Come. Dawn is not far off. Let us see what these Iceguard fools are about.'

The twilight was drawing to a close, the eastern sky beginning to brighten when Luxor was roused from sleep. Around him, the camp of Moonguard and Barbarians remained asleep, save for the sentries posted around the boundaries. The Forest of Thangrun was a wholesome place, and the trees were spaced out, affording easy travel, good camping and a view of the stars at night.

Luxor sat up, rubbing the weariness from his eyes. There was an elusive taint upon the air, almost like a scent of something fresh and invigorating. He frowned for a moment, before recognising the sensation.

The Moon Ring! Someone has pledged their loyalty to me ...

He directed his vision towards the east, sweeping across hills and plains, seeking out the source of new connection. Within moments he felt drawn into another forest where a proud city stood in a fair valley.

The image of a Fey, old, grey and bearded, with a stern yet wise expression, appeared in his mind.

Luxor, the Moonprince, it is an honour to meet you.

'The honour is mine,' Luxor whispered, feeling the Moon Ring pulse upon his finger. 'To whom do I speak?'

I am Imorthorn, Lord of Fangrim, master of the Fey of Icemark. I have received a visit from a young Lady known to you ...

'Tarithel!' Luxor exclaimed.

She has spoken much about you and your travails, and she has commended both herself and you to me through her conduct.

'I am gratified to hear that,' Luxor answered. 'Tarithel is very dear to me.'

Yet I have news of her which you may not be pleased to hear.

'Of what do you speak?'

Tarithel continues on her quest, Moonprince. She is quite a determined young woman. She seeks her betrothed and would not tarry.

'I told her to wait for me,' Luxor rumbled. 'I am sworn to see her safely back to her father in Midnight.'

I deem a higher purpose calls her. Whilst in my realm she spoke to the spirit of the forest here. It revealed her purpose in all this, not only to rescue her betrothed, but also to seek the demise of the Heartstealer, that same evil that taints the Icemark and holds your son captive. She has been called … and she has gone.

Luxor was about to retort, but then he remembered the stories of what Tarithel had done in defence of the Citadel of Dreams in the battle for Midnight, remembered how her father had spoken of her strange gifts and how she had somehow eluded even the attention of Lorgrim the Wise on her flight north.

And yet …

'The demise of the Heartstealer?' Luxor repeated. 'To rescue Morkin would seem perilous enough and yes, she commands a measure of power … but how can she hope to defy that evil? Shareth has vast resources at her disposal, men, armies, the machinery of war …'

I do not have the answers, but it would seem the two quests are bound up with each other. Shareth stands between Tarithel and her betrothed. I did try to counsel against such a course, but the spirit of the forest seems clear … and Tarithel has very much made up her mind.

'She is stubborn, brave and forceful to a fault,' Luxor muttered.

Yet I found her good, generous and loyal. She knows her foe is Shareth the Heartstealer. And it will not be long before Shareth becomes aware of her, if she is not already. There are powers at work here, Moonprince, greater than you or I.

'And I am not pleased at being manipulated by them once again,' Luxor rumbled.

But by such things are great deeds done, so my histories tell me.

'Great deeds … ' Luxor sighed. 'I would prefer an honest

fight without this … this weight of some untold purpose hanging over me.'

I fear that fight will come, honest or not. But, Moonprince, I know you dispatched the Witchking. So tell me, what do you now intend here in the Icemark?

'I must consider what you have told me,' Luxor said. 'And I shall have words for Tarithel too, no doubt! For now, I travel north-west, in the company of the Barbarians of this realm, to seek audience with their leader, Imgorad. To gauge what support I might gain from the people of Icemark.'

Then you have already achieved much that I could not. The Barbarians and my people are long estranged, Moonprince. But I can give you something to aid you in rallying support for a stand against the Heartstealer. Tarithel has been a fair and honest envoy. The Fey of Icemark will stand with you against her evil, should you desire it.

'This is welcome news, Imorthorn of Fangrim.'

We are not as mighty as you might hope. Certainly we cannot defy the Heartstealer on her own, but combined with others, there might be a chance. Chance enough to give Tarithel time to fulfil her own quest. If you would have it, I will summon our strength.

'I would have it, and be most grateful for it.'

Then it shall be done. I pledge myself to this purpose, as the Moon Ring requires. Dawn breaks, Moonprince. May the sun shine on your endeavours …

The tingle of the Moon Ring's influence faded away, leaving Luxor staring at the glowing sky on the eastern horizon.

He took a deep breath, sensing a presence behind him. He turned to see Rorthron standing there.

'We need to talk.'

Dawn broke across the Forest of Fangrim, bright ribbons of orange and red cloud streaking from the eastern horizon. Imorthorn watched as the sun crept above the horizon. The day was clear, as if a faint hint of summer was on the air. Imorthorn took a deep breath.

She is gone now, I have spoken to the Moonprince. My decision is made. The wrath of the Heartstealer will be kindled further. Flame and war is coming. The fragile peace of the Icemark is at an end.

He turned and strode from the balcony that overlooked the city. He had summoned the other Fey Lords for a breakfast council. They were all awaiting him within the hall.

All three, the brothers Carorthane and Carorthand alongside Imgorthand, stood up as he entered.

'Is the Lady Tarithel not joining us?' Imgorthand asked.

'She is not,' Imorthorn replied.

'But, she did return from her ride into the forest?' Imgorthand continued. 'Somewhat overwrought, so I heard.'

Imorthorn looked at him for a moment. 'She did.'

'I would hear what she has to say,' Imgorthand said.

Imorthorn sat down and helped himself to a plate of meats and fruits.

'That will be difficult,' Imorthorn said. 'She is gone.'

'Gone?' All three Fey said in unison.

'I have sent her on her way,' Imorthorn said. He stopped eating and looked at them. 'Time for debate is over. It is by her hand that the Heartstealer is to be defeated. The Fey will see this done.'

'You would pitch us against the Heartstealer?' Imgorthand cried. 'Sending a girl, undefended into the north? She'll be waylaid by brigands within a day of leaving our lands.'

'She eluded our best guards,' Carorthane said. 'She has nothing to fear from brigands.'

'And if she reaches Shareth, what then?' Imgorthand

continued. 'She will die, slowly and horribly in some foul way, and Shareth will know it is the Fey of Fangrim who sent her. She will come and wreak her fury upon us. This is madness!'

'Shareth is coming anyway,' Imorthorn said. 'Whether we hide within our forests or not.'

'You've forced her hand,' Imgorthand said. 'She will not forgive us.'

'She never bore any love for the Fey,' Carorthand said. 'She plays a long game, sapping our strength away in petty disputes with our neighbours. Once we are all weak enough …'

'Yes,' Imorthorn replied. 'Long we have slumbered and left her unopposed. Our strength has diminished and hers has grown. Soon we will be too weak to have any choice in the matter.'

'But a girl, alone?' Imgorthand spluttered. 'Walking into a trap. Is that to be the sum of our strategy?'

'To take on the might of the Heartstealer?' Carorthane said, with a nod. 'I do not doubt her bravery, but how can she hope to succeed? How can you place such confidence in her? Plunging us into war if she makes it that far?'

Imgorthand looked across at Carorthane in surprise, the two of them hardly ever agreed on anything.

Imorthorn leant back in his chair.

'Fangrim spoke to her,' he said, his voice a whisper. 'Fangrim itself has spoken to Tarithel and placed a burden upon her.'

'Fangrim?' Imgorthand asked. 'What do you mean?'

'The girl has a power,' Imorthorn said. 'We might call it sorcery. Before my eyes she brought flowers to life. She tells how the forest of her homeland came to her aid in the battle against the Witchking, at her bidding.'

'Sorcery indeed,' Carorthane said.

'And how do we know she hasn't bewitched you?' Imgorthand said. 'We have known this girl but two days. She comes from a far off land, who's to say what she really intends?

More likely this Moonprince seeks to hide behind us, using what little of our might remains to delay the Heartstealer whilst he fortifies his homeland at our expense!'

'Imgorthand …' Carorthand said.

'And he sends a pretty girl with parlour tricks to woo us into a confrontation we cannot hope to win,' Imgorthand finished. 'It will go the worse for us. Mark my words.'

'I trust I am old enough and wise enough not be taken in by the charms of a young woman,' Imorthorn said, with a chuckle. 'I tested her integrity. She passed that test. I urged her to seek out the wisdom of the forest. She had the chance to run away, yet she came back to me.'

'And what was said?' Carorthand asked. 'Fangrim spoke? Truly?'

'She went to the Stones of Sirium,' Imorthorn said. 'Or she was led there. It seems that Fangrim itself fears the advances of the Heartstealer and would see her countered. Fangrim told Tarithel that she might be the means by which the Heartstealer would be defeated. A sorceress against a sorceress.'

'And you have sent her where?' Carorthane asked.

'First to Thormand,' Imorthorn said. 'He knows the road northwards better than any and can advise on approaching the Dwarves. She will have to travel through their realm regardless.'

'We cannot help her beyond our borders,' Carorthand said. 'Once into the realm of the Dwarves, what then? Is her stealth, her power, sufficient?'

'A lone traveller is hard to spot,' Carorthane added. 'She has that advantage at least.'

'The forest itself is at her call,' Imorthorn said. 'Secrecy and speed is her greatest ally. The Heartstealer does not know where she is. That must remain so for as long as it is possible.'

Carorthane and Carorthand nodded, Imgorthand shook his head.

'Then it is cast and done,' Imgorthand said. 'I still call it folly, trusting in imaginary words from the forest and a strange girl from a far off land, but little can be done now. We risk enflaming Shareth's wrath against us – mark my words! I fear we will hear no more of Tarithel from this moment forth. She'll probably be dead within the moon. Yet if, by lucky happenstance, she does reach the domain of the Heartstealer, what are we to do in the meantime?'

Imorthorn smiled. 'More sorcery I'm afraid.'

The three Fey Lords looked at him in surprise.

'Luxor, this heralded Moonprince of Midnight, bears a ring,' Imorthorn said. 'A war ring of that realm. It allows him the means to communicate with those who share his aims and ideals. I have spoken to him via it.'

'And?' Imgorthand asked.

'I have told him Fey will stand with Luxor,' Imorthorn said. 'He intends to rally the peoples of Icemark. Even now he has secured an audience with Imgorad of the Barbarians, perhaps he can succeed where others have failed. If the Icemark is being roused anew, we Fey will do our part when called.'

Imgorthand looked concerned, but Carorthand and Carorthane were nodding.

'About time we took a stand against her,' Carorthand said.

Imorthorn nodded. 'And convenient that we were all assembled when Tarithel arrived. Now I despatch you with an urgent mission. Assemble our strength, Carorthane to the west and Carorthand to the east. Imgorthand, rally your folk of the far south. Our armies must be prepared and mustered for battle within the moon. Ride swiftly!'

Chapter Eight

Glormane the Dwarf stands in the City of Glormane looking east to the Hall of Malorthuk.

Glormane pulled his cloak tighter about himself. A fierce wind was whistling across the walls of his city, blowing from the north-east from the nearby hills. Above him fluttered many of the banners of the greatest Dwarf lords of the realm.

Imgorarg.

Glormane could see his banners borne aloft outside the city gates. Imgorarg had camped outside, ensuring he could meet all the dwarven lords as they approached.

A cunning ploy. He seeks to bend ears to his will ahead of the Summons.

Glormane narrowed his eyes as he peered into the blustery gale. He'd made mistakes. He'd be the first to admit it. Their borders weren't as secure as they could have been. Incursions from the Giants and the Barbarians in particular hadn't been repelled as he would have liked. To the south the Fey lurked in their forests. They were the most peaceable, but doubtless they cast their spells and mischief as ever.

Yet I fear the north more than any other threat.

The Heartstealer and her Icelords had been conspicuous by their absence of late. There had been no reports of skirmishes around the mountains of Anvulane, that vast and almost impenetrable range of sharp jagged peaks that curled through the middle of the Icemark like a scythe. It was

Imgorarg himself who held those borders, though Carorthay also kept a close watch on the eastern roads.

Never trust an Icelord. That is what my father used to tell me. Giants are fierce but predictable, Barbarians reckless but bold. The Fey will work their magic, but will always hide amongst the trees when threatened ... just never trust an Icelord.

This day the Dwarves would have their say and have their vote. Glormane's father had passed on into the next life. The mantle of leadership lay with him now, the Summons should ratify that in front of all the dwarven people. Many had concerns and were here to lobby him for their agendas. He would listen and act accordingly.

But Imgorarg.

The surly Dwarf lord from the north was a threat to the peaceful conduct of the Summons. Glormane had seen him foment hatreds before, always pushing for the Dwarves to go on the offensive and wrest land and territory from the other races. He had been a constant irritant to Glormane's father. Worse still, on occasion, Imgorarg had been in the right, a stiffer defence and the occasional attack were warranted when the other races pushed too far. Many shared his views now; Glormane had often heard the grumbles of discontent.

But we are not strong enough to take on more than one of the other races, barely strong enough to hold our own. We must always tread a delicate balance between diplomacy and aggression, caught as we are between all the others in the midst of the Icemark. Anger any others too much and an alliance of foes might wipe us out. Imgorarg's war mongering would end our people in short moons.

Glormane would have to bring him under control for the benefit of all.

Luxor had led Rorthron some way from the camp of the Barbarians. The glow of the dawn was growing, it would not be long before the sun rose.

'I have received a pledge from Imorthorn of the Fey of Fangrim,' Luxor said. 'The very one who first warned us of the danger Shareth posed.'

'Tarithel reached him then,' Rorthron observed.

'Yes,' Luxor said. 'Imorthorn puts the Fey of his realm at our disposal should we wish it.'

'Welcome news,' Rorthron replied.

'But there is more,' Luxor grumbled. 'Tarithel continues on against my command. Imorthorn reports that she intends to ride to rescue Morkin.'

'Her love for him is motivation enough,' Rorthron said. 'Love is a powerful force, especially in one so young.'

Luxor pursed his lips.

'Imorthorn talked of some strange spirit of his forest revealing a greater purpose to Tarithel's quest,' Luxor said, his voice low. 'Not only does she intend to return my son, but somehow defy that hagspawn herself. Much as I admire her spirit ...'

Rorthron didn't volunteer a response.

Luxor glared at him.

'I am not a fool, Rorthron the Wise,' Luxor said. 'I saw your face when you learned that Tarithel had forged a path through to the Gate of Varenorn alone and unaided. I heard tell of what she did in the defence of Dreams in our struggle against the Doomguard. She is no mere Fey. You know more of this than you have told me.'

Rorthron rubbed his chin.

'Suspicions only, my dear Moonprince.'

'Then tell me what you suspect,' Luxor said. 'For a guess from you seems likely to be something I might rely on more than the firm convictions of others.'

Rorthron nodded.

'The girl has a power,' Rorthron said. 'That cannot be denied. Few even of the Wise could have forged such a path through the Frozen Wastes and certainly none of the Fey could have managed such a feat alone. Lorgrim was quite alarmed and befuddled by it. Quite how she did this, even I cannot say. I made some subtle enquiries whilst we sojourned at the Citadel of Dreams and it seems that Tarithel demonstrated nothing unusual in her ways and behaviour until she was granted the rank of Lady of the Forest by her father, a title all the Fey considered to be nothing more than an honorary position amongst their people.'

'And after this she was able to command the forest in some fashion?' Luxor asked. 'I heard the very trees came to her call when she summoned them against the Doomguard.'

'It would seem so,' Rorthron replied.

'This power she has then,' Luxor said. 'Might it be fully enough, when measured against the Heartstealer?'

'That I cannot say,' Rorthron replied. 'Without knowing precisely what it is … and I do not know. Certainly, there are powers in these lands that might be strong enough to defy Shareth …'

Rorthron's voice tailed off and he looked up to the horizon.

'You have a story to tell,' Luxor said. 'I know that expression.'

Rorthron turned back and smiled. 'It is incomplete and I have told no others of this. It is not a story of which you will be fond, Moonprince, as it involves powers which exist beyond the reach and knowledge of men. Magic, as your men of the Free would call it.'

'Such things I seem cursed to be a part of,' Luxor said. 'Tell me nonetheless.'

'Very well,' Rorthron said. 'Much of what I am about to say

is known only to the Wise themselves and forms the ancient history of our race. You recall the tale of Ushgarak and Gryfallon of course, the construction of the Ice Crown, forged in the Frozen Wastes in the very depths of winter?'

'I am unlikely to forget it,' Luxor replied.

'Would you be surprised to learn that there are other Crowns?' Rorthron said.

Luxor's face blanched.

'Not like unto the Ice Crown,' Rorthron said. 'Do not concern yourself about the return of the Ice Fear, that was a pallor unique to the Witchking's own foul enchantments.'

'I will start to breathe once more,' Luxor said, with a chuckle.

'You know that long ago the Wise were pledged to the protection of all these realms … Midnight … Icemark … and beyond,' Rorthron said. 'A duty in which they failed, holing themselves up in their towers and washing their hands of responsibility. The rise of the Witchking was one outcome of that. Perhaps you have wondered why the Wise were unable to counter him.'

'I have often asked why that should be,' Luxor said. 'The Wise, if the number of towers they built is any guide, would seem numerous enough.'

'They were once many,' Rorthron said. 'Most are now moribund beyond recall, their towers locked and inviolable. Long before I was born the Wise were great and powerful, deeds such as you have seen me perform are but the faintest echo of what my people could once attain … but you see, all those powers were lost.'

'Lost?'

Rorthron nodded.

'It is a story of perhaps the greatest folly of all the lands,' Rorthron said. 'The Wise were concerned that these powers … they called it the "First Power" … would be abused, that the Wise would come to be despots, enslaving the other races about them, so they determined to spread that power in such a way that no single individual might wield enough to set themselves above others.'

'I would likely approve of such a thing,' Luxor said. 'But continue …'

'The Wise took their powers, and split them.' Rorthron said. 'They crafted Talismans of great potency and channelled their powers within them, giving them to Kings and Queens, Lords and Ladies … and the leaders of other races … thinking to empower them to govern their affairs in an orderly way. The First Power was broken asunder to do this.'

'These Talismans,' Luxor echoed. 'They still exist?'

Rorthron chuckled. 'They do indeed. You have encountered two already, Moonprince. One your son destroyed …'

'The Ice Crown.'

'And another you bear upon your finger even now.'

Luxor looked down at his hand, seeing the Moon Ring on his finger. The ring pulsed with energy.

'Something so potent could only be such a Talisman,' Rorthron said. 'The gift of far-seeing, the ability to spread the warmth of your mind across the realm? These are, in fact, the true powers of the Wise as they once were. I guarded it for hundreds of moons until your line of descent became clear to me.'

Luxor turned his hand back and forth, appraising the ring anew.

'Then there are others too?' Luxor asked.

'There are,' Rorthron replied. 'Midnight was not the only realm so blessed … or cursed might be the better word perhaps. Other Crowns were forged, and beside them other Talismans of power. There were hundreds so I understand, but most have doubtless been lost beyond recall in the long years since they were made, but a few will still be present here in the Icemark. Where they might yet be, I cannot say, but they remain and they are potent.'

'But Tarithel bears no Talisman,' Luxor said, with a frown.

Rorthron smiled. 'Perhaps she does.'

'The jewel?' Luxor said, looking up with a flash of realisation. 'The jewel that Tarithel was given … might it be one as well?'

'It is at least possible,' Rorthron replied. 'According to the Lord of Dreams Tarithel was given that jewel to wear to mark the occasion of her becoming Lady of the Forest. Perhaps the jewel was more potent than the Fey knew. It would explain much.'

'It would,' Luxor mused. 'Yet, that jewel was an heirloom of their house, was it not? Why Tarithel, and why now? Her mother bore it for many years …'

'Without any indication of such powers,' Rorthron said with a nod. 'Yes. A shrewd observation. That the jewel is able to manifest its powers through Tarithel, marks her out for great things I suspect. There is certainly more to her than meets the eye.'

'But these abilities are not without penalty,' Luxor muttered. 'This ring gives me great abilities, but at the cost of my own strength at times. What power might that jewel give her and at what detriment?'

'I cannot be sure of any of this,' Rorthron replied. 'You asked me to guess, and so I have. I do not think it is an accident that Tarithel has been gifted this jewel, likewise you were supposed to bear the Moon Ring. Shareth may also have Talismans at her disposal, she would certainly have known about them from her father.'

'And this … spirit of the forest that Imorthorn talked about …'

'As you recall,' Rorthron said. 'The Forest of Dreams came to the aid of Tarithel when her Citadel was besieged. Corleth also told me that he was freed from Dregrim by the actions of the Forest there. Perhaps that potency exists in the Forests of Icemark too and Tarithel is able to command it …'

'Or be led by it,' Luxor said. 'These Talismans are not merely tools, at least, that has not been my experience. Often this ring you gave me seems to have a will of its own, guiding my hand, or suggesting some preferred outcome.'

'You speak wisely,' Rorthron said, with a chuckle. 'The Wise feared the First Power for some reason, hence they broke it up. Lorgrim himself believed that the Witchking was searching for the Talismans, perhaps to reunite them and thus bend them to his own will.'

'I remember the Witchking's glee when I confronted him,' Luxor said, with a frown growing on his features. 'He seemed pleased … delighted … he said … the Moon Ring I have long sought and you have brought it direct to me!'

'Yet his perfidy was undone,' Rorthron said.

'Yes,' Luxor said. 'And the Moon Ring aided me in that objective … and when that was accomplished, I vividly recall the Moon Ring cooling upon my finger, its fires and potency waning, as if it knew it had accomplished its task. Only to be reignited once more once knowledge of Shareth came to me …'

Rorthron nodded.

'Then these Talismans do know their own minds,' Luxor mused. 'And if they are all remnants of this First Power of which you speak … might that Power not have some greater purpose?'

'The Witchking seemed to believe so,' Rorthron replied. 'He sought to steer them to his own will. His daughter may harbour a similar thought …'

'To gather together the remnants of this First Power,' Luxor whispered. 'To what end?'

'At the very least, the Talismans magnify the attributes of those that bear them,' Rorthron answered. 'In her case …'

'Cruelty, misery, suffering and enslavement,' Luxor said. 'If she grows yet stronger, her potency enhanced by ancient powers … we will not be able to stop her. The Witchking had but one Talisman …'

'And a lesser one,' Rorthron answered. 'The most recently crafted of all, in many ways a poor imitation of that ancient art.'

Luxor took a deep breath.

'Then I must speak to Tarithel.'

Tarithel reined in Álainn as a presence filled her mind. She had been dreading the communication.

'My Lord Luxor,' she said, bracing herself for his wrath.

Tarithel. I have spoken to Imorthorn and …

'Let me explain!' Her voice was a near shout, surprising her with its volume. 'My Lord … there is much to tell you.'

I know you venture north against the instructions I gave you …

'I have good reason!'

I know.

Tarithel gasped and the words she was about to utter died on her lips. There was no anger present in Luxor's tone, only a feeling of regret.

'You will not forbid me to go?'

Now there was a faint sense of amusement that floated about her for a moment.

Would it avail me much?

'No,' Tarithel answered.

I thought so! I have learnt from Imorthorn of what has been told to you by the spirit of the forest, and Rorthron has confirmed many of my own fears regarding the strange powers that seem to exist about us. But I would hear it from you.

Tarithel took a deep breath.

'My Lord,' she said. 'Imorthorn speaks truth. I did intend to follow your wishes, truly I did! But the Forest here, Fangrim it is called, spoke to me, clear as day. I am to seek out Morkin and rescue him from the clutches of the Heartstealer, but I am bound also to confront this witch. The power of the forests of Icemark and Midnight accompany me and guide me onwards.'

Your fate seems directed by powers beyond my reckoning … as does mine. I do not pretend to like it, but it seems the Witchking has forced us all down a road that now his daughter follows too. If she is not vanquished, Icemark and hence Midnight will be assailed by not only great armies and great wrath, but the potency of ancient magic too. With great reluctance I must defy your father and encourage you upon your way.

'My father will forgive us both,' Tarithel answered, tears coming to her eyes. 'Surely he will.'

For my part, it seems I must attempt what I have already been told is impossible, to rally the disparate races of the Icemark to stand against this cursed hagspawn in battle.

'You have rallied great forces before,' Tarithel said. 'You can do it again. I know you can!'

I thank you for your confidence! Yet I counsel great caution. I have borne this Moon Ring for some time and know its potency well, it is not all it seems to be. The jewel you bear, if it be at all similar to the Moon Ring … treat it cautiously; use it only in extreme need. I fear these Talismans seek to use us, rather than the other way round.

Tarithel shivered. She rolled the jewel between her fingers.

'I have wondered the same,' she said. 'I will be mindful of what you have said.'

Ride on then Tarithel. Ride on! Find Morkin, free him … I would have us all stand together once more in defiance of this accursed Heartstealer. Always remember that we have already defeated her father … and we will be victorious once again. Last time it was Morkin that left on a lonely quest into the un-

known, now that fate has befallen you. He succeeded … and so shall you!

Tarithel could not find words to reply, but a furious sense of exaltation surged through her. She spurred Álainn and yelled at the top of her lungs, charging off through the forest at a furious pace.

Imgorthand had ridden out at Imorthorn's request. His army, a small group of one hundred Fey at arms rode with him, heading back towards his own city far to the south-east, beyond the eaves of the Forest of Fangrim. The easiest route took them out of the valley and then on to the Plains of Faray.

Alongside him rode Morildrane the Fey.

'Imorthorn sent the girl off without consulting the council?' Morildrane asked.

'Yes. He said not one word to us,' Imgorthand replied. 'None of us were too impressed with that, I can tell you.'

'Did he explain himself?'

'Only to say that leaders must sometimes act quickly,' Imgorthand said. 'He would take no questions on the matter. He told us that the Fey have aligned ourselves with this Moonprince of Midnight from the southern realms.'

'And thus against the Heartstealer,' Morildrane replied. 'Once she find out things will not go well for us. It seems …'

Morildrane's voice tailed off.

Imgorthand turned to look at Morildrane.

'You can say what is on your mind, have no fear.'

'It seems … well … so reckless!' Morildrane answered, his voice low. 'Pitching us into conflict with the Heartstealer on the word of a girl and a warrior from another land we haven't even met? Embroiling us in a conflict we neither started nor stand to gain anything from? Who is to say what kind of character this

Luxor really is? Shareth we know, both her power and her habits … what will the Barbarians make of this? The Giants and the Dwarves? This plunges us into uncertainty on all sides!'

Imgorthand nodded. 'I hear your words. But we have all been assigned our duties. We are to rally the Fey to the banner of the Moonprince. Imorthorn has decreed it.'

Morildrane grew silent, thinking it through.

'We must apportion this duty,' Imgorthand said. 'We will ride together until we reach your fortress. Then I must send you south to speak to Berormane, Lorangrim, Tharand and Imorthesh. I will ride on east to summon Lorangriel, Thorthand, Ingormiel and Thigrand.'

Morildrane nodded. 'Fear not, my Liege. We will ride as swiftly as we may.'

'We will arrange to meet at the city of Lorangriel before the moon is out,' Imgorthand said. 'Our orders would have us rendezvous back at the City of Imorthorn as soon as can be arranged.'

Morildrane nodded and they rode on in silence for a time. The forest around them seemed subdued.

'Imorthorn places great faith in this girl,' Imgorthand muttered. 'But I fear you may have spoken the truth.'

'He has sent her on her way you said?' Morildrane asked. 'Do you know to where?'

'She rides towards Thormand as we speak,' Imgorthand said. 'Imorthorn seems swayed by some nonsense about her hearing the voice of Fangrim of all things.'

'The voice of Fangrim?' Morildrane asked. 'The forest has a voice?'

'Imorthorn sent her into the forest,' Imgorthand replied. 'She claimed the forest spoke to her, and set her on a path to confront the Heartstealer herself. Imagine that, a girl, facing down that fell sorceress with nothing but a pretty smile and a toss of her red hair!'

'She does not know of the danger?'

'Oh, she knows alright,' Imgorthand replied. 'But she has gone anyway. I imagine she will be set upon a few days after she wanders into the realms of the Dwarves. They will have some sport with her and that will be that. Perhaps that will change Imorthorn's mind.'

'Would it not have been better to keep her with us?' Morildrane asked. 'If she truly does have powers of some merit, they could have been used in the defence of our realm, not on some foolhardy quest.'

'I don't disagree,' Imgorthand said. 'It seems folly of the utmost kind to me too.'

'Such powers as she had,' Morildrane said. 'Did Imorthorn say what they were?'

'Some flight of fancy, bringing flowers to life or some such,' Imgorthand said. 'Sorcery he called it. She will have to do better than that if she wishes to defeat the Heartstealer.'

'But if she is captured …'

'Aye,' Imgorthand acknowledged. 'Precisely the point I made. Imorthorn pitches us against the Heartstealer where we would be better advised to stay out of her affairs. Well … it is done now. He claims he has spoken to this Moonprince and pledged our support.'

'How so?' Morildrane asked. 'The Moonprince is leagues away to the west is he not?'

'More of this untrustworthy magic for you,' Imgorthand said. 'This Luxor bares a ring of some potency. It provides a means for him to speak and hear across the Icemark. Imorthorn speaks to him thusly.'

'And this … magic,' Morildrane said, pursing his lips. 'I wonder should we trust it. Is it wholesome?'

'That, my friend,' Imgorthand said. 'Is a very good question indeed.'

The great hall of the city was filling rapidly, the buzz of heavy conversation echoing off the ancient rafters that hung low across the ceiling. The hall was roughly hewn, unfinished wood in the fashion of the Dwarves. Little decoration save helms and weapons adorned the walls. Tables and chairs were likewise stout and free from embellishment. Dwarven lords and their entourages were crowding inwards, pushing and shoving for position amongst the melee. It was the dwarven way.

Imelorn and Imulorn pushed through the raucous crowds, making their ways towards the front where Glormane could be seen, one foot resting on an ancient tree stump placed at the far end of the hall. An axe was buried in it. It was said that the first king of the Dwarves had felled the tree with his axe, thus establishing the kingdom. Whether that was really true, nobody knew, but in living memory, the affairs of the kingdom had been conducted in its presence. Nothing was decided until it was 'stumped'.

'No ale,' Imelorn grumbled. 'You'd have thought they would have provided a repast at the very least.'

'That comes later,' Imulorn replied. 'Once business in complete, otherwise half the lords will be in a stupor before the vote. Ale and politics don't mix well … or perhaps they mix too well!'

'I don't see Carorthay,' Imelorn said, looking around him.

Imulorn nodded. 'Yes, he should be here by now, something has delayed him it seems. It's a long march from the east of the Kingdom.'

'I'd hear what he has to say,' Imelorn muttered.

'We should pay attention to what Imgorarg says,' Imulorn replied, giving his brother a nudge. 'Look …'

At the rear of the hall they could see Imgorarg and his entourage striding through the double doors. Imgorarg paused on the threshold, eyeing those about him. Conversation petered out. The two brothers saw Glormane straighten. For a moment the two Dwarves locked gazes, but the moment passed without either saying anything.

'Lords, Warriors, Friends,' Glormane began, raising his voice over the remaining buzz and looking around at the assembly. Silence settled around him as he spoke. It was the traditional dwarven greeting favoured by the older generation. 'My father is dead and the mantel of leadership must pass on.' Glormane rested his hand upon the axe embedded in the stump. It, too, was ancient, the one which had felled the stump according to dwarven lore, its handle decorated with many runes and carvings.

'We stand, as always, at a crossroads. Decisions must be made about the future of our kingdom. Our lands are central in the Icemark, bordered by the other races which vie for trade and land about us. Some of you have told me we do not defend our borders adequately …'

There was a rumble of agreement from the ranks of the Dwarves. Imulorn saw nods from Gloruk, Berangrorn and Thelak, Lords whose fortresses in the west had often been involved in skirmishes with the Barbarians and Giants in the last few years.

'… I will heed these warnings,' Glormane said. 'Trade we must protect and peace I will pursue, but not at the cost of our own security. Our borders remain our borders and we must defend what is ours …'

'Pretty words.'

Heads turned to the back of the hall. Imgorarg stood there, his own axe head down on the floor, his hands poised on the top of its shaft.

'You have something to say, Imgorarg of the northern

reaches?' Glormane said, his voice low as he used the formal way to recognise the other Dwarf.

Imgorarg didn't respond for a moment, but picked up his axe and then dropped it head first on the floor of the hall. The symbolism wasn't lost on the Dwarves around him.

'Under your father's … leadership,' Imgorarg rumbled. 'I have seen Barbarians ride up the gap of Carormarg unchallenged to our very front doors. I have seen the Fey dazzle our people with trinkets, soft silks and idle finery in exchange for hard won gold. I have heard the Giants scorn us to our faces and not heard us make a response.' He paused and leant forward. 'I have seen us grow weak.'

'Our borders remain ours,' Glormane replied. 'I would see them strengthened as I have already stated. Thus it will be.'

'We will need more than words to hold our borders,' Imgorarg replied. 'We will need sharpened axes and a willingness to use them, or the flags of the Fey will flutter in the south and those of the Barbarians in the west where once all was ours.'

'We will hold what is ours,' Glormane said. 'But I will not countenance outright war with those around us. We remain strong, but we cannot fight a battle on more than one flank, this has always been our way. Fight the Fey and the Barbarians invade, fight the Barbarians and the Giants stride through the mountains …'

Imgorarg nodded. 'You speak wisely, Glormane of the central plains. But what of alliances? Alone we wither, do we not?' Imgorarg spread his arms wide, stepping around his axe, looking at the Dwarves beside him. 'Why not seek to forge a greater strength?'

'With whom?' Glormane said. 'The other races are no friends of ours. Barbarians? Fey? Giants? All seek what is best for their peoples alone …'

'Which is where your wisdom falters,' Imgorarg growled, turning back to face Glormane. 'I speak of a greater power.'

A low murmur hummed across the assembled crowd. Glormane could see the Dwarves muttering to each other, but they had all turned to Imgorarg to hear what he had to say.

Glormane stepped away from the stump, his hands on his hips.

'We do not speak of them. Their treachery … her treachery! It is well known. Our fathers knew this … and their fathers before them. That wisdom does not die.'

'So you say,' Imgorarg said. 'But you speak of ages past, moons long consigned to the annals of history. Why, when last did the Iceguard sully our borders, eh? When? I have read the history books. Battles with the Fey, the Barbarians and the Giants are all recounted in recent tales … those of the Iceguard? No, they have not been our foe for long, long moons.'

More mutterings filled the hall.

'We will have no dealings with the Heartstealer!' Glormane cried, raising his voice. 'Never trust an Icelord.'

This was greeted with nods of approval from the older Dwarves.

'Aye,' Imgorarg said with a smile. 'I remember that lesson, pounded into me as a child by the old seers. I never thought to question it until I saw it for the indoctrination and hide-bound thinking it truly is.'

'Treat with the sorceress?' Glormane asked. 'Her evil is spread across her lands like a plague. Fell and black arts are her ways, treachery and lies! Darkness and gloom accompany her at all times. Her Icelords slaughtered thousands of our people …'

'Evil is but a point of view,' Imgorarg replied, waving his arm in a dismissive gesture. 'And we slaughtered Icelords in the same numbers, do we not celebrate our glorious victories at their expense? Ancient history is long behind us. The future of our kingdom is what is at stake.'

'I will countenance no deal with that hagspawn,' Glormane rumbled.

'But I would,' Imgorarg replied, his voice low.

Silence fell in the hall. The Dwarves looked back to Glormane.

'So,' he said, after a long moment had passed. 'You challenge me for the leadership of our Kingdom, flouting our traditions and our ways for your own advancement?'

The older dwarven lords nodded in agreement at Glormane's words, casting disapproving looks in Imgorarg's direction.

'I care little for advancement,' Imgorarg replied. 'I care only for the fate of our Kingdom. I would not see our lands lost piecemeal and our people enslaved for the sake of old thinking and slavish adherence to tradition. New thoughts, new ways! Let us look to the future and not to the past!'

The younger Dwarves in the hall cheered at his words. Glormane could see they outnumbered the older ones by two to one.

'But you're right in one thing,' Imgorarg said as the cheers subsided. 'I do challenge you.'

The hall descended into confusion, angry shouts filled the air and all semblance of order was lost. The Summons was over, and inconclusive.

Imelorn looked across at his brother. Imulorn had been watching the altercation with growing dismay.

'This is getting interesting,' he shouted in his brother's ear, struggling to be heard over the din. 'Time for that ale?'

Luxor blinked. Whilst he had been talking to Tarithel by the strange potency of the Moon Ring, the sun had risen over the distant hills. Before long, the Barbarians would be stirring and the camp would be broken.

'You spoke to her?' Rorthron asked.

'I did,' Luxor said. 'She is as determined as I thought she would be, and related the same tale as Imorthorn. She goes to rescue Morkin and defy Shareth, with the spirit of the forest, whatever that might be, the power behind her motivation.'

'And …?' Rorthron asked.

'She cannot defy the Heartstealer alone,' Luxor answered. 'Therefore if I am also to defy that wretched hagspawn, I cannot do it with one mere garrison of moon guard, however skilled and loyal. I must do what the Fey and these Barbarians have told me is impossible. Rally the Icemark to my banner.'

Rorthron nodded.

'And such a thing has always been your intent,' Luxor said, giving Rorthron a glare. 'Has it not?'

Rorthron regarded him from under his bristling eyebrows for a long moment.

'I have always believed that evil should be countered, ere it grows stronger,' Rorthron said. 'The end of the Witchking availed us much, but his daughter is a weed of the same type. Unchecked, that malevolence will grow back swiftly and be worse than before. Save Morkin, you are the last of the House of the Moon. Perhaps it is your fate to combat such wickedness.'

'I do not like being an instrument of fate,' Luxor grunted. 'Nor having my paths decided for me by you or anyone else!'

'You will have much need of your own skills in the days and moons ahead I think,' Rorthron replied. 'Convincing the Barbarians will not be easy.'

'And you?' Luxor asked. 'How do you intend to occupy yourself whilst I play the diplomat?'

'I shall do what I have always done,' Rorthron replied. 'I will seek answers to the mysteries that befuddle us. I will look for knowledge of these Talismans, what they can do, where they might be found.'

Rorthron cast a glance to the south-east, where the tower they had passed on the previous day could be seen, casting a long shadow in the first rays of dawn.

'You have been eyeing that tower for the last two days,' Luxor observed. 'Ever since it came into sight. It looks the same as any other to me.'

'Aye,' Rorthron replied. 'It does, but something calls me to it. Perhaps there is something there which might enlighten us.'

'You wish to depart now?' Luxor asked.

'I do,' Rorthron replied. 'There is a sense of urgency, or perhaps uneasiness is the right word … for which I have no explanation.'

'We should ensure you take your leave of our hosts,' Luxor said. 'I cannot afford to risk their good will.'

'Indeed not,' Rorthron said. 'I will be as swift as I can and will return here the very next day.'

'Very well,' Luxor replied. 'Do not be late!'

'Do not fear,' Rorthron replied. 'With that accomplished I will seek to extend your influence to more distant lands. The Giants of this realm might be a potent ally. Thus, once we have settled our affairs with the Barbarians, I will venture further north.'

Luxor nodded.

'And Tarithel now goes to the Dwarves. Perhaps we will find some allies amongst these estranged people.'

'Let us hope so, Moonprince,' Rorthron said. 'Much depends upon our combined actions ere the moon is out.'

The skies above the Fortress of Kahangrorn were grey and gloomy, but the storms that had raged above its dark walls had spent their fury and dissipated. Shareth was elsewhere.

CHAPTER EIGHT

Beyond Kahangrorn, to the south and east lay a dismal clump of forest. Shareth had ventured within, coming at last upon an austere construction tangled with vines and twisted creepers. Long ago it had been a place of worship to priests, priestess and acolytes, all serving some long forgotten religion. Now its potency had been discovered once again, but harnessed by dark and mysterious forces.

The Temple of Obenad.

There were many such constructions through the Icemark, ignored through fear by the inhabitants. None ventured within them, rumours of evil traps that snared the unwary abounded and grew more terrifying with each recall. Shareth had done nothing to assuage such rumours, they served her purpose well.

Yet, she alone amongst all of Icemark, had discovered their purpose and subverted it to her will. She had ventured down the long abandoned walkways, mapped the labyrinthine halls, confronted such powers as still resided there, overcome them and divined their secrets. Her power grew all the greater, her reach and vision longer and clearer.

Within, the shadowy corridors were silent save for a faint rumble that echoed out of the hollows far below.

Through many levels of stone lay a chamber, carved out of the bedrock upon which the temple had been constructed long ago. There were no torches, the room was shrouded in darkness, a blackness impenetrable to the eyes of those who lacked the skills to appreciate the elemental arts that had been twisted together during its formation. She had unlocked its secrets.

To Shareth, its contours were familiar, she moved with ease, her vision augmented far beyond the mere visible.

At the centre of the chamber strange icons, texts, runes and markings were carved into the floor. She stepped inside their boundaries, a faint red light flickering around her.

She gestured and cyan flames licked through the carven shapes, fire fed by some unseen source. Yet there was no heat, only a blaze of colour. Fire ran up her robes, but no harm came to her.

Images flickered before her, taking form within the colours of the flames.

A Fey, a Dwarf and a Barbarian.

Their features were indistinct, but she knew who they were. This was not the first time she had contacted them in this manner. They were awaiting her instructions.

'What news from Fangrim?' she demanded.

The image of the Fey turned to regard her, bowing low. Far to the south, in a temple of similar construction, the real Fey saw an image of her in turn.

'We have had a visitor,' he said. 'A young Fey-girl from the land of Midnight.'

'As expected, she went to the Fey first,' Shareth said.

'Imorthorn is bewitched by the girl,' he replied. 'She has turned his ear and addled his mind. He has sent her away whilst he rallies his people to stand with the Moonprince from Midnight. He speaks to the Moonprince via a war ring of Midnight.'

Rage blazed from her, the flames around her leaping high, but they were soon brought back down as Shareth considered the news.

'A war ring, yes, my father mentioned this Talisman … I expected little else of Imorthorn,' she said. 'Long he has resisted my rule, but his undoing is close now and a stand with the Moonprince will be the last in a long line of poor choices. The girl, when did she leave and where was she bound?'

'Yester eve she left the city,' the Fey replied. 'But her movements were a closely guarded secret, none knew save Imorthorn until after the event.'

'So,' Shareth said, a smile crackling across her features. 'Imorthorn doesn't even trust his own people.'

'But he sent her northwards,' the Fey added. 'For all others were sent in different directions.'

'And do all agree with Imorthorn's decision?' Shareth demanded.

'Most, but there are rumbles of discontent,' the Fey replied.

'Then fan those flames,' Shareth said. 'Imorthorn's gaze must be turned inwards, not outwards. Let Fangrim ring with turmoil.'

The Fey nodded.

'More of this girl.' Shareth demand. 'Tell me of what you have found out.'

'She calls herself Tarithel and bears the title 'Lady of the Forest'' the Fey said.

'Tarithel ...'

'She hails from the same realm of Midnight as does the Moonprince,' The Fey continued. 'She has some allure about her, some power ... and she wears a bright green jewel about her neck. She entered our realm secretly, eluding our guards, coming to the very city before she announced her presence. Some magic surrounds her. Imorthorn is quite besotted with her.'

'An enchantress,' Shareth mused. 'And Lady of the Forest? I know a little of Fey lore, such titles are granted to those that tend the Forests of their realms.'

And the jewel? Could it too be a Talisman?

'Imorthorn sent her into the forest,' the Fey continued. 'Shortly after her return she was sent onwards. I would surmise she is heading into the realm of the Dwarves by now.'

'You hear that?' Shareth said, turning her attention to the image of the Dwarf alongside.

'I do, glorious Empress of the Icemark,' the Dwarf replied. 'If we should find her?'

'Kill her,' Shareth said, her lip curling with distaste. 'And bring me her carcass, for I will decorate the walls of

Kahangrorn with her flayed skin. Mark the jewel she wears, retrieve that for me, I wish to possess it.'

'It shall be done as you say,' the Dwarf replied, with a bow.

'What news of Glormane and his fall from grace?'

'Everything is in place, Empress,' the Dwarf replied. 'He is weak and weakened further, it will not be long before the Dwarves all pay homage to you …'

'As it should always have been,' Shareth snapped.

'Your majesty …' the Dwarf replied, bowing even lower.

'And from the Barbarians?' Shareth asked, turning her attention to the third figure.

'We have seen this Moonprince,' the Barbarian replied. 'He arrived as you warned us he might, stealthily, via the Gate of Varenorn. Our kindred already intercepted him; he journeys towards Imgorad in the company of Careneon, Torinarg and an old man in a deep purple robe.'

'Rorthron of the Wise is he,' she said. 'Assail him not, he is a foe beyond your power. I will put an end to his mischief in time. Where is the Moonprince bound?'

'They turned aside on the edges of my domain, heading north-west,' the Barbarian replied. 'They travel towards Imgorad himself.'

Shareth nodded.

'So the Moonprince turns the Fey to his whim, seeks an alliance with the Barbarians and sends his Fey-girl to the Dwarves. He will find his ambitions thwarted within the moon.'

'Imgorad will likely grant him an audience,' the Barbarian said. 'He is wily and wise, and will perceive the opportunity the Moonprince's arrival gives.'

'Then he must be made aware of all the facts,' Shareth said. 'For the Moonprince is no ally of the Barbarians … behold!'

Shareth gestured again and another image took form, this time of a battle ravaged Citadel. Armies stood facing each other, the three watchers could make out men alike to the Iceguard, and others holding to the defence of the Citadel.'

'Behold the true colours of the Moonprince,' Shareth yelled. 'See here his betrayal! What you see before you is the Citadel of Xajorkith, far to the south in the realm of Midnight. Here is your ancient kin, the Utarg of Utarg, come to parley with the Moonprince. See how the Moonprince treats with him.'

Before them, the image shifted. A huge man, clad in the manner of the Barbarians strode forth, gesturing to the armoured men before them. Yet a woman stood in his way. The woman raced towards him, knives raised. A fierce battle ensued, but before a minute had passed the man lay dead or dying at the woman's feet, her knives slick with his blood.

'Murdered by one of his sorceress lackeys in cold blood at his command,' Shareth said, her voice a whisper. The image of the citadel faded away. 'The Moonprince is no friend of the Barbarians. He will bring the Fey against you, just as he did in Midnight before he slew my father. Tell Imgorad of this perfidy, then let him decide whether to ally himself with such as him.'

'It shall be done,' the Barbarian replied.

'And what of the Giants?' the Fey demanded.

Shareth turned upon him and he quailed at the vengeful look upon her face.

'Their demise is at hand, and their lands ripe for the taking,' she said, a cruel smirk twisting on her features. 'It will not be long before I have new instructions for you. Heed them when they come, report on the puerile antics of your current leaders, follow my commands and it will be you who will soon have dominion over your lands within my empire. Once all is subdued, other lands beckon for our control and they shall fall as swiftly as the Icemark. I have deemed it, so shall it be.'

'So shall it be,' the three figures echoed.

'You will have need of power in the days ahead,' Shareth said, gesturing in the air with an outstretched finger. A strange cyan glow followed her movements and a sphere of malevolent light hovered before her. She reached within it, plucking out what seemed to be a number of golden chains with an obsidian gem affixed to each of them.

'These will give you the power to both sway minds and influence those about you,' she instructed. 'And in time of need you may use it deal with my foes. Take them and spread my will about the Icemark!'

With another gesture from her, the golden chains floated towards the darkened images of those she spoke to. She saw them reach up and grab them, placing them around their necks.

'A great honour, Empress of the Icemark,' they all intoned.

'Go now,' she said. 'There is much to be done!'

Shareth dismissed them with a final swing of her arm. Their images faded into the darkness.

She staggered back, steadying herself against the wall before sinking to her knees.

These spells, they cost me ...

She stayed that way for long minutes, her head bowed.

Then she laughed, and her mirth echoed through the ancient temple, crescendoing with glee and delight.

She made her way upwards, following the ancient pathways, bypassing the feeble traps left for adventurous fools who might venture within, arriving at the surface once more.

It was midnight, the stars clear in the firmament above. Two Iceguard warriors stood waiting for her. She beckoned them across.

'I return to Imiriel now,' she said. 'It is time. You know what must be done to the west. Issue the orders as I have directed and move upon the dawn. There must be no mercy, it must be swift, deadly and overwhelming. We have lulled them into expecting more foolish posturing. They will not understand their fate until they are already doomed.'

The warriors nodded.

'It will be done,' they both echoed.

'Make haste,' Shareth said. 'Ride through the night to Kahudrun. At dawn break on the morrow, it begins. Long I have prepared for this, the fall of the Icemark! All of it shall be mine, all of it!'

She watched as they mounted their dark steeds and rode off towards the forest boundaries, disappearing from sight in moments. Shareth waited until they were gone before looking to the horizon.

Out of the darkness her own horse moved to her, its outline just discernible in the starlight. She mounted it and spurred it around, heading northwards at a gallop, its hooves catching cyan sparks in the darkness.

Chapter Nine

Shareth the Heartstealer stands in the City of Imiriel looking south to the Frozen Wastes.

Dawn broke across the plains of Morormarg, red light spilling across the great Giant fortress of Ulformane. It stood in the midst of the Morormarg, an empty desolate land that separated the realm of the Icemark to the east from the lands of the Giants in the west. It had long been in contention between the two races.

Light flickered from halberds, swords and spears. Bows were strung, quivers filled. Before the gates of the fortress an army stood, arranged in neat ordered rows, shields held firm before each man.

Beyond them, across the plain, mist lay heavy and thick all about, swirling with restrained menace.

Carangrane looked down upon them from the walls of the fortress, Varangrim beside him.

'I see the banners of Kahudrun, Kahangriel and Imgasharg,' Varangrim said, looking at the devices on the dark hued flags waving in the occasional breeze. 'Some five thousand strong give or take. Enough to take this fortress had we not been here to defend it.'

Carangrane nodded. 'Yes. I find it hard to believe that was their intent though. A declaration of war, unprovoked? Come, let us see what they are about.'

The two giants made their way down to the outside wall.

There, a pair of great stone doors were pulled aside by teams of soldiers. Carangrane and Varangrim were joined by Fenorn, Anvildrak and Ulformane.

'We will parley with them,' Carangrane said, raising his voice. 'Do not provoke them. I would have them walk away, tails between their legs like wolves routed from a rotting carcass. Is that understood?'

Varangrim looked around at the other three giants, who nodded their acquiescence.

Carangrane turned about and trudged forward, the others fell in behind him, to either side.

The giants carried no banners, nor did their armour or clothing carry rank or means to identify them to outsiders. The giants knew who was in charge; that was sufficient.

The five giants strode towards the army, stopping as they topped a rise beyond the road that led to the fortress. The Iceguard army stretched out before them, standing at attention.

Before them, the banners of the Icelords moved. Horses emerged from the ranks of shielded men.

Three lords on horseback came towards them, a rider at each side holding the banner aloft making a total of six.

The Icelords slowed their steeds and drew close. On horseback they were almost able to see eye to eye with the Giants, though their faces were obscured behind dark metal helmets. They waited a dozen paces away, making the Giants come to them.

Carangrane covered the distance in a few great strides.

The leader turned his horse to one side adjacent to Carangrane, the horse snorted and stepped sideways at a deft touch on the reins. Carangrane recognised him.

'Imgasharg,' Carangrane rumbled. 'Your domain lies far to the north and east of here. Are you lost?

'Are we not free to patrol the plains of Morormarg?' Imgasharg replied.

'Patrol, yes, but since when have Iceguard patrols been five thousand strong?'

'These are treacherous times,' Imgasharg returned.

'Are they?' Carangrane replied. 'If so, the treachery is not of our making.'

Imgasharg laughed.

'No, I suppose not. But treachery nonetheless.'

Mist billowed around them. Out of the ground, men lurched to their feet, dozens of men, men with crossbows ...

Bolts thudded out around the giants. They yelled in alarm.

The Iceguard soldiers had one target.

Varangrim grabbed at Carangrane, seeing to his dismay that his chest was riddled with crossbow bolts, torn, ripped and bloodstained. Carangrane sank to his knees as Varangrim tried to pull him back.

Assassins! Treacherous cowards!

From behind him Varangrim heard a sound, a low sonorous call. Out of the corner of his eye he saw Fenorn with a horn raised to his lips.

A battle horn, summoning our folk! No! Stay within the fortress ...

The sound of the horn was repeated from the battlements of the fortress. Already giants were surging from the open gates, swords and cudgels held aloft, charging down towards the ranks of the Iceguard warriors.

The Icelords saw the oncoming hordes, signalled to their men and turned their horses about, galloping away.

Carangrane collapsed on to his back, his eyes closed.

'Avenge the fallen!' Fenorn yelled, his voice echoing back from the rocks and walls of the fortress. Anvildrak was at his side, a huge two-handed hammer held in his hand.

'Hold!' Varangrim cried. 'This was their plan ... to goad us ... it is a feint!'

The first of the giant soldiers reached them and then there

were dozens of them all about, led by an enraged Fenorn and Anvildrak, charging down the hillside towards the massed ranks of the retreating Iceguard. Then the Iceguard came about, dropping into battle formation; halberds, swords and spears at the ready; organised, disciplined and holding firm.

Varangrim raised his head, seeing the first line of giants cut down by arrows loosed from concealed bows. The giants' attack was haphazard, frenzied and uncontrolled.

'No!'

He felt a hand grasp his arm. He looked down to see Carangrane gazing up at him, blood seeping from the corners of his mouth.

'Lead them! You … must … lead …'

Carangrane's head fell back, his body lifeless and still as the battle raged towards him. Before he had a chance to react, Varangrim heard more horns blowing from the fortress behind him. He turned seeing giants along the walls gesturing and pointing to the north.

He squinted in the direction they were indicating.

Shadows out of the distant mist. Mist which was now evaporating as if by magic, revealing …

More men, more Iceguard.

As he watched, armies could be seen charging across the now fully visible plains of Morormarg, thousands strong.

The forest thinned. Tarithel reined in Álainn and stopped to look, the pair of guards either side of her doing likewise. Before them a small fort guarded a pass out of the forests and on to a mist-bound plane.

It was the second day of travelling since they had left the city of Imorthorn and ridden northwards through the forest of Fangrim. Tarithel instinctively knew the way, the route through the forest was obvious to her. They had made good time.

'The Fortress of Thormand?' she asked.

The guard to her right nodded.

'Yes, my lady,' he said. 'The north of our realm. Here Fangrim ends. Beyond are the plains of Thoriel. Dwarf country.'

The guard's voice had a disparaging tone.

Another hour saw them reach the fortress. The gates were open; they had long been seen by guards upon the walls. Thormand was waiting in the forecourts even as the heralds announced their arrival.

Thormand was tall and fair in the manner of the Fey, with a shock of long black hair that trailed beyond his shoulders. He was not dressed in armour, but in lighter more colourful garments reflecting the colours of the forest nearby. A warm smile greeted Tarithel and she smiled in return as he took her hand and bowed.

'Lady Tarithel of Dreams and of Midnight I presume,' Thormand said. 'News of your arrival in our lands has travelled swiftly; it is a great honour to have you visit our humble outpost.'

'Lord Imorthorn speaks most highly of you,' Tarithel replied, with a formal curtsey. 'He bade me give you this.'

She handed him a rolled paper, sealed with wax. Thormand took it, nodding to the pair of escorts and raising his voice.

'See to their needs. Wine, food and fruits as they desire.'

The pair of escorts moved aside. Thormand gestured to Tarithel. 'Come, refreshment awaits within. Hot water and a change of clothes. You must be tired.'

'You already anticipate my wishes,' Tarithel said with a smile. 'I am most grateful.'

'I will have dinner ready within the hour,' Thormand said. 'We will talk in private then. With your leave?'

Tarithel nodded. A maid was summoned and led her within the fortress. Thormand was as good as his word, by the time the gong sounded for dinner Tarithel was cleansed and dressed in fresh linen.

She entered the hall where a small table had been set. Meats, vegetables and fruits were placed before her, with wine and pressed juices. Thormand stood up as she entered and pulled out a chair, gesturing for her to sit down. She did so and he returned to his own seat.

'Do not stand on ceremony,' he said, with a smile. 'Our manners here in the outposts are rather coarse when measured against those of the great cities of the south …'

'Your manners are more than satisfactory,' Tarithel replied, taking a generous portion of food on to her plate. 'I'm starving!'

She ate with relish, much to Thormand's surprise. He grinned and began to pile his own plate high.

'The missive from Imorthorn was straight and to the point,' he said. 'I am to serve you in any way that you might desire, support your intentions, but not speak a word to another soul. It's all very mysterious, is there anything you can tell me?'

Tarithel finished a mouthful and wiped her lips with a napkin.

'I ride north,' Tarithel said. 'And I must go alone.'

Thormand choked and stopped in mid chew.

'You surely know that is the realm of the Dwarves,' he said, wiping at his mouth. 'Our lands stop here, the Fey are not welcome there.'

'So I have heard,' Tarithel said. 'But it is not to the Dwarves I go.'

'Then where?'

'I seek the sorceress Shareth, that you call Heartstealer.'

Thormand dropped the fork he'd been holding and stared at her for a long moment.

'This is not in jest is it?'

She shook her head.

Thormand took a deep breath.

'My Lady … Shareth, she is … simply evil. There is no other word for it. I am not old as the Fey reckon things, others older and wiser than I will tell of her motives and ambition, all I have seen is rampant hate and destruction in all my moons. She calls herself Empress of the Frozen Empire. Her powers are great … greater than any other in the Icemark I am sure. Venture into her clutches and you will not return …'

'I must go.'

'My Lady, it is certain death!'

'I must go.'

Tarithel's voice was quiet and firm. Thormand looked at her, seeing the determination etched on her features.

'But why?'

'She holds my betrothed in her enchantments,' Tarithel replied. 'Only I can release him.'

Thormand studied her expression for long moments.

'And you know where he is held?'

'A city called Imiriel,' Tarithel said. 'I do not know where it is.'

'I have heard the name,' Thormand mused. 'And you are right, it does lie to the north, many weary leagues of travel. Shareth's territory is a long way from here through unfriendly lands.'

'I have already come many leagues,' Tarithel said. 'If my horse Álainn could speak, she would tell you of the hardships I have put her through.'

Thormand chuckled.

'From Midnight,' he said. 'Far to the south I understand. A journey that would give me pause for sure. Yet I daresay it will be a harder and bleaker road to the north.'

'I must take each step as it comes,' Tarithel replied. 'Starting out from here. Imorthorn said you could guide me, will you do so?'

Thormand looked at her for a moment and then raised a glass to her.

'I will,' he said. 'This … betrothed of yours. He must be a special man.'

'He is,' Tarithel said, her heart aching in her chest as Morkin's face came to her mind. 'Morkin, son of Luxor, Moonprince of Midnight. By his hand was the Witchking's Ice Crown destroyed.'

'The Witchking?' Thormand said. 'I have heard tales of this even here. Doomdark was the name by which he was known in these parts.'

'Shareth is his daughter,' Tarithel replied. 'She was long tutored in his fell powers so I have learnt.'

'And you would risk your life to set your betrothed free?' Thormand asked. 'Because that's exactly what you will be doing.'

Tarithel nodded. 'Of course.'

Thormand took a sip from his wine.

'Then I hope he knows how lucky he is to have earned your affections,' he said.

Tarithel smiled, but didn't answer.

'My duty is clear,' Thormand said. 'Though I cannot profess to like it very much. I am bid to speed you on your way, as secretly as possible.'

'Any assistance you can give me is very much appreciated,' Tarithel answered.

'Well then,' Thormand said, leaning back in his chair. 'I can tell you a little of the road that lies before you. To the north beyond Fangrim are the southern realms of the dwarven Lords. We are generally at peace with them, with only minor quarrels along the borders. I do not think you will have too much difficulty at first. They are not exactly friendly, but they will suffer you to pass through their lands if you respect them. The realm through which you will first travel is under the watch of a Dwarf called Thigrak. He is old and cantankerous, but you can reason with him. Two brothers support his rule, Imulorn and Imelorn… yes, I know, the names get confusing. Both are worthy, but of the pair, Imulorn is the wiser, with Imelorn trusting more in the sharpness of his axe than his wit.'

Tarithel tried to commit the names to memory.

'After a day's ride you will reach the forests of Glorthorn. I have been there upon occasion. The Dwarves do not care for their trees as we do, seeing them only as wood to be called upon as required. Beyond that, the road leads to the city of Glormane himself, which serves as the capital of the whole dwarven kingdom. You will not be able to avoid being seen, those roads are well travelled. Glormane himself is the current leader of the Dwarves.'

'This Glormane, can you tell me of him?'

Thormand nodded. 'I have met him twice and he also seems of reasonable character. Imorthorn and he even shared a meal and ale once not so many moons ago. He will hear you out if nothing else.'

'These Dwarves do not seem to be the fierce enemy I have been warned of,' Tarithel said.

'I have told you only half the story,' Thormand said. 'It is fair to say that the southern Dwarves are not often ill-deposed to the Fey, we even trade with them occasionally, but those of the north are far less accommodating. The Dwarves are not united as we are. There are distinct factions, with tensions that run far deeper than those found amongst the Fey. Glormane's hold on power is tenuous, others vie for his position and would take control if they could. I do not know for certain what you will find if you reach the City of Glormane, but it will be politically tense. You must be cautious.'

Tarithel nodded. 'I am no stranger to politics; my father schooled me at length. The lessons were dull and tedious, perhaps they will have a use at last! Beyond that, where am I bound to go?'

Thormand shrugged.

'I have never ventured further north than the City of Glormane,' he said. 'My knowledge of those lands is poor I'm afraid. I know the way north is barred by the Mountains of Anvulane …'

'Anvulane,' Tarithel echoed in a whisper. 'This is a name I have heard …'

'A vast chain of mountains which stretches most of the width of the Icemark,' Thormand said. 'Stories tell that they cannot be crossed, but I am sure the Dwarves must know a way. Beyond them …'

'Yes?'

'Is the realm of the Iceguard … and Shareth herself.'

Tarithel couldn't repress a shudder.

'I would not trust the northern Dwarves,' Thormand added. 'We Fey have made poor choices in the past, antagonised and provoked them, but I have seen real treachery from the northerners. They live on the borders of the Frozen Empire and are tainted by it. If the northern Dwarves learn of you, it will not be long before Shareth also knows. They might even be in league with her already. I do not see how you can keep yourself hidden from her.'

'Is there no other way?' Tarithel asked.

Thormand shook his head. 'I think not. To veer west of the Mountains of Anvulane you would have to travel through the realms of the Barbarians and the Giants. They are no more well-disposed to the Fey than the Dwarves, perhaps less so – and they are constantly at war! You could strike east I suppose, follow the borders of Fangrim almost to the edge of the Frozen Wastes before turning north, but those lands are desolate and bare, the way brutal and hard with little sustenance to be found, it might take you many moons of travel …'

'And I do not have the time,' Tarithel said. 'Shareth suspects my presence I'm sure, and she must know that Luxor himself has arrived within the Icemark.'

'Doubtless she has spies who will soon tell her,' Thormand agreed. 'Her magic reaches far and wide I'm sure. She may not know your intentions though, nor where you currently are in any detail. I would say that you are hidden from her sight whilst you remain within the borders of Fangrim.'

'But I cannot tarry here.'

'No indeed. I would say your best hope is to go to the Dwarves and hope you can persuade Glormane to help you,' Thormand said. 'Succeed with him and you have a chance to slip into the Frozen Empire unnoticed. From there …'

Thormand's voice faded away. The look upon his face said more than his words.

Tarithel nodded, a sigh escaping her. Then she looked up. 'Imorthorn said you would guide me and so you have. Fangrim itself has spurred me on to challenge Shareth and challenge her I shall! You say there are forests on my route, I shall hope that the ancient trees of Icemark will sustain me through my journey. I will go to the Dwarves as you direct and convince them to help me.'

Thormand looked back at her.

'I pray you will succeed,' he said. 'But know that none can come to your aid so far to the north. We cannot send armies to you to protect you; that would risk a war we could not win.'

'If I do reach my betrothed it will not be by force of arms,' Tarithel replied. 'Such things have their place, but battle is not my way.'

'Then here's to you, Lady Tarithel of Dreams and of Midnight,' he said, raising a glass to her. 'All the blessings of the Fey I can muster I bestow upon you. Ride swiftly.'

Twilight was upon the lands of the Icemark, the last vestiges of sunlight spilling blood red over the snow. A thin smattering of ersh floated through the air, swept down from the razor sharp edges of the Frozen Wastes.

A traveller unfamiliar with these parts would look about themselves in utter dismay. To the north, the Frozen Wastes lay across the horizon, stretching out in an unbroken line. Yet, to the east and west their boundaries curved around a valley, enveloping it in their embrace. Even to the south, a line of their icy daggers protruded up above the horizon. The valley was surrounded by the ancient, impassable boundary, cut off from the rest of the realm. It was the utter icy core of the Frozen Empire.

This was the Vale of Anvoril.

Long ago, before the evil of the Witchking and the tyranny of his daughter's reign, it had been a fair valley, green and pleasant. A city lay here, constructed in a manner unique to the Icemark, hewn of crystal and marble spires and minarets. It still remained, now long since abandoned by those who had once lived here, its elegant streets and ornate architecture no longer appreciated, for none could find their way into the vale, with its borders closed by the Frozen Wastes. Few even recalled it existed and none had been able to find their way here in many lives of men, Dwarves and giants. The Barbarians knew nothing of it, and even the Fey had few recollections, given its remote distance and long abandonment.

Yet it remained, standing tall, proud and fair against the snowy landscape, glistening in the fading light of day. It remained a testament to those who had built it long ago in the far north of the Icemark.

CHAPTER NINE

The crystal city of Imiriel; it was as remote and as inaccessible as a dream, yet solid and real.

No common folk of Icemark lived here now; the vale was silent. Yet, as if summoned by some strange power, lights flickered from the soundless towers.

Something yet stirred.

The gates to the city opened, swung back by an inaudible and invisible command. Before them, stood a tall woman, dressed in furs, her arms outstretched, a diadem upon her head.

She walked within the threshold of the city, lowering her arms as she did so, the great gates closed behind her with a rumble and a thud.

Shareth the Heartstealer had spared no concern over those that had once dwelt here, she could not even recall if she had evicted them or slaughtered them. People mattered little to her, unless they had some use to which they could be put, but she appreciated craftsmanship and beauty. Many fortresses and cities of lower design she had razed or sacked, but Imiriel … such a thing would be a crime, even to her. It was majestic, beautiful and awe inspiring.

And it was hers.

If any place held affection in her icy heart, it was Imiriel.

She had not altered it, defaced it or changed it in anyway. Its streets, buildings and towers remained, preserved for all time by her own mystic arts against decay and deterioration. Here she had solitude, a place unassailable to any army, any enchantment or device. It was her utter sanctuary, beyond the reach of anyone without the knowledge of how to counter the barricade of the Frozen Wastes.

For there was a way, known to her and only a handful of trusted others.

Imiriel held other secrets too. Shareth smiled to herself as she strode within the vaulted arches of the city centre, taking in the sculpted curving flow of immense staircases and sparkling chandeliers. At another brief gesture, fires erupted in great oil burners, lighting the interior with a lurid orange glow. Warmth pervaded the crystal halls. She shrugged off her outer garments and they faded into nothingness behind her, unwanted for now, but ready to be summoned back at a moment's notice.

Down the colonnades she walked, doorways opening to her and swinging back at her very presence, until she stood in the very centre, at the base of the tallest tower in the city.

She spared a look upwards at the architecture, rising tier upon tier above her, now lit by torchlight at the base where she stood, but, due to the craft and expertise of its builders, capturing both moonlight and starlight in traceries of light above her. Even the faint scattering of the Roads of Light across the heavens was caught in those crystal spires.

Shareth stepped forward a pace.

Architectural wonders notwithstanding, before her was the true secret of Imiriel.

A crystal pedestal was placed under the focal point of the tower, rising perhaps a yard from the smooth marble floor. Placed on it was a purple cushion, edged with golden thread. Upon that sat a crown, sparkling before her in the light snatched from above.

Shareth smiled.

The Crown of Imiriel itself. The first … and the last gift my wastrel mother ever gave me!

It was the source of her ambitions. Long ago it had been forged. It was far older than the Talisman her father had wrought and used to cause so much destruction in the realm of Midnight. The Ice Crown had been created by her father Gryfallon, made of ice and cold and malice in the depths of winter to focus and magnify his own power.

She ran her fingers over the untarnished metal of the crown, caressing its smooth surface under her fingertips.

His reach exceeded his grasp; I shall not make the same mistake.

The Crown of Imiriel was far older, created before Shareth existed, before her father Gryfallon the Witchking rose to power. It was a gift of the Wise to the people of the Icemark.

The Wise! The Fools would be a better name! They willingly broke their power and divided it up amongst the unworthy, giving these Talismans to the lowly kings, queens and leaders of the realm. In their folly, they diluted their influence and left the stage for those of us who had the will to take their place.

Her mother had been one such queen. Gryfallon had courted her, seduced her and married her out of lust, not for her, but for the Crown she bore.

And when I was old enough …

Shareth smiled at the memory. Bloodlust had always been strong in her, she had learnt to maim and kill animals under the tutelage of her father at a young age. Slitting her own mother's throat at her father's instruction and watching the life drain out of her as realisation of treachery dawned in those final moments had been so satisfying. Thus she was crowned … not mere Queen, but Empress of the Frozen Empire.

My father divined the potency of the Talismans, and tasked me with finding those scattered remnants of the power of the Wise throughout the Icemark … they called it the First Power … but now they will come to fear it as Shareth's power!

She stretched out her fingers, the tips flexing before her.

Alongside the pedestal, four other pedestals appeared out of the marble, rising into place without a whisper of sound. Atop them were identical purple cushions to the first. Upon the one to the immediate right of the Crown of Imiriel was another crown, but the other cushions bore no contents. They were empty, awaiting their task.

Shareth smiled to herself.

My father hoped to take these Talismans and harness their power. He tasked me with finding them, little did he know that I had already retrieved two! He trusted me, and that would have been his undoing had that squalid Moonprince not usurped my own vengeance. My crowns, my power! Here at the City of Imiriel lie both the Crown of Imiriel and the Crown of Carudium!

Her mirth passed.

Yet there is another crown I have yet to find. The Crown of Varenand eludes me still ... yet I know it lies within the realm of the Giants, secure in their capital no doubt! Also lost are the Runes of Finorn and the Spell of Thigorn. These are all that remain of the foolish decree of the Wise so long ago here in the Icemark. It has taken me long years to find and master the powers afforded by these Talismans, how much more potent will I be once I have all five! A power my father could only imagine in his wildest dreams will be mine. I will take all Icemark, then Midnight will fall and I shall wrest the Moon Ring from that upstart Moonprince! Onwards then to Varangor, to Bloodmarch, Merineth, Ustor, Erandor, Valahar, Berin, Arillon and Isheril. All power shall be mine! All lands will bow in homage to me, forever. I will sweep all before me, unassailable and irresistible in will and purpose.

The two crowns before her sparkled in the light from above, imbued by powers too immense for mortals to bear.

But I alone am worthy to command them. Eternal and forever. I am Shareth.

She licked her lips.

And ... irresistible? Yes, that gives me another idea!

She smiled to herself.

With an imperious gesture she dismissed the five pedestals and they sank into the pearlescent floor and were lost from view, the surface smooth and unblemished as if crafted from solid marble.

She turned and followed the sweeping staircases of the tower until she reached its uppermost height. Here were her most private chambers, the ultimate seclusion from the world outside.

The rooms were lush, appointed with ornate chairs and chaise-longues, rich tapestries hung upon the walls and carpeting the floors. Mirrors, oval and full-length were positioned so that she could always catch a glimpse of her form at any point within.

She wandered through, admiring priceless works of art and sculpture that she had taken in her many conquests, there were items from all the kingdoms of Icemark on display, with some from even further afield – a dragon's claw from Varangor, jewels from the Bloodmarch. Her wealth was conspicuous, but it was the possession of such items that meant the most to her, the cost was immaterial, that someone else had been deprived of their ownership and mourned their loss made her preen with greed and satisfaction.

Shareth laughed to herself and walked further into her chambers, stopping at her large four poster bed. There she sat upon the edge, cross-legged and thoughtful.

And deprived that tawdry Fey maiden shall be too!

She stood up, spinning around. Her travelling garb was replaced by a sleek close fitting milky gown, feather light and low cut. Flames rose from oil burners around the room, heating the interior. She pulled at the cords that bound her hair in place, letting her long, dark locks fall around her pale face.

She gestured, her fingers drawing faint cyan circles in the air.

Before her a young man appeared, blonde-haired, tall and fair, strong in the manner of the men of the Free of Midnight. His hair was held in place by a braided band around his forehead. Shareth appraised him for a moment as he looked about himself, confused.

'Mistress?'

'Yes, sweet boy,' she said, uncrossing and crossing her legs. 'I have summoned you, come hither.'

For a moment he resisted, Shareth's eyes narrowed.

'Hither!' she snapped.

He came to her then, striding forward to stand before her, looking down at her.

She smiled and stood, staring into his eyes.

'Who is your liege, Morkin son of the Moonprince?'

Morkin looked at her.

'You are my Liege, Mistress. My loyalty lies ever with you, glorious Empress of the Frozen Empire.'

She rested a hand on his shoulder and moved around him. She stayed close, her breath hot on his neck. Her words now whispered.

'And you have forsaken all others for me?'

Again came the pause. She stroked a fingernail across his cheek.

'Answer me, sweet boy …'

'There are no others but you, my mistress.'

'Not even some fawning Fey-girl with red hair and green eyes?'

'She comes not to my mind,' Morkin replied.

'Then you will give yourself to me,' Shareth whispered. 'Without let or hindrance?'

'My body is yours,' he replied.

'So it is …'

Shareth pulled him close, her voice breathless with lust, her clothing glistening and then fading away.

'Then let us wait no longer,' she said, in a whisper. 'Let me show you everything a young squire ought to know …'

Tarithel had ridden on from Thormand's fortress. Following his directions, she had stopped at the Fountain of Berenial, finding herself refreshed by its waters. The fountain itself was sited on the source of a natural spring according to Thormand. It was a bleak structure, old and crumbling in parts, its facades tarnished and covered in mildew. Tarithel wandered around it for a few moments, wondering who had built it and what stories it might have to tell about the people who dwelt in this land. She knew the Icemark to be somewhat larger than the realm of Midnight, but the land seemed even more desolate and inhospitable, with even fewer inhabitants, its monuments less cared for … older and more careworn.

To the west she could see the Dwarven fortress of Varatrarg, but Varatrarg himself was not at home, no banners were flying.

Away to the north for the Dwarven gathering I should guess.

Before her, a mountain range bordered the lands to the north-west. According to Thormand, the City of Glormane was two days ride to the north. The sun was already burning away the morning mist. Tarithel walked back to Álainn, mounted and spurred her onwards.

She spared a glance behind her, watching the Forest of Fangrim receded as she rode on across the plains. She shivered, remembering what the spirit of the forest had told her.

Spirit of the forest … a power stranger and older than any other I have felt. Fangrim has its own will, it is an ancient realm, older even than the Fey.

She didn't know how such knowledge had come to her, only that it had and there was no doubt in her mind.

Fangrim itself wishes to resist the Heartstealer, that much is clear.

The forests of Midnight had come to her aid against the Witchking and his hordes of Doomguard, but she had felt she had some measure of control over that altercation. Even the whispered thoughts in her mind from the Liths of Midnight were subtle and suggestive rather than controlling and dominating.

Yet here ...

She shivered. Even Imorthorn knew more than he was telling when he sent her into Fangrim.

He suspected something. What? That I would awaken the spirit of the forest somehow? If so, that seems to be what I have done. Is that power mine to command, or am I a tool for it to use as it desires?

She rode unchallenged across the plain, stopping only at intervals to rest Álainn. The land rose and fell around her, but there was no sign of any patrols or travellers. As the day wore on she spotted a fortress nestling at the base of some hills to the east. From Thormand's map she could see it was the Fortress of Imulorn, one of the Dwarves she had been advised of.

Her destination for today lay in sight. She could already make out the eaves of the Forest of Glorthorn in the distance to the north. She rode on.

By the time she reached its edge the sun was dropping into the west, settling beyond the mountains. Their shadows reached far across the plain. She had been following a path that ran northwards, but decided to venture away from it in the final league of her travels, ensuring she was unlikely to encounter any others who might come this way. She led Álainn within the forest, stopping at intervals to listen. The normal sounds of the forest at sunset reached her and she sensed nothing untoward within, little of anything at all in fact.

She made herself a small fire and broke out her provisions, making a frugal meal. Looking south through the boughs of the trees she watched as dusk crept across the plain she had travelled across. Mist rose, faint traceries at first, before thickening into a swath of cloud that blocked her view.

She turned her thoughts to Luxor, trying to make contact with him via the Moon Ring. Yet somehow she could not hear him.

Perhaps these mists … her sorcery … might they prevent the Moon Ring from working?

The mists swirled around with a mind of their own, as if they were searching for something.

Does Shareth know of my intentions? My whereabouts? Fangrim wants me to confront her, but how can I stand against her power? She was long tutored by her father, the Witchking. Rorthron told how he was one of the Wise long ago. She is a sorceress of great power!

Tarithel felt panic begin to seep into her soul. She had been foolhardy, leaving all escorts behind her, running off on this quest.

Despite what the forest told me I am just a foolish girl! How can I hope to find Morkin without help? Surely I am just walking into a trap, perhaps even one Shareth has set for me …

The Barbarians had ignored her as she slipped through their southern territory. The Fey, for the most part, had accommodated her and sped her on her way, but ahead …

Few of the Dwarves will be friendly, beyond them lies the realm of the Icelords themselves, I will find no friends there. How can I elude captivity in such hostile lands? A lone Fey travelling in enemy territory?

She had no answer to that question, but even as fear arose in her, chilling her heart and making her break out in a cold sweat, something else stirred.

Morkin's face came to her, bereft, alone. She felt her heart leap at the vision of his face.

My love! I will not abandon you, I will die first.

And then there was the reassuring comfort of the trees around her. It was nothing like the strength of Fangrim, but even here, the trees felt like allies, as if they would somehow stand alongside her and guard her. She took a series of deep breaths, feeling her heart slow within her.

I cannot turn back, I must push onwards. I will go to the Dwarves. I will make my case to them and I will show no fear. I have come this far!

Tarithel extinguishing her fire before climbing a tree to sleep.

Rorthron had left them after the camp had been struck. Careneon had accepted Rorthron's request with a proviso, that a small company of Barbarian riders would escort him to the tower and back again to the City of Imgorad.

'The Outlands can be dangerous,' Careneon had said, giving Rorthron a wary look. 'I would not want any harm to come to you on my watch.'

Rorthron had chuckled.

'Your hospitality and concern for my wellbeing are noted.'

Now the sun was sinking towards the horizon as the men of the Moonguard and the Barbarians rode onwards through the forest. Luxor, Careneon and Torinarg rode at the fore. A valley was opening before them, split by a sinuous river which led up to the walls of a city. Its buildings were cast in shadow by the setting sun, already fires could be seen illuminating the ramparts, with buildings lit from within as the light faded.

Luxor studied the city as they drew closer; it was unlike the Citadels of his homeland, with their lofty walls and high parapets. The Barbarians spent their time and effort on weaponry. The city was festooned with all manner of contraptions and bristled with trebuchets, ballistae, catapults, towers and many other devices he was unfamiliar with. Within the walls the buildings seemed placed at random, with no obvious thought to their location or purpose. Luxor could see that many were damaged and others had been repaired without effort spared on making them look whole again.

'It seems that war truly is a constant threat in the Icemark,' he muttered.

Beside him Careneon nodded. 'Peace is but an interlude in these lands.'

He raised a hand and the combined armies drew to a halt.

'The City of Imgorad,' he said. 'The capital of our realm you might say. Our presence will have been noticed, but tradition dictates that I announce our arrival.'

With that, Careneon pulled a horn from his belt and blew three blasts upon it. The sounds drifted over the cooling air of the valley. After a moment's pause two deep, sonorous tones answered from the city.

'We may approach,' Careneon said. 'Imgorad awaits us.'

Careneon gestured and his banner and that of Torinarg were raised. Luxor signalled for his own men to do likewise. The armies moved off, heading towards the city.

Luxor concentrated for a moment, searching out Rorthron's presence via the Moon Ring. The answer was swift.

My Lord, Moonprince?

'Have you reached the tower?' Luxor asked, his voice low.

Almost. I would have been swifter had I not had my 'protective' escort.

Luxor chuckled.

'They are wise to be cautious,' he said. 'I am sure I would not want someone as powerful as you wandering around my domains unsupervised ...'

Were I a man, I might be offended ...

A vague sense of amusement filtered back through the link.

And you, Moonprince?

'We approach the city of Imgorad,' Luxor replied. 'It is impressive, if war and battle is your only concern.'

It may be wise not to mention the Fey immediately. There is much animosity there ...

'I thought as much myself,' Luxor said. 'Let this Imgorad decide on his own course of action. There is enough animosity in the Icemark without us fanning it into flame. It was hard enough to bring Fey and Free together to confront the Witchking, let alone navigate the politics of these lands.'

I would judge that the Barbarians are more akin to the Free than you might think.

'Really?' Luxor asked in surprise.

Proud, stubborn, obsessed with warfare ...

Luxor laughed. 'Lord Blood might enjoy their company I suppose. He would find much to his satisfaction with all those weapons I see arranged before us.'

But they are men. Perhaps kin of the Free many moons ago, despite being long separated. They are more likely to see things as you do, more so than the Giants and the Dwarves at least.

Luxor nodded. 'They seem straightforward enough folk thus far.'

Yet we must seek alliances everywhere, if we wish to defeat the Heartstealer. And safeguard Tarithel as best we can.

'It goes against all my instincts to let a young woman go alone into such danger,' Luxor muttered.

Young she might be, but she has faced the evil of the Doomguard before and not cowered before it. By her father's account it was her, not he, that roused the Fey of Midnight to war. More likely she is concerned for our fate.

Luxor smiled.

'Perhaps you're right,' he said. 'She is headstrong and bold, much like my own son.'

They will be quite the match. And they will be together. Morkin will be returned to her ... and to you.

Luxor nodded.

'Your words are a comfort,' he said. 'I will hold you to them.'

Luxor looked northwards through the forests, wondering what sights greeted Tarithel's eyes as she made her own way through strange lands.

'She heads directly towards Shareth,' Luxor whispered. 'That the two will meet seems certain now. Can there really be hope she can prevail, find Morkin and release him from that sorceress' witchcraft?'

Shareth's power is bound up in her own self, not focussed through a Talisman as was our previous foe. There is no Ice Crown to be destroyed, but there are other Talismans in the Icemark, as we know. To defeat Shareth ... Shareth must be killed. Set against that is your daughter-in-law to be, and the limit of the powers she can command is yet to be tested. Remember, once Morkin was lost, her flight northwards was as swift or swifter than the Wise might travel. She had visions of where to go and what needed to be done. The spirit of the forest guides her, Moonprince ... not us ...

Luxor shivered.

'I still dislike the thought of brooding intelligences lurking unseen and directing us hither and thither for purposes unknown,' he said. 'I prefer a straight and honest fight with swords raised.'

Yet, here you are, with a magic ring upon your finger, in the company of the Wise on a quest against a sorceress, speaking to me from afar ...

Luxor grunted in response.

And, as I recall, my counsel during our struggle against the Witchking was that swords and shields could not defeat him unaided. I believe I was proved correct, was I not?

'You were,' Luxor said. 'At much risk to my son.'

Who took the task willingly, and not at my direction.

'And he now lies in the clutches of that same evil,' Luxor said.

Such things are bound together, Moonprince. All of them. I will seek out more knowledge of that which is doing the binding;

perhaps that will help us divine its purpose and allow us to achieve our goals.

'Do what you must,' Luxor said. 'I can only do what I have the wit for. Armies, tactics, stratagems and negotiations I can cope with. I leave the mysterious arts and ethereal magic to you.'

And with that, I approach the tower. Good luck to you, Moonprince.

'And to you Rorthron of the Wise,' he muttered. We spread ourselves thinly. But I suppose it must be so.'

Your focus is rightly with the Barbarians. Your next challenge awaits. I will join you as soon as I am able. Success to you.

'Thank you,' Luxor muttered, and the influence of the Moon Ring ebbed away. Luxor raised his gaze to the city.

A phalanx of Barbarian warriors blocked their route towards it. As they watched a tall man in a horned helmet stepped through their ranks and strode forward.

'Careneon, Torinarg,' he called in a deep loud voice. 'Your banners I know. But there is a third I do not recognise.'

Luxor climbed down from his horse and walked forward.

'It is mine,' he said.

The Barbarian stepped forward. He was taller than Luxor by several inches, heavyset, strong and powerful.

'And you are?' he rumbled.

'Luxor, Moonprince of Midnight, slayer of the Witchking of that realm.'

There was flicker of reaction in the face that stared back at him.

'And what is your business here, Luxor, Moonprince of Midnight?'

'I seek an audience with Imgorad, Lord of the Barbarians himself,' Luxor said, his voice loud and clear. 'To seek his support in a stand against the so called Empress of the Frozen Empire, Shareth the Heartstealer.'

'A stand against the Heartstealer is brave,' the man said. 'Brave, but foolish.'

'Every man is fool at times,' Luxor replied. 'Wisdom is found in not being a fool too often.'

The man laughed. 'You are right in that. Welcome, then Luxor of Midnight. I will hear your words, for I am Imgorad of the Barbarians. Come within! Meat first, then we will talk.'

He gestured, throwing his arms wide.

Luxor looked across at Careneon who nodded by return.

'A fair start,' Careneon said, with a faint smile.

Chapter Ten

Lorelorn the Icelord stands in the City of Lorelorn looking north into the mist.

As ever, the mist lay deep and heavy upon the Forest of Farorn. Some held it to be the source of the mist that often plagued the lands of the Icemark, formed by some ancient malice amidst the dark and twisted trees and then leaching out across the lands, coerced by the will of the Heartstealer. It was a forbidding place, its eerie eaves and twisted branches as formidable a barrier as any other natural obstacle in the lands.

Farorn was one of the great Forests of the Icemark, second only in size and stature to Fangrim, the home of the Fey far to the south. It covered a full third of the realm of the Icelords, with many of their fortresses built within its vast expanse.

The forest was the territory of Lorelorn the Icelord, one of the six trusted warlords of Shareth herself. His own city was built to the north of the forest and he had lived there all his days.

When he was a young man he had ridden far and wide within the borders of the forest, learning its ways and whims. He was no Fey, but the forest was familiar to him and he understood it well enough.

As was his habit, he had ridden out early to take the morning air before the pressures of the day and the administration required of him took its daily toll. The forest was as gloomy as ever, but it was at least at peace, a commodity he valued.

His vassal, Talorthane, was due to arrive later that day with reports from further afield.

A well ridden circular route had taken him some leagues from the city and he was now returning by ways less well trodden, routes that he alone had forged through the thick boughs and dense undergrowth.

The foliage crowded about him, tinged here and there with ersh, the fine powder snow of the new moon. His thoughts were occupied with the news filtering back from the realm of the giants when his concentration was disturbed.

It took him a few moments to realise what had caused it. He looked around him in confusion, uneasy.

A scent. A scent upon the air.

He reined in his horse and dismounted, sniffing the air.

The scent was fragrant, fresh and clean, with none of the tang of rotting or damp vegetation as was usual on the muddy pathways.

Tying his horse to a tree, he stepped forward in search of it, making his way in the gloom. The scent grew stronger as he moved.

He walked further on.

And was brought up sharp.

He'd stepped around a fallen tree, its roots exposed and clawing upwards. As he'd done so, bright sunlight flickered about him. He looked up to see blue sky and sharp-edged billowy clouds such as he'd never seen before. The blue was striking and intense. With it there was unfamiliar warmth upon his face.

He blinked in surprise and looked about him.

The view that greeted his eyes drew a gasp from him.

Gone was the bleak darkness of the forest he knew, replaced instead by a glade of fresh wild flowers and overwhelming greenness. Birds and small insects flitted this way and that about him. The snow was gone, banished in the unfamiliar warmth. Somehow it seemed wholesome and appropriate, despite its impossibility.

What is this? What magic?

He knelt down for a moment, taking off his gloves and running his fingers through the rich, green grass, the scent almost overpowering. It felt real enough. He looked over his shoulder, seeing the deep darkness of the familiar forest behind him.

I have been this way a hundred times and never spied such a thing. Some mischief is at work!

Lorelorn replaced his gloves and drew his sword.

'It is not mischief, Lorelorn of the Iceguard.'

Lorelorn turned, raising his sword to strike at the owner of the voice.

A man stood, some twenty yards away, his back turned to Lorelorn.

'Name yourself, stranger,' Lorelorn called. 'You trespass in my lands, thus you answer to me.'

The man turned. Lorelorn looked at him in puzzlement. He was no Icelord, but his bearing and countenance was of the gentry, with the dress and appearance of authority and rank. A Lord perhaps, but not one of the Icemark.

'Your lands?' The man said with a smile. 'I suppose they are at that. Your people have resided here for many moons, have they not?'

'I demand to know who you are,' Lorelorn called.

'I have many names,' the man said. 'But here I shall go by the name of Lord Midwinter; that still seems appropriate.'

'And where are you from, Lord Midwinter?' Lorelorn demanded. 'I know of no such kingdom. Where is your home?'

Midwinter smiled. 'Always so many questions! Why not stop warmongering long enough to appreciate the world set before you? The Icemark can be quite beautiful, can it not?'

Lorelorn raised his sword.

'You cross my lands without permission. You will come with me back to my City and submit to …'

Midwinter gestured and Lorelorn found his body sluggish, as if it was no longer quite his to command. He stood, almost immobile, his sword arm lowering itself.

'That is enough,' Midwinter replied. 'Know first that I mean you no harm. I stand here in your lands … but these are lands I have given to you, though you will not understand how that has been done.'

Lorelorn found he could still speak. He blinked, only to find in that moment that the mysterious Lord was standing close to him, staring at him.

'Who … or what are you?' Lorelorn managed. 'Why are you here?'

'I am here to seek the safety of the Icemark as I sought the safety of Midnight,' Midwinter replied. 'Such things are important to me.' The man's voice was distant, subdued all of a sudden, as if his thoughts were consumed by some great preoccupation that lay beyond sight. 'Yes, very important indeed. Wrongs need to be set right, things are not as they should be.'

'What do you mean?' Lorelorn asked.

'Your mistress,' Midwinter replied. 'She sets herself against all I hoped to see for this realm. War and conflict is not what I intended. I know you well enough, Lorelorn of the Iceguard and master of the Forest of Farorn. You have seen this too. I know your heart.'

Lorelorn frowned.

Midwinter nodded. 'Yes. I see it in your eyes. The Icelords are caught in service of one whose whims cast pain and suffering across these lands. I would see that undone.'

'You set yourself against the Heartstealer?' Lorelorn asked. 'Such a path is of the greatest folly. She is powerful beyond measure …'

'The mightiest avalanche can be started by the smallest

pebble,' Midwinter replied. 'Change is upon you, Lorelorn of the Iceguard. The balance of events could go either way and there are other powers beside the Heartstealer.'

A joyful cry reached Lorelorn's ears. He turned to see a young maiden running through the lush foliage, a smile upon her face, her bright red hair flowing in the breeze, a bright green jewel about her neck. For a moment she stopped in her headlong rush, turning around and looking at him as if she saw him. She smiled, but then faded from his sight.

From the opposite side of the glade Lorelorn saw a vision of his mistress, Shareth herself. She stood not far from him, ephemeral yet still present. Her features were twisted in a callous glare, her arm outstretched. Her fingers pointed at him before she too faded away.

'A choice will come your way,' Midwinter said. Lorelorn looked back at him, startled by the depth of the man's gaze and the surety behind it. Somehow Lorelorn could sense complete sincerity, his instincts of distrust overwhelmed by the strange man's presence. 'A choice which will have great impact on these lands.'

'You speak like an ancient seer, or perhaps you are one of the Wise,' Lorelorn replied. 'What is this choice you speak of?'

'You will know,' Midwinter replied. 'If you are honest with yourself, you already do. You must seek your own answers.'

Midwinter turned away, returning to the position he was standing in when Lorelorn first saw him. Somehow Lorelorn knew the meeting was at an end. He had been dismissed, yet he did not feel anger or even in the least bit slighted … but a sense of loss, as if he'd been in the presence of one far greater than he and would not know that presence in his life again.

'I wish we could speak further,' Lorelorn managed to utter.

Midwinter shook his head. Lorelorn knew it was coming, but the refusal shook him to the core, causing him to clench his jaw firm and close his fists to clamp down on the feelings of sadness and loss that rose within him.

'But I will always be here for those that remember the Icemark,' Midwinter said.

He turned his head and smiled.

'Farewell Lorelorn, Lord of the Forest of Farorn.'

Lorelorn stumbled back. The light about him faded. As he looked up, the strange green glade had vanished beyond recall and the dreariness of the forest was all about him once more. He cast about him in surprise, but there was no sign of the strange Lord, nor the warmth of the mysterious glade.

The whinnying of his horse turned his attention back the way he had come and he traipsed back, sombre and thoughtful.

Tarithel roused early, stretched and climbed down from the tree. Dawn was glimmering in the east, the light of the sun just flickering between the trees. Looking south the plains were still shrouded in mist, but it was easing, the sky above clear and blue, the day promised to be fair.

Tarithel pulled her clothes tighter about herself and went to see to Álainn. The horse nuzzled against her, seeming little worse for wear after its long journey.

'Come, my friend,' she said, 'We still have many leagues to travel.'

She led Álainn by her reins through the forest, returning to the path she had abandoned the previous day. There seemed to be no travellers about, though the path was well-tended. Turning northward she led Álainn on. Two hours of walking saw her reach the boundary of the trees, the land opening out before her.

She found herself in a vast valley, with mountains visible to her left and her right, fading away into the distance. Despite the cold and the ice, that land had a welcoming air about it, she could tell it had been tended and that people lived hereabouts. The path snaked away from her, dropping down through a series of switchbacks on to the plains ahead. She consulted the map Thormand had given her, spying a forest on the horizon. According to the map, the City of Glormane lay just east of it, but even with her keen eyesight, she could not make it out.

'The Kingdom of the Dwarves,' she said to herself, drawing a deep breath. 'I have truly left the realm of the Fey now …'

She mounted Álainn and turned her to follow the path down the side of the valley until they reached the floor. The sun was warm on Tarithel's face now, a gentle breeze blowing from the east growing stronger as the sun rose higher. The road wound northwards for league after league until she could see a mound of earth rising up some distance off to her right. Her curiosity piqued, she guided the horse towards it and dismounted nearby, scrambling up the gentle slopes.

As she reached the top she was surprised to discover it was deep pit. She reached its rim and staggered, only just regaining her balance in time to stop herself falling down the inside slope, which was far steeper.

The slope sank away deep into the ground. Peering over she couldn't see the bottom, it was hidden by the shadow cast by the rim, but she could make out a thin rough passage cut into the slopes, spiralling down from the opposite side of the rim into the depths below.

I wonder where that goes?

There was a faint smell drifting upwards from the gloom below, Tarithel sniffed and recoiled. It did not smell wholesome, but dank and unpleasant, reminding her of the tunnels through to the Gate of Varenorn now far behind her to the south-west. She shivered despite the warmth of the sun.

Best to leave well alone I think!

Carefully, she made her way back down and re-joined Álainn, riding down the path. The forest she had seen on the map was clearer now, closing in on the path from the north-west. The path veered north-east and Tarithel could see a huge wall rising out of the plain.

She realised that this was the City of Glormane. It was unlike any city she'd visited before. From the plain she could see no sign of the buildings within, the wall obscured everything. As she drew closer she could see banners fluttering above the wall, snapped taut in the breeze that now blew across the plains.

Still she could see no one in the lands surrounding the city; it seemed as if all must be inside the walls: no farmers, no soldiers, no other travellers. The forest was close to the path now, overhanging the path on the left hand side.

Surely some guards have seen me? Will they not remark upon a Fey in their realm? Challenge me perhaps?

But there was nothing. It seemed the Dwarves trusted in their walls alone.

Tarithel sighed in frustration. This was not what she had expected. At best she had hoped for a cautious welcome, at worst being accosted and attacked, but to just be ignored … it was, strange and unnerving.

Where is everyone? Something is wrong.

She reined in Álainn. The city was perhaps a league away, visible around the edge of the forest. She got down, looking back the way she had come.

The forest seemed still too. There were no birds, no sounds of animals. She felt the hairs on the back of her neck stiffen and a shiver ran through her. She heard Álainn snort and shuffle her hooves behind her. She whinnied and backed away. Tarithel turned.

'Easy …' Tarithel called. Álainn shook her head, her nostrils flaring, refusing to move onwards.

Now what?

She stepped towards the forest, trying to see within the overgrown trunks.

Something grasped at her foot. She looked down, seeing a rope snap tight around her ankle. It yanked hard, pulling her off her feet. She screeched in surprise and fear. She heard Álainn whinny, followed by the sounds of galloping. She hit the ground hard, falling on her back, the breath knocked out of her. Before she had a chance to react she was pulled into the undergrowth, twigs and thorns scraping at her as she was dragged away. She flailed, trying to claw at the binding around her ankle, but it was impossible. She only managed to twist herself over, seeing Álainn bolting away down the path before she was lost to sight.

The wrench on her ankle eased and she slid to a halt. She rolled herself over and made to sit up, only to find a series of spear points mere inches from her face.

'A Fey!' someone spat. She tried to turn but she could barely move, the grip on her was strong.

'I seek Glormane,' she cried. 'Glormane, leader of the Dwarves. Peace to you …'

There was a mutter from all about her, a coarse laugh.

Something shuffled behind her. A coarse hessian bag was forced over her head and she was wrenched up, the bag tightening around her neck, almost cutting off her breathing. She could just make out the blurred outlines of figures gathering about her, hooded and cloaked, all holding torches.

She was pulled forward and up, finding herself on her knees.

'Please! I must speak to Glormane …' she called out.

'Just as we were told. Treachery from the Fey! Bring her.'

Before she could say another word something struck her on the back of the head. Stars danced in her vision for a brief moment before everything went black.

Rorthron had ridden as swiftly as he could with the Barbarians beside him. At first there had been ribald comments about babysitting an old man, but these were replaced with first admiration and then astonishment as Rorthron rode hard across the plains of the Icemark. Any thoughts of an easy but dull and boring duty had been banished from the minds of his escort.

And any power that sought to stand against me would not be fazed by half a dozen Barbarian riders! Yet, such is the cost of diplomacy. We cannot afford to break our trust … and we travel across their lands freely only with their leave.

The Wise had long been estranged from the other races of both Midnight and Icemark. Rorthron knew well the history of his own land, having been there in the younger days of Midnight when Gryfallon the Stargazer first came into the service of Lord Ushgarak, before usurping his throne and becoming corrupted by his own power. Gryfallon had transformed into the Witchking, and Midnight had been cut off from other realms by the unrelenting frigidity of the Frozen Wastes. Thousands of moons had passed before Midnight was set free by the actions he had helped initiate.

Yet here … in the Icemark …

The Frozen Wastes remained on the borders of this realm, doubtless their magic held intact by the fell arts still practiced by the Witchking's daughter, Shareth. But the Wise lived in the Icemark too. Rorthron had seen the familiar towers on his journey north with Luxor, their architecture subtly different, but he could sense the power that lay within.

Are they the same as my slumbering brethren to the south? Unwilling or unable to rise to meet the challenge of evil? Do they, too, wait for some unspoken signal to join again in the af-

fairs of the lands in which they reside? This I must know. Luxor's quest to counter Shareth is part of this puzzle, but there are greater forces at work here … Lorgrim's revelation of the First Power … Icemark holds the answers!

Across the plains the party rode onwards, heading south-west.

Rorthron had been aware of something the moment he set foot in the Icemark. It was impossible for the Wise to fully conceal themselves from each other and there was a definite sense of presence, a taint of enchantment perhaps, which portrayed the presence of another of his race. Rorthron had memorised the maps he had seen thus far and knew the Tower of Zarorthane lay five leagues away, they had marched past it on the previous day.

I did sense something, something I must inspect! It was concentrated there …

The crescent moon was already close to setting before Rorthron called a halt to the ride. The Barbarians reined in their horses, glad of the change of pace. A low line of hills lay to the south, but a plain stretched to the east with the Tower clearly visible. It stood, sentinel dark, against the eastern horizon, a faint line of twinkling stars framing its outline in the frosty air.

They rode on at a more measured pace, closing the distance to the base of the tower. Rorthron could see snow drifts piled around the perimeter. He brought his horse to a halt and dismounted, sensing something ahead. As he approached he could see that the snow was halted by some invisible barrier, the craft of the Wise, it encircled the tower at a distance of a hundred yards. None but the Wise could traverse this, but such enchantment was familiar to Rorthron.

Rorthron could see the Barbarians looking apprehensively around them.

'Wait here,' he instructed. 'I will leave my horse in your

keeping until I return, I should be no more than a day at most. Set a camp and wait for me.'

'Our orders are to watch you at all times,' the leader of the Barbarians said.

'You cannot approach the tower,' Rorthron said and then lowered his voice. 'I would not advise you to try.'

The Barbarians swallowed.

'I give you my word that I shall return to you,' Rorthron said.

The Barbarian nodded. Rorthron turned back to the invisible barrier.

He held out his hand as he walked forward, his steps light upon the snow, barely dinting it. A warm, glowing magenta aura spread before him, highlighting a circular ring in the air where the barrier stood. He heard the Barbarians gasp in surprise and dismay. Rorthron paced forwards without hesitating, walking through the opening and stepping down to the ground beyond, clear of the drifting snow. He looked back and gestured with his hand. The circular glow shrank and faded away behind him. The Barbarians remained, watching him, but maintaining a safe distance.

'Trespasser!'

Rorthron whirled around to be confronted by a figure, stood mere feet away, glowering at him. The face was old and careworn, much of it hidden in dark grey robes.

Wind blustered around Rorthron, whipping his long cloak around him in a frightful gust. Snow blew in the tempest. The figure spoke, its voice a cacophony of noise and unearthly yelling.

'Be gone, or you will be smited on the very ground upon which you stand! Do not defile this place, flee now!'

Rorthron braced himself against the gusts and they subsided in a moment. The figure before him remained unmoved.

'I daresay that works rather well for the simple minded,' Rorthron said. 'But I am made of sterner stuff.'

The figure remained unmoved, but it spoke after a moment.

'You have surmised I am but an image,' it said, its voice cracked and worn. 'It's traditional to knock if you are an uninvited guest.'

'Difficult to knock if one cannot approach the door,' Rorthron returned.

'Precisely the reason for having the barrier,' the figure replied. 'Dare you disturb the repose of he who lies within? You are required to explain yourself, Rorthron of the southern Wise.'

'You know my name,' Rorthron replied, 'I surmise yours to be Zarorthane, of the Wise of Icemark.'

'As I stated, I am but an image of his great majesty, here to guard the boundary of his magnificent realm. You must pay homage to he that is great amongst the Wise of Icemark, he who holds the very secrets ...'

'Enough,' Rorthron said. 'I will not parley with an image ...'

Rorthron gestured with an outstretched arm and the image flickered and disappeared in the midst of its outburst.

Rorthron walked the short distance to the tower. He paused upon the threshold, divining the magic that held the door closed. With that small task accomplished he opened the door and moved to the centre of the ground floor, his footsteps echoing above him. Everything was coated in a thick layer of dust, undisturbed for uncounted moons. It seemed that the Wise of Icemark had been longer in their slumber than even those of Midnight.

Above him a staircase wound upwards out of sight. He stepped upon it and followed it through its many turns. In layout it bore a great similarity to the Towers of Midnight, including Rorthron's own abode, the Tower of the Moon, now hundreds of leagues to the south. Rooms opened off the staircase through low stone archways, but where Rorthron's own tower would have been crammed with books and warmed by roaring fires, here the rooms were bare and cold, caked in dust.

'Visitors are few then,' Rorthron remarked, as he marched ever upwards. 'For the better I vouch.'

After a lengthy climb he emerged at the topmost height of the tower. Rorthron could see the land of Icemark laid out below him, lit by the light of the crescent moon and the bright stars through crystalline windows. This room bore a little more decoration. A pedestal stood at the centre, topped with a diamond that gave out a faint, magenta light. Mirrors hung on the walls, but they did not reflect the contents of the room, rather they seemed to show the interior of other towers, those equally as quiescent as this one. There was an alcove in the northern wall.

He stepped closer to it, seeing a statue of an old man. It was exquisitely detailed, the carving intricate, a work beyond the best masons of Midnight.

Too intricate ...

Rorthron chuckled.

'So, Zarorthane the magnificent I assume,' he murmured to himself, taking a closer look. Rorthron was not sure quite how the Wise had cast themselves into their long slumber, it was a secret he had never been told. It preserved them, inviolate and eternal, whilst they reposed within it, disconnected from the world. Zarorthane's skin was as stone, protected from the long count of moons.

And when might the Wise reawaken? What event might finally persuade them to re-join us? Not the threat of the Witchking, nor his daughter so it seems.

An empty hearth, long cold and dead, was the only other object of note within the chamber.

Rorthron walked back towards the centre of the room, where the magenta light of the diamond pulsed. Looking closer he could see that a book was placed upon the pedestal, with the diamond on top of it.

He circled it, gesturing whilst muttering soft words as he probed it.

He heard a faint whisper, not so much a voice, more an impression of such, pressing at his mind as he tried to approach the diamond. It flickered as he did so.

Your purpose here, Rorthron of the southern Wise?

'I came here in answer to a summons,' Rorthron replied, looking around him. 'Or, at least, so I surmised.'

You come here in the company of a Moonprince …

'Luxor of Midnight,' Rorthron replied. 'Indeed yes. He seeks …'

The demise of the Heartstealer, daughter of the Witchking he has already slain. Quite the hero of the Free.

'Who are you?' Rorthron demanded.

I am what I am.

'Riddles rarely help,' Rorthron chided, 'Are you Zarorthane himself?'

No, he slumbers as do all the rest. I am much less … and much more. A guardian he placed here to act in his name. Whilst he slumbers, here at the Tower of Zarorthane reside both the will and the wisdom of the Wise of Icemark …

'Then what is the intent of the Wise of Icemark? Why did you summon me here?'

The crystal flickered before Rorthron sensed a response.

The Wise of Icemark will play no part in the conflict that is brewing. Yet, you know the lore, Rorthron of the southern Wise. You know of the Moon Rings and the lay of Yanathel. You witnessed Luxor's son find a way to undo the magic of the Ice Crown. Shareth's wrath at the death of her father was a fearsome thing. The Wise cannot change this, not now, not with so much lost …

'The situation is not so simple,' Rorthron said. 'Luxor's son, Morkin, has been abducted by Shareth. Luxor will not abandon him … he seeks his return.'

He would do well to consider him lost. None of the Wise dare to defy Shareth, she has her father's might – the power of the Wise, and none of his discipline. Shareth wishes nothing more than to avenge herself upon him. Doubtless she makes plans to that end.

'I'm sure she does,' Rorthron answered. 'Luxor is fully aware of that fact. I am here to help him and make sure her wishes are not granted.'

Have you faced the Heartstealer?

'Once,' Rorthron said, with a shiver.

Her powers are stronger than you realise. Her arts are not just of the Wise, she has subsumed evil and cunning from many sources, combined with her own rage and self-obsession. She is a wild and dangerous sorceress, more so than her father. None of the Wise can stand against her ... unaided.

'Unaided?'

We studied the lore and history of the Icemark in great detail. Zarorthane himself may be, perhaps, the greatest historian that remains. There are other powers at work in these lands, Rorthron, older than Shareth, older even than the Wise themselves ...

'You speak of the First Power,' Rorthron said.

You know of it?

'A little,' Rorthron replied. 'The folly of the Wise, so I was told. Talismans crafted in the depths of time, sundered now and lost ...'

Your Gryfallon studied those arts and forged the Ice Crown with that knowledge. But before then many others were created. Combined, their powers would be immense, beyond anything that could be wielded by any of us today. Yet, some still exist.

'You know of them?'

We know of the Talismans that still lie within the bounds of Icemark ...

'And will you tell me?' Rorthron asked.

To what purpose would you put such knowledge should we give it to you?

Rorthron thought for a moment.

'I would attempt to safeguard the legacy of the Wise,' he replied. 'To ensure the powers we once had are not used for ill.'

A good answer. Spoken by one who has felt the fell taint of the Ice Fear first hand, no doubt. And the Heartstealer?

'I seek to aid Luxor in his struggle against her.'

Very well then ...

The light of the diamond faded and it rolled to one side with a gentle thump upon the book. Rorthron waited a moment before he stepped forward.

Within this diamond lies the will of the Wise of Icemark, this book ... this contains the knowledge of the Wise of Icemark ...

There was no sound, no movement other than his own.

Gently, Rorthron picked up the diamond and turned it around in his hand.

Magic being contained, or perhaps constrained, within an object. The arts of the Wise, sometimes put to good use, sometimes not? Talismans indeed ...

He placed the diamond on the floor before returning his attention to the book upon the pedestal.

The knowledge of the Wise of Icemark!

The book was old, leather bound and secured by thick, metal clasps. There was no front cover as such, no runes to be deciphered, it was plain and ordinary. Rorthron unpicked them and pulled the binding open.

The book creaked and then lay open to his inspection. The first page was covered with symbols. The text was peculiar, hard to see and difficult to make out. It was in no language that Rorthron knew and yet ...

Words formed at the top of the page in a language he could make out.

Yes, you begin to understand, Rorthron.

Rorthron jolted back in surprise, looking around the room before returning his attention to the book.

Seek the knowledge you desire. If it is known, so shall it be revealed.

'I seek …'

More words formed, somehow now intelligible, on the old worn pages of the book.

These are the annals of one Zarorthane, held in great esteem by those learned in lore, history and the affairs of the Wise of Icemark. He alone across all time and in …

'Yes, yes, yes …' Rorthron muttered. The text reformed itself.

You have heard tell of the folly of the Wise. How, long ago, we feared that too much power was concentrated in one place and that if any one individual sought to control it … Long before that, before the races of Midnight and Icemark came to these lands, before the Free, before the Fey … we were. The Wise lived here long before anyone else. Much we achieved in those times, before our folly overtook us.

'Our folly?'

We sought too much, the power of the world as divined by our curiosity and found to be imbued in every part of nature was never supposed to concentrated in one place, but spread out through the lands, thinly, like a veneer, holding things in place and shaping them. But we had, over the course of so many moons, pulled it together. It was potent, enabling many amongst us to achieve greatness beyond anything ever achieved before or since.

And not just strong, it became wilful, mischievous even, having its own whims and intentions. It enticed, teased and misled our folk, promising them power through dreams and visions, furthering its own ends. By the time we divined its intents, it was almost too late. We think that the magic of these lands was deliberately spread out in this fashion, to prevent such a thing occurring.

'By whom?'

By one, or by many, we never found out. Perhaps the Temples of this realm may hold a clue to their identity. If they were even a people, they would have been masters of us all. Whoever they were our own meddling undid their intentions. We called it the First Power and it began to dominate the will of the Wise; so much for our much vaunted wisdom. The result was war.

Rorthron paused for a moment and sighed to himself.

'War … the price of magic, or merely an inevitability?'

A great war, fought between the Wise for control of that power. The great mountains of Midnight and Icemark, forged in the heat of those battles. Chasms were wrought, valleys carved, lakes flooded into great depressions – blasted into the ground, the lands forever changed. You wonder how the deep places of our lands came to hold strange powers? The ability to gain a day or summon the night, the invigorating potency of the lakes and springs? The Liths and the Stones? Those powers are the latent remnants of that battle fought between those who wished to return things to how they were, and those who thought they knew better.

Some of that power remained concentrated, not to the same degree of potency for certain, but strong enough to be meaningful. In the war much of the magic had been captured, sealed within precious objects crafted by the Wise for that very purpose.

'So, we come to the Talismans,' Rorthron said. 'For this is the lore I need to know. That there were Crowns I already know but …'

It was an art form, to shape and mould such an unruly force and keep it thus contained, but such was our skill in those days. The result was a craft and the outcome of that craft. These were the Talismans.

Hundreds there were, mostly of lesser worth and potency. These are scattered throughout the Icemark or buried deep in long forgotten snows. Bows, spears, swords, hammers and axes. Do not trouble yourself with these trinkets.

Concentrate on the greater powers, first the Spells. These might have many purposes from the changing of time, to revealing secrets paths, travelling swiftly and other such influences. Many of them were dark and twisted, draining the soul of vigour or summoning the darkness. Most are lost now, or diluted within the stones or temples of the Icemark where even the commoners of the realm may still chance upon them.

Then came the Runes. They were of a greater potency than the Spells and many were wrought. They could grant their bearer protection from harm and at the same time imbue those nearby with great strength and fortitude.

Then came the Crowns; they that were the most powerful. They had the ability of transportation, much like the hidden walkways of the Liths and Stones, but the bearer could both move to a place of their choosing, or summon those far away to them. They were mighty in the deeds of warfare, used strategically to foil the plans of a foe.

All were perilous to use, even for the Wise, but separate in this fashion they were at least manageable, and the intent and will of the First Power was no longer manipulating us.

'And they were sown amongst the people of Midnight and Icemark?'

Yes, and further afield as well.

Rorthron frowned.

'The Moon Rings … and Tarithel's gem perhaps?'

That lore is not known to us here in the Icemark.

'Then speak of what you do know.'

The Wise knew they could not be trusted with such power, the Talismans grew ever more potent in our hands. We thought they would be safer with those of lesser abilities, amongst the Free and the Fey.

'Quite the assumption.'

Yes, and an erroneous one. The Wise watched as Kings, Queens and mighty Lords and Ladies arose bearing those Talismans. Bloody empires expanded, each one more dreadful than the last.

'Did we not intervene?'

The Wise sought their own counsel and tried their hand. After countless moons they learnt their hardest lesson. Their interference only made things worse. Ironic is it not, they were called the Wise, yet the outcome of their works shows that they were never so. Ultimately they determined that keeping themselves distant from the affairs of the races of the lands was the safest course of action. And it worked. Over time most of the Talismans were lost in battle, forgotten, mislaid or buried deep beyond recall. Only a handful now remain, and of those, one your Moonprince has already destroyed.

'The Ice Crown,' Rorthron said.

Yes, the Ice Crown forged by Gryfallon. He was seeking more than just a crown or domination of Midnight. He uncovered quite some potency of the First Power, corrupted by it though he was. He sought to unify the remaining Talismans in order to further increase his grasp.

'And how would he have done so? How would he accomplish such a task?'

We do not know, but such knowledge was once written down long ago.

'Where?'

In the Last Book of the Wise.

Rorthron gasped, pondering this new revelation.

'And where can I find this tome?'

Alas, we do not know ...

Rorthron watched, but no more words formed on the page.

'So,' he said, straightening and easing the strain on his back. 'Gryfallon sought the Talismans to bolster his own powers, knowing that the First Power would give him abilities beyond any control of the Wise. Shareth now takes on his mantle … does she seek the same?'

A faint breeze rustled the book and a page was turned. Writing appeared on the revealed paper.

She must not be allowed to possess them all. At this time she does not have the power her father had, but she has the potential to be far more destructive than he. If she can, she will embrace the First Power and it will wield a terrifying force through her, enough to lay waste to Icemark, Midnight and more besides.

'And that must be prevented,' Rorthron muttered. 'But what Talismans are there? Where do they lie?'

Five Talismans of note remain in the realm of Icemark. Learn now of the Spell of Thigrorn, the three Crowns of Varenand, Imiriel and Carudium, and the Runes of Finorn. These are all that remain of the many that were forged. Of the Crowns, two Shareth already has in her grasp, those of Imiriel and Carudium. A Crown, a Spell and a Rune remain at large.

The Spell is the least potent of them all, but still able to take the bearer to a location of their choosing. The Crowns have the power of displacement, they are imbued with the strength and fortitude of the Liths, able to summon those brought to mind to the location of the bearer.

'And the Rune? What of the Rune?'

The Rune's power takes the strength and emotive force of the one who possesses it and magnifies its force, granting peace, health and rest or angst, illness and anguish depending on the measure of the bearer. Regardless, whosoever holds the Runes will be granted much protection from their foes.

This knowledge must not be used lightly. Within the hands of those who strive for good it would aid their quest, but should such knowledge be discovered by those who wish others ill, it would speed their own ambition and bring an everlasting languor upon our lands …

'But where!' Rorthron roared. 'Where can these Talismans be found?'

You have found guidance. Seeking the Talismans of the Icemark? In the realm of the Giants shall you find the Crown and the Runes. Carangrane the Giant stands at the Fortress of Ulformane. Looking for the spell of Thigrorn? It lies deep within the Forest of Farorn.

Rorthron gasped.

One last thing, Rorthron of the Wise. The Wise of Icemark have kept this secret for uncounted moons, but Shareth is no fool. She has ways and means to discover such truths and discover them she has. Even now her forces march on the Giants … surely she seeks the remaining Crown and the Runes. The Talismans must not be unified. The First Power must not be unleashed upon the lands again … Such is your quest and your charge from the Wise of Icemark.

The words ended and as Rorthron watched, the book snapped shut, the clasps buckling themselves in place. Once more the diamond lit up with a fierce magenta glow and floated above it once more.

Rorthron was left alone in the cold and desolate chamber.

'The Runes and the Crown first then,' he said. 'Shareth cannot be allowed to possess them. To the Giants!'

On the horizon the dark smoke could be seen drifting into the sky, visible for leagues and leagues across the plains of Morormarg. The smoke was lit from below by fiercely burning flames. The Fortress of Ulformane had been sacked and razed, its occupiers forced to retreat in ignominy.

A trail of dead soldiers, broken swords, spears, shields and clubs led away from the Fortress heading south-west abating only when it came upon the lands belonging to another

Fortress, that of Thorarg. There had the armies of the Iceguard veered aside, riding back the way they had come, slaughtering any of the wounded or infirm they found.

A massacre.

Carangrane, leader of the giants, was dead, slain by the soldiers of Imgasharg the Icelord.

Thorarg had ridden out to meet those that had survived. Of the leadership of the giants, Varangrim stood alone, injured and bleeding from a dozen wounds.

'See to my men,' Varangrim called, gesturing to those staggering around him. 'I will have no one tend to me whilst they suffer.'

'What happened?' Thorarg demanded, gesturing to his own men to help the injured. 'We received orders from Carangrane himself to remain at our posts …'

'Carangrane is dead,' Varangrim muttered. 'He will be giving no more orders.'

'My Liege,' Thorarg said, his voice a low whisper. 'What can be done?'

'Have your people make preparations to leave.'

'Leave?'

'Yes, leave!' Varangrim shouted. 'An army of Iceguard warriors more than five thousand strong lies a day's march north-east of here. Our forces are in disarray, weakened and broken. If we do not retreat by nightfall we will all be slain …'

Varangrim staggered and would have fallen had Thorarg not caught him.

'I will make preparations. You need rest, my Liege.'

'There is no time, listen to me …'

In a jumble of words, Varangrim recalled the treachery of the previous day.

He had watched as the giants, enraged by the attack and spurred on by the battle cries of Fenorn and Anvildrak and charged from the safety of the fortress, descending in wrath upon the armies of the Iceguard.

For a moment, victory had seemed certain. Imgasharg and his troupes of Iceguard had retreated before the rampaging might of the Giant.

But Varangrim had seen it for what is was. A feint, a tactic long thought through.

Even as the warriors of Imgasharg retreated before them, other armies were circling in from the side, obscured in the treacherous mists of the Icemark. The giants found themselves exposed on three flanks, their fortress abandoned and their safety lost.

Varangrim had yelled and cried for retreat, but few had heeded his words except those from his own command. He had watched in dismay as the greater part of the warriors of Fenorn, Anvildrak and Carangrim had been encircled by the strengthening Iceguard forces, hemmed in by a ring of steel; a trap that was sprung and snapped closed.

The giants within were encircled, outnumbered three to one.

In desperation Varangrim had led a charge at the wall of Iceguard warriors, seeking to free his comrades in arms, but it was in vain. Even as they did so, more Iceguard warriors rode to flank them seeking to cut off any chance of retreat.

Varangrim had seen the day was lost.

'We fled,' Varangrim finished. 'With those cursed Iceguard at our heels, laughing at our misery as we ran. They had their sport with us, cutting down the injured and the weak. Then they let us go.'

'We must teach them a lesson!' Thorarg cried. 'Have vengeance upon them for the sake of our lost cousins. We are giants …'

Varangrim shook his head. 'Did you not hear what I said? Carangrane is slain. Fenorn and Anvildrak with him, Ulformane too. If war has been kindled against us, we have already lost. We must ensure we save our homelands to the west. The Icelords have long been waiting for this moment. Shareth has lulled us into carelessness and we have fallen for her plan. We must consolidate ...'

Varangrim's eyes glazed over and he sank back against Thorarg.

'Healers! Healers!' Thorarg yelled.

Luxor and the Barbarians were gathered in the expansive halls of the City of Imgorad. It was far larger than the halls of the Fortress of Careneon. The room had high ceilings, lit by a huge fire in the centre above which were strung a series of boars, spit roasted. About the room were hung skeletons of beasts of many kinds, few of which Luxor recognised, their bones blackened by the smoke and haze that lay heavy in the room. Luxor's men sat alongside the Barbarian warriors at rough wooden benches arranged around the fire, helping themselves to battered, metal plates filled to the brim with meat and gravy alongside vast tankards of beer. The Barbarians traded lewd jokes and ribald tales with the men of the Free.

Luxor sat at a table overlooking the raucous proceedings, alongside Imgorad, Careneon and Torinarg. Beside them were other Barbarians of the nearby realms. Luxor had been introduced to Firak, Anvorthun and Thangrad. All had acknowledged his presence with a nod, but had said nothing. It seemed they all awaited their leader's verdict.

'I am gratified to see your men can drink,' Imgorad said, with a chuckle. 'I feared the men of the southern realms might not care for our ale.'

Luxor took a pull from his own tankard. The ale was rough and strong, but not unpleasant.

'My men and I find much to our liking in your realm, my Lord,' he replied. 'Not least your hospitality.'

Imgorad chuckled. 'It is said you come with a smooth tongue,' he said. 'But I do not find you unwholesome to behold. A mighty warrior so I hear, your reputation precedes you.'

'I am but a man,' Luxor replied. 'If I have done great deeds, then it is because I have stout support from my men, loyalty and a measure of luck alongside.'

'I hear that it is you that slew the father of our dear Heartstealer,' Imgorad said.

'It is as you say,' Luxor answered. 'A mighty host of Midnight was roused to assail the gates of the Witchking's fortresses. We were sore pressed, but his evil was cast down and he was slain where he stood. Our land was freed from his evil. Even his foul magic was dispelled and the long winter broke into spring …'

'And it enflamed the wrath of she who desires to rule us here in the Icemark,' Imgorad said, his voice deeper.

'I had no knowledge of her nor these lands at the time,' Luxor responded. 'I thought we had vanquished all evil and that we might beat our swords to ploughshares at last. Yet, his reach was far greater than we thought. The people of Midnight intended no harm to come to those in the Icemark.'

Imgorad nodded. 'And you have dispatched your evil,' he said. 'Ours remains.'

'Then you do stand against the Heartstealer?' Luxor asked.

'We neither stand with her or against her,' Imgorad said. 'She is fickle and sly, but at times generous and accommodating, whether her whims depend on the moon or the weather I do not know, she is unpredictable.'

'But you say she is evil,' Luxor pressed.

'She commands powers which I have seen no others use. Sorcery some call it, perhaps drawn from the dark realms beneath the Icemark, I don't know, nor much care. She plays the races of Icemark against each other, fostering hatred and enmity here, truces and pacts there. Her intent is doubtless to rule all the Icemark, but that remains beyond her powers … unless there is something I do not know.'

Imgorad turned to look at Luxor.

'She swore an oath to one of my companions,' Luxor said. 'That she would lay waste to Midnight and push onwards through the southern parts of our realm to lands beyond. She seeks her revenge upon me for the death of her father.'

'A daughter's prerogative I deem,' Imgorad answered. 'But if she seeks to subdue your lands, she must traverse mine, is this what you are saying?'

Luxor nodded. 'Yours and others. I hear tell of Dwarves, Giants and Fey besides amongst the people of the Icemark.'

'You have heard true. They fight their own battles, often as not against us,' Imgorad rumbled. 'I care little for the other races, but your presence here changes things. The Heartstealer desires your death no doubt, I could do worse than hand you over to her, our standing with her would improve in great measure.'

Luxor didn't answer.

Imgorad glared at him for a long moment, taking a pull from his tankard, before laughing and punching him in the shoulder. Luxor joined in the laughter.

'Fear not, man of the south,' Imgorad said, wiping his mouth with the back of his hand. 'We bear little love for the Heartstealer in these parts, yet she is a fearsome combatant that it is not wise to cross unless there is sound cause. We even had a treaty with her not so long ago. There are none who have taken a direct stand against her and survived long.' His gaze hardened. 'But I would hear your words on why I should not hand you over to her.'

'She is wrought of the same evil that cursed our realm to winter for a thousand moons and more,' Luxor answered. 'The same evil resides here, your lands are snow and frost bound, your people shiver in a cold that will never be revoked until this evil is vanquished. She takes each one of you: Fey, Giant, Dwarf and Barbarian and plays you off against each other, keeping you strong enough to prevent others getting an upper hand, but never so strong that you can rise up against her.'

Imgorad looked at Luxor, his eyes narrowing. 'Go on …'

'I've heard tell of allegiances tried and stands taken here in the Icemark,' Luxor said. 'All have failed. The races of the Icemark do not trust each other … yet far in the south, the men of the Free and the people of the Fey, long estranged so they were, put aside their differences and stood against the evil as one. We cast him down. The same can be done against this Heartstealer; that is my belief.'

'Perhaps the animosities your people bore against the Fey were not so great as the enmity that exists here,' Imgorad said. 'Wars have been fought in times not long gone. Hostility remains, and skirmishes are renewed every new moon. I do not doubt your sincerity, Moonprince. But this is the Icemark, not Midnight.'

'Then Shareth's hold over you will never be broken,' Luxor said. 'I bore the Fey little love in my homelands, treacherous and fickle I thought them, but we found a way to look beyond our differences and I learned all was not as I first thought. I understand there are grievances, border disputes, old scores to settle, but is not Shareth the greater evil? She is coming and her passing will not be peaceful.'

'In that regard I hear your words,' Imgorad rumbled. 'She has sent armies south in the past, doubtless to support her father's work in your lands.'

'She will not be satisfied with what she has,' Luxor answered. 'With her father's death, she considers Midnight … and the Icemark, her inheritance. She will take it all sooner or later, unless she is stopped.'

Imgorad nodded and then pursed his lips.

'All this I can accept,' he said. 'But it is not the whole truth, or perhaps even the main part of it. Why trouble yourself with the affairs of a distant land, when there must be work enough in Midnight to repair the damage caused by your recent conflicts? Why are you really here, Moonprince?'

Luxor smiled.

'Careneon told me you were wise and insightful,' he said. 'Your countrymen speak both well of you and truthfully.'

'Well they might,' Imgorad replied, with a chuckle. 'They know what would happen otherwise.'

Luxor smiled and then grew serious. 'The Heartstealer, Shareth … she has taken my son.'

'Your son?' Imgorad asked. 'How so?'

'Spirited him away by means of her fell sorceress powers,' Luxor answered. 'I only know she has him captive and has turned his mind from his natural loyalties, bewitched and cursed.'

'And you mean to retrieve him,' Imgorad said.

'Wouldn't any father seek to do the same?'

Imgorad regarded him for a moment. 'He would. If he had any honour about him.'

Luxor sighed. The pair exchanged a long look.

'You speak enough truth, Moonprince,' Imgorad finally said. 'And what you say tallies well with what my emissaries and messengers tell me of what takes place in other realms. Iceguard patrols have been seen in many places uncontested, and Shareth interferes in the politics of the Dwarves and Giants from what I have gleaned. If I should be so inclined, what is it that you ask of me and mine?'

Luxor raised his fist and extended his hand, the one that bore the Moon Ring. Imgorad and the other Barbarians looked at it, seeing a red glow emanated from the golden band.

'I was given this Talisman by Rorthron of the Wise,' Luxor said. 'It is the last war ring of Midnight, a heirloom of my house, the house of the Moon. It gives me the power of far-seeing, I can roam the landscape of Midnight or Icemark through the eyes of those who swear loyalty to me. With that, I can coordinate strategy, tactics, ventures … and attacks.'

'Such a power would allow us to co-ordinate strikes against the Heartstealer,' Imgorad whispered. 'Barbarian, Fey, Giant and Dwarf alike …'

'It is so,' Luxor said. 'And I have already sent an emissary to both the Fey and the Dwarves. The Giants will not be long delayed. Together we are powerful enough to unseat this hagspawn and her Icelords. You ask me what I ask of you … I ask that you pledge the allegiance of the Barbarians to my cause … and vow to see the end of Shareth, Sorceress, Heartstealer of Icemark.'

A rumble of anticipation rolled around the hall. All conversation stopped as attention was focussed on the top table and the interplay between Luxor and Imgorad.

Imgorad took another pull from his tankard, but said nothing.

Imgorarg and Glormane. The two Dwarves faced each other across the ancient tree stump of their people, whilst their entourages jeered and heckled all around them.

'I say your family has led the dwarven people to ruin,' Imgorarg sneered. 'And that you continue your father's legacy of weakness, letting the Barbarians and the Giants nibble away at our borders.'

'And you would have us ally with a sorceress?' Glormane countered. 'Become a lowly vassal of the Heartstealer, our lands crushed under the booted feet of the Icelords, of lower standing than the Barbarians and the Giants? Is that what you promise us, Imgorarg?'

Jeers from one side of the hall, cheers from the other.

Imulorn looked across at his brother, who had managed to procure an ale from somewhere and was busy downing it.

'This is going to get ugly,' Imulorn muttered.

Imelorn shrugged and patted his axe. 'Just tell me who to swing this at, brother. You can choose the side, it all sounds about the same to me.'

'You're not worried about aligning ourselves with the Heartstealer? She who has been the death of so many of our folk?'

Imelorn shrugged. 'My friends and family have died at the hands of Barbarian, Giant and Fey. I see no difference. Ally with whomsoever seems the strongest would be my suggestion – just keep an axe and shield to hand!'

Imulorn sighed. 'Need I remind you that our liege, Thigrak, instructed us to vote in favour of Glormane?'

'Even Thigrak would not risk the Dwarves becoming weak,' Imelorn returned. 'Glormane seems less of a leader than we were led to believe.'

The brothers turned to regard the ongoing argument. Imgorarg had stepped forward, placing one foot on the stump, glaring down at Glormane. He was the bigger and stronger of the pair.

'At least I have the courage to openly state my intention to court a sorceress,' he growled. 'Unlike you.'

Glormane didn't answer. Imulorn could see the confusion on his face.

'What's he saying?' Imelorn asked with a frown. 'A sorceress? This is news …'

Imulorn shook his head. 'I'm not sure. I don't think Glormane does either …'

'What nonsense is this?' Glormane demanded. 'I court no sorceress. I will have no dealings with the fell arts of magic.'

Imgorarg straightened and clapped his hands.

'He claims he knows not,' Imgorarg said, stepping back and gesturing around the hall with outstretched arms. 'I call you all to witness his perfidy. While he claims to have our best interests at heart, he forges alliances in secret!'

Glormane was staring at Imgorarg, his mouth open.

The doors to the hall swung back. The Dwarves turned as one, to see a troupe of soldiers march in, dragging a body behind them by means of a rope. The body was dressed in grey travelling garb, its arms outstretched and tied at the wrist.

It was a woman, her head adorned by striking red hair.

Imgorarg grunted and the soldiers hoisted her up, pulling her head back to reveal her features. A rumble of discontent buzzed around the hall as the Dwarves took in her elegant features and sculpted ears. Bruises were visible on her cheeks. She was in a faint, blindfold, her body slack in their grasp.

'Fey!' someone shouted.

'Yes,' Imgorarg rumbled, stepping around the stump to stand before the woman. 'In our very midst.'

'I do not know this woman,' Glormane laughed. 'You kidnap some random traveller in the wilderness and bring this as evidence? Your wits desert you Imgorarg. I'll give you credit for staging an amusing play, perhaps you missed your calling as a court jester ...'

Imgorarg ignored him, instead lifting a hand and slapping the woman across the face. She yelped and jolted in the grasp of the soldiers. Imulorn and Imelorn saw her struggle for a moment before gaining her footing.

Imgorarg leaned in close.

'Who are you?' he demanded.

'I am Tarithel,' the woman gasped, turning her head on hearing his voice. 'A traveller. Please, I mean no harm. I have come to speak with the Dwarves.'

'From Fangrim?' Imgorarg said, a smile upon his face.

'Yes, Fangrim,' Tarithel said. 'I have travelled far to reach you, seeking peace and your help ...'

'And whom do you seek?' Imgorarg said.

'I seek Glormane,' Tarithel said. 'For this is his city ... is it not?'

A further rumble of muttered conservation travelled around the room.

'Know her not then?' Imgorarg asked, turned to face Glormane.

Glormane shook his head. 'I have never seen her before. You know well enough that we haven't treated with the Fey in many moons.'

'You still claim that?' Imgorarg shouted. 'Yet she speaks your name?'

'Many know my name,' Glormane retorted. 'State your case, if you have one.'

Imgorarg scoffed.

'Then it is as well I have been warned of who she is,' he said, turning to face the assembled Dwarves. 'This Fey. She is no traveller, she is a sorceress aided and abetted by the treacherous Fey of Fangrim ... but she does not hail from those lands ... oh no ... she comes from further beyond. She comes from the realm of Midnight!'

'Midnight?' Glormane demanded. 'Now your fantasies lead us to madness ...'

Imgorarg continued on. 'With her magic she has forged a path through the Frozen Wastes themselves!' Imgorarg grabbed his axe, turned on Tarithel, grabbing her by the chin and lifting her head. The axe blade was at her throat.

'Speak the truth Fey, or do you deny it?'

'It is true I come from Midnight,' she cried. The Dwarves about could hear the fear in her voice.

'You are in league with a despotic Lord of that realm!' Imgorarg roared. 'We have heard of the plight of Midnight, how an unholy alliance of Fey and Men attacked, without provocation, the ancient home of Shareth's father and slew him! Now you seek more allies for your rampant lust for blood and war … intending to recruit us to your cause and wreak your war across the face of the Icemark, with the Dwarves to be sacrificed in the front line!'

'No …' Tarithel sobbed. 'This is lies!'

'And you are a sorceress,' Imgorarg cried. 'Behold!'

He grabbed at her neck, pulling at the necklace that hung there. As he did so, the stone suspended upon it was brought into view. He held it up and a strange green light was cast about the hall. The Dwarves shrank back, many collapsing to their knees in abject fear.

'Witness her magic!' Imgorarg continued. 'She seeks to enchant us even now. Shareth has warned us of this treachery. This woman is a sorceress of the Fey!'

He leaned in on Tarithel, his face close to hers.

'Deny it!'

Imulorn and Imelorn watched as Tarithel shrank back from Imgorarg's yells, but she did not answer.

'You see?' Imgorarg shouted. 'She cannot, for it is the truth! And it is the Queen of the Icemark who holds our salvation, not this evil from the Fey!'

'Slay her!' Someone yelled.

Tarithel struggled, but there was no escape from those that held her.

'Slay the sorceress!' Imgorarg roared, before turning on Glormane. 'And slay those who brought this evil upon us.'

The chants in the hall were rising.

'We cannot let this happen,' Imulorn said. His brother grabbed his arm.

'Glormane has already lost,' Imelorn replied. 'There's no saving him or that Fey-girl now …'

Imulorn turned to see Glormane had been grabbed by

more of Imgorarg's soldiers and wrestled alongside Tarithel. Axes, their polished blades glittering in the firelight, were poised at their throats.

'For high treason and treachery, we end you now,' Imgorarg said, gesturing to his soldiers.

The axes swung back, ready to fall and hew.

Chapter Eleven

Imgorad the Barbarian stands in the City of Imgorad looking east to the Forest of Thangrun.

Rorthron and his escort of Barbarians were riding back north-west towards the city of Imgorad when he felt the presence of the Moon Ring about him. He kept his horse cantering on-wards at an easy pace as he focussed his mind.

Rorthron!

Rorthron recognised the touch of the Moon Ring upon his mind.

'My Lord, Luxor?'

You ride to me?

'I do … I have found out much …'

Rorthron allowed his thoughts to expand within his mind, giving Luxor an understanding of what he had found back at the Tower.

More magical mysteries I see. Talismans and spells … at least the Wise of Icemark are able to tell us something useful!

'Useful yes,' Rorthron replied. 'But more to worry about too …'

This book? The Last Book of the Wise?

'Yes,' Rorthron replied. 'A question for Lorgrim when and if we return from our current travails.

Luxor's mental voice was strained.

'How goes the negotiation with Imgorad?'

He considers what I have said, I hope I made my case well

enough. He seems a practical and wise enough leader, but what I cannot tell is whether he has the desire to put himself against the Heartstealer, or whether he will prefer to maintain things as they are.

Rorthron nodded.

'In the meantime, my own quest here is placed before me,' Rorthron said. 'The Wise have revealed that both the Crown and the Runes lie within the Kingdom of the Giants. I have a name and a location. Carangrane the Giant and the Fortress of Ulformane. I do not know where they lie, but I dare say it is far to the north.'

You must first return to Imgorad and seek his permission to cross his lands. They may even know where this place can be found.

'Of course,' Rorthron replied. 'My escort will be sore weary by the time they return. I am sparing little speed.'

I look forward to seeing you once more.

'Haste is called for,' Rorthron added. 'I also learnt that Shareth already possesses two of the three crowns herself. Doubtless she seeks for the last as we speak. We must find both the remaining Crown and the Runes before she does …'

Or she will be unassailable.

'I fear you speak the truth.'

Ride swiftly then, Rorthron. I will see you soon.

The uproar continued in the hall of the Dwarves. Voices shouted and Dwarves jostled for position around the two protagonists.

'No last words?' Imgorarg said with a laugh. 'You and your Fey mistress?'

'I truly fear for our Kingdom when it can be won over with force and lies,' Glormane retorted. 'When none will stand for truth, we do not deserve to prosper. How many have you bribed, Imgorarg? What have you promised?' He raised his voice. 'To all of you I say this, the Heartstealer will betray you all, deep in your hearts you know this. I only hope you see the error of your ways before our Kingdom falls!'

'Pretty words,' Imgorarg replied. 'But idle ones.'

'I will serve my people to the end,' Glormane spat. 'Unlike you.'

'Then your last service to us is of some merit,' Imgorarg snarled, gesturing at the Fey-girl, who was still held slumped in the grasp of his companions. 'You have bought a spy to us. Shareth herself sent word to watch for this Fey maiden, this sorceress, set on our destruction! And here she is. She will make a perfect gift to the Heartstealer, and Shareth will be forever grateful to the Dwarves.'

'Hand her over and you spill innocent blood,' Glormane replied. 'You will set us on a course of war with the Fey. They will not forgive you if you kill her!'

'The dwarven people have made their choice, Glormane,' Imgorarg said. 'We stand with the Heartstealer, not with the Fey. Or do you not heed the will of the people?'

'The will of the people?' Glormane retorted. 'All I have heard is the will of Imgorarg. Where is Carorthay? Would he not have something to say in all this?'

A mutter of approval ran around the hall. Imulorn stepped forward, pulling away despite Imelorn trying to restrain him.

'Yes,' Imulorn said, pushing to the fore through the crowd of Dwarves and seizing his moment. 'I would hear Carorthay's wisdom. All should hear his words before this is all decided. Where is he?'

'Carorthay did not respond to the summons,' Imgorarg replied, glaring at Imulorn. 'Thus he must abide by the decisions made in his absence.'

There was a thump from the other end of the hall followed by three heavy knocks at the closed doors.

The assembly turned as one as the doors were pulled back.

'I see everyone is behaving themselves as well as ever.'

The voice was deep, old but penetrating. The Dwarves paused in their clamour, muttering amongst themselves.

Another Dwarf stood in the entranceway to the hall, standing, somewhat nonchalantly between the stone pillars that marked the threshold. He pulled back a cowl, revealing an old and careworn face, grey bearded but with dark eyes hard as flint.

'Carorthay!' Imgorarg exclaimed in evident surprise.

'Surprised to see me no doubt, Imgorarg?'

Gasps went up from the assembled throngs of Dwarves.

'That summons you mentioned, Imulorn,' Carorthay said, making a show of removing his armoured gloves. 'I never received it.'

His voice was deep, rumbling from his throat, deeper even than Imgorarg's.

'And the reason for that,' Carorthay continued, stepping forward towards Imgorarg, 'Is that Glormane's messengers were waylaid upon their route and killed by rogues in your employ. My folk found them … let's just say that appropriate justice was meted out by me.'

Carorthay glared at Imgorarg.

More gasps erupted from the Dwarves.

'And had I received the summons,' Carorthay said, his voice steady. 'I would have made a more timely report of the treachery of your beloved Heartstealer. The Icelords on our north-eastern borders are ready for war. She seeks for a civil war amongst our people, a war that would weaken us and leave us open to be conquered. This is the path you have led us to, Imgorarg. The only question that remains in my mind is whether you have done this willingly or not …'

'Lies!' Imgorarg roared. 'Your mind is already bewitched by this Fey sorceress.'

'If we are to be bewitched by a sorceress,' Carorthay said, sparing Tarithel a glance. 'This one seems more fair to me than that hagspawn from the cursed north.'

'The dwarven people have made their choice,' Imgorarg said. 'Slay her, take them!'

The assembly fell into chaos, Dwarves shouting and gesturing at one another.

Imgorarg's Dwarves charged forwards, axes raised. A wild blow from the haft of one toppled Tarithel and sent her spinning to the ground.

Imulorn picked up his own axe and made ready. His brother stood at his side.

'We're with Glormane and Carorthay in case you were wondering,' Imulorn yelled to his brother.'

'Right you are,' Imelorn said, hefting his axe and wading into the fray.

The hall rang with the sounds of battle.

Varangrim stirred, his body stiff and sore. The great giant propped himself up, grimacing against the pain, seeing his limbs bound with bandages. He was lying on a makeshift mattress made of dried rushes. Around him lay many of his men, tended in the same fashion.

'My Liege!'

Varangrim looked up, weariness almost swamping him.

'Thorarg,' he acknowledged. 'What news?'

'I have made preparations such as you asked for,' Thorarg said. 'I have sent word to Torelak and Ganigrorn. We are prepared to retreat to the city of Imgenarg.'

Varangrim nodded. 'It still stands?'

'It does, my Liege.' Thorarg looked downcast.

'What is it?'

'There is more news,' Thorarg said. 'Runners arrived during the night. The Iceguard have moved against us all along our eastern borders, their armies moving swiftly from the cover of the Forest of Farorn. It was not only Ulformane that fell, but the fortresses of Glortheon too. Armies loyal to the Heartstealer have been seen crossing the Hills of Anvormand ...'

'Towards my own city,' Varangrim said. 'It is well defended, and with Imatron and Thormuk nearby. We must know what the Iceguard are doing. The invasion we long feared now seems to be upon us and we are not prepared for it.'

He leant forward, staggering to his feet.

'You are hurt ...' Thorarg said.

'I have strength enough,' Varangrim said. 'I fear this is no skirmish this time. The Heartstealer has our lands in her sights.'

'There are Iceguard armies gathering still on the Plains of Morormarg,' Thorarg said. 'In greater numbers than a single fortress can withstand.'

Varangrim nodded. 'Then we retreat now,' he said. 'Give the word, take everything of value that can be taken, weapons, provisions, livestock. We will rally at the City of Imgenarg in the shadow of Anvormane. Those mountains have always been the backbone of our people, they will be so again.'

Rorthron and his escort of Barbarians rode into the City of Imgorad. The horses were sweating, their coats slick having ridden hard for hours. Rorthron and the Barbarians dismounted, handing the weary beasts over to the stable hands.

Luxor and Imgorad were waiting for him.

'He rides well, for one so old,' Imgorad said, noting the exhausted faces of his men.

'The Wise have great fortitude,' Luxor replied. 'And the weather seems to part before them. Rorthron rode the length and breadth of Midnight is his quest to rid the land of the Witchking. He is tireless in pursuit of the truth.'

'A worthy companion,' Imgorad said, with a nod. 'And a means to spy out the lands in haste.'

'Rorthron is no spy …' Luxor begun.

'Perhaps,' Imgorad said. 'I understand your position well enough, Moonprince. Knowledge is power; that I do know. All I ask is that you tell me of what you learn whilst within my realms.'

'That I am happy to do,' Luxor replied.

Rorthron walked up to them, unwearied by the long ride that had exhausted the Barbarians who'd ridden with him.

'My Lords,' he said, with a bow.

'Rorthron,' Luxor acknowledge, extending his hand. Rorthron shook it. 'It is good to see you once again. What news?'

Rorthron looked at Imgorad for a moment, before looking back to Luxor.

'It is all right,' Luxor said. 'We stand in the Outlands of the Barbarians by their good will, anything we know we should trust them to hear too.'

Rorthron nodded. 'Very well. I have learned that the Heartstealer does indeed have a plan for domination of the Icemark. Not only has she gathered much strength in the form of the armies of the Icelords, but she also controls Talismans … the like of which our former foe also held in his grasp.'

'Talismans?' Imgorad asked.

'The Witchking held the Ice Crown,' Luxor answered. 'A fell weapon indeed, it struck fear into the hearts of Free and Fey alike, rendering them cowards, crying piteously for the mercy of death. We were sore pressed to counter it.'

'Crowns, spells and runes,' Rorthron said with a nodded. 'Such powers are aboard in this realm too.'

Imgorad looked thoughtful for a moment. 'I believe what you say. There has been talk of Crowns and such like in the stories of our ancestors. The bards would know more, they are ancient tales. Few give them much credence, but they always had the ring of truth about them.'

'Shareth does not control them all,' Rorthron said. 'At least, not yet. But she seeks them. Already she possesses two … if she finds more her power will likely grow beyond our ability to counter.'

'And so you will urge me to join you in countering her,' Imgorad said with a chuckle. 'There is a surprise.'

Rorthron's eyes narrowed.

'She will seek to implement her plan regardless of what we do,' Rorthron said. 'Our choices will influence the outcome … either way.'

'What do you suggest?' Luxor said.

'I believe the Wise of this realm will aid me,' Rorthron said. 'I am, after all, kin to them, if long estranged. With your permission I will seek out the fate of the other Talismans. If they do exist, I will put them beyond her grasp.'

'Such power might be best used against her surely?' Imgorad asked.

'Perhaps,' Rorthron said. 'But without knowing the potency or capability of these devices, I would not trust them to be used. Such things are prone to misuse, and oft turn to evil. Better that we keep the power from the Heartstealer and only use them at greatest need.'

'Then what do you ask of me?' Imgorad asked.

Rorthron looked at Luxor again. 'What I have learned indicates that news of the Talismans might be found in the north of Icemark. I ask for permission to cross your lands for this very purpose.'

'The north?' Imgorad answered. 'You will find the Giants in that direction. I cannot say whether they will permit you to cross their lands. Association with us may taint your reputation before you can even speak to them.'

'I will have to trust in my diplomatic skills,' Rorthron replied, with a smile.

Imgorad thought about it for a moment.

'I will permit this,' he said. 'But there are conditions.'

'Name them,' Luxor said.

'Any knowledge you gain as to the whereabouts or disposition of these Talismans,' Imgorad said. 'You will report back to me. You may cross my lands, but you do not represent the Barbarians … once you are beyond our realm, your conduct speaks only of your Moonprince, not of my people.'

'Acceptable,' Luxor said. 'You will find us true to our word, Imgorad. I hope that will prove our good intentions to you.'

'When will you depart?' Imgorad asked.

'Immediately,' Rorthron replied. 'Time is of the essence.'

'Now …' Imgorad said, 'Without rest? Why you only just …'

'The Heartstealer will not be idle,' Rorthron replied. 'And thus … neither must I.'

Imgorad raised his hands in acknowledgement. 'So be it. I can provide you with an escort to the border if you desire.'

'They will only slow me down,' Rorthron replied. 'I will be swifter alone.'

'You ask me to trust you … very well. I shall.' He paused for a moment, before fixing Rorthron with a stern glare. 'Your conduct will reflect upon your Moonprince here. The trust of the Barbarians is not often given and is dangerous to betray.'

'You will not find it misplaced,' Rorthron replied.

'Then I give you leave to seek,' Imgorad said, before turning his attention to Luxor. 'Come then. You and I will discuss our situation further.'

Luxor nodded and gave Rorthron a pointed stare.

'My Lords,' Rorthron said, bowing to both of them.

'Be both safe and swift,' Luxor said.

'We will speak again soon,' Rorthron replied.

'It seems she will live.'

Footsteps. Fire crackling.

The smell of smoke and cooking meats.

Tarithel's head was pulsing with pain from where she'd been hit. She tried to move but found her knees and ankles were bound, with her hands tied behind her back. A foul smelling rag had been tightened around her mouth and she was still blindfold. She wriggled, testing the bounds, but they were firm and secure.

'She was alone?' The second voice was more refined than the others. It sounded familiar.

'Seems that way,' the first replied. 'Imgorarg's men claim to have found her travelling the forests. A lone Fey, travelling unescorted as far as we can tell. They caught her unawares, which seems strange if she truly is the sorceress they called her.'

'She doesn't look like a sorceress …'

'And how many of them have you met?' the first asked with a laugh. 'She's a Fey and she wears the colours of Fangrim, that will do for a start …'

'We need to know the truth,' the refined voice said.

The footsteps shuffled nearer.

'Wake her,' said the first voice.

Tarithel felt herself prodded. She moaned, but couldn't speak.

'So … she's been listening,' the first said. 'Let's hear what she has to say for herself.'

Tarithel heard someone shuffle closer. She moaned again and tried to wriggle away, but someone took a firm grip of her neck and slid a cold blade against her skin. A moment later the gag in her mouth was released. Tarithel spat out the foul taste in her mouth.

She was wrestled into a kneeling position and the blindfold pulled from her head. She blinked in the bright glare of flaming torches. Two Dwarves were looking down at her.

'As you've seen, you've chosen a poor time to visit this land, Fey-girl,' the nearest said.

Tarithel looked him in the eye. He was the eldest of the pair and dressed in rather more flamboyant furs and leather than his companion. His voice was the more elegant and refined.

'The manner of my welcome left something to be desired,' Tarithel replied, wincing at the throbbing in her head.

The second and elder of the two Dwarves chuckled at the aggrieved tone of her voice.

Tarithel looked around her. Slumped by the fire were several other Dwarves, some on their backs, some on their sides, all clutching an assortment of weapons; axes, swords and spears. Many bore the marks of fighting, with injuries bound up in bloodstained rags.

What happened? I could see nothing! I remember an argument ... a fight ... I must have been hit. Those Dwarves were going to kill me ... then who is this who has me captive now?

'You're no peasant girl then,' the first Dwarf said. 'I'm sorry we fall below your obviously high standards. Can I offer you wine my Lady, or a bath perhaps, maybe even Shareth's crown?'

Tarithel glared at him. The Dwarf stood before her, placing his axe blade close to her face.

'Or better still,' he said, looking down at her, 'let's hear your explanation as to why you're travelling in this realm, why

Imgorarg claimed you were sorceress and whether there is any truth in his claims. I suggest you're both honest and swift about it.'

Tarithel stared the Dwarf, shrinking back from his fierce visage.

'I came seeking Glormane of the Dwarves,' Tarithel said, summoning her own strength. 'He was here, in this very fight! Where is he? Lord Imorthorn told me that he was a Dwarf of great honour. He is held in high regard by the Fey of Fangrim.'

The Dwarf looked surprised and looked across to his companion. Tarithel saw the elder Dwarf's eyebrows rise.

'Is he indeed?' the second Dwarf said. 'Well, there's a thing!'

'He is,' Tarithel said. 'And I expect he'd have something to say about how visitors in his realm are treated, doubtless he would have words for brigands, accusing travellers of evil, kidnapping them, beating them about the head and tying them up!'

The elder Dwarf looked at his companion. Tarithel caught the glance.

'And you are Tarithel, sorceress of the Fey?' the elder Dwarf asked.

'My name is Tarithel,' she replied, glaring at him. 'I am Lady of the Forest. I have travelled the road from Fangrim. But I will tell you nothing else. I demand to be taken to Glormane, he will receive me. I have a message for him and for him alone.'

The elder Dwarf stepped back and then gestured to his companion and to her with a nod.

The other Dwarf knelt behind her and undid the ropes that bound her. Tarithel rubbed at her wrists, trying to ease the soreness.

'Very well Tarithel of Fangrim, Lady of the Forest,' the Dwarf said. 'I do not need to take you to Glormane, you can make your complaints to him directly. I'm sorry my hospitality isn't what you expected.'

Tarithel blinked.

'You?' she asked. 'You're Glormane?'

Glormane nodded. Tarithel looked around her again, looking now at the elder Dwarf.

'And I am Carorthay,' he said, by way of introduction. 'Of the Eastern realm.'

'But you're not wrong,' Glormane said, gesturing around him. 'The quality of my court is rather reduced of late. I apologise for the manner in which you were captured. You can thank Carorthay here that you live at all … as do I.'

Tarithel swallowed.

'My thanks then,' she answered. 'To both of you.'

'Tell us then,' Carorthay said. 'Imgorarg claimed you were a sorceress. Should we fear you, or bow down before you perhaps?'

Tarithel shook her head.

'No, my Lords,' she answered. 'If I am a sorceress, I am a poor one! I have left the realms of the Fey to travel northwards into the Frozen Empire. My betrothed is caught by Shareth and I must set him free.'

'You seek Shareth?' Glormane asked, his mouth dropping open.

'I must,' Tarithel answered. 'She holds him in the City of Imiriel, far to the north. That is where I must go and why I have travelled here.'

'She will have you slain and mounted on a wall the moment you set foot in her domain,' Carorthay said. 'She will not suffer you to pass. Imgorarg planned the very same fate for you just an hour ago.'

'I must go …' Tarithel replied.

'And Imorthorn sent you to us?' Glormane asked.

Tarithel nodded. 'I came here on his guidance, and that of

Thormand the Fey, that you might be able to guide me on my quest.'

Carorthay and Glormane exchanged a glance.

'Well, she doesn't seem all that terrifying,' Carorthay said. 'I think we can trust her for now.'

'Aye,' Glormane said.

Glormane held out his hand, helping her to her feet. She was surprised to find she was taller than him. None of the Dwarves came up to her chin, but all were at least twice as wide as she was.

Tarithel frowned, noticing the injured Dwarfs all about the hall.

'My Lord …' Tarithel stammered. 'But, what has happened?'

'My lady, you're looking at what remains of my court,' Glormane said. 'There has been something of a shift in power in the kingdom of the Dwarves. Like I said, you choose a poor time to visit us.'

'I don't understand,' Tarithel said. 'This is your city … that other Dwarf? Imgorarg? He's in the service of the Heartstealer!'

'Internal conflict,' Glormane said. 'Civil war is upon us. Though there is little civil about it.'

Tarithel swayed. Glormane helped steady her, passing her a tankard. She sniffed, it was some kind of rough ale.

'It's better than the water,' Carorthay said with a chuckle. 'Trust me.'

Tarithel took a sip and almost choked on the strong taste.

'Know you much of Imgorarg?' Glormane asked.

'I had been told the name,' Tarithel said, shaking her head to clear it. 'That he was not so trustworthy. But, until that fight …'

'A Dwarf from our northern realm,' Glormane said. 'It is he who commands the majority of the Dwarves now. We are …' Glormane gestured to Carorthay, 'somewhat out of favour.

If safe passage through our lands was your desire, I fear you have come too late.'

'I must make my way through,' Tarithel said. 'I came to ask for your help. I have no choice. Imorthorn himself recommended you to me … I have nowhere else to go.'

'Imorthorn is a good Fey,' Carorthay said. 'If such things exist.'

Tarithel looked at him. Glormane chuckled.

'I jest,' Carorthay said. 'Our people have had our differences, but Thormand and Imorthorn have always been true to their word. If they have sent you, then we will do what we can.'

'That will not be much,' Glormane added. 'Given what has happened here.'

'And what exactly has happened?' Tarithel asked. 'The fight began and then … ' She rubbed at her forehead, feeling a throbbing bruise.

Glormane stopped and put down his axe, leaning on the handle.

'I have lost the leadership entrusted to me by my father,' he said. 'Four generations of my line and it comes down to my foolishness.'

Tarithel didn't answer.

'I underestimated my opponent,' Glormane continued. 'And the wave of frustration that has built up regarding the constant skirmishes around our borders; the dissatisfaction of my people. I was a fool and I have paid for my foolishness.'

'And this, Imgorarg, is your opponent?' Tarithel asked. 'He leads the Dwarves now?'

'He does, my people have been persuaded to follow his lead over mine.'

'Then I must go to him,' Tarithel said. 'And make my case there.'

'We only just prevented him from slicing your head from

your neck,' Carorthay said. 'He will slay you and take your remains to her!'

'Imgorarg is no friend of the Fey,' Glormane said, turning to her. 'He is in league with the Heartstealer. Of her, you clearly know enough already.'

'I do,' Tarithel said. 'But it is to her I must go.'

Glormane stopped, shaking his head.

'Start this again,' Glormane said. 'It makes no sense to me. Your betrothed? What interest does the Heartstealer have in him?'

Tarithel sighed.

'It is a long story …'

'Time for you to tell that story I think, Lady of the Forest,' Carorthay said. 'A Fey alone is an unusual sight in our lands, a woman more so … a woman of rank … that has never happened before to my knowledge. Clearly you risk much on this quest. Imgorarg accused you of coming from afar, being in league with some warrior of the southlands.'

Tarithel took another gulp of the ale before continuing.

'I am not of Fangrim,' Tarithel said. 'Though I have ridden the long road from that great forest, sent onwards by Imorthorn and Thormand as I have said. My home is much further away, beyond the Frozen Wastes.'

'Beyond?' Glormane said. Tarithel saw his eyes narrow. 'There was truth in Imgorarg's tale?'

Tarithel nodded. 'I hail from the land of Midnight, not the Icemark.'

'Midnight?' Carorthay echoed, his expression creasing into a frown. 'I have heard tales told of it. There were a few rumours from the Fey, a great battle fought in that land where its people overthrew the might of the Witchking.'

'It is true,' Tarithel said. 'Not three moons ago the Witchking was defeated … slain.'

'By some mighty warrior of those lands?' Glormane asked.

Tarithel nodded. 'You speak of my Liege, Luxor Moonprince of Midnight. Even now he rides through the Icemark to the south. The Witchking's power was laid low by the hand of my betrothed, Morkin, Luxor's son.'

'How so?' Carorthay demanded.

'He was able to steal away the source of the Witchking's power, the Ice Crown, and destroy it.'

Glormane and Carorthay looked at each other.

'If that mighty he is, how came he to be in the clutches of the Heartstealer?' Glormane asked.

Tarithel looked away.

'She stole him away by her sorcery.' Her expression hardened. 'And I didn't come all this way to turn back now. I will find him and I will release him. Will you let me go? Will you guide me onwards?'

Glormane stepped back from the fierce and determined expression on her face.

'If it were up to me I would speed you on your way,' Glormane said. 'But my powers are now not what they were. We cannot guarantee you safe passage northwards, not while hostile forces camp around our gates. Even now Imgorarg holds the plains beyond my city.'

'Eastwards perhaps,' Carorthay said, 'But it would not be easy to smuggle you past.'

'But north is where I must go,' Tarithel said.

'Imgorarg will not permit it,' Carorthay said. 'You would be caught the moment you set foot outside of these walls. The dwarven kingdom belongs to him now, and thus, to the Heartstealer.'

'A fell day for the Dwarves,' Glormane agreed.

'Would you not take back control?' Tarithel asked.

'You do not understand our ways,' Carorthay said. 'The Dwarves rule by strength and consensus, not by decree. Imgorarg has the support of the majority of the Dwarves.

The vote has been cast. Imgorarg has left the city to rally his forces; it is only a matter of time before we are defeated and the city taken. There is no escape.'

Something stirred in her, a green fire that began to smoulder in her heart. She felt, rather than saw, the jewel around her neck begin to pulse with light.

The spirit of Fangrim …

'You say this Imgorarg is allied with the Heartstealer?' Tarithel cried. The words did not seem to be wholly her own, though she agreed with them. 'Do you not know of her evil?'

'Oh, I am well aware of it,' Glormane replied.

'And you would leave it there?' Tarithel demanded. Anger rose within her, a sudden uncontrolled rush of rage. A green fire lit her from within. 'Your kingdom a vassal of her evil and witchcraft?'

'You do not understand …' Carorthay began.

'I understand well enough,' Tarithel answered. The fury swirled within her, boiling upwards. It felt strange, as if she were somehow watching from afar, but it grew, burning hot, filling her body and mind with wrath. 'I have seen this everywhere I go in the realm of Icemark; a lack of will and courage! Will none defy the Heartstealer? Shareth is her name! She is not all powerful. It is you, you're all cowards!'

Her words shocked her, but the anger still ruled.

Carorthay recoiled, anger growing on his face. Glormane hefted his axe.

'You dare insult me to my face in my own hall …' Glormane rumbled.

Tarithel felt fear, but it was subsumed by the fury that was blazing through her, so powerful now that she could not resist it. It gave her a confidence and assurance that was not her own.

'Oh,' Tarithel cried. 'So you would take an axe to an undefended Fey maiden would you? How very brave of you. This maiden is not without her own powers. Behold!'

Glormane snarled and brought the axe around. Tarithel stepped back, the jewel around her neck glowing with a fierce, green light that shone all around them. It was blinding, causing the wooden beams of the hall to cast shadows all around her, shifting as she moved. From the corner of her eye she saw movement and heard the other Dwarves running towards her, yelling out as they came.

Roots sprouted out of the ground before her, smashing through planks and rending aside the floor of the hall, spiralling up and twisting about Glormane. The axe was wrenched from his hands and flung aside, thudding into the panelled walls where it stuck fast, vibrating.

'She must be defied!' Tarithel's voice was a sudden roar. 'She must be stopped!'

A pulse of green light flickered out from her, dancing around her. The Dwarves were cast upon the ground, stunned.

The trek through the Hills of Glorthay and towards the Plains of Thigrim was a weary undertaking for the disheartened giants. The weather turned foul, wind wiping through the hills, with a cold icy drizzle that soaked through clothing and leeched the heat out of flesh. The giants trudged onwards, heading west.

Varangrim had hopes of reaching the city of Imgenarg within two days, but the road grew poorer. Wagons and carts were overturned. Mud splattered everything and the progress of the armies that had survived the attack was slow.

'Even the weather seems set against us,' Thorarg said, squinting through the gloom.

Varangrim grunted in response. 'I wouldn't put it beyond the powers of the Heartstealer.'

A squall buffeted them, whistling through the hills and cutting off their conversation.

The camp that night was a miserable affair, it seemed no one could persuade a fire to stay lit, and everything was soaked through. The temperature stayed just above freezing and the wind blustered to and fro all throughout the night.

Dawn broke, and with it somewhat better weather. The drizzle was replaced with high grey clouds but no sight of the sun. The giants struggled onwards.

Passage across the plains was a little easier once they had left the hills. The ground underfoot was firmer, dusted with snow. Their pace quickened.

Imgenarg's banners were still flying over his city and they could see others besides. Varangrim recognised those of Torelak and Ganigrorn.

'Ganigrorn has been swift indeed,' Thorarg said. 'To have reached the city ahead of us.'

Varangrim nodded. 'Let us hope they have better tidings than we do.'

With the city in sight the pace of the giants increased further. Imgenarg's city was built into the steep sides of the mountains of Anvormane, a natural and intimidating defence against any attack, unlike the more vulnerable fortresses that dotted the plains. Varangrim gave a signal and the banners of his own army were unfurled and hoisted, alongside those of Thorarg.

Deep trumpets sounded from the city.

Another hour saw them reach the ramparts. From there they ascended the stone pathway upwards to the gates which were swung back to welcome them.

Imgenarg was waiting.

'Varangrim!' he called. 'It is good to see you. The runners; the news. Tell me it is not so.'

Varangrim looked wearily at him.

'Carangrane slaughtered by the treachery of the Heartstealer?' Varangrim replied. 'Alas, I saw it with my very eyes. He is gone. Anvildrak and Fenorn with him.'

Imgenarg sighed. 'This is evil news. I had hoped it might be a fanciful story. But tidings are foul, in more ways than one.'

'There is other news?' Varangrim said. 'You must tell me.'

'You're exhausted. Food, wine and talk,' Imgenarg said. 'In that order.'

Varangrim nodded.

Rorthron had ridden hard from the City of Imgorad. His path tracked ever northwards, crossing hills and plains in a rush, his flight assisted by his knowledge of the Wise, his passing unseen to any that might be watching.

Before the day was out he was already far to the north of the Barbarian city. Mountains had appeared before him, rising up from low foothills as the sun began to set in the west. Rorthron knew them to be the southern tip of the Mountains of Anvormane, a range of sharp peaks that extended northwards across the Icemark for many leagues. If he followed them on his journey, he would be led into the realm of the Giants.

There to seek news of Carangrane … and the Talismans!

He was nigh on to their territories now, the realms of the Barbarians falling behind him. From what little his previous Barbarian escort had been able to tell him, it seemed these lands were often in dispute between the Giants and the Barbarians, even the Dwarves to the east laid claim here. Many battles had been fought, all inconclusive. The graves of many a warrior were buried in the lands before him.

The Hills of Carangruk were falling away by the close of

day as he rode onwards into the Pass of Carormarg. His destination was not far ahead and before the twilight had faded he reached it, yet another Tower of the Wise. Like all the others it was closed, locked and forlorn. He rested his horse and stood in the darkness, meditating on his next move. The stars wheeled in the heavens above as he stood motionless. Another day would see him enter the realm of the Giants.

Perhaps we will have some news then. It is to be hoped!

Glormane fell to his knees.

'Who are you?' he gasped.

The green light faded. Tarithel staggered to one side.

'No … I am Tarithel, daughter of the Lord of Dreams,' she whispered, confused and bewildered. 'What was … I don't know …'

'You are a mighty sorceress,' Glormane said, still prostrate upon the ground. 'What do you ask of us?'

Tarithel's thoughts were awhirl. The power had left her now, leaving her feeling exhausted, dizzy and unsure.

'I'm sorry!' she cried. 'I didn't mean …'

Glormane scrambled away, terror etched on his features.

Tarithel sank to her knees, gasping for breath, tears coming to her eyes. Then a wave of despair crept over her.

Morkin lost! Here I am far from home, lost amidst a land of strangers, coerced by strange powers, facing certain death or worse … what am I doing? I'm just a girl, a fool … they will set upon me and kill me …

'Who are you?'

Tarithel looked up to see Carorthay standing over her.

Tarithel had no words for him.

'I have seen such powers only once before,' he whispered.

'And they were used by she who casts her evil sorcery across this land.'

'I am not she,' Tarithel replied, shaking her head.

'Then who are you?' Carorthay whispered. 'The truth now … all of it.'

'I am just Tarithel,' Tarithel replied, her voice hollow. 'Truly I am. This power I do not fully understand. It comes from the forests of this realm. I don't know why I have it! Only that I must use it to save my beloved … and defeat the Heartstealer.'

'Do you believe you can?' Glormane asked.

'I can. I must!'

Carorthay nodded and then held out his hand, helping her to her feet.

'Then what would you have us do?' Glormane asked, stepping up behind Carorthay.

'Do not give up on your kingdom,' she said, the words coming to her mind. 'We must all do our part to resist the Heartstealer. This is how she destroys everything; stealing away our will, our hopes, our friends. She means to take away everything good from all of us. She can only do so if we let her.'

Carorthay and Glormane exchanged a glance. Glormane looked her in the eyes, Tarithel saw the hope kindle there.

'Defy her? Defy Imgorarg?' Glormane asked. 'It will mean certain death. We're outnumbered, we cannot win …'

Tarithel took his hand in both of hers. 'No. Do not believe that. I have prevailed against this evil before, despite insurmountable odds. My liege and my beloved defeated the Witchking himself, father of this awful Heartstealer. My own home Citadel was sorely oppressed in the struggle against the Witchking, but we prevailed. We will prevail again!'

She smiled.

Around them, the other Dwarves were getting to their feet, keeping a respectful distance.

'I do not see how,' Glormane said. 'But you have a power that cannot be denied. You are right. I have cowered in my defeat and given up without a fight. I will return to the fray. Will you stand with us, Lady Tarithel, sorceress of Fangrim?'

Tarithel grinned at him.

'It is your city, Glormane. Defend it and I will help you in any way I can!'

Chapter Twelve

Varangrim the Giant stands in the City of Imgenarg looking north-east to the Plains of Thigrium.

Imgenarg sat at a table within his hall. Many other giants were assembled alongside. Varangrim, Thorarg, Torelak and Ganigrorn sat with him. Meat was piled high on huge metal platters and the giants ate vigorously. Wine accompanied the meal.

'Your hospitality is welcome,' Varangrim said. 'But tell me, what news from afar?'

Imgenarg wiped his lips with the back of his hand.

'The news is grim, my friend.'

Varangrim set down the tankard from which he had been drinking.

'Go on.'

'News of your battle reached us three days ago,' Imgenarg said. 'But since then runners from further afield have reached us. The Heartstealer has not been idle. She has moved against us across our entire eastern border.'

Varangrim's jaw tightened.

'I feared it was so.'

'Armies have swept westward, striking from concealment within the Forest of Farorn,' Imgenarg said. 'Sweeping all before them. Thormuk, Imatrorn, Glortheon …' he sighed, looking at Varangrim. 'And the City of Varangrim itself. All fallen to the foe.'

Varangrim flung his tankard away. It clattered to the floor. He got to his feet and paced around.

'How can we have been so blind to her stratagems?' he yelled. 'Carangrane … I trusted his wisdom, but it has gone awry. The Heartstealer has led us astray for years, posturing and posing before us like some common whore, yet … she has the greater strategy … and now she has struck what may be a mortal blow!'

'Her reach grows long,' Imgenarg continued. 'Imgormad and Glormeon I have not heard from, thus I fear the worst. We cannot reach them, nor do we now have the strength to go to their aid. Runners from Oborthar and Obigrorn report armies of the Heartstealer camped in the Plains of Thirim, ready to attack.'

'Gateway to the Vale of Thudrane,' Torelak gasped. 'Our heartlands.'

'Carangrane counselled to leave her be,' Varangrim said, his voice heavy. 'All through my days I have respected his choices and thought he spoke wisdom. We lost too many of our folk to foolish border fights. Yet now … she lulled us … lulled him into inaction. All this time she has been planning our demise, waiting until her army of foul Icelords were strong enough. Now, she has struck a decisive blow against us.'

'On receipt of this news I have sent runners through the mountains with instructions to prepare for siege,' Imgenarg said. 'To Carangrane, to Finorn and Thangrorn.'

Ganigrorn leant forward.

'There is news from the south too,' he said, his voice deep. 'I have left a watch on my own fortress and brought only those warriors I could spare. The Barbarians have been disturbed by news from afar so it seems.'

'What news?' Varangrim demanded.

'Some mighty warrior joins their ranks,' Ganigrorn said.

'I've heard only rumours, but they speak of magic, mighty deeds and power.'

'A newly invigorated foe to the south is further news we do not need,' Varangrim replied. 'Can these days grow darker yet?'

'We must be mindful of it,' Imgenarg countered. 'If the Barbarians sense our weakness, they will likely move against us too.'

Varangrim nodded.

'It may already be too late for that,' he said. 'The Heartstealer is cunning. She will find ways to let them know.'

'Then we have enemies upon all sides,' Imgenarg said. 'We must defend what we have or all is lost. What must we do? What is our strategy? What is our plan?'

The giants all looked at Varangrim.

He swallowed.

'I have no answer for you,' he said at last. 'All is ruin.'

Lorelorn the Icelord had ridden back to his city. Everything was as he expected, as he had commanded and as it should have been.

Yet he remained unsettled by what he had witnessed deep in the forest.

He shrugged off his riding gear and handed it to his servants, striding through into the inner rooms of his halls within the city.

'Is Talorthane here yet?' he demanded.

'Arrived just an hour ago, my Lord,' the nearest servant replied, bowing low.

'Send him to me immediately,' Lorelorn snapped.

Lorelorn did not have to wait for long. Talorthane, a worried look upon his face, marched into the room within minutes.

'My Lord,' Talorthane said. 'Had I known you …'

'Never mind that,' Lorelorn said. 'Close and lock the door … then join me.'

Talorthane frowned, but did as he was bid. Lorelorn pulled up two chairs, close by a roaring fire. He sat in one, and gestured for Talorthane to sit in the other.

'News?' Lorelorn demanded.

'The attack on the Giants has begun,' Talorthane said. 'And it has gone as Shareth planned it, too. The giants fell for her subterfuge. We were cunning, if dishonest. The City of Ulformane has fallen and our forces have struck west across as vast swath of their territory. It seems she picked the moment well.'

'Shareth always had a sound head for strategy,' Lorelorn acknowledged. 'What of our borders?'

'Guarded and patrolled as directed,' Talorthane answered. 'Weapons were made ready and provisions stockpiled as instructed … is there … something amiss, my Lord?'

Lorelorn sighed.

'I recall,' he said, his voice hushed. 'You voiced some misgivings over our rush to war when last we spoke.'

Talorthane looked pale. 'The misgivings of foolishness I assure you, idle musing, nothing more …'

Lorelorn held up a hand and looked Talorthane in the eye.

'I share your concerns,' he said.

'My Lord?'

'I have ridden into battle many times against Giant and Barbarian, Fey and Dwarf,' Lorelorn said. 'Each time I felt there was a valid reason; the fate of a City, a strategic bulwark against invasion, punishment for damage or avenging a loss …'

'And now?'

'You yourself said it,' Lorelorn continued. 'There is more to this than meets the eye.'

'We have struck hard at the Giants,' Talorthane said, his

voice hushed. 'At Shareth's instruction no mercy has been shown; their cities are aflame. She has fomented civil war amongst the Dwarves and curried peace with the Barbarians. Only the Fey are too far away for her to directly engage … for now anyway.'

'The death of her father has spurred her to this,' Lorelorn said. 'We know she has abducted the son of this Moonprince and thus forced him to march upon the Icemark, with this Fey-girl spy sent in an attempt to retrieve him presumably …'

'Shareth risks much.'

'Too much,' Lorelorn replied. 'She risks over extending our forces, fighting a war on many fronts … something we have avoided, rightly, for many long moons. The question is … why now?'

'Revenge for the death of her father, surely?'

'That makes no sense,' Lorelorn replied. 'Her fury is with the Moonprince alone. She has him here in the Icemark. Send a small group to abduct him or murder him; that is the sensible thing to do. She spirited away his son, why can she not do the same to him? Then she can torture him to her heart's content as she has done with so many others. Nothing about the dispositions of our armies or borders needed to change. Yet she abducts his very own son, holds him captive, forcing the Moonprince to confront her. Whilst this uncertainty is at play, she decides the time is ripe to sweep all of Icemark before her with military might? No … there is something else going on, some urgent need she has not shared with us …'

Talorthane took a deep breath. 'Then what are we to do? We cannot disobey her … the very thought is …'

'War is an art,' Lorelorn said. 'It seems likely we will soon be called to butchery, the slaying of men, women and children of the other races. Some of our ranks have no qualms about such behaviour, Imgasharg for example … but I am not enthused … and neither, I believe, are you. Is that a fair assumption?'

Talorthane nodded. 'I will gladly fight for sound reasons, but needless slaughter? I find that hard to stomach even if in the defence of our own.'

Lorelorn nodded.

'We need to understand the stakes involved and I have …' Lorelorn paused, remembering the strange vision he'd received in the forest. He sighed.

'My Lord?'

'This Fey-girl we were asked to seek,' Lorelorn asked. 'She was red-haired, was she not?'

'So you described her to me, my Lord.'

'And she has not yet been found?'

'Not that I've heard.'

Lorelorn pursed his lips and thought for a moment. 'Then I wish for her to fall into my jurisdiction,' he said. 'I will still honour Shareth's wish to execute her, trespass alone is a crime worth such punishment, but … from her we might extract some answers first. Doubtless she knows something that we do not and Shareth's unique interest in this girl means it is something profound. Time is short. Shareth is bound to order us all to outright war before long.'

'Then what would you have me do?'

'Ride south to the borders of my lands and that of the Dwarves,' Lorelorn said. 'Search for her. If you can, find this Fey-girl and bring her to me discretely – take only those men you utterly trust. We will have little time before we will have to take her carcass to Shareth. Then at least, we can decide what to do based on what she might reveal.'

Within the hall of the Barbarian city of Imgorad, there was a commotion from the doors. Two Barbarians pushed through, striding forwards and then lowering themselves before Imgorad on bended knee. Luxor saw that the first wore an ornate golden necklace from which dangled a large, dark gem.

'Noble Imgorad,' the first said, looking up. 'We come bearing urgent tidings.'

Imgorad got to his feet, signalling for the two newcomers to do the same. It was clear they were brothers, so alike were their features.

'Kahudrarg, Kahudrak?' Imgorad asked. 'You are tasked with the patrol of our borders with the Fey to the east. What brings you here?'

'Not the Fey my Lord,' Kahudrak replied. 'Not this time. We come to report perfidy closer to home. We have news of great import … missives of treachery no less!'

'Treachery?' Imgorad demanded. 'Speak, man, speak!'

Kahudrak exchanged a glance with his brother, who nodded encouragement.

'We intercepted an Iceguard patrol in the near the Mountains of Imorthay, nigh on the edges of the territory of the Dwarves,' Kahudrak said. 'They were searching for this Moonprince we have heard so much about. We interrogated them as well we might, since they trespassed into our realm. They claimed he sought war against the Heartstealer and was rousing the Fey against her.'

'I have seen the Fey making ready at the Fortress of Berormane,' Kahudrarg added, stepping up alongside. 'They make preparations for war.'

Imgorad looked at Luxor.

'As well they might,' Luxor replied. 'My emissary has warned them of Shareth's increasing wrath.'

'They make not ready for war on the Heartstealer, my Lord,' Kahudrak said. 'But on us!'

Shouts erupted all around the hall. Imgorad thumped a fist on his table and the noise subsided.

'Know you of this?' Imgorad asked, glaring at Luxor. 'Have you gone to the Fey and instructed them to rally for war against we Barbarians?'

'For myself no,' Luxor retorted. 'Though as Careneon will tell you, it was my intention to visit them. That is no secret. I have sent an emissary to them and the Fey have pledged allegiance to my cause. But that cause is against the Heartstealer, not against the Barbarians. I tell you truly, I am here to seek your friendship.'

'He lies!' Kahudrak cried.

'You have more?' Imgorad asked, looking around at Kahudrak.

'There is traffic between the Fortress of Berormorn and the City of Carorthane,' Kahudrak said. 'Something has roused them along our borders …'

'And it is your duty to guard those borders,' Imgorad said. 'Have they crossed our lands? Laid siege to our own dwellings?'

'No, my Lord …'

'Then there is no war with the Fey …' Imgorad rumbled.

'Noble leader,' Kahudrak said. 'These Iceguard in our custody … they told us something of the wars in the south. A mighty host of Men and Fey that swept all before them, conquering Midnight and subduing it. No mercy was shown to the enemy, they were all slaughtered mercilessly.'

'Such is the nature of battle,' Imgorad said, with a shrug. 'Your point?'

Kahudrak straightened.

'They also told of the Barbarians of that realm,' he continued. 'How they were killed at the hands of those loyal to the Moonprince …'

A rumble of discontent erupted in the hall, growing in intensity.

'Silence!' Imgorad called. 'Speak plainly.'

'The Iceguard told us that Shareth's father, the Witchking sued for peace and the Barbarians of Midnight tried to broker that peace, but their leader was cut down by those loyal to … him!' Kahudrak pointed at Luxor. 'This Luxor, Moonprince of Midnight, is an ally of the Fey alone … and no friend to the Barbarians!'

Again the hall erupted in shouting.

Imgorad banged a fist on his table once more and the clamour subsided.

'You make a serious accusation against our guest,' Imgorad said. 'Do you understand the import of what you have claimed?'

'I do, noble leader.'

Imgorad turned to Luxor.

'Is there truth in what he claims?'

Luxor took a deep breath.

'There is some truth,' he said.

Mutterings flickered around the hall.

'But only part of it,' Luxor said, raising his voice. 'The Witchking never parleyed with us, Fey or Free. He sought only our destruction, as the Heartstealer does here in the Icemark. As for the Barbarians of my realm, we do not call them that. The Targ, they call themselves. They are few, and live in desolate lands to the east of Midnight. Their leader was a mighty warrior who called himself Utarg of Utarg. I sent an emissary to him as did the Witchking, requesting his aid in battle.'

'And …?' Imgorad prompted.

'He came to the Citadel of Dawn,' Luxor said, 'where we made our second failed attempt to defy the progress of the Witchking. There he declared for the Witchking, slaying the Lord of Dawn before our eyes. We lost that Citadel, it was razed. Those Barbarians fought for the Witchking despite our entreaties. We were beaten back to our last stronghold, that of Xajorkith on the southern borders of Midnight. There a mighty host of Doomguard assembled, the Barbarians of the Targ amongst their numbers. We prevailed and they did not. Utarg was slain by a valiant warrior of the Free, the Lady of Silence.'

'A woman?' Imgorad asked.

'Aye,' Luxor said. 'But she lives no more, she gave her life in the last battle against the Witchking.'

Imgorad nodded and then turned to Kahudrak and Kahudrarg.

'Your message is timely,' he said. Both Barbarians bowed low once more.

He looked at Luxor.

'It seems the Barbarians stood against you in the past,' he said. 'And what happened to them after the Witchking's defeat? Did you slay them in vengeance for their choice?'

'No. They retain their lands,' Luxor said. 'The realm of the Targ is not large, but it is theirs. I did not hold their leader's stance against the lives of his people.'

'And yet your vassal, this women, this Lady of Silence,' Imgorad rumbled. 'Slew one of my kinsmen?'

Luxor tilted his head back, but looked Imgorad in the eye.

'It is as you say.'

Imgorad's eyes narrowed and he stared at Luxor for long moment. Neither moved. Silence fell in the hall as all regarded them.

'So I have a choice it seems, just like this distant cousin of mine,' Imgorad said. 'To pledge myself to you Moonprince and go to war with the Heartstealer … or not.'

'The Witchking broke all promises he made,' Luxor replied. 'Shareth will too. I stand before you now and swear I will not.'

'So you say,' Imgorad said. 'I will consider carefully what

has been said. I know the Heartstealer well, Moonprince. You, I have met just this day. Trust and experience will guide me. My answer will not be long delayed.'

Dawn broke across the realm of the Dwarves. Light blazed across the City of Glormane, blood red in the first rays of sunlight.

'I'm not sure Thigrak foresaw all this,' Imulorn said.

The two dwarven brothers were standing on the walls of the City of Glormane, looking eastwards across the plains towards the Hills of Haginorn, squinting into the sun. Below, perhaps a league or so away, banners could be seen being hoisted aloft.

'As far as I can see it was inevitable,' Imelorn replied. 'Imgorarg wants us to ally with the Heartstealer and Glormane and Carorthay want to preserve things in the manner our fathers managed the affairs of the realm.'

Imulorn looked at him in surprise.

'Either way,' Imelorn added. 'It always comes down to who can swing their axe better. Look out there, all the usual suspects from the north, spoiling for a fight. I see the banners of Imgorarg, Torormarg, Berangrorn and Anvarorn. More than enough strength to overcome us.'

Not far away, Carorthay and Glormane stood, deep in conversation. Alongside them was the willowy Fey-girl, her red hair glowing bright in the sun's rays, streaming away from her face.

'And we ally ourselves with a sorceress regardless of the outcome,' Imulorn mused. 'Strange times. Yet, given a choice between the Fey and the Icelords …'

'The old wisdom holds true?' Imelorn chuckled. 'Never trust an Icelord?'

'Fey magic holds little appeal for me either.' Imulorn said. 'But it seems of a more wholesome type than that of the Heartstealer. I deem this Fey-girl means us no harm.'

'Never trust a pretty girl either,' Imelorn said, with a grin.

'There is some wisdom there too,' Imulorn chuckled. 'Come, let's see what our strategy is.'

The pair walked across to the dwarven leaders. Glormane acknowledged them as they approached.

'You've seen the banners?' he asked.

'We have,' Imulorn replied. 'A sizeable force.'

'More than enough to overwhelm the city,' Glormane replied. 'Imgorarg has not been idle overnight.'

'And of the others?' Imulorn asked.

'Torelorn and Thatruk have declared themselves neutral in this contest,' Carorthay said. 'And will support the victor. Thudrun likewise. We have not heard from Lorangrarg or any others, but history tells me their attitude will be similar.'

'Then what strength we have is already here,' Imulorn said.

Glormane regarded him.

'I do not demand you fight at my side,' he said. 'With the precarious position of the leadership, I do not have the right. I can only ask it of you … and your brother.' He looked across at Imelorn. 'For the sake of the strong friendship that existed between my father and your liege, Thigrak.'

Imulorn nodded. 'Thigrak instructed us to support you. I have no intention of disobeying his wishes.'

'Just tell me which neck to hew,' Imelorn said. 'I'll see it done. But we cannot summon our own armies from the far south in time to help.'

'Aye,' Carorthay said. 'This will be decided today, one way or another.'

'What strength do we have?' Imulorn asked.

'Carorthay and I have near a thousand warriors apiece,' Glormane replied. 'Thelak is here too, and supports us with his men. With the other loyal entourages we have just over three thousand all counted.'

'Set against more than five for Imgorarg, I'd wager,' Imelorn said.

Glormane nodded. 'We have the city and we have our own sorceress …'

The Dwarfs turned to look at the Fey-girl. Her expression was pensive and they saw her wince at their description.

'On the testimony of Imorthorn and Thormand,' she said. 'I will fight alongside you, Glormane of the Dwarves. Should we be victorious, I require something of you in return.'

Glormane raised an eyebrow.

'And what would you ask of me?'

'Two things,' she replied. 'First, that you will pledge your loyalty to Luxor, Moonprince of Midnight and help him in his fight against the Heartstealer.'

'And second?' Glormane asked.

Tarithel swallowed.

'Safe passage for me northwards and a guide through the Mountains of Anvulane nigh to the edge of the Heartstealer's realm. Will you agree?'

Glormane regarded her for a long moment.

'No,' he said.

Tarithel frowned.

'We Dwarves will settle our affairs without recourse to pledging fealty to whatever new power deems itself fit enough to rule,' he replied. 'We are masters of our own destiny.'

'Luxor does not seek to rule,' Tarithel countered. 'Only to defy the Heartstealer and unite the Icemark against her.'

'I have enough troubles keeping my homeland in one piece without encouraging further battles,' Glormane answered. 'However, your second request I will mostly certainly grant.'

Tarithel pursed her lips, but said no more.

'And … if we all die upon this battlefield like I suspect we will,' he muttered. 'It matters not at all.'

Rorthron had ridden onwards even before the sun had risen, the warm pinks and oranges of dawn had burst upon the plains finding his horse already at full stride, galloping onwards, his route unerringly northwards.

The leagues fell away as the sun rose, both he and his steed invigorated far beyond the endurance of normal flesh and bone. Mountains had now risen up both to the east and the west, the twin ranges of Anvormane and Anvulane, confining his progress to a valley just a few leagues across. Here he knew was one of the great strategic points of the Icemark. To the north, the land of the giants, to the south the Barbarians … and now, to the east, through a narrow gap in the Mountains of Anvulane known as the Pass of Carormarg, lay the lands of the Dwarves.

At this crossroads stood the Fortress of Thortheon, the northernmost outpost of the Barbarians and the end of their influence. Most travellers would have been forced to stop at the fortress, there to be questioned on their routes and affairs, and taxed into the bargain. Thortheon doubtless would make it his business to know everything that transpired hereabouts, well aware that his fortress lay at such a crucial location.

Rorthron, however, had the means to remain hidden when required and passed by without alerting the people of the city. He could see all manner of preparations underway, it seemed the city was being readied for some potential conflict, perhaps with the Fortress of Ganigrorn, mere leagues away to the North, held by the Giants.

Yet Rorthron did not tarry, once again he plunged onwards, riding north through forest, across plain and hills, stopping only to refresh himself at a spring he spied on the edge of a forest. He recognised the power of the Wise in its construction, the waters clean and invigorating, energising the flesh and restoring the soul.

He kept to the forest paths where he could, it was easier to stay concealed here. He lost little speed, well versed in the arts that the Wise had in common with the Fey in such places. As the sun began to fall into the west once more, the forest came to an end and the realm of the Giants was laid open to him. The mountains to the east had fallen away below the horizon, but those to the west seemed stronger and taller than ever. Nestled against their flanks was a vast city.

Even from this vantage point Rorthron could see guards upon the walls, towering into the air, far taller than the men of the south.

Giants indeed!

He spurred his horse onwards once more.

Not far from the route Rorthron had taken, two riders turned their horses at the edge of the Forest of Firun. They were a pair of Barbarians, on a regular patrol in the northernmost part of the realm, keeping an eye on their border with the Giants.

'They are on the move,' the first said.

Both riders squinted into the morning mist across the Plains of Thenorn toward the Fortress of Ganigrorn. As they watched they saw an army leaving the gates, banners raised high, with wagons and other folks besides.

'Not just on the move,' the second replied. 'They are evacuating their fortress. Look, even now they are turning north-west, not towards us. What can be happening? Where are they going?'

'It's an opportunity to be taken,' the first said. 'We must inform Thortheon immediately. Ganigrorn lies open to any who would take it, there cannot be much more than a small garrison left to defend it.

'It could be a trap,' the second said.

'Or the Giants have more serious issues to deal with in the north.'

'Either way, Thortheon must know. Let us ride swiftly back.'

'Agreed.'

The two riders turned and spurred their horses back through the trees.

In the realm of the Dwarves, the armies of Imgorarg, Tarormarg, Berangrorn and Anvarorn were arranged before the City of Glormane. They were prepared for a siege, having worked through the night to arrange their weapons and construct hastily prepared ladders.

Glormane, Carorthay, Imulorn, Imelorn and Tarithel walked out to meet them before the gates of the city, surrounded by their own armed escort of Dwarven warriors. They stopped a hundred yards from the gates and waited as Imgorarg and his entourage closed the distance between them.

'You stand before my gates prepared for war,' Glormane called. 'Swear fealty to me, acknowledge me as leader of the Dwarves, disband this alliance and return to your own lands. I will be merciful.'

Imgorarg laughed.

'You are no leader of the Dwarves,' he mocked. 'And I dispute your right to call yourself such. The people have chosen me, not you. Surrender the title, swear fealty to me and I will let you live.'

'And what of my guest?' Glormane asked. 'Tarithel of the Fey?'

'She is an enemy of the Dwarves,' Imgorarg said. 'She will be executed for being a spy in our realms, and using sorcery against us.'

'And yet you would have us bow the knee to another sorceress,' Glormane observed. 'The dwarven people a lackey of the Heartstealer?'

'The Heartstealer respects our strength and will enhance it,' Imgorarg replied. 'At the expense of these foul Fey.'

'Her lies are enticing,' Glormane replied. 'As all lies are …'

Imgorarg hefted his axe, and all about them did the same.

'Will you surrender the title?' Imgorarg demanded.

Glormane shook his head. 'I will not.'

'Then you will rue the day,' Imgorarg said. 'The will of the dwarven people will be done … and you …' He turned to regard Tarithel. 'You will be cut down, your skin flayed from your body and your carcass sent to Shareth as an offering, Fey-girl.'

He chuckled at the look on her face and spat on the ground before turning away. His men followed him.

'Charming fellow,' Imulorn said, once Imgorarg was out of earshot.

'See to the final preparations in defence of the city,' Glormane said. 'It will not be long now.'

Within the hour, flags were raised by the armies surrounding the City of Glormane, Imgorarg's banners in the fore. Tarithel stood on the battlements looking east, alongside Glormane, Carorthay, Imulorn and Imelorn. Arrayed along the walls were Dwarves loyal to the east and the south of the dwarven realm.

Chants rent the air, coarse cries and yells echoed across the plains before the city.

'They outnumber us nearly two to one,' Carorthay said.

'The walls are strong,' Glormane replied. 'They will hold. This city has not been taken before.'

The chants from the armies below faded away, replaced by a regular thump of axes being beaten against shields. At some command, the northern Dwarves began marching forward.

'We should cut them down with our archers whilst we have a chance,' Carorthay said.

Glormane shook his head. 'I will not cast the first stone, not on my country folk. These are not Giants, or Barbarians or even Fey. They are our kinsmen. They must attack, we must defend.'

Carorthay sighed, but nodded, turning to Tarithel.

'You should seek shelter within,' he said. 'This will be bloody and uncouth. Dwarves do not fight with the swiftness and precision of the Fey. We can better protect you if you stay inside the city.'

Tarithel regarded him.

'I am no stranger to warfare,' she answered. 'I stood on the parapets of my home citadel as the Doomguard of the Witchking tried to raze it. They could teach the Dwarves brutality, I am sure.'

Tarithel unslung her bow, strung it expertly and notched an arrow.

'And I might surprise you with my own expertise.'

Carorthay noted the knives tucked into the belt at her waist. He smiled and bowed.

'Here they come!' Imulorn called.

A mass of arrows rose from the ranks of the armies below, scattering off the stone of the City defences, but cutting down several of the Dwarves along the walls.

Glormane raised his arm and then, with a heavy sigh, snapped it down.

'Loose! Away!'

Archers behind the walls shot their own arrows, returning

the attack. Catapults on the walls launched stones into the air, which then cascaded down, striking dozens of Dwarves on the fields below.

Already the attacking armies had reached the foot of the walls. Roughly hewn ladders were crunched into the foundations, ropes with grappling hooks were launched through the air, too many to count, securing themselves to the crenellations of the city whilst the Dwarves on the walls tried to hack them loose. Many were cut, but many more remained secure as the great ladders were hoisted into place, Dwarves clinging to them.

Another volley of arrows was shot through the air. Two ladders were smashed into kindling by volleys of catapult launched rocks, but then the northern Dwarves were falling upon the defenders on the walls, axes swinging.

Blood flew. Dwarves were hewn where they stood, some pushed back and fell to their deaths inside and outside the walls. Yells punctuated the air, often turning to screams that were cut with a ghastly thump as bodies hit the ground.

Tarithel shot two Dwarves who came at her, but then found herself pushed back alongside Imulorn and Imelorn as the press of the attack increased. It was too close for her bow, she pulled the knives out of her belt and avoided being decapitated by the swing of an axe. Her assailant had no time for another blow, he died with a stab to the heart, the Fey blades unfazed by the dwarven armour he wore.

Yet the walls were already lost. Imulorn pulled her back as Imelorn stood guard. There was no sign of Carorthay or Glormane, the battle was everywhere.

'We must retreat, my lady!'

Tarithel nodded and backed away alongside the two dwarven brothers.

'There she is! Take the Fey-girl!'

Tarithel recognised Imgorarg's voice. The big Dwarf was fighting his way towards her.

'Stay back!' Imelorn growled. 'He's mine!'

Imelorn strode forward, his axe raised. As he did so, Tarithel saw Imgorarg pull something from his tunic. She saw a heavy gold chain about his neck, a gem of obsidian dangling from it. As she watched Imgorarg raised the gem before him, his eyes closed, muttering words under his breath.

Light and movement pinched around the gem. A wave of terror surged outwards, slashing at the minds of the dwarven defenders all about her. Tarithel heard their screams of fear and agony as the enchantment battered their minds.

BOW BEFORE YOUR EMPRESS! I AM SHARETH!

The power was unrelenting. Dwarves fell all about her, clutching at their heads whilst Imgorarg walked forward undeterred. Alongside him, somehow protected from the effects of the spell, his companions hacked and slashed at the helpless all around.

Imulorn and Imelorn were prostrate upon the flagstones of the wall, Imgorarg was walking towards them. None could withstand the fell magic of the Heartstealer. Darkness fell, despite the bright sunlight, mist erupting out of nowhere and smothering everything.

DEFIANCE IS DEATH!

Tarithel had heard those words before.

I have defied you! I will defy you further! I am the Lady of the Forest!

Pain crushed around her as the darkness sought her out. But she was ready for it. Her own pendant was raised before her and bright green light pierced the darkness.

Fear, as awful and terrible as the Ice Fear she remembered afflicting Midnight, battered against her. She drew up the shutters of her mind, concentrating only on halting Imgorarg's approach. He pressed forward, gesturing with the black gem, thrusting it towards her. Its power was magnified as he did so. Tarithel cried out as terror began to overwhelm her.

Despair clutched at her mind. As it did so, an image of a

woman appeared behind Imgorarg, huge and looming over him, writhed in blackness and soot. Her face was sharp and angular, but beautiful, the skin pale and the eyes like sparks of fire in the darkness.

SUBMIT FEY-GIRL!

I will not submit to you, Shareth Heartstealer!

Shareth laughed at her. About Tarithel, the movements of the Dwarves slowed and came to a halt. Tarithel looked around, seeing some frozen as they fell from the walls, others held fast even as they were hewn by the axes of their enemies, splashes of blood motionless in the air.

Shareth stepped forward. She was taller than Tarithel by perhaps half a foot, dressed in a black gown with silver edging, her cloak billowing out behind her in a non-existent wind. Her skin was so pale as to be almost white, Tarithel could see her fingernails were painted black to match her attire, her lips a dark, malevolent red.

Shareth didn't speak, but her voice reverberated inside Tarithel's head.

YOU DARE TO STAND BEFORE ME?

I do!

LACKEY OF THE HAPLESS MOONPRINCE!

Tarithel summoned her thoughts, concentrating as hard as she could, trying to free her mind from Shareth's baleful influence. For a moment she succeeded, but then the cold and fear rushed back, forcing her stagger back.

YOU CANNOT HOPE TO MATCH ME, FEY-GIRL.

Laughter accompanied the words. Tarithel found herself on her knees, looking up at Shareth.

I am not scared of you!

More laughter.

I DO NOT NEED YOU TO BE SCARED … DESPAIR WILL WORK WELL ENOUGH FOR ME … BEHOLD!

Before Tarithel an image of Morkin appeared alongside

Shareth. Tarithel gasped out loud, his fair face at once so familiar to her and so long missed. He was dressed as she had last seen him, standing on the parapets of the Citadel of Dreams, before he had been spirited away.

Morkin!

As she watched he regarded her, looking her up and down as if appraising her, but with no recognition, no care or concern on his features. He moved forward, looking down on Tarithel, stepping alongside Shareth.

'This is the girl you spoke of?'

Tarithel gasped at the cruelty and indifference in his voice.

Morkin?

THE SAME. THE TAWDRY FEY MAIDEN WHO FAWNED OVER YOU.

Morkin's lip curled in a sneer, looking straight at Tarithel.

'I care not for you,' he said. 'Girl child, fickle Fey that you are. I have found a real woman, experienced in ways you will never know. She is my desire …'

Morkin, no! I love you!

Tarithel cried out, her heart clenching in her chest, her breathing coming in short, sharp gasps, an agonising pain spearing through her midriff.

Morkin moved closer to Shareth, taking her in his arms and pulling her into a languid sensuous kiss, his hands roving over her voluptuous body, revealed as the cloak she wore was cast aside. Shareth returned the embrace and then grasped Morkin tighter still, pushing him down and clasping his head tight to her bosom before looking back at Tarithel.

HE HAS GIVEN HIMSELF TO ME DESPITE YOU, WILLINGLY! YOU HAVE SEEN IT …

Whether it was grief or heartbreak, anger, passion or fury, something snapped in Tarithel's mind. She found herself on her feet, arms outstretched, a wrath burning through her brain and outwards through her arms and hands. Green light crashed and flickered around her, her features and outline crackling with energy.

Seen it?

The green light burst forth. Tarithel, in her rage, ran at the static figure of Imgorarg. Grabbing an axe from an immobilised Dwarf beside her she ran at him, swing the heavy axe around. It was as much as she could do to wield it, but she managed to wrestle it above her head.

NO!

She brought the axe down.

The blade crashed into the obsidian gem, which flew asunder with the blow, fragments crackling and spinning away as she watched. About her the images of Shareth and Morkin flickered and faded away, the darkness dispelled, the light returning about her. The screams of the injured and dying reached her ears and the battle raged once more.

But for only a few moments.

Gasps of surprise, delight and dismay sounded about her, for long moments she could not understand what was happening, her own vision swamped by flashes of green light and black shadows.

Then her vision cleared. She was still holding the axe. Before her Imgorarg was on his knees, staring at her in shock and bewilderment. Her eyes travelled down to his chest, the axe blade was embedded in it up to the haft. Blood spurted across her, covering her face, arm and hands with lurid red.

Imgorarg tried to say something, but it was lost as blood pooled in his mouth and he slipped sideways to lie motionless on the blood-stained paving of the wall. The axe was wrenched from Tarithel's hands.

She stumbled back, only just aware that someone was pulling her back away from the edge of the wall. She was shaking, gasping for breath.

Darkness closed about her once more.

Far to the north in the mighty Fortress of Kahangrorn, a shrill scream split the air. Crystals of ice froze in the air, spiralling down to smash upon the iron hard ground. The very foundations of the fortress trembled at the onslaught.

HOW DARE SHE!

The blast of hatred and anger washed out across the plains in an ever-widening circle. Within the dark, ill-lit halls of the fortress she brooded, plans forming in her mind, each one more unpleasant than the last.

SHE DEFIES ME!

Shareth's rage grew once more, the doorways flew open at the slightest of her gestures, slamming back against their stops with an echoing clang.

WHO IS SHE TO DO SUCH A THING?

She moved down the shadowy corridors, wraith-like, making no sound nor leaving any trace of her passing. She reached the carved balustrade at the end and looked out over it, south across the plains to where she knew the wretched Fey-girl must have been, far beyond the mountains to the south. Still raging she thrust her arm up, clenching a fist.

Lightning crackled and flashed, followed by an echoing roll of thunder. Rain cascaded down in thick sheets.

Shareth stood there for long moments as the rain fell about her. It did not have the temerity to touch her, merely splashing at her feet. The air cooled her ire and she took a deep breath, her anger subsiding.

SOME POWER SUPPORTS HER, SUCH STRENGTH! WHAT CAN IT BE?

Shareth replayed the confrontation in her mind. The Fey-girl had not succumbed to the power Shareth had imbued within the gem she had given to Imgorarg. It had the desired effect on the pitiful Dwarves, either blinding them to their own consciences or rendering them impotent before its power.

BUT HER …

The girl had been able to resist. Moreover she had been able to counter the spell, turn aside its potency and strike back with devastating effect. Shareth flinched at the memory of the strange green light that had surged around the girl, empowering and protecting her. She was no mere Fey, she was a sorceress herself.

HER POWER, I MUST DESTROY OR POSSESS IT!

The Dwarves should have fallen upon each other in civil war by now … the girl had thwarted her plans.

Rage grew in her again. Vengeance flickered in her mind and a new plan formed.

IF THEY WILL NOT FIGHT EACH OTHER, THEY WILL SUFFER IN OTHER WAYS!

She issued orders and her minions and slaves scurried to enact them. Soon her will would be forced upon all the Icemark. The Dwarves were a setback, but the intervention of the Fey-girl would change nothing.

Chapter Thirteen

Morildrane the Fey stands at the Fortress of Morildrane looking north-west into the mist.

The forces of Torormarg, Berangrorn and Anvarorn had surrendered on news of Imgorarg's death. Glormane and Carorthay put a stop to the fighting and ensured that both sides saw to the needs of the injured, regardless of where they had fought. Vows of loyalty were demanded and sworn before Glormane. The civil war was over almost as quickly as it had begun.

'Well,' Imulorn said, looking at his brother. 'If we had any doubt upon whether we should side with the Heartstealer, I think such doubts are now dispelled.'

Imelorn staggered up to him with a groan. His face was smeared with blood, one eye was swollen and his armour was rent in many places.

'We've sent a message, for sure,' he muttered. 'We hold our independence in high esteem I would say.'

'Yet we are in the debt of a Fey sorceress,' Imulorn said. 'We would not have won without her magic.'

'No indeed,' Imelorn replied. 'And what will that debt cost us I wonder?'

'It will cost you nothing other than what I already agreed with Glormane.'

Both Dwarves turned to see Tarithel regarding them. She looked haggard and drawn, as if something had sucked the very life out of her. Imelorn regarded her.

Imgorarg had some magic crystal with him. There was a scream of noise, a howl of fear. I remember clutching my head as pain smote me, but then it was gone and I looked up to see her holding an axe embedded in Imgorarg's chest! A killing blow any one of us would have been proud to have dealt! I would not have thought such as she could wield an axe in such a way!

'I am no envoy of the Fey of Icemark,' she said. 'I do not speak for them. I seek the downfall of the Heartstealer and the return of my betrothed from her clutches. All I ask of the Dwarves is what we agreed. Safe passage north, into her realm.'

Tarithel's voice was uncertain and toneless.

What happened to her? There is more to this than meets the eye.

'You really mean to carry on?' Imulorn said, looking at her in surprise. 'She doubtless knows of you now. Imgorarg had some magic given by her, doubtless she will know of what you've done here. She will seek you out. You are in great peril!'

'I have been in great peril from the outset,' Tarithel replied, her voice hollow. 'Nothing has changed in that regard, I am merely closer to my fate. I must go on. Haste will serve me now.'

Glormane strode over to them followed by Carorthay.

'We have won the day,' he said. 'I am duty bound to honour my word. I would have it no other way. We will see you to the Heartstealer's domain, if that still be your wish?'

'It is,' Tarithel said, 'But will you not reconsider a pledge to my liege, Luxor?' Tarithel asked. 'Shareth will attack you all, together you will be stronger. Already the Fey have sworn their allegiance ...'

'I have already spoken on this,' Glormane said. 'By your power you have delivered my people from a great calamity and I am grateful. But Dwarves decide their own paths.'

Tarithel saw the looks exchanged between Imulorn and Carorthay, but neither spoke.

'Then I must carry on,' Tarithel said.

'I would not see you perish,' Glormane said. 'Will you not reconsider this flight northwards?'

Tarithel regarded him. A faint smile touched her features for a moment.

'This Lady must also decide her own path,' she said, before her features faded into melancholy once more.

Glormane sighed and then nodded.

'I have friends here,' she said, looking at each one in turn. 'Friends unlooked for, amongst a people I did not know. Your words would seem like wisdom, but my heart tells me it cannot be so. I understand my choices better now; these powers I have been gifted … they can only be used to further my quest to defy Shareth. If I shrink from that duty, they will desert me. I must press on.'

The Dwarves looked downcast. None spoke.

'Then,' Carorthay said, after a long moment. 'If you are to continue, we must do our best to ensure you remain hidden for as long as can be. I hold the lands to the east, it is the obvious way to travel, therefore you cannot go that way.'

'Imorthorn advised me to cross the mountains of Anvulane …' Tarithel began.

All four Dwarves snorted in unison.

Glormane took pity on her. 'You don't cross the mountains of Anvulane,' he said. 'They host a cold that matches that of the Frozen Wastes, treacherous paths and wild wolves infest their reaches. We do not venture there, not even the Icelords would dare cross those mountains. They are a formidable barrier … something that has served as well as a backstop against the Heartstealer's whims.'

'Then west?' Imulorn asked. 'Through the Pass of Carormarg. Gloruk will receive us at his Fortress, she can venture northwards from there.'

'A long route in the wrong direction,' Glormane countered.

'And into the realm of the Giants. Our scouts report the Heartstealer holds much of those lands already. War is kindled there. That route would be fraught with danger.'

'Then, not north, east or west,' Tarithel said. 'Then where?'

Glormane, Imulorn and Imelorn muttered amongst themselves, arguing the pros and cons of the routes over and over again.

Carorthay coughed. All of them turned to regard him.

'Down,' he said.

'Down?' Tarithel queried.

Carorthay nodded.

'Those roads are closed to us,' Glormane said, his voice a whisper. 'You know what happens when our folks have ventured beneath the ground ...'

'Closed to us perhaps,' Carorthay said. 'But to a sorceress?'

'What are these roads of which you speak?' Tarithel asked.

Carorthay rubbed his beard.

'Below the Icemark are tunnels,' he said. 'You came through such a passageway yourself when you came from Midnight. For what purpose and by whom they were constructed none now know, but they are there. Beneath the plains, beneath the forests ... and beneath the mountains.'

'There is a pathway ... under the Mountains of Anvulane?' Tarithel asked.

'She cannot take that path,' Imulorn said, shaking his head. 'Those ways are dark and perilous. There are ... creatures ... wraiths ... who knows what evil invests those places! You would be better off facing Imgorarg's armies than following that route.'

'Wraiths ...' Imelorn laughed. None of the other Dwarves shared his mirth.

Glormane was nodding. 'We do not go there, those places are best avoided. Carorthay ... to suggest such desperate choice ...'

'If Tarithel goes east she is caught by Imgorarg's people and handed to Shareth,' Carorthay answered, his voice stern. 'If she goes west she rides into war with the Giants. Anvulane is impassable to the north. I dare say she will not give up and ride south! The passageways can take her to the Frozen Empire unseen and undetected.'

'Do you know the way?' Tarithel asked.

'I know of a passage,' Carorthay said. 'I have not taken it, nor do I know any who have in living memory … but it is there. A passage is said to run from the Temple of Theleon, northwards, under the mountains to the Palace of Lorigriel on the edge of the Frozen Empire.'

'That must be fifteen leagues as the crow flies,' Imulorn said. 'A weary traipse if nothing else.'

'I will take that road,' Tarithel said. 'Will you take me to this Temple? I will find my way from there, I'm sure.'

'I will take you myself,' Glormane said.

Carorthay shook his head. 'Your duty is here, sire. The leadership remains fragile, you must secure it. I would go myself …'

'If I am needed, so are you,' Glormane replied.

There was a pause. Tarithel looked at them all.

'Very well,' Imelorn said. 'Dangerous dark tunnels, evil magic, fearsome denizens of the deep. My axe remains sharp enough, when do we depart?'

Tarithel smiled.

'We'll need some brains in the expedition too,' Imulorn said. 'We will both see this done.'

'I cannot ask this of you,' Tarithel said. 'I will not.'

'My Lady, it will be our honour,' Imulorn said. 'With your leave, sire?'

Glormane nodded.

'Then we will take this dark road and see you to the edge of Shareth's realm,' Imulorn said.

'Or die trying,' Imelorn replied with a laugh.

Tarithel pursed her lips.

The riders of Imgorthand and Morildrane had crossed back into the Forest of Fangrim, arriving at Morildrane's Fortress on the morning of the second day of travelling from Imorthorn. Morildrane had sent riders ahead and the Fortress was ready to welcome them in. Food and drink were arranged and fresh horses prepared.

The two Fey leaders sat across from each other within the halls of the fortress.

'We will ride on after luncheon,' Imgorthand said, helping himself to a plate of meats and vegetables. 'It will not do to keep Imorthorn waiting. If war is being kindled on our borders we will have to ready our warriors as soon as we can.'

Morildrane nodded.

'It will be sad to see our forests and lands put to the torch once more, but if our leader calls for war, who are we to argue with him?'

Imgorthand sighed, his expression grim.

'But let us talk of happier things,' Morildrane said, his voice lighter. 'I have a gift for you.'

'A gift?' Imgorthand said in surprise. 'What have I done to warrant a gift?'

Morildrane smiled. 'It is but a small token of my appreciation. You of all the great Fey lords of this realm have been responsible for the restoration of my house and the honour of my family. You spoke up for me when others would have let my name slide into ignominy. For that, I thank you.'

Morildrane brought a box out from underneath the table. It was wrought in the Fey manner, made of several different types of wood, blended with craftsmanship and skill, edged with silver traceries and set with runes.

'For my part I did what I felt was right and proper,' Imgorthand said. 'Your father's faults are not yours.'

Morildrane nodded and placed the box before Imgorthand.

'Still, you have my thanks and gratitude.'

Imgorthand opened the clasps that held the box closed and then lifted the lid. He gasped in appreciation, lifting out a thick golden necklace with a dark gem dangling from it.

'Such a gift!' Imgorthand said.

Morildrane bowed his head before looking up once more.

'My Liege,' he said. 'A measure of the esteem in which I hold you.'

Imgorthand turned the necklace about before placing it over his head.

'How does it sit?'

'It marks you out for greater things,' Morildrane replied. 'Great amongst the Fey will you be!'

Imgorthand nodded, not noticing the slight flicker of cyan light that emanated from the gem. Morildrane sat back, a satisfied look upon his features.

'But back to business,' Imgorthand said. 'These are disquieting times. And you're right to voice your concerns to me. But I see no way we can refuse Imorthorn's request. He is our leader and he has not led us astray yet.'

'Not yet,' Morildrane replied. 'Let's hope, not ever. But there could be precautions we could take.'

'Precautions?' Imgorthand asked.

Morildrane nodded.

'The southern Lords of the Fey have you to thank for the safety of their lands, your leadership has been exemplary and they will doubtless share your concerns over these orders and the threat of war.'

'What are you saying, Morildrane?'

'Only this,' Morildrane said, rubbing his chin. 'Imorthorn might not listen to a few, but he cannot ignore the voices of many. Let us recruit the leaders of the Fey as Imorthorn desires, but have them swear allegiance direct to you in these matters, gather them under your banner. It will give you leverage with Imorthorn and a chance to sway the outcome if wisdom strays to folly.'

'I cannot and will not defy Imorthorn!'

'Of course not,' Morildrane answered. 'There's no question of anything but our unerring support for his leadership, but if many voices cry out the same concerns, perhaps his outlook could be swayed more toward peace and less towards war.'

Imgorthand thought for a moment.

'As usual, you speak with a wise head, untroubled by past loyalties and traditions,' Imgorthand answered. 'It is too easy to become mired in hidebound thinking. It is good that you speak clearly into these situations, my friend. Yes. We will do as you suggest. Perhaps Imorthorn can be gently persuaded to take another path than one that leads directly to war.'

'Your wisdom exceeds mine,' Morildrane answered. 'But if war is to be averted by your hand, the Fey people will not forget your skill and statesmanship, my Liege.'

Imgorthand smiled. 'I'm sure you're right, Morildrane, yes indeed!'

Luxor strode back and forth within Imgorad the Barbarian's hall, awaiting news. Imgorad had been in counsel with Kahudrak and Kahudrarg for some time behind closed doors. Food and drink were still being consumed by both Imgorad's men and his own Moonguard, but Luxor no longer had an appetite.

The Moon Ring pulsed upon his finger.

Luxor?

'Tarithel!' Luxor recognised the distinctive precise tones of the young Fey woman. 'I have hoped to hear from you for some time ...'

Time is short, and my adventures have been many since we last spoke. I have reached the Dwarves.

'And how have you found them?' Luxor asked. 'Have they received you peaceably?'

In a word, no! There has been much strife and battle here between rival factions. The leadership of the Dwarves rests with Glormane now, though, who is good and true ... yet I was unable to persuade him to pledge his allegiance to our cause ... I'm so sorry!

'You have done enough,' Luxor said. 'You're safe though ... you spoke of battle?'

I am fine ... Luxor, Shareth meant for the Dwarves to fall to fighting amongst themselves. She gave our foe, Imgorarg, some strange Talisman ... a black gem imbued with her fell magics ...

'A black gem ...' Luxor frowned.

But we were victorious. The power of the forest helped us to defeat him. For now the Dwarves have agreed to escort me northwards ... they know a route past the mountains that Shareth cannot spy. I hope to enter her realm in secret. How are you and Rorthron?

'Rorthron rides north to seek answers and take my missives to the Giants,' Luxor replied. 'I await the decision of the Barbarians even as we speak.'

That is good ... I ...

Luxor frowned, sensing a tremble of strong emotion through the Moon Ring.

'Tarithel? What is it?'

For a long moment no words came back to him. Luxor realised Tarithel had dissolved into tears. A sense of heartbroken grief came across the link between them, mixed with despair and anguish …

Oh my Lord Luxor … forgive me … I mean not to add to your burdens …

'Tell me,' Luxor coaxed.

In the battle … I saw her … saw Shareth! The foe against which we fight. She spoke to me, taunted me. She has Morkin in her grasp and … I saw him turn to her. She has stolen his heart away from me …

'Listen to me,' Luxor said, a sterner note in his voice. 'This sorceress will twist anything to her advantage. She can doubtless conjure an image to create any vision she wishes to portray. Trust not in what she shows you. She is a liar through and through …'

What you say is true, but if she has seduced him, poisoned his mind against me as she says, can I ever win him back?

'Morkin loves you, Tarithel,' Luxor said. 'Such love as I saw between you is not subject to magic and spells. You will find him, you will undo the webs and deceits she has spun about him and you will be together.'

As he said the words, a great door at the end of the hall opened and Imgorad emerged.

'The decision of the Barbarians comes now … farewell Tarithel and take great care!'

I will dear Moonprince! And thank you!

Thorarg looked across at where Varangrim stood, arms crossed behind his back, staring into the fire. Varangrim had not moved for an hour or more.

'I've seen this look before,' Thorarg said, with a heavy sigh. 'It is defeat.'

Torelak sighed, 'There has been enough of it around. The

death of Carangrane, of Fenorn … Anvildrak … this responsibility weighs heavy upon him and there was no time to prepare.'

Ganigrorn nodded. 'But the Heartstealer will not wait for us while we indulge in idle thinking of our mistakes. We need to respond, plan a defence … rouse our people.'

'What is our strength?' Thorarg asked.

Torelak ran through the roll call of the Giant's cities.

'It makes for a grim report,' he said. 'Nearly half our fighting force is either destroyed, put tactically beyond our reach or cannot be spared in the defence of our heartlands. There is no way we can mount an offensive with any hope of success.'

'Defence then?' Thorarg queried.

'If we deploy our forces in the Valley of Thigrium, we can hold the Iceguard there,' Torelak said, 'But that would mean abandoning our lands to the East.'

'I will not see my city fall to the Heartstealer without a fight,' Imgenarg rumbled.

'Nor I,' Ganigrorn added.

'If the Heartstealer reaches the Valley of Thigrium before we do,' Torelak replied. 'She will split our defence in two … she will take our lands from us, east and west of the mountains of Anvormane. We have lost the east already. We must consolidate our forces as soon as we can or the west will follow.'

'It is two days march,' Imgenarg said. 'I say we make a stand here against the Heartstealer, push back the filth from our lands!'

'We are all that is left of our eastern strength,' Torelak replied. 'We cannot stand alone, we have not the numbers. Without us, the western cities will not stand against the Heartstealer's newfound strength. A stand here will result in the end of our race!'

'What say you, Ganigrorn?' Imgenarg asked.

The southern giant placed his hands on his hips, straightening to his full height.

'I fear Torelak speaks wisdom,' he said. 'We no longer have the might to take the attack, we must defend our homeland from the Heartstealer and perhaps the Barbarians too.'

'You would give up your fortress?' Imgenarg said.

'Not willingly, but for the sake of our survival?' Ganigrorn replied. 'Of course.'

Thorarg stood up from the table.

'Varangrim,' he called, raising his voice. 'We must decide. We must decide now.'

Varangrim turned, looking at each of them in turn before striding back, his form silhouetted for a moment by the glow of the fire. As he approached, the other giants could see his skin was grey and his features downcast.

'The choices before us are both evil,' Varangrim said at last. 'Retreat north and hope we can intercept the Heartstealer's forces before they strike our homelands, or march upon them here.'

'The longer we delay, the closer to our homelands they get,' Torelak insisted.

'My forces are at your command,' Ganigrorn said. 'I served Carangrane, I now serve you.'

Varangrim nodded.

'Yet I am not Carangrane,' Varangrim said. 'We have limped to the edge of destruction under my leadership.

'All the more reason to act decisively now!' Torelak yelled.

Thorarg stepped forward.

'There is another course,' he said, his voice low. 'A way that might spell survival for both the east and west of our realm.'

The other giants looked at him in confusion.

'We sue for peace,' Thorarg said.

'Peace?' Varangrim echoed. 'After the slaughter of our comrades and the destruction of our lands?'

'Shareth is no fool,' Thorarg said. 'She knows that defeating us will sap her strength. Her goal is not our destruction, but the subjugation of the Icemark and the lands beyond. She will march upon the Dwarves and the Barbarians in time … and then the Fey of the south. We might be part of that achievement, or just a passing note in the history books.'

'I will not countenance an alliance with her,' Varangrim said. 'Everything we stood for … everything Carangrane intended …'

'Carangrane is dead,' Thorarg said. 'The future of our people … their very existence is at stake now. If we fight, Shareth will have no choice but to exterminate us. The Barbarians will scent blood before long, if they haven't already. They will attack from the south, aiding our destruction and weakening themselves so she has an easier time of marching onwards.'

'What are you saying …?' Torelak said.

'What I am saying is that the Heartstealer has already won,' Thorarg said. 'We can resist for a while, honour those who have fallen … and be destroyed. Or we can sue for peace, listen to her demands and save our people from certain extermination.'

Varangrim sighed, pacing around for long moments.

'Ganigrorn, Torelak,' he said. 'You must see to the southern defence. The Barbarians must be thwarted in any ambition they have for our lands. Go back to the Fortress of Ganigrorn and defend it. If they attack you are to hold the line. It cannot be breached, do you understand?'

The two giants nodded.

'The rest of us go north,' Varangrim said. 'We will meet the Heartstealer, we will see if she might give us terms we can accept.'

Luxor watched as Imgorad walked into the hall with Kahudrak and Kahudrarg and stood behind the top table at the front of the hall. He didn't miss the aggressive looks that were sent in his direction by the pair of brothers. As he watched another Barbarian entered the hall from a side door. Luxor didn't recognise him. He strode towards Imgorad and bowed low.

'Great leader,' he said. 'I have news from the north.'

Imgorad turned and gestured to the man.

'Rise Thortheon of the northern realms,' he said. 'It seems this is a day of great tidings both good and evil. What news?'

'My scouts report great activity in the realm of the Giants,' Thortheon replied. 'The Fortress of Ganigrorn has emptied, its army marching swiftly northwards. My scouts followed them as far as they could and it seems the Giants have been beset by the forces of the Heartstealer. From what we can determine she wages a major offensive against them in their realms to the north.'

'They have left their southern realms unguarded?' Imgorad said, his eyes narrowing.

'Not unguarded,' Thortheon said. 'But certainly weakened. Riders from Carormand confirm the same from the western reaches.'

Imgorad nodded and beckoned to Luxor. Luxor stood before the table, with the Barbarians lined up upon the other side.

'So Moonprince,' Imgorad said. 'What know you of this?'

Luxor looked surprised. 'Of the woes of the Giants? Nothing at all. Though it does not surprise me that Shareth makes war upon them. She will bring such attacks on all the people of Icemark in time.'

'Yet you sent Rorthron to them not a day ago, did you not?' Imgorad asked.

'Rorthron of the Wise rides to them as you say,' Luxor replied. 'But he has told me nothing of their situation as yet.'

Imgorad grunted in response.

'Here are my orders,' he said. 'I see an opportunity before us. The Giants are weakened, struck down by the Heartstealer. We can reclaim lands long ago taken from us. This we will do. Prepare our forces for an offensive, but keep a strength upon our eastern flank, we will risk no perfidy from the Fey. We march as soon as we are ready.'

Luxor's expression fell. 'Great leader …'

Imgorad turned to him.

'As for you Moonprince of Midnight,' he said. 'I hear your words and they are fair to my ears … too fair. You speak of what you do not know. There is no defeating the Heartstealer, we can only side step her wrath, bargain and negotiate. Taking lands from the giants gives me more power to negotiate with her … she respects strength … and we will be all the stronger.'

'You must resist her!'

'My people will not be a pawn in your conflict,' Imgorad replied. 'We Barbarians look to our own interests. If you seek her demise then trust to your Fey friends alone. I will not ally myself with the likes of them.'

'You should know that the Fey have already pledged themselves to this end,' Luxor said, standing straighter. 'They will take a courageous stand against evil … yet you say the Barbarians will not?'

Conversation became muted within the hall, only the faint mutterings of some could be heard as all eyes focussed on Luxor and Imgorad.

'Such decisions as I make are for the good of my people and my people alone,' Imgorad rumbled. 'Take a care not to outstay your welcome, Moonprince of Midnight. We are still friends, for now …'

'I would be a friend to all peoples of the Icemark,' Luxor replied.

'And yet my countrymen have been slain at your behest,'

Imgorad said. 'It is to your credit that you have spoken the truth of the matter, Moonprince, otherwise I would have you slain as you stand before me, or perhaps handed to the Heartstealer as a prize.'

'I was assured the Barbarians had more honour than that,' Luxor replied.

Imgorad raised himself up to his full height, looking down upon Luxor. The pair stared into each other's eyes for long moments.

'You dare to impugn my honour,' Imgorad growled.

'I question it,' Luxor replied.

With a roar Imgorad upended the table. It crashed down before Luxor, who stepped backwards, his hand on the hilt of his sword. Behind him, Luxor heard his own men and the Barbarians leap to their feet.

The moment passed. Luxor held up his hand for calm.

'You will leave upon this day,' Imgorad said, his voice low. 'You are banished from my realms. Go to the Dwarves or the Fey if they will receive you. If we meet again it will be as enemies, Moonprince of Midnight. Mark my words.'

Luxor paused for a long moment, but then he sighed and fixed his gaze upon Imgorad once more.

'You will regret this decision,' Luxor said. 'Mark my words, the Heartstealer will betray you, sooner or later.'

Tarithel's horse, Álainn, had been found, brought back to the city and saddled anew with provisions for the journey ahead. Imulorn and Imelorn stood nearby, waiting for her.

She turned to Glormane and Carorthay, curtseying.

'My Lords. With your leave I depart. I cannot thank you enough for what you do for me.'

Glormane sighed. 'I would rather not send you away. Your

actions may have saved the Dwarven kingdom from destruction, my Lady. These are strange words for a Dwarf to utter, but we will miss you greatly, Tarithel of the Fey.'

'I wish you all good fortune on your quest,' Carorthay added. 'Come back to us sweet Lady of the Forest.'

'I intend to,' Tarithel answered. She reached out, pulling both the Dwarves into an embrace. Both looked astonished for a moment.

'I will always speak well of the friendship and honour of the Dwarves,' she said as she pulled back, tears in her eyes.

Glormane coughed, rubbing at his beard, blinking.

'I will try to speak less harshly of the Fey,' he managed. 'When I next meet Lord Imorthorn ... well ...'

Glormane coughed again.

'We will look upon the Fey as friends once more,' Carorthay said.

Glormane nodded.

Tarithel nodded and wiped away her tears.

'Until we meet again.'

She walked to Álainn. Imulorn and Imelorn bowed to Glormane and Carorthay and began marching away from the city. Tarithel mounted Álainn and turned her after them.

'I sincerely hope that is not the last we see of her,' Glormane muttered.

Carorthay nodded. 'She goes to an uncertain fate,' he said. 'For her ... and for us all.'

Glormane sighed. 'We have done what we can. I must see to my City for now ...'

'And me to mine,' Carorthay replied. 'I fear mischief upon our eastern borders.'

'Yes,' Glormane replied. 'The Icelords may seek to exploit our weakness. Defend the east my friend, as you have always done.'

Carorthay bowed and departed.

The garrison of the Free that had journeyed many hard roads in the service of Luxor Moonprince of Midnight, now trudged onwards east and south, flanked by the armies of Careneon and Torinarg.

Luxor rode at the head of his men, peering into the distance as the landscape unrolled about him. The Forest of Thangrun had been left behind and the plains now opened before him. Mountains were rising on the eastern horizon.

Curse the arrival of Kahudrak and Kahudrarg. Such unfortunate timing! Are they in the pay of the Heartstealer perhaps? Was there something else I could have said to win the day?

He turned the events over and over in his mind, rueing the outcome.

I have failed to gain the support of the Barbarians, and the Dwarves could not be persuaded either ... without both their pledges the Fey do not have the strength to counter Shareth by all accounts. If we cannot win, allegiances will falter and we will be back to where we started, with Shareth all the bolder and no close to rescuing my son!

Thoughts of Morkin led him to thoughts of Tarithel.

She has done better than I, we have the Fey at least! Perhaps I should have sent her to talk to Imgorad too!

He sighed, replaying events over and over in his mind. Yet Tarithel was far away now, soon to be deep in the heart of the lands of their sworn enemy.

Does she have a hope? Perhaps I should have tried harder to stop her, hold her at Imorthorn's city.

He sighed.

No, she loves Morkin, as much as I. She would not have waited. Why is this world so cruel that it allows young folk to shoulder such burdens as these?

He called to mind Morkin's quest to destroy the Ice Crown. He'd left a young man and a squire, only to find him grown, seasoned and scarred by his experiences in defying that great evil.

And what will become of Tarithel? A young maiden, beautiful and carefree she was ... so it seemed to me. What will this journey have done to her? What price will it demand of her before all is ended? She goes ever nearer this same evil that has plagued us.

There was little he could do for her now. She was far beyond his reach, as Morkin had been beyond his before. Now both were lost, their fates entwined together.

Luxor could see Torinarg's banner fluttering on the right flank of the armies. Careneon's was to the left. Luxor could see that it was turning towards him. Careneon approached.

Luxor held up his hand and his men came to a halt. The Barbarian rode up to them.

'My Lord Luxor,' Careneon called. 'We ride soon into lands disputed between ourselves and the Fey. We must leave you on the morrow.'

Luxor nodded.

'You have followed your orders as does any good soldier,' he said. 'I commend you for it. I only wish we were able to draw our swords together as allies against the evil I know is coming.'

Careneon fixed him with a long look and then dismounted from his horse.

'We should set camp,' Careneon said, looking to the west. 'Only one hour of the day remains and it has been a long ride.'

Luxor nodded and his men went about their tasks. Soon fires were burning and provisions broken out. Careneon remained nearby.

'You have something on your mind?' Luxor asked.

Careneon sat down opposite him, his eyes glinting in the light from the fire.

'I am greatly saddened at the way things have transpired,' he said, in response to Luxor. 'I am bound to my orders, this you know, but that doesn't mean I am happy at the prospect.'

Luxor nodded.

'That is good to know,' he said. 'Perhaps I underestimated the task I had. Loyalty was pledged more straightforwardly in my home land of Midnight. The issues perhaps more clearly defined. The Witchking was evil and we fought against him. There was little room for ambiguity. Here in the Icemark …'

'It is difficult to see who might be a friend and who might be a foe,' Careneon answered. 'All are wary and suspicious. Motives are questioned, truth is elusive. Imgorad is not evil, Luxor, but he has but one overriding concern, the future of his people.'

'These are things I do understand,' Luxor said.

'If he feels defying the Heartstealer endangers us unduly …'

'She will betray you all in the end,' Luxor said. 'This seems to be her game, and a cunning strategy it is, to keep all races in this land at odds with each other, never able to counter her. She need not fight when you all do her work for her.'

'The Barbarians are not allied with the Heartstealer,' Careneon retorted.

'No?' Luxor said. 'Yet, here I am, her sworn enemy, banished from your lands. Likewise the Dwarves will not swear their loyalty to me, despite my envoy helping with them their woes. Who does that favour, my will, or the Heartstealer?'

Careneon rubbed his chin.

'Despite Imgorad's proclamation,' Careneon said. 'I would not want us to part as enemies. I am not Imgorad, nor do I speak for the Barbarians, but if I am any judge of character, I see you as an honourable man, Luxor, Moonprince of Midnight. Given time, I would hope to be your friend.'

Luxor smiled and held out his hand. Careneon grasped it tight and a fierce shake was exchanged.

'The realm of the Fey lies yonder,' Careneon continued, pointing into the gloom to the east. Night had fallen and the sky was grey with cloud, little could be seen. 'We will reach the Tower of Thorthorn early tomorrow. The Fey claim everything east of that to be theirs. I might dispute that, but it does not seem the right time for such petty squabbles, so I will respect it for now. There we must leave you. Proceed four leagues or so and you will find the City of Carorthane, he is great amongst the Fey so I understand. Your welcome there should be warmer than of late.'

'I thank you for your words,' Luxor said. 'But nothing more can be done now, let us talk of other things whilst we can enjoy each other's company. Tell me of some legend of the Icemark ...'

'I am not a storyteller,' Careneon answered. 'I should summon a bard.'

'Surely you know a tale or two?' Luxor said. 'I will start with one of mine ... did you know that we have ships in Midnight?'

'Ships?' Careneon asked in surprise. 'Ships that sail? Has the ice retreated already?'

'It has now,' Luxor answered, 'but we had them even at the height of the ice, preserved from time before the Witchking cursed our lands into everlasting winter. There is a city to the south of Midnight; Xajorkith is its name. It was once upon the coast of the sea, at the mouth of river. Great trade between Midnight and the lands further south took place in those days, with ships laden with all sorts of wonderful items. All that was lost when the ice came of course. The river froze first and then the oceans. Midnight was cut off from other lands, much as the Icemark was.'

'Most ships were destroyed. They were useless of course

and a source of wood for the fires, but one was returned by the Lord of that city.'

'But why?' Careneon asked.

Luxor smiled. 'I asked the very same question when first I beheld it. Xajorkith was threatened by destruction and yet there, still preserved and tended lay this ship … this useless ship! The answer was simple … hope.'

'Hope?'

'Yes, hope. Hope for change, hope for better days when the ice would retreat and the ship might make its way once more. Such a thing we could hardly conceive of course, the Witchking's power waxed to its greatest extent, his hordes laid siege to the city and all looked lost. Yet … we prevailed, the city survived, and now the ice retreats. Even now that ship might yet be sailing upon clear blue water, perhaps it will even take us to the southern lands as once it did.'

Luxor stopped.

'If I could find a way to stop this evil from spreading once more,' he muttered. 'Ah well …'

'A heart-warming tale,' Careneon said. 'I should like to set foot on a ship and sail to lands beyond the horizon, it is good that Midnight can still tell such stories, I fear it will be far longer before the Icemark can look forward to such things.'

'There must be tales here,' Luxor said. 'Some stories you tell to cheer yourselves in the depths of winter, surely?'

Careneon chuckled. 'Well, there is one I can recall, have you heard the tale of the Crowns of Icemark?'

'Rorthron has mentioned them,' Luxor said, pulling himself up into a more comfortable position before the fire. 'But I know little more.'

'As it was told to me,' Careneon said. 'Long ago, before the ice and snow, Icemark was fair to behold. It was said the Wise went to and fro amongst the people and the races were not at constant war with each other as they are today. A child's tale no doubt, meant to ease the fears of the young.'

'It starts well enough,' Luxor said.

'The Wise were pleased with what they saw,' Careneon said. 'And they gave great gifts to those they thought worthy, Talismans of power imbued with the magic of the Wise. Least amongst these were spells. It was said they could swiften the steps, or embolden those who knew them, making them fairer or more courageous. Even today spells are spoken at weddings and funerals. They don't work of course, but tradition is … well, tradition.'

'But, so the story goes, the Wise wanted to give the leaders of the races greater powers, so as to maintain the peace they saw around them. To each race they gave a crown, each imbued with its own powers and charms. Depending on who the tells the story, the crowns have different names and different powers, but there is one that seems to be the same regardless of the story teller. The Crown of Varenand.'

'Varenand?' Luxor echoed. 'Is that a place, or a man?'

'Supposedly he was the first leader of our people,' Careneon answered. 'Perhaps five thousand moons ago or more. He is said to have unified our warring clans and turned our thoughts outwards rather than inwards. The Wise were said to have been impressed with his conduct, and thus gave him their blessing. The Crown was said to be the source of his power, and through it he was able to govern fairly and wisely for a hundred moons or more. The Crown was said to have been held by many of our leaders afterwards, but at some point it was lost when we found ourselves in conflict with the Fey and the Giants.'

'And you think this crown is real?'

'Do not put much stock in such fancies,' Careneon replied. 'Varenand is more of a legend than reality. A golden age of myth we look back on with fondness … that almost certainly never took place!'

'Legends and myths always have a kernel of truth though,' Luxor said.

'Perhaps,' Careneon admitted. 'And this crown features in many of our old tales. Some give it strange powers, it is said that it would give whomsoever wore it the power to summon friends to their aid, wherever they might be. Fanciful stuff.'

'But not impossible where the Wise are concerned,' Luxor said. 'In my homeland we have strange Liths, standing stones which have magical properties if one knows how to access to them. Rorthron himself used them in our struggle against the Witchking. Armies were transported at great speed across the realm of Midnight, far faster than any horse could gallop.'

'I will take your word for it,' Careneon said, with a raised eyebrow. 'Anyway, the Crown of Varenand, and all the other crowns were lost over time. It is said their powers changed those who bore them, making them arrogant and fractious. War and conflict began in the Icemark, the crowns destroyed or lost in the process. The Wise, dismayed at what their gifts had done, drifted away and were seen no more, only their towers now remain, locked and impenetrable. It is said that there will be no peace in the Icemark until that crown is found once more.'

Luxor nodded, deep in thought.

Rorthron believes these crowns still exist. Is this the means by which we might kindle hope? Imagine if we found the lost crown of the Barbarians! Would that change their minds?

'I'll admit, not so uplifting as your story,' Careneon said. 'But such are the tales of the Icemark. The races hereabouts have been so long in conflict that it is hard to imagine it being any other way.'

'But you still have hope,' Luxor said. 'That can only be a good thing.'

Chapter Fourteen

Tarithel the Fey stands in a tunnel looking east.
Six hours of the day remain.

The road from the city wound up into the hills as dusk turned into night. Imulorn and Imelorn had deemed it safer to travel under cover of darkness. The moon was now half full, illuminating their way. The bright Moonstar glimmered in the eastern sky.

'If we can reach the Forest of Torangrim before dawn we will stand a good chance of not being spotted,' Imulorn explained. 'The Temple of Theleon is nestled up against the eastern flank of the mountains, the forest will cover our movements during the day.'

Tarithel nodded.

'These … stories of the passageway,' she asked. 'Are they true?'

Imelorn chuckled. 'I doubt it, those sort of stories never are. The odd wyvern I might grant you, a skulkrin or a troll perhaps will lurk in those places. Nothing more dramatic than that I'm sure. The stories tend to grow in the taverns, particularly when good ale is involved. Most of those tunnels have collapsed over the years anyway, let's hope this one is still passable.'

'You don't believe in the tales of evil wraiths then?' Tarithel asked.

'I've never met anything that I couldn't hack apart with a good axe given a decent swing,' Imelorn replied.

'The tales have some truth about them,' Imulorn retorted. 'And these temples and palaces, they were wrought long before any other folks lived in the Icemark, they represent something that used to be here. The stories don't just tell of creatures, but powers that bring night upon you without warning, or drain you of your strength …'

'Just stories …' Imelorn snorted.

'Oh no,' Tarithel replied. 'I quite believe them. I have seen such things myself.'

'Truly?' Imulorn asked, his eyes wide.

Tarithel nodded. 'Once, when I encountered Rorthron the Wise for the first time in the snows of my homeland, he gave me a cup. When I drank from it, the sun changed position in the sky, granting me many more hours of the day. I can't explain it, but such things can happen.'

Imulorn gave Imelorn a look. Imelorn scoffed.

'I'll believe it if I see it,' he said.

The hills came to an end and they made their way out of a gentle valley. Before them the trees of the forest could be seen, a line of darkness blocking their way ahead.

'I dislike the forests at night,' Imulorn said, with a shudder.

'The forests are the safest place you can be,' Tarithel said, climbing down from Álainn.

'For the Fey, perhaps,' Imulorn replied.

'We have a kinship with the trees, it's true,' Tarithel said. 'We care for them, in turn they care for us.'

She led them within the boundary of the trees, her eyesight keen and able to find a way that they could not see. Before long she came to a halt.

'Here is a good place,' she said.

Imelorn looked about him. The forest seemed dark and unwelcoming to him, still and oppressive.

'I fail to see what delights you Fey so,' he grumbled.

Tarithel smiled at him in the gloom.

'Watch!'

She knelt down and touched the mossy ground around them. Both of the Dwarves saw the jewel she wore about her neck begin to glow, illuminating the mysterious Fey-girl with a wholesome but unnatural green glow.

As they watched, the glow seemed to spread to her fingers, the moss and ferns around her responding to the light and emitting it themselves. About them a glade was revealed in the darkness, lit by sparkles of green light across the moss, the bark of the trees and the leaves overhead.

Imulorn and Imelorn turned around in wonder, looking about themselves. They heard her sigh and sit back, holding her head in her hands.

'Tarithel?' Imulorn asked.

'It's all right,' Tarithel replied, with a smile. 'This jewel ... it is wearisome to use, that's all ...'

'It is magic,' Imulorn said, looking at his brother. 'I told you ...'

Imelorn coughed and muttered something that might have been acquiescence.

'Very pretty,' he said. 'But I daresay yonder pretty lights won't cook a decent meal, will they?'

Tarithel laughed.

'No,' she said. 'You must resort to your own skill for that.'

They ate a meagre meal and settled down to sleep.

Before dawn broke, they set off continuing to make their way north-east through the forest. As before, Tarithel had a skill of finding paths where none seemed to be, and, after a while, the pair of Dwarves let her lead them on.

The faint light of sunrise was beginning to creep up around them, turning the dark gloom of the forest into a brightening grey, until the first beams of light flickered through the thickset trunks of the trees.

'Not far now,' Imulorn said, peering into the brightness

ahead. The forest ends within the league and the Temple will not be far.'

Tarithel nodded.

They continued onwards as the sun rose before them. The forest thinned and they slowed their walk through the trees.

Before them they could see the Temple, a vast edifice rising out of the plain, almost as high as the mountains that formed an imposing backdrop to the spectacle, their shadows reaching across the plains beyond the Temple itself. Tarithel looked to her left and right, seeing the mountain range extending north-west and south-east as far as she could see.

'Anvulane,' she whispered.

'Aye,' Imulorn said, drawing close alongside her. 'The greatest mountains in all of the Icemark.'

Tarithel shivered. The mountains, cast into shadow by the rising sun, seemed bleak, grey and threatening. Their heights were snow-capped, but mist and cloud writhed around the highest peaks. Their slopes were cliff-edged in many parts and their ramparts steep and sheer. It was not difficult to believe they were impassable.

The Temple was nearby, perhaps just a few hundred yards away.

Both Imulorn and Imelorn were looking about them.

'Few people come this way,' Imulorn said, 'I think it's unlikely that this place would be watched, but we should not tarry for long. We are not that far from the City of Imgorarg itself and I doubt his people will have much hospitality for us after the war.'

Tarithel nodded and they walked down the slopes of the gentle hill upon which the forest boundary lay, dropping down towards the plain, and the lonely Temple that rose before them.

Within a few minutes they stood in its shadow, shivering in the cold dawn air, its bulk stretching above them. Up close the skilled stonemasonry of the construction was plain to see. Vast, carved stone blocks formed the build, towering high, layer upon layer like an enormous flight of stairs, though with each step taller than they were. Tarithel led them around the base, looking for a way inside.

'Is there no entrance?' she asked.

'There will be,' Imulorn said. 'A great gate set precisely in the centre of one of the sides. Why this should be I know not. None know by whom these Temples were built, nor for what purpose. They are ancient beyond our reckoning.'

'A waste of good stone that could have been much better used to build fortresses and cities,' Imelorn said.

'You said this was the Temple of Theleon,' Tarithel said, running her fingers over the stonework, feeling the smooth surface beneath her fingertips.

'And we do not know who he, she or they were either,' Imulorn said, chuckling. 'Icemark is full of such mysteries, more than can be counted.'

'Then where do the names come from?' Tarithel asked.

'Old maps for the most part,' Imelorn said, striding ahead. 'And of those some are right and some are wrong and all are incomplete. Does it matter? No, it does not!'

Tarithel exchanged a look with Imulorn, shrugged and then followed, pulling Álainn along beside her.

They rounded the south-east corner of the Temple and were able to see its easternmost flank. There, after they had walked halfway up its length, stood an imposing entranceway, a huge lintel supported by two enormous columns. The entrance matched the austere architecture of the temple itself, there were no curves in evidence, both the lintel and the columns were plain, rectangular and undecorated.

They were also unmarked by time. There were no stains upon the stonework, no chips or scratches, no crumbled edges. Everything seemed new and fresh as if the stonemasons had departed only the night before.

The entranceway was perhaps ten feet across by thirty tall. There was no door, just an empty space. Tarithel tried to peer inside, but despite the bright sunlight now shining behind her, the interior seemed inky black.

'According to Carorthay,' Imulorn said, standing alongside her. 'The entrance leads down to an underground tunnel. We can take that northwards under the mountains.'

Tarithel nodded, shivering, still looking at the darkened portal of the Temple.

'Come, come,' Imelorn said. 'Time is wasting. If we want to get you through the mountains this is our route …'

He strode forward, Imulorn following close behind. Tarithel made to go after them, but her legs and arms felt heavy and unwilling.

'No wait!' Tarithel called. The jewel around her neck pulsed. She felt a great aching weariness steal over her.

Imelorn stomped into the entrance, his brother close behind them. Tarithel saw them swallowed up by the darkness, hearing a muffled yelp from within. Álainn whinnied in alarm. A sense of impending dread and terror rose about her.

'Imulorn! Imelorn!'

She dragged herself up to the threshold of the Temple, trying to see within, it was still pitch black, as if there was a wall of darkness thrown up at the entrance. It was like the deepest shadow, impervious to the light of the sun.

She stretched out her fingers towards it, reaching forwards, flinching back as she did so, squinting, fearing some calamity she could not articulate.

Her fingers touched the blackness. Tarithel screamed out loud as a sepulchral voice echoed in her head.

You defile this holy place? Such a curse tells of a fall from grace.

We steal from you your very breath, and take your strength with the languor of death!

The jewel around her neck burnt hot against her skin and

the words turned into a tormented scream. She stumbled back, falling back on the barren ground outside the temple, scrambling backwards, her heart pounding in her chest.

She was trembling from head to foot.

Some ancient power, not like Fangrim or even Shareth, older, hostile, implacably evil! What was it?

Her vision cleared, she blinked, trying to get her heart to stop its headlong rush. For long moments she felt dizzy and ill, struggling to avoid being sick. She took several deep breaths. She felt tired, as if she'd walked some great distance, her arms and legs ached.

She struggled to her feet.

'Imulorn, Imelorn!' she called, staggering towards the entrance.

The strange darkness was gone, the light of the sun now illuminated a passageway that led within the Temple. Sprawled on the floor before her, Tarithel could see the bodies of the two Dwarves.

She ran forward, still calling their names.

Both seemed insensible, but both were breathing. She tried to rouse them, but neither responded.

'Wretched Dwarves!' she called.

She grabbed hold of Imulorn and heaved, trying to pull him back outside. He was heavy and she slipped and slid as she struggled. By the time she had pulled Imelorn back out she was exhausted and sank to the ground.

My strength … all stolen away somehow. What was that? Some spell of ancient power we disturbed? If that guarded just the entrance, what other horrors might we find within?

The sun rose further in the sky, warming her. The terror of the entrance began to recede. She soon felt better, the dizziness passing.

She turned her attention to the pair of dwarven brothers, shaking them, trying to get them to wake up.

With great reluctance they opened their eyes.

'Tarithel?' Imulorn croaked.

His eyes were heavy, rolling in his head as if he were struggling to stay awake. Twice Tarithel had to rouse him again.

'So … tired …' he managed to utter.

'Can you walk?' she asked. 'We can't stay here in the open … Imgorarg's people might see us!'

Imulorn struggled to get to his feet, with Tarithel pulling up Imelorn beside him. Both Dwarves staggered drunkenly, propping each other up.

'Can't walk,' Imelorn muttered, sinking back to his knees.

'Inside the Temple then!' Tarithel instructed.

She pulled and cajoled the pair along and they made their way inside, both Dwarves collapsing when inside the entranceway, propped up against the walls.

'What happened?' Imulorn whispered, his eyes closing again.

'Stay awake!' Tarithel hissed. 'Some kind of spell. I heard some fell voice in my mind. It was a curse.'

'I have heard of … such things,' Imulorn said. Beside him Imelorn slumped down, asleep once more.

'We need to keep moving,' Tarithel said, pulling at him. 'Come on! We can't stay here!'

'It has robbed us …' Imulorn gasped. 'Of strength … all we can do … is rest. We cannot … carry on. You must … leave us …'

'I'm not leaving you!' Tarithel said. 'I need you … I can't find this path alone!'

But Imulorn had slumped alongside his brother. Tarithel shook them again and again, but neither would rouse.

She threw herself down across from them, holding her head in her hands.

I knew something was awry, I should have been more careful! Now my friends are cursed …

She heard something. Voices.

In a panic she pulled Álainn further into the passageway, out of the light of the sun, deeper into the shadows. Then she returned and crept toward the entrance, straining her hearing, peering out.

Nothing was ahead of her, but a snatched look around to the north revealed as a small troop of Dwarven warriors had emerged from the hills to the north. They were heavily armed and dressed for war. She retreated back into the entrance, considering her options.

Dwarves from Imgorarg's city no doubt. If they find us here …

The voices were getting nearer. She thought about making a run outside, but there was no way she'd be able to hide in the forest before the Dwarves saw her. She'd seen how handy they could be with knife and axe, she'd be lucky to get away with her life.

She retreated further into the passageway, Álainn snorting in agitation beside her, wondering if she could somehow shift the pair of brothers further away from the entrance. Just as she was thinking about doing so, silhouetted figures appeared in the entrance. She could hear their voices.

'Look … footsteps … they've been this way. They could be within!'

'Careful … these Temples are cursed!'

'Bring a torch,' said the first. 'Let's see what we're about, there's a pretty reward for that Fey-girl and I want it.'

At their words Tarithel retreated further in along the passageway, holding close to the rough stone edges. A cold wind blew from behind her, ruffling her cloak and hair.

Fire flickered ahead of her and the other Dwarves stepped within. It took them only moments to discover the unconscious bodies of Imelorn and Imulorn.

'Southern Dwarves,' one said, spitting on the floor. 'They're going to be sorry they came this way.'

'Haul 'em out,' said another. 'Go further in, it's the Fey-girl we're after. Don't hesitate to kill her, don't let her enchant you first …'

The Dwarves were getting close, the torches held aloft. They would see her in moment. Tarithel had only one option left. She turned and ran.

'There!' someone shouted from behind her.

A knife slashed through the air nearby, ping off the rocky wall. Tarithel struck her foot against some hidden rock and went sprawling to the rough floor, holding out her hands to stop her. She felt the skin of her palms scratch and bleed.

She struggled up. Álainn was whinnying in alarm somewhere in the darkness, but Tarithel couldn't see her.

'It's her, get her!'

Tarithel couldn't see where she was going. Cold wind blustered around her, the sound of her footsteps echoing.

Her feet found an edge and she tottered there for a moment, trying to find her balance in the darkness.

It was no good.

With a shriek of fear that reverberated around her, Tarithel fell into oblivion.

Shareth's ire had not cooled, yet sanity had returned as it always did. Her wild emotions gave her great power, but she was wise enough to know that she could not afford to let them rule her. She stood on the great battlements of the Fortress of Kahangrorn, looking south through the mist that writhed around its base like a tortured wraith given icy form.

Her fist, clenched, was held before her. By a conscious effort she relaxed her grip, watching her fingers uncurl. She looked to her left, seeing that the gibbous moon had risen above the battlements. It was close to full, blood red, low in the sky, matching her mood.

IT IS TIME. I MUST KNOW!

With imperious strides she took herself down through the gates of the Fortress, passing the guards and the armies surrounding it. She made her way unseen through the dark boughs of the Forest of Carenak. By the time the full moon had risen in the sky to cast its pale pearly glow across the bleak landscape, she had reached her destination.

The Temple of Obenad.

She descended through shadowed staircases and dark marbled halls. Torches sprung to life as she walked forward, illuminating her progress, snuffed out in puffs of smoke as she passed, until she reached the inner chambers, secrets locked away from mere mortals through ancient enchantments of woe and terror. Even Shareth knew to be wary, there were greater potencies than herself at large in the Icemark, some even older than her father had been.

But she had twisted some of these powers to her own use, and the inner sanctum of the Temple was one such place.

Across the ornately carved stone flooring she stepped, her feet marking out a rhythm and a spell. Cyan light flickered around her and shadows appeared. Two figures, only their outlines visible in the faint glow.

As she watched she saw them bow low before her.

'Much has happened since our last conversation,' Shareth said. 'You will note that one of our number is missing.'

The shadows resolved into the forms of a Fey and a Barbarian. The Barbarian spoke first.

'There is news from the Dwarves?'

'There is,' Shareth said. 'News that displeases me. My servant within their ranks has met their end.'

The two figures looked at each other.

'My plan to kindle a devastating war amongst the Dwarves

has been thwarted by the actions of that … emissary … of the Moonprince.'

'Emissary?'

'The girl,' Shareth said. 'Tarithel, the Lady of The Forest as she was described. It seems she did indeed arrive in the realm of the Dwarves. War was kindled as I desired, the Dwarves at each other's throats … yet she intervened. I have tested her strength and it is considerable. She bears a power, and wielded it against my interests. Glormane regains his ancestral seat of power in their Kingdom.'

'Then …' the Fey said, his voice tremulous. 'What of your plans?'

'They remain,' Shareth said. 'For the Dwarves still fought and remain in some disarray. Glormane will have little time to enjoy his new found leadership before a great calamity is unleashed against him. For if the Dwarves will not align with me, they will fall before me. They are weaker than they have ever been, reeling from their internal bickering. The girl may even have done me a service, sowing confusion and chaos in her wake. It is of no matter now, the Dwarves will fall.'

'What of the girl herself?' The Fey asked. 'If she is indeed powerful as you say … more so than we first suspected …'

'Leave her to me,' Shareth said. 'She travels northwards towards my realm, she need not concern you any longer. Once she is found she will be killed by my own and that will be the end of her mischief. Now … tell me of news from the south. Is dissent fostered amongst your people?'

The Fey straightened.

'It is indeed Empress,' he replied. 'The eastern Fey are much vexed by the orders of Imorthorn. They assemble to ride according to his orders as they must, but their leader is not happy with the justification for war. I have enflamed his doubts and sought to lead him to a path of reconciliation with the Frozen Empire. This will put him at odds with Imorthorn when all are assembled. The Fey will lock themselves in endless debates and a challenge for the leadership will be the outcome. The Fey will be paralysed; they will mount no effective force on behalf of this Moonprince, and present no threat to you.'

'Make sure it transpires as you have described,' Shareth replied. 'I will expect to hear of Imorthorn's demise or disgrace at our next encounter.'

'I will make all endeavours to that end,' the Fey replied.

'And of the Barbarians?' Shareth asked, turning her attention to the other figure.

'This Moonprince has arrived in the court of Imgorad,' the Barbarian replied. 'He is as you described, eloquent and convincing. Imgorad has heard his case.'

'You explained his true intent and his attitude to the Barbarians in the past?'

'I did indeed,' The Barbarian replied. 'And much consternation it caused, but Imgorad is not one to be swayed easily. He took all news from near and far into consideration before he made his decree.'

'And?' Shareth demanded.

'You will be pleased to know he has banished the Moonprince from our realms,' the Barbarian answered. 'Even now our people march him from our land under escort towards the realms of the Fey. Imgorad even pronounced death upon him should he attempt to return. The Barbarians are true to you, Empress of the Frozen North.'

Shareth cried out with glee.

'Ah, this is fair news indeed!' she yelled, spinning around in a brief moment of joy. 'You have done well, well indeed! Luxor is forced to backtrack! Tail between his legs. Sweet news!'

Her laughs echoed around the chamber for long moments.

'There is more,' the Barbarian said.

'More?' Shareth asked. 'Is that not enough?'

'Imgorad received further missives from the North,' the Barbarian answered. 'Word has reached him of the damage inflicted upon the forces of the Giants by your own assault. He perceives this as an opportunity to tackle them, reclaim long lost territories and expand his realm. He marches upon their southern borders even now.'

'Imgorad is no fool,' Shareth said, a grin crossing her features. 'The Giants crushed between two anvils; this does not displease me. I see no reason to thwart his efforts. Let him take them if he can.'

The Barbarian bowed.

'So then,' Shareth said. 'The Dwarves weakened and soon to be brought low for their perfidy. The Fey locked up within Fangrim caught in their own turmoil, awaiting a leader who will see the sense of cooperation with the Frozen Empire, the Giants on the verge of extinction and the Barbarians evicting the Moonprince from their lands. Today has been a day of welcome news. Continue your good works my loyal servants, your rewards will be all the more plentiful.'

Both of the shadowy figures bowed low once more.

Shareth waited until their outlines faded into the gloom of the chamber.

She smiled.

'And little do you know my real plans.'

A giggle, almost girlish in its lightness, escaped her lips and she turned and made her way outwards once more.

The first thing she sensed was an awful throbbing in her head. Tarithel moaned and stirred. As her memory came back to her, she propped herself on her hands and knees. She felt dizzy and sick, but she was surprised to still be alive.

Then something licked her face.

She spluttered, rolling over, seeing the dim outlines of a large muzzle and two damp nostrils.

Álainn!

Álainn pawed at her and Tarithel pulled herself upright using the horse's bridle.

I fell! What happened?

She looked around her, able to make out a few details in the gloom. There was a faint brightness all around her, as if the rocks themselves were glowing in the darkness. It was enough to make out their outlines, but she couldn't see far.

Seeing nothing of any note she looked upwards. Stretching away as far as she could see was a cavern, its walls made of smooth, carved rock. There was no sign of any daylight. She stroked the horse's muzzle.

How did I survive that fall? And how did Álainn find her way in here? This horse is such a loyal companion, nothing can separate her from me!

She sat herself upright, checking herself for injuries. She was bruised for sure, but there were no broken bones.

And what happened to Imulorn and Imelorn?

She got to her feet, wondering if she could climb back up the steep sides of the cavern. She shook her head to clear it and regretted it. The dizziness swirled around her and she staggered, leaning against Álainn to steady herself. She was still weary, but nothing like the utter exhaustion thrust upon her by the temple curse.

After a moment, she took stock of her situation. She had her clothes, shoes and a knife in her belt, her provisions and water were still slung upon Álainn's back. There was no sign of Imulorn or Imelorn, and no noise she could hear. She was alone.

I daren't call out ... who knows who ... or what might be listening?

She looked around again, seeing fresh rubble on the uneven floor. She traced it back to one side of the cavern.

It caved in?

She couldn't tell for sure, but it seemed as if there had been a proper passage out of the cavern not far from where she had fallen, a wide hallway with a gentle slope to it. Rocks were now piled before her, the way back was blocked.

Deliberately perhaps?

She must have fallen down some kind of opening in the floor of the passageway above, but there seemed no way she could climb back up, the walls of the cavern were smooth and sheer.

How did Álainn find me? It's impossible ...

There were no answers to be found. She was underneath the temple, now she had to find her way out again. She had no idea which direction to head, so she moved to the nearest wall and followed its edge along. It formed a rough arc on her right side and she walked around. The cavern wasn't large, she soon found a passageway leading down and away from the open space.

Peering at the rocks she could see that there were faint sparkles of light that were providing the dim illumination around her. She scratched at the surface of a rock and found the little pinpricks came away, glowing in her palm for a few moments before fading away. They seemed to be present all around, allowing her to see a little ahead.

As she did so, she was conscious of a whisper of movement in the air, a damp chillness that made her shiver. She looked around, seeing nothing. Alongside her, Álainn snorted and shook her head.

'You feel it too, do you?' she asked. Her voice sounded frail and scared in the gloom.

She pursed her lips.

Nothing else I can do ...

She took up Álainn's reins and stepped forward into the passageway, the horse trotted behind, their footsteps echoing about the stony walls. Dust blew across the floor, as if following them.

Far to the west, in the realm of the Giants, Ganigrorn and Torelak had already departed, marching south from the City of Imgenarg. Imgenarg himself, along with Varangrim and Thorarg, had seen to the preparations of the remaining force of Giants, readying them for a long march north. After a day's long work, the three Giants stood in Imgenarg's hall once more.

'Ganigrorn and Torelak are dependable,' Imgenarg said. 'I have fought with them many times. If there is a way to prevent the Barbarian ingress, they will find it.'

'If there truly is to be a Barbarian ingress,' Varangrim said. 'If there is no threat, we have sent forces south needlessly, forces which might turn the battle in the north, or give us more leverage over the Heartstealer.'

'We must defend our borders,' Thorarg said. 'We cannot risk an assault on two flanks.'

'A decision made in haste …' Varangrim began.

'May oft go astray.'

Another voice echoed around the hall. The three giants turned in surprise and stepped back in alarm and suspicion.

A man stood alongside the fireplace, leaning on a staff and dressed in purple robes. By the standards of men he was both tall and old, though he stood far shorter than the giants.

In moments, spears were grasped and the three giants advanced on the man, surrounding him in a ring of steel.

'Who are you?' Imgenarg demanded. 'And what business have you in my hall, unannounced and uninvited?'

'Peace,' the man answered, his voice deep and commanding. 'If news from the south is what you desire, news from the south is what I can provide.'

'Your name, stranger!' Varangrim roared.

The man gestured with his staff and the fire crackled and died down, hissing and spitting. A gloom settled across the room and the air seemed to thicken around them. The giants took a step back as the tip of the staff crackled with bright flashes of light.

'I am Rorthron of the Wise, here to bring you counsel in dark days,' the man said. 'Will you receive me, giants of the north?'

The giants looked at each other, exchanging confused and bewildered glances. Varangrim recovered first.

'The Wise?' he demanded. 'We have heard nothing from the Wise in years beyond count and I have heard of none hereabouts with the name you claim. Where are you from?'

Rorthron lowered his staff. The brightness of the room returned to normal and the fire sprang back up in the hearth.

'I am not of this land,' Rorthron replied. 'I hail from the realm of Midnight, far to the south of Icemark, hundreds of leagues away. I come to parley with the leader of the Giants, Carangrane is his name I am told.'

The Giants looked disconsolate.

'Carangrane is dead,' Varangrim said. 'Slain in battle two days ago. I am the leader of the Giants now.'

Rorthron frowned. 'Dead … this is evil news. Slain by the Heartstealer's forces?'

'Aye …' Varangrim said. 'Treachery on her part … foolishness on ours.'

'Regardless,' Rorthron continued. 'I come as an emissary from the realm of Midnight. Perhaps you have heard of our struggles against the Witchking?'

'Rumours,' Varangrim answered. 'Vague tales perhaps.'

'They are true,' Rorthron announced in ringing tones. 'My Liege, Luxor Moonprince of Midnight despatched the Witchking and broke his curse upon our lands. The

Witchking's daughter, much aggrieved, has sworn bloody vengeance upon him … it is she who now makes war upon you.'

'The Heartstealer!' Imgenarg called. The giants muttered to each other.

'Aye,' Rorthron replied. 'She saw both Icemark and Midnight as her inheritance, thus far that has been denied her, and her wrath grows hot as a result. This, I think, you have already seen.'

'She has laid waste to our lands to the north and east,' Varangrim replied. 'Already she advances on our homelands.'

'Then it is not too late to stop her,' Rorthron said.

'Stop her?' Thorarg scoffed. 'There is no stopping the Heartstealer now. Our forces are scattered, we can barely hold what remains to us.'

'Alone perhaps,' Rorthron said. 'But in concert with others. There is strength enough in Icemark to resist both her and her armies.'

'So you say,' Varangrim said. 'What strength can you command, Rorthron of the Wise? Perhaps you can conjure armies out of the mist, or perhaps you can face Shareth herself, commanding the strength of the towers your people have hidden in since time immemorial?'

'Luxor has the support of the Fey of Fangrim,' Rorthron said. 'And has sent an emissary to the Dwarves. I stand before you now asking for the same. Luxor has overthrown the Witchking, Shareth's father, he will do the same to Shareth.'

'And what of the Barbarians?' Imgenarg demanded.

'Luxor seeks their support even now,' Rorthron answered. 'They are a stubborn people. But the same choice presented to them I now present to you. Shareth is treacherous and evil, whatever promises she makes to the people of the Icemark they will be overturned eventually. She desires nothing less than dominion over all, she has pledged to take Midnight in her father's place and continue onwards to lands further south. Her plans unfold already, what you have seen thus far is nothing compared to what lies in store … unless she is stopped.'

Varangrim looked at Imgenarg and Thorarg.

'Then our choice is simple,' he said. 'We are poised between Shareth and this Moonprince of the southern realm of Midnight. Shareth we know, but this Moonprince we do not, save this emissary of the Wise. I'd hear your thoughts.'

Imgenarg cleared his throat.

'Shareth has laid waste to our lands and slayed our kin. What alignment can there be between us? We should be crying our vengeance upon her and marching against her foul Iceguard.'

Varangrim nodded and turned to Thorarg.

'Shareth's strength we know, at great cost,' he said. 'Can this Moonprince do what he claims he can? If we pledge our fealty to him and his might is not what is claimed, what then? Shareth will have no mercy.'

'Has Shareth shown us any mercy thus far?' Varangrim answered. 'All we have received is treachery and death, our cities destroyed and our people slain. I'd consider treating with her if there were no other choice, but now there is. This decision I will not make lightly, but the leadership of the Giants has fallen to me in these dark times.'

'And we will honour that decision,' Imgenarg rumbled, looking at Thorarg. Thorarg took a deep breath, but then nodded.

'You lead and we will follow,' Thorarg said.

Varangrim turned back to Rorthron.

'If your Moonprince succeeds in his aims,' he said. 'Defeating Shareth, what then? Where do the Giants and all the other races then lie in his judgement?'

'Luxor is no tyrant,' Rorthron said. 'He is a Lord of Midnight, not of the Icemark. He would see you at peace, not rule over you. Shareth has sworn to lay waste to all of Icemark, Midnight and other lands besides. Luxor would see this stopped and his own son freed from her clutches. If that can be achieved, then he will look to establishing a peace in the Icemark, as he did in Midnight. We both know there are many grievances between the races here, but diplomacy and negotiation will be his tools, not the iron rod of a new king or despot.'

'And will he punish the other races for their crimes against the Giants,' Varangrim asked.

'He might,' Rorthron said. 'And likewise the Giants too, if the testimony of other races is to be believed.'

Varangrim smiled.

'I think I like him already,' Varangrim said. 'Well then. It seems we have the choice between a rapacious sorceress bent on our destruction, or the virtuous Moonprince of Midnight.' His eyes narrowed. 'Yet, I am sure such things are not quite so clear cut.'

'Luxor would be the first to admit he himself is not faultless,' Rorthron replied. 'But he is a good man.'

'So it seems,' Varangrim answered, pacing away to the fire. He stopped there for long moments before turning back.

'Such things need much consideration,' he said. 'Walk with me, Rorthron of the Wise and we will see what is to be done.'

Imulorn roused, struggling to move. His hands were bound and he was lying on his side on the cold, hard ground. Looking about him, he could see a rough camp set about him. A fire was burning, over which a cooking pot was slung, steam rose from it, along with an enticing smell. Beyond that, he couldn't see much more than a featureless plain. He couldn't tell where he was.

The low tones of conversation reached his ears, the northern Dwarf dialect obvious.

He stayed still, not wanting to draw attention to himself. From his position he couldn't see his brother.

And Tarithel? Did she escape?

He cast his mind back. The overwhelming need to sleep due to the curse in the temple. Trying to tell her to leave them …

Did she?

He concentrated on the voices around them. It was hard to make them out.

'… not interested in Glormane for now, that'll come later … mark my words.'

'About time too, who will it be? Imgorarg being dead and all.'

'My coin is on Torormarg, he was second in command. Anyway orders are orders. Let's get these two back to the city, then we march, don't want to miss the end of Carorthay do we? We only have two days.'

'Yeah well … sun's rising, we'd better be moving …'

Imulorn sensed movement and heard orders being barked. Something prodded him.

'Wake 'em,' a voice said.

He was wrestled up by a pair of strong hands and found himself starring into the eyes of a Dwarf he did not know.

'On your feet, southerner!'

Imulorn looked about him to see his brother hoisted into place beside him. He looked in a bad way, with a bruise on his forehead and congealed blood across his face. The other Dwarf moved away and resumed packing his provisions.

'Imelorn!' Imulorn whispered. His brother looked up at him.

'Still alive then … small mercies I guess.'

'Did you see what happened to Tarithel?'

Imelorn shook his head. Imulorn sighed.

The northern Dwarf strode back and stood before them.

'No talking.'

'You don't give us orders,' Imelorn retorted.

The blow was obvious, but Imelorn took it regardless. He staggered, going down on one knee.

'I do give you orders,' the Dwarf said. 'Best you be remembering that. Traitor!'

'Traitor?' Imelorn scoffed. 'You don't remember your masters turning on our leader then?'

'You're allied with the Fey,' the Dwarf retorted. 'Weak and craven.'

'You didn't find her, did you?' Imelorn managed a toothy grin.

'She was caught in the temple,' the Dwarf replied. 'A thousand tons of rock collapsed on top of her. We heard her screaming. She's been buried alive, the right end for a Fey spy.'

'You …' Imelorn struggled to get up. Another blow crushed him down to the ground.

The Dwarf pulled Imelorn back to his feet.

'And you are Glormane's lackeys,' he said, spitting at his feet. 'Those loyal to Imgorarg will prevail in this fight. And you … you'll be made an example of when we reach the city. Now march!'

Both Imulorn and Imelorn were shoved in the back and forced forwards amidst their captors.

They were marching north-west. Imulorn could see the Temple of Theleon a league or so behind them. Ahead, hills were rising against the horizon. Imgorarg's territory. His city could only be five or six leagues away.

'Maybe Tarithel eluded them,' Imulorn said. 'Found a way into the tunnels below …'

'Let's hope so,' Imelorn said. 'Either way, we can't help her now. We need to find a way to escape before we get to the city, or …'

Imulorn nodded.

The fires had burnt low and most of the riders of the Barbarians and the Moonguard had turned in for the night. Luxor pulled his cloak tighter about his shoulders and stood alone, looking up at the bright stars in the sky. They seemed cold, hard and indifferent to his plight.

I have failed to gain the support of the Barbarians, likewise Tarithel was unable to turn the Dwarves … is this quest doomed to failure? I am assured that without their support we will not be able to challenge Shareth. What else can I do? Now I am banished from the lands of the Barbarians …

He turned the conversations over and over in his mind, wondering if there was something else he could have said or done to change the outcome.

Curse Kahudrak and Kahudrarg … surly and ill-tempered they were … servants of evil if ever I saw one!

The Moon Ring tingled upon his finger and he felt his strength ebb further. A voice formed in his mind.

Moonprince?

'Rorthron?' Luxor exclaimed. 'How have you fared?'

I have reached the realm of the Giants, but Shareth has already attacked them. Their leader, Carangrane, whom I sought to find, has been slain in battle and much of their territory has been seized. It seems Shareth moved in great force against them. I fear she is aware of the same information vouchsafed to me regarding the Crowns, Runes and Spells and moves to find them.

Luxor rubbed his forehead.

'Our troubles grow apace,' he said, with a heavy sigh.

Am I to assume that the Barbarians have not sided with us?

Luxor nodded. 'Imgorad is stubborn and firm of will, but Shareth must have divined my intent. Two Barbarian brothers, armed with stories of how the Utarg was slain by the Lady of

Silence arrived unannounced and they claimed kinship with the Utarg.'

The Witchking must have somehow shown Shareth that battle … her reach is indeed long. Take heart, Moonprince. Imgorad may already have made his decision long before we even arrived. The enmity between the Giants and the Barbarians is deepest of all.

'Either way, the story was enough to turn away Imgorad's favour,' Luxor said. 'We are banished from his lands. I now travel with an escort to the borders of the Fey. Be wary on how you return …

I will.

'Tarithel has told me that the Dwarves received her too and are assisting her with entering Shareth's domain, but they will not pledge to me either.'

These races are stubborn and slow to trust.

'Indeed. What of the Giants …?'

I have not yet succeeded in gaining their pledge either, alas. They are even considering treating with the Heartstealer on account of their losses. Their new leader, Varangrim, is weighed down with the responsibility he has inherited and their homeland is under threat from the Iceguard forces …

'Perhaps we have come too late to this conflict already. Shareth has foreseen our plan and stayed one move ahead … perhaps it was never possible to save the Icemark from her.'

She is both wily and cunning, but do not give up hope just yet, Moonprince. Treachery may be its own worst enemy. The dark is strong, but dawn is not far away.

'If we can secure the Giants, with the Fey perhaps it will be enough,' Luxor muttered. 'But our strength is marginal to say the least.'

We must consolidate what we do have. Shareth will betray the Barbarians and the Dwarves eventually, we must be ready to receive them when that happens.

'Aye,' Luxor replied. 'But that may be too late in the day to stop her. Good fortune to you Rorthron, and I wish you success with the Giants. We desperately need their pledge if we are to make any headway!'

Tarithel trudged on for weary leagues, leading Álainn through the underground gloom. The tunnel twisted and turned a little, but ran true to its original direction, though she had no idea which way that was. There had been no alternative routes, no splits of the pathway one way or the other. The passageway continued on, mile after mile, league after league.

The going was easy for the most part, the passage was carved out of the rock, not hewn by tools or paved with brick. Quite how it had been constructed she couldn't surmise, but she was grateful for the smooth surface and lack of protrusions. She had been walking for several hours before she noticed that the passageway had taken a downward turn and was descending further into the depths.

I'd hoped to be going up, not down!

As she was pondering this, the passageway opened before her into a large space, a cavern much like the one she had left underneath the Temple. The faint illumination flickered around her, showing her the outlines of a passageway on the far side.

All was silent.

She stepped forward, looking about her.

With a thump of ignition, flames erupted nearby. She shrieked in alarm, causing Álainn to snort and stamp her hooves.

Adjacent to the entrance she had emerged from, two enormous metal oil burners stood on each side of her. Atop them were upturned bowls from which flames were leaping, casting a bright glow around the cavern. As she watched she saw four more of them burst into flame, marking out two exits from the cavern; the one before her she'd already seen and another one to her left.

The flames sensed me somehow? There is magic here … and I'm not sure it is wholesome!

The flames were sharp and bright, lighting up the cavern for her. She spied a mural on the floor and went over to look at it, leading Álainn behind her. It was a four-pointed design, carved into the stonework and decorated with many symbols she didn't recognise, but some she did.

A compass rose!

She had come from the west and had been heading east, if the design was to be believed. Now she had a choice of continuing east, or turning north.

North then. Easy enough.

She took a moment to give Álainn some water and gulp a little down herself. Glormane and Carorthay seemed to think that the tunnels ran all the way under the mountains. If that was so, she still had a weary way to go, but if the tunnels continued to be as well-kept as the ones she had used so far, she would make good progress. It was perhaps three or four leagues to the mountains and then another six to traverse them to the other side.

I have come at least two leagues already, another two to the north should see me right under their roots. That will have been a day's march, if indeed it is still day – I cannot tell! I will rest then, and see if I can march beneath the mountains tomorrow. With luck, perhaps I can escape from the dark in a day or two, with the mountains of Anvulane finally behind me!

Tarithel pulled on the horse's reins, leading it forward once more, turning towards the north exit from the cavern. She stepped within the passageway.

As she did so, the flames flickered and died behind her,

she felt a cool breath of wind against her cheek. She stopped and looked around, straining her ears. Other than Álainn and herself she could hear nothing at all.

She shivered.

But we're not alone down here.

They stood before her in answer to the deafening summons that had echoed through their minds. Shareth had no need of messengers for her trusted warlords, once her will was decided and if she meant them to partake in it, they knew.

The greatest leaders and most dread Iceguard warriors of the Frozen Empire stood before her, silent and as motionless as stone statues as they awaited her pleasure.

They had ridden in from all corners of the Icemark, their horses' hooves pounding the frozen ground in their haste to answer her call. That call had been urgent, imperative, there could be no delay.

Now they stood in line within the courtyards of the Fortress of Kahangrorn, waiting, the wild whipping their dark cloaks around them, the sky overhead twisted and hung low with dark heavy tumultuous clouds.

Imgaril, Zarashand, Glormarg, Fangrorn, Anvireon and Lorelorn.

At their command lay all the fearsome might of the Frozen Empire, a military might more than the equal of any of the other races of the Icemark, more powerful than many of them combined. Their warriors were well trained, seasoned, armed with swords of strong steel, deadly bows, pikes and halberds. Their armies were equipped with siege weapons and all manner of intricate weaponry to bring to bear on any who defied their will.

The Iceguard were feared throughout the Icemark. Few

ever fought lengthy pitched battles against them, such an attempt was folly.

'Prepared to do her bidding I hope?' Anvireon said. His voice was sly.

Imgaril turned to regard him.

'Loyal subjects such as we are always prepared,' he replied. 'What news of the far north, Anvireon, jailer of Icemark?'

'I speak on to her to whom my loyalty lies,' Anvireon replied. 'And only to her. I would not entrust such potent information to a mere lackey such as you.'

Imgaril went to draw his sword, but Zarashand held him back.

'Leave him,' Zarashand said. 'He is not worth the effort you would expend. We all know why the Heartstealer keeps him far away from the battles that must be fought …'

That provoked a chuckle from Lorelorn and Fangrorn.

'You pride yourself in your wars and skirmishes,' Anvireon replied. 'Yet, it is I who guard the true treasures of the Empress, I alone.'

'And alone you will remain,' Imgaril said.

Before the warriors, the inner doors of the fortress opened of their own accord, swinging back and crashing into place with an echoing clang. She stood within the threshold, the same as ever.

In form she remained a beautiful young woman, well-endowed in her feminine charms, disarming and alluring. Her skin was pale and flawless, only her eyes gave a suggestion that many more years lay upon her that might be perceived at a casual glance. She tossed her hair and then strode towards them.

As one they bowed the knee before her.

Lightning crackled overhead.

'Rise,' she commanded, gesturing with one hand.

They did as she bid.

'I have new instructions for you,' she said, pacing before them, a habit they were long familiar with.

They all bowed their heads as they knew she expected.

'The time to subdue the Icemark is come,' she said, her voice proud and haughty. 'The Fey are impotent within their precious forests, squabbling amongst themselves. The Dwarves have been riddled by civil war and weak leadership. The Giants reel from the attacks we have already subjected them to and the Barbarians nibble at their borders …'

None of the Iceguard warriors spoke a word, but the question was within all their minds.

'Yes … you would do well to ask,' Shareth laughed. 'What of the hated Moonprince who slew my father? He has tried and failed to turn the people of Icemark to his whim. The Fey you might expect to be well deposed to him and so they were, but they are weak and craven. To the Dwarves he sent his emissary, but all she did was weaken their resolve. He never reached the Giants, for the Barbarians have defied him and banished him from their lands. His quest is in ruins before it has even begun. Now it is time to take advantage of his failure.'

The warriors didn't respond, Shareth's own euphoria was powerful enough.

'Icemark is ripe for the taking,' she said, stopping in her pacing and turning to face them. 'The time is now. Listen to my orders and carry them out immediately.'

The warriors nodded in accord.

'Imgaril, take your forces to the west. Consolidate our gains there and harass the Giants further, I want them to know no peace. They will have to contend with attacks from the north and south. If you take a fortress or city, then raze it! Burn the ground. Your objective is to take the City of Carangrane. There you will search for the Crown of Varenand, it must lie in that fortress! Where else could the giants have hidden it?

Find it and bring it to me. My powers will then be beyond the reach of any others.'

'Zarashand, Glormarg, you will take your forces through the lands we have conquered, down between the arms of the Mountains of Anvulane and Anvormane, pushing the Giants before you, this will force them into the clutches of the Barbarians. But then we will pause, not stepping a foot into the Barbarians lands, old or claimed. On the Plains of Thenorn we will halt. Let the Barbarians do our work for us ...'

Shareth paused for a moment.

'Fangrorn, your task lies to the south and east. Assemble your armies and invade the realm of the Dwarves. I will punish them for not turning to my side when they were given a clear choice. You will sweep through the Plains of Imoril and take the City of Carorthay, he has long stood against my plans and now gets his reward. Then take the realm of the Dwarves by proceeding west through their lands. They will not have the time to prepare a defence. Destroy their capital Glormane! Continue on until you reach the Pass of the Carormarg.

Fangrorn nodded.

'Lorelorn, in your hands I leave the defence of my homelands. Guard the Frozen Empire in case of any treacherous attacks or strategy I might have overlooked.'

Lorelorn bowed in acknowledgement.

She paced to the end of the line, looking at Anvireon for a moment, before turning back to the others.

'And of the Fey-girl,' she asked. 'Has she been found?'

None of the Icelords responded.

'Then where is she?' Shareth hissed, pacing back and forth before them. 'She seeks to find my treasure no doubt, she will head ever northwards.'

'Shall we organise patrols and search for her?' Imgaril said.

'I have resources in the south of my realm,' Lorelorn said. 'I can cover all the lands north and west of Anvulane. If she seeks the boy and is being led towards him, surely she must come through my lands … through Farorn.'

'Yes,' Shareth replied. 'She may already be within my domains and she must be found. Lorelorn! It is your responsibility to find this girl. The rest of you will subdue the Icemark as I have ordered.'

Lorelorn bowed again.

'You will seize her,' Shareth said, pointing to Lorelorn. 'Find her and end her, I want the jewel she carries, nothing more.'

'You say she is a sorceress herself,' Lorelorn said. 'Can she be seized if she has such powers?'

'Scared of a Fey-girl?' Imgaril asked, under his breath.

'No bickering,' Shareth snapped. 'I expect better of you all.'

Imgaril subsided.

'Lorelorn is right to question this,' Shareth said. 'She is no mere Fey-girl, her powers are strong enough to have wrecked my plans for the Dwarves.' She smiled and looked at Lorelorn. 'But fear not. I have the measure of the girl now, and I will provide you all with what you need to carry out my orders.'

Lorelorn bowed low. After a moment the other Icelords did the same.

Shareth took a deep breath, her eyes closing and her fists clenching tight. As the Icelords remained bowed before her she trembled as if with fury, her face contorting with pain.

A cry escaped her lips as she wrestled with elemental powers known only to her.

With a shrill yell, Shareth gestured in the air. A flickering sphere of cyan light pulsed before her. She reached within it, plucking out golden chains with dark gems dangling from them, gasping with the effort.

One by one she draped the chains over the necks of the Icelords. The gems hung low and heavy on them, dark hued obsidian, but with the barest flicker of cyan sparkles scattered about them.

'I have given you all a measure of my powers,' she said, her breathing still laboured. 'These are potent indeed. You will use them to subdue our enemies. The gems will respond to your commands as they respond to mine. This will aid you in battle, or in the pursuit of this errant sorceress. Guard them with your lives, for they are perilous.'

She gestured for them to rise.

'We thank you and will do as you command, Empress,' they all intoned.

Shareth took several deep breaths before standing straight once more.

'And how is my treasure?' she asked, turning her attention to Anvireon. 'Does he pine still?'

'His cries are piteous,' Anvireon said. 'You have beguiled him with your beauty and charm, my Empress.'

'Of course,' Shareth replied. 'And if this Fey-girl does ever see him again, she will find that he no longer has space in his heart for her, and she will discover more about him, even less to her taste.'

Shareth ran a hand across her midriff and laughed before turning around, her cloak billowing out around her.

'So finally … here are my orders for you,' she said, pointing to Anvireon. He moved to her and she whispered in his ear, the sound of her words like the hiss of a snake.

'It shall be done,' Anvireon answered, as he stepped back

The Lords bowed once more.

'Zarashand, Glormarg – I shall join you in the attack on the south, but we will hold back, letting the Giants and the Barbarians fall upon each other until both sides are fatally weakened. Only then will I give the order to proceed. Yes, I will be with you, our enemies will have seen no wrath the equal of what I intend to unleash upon them. They will perish amidst their fear, only now realising who they should have sworn loyalty to!

'Imgaril will then join us fresh from the demise of the Giants, and then our strength shall be deployed against the Barbarians themselves. Fangrorn, having despatched the Dwarves will join us as we enter the realm of the Barbarians. With our full might combined, we will sweep through their lands and subjugate them. The City of Imgorad will fall and their power will be broken forever!

Shareth raised her arms.

'Then all that remains will be the hated Fey and their idle Moonprince. We will burn their precious forests and torch their sacred places. With no allies they will no longer have the strength to resist us. Icemark will belong to me. With all potential sources of support cut down, will I have my vengeance upon this Moonprince! I will wreak devastation on all he holds dear. Only then will my father's revenge be assured. That will be sweetness itself to savour.'

She stepped back.

'Go now! You have your commands! Subdue the Icemark!'

Chapter Fifteen

Rorthron the Wise stands in the Mountains of Anvormane looking north-west.

Far to the south, the sun was rising on the City of Lorangriel. As befitted a city of the Fey it was ornately wrought with lofty spires and minarets, its walls bright white in the early sunlight. The sky above was clear and blue.

The vale in which the city stood was both peaceful and pastoral. The area had never known much in the way of strife, shielded from the wars in the north by the entire bulk of the Forest of Fangrim and bulwarked from the east and south by mountains and the Frozen Wastes. The greater extent of the realm of the Fey lay between the city and the Barbarians to the west and no Barbarians had ventured this far east in living memory. Little conflict of any kind had ever reached these parts, the fortresses hereabouts guarded by only a few warriors out of a sense of duty and respect to tradition.

Here the Fey were at peace, the rumours of war and conflict far away.

Thus it was, with some surprise, that Lorangriel himself saw the banners of a Fey army approaching his city. The devices emblazoned upon them were easy enough to read, the banners of Imgorthand himself, leader of the south-eastern Fey, stood at the fore.

Orders were given to make ready for surprise guests and a sense of anticipation filled the corridors and streets of the city. Lorangriel knew that Imgorthand had been summoned to a Fey council by Imorthorn himself. Some decisions had been made.

Imgorthand rode in at the head of the army and Lorangriel went to meet him, bowing low in the custom of the Fey.

'My Liege,' Lorangriel said. 'You've returned early from the Council of the Fey.'

'I have,' Imgorthand said. 'We have work to do. First, I have hungry Fey here and weary horses. Let them be seen to and we will talk further.'

Lorangriel summoned servants and soon the city was busy attending to the visiting army. Imgorthand and Lorangriel retired within the city, walking up to Lorangriel's chambers.

There, before a roaring fire, they both took food and wine, before Imgorthand explained his purpose.

'War?' Lorangriel echoed in dismay. 'With the Heartstealer? Open warfare? Has Imorthorn taken leave of his senses?'

'A question I suggest you do not repeat in his company,' Imgorthand answered, raising his eyebrows.

Lorangriel nodded. 'Forgive my impertinence, but … this tale. A strange girl out of the south with magical powers, sent off on a quest into the very realm of the Heartstealer … a Moonprince from a forgotten land … my scribes, bards and scholars could not write such an entertaining fiction even if I asked them to … and yet you believe it is true?'

'The girl I met,' Imgorthand said. 'She was real enough. As for the Moonprince, Imorthorn has decreed it, thus is it true … unless we choose to defy our leader.'

'Of course not,' Lorangriel replied. 'But to pitch us in direct defiance of the Heartstealer … we do not have the strength! What is the strategy?'

'Imorthorn claims that this Moonprince rallied the forces of his homeland,' Imgorthand explained. 'A land called Midnight beyond the Frozen Wastes to the south. There he struck down the Witchking of that realm, slaying him and freeing their land from tyranny. It seems the Witchking was none other than the Heartstealer's very own father.'

'And he seeks to do the same here? Vanquishing … her?'

'So it seems.' Imgorthand said. 'I counselled restraint, but … well …'

Lorangriel sat back in his chair. 'But we don't have the strength to contest the Iceguard … and there are many weary leagues of hostile terrain between us and them. What of the Dwarves, the Barbarians … the Giants?'

'This Moonprince sends envoys to them too. As I departed I heard he had already reached the Barbarians.'

'You think he can convince them to rally to his banner?'

'I have no idea,' Imgorthand answered. 'Imorthorn seems convinced, he is the only one of us who has spoken to this Moonprince … Lord Luxor is his name.'

'This Luxor came to the City of Imorthorn?'

'No,' Imgorthand replied. 'More magic it seems. A ring of some potency worn by Luxor gives him the power to vouchsafe messages at great distance. No, I don't understand more than that.'

'I have heard rumours and ancient tales of such Talismans,' Lorangriel said. 'But to hear that our fortune may depend on such a thing …'

'Leaves me in some disquiet,' Imgorthand said. 'But we have our orders.'

'My Liege?'

'We are to summon our forces and assemble at the City of Imorthorn as soon as they can be mustered. Send riders to Thorthand, Ingormiel and Thigrand instructing them to assemble their armies and ride swiftly here. I have sent Morildrane to do the same with the other southern Fey. We must be ready to ride back to Imorthorn before the moon is out.'

'It will be done as you say,' Lorangriel answered, pulling a cord to summon his servants. 'What do you think awaits us?'

Imgorthand sighed. 'I know not,' he answered. 'But it will be the severest test of Imorthorn's leadership, no doubt.'

Imulorn and Imelorn struggled on, pushed and cajoled from behind by their captors. They were forced on throughout the day, not being given food or water as they were marched into the hills.

Imelorn was struggling. He stumbled, falling forwards on his side on the dusty path only to be wrestled back up and forced on. Before long, he stumbled again.

'He needs a rest!' Imulorn yelled at the Dwarves who tried to get him back on his feet. They looked over to their leader, who nodded. Imelorn and Imulorn were left alone as the other Dwarves shared out water and food.

'How are you?' Imulorn asked, keeping his voice low.

Imelorn looked at him. His face was a mess, the wound in his head had opened again and was bleeding, one eye was almost swollen shut.

'Never better.'

'What happened to you anyway?' Imulorn asked.

'Whilst you were snoring away, I tried to escape,' Imelorn replied, with a wince. 'Didn't quite go to plan.'

'Well, we're going to need a better plan,' Imulorn muttered looking around himself. 'Once we're inside the city, we won't be coming out.'

'How many of them are there?'

'I counted eight.'

'Not good odds,' Imelorn replied.

'It's not just about us,' Imulorn whispered back. 'I overheard them talking, some kind of attack on Carorthay is planned in the next few days. Could be these northern scum, or it might be the Icelords … either way we've got to get a warning out.'

Imelorn nodded. 'Can you get free?'

'I'm working on it.'

'When you do, I'll be your distraction.'

Imulorn looked at him. 'We're both getting out of here.'

Imelorn chuckled. 'Brother, we both know that's not going to happen. I can barely walk. I won't get far even if we did manage to escape … but I'll take down as many of these hagspawn traitors as I can.'

'I'm not leaving you behind,' Imulorn snapped.

'Then the warning isn't going to reach Carorthay, is it?' Imelorn answered. 'Don't be a fool. You know what's got to be done.'

Imulorn looked away and shook his head.

He's right …

In the far north of their realm, Obigrorn counted the warriors of the Giants who assembled. Backed by a small ridge of mountains, Obigrorn's fortress guarded access into the heartlands of the Giants, the narrow Vale of Thudrane. There was no other way around to the north or the south. The mountains of Anvormane, impassable as they were, saw to that. For an invading force, only this route was possible. To take it would require a massive force of arms.

Which is precisely what the Heartstealer deploys against us!

Obigrorn had received missives throughout the day, each one more depressing than the last. It seemed the Heartstealer's forces, army upon army of Icelord warriors had swept out of the east in a well co-ordinated and lethal strike against the defences of the giants. Word of the defeat at Ulformane had come first, with the evil news of the death of Carangrane himself.

Then came news of the collapse of the eastern defences. Thormuk, Imatron and the City of Varangrim, all had fallen to the Icelords within days, overwhelmed by sheer numbers. Some accounts suggested that the Heartstealer herself had accompanied her forces to Varangrim. There was talk of magic and fell powers, evil sorcery, darkness and death.

Of their realm to the far north, Obigrorn had heard no news. The fate of Imgaron, Glormeon and Asorthane was unknown. No word had been received. Obigrorn feared the worst.

News from the south was no more encouraging. The defeated forces from Ulformane had rallied and assembled at the City of Imgenarg, under the leadership of Varangrim, but they were two days march away and still pursued by the forces that had already defeated them once. The giants were out manoeuvred and outnumbered, caught between the crushing jaws of the Heartstealer's forces.

Obigrorn marched about his fortress, taking stock of numbers, provisions and weapons. The news was dire. Scant thousands had managed to escape from the battles to the east; all bore tales of defeat and destruction.

Worse, the armies of the Heartstealer were converging on his fortress. He had perhaps a day before his lands, deep in the heart of the realm the Giants considered completely safe only scant days before, would be the frontline of the invasion.

Three thousand, no more ... and all weary and ill-provisioned. We have lost perhaps a third of our territory already. Long she has planned this ... but what does she hope to achieve?

Obigrorn had sent out runners to gauge the size of the incoming force, but he did not expect the news to be any better. The armies of the Heartstealer were circumnavigating the Forest of Felun, approaching from the north and south, converging on his position.

And if Shareth does ride with her armies against us … if she accompanies them surely she intends to cast us down, eradicate us completely!

By noon some of the runners had returned. They looked weary, having spared no speed in bring back news of what they had seen. Obigrorn listened, with a grim expression.

'They ride swiftly,' one said, reporting on events in the north. 'They number ten thousand strong at least, with siege weapons in their midst and supplies running back and forth to the Forest of Farorn across the hills. They are led by one of Shareth's own, Imgaril himself! The City of Varangrim is lost and nothing stands between them and us. They ride direct to us, and they will be here by dawn tomorrow.'

'Ten thousand …' Obigrorn muttered in dismay.

The runners from the south had little comfort either.

'Varangrim himself remains alive,' he said. 'A remnant of our forces has reached Imgenarg and still holds that City, but another army of the Heartstealer's forces have cut off their passage north. They cannot reach us with that army between us and them.'

'And how strong is that second force?' Obigrorn asked.

'Eight thousand at least,' the Runner replied.

Obigrorn sighed. 'Then we cannot reach them either. If we attempt to do so, we leave the gateway to our homelands wide open.'

Obigrorn thanked them both. He sat down upon the stone throne that his grandsire had hewn long ago. His father had sat upon it before him … and now it was his.

The Heartstealer extends her claws. I can defend my Fortress as tradition dictates … but the armies of the Heartstealer will doubtless combine … I cannot prevent that. With such power at her command we will fall, it is merely a matter of time. With this fortress fallen … what then? The Heartstealer marches into our lands and takes them forever. This is the end of the Giants! This cannot be allowed.

He could think of only one alternative.

Strength remains in the City of Carangrane. It is difficult to assail, high in the mountains, perhaps the last refuge of our might. If we could consolidate what forces remain to us ... perhaps we have a chance to resist her ... a fairer chance than we stand here at least, outflanked and outnumbered.

Obigrorn looked about him. The stone visages of his ancestors, carved back through history looked down upon him, but they were mute and offered no advice.

To save my people I must abandon my home ... and leave it open to desecration by the foe. Yet, I do not see another choice ...

'I must ask for more messages to be sent,' he said, after a moment. 'Arrange for runners to be sent to the cities of Carangrane and Anvildrak and the fortresses of Berorthim, Thangrorn and Finorn. Summon all able bodied warriors to the last defence of Carangrane. We will rendezvous there and thus make our stand against this foe. Run also to Imgenarg and advise Varangrim of what I have decided.'

'Yes, Great One.'

'Announce to all here that we march for Carangrane. The Fortress is to be emptied of weapons, provisions and anything that might be useful to the Heartstealer by nightfall. Then we march as well. See to it.'

The runners nodded and left him.

Obigrorn looked once more at the graven statues of his ancestors.

'Forgive me,' he said. 'Evil times require evil choices.'

Tarithel continued her weary walk through the dark tunnels

of the Icemark. The journey through the passageway was dull and uneventful. The smooth floor continued throughout, making no obstacle to her progress. As far as she could tell, though there were a few twists and turns, the passageway ran true to the north.

I wonder why these passages were built, and by whom? Whoever they were, they had some great skill to cut the rocks so smoothly.

The passageways showed little signs of use. There was dust on the ground, undisturbed until she and Álainn made their imprints in it. Nothing adorned the smooth walls. Here and there she could see different types of rock that made up the sides of the passageway, curious undulations and twists and folds in the rock itself. The passageway ignored them though, ploughing on straight into the rock.

There was nothing to hear either, not even the faint trickling of an underground spring or the creak of a shifting rock.

She was beginning to wonder if the passageway would ever come to an end when she found herself noticing some faint footprints in the ground beneath her feet. Here and there, the dust had been disturbed.

Others have come this far at least. But when? It could have been years ago …

She stopped for a moment to listen, but still could hear nothing. She pushed on, staying more alert.

Within a few hundred yards she emerged into another cavern, the large metal oil burners leapt into life once more, bathing the area with torchlight from their flames. It seemed indistinguishable from the last cavern she had been in, giving Tarithel the unsettling impression that she'd been walking in circles for hours.

There was another compass rose on the floor, but this was one was scuffed and marked with usage. There was a tunnel to her left, heading west, another one led northwards. It seemed most of the traffic had gone that way. The dust was still thick though, whoever had come this way had not done so recently.

But it was used … why isn't it any longer? Perhaps the entrances are closed …

That gave her a chill. Suppose the exits had collapsed like the one she had come through? There was nothing she could do but go on and find out.

Tiredness had crept up on her through the last few hours. She couldn't tell what time it really was, but she must have been walking for hours and hours. She was weary and so was Álainn. It was time to stop and rest.

She saw to Álainn first, feeding her with a bag of rolled oats she had brought along. Álainn looked mournfully at her and she patted her flank.

'I'll find you some kind of meadow once we get out of these benighted tunnels,' she said. 'Sorry there's nothing comfortable to sleep on.'

Álainn still looked miserable; she stood where she had stopped, appearing to doze. Tarithel felt the same.

She ate a meagre meal and then broke out her sleeping mat and blankets, arranging them in the corner of the cavern just away from the southern entrance she'd come through. If anybody did come through the other passageways that would at least give her a little time to react. She placed her knife beside her and curled up in the gloom, exhausted, drifting into an uneasy sleep.

A cold wind blew through the Hills of Thashil in the far north of the dwarven realm.

'Up and on your feet!'

The northern Dwarves were back on their feet and getting

ready to resume the march.

'You get your hands free yet?' Imelorn whispered.

Imulorn shook his head.

'Time is running out, brother.'

'I know, I know …'

'Get moving!'

Imulorn and Imelorn were shoved along, stumbling forward in the midst of the other Dwarves. Even as they did so, they heard snatches of conversation.

'… been spotted!'

'Not going to outrun them on this terrain …'

The path they were following was winding up the side of the hills, with a precipitate drop growing on their right, falling away into the valley below. Both were shoved in the back and pushed onwards.

Imelorn tilted his head, raising his eyebrows and gesturing at the drop.

Imulorn sparred it a glance.

'Are you insane?' he said back.

Imelorn grinned, faked a stumble and then threw himself over the edge.

'Damn you!' Imulorn cursed, yelled and hurled himself after him.

For a moment he heard shouts and yells, but then he hit the ground hard and started rolling, unable to stop himself, his arms still tied behind his back. The world spun about him in a dizzying way … ground, sky, rocks, clouds. Everything was a blur of motion.

Rocks!

The impact knocked the breath from him, pain shocking up his chest and shoulders as they took the brunt of the force. He tried to shield his head as best he could.

The whirling motion came to an abrupt halt when he plunged into a thicket somewhere down the hill side. He landed hard on his front, gasping for breath, but relieved to find himself intact. There was pain everywhere, but none of it seemed to indicate a broken limb. He lay still for a moment as the landscape continued to spin about him, clenching his eyes shut as the nausea swirled.

After a few deep breaths he raised his head and looked around.

'Stay down!'

Somehow Imelorn was nearby. A moment later they were side by side, hidden in the dense undergrowth.

Imulorn frowned. He could hear shouts and screams from somewhere above them.

'What's going on?' he asked.

'Nothing good,' Imelorn replied.

Now they could hear the clash of axe and shield, the sounds of battle ringing from somewhere high above them. It continued for a minute and then went quiet, with only the faint sounds of distant spoken words drifting over the wind.

Then footsteps, growing closer. The brothers crouched as low as they could.

'Bit late for that,' a new voice said. 'You can come out of hiding now.'

Imulorn looked at Imelorn, who shrugged. They were in no shape to escape again. Slowly, they got to their feet.

Another Dwarf was standing just beyond the thicket, hands at his hips, regarding them from under bushy eyebrows.

'Thought I saw you two in the midst of that pack of northerners,' he said, a grin twisting his features. 'I'd recognise those bellies anywhere!'

Imulorn and Imelorn stared in shock, surprise and increasing joy. The face was a familiar one, a leader of the eastern Dwarves and a friend of their liege, Thigrak himself.

'Hagudril!' they both yelled.

'Aye,' Hagudril said. 'And Thigrak will not be best pleased

to note the company you've been keeping, what are you doing here in the north?'

'It's a long story,' Imulorn said. 'And we have much to tell.'

Varangrim and Rorthron stood on one of the towers of the Fortress of Imgenarg.

'We have not had any of the Wise visit us in living memory,' Varangrim said. 'Our erstwhile leader, Carangrane, may have done, but his wisdom has failed now and our people …'

'The Giants will endure,' Rorthron said.

'You have given us hope in a dark time,' Varangrim said. 'I have inherited his legacy, I would not like to preside over the end of our people.'

'I am sorry for his death,' Rorthron acknowledged. 'I very much hoped to meet him, he might have had clues to a riddle in which our salvation lies.'

'How so?' Varangrim asked.

'I uncovered ancient knowledge of the Icemark from the Wise of this land,' Rorthron said. 'It sent me on this quest to you. A legend of Icemark I suppose it would seem to you. I hoped to find it, to further thwart the Heartstealer's rise to power. I was told it lay in the hands of Carangrane.'

'Then tell me,' Varangrim said. 'If it's within our power, we might still achieve it.'

Rorthron nodded. 'Have you heard of the Crowns of the Icemark?'

'Old stories,' Varangrim said. 'Magic and strange tales for the campfire …'

'They are real,' Rorthron answered. 'Much of Shareth's power is provided by these … they are called Talismans by the Wise. There were many of them long ago, given to kings, queens, lords and ladies. Most are lost, but two she has in her possession.'

'Magic Crowns?' Varangrim echoed.

'And in the hands of a sorceress, potent indeed.'

'What does this have to do with Carangrane?'

'I was told,' Rorthron said. 'He had one in his possession. It is likely the reason that Shareth moved so swiftly and harshly against your folk. She, too, must have learned that it lay within your lands ...'

Varangrim stared at Rorthron.

'Then our people are being slaughtered for some bauble of the Wise?'

'Shareth's lust for power consumes her,' Rorthron said. 'I have fought this evil before, it cares not for people of any race.'

Varangrim sighed.

'If Carangrane did possess such a thing,' he answered. 'He never mentioned it to me. A giant would never wear a crown anyway, such trinkets are the delight of Barbarians and Dwarves.'

Rorthron sighed. 'Then any knowledge he might have had died with him. Such a Talisman might turn the tide of this conflict. Even merely keeping it from Shareth would be a boon.'

A runner approached them with a message. Varangrim took it, pondering its contents.

'More tidings?' Rorthron enquired.

'A missive from Obigrorn,' Varangrim replied. 'The Heartstealer's forces move against him and he has decided to retreat to the city of Carangrane to make a stand against them rather than fight in the open. He has little choice in the matter. He will soon be besieged.'

'Carangrane's own city?' Rorthron asked. 'Then Shareth's intentions are clear. She must be stopped.'

'Carangrane did tell me that Shareth once went freely about

our lands long ago,' Varangrim said, 'in the time of his grandsires and beyond … and that she was seeking something. He did not know what it was, but …'

'Then she did know even then,' Rorthron murmured. 'Or suspected at least.'

'Our grandsires grew suspicious by all accounts,' Varangrim continued. 'They stopped her and I heard tell she was not pleased about it. So she has laid her plans for many moons, building up her strength whilst ours ebbed … until she was ready.' He looked aside for a moment. 'Carangrane did speak of treasures though, ancient artefacts …'

Rorthron looked around.

'Where?'

'In the vaults of his city,' Varangrim whispered. 'The City of Carangrane.'

'Then I must go immediately,' Rorthron answered. 'If there is the slightest chance that …'

'It will be besieged by the Heartstealer's forces before you can reach it,' Varangrim said. 'She holds the lands to the north, the only way into our homelands is via the Vale of Thudrane and she has much strength deployed there according to Obigrorn. Even now, the forces that defend that area are forced to retreat against her overwhelming strength. We have lost the north of our realm already. You cannot hope to reach it in time.'

'Show me a map,' Rorthron replied.

They retreated indoors, Varangrim gestured to a mural on the wall which depicted the land of the Giants.

'We are here,' Varangrim said, jabbing a huge finger at the map. 'Carangrane lies directly west as the crow flies.'

'Then it is not far.'

'You cannot cross the Mountains of Anvormane,' Varangrim said. 'That is certain death, they rival the desolation of the Mountains of Anvulane themselves. They are impassable, and have long been a great defence for us against the powers of the east.'

'Not for you perhaps,' Rorthron said with a smile. 'But the Wise have ways to travel swiftly and unseen. I can reach that city ere the Heartstealer's forces arrive.'

'Then you must be swift indeed,' Varangrim said. 'I will give you leave to do so and missives to take there, if you will. A message to our kin delivered in time might even save our homelands, or give them some fresh hope at the very least.'

'Of course,' Rorthron said. 'Then my course is set. Write what you will, I will leave before the day is out.'

'And what would you have us do?' Varangrim asked.

'I am not sure,' Rorthron replied. 'I would hold this city for now, but whilst the situation with the Barbarian's remains undecided it will be best to wait. I will do whatever I can to safeguard your homeland from the Heartstealer and prevent the Talismans falling into her clutches. If we prevail I will bring back what strength I can.'

'If you manage all that,' Varangrim said, with a nod. 'Then the favour of the Giants will be upon you forever more. Save my homeland and the pledge of the Giants will be made to this Moonprince of yours. All speed and power to you, Rorthron of the Wise!'

The army of the Free and the army of the Barbarians stood not far from the Tower of Thorthorn, its shadow long in the morning light. Hills rose behind the tower to the east, with mountains to the north and the south. Torinarg and Careneon faced Luxor.

Careneon stepped forward.

'Here I must take my leave of you,' Careneon said. 'The lands further east are in dispute and I will not provoke the

Fey at this time. They regard these places as their own.'

Luxor nodded in response.

'I will speak well of your conduct in this matter when I reach them,' he said. 'Your conduct has always been honourable.

Careneon sighed.

'I wish you well, Luxor, Moonprince of Midnight,' he said. Torinarg bowed beside him. 'Yet by decree of my leader Imgorad, you are forbidden from entering our lands again on pain of death. You understand this?'

Luxor nodded.

'I do.'

'Farewell then,' Careneon said.

Luxor took a step forward.

'She will betray you,' he said. 'Perhaps not this day, but in a day that will not be long delayed. Beware the evil tongues of Kahudrak and Kahudrarg. Your people will suffer at the Heartstealer's hand. I know the evil that drives her, I have battled it for many moons in my fight against her father. It is … not of this world … unrelenting, unresting. It will not stop until she has everything she has sworn to take, or she lies slain upon the field of battle.'

'I do not doubt your words,' Careneon said. 'But my hands are tied.'

'I will respect Imgorad's decree,' Luxor said, 'But should he reconsider, there will be no hesitation from me. I would stand with you all against her, should you let me.'

Careneon took a deep breath.

'Then …' he said. 'I hope … and fear … that our next meeting will not be long delayed.'

Luxor nodded. Careneon and Torinarg turned and walked away, their armies making ready to depart. Luxor watched them go with a downcast look upon his face.

Hagudril had seen to Imulorn and Imelorn's injuries as best he could in the wilderness. They were cleaned, treated with salve and bandaged up. The elder Dwarf stood with perhaps a hundred of his warriors in a camp below the hills.

'You were fortunate I was patrolling my lands to the north,' Hagudril said. 'I only go as far as the Stones of Asudrane, but since the battle at Glormane's City everyone has been restless. I saw smoke not far from the temple and decided to investigate. As well for you I did. You led us on a merry chase.'

'We are grateful,' Imulorn said, 'But we have urgent news. We overheard conversations. The northern Dwarves were speaking of an attack on Carorthay within days ...'

'By whom?' Hagudril asked.

'It wasn't clear,' Imulorn replied. 'But they seemed confident enough.'

'Icelords perhaps?' Hagudril said, after pondering the news for a moment. 'The Heartstealer will doubtless have heard about our squabbles and perhaps considers us an easy target. Anvarorn fought against Glormane so I heard ... if he sides with the Icelords then Carorthay could easily be threatened ...'

'Either way we'd best march quickly to Carorthay,' Imelorn grunted.

Hagudril whistled and two young Dwarves approached.

'My fastest runners,' Hagudril explained and directed his conversation to them. 'Run straight to Carorthay but stay south of the Mountains of Kahorthak, stop for nothing. Tell him to prepare for an attack and that we will march to him as soon as we are able.'

The two Dwarves bowed, grabbed a pack of provisions each and made off across the plain.

'They should reach him before the night is out,' Hagudril said. 'They are swift enough. We will march too … if you're ready?'

'We must be,' Imulorn said, looking at his brother. 'Time is short.'

'We'll reach my Fortress today and summon my entire army,' Hagudril said. 'Then we'll see if that's enough to prevent this attack … wherever it comes from.'

Tarithel woke in the darkness. For a moment panic seized her, she couldn't remember where she was. The blackness around her was complete. Her heart hammered in her chest and sweat chilled on her skin. She sat up with a shriek that echoed back to her from the gloom.

The faint illumination that had accompanied her in her travels underground flickered back to life around her, revealing the soft outlines of the cavern.

It seems to sense there's someone here …

Memories came back, the Dwarves, Imulorn and Imelorn, who had escorted her to the entrance of the underground passageways.

I hope they're all right!

Then the weary trudge through the passageways themselves.

A day already I guess … is it morning outside? It's impossible to tell.

Álainn nuzzled her and she patted her muzzle. As she sat up, the hairs on the back of her neck rose and she froze for a moment.

Something woke me …

There was a sound, on the edge of hearing. Tarithel strained to listen, wondering for long moments whether she was hearing something real or not, but after a few moments she was sure.

Something is in the tunnel.

Whatever the noise was, it was coming from the southern tunnel, the one she had walked through before she'd slept. It wasn't footsteps, voices or anything she recognised, but some kind of faint, keening wail, rising and falling in pitch.

For a moment she thought it might be the wind whistling through the rocks … but there wasn't a breath of motion in the air around her.

It was getting louder. Soon there could be no doubt she was hearing something and it was heading toward her.

Tarithel gathered up her things and arranged them on Álainn. The horse was stomping its hooves in agitation, its hair soaked with sweat and its eyes wide with fear.

I think we should go!

She led Álainn onwards into the north passageway, walking as fast as she dared in the dimness. The noise faded behind her and was soon lost in the dark.

Rorthron's journey had taken him deep into the mountains. He had been forced to leave his horse behind, there was no path that it could take; the way was obscure and treacherous. Snow blustered around him in a freezing gale, the tumultuous wind threatening to cast him from the precipitous heights.

The weather was fickle, damp and rain swept one moment, misty the next, then snow-laden storm clouds would descend and wreak their fury upon him. No others could have survived such a passage, there was an ancient power upon the mountains that was laced with a malevolence older even than the rocks that composed the craggy outcrops he had to negotiate.

Even with his great reserves of strength his progress was slow and the will of the mountains indomitable. They had existed long before the peoples of Icemark and they would exist long after they had all perished. Such fury as they could muster resided deep within their very cores and was inexhaustible.

Yet, step by step, yard by yard and league by league, Rorthron made his way onwards, his own spirit defying the will of the mountains. Whether it was the will of the Wise of Icemark that helped him on his way, or whether by his own reserves of courage and conviction, Rorthron gazed upon a fair valley with the mountains behind him to the east and dappled sunlight playing on more pleasant lands.

As he descended to the foot hills, the snow released its grip. A forest stretched out before him, but above that, nestled in the sides of the mountains themselves, Rorthron could see a city.

That it was built by the Giants was unmistakable, the lack of curves, the sheerness of its construction and the blocky robust design gave it away.

The City of Carangrane!

Rorthron squinted into the distance. A dark stain could be seen on the valley before the City, perhaps two or three leagues beyond it. Rorthron was familiar with such sights, having seen them many times before. An army, vast in number, seen at a great distance.

The bloody sword of battle will soon bring death in this domain, I have no time to rest!

Tarithel hurried on through the tunnel, leading Álainn behind her. The tunnel had twisted and turned at intervals, but she'd had no choice in which way she went. Now though, the passageway was rising at last and she noticed that the rock she was travelling through was different, more coarse and sandy than the smooth rock below.

Rising can only be a good thing. I hope there is a way out somewhere soon!

The darkness was playing on her nerves. She was conscious of the weight of rock and stone all about her. She found herself ducking for no reason, as if the vast mass above her were poised to crush her. Her body was trembling and the urge to run ahead in a panicked rush just to get out of the tunnels was growing to fever pitch.

She forced her feet onwards, concentrating on placing one foot in front of the other, step by step as the oppressive darkness tore at her mind and thoughts. Fear was gnawing at her. It seemed irrational, growing throughout the long hours of trudging through the mind-numbing tedium of the tunnels. She couldn't stop from shaking. It was taking all her concentration just to keep walking and leading Álainn onwards.

It came as a blessed relief when she stumbled out into another cavern. Flames leapt alive around her as before, illuminating yet another of the junction points for the tunnels, complete with the compass rose on the floor.

This one seemed unmarked, the dust heavy on the floor. She had to sweep it aside to gauge where she was. Before her, a rough stairway led upwards out of sight.

She stopped to give the horse some water and then drank a little herself, feeling a little better.

But where am I?

She took the roughly drawn map the Dwarves had given her and inspected it. From what she could make out, she had crossed underneath the mountains. The compass rose showed exits east and west.

Which means this exit is not the one I must use! It rises right into a fortress of the Iceguard!

She squinted at the map in the faint light.

Thildresh, whoever he might be ... he's best avoided. I must seek the palace the Dwarves spoke of ... Lorigriel.

If she was reading the map correctly, the Palace lay south and west of where she was.

But only a couple of leagues. I wish I could rest, but the thought of being out of these awful tunnels ...

Without hesitation she plunged onwards, following the left tunnel and heading west.

About the City of Lorangriel, the Fey of the south and east had mustered. Warriors both on horseback and on foot were camped around the City and all manner of provisions were being made ready for the long march north-west to Imorthorn. As the Fey outside the walls prepared their weapons, arms and equipment, their leaders were ensconced within the City, discussing their plans.

The full might of the south-eastern Fey was represented. Imgorthand had authority here and those loyal to him stood around him in the hall. Here was Lorangriel, owner of the City itself, alongside Thorthand, Ingormiel and Thigrand. Morildrane stood alongside his liege, having brought Berormane, Tharand and Imorthesh with him in answer to the summons. In total, some ten thousand Fey warriors were represented.

Greetings were perfunctory; the leaders of the Fey armies had many questions.

'Morildrane summoned us with little explanation,' Berormane said, his voice gruff. 'Rumours of war, freshly kindled ...'

'I heard we have declared war on the Heartstealer!' Tharand cried, his voice high and tremulous. 'Say it is not so?'

Imgorthand looked at Morildrane. 'You have not explained the summons?'

'I thought it best to leave that to you,' Morildrane answered. 'For clarity.'

Imgorthand nodded. 'Very well then,' he said, raising his voice and signalling for attention. 'My country folk, here are the facts as they are known.'

The hubbub died down in anticipation.

Imgorthand took a moment before he spoke.

'Several moons ago, a great storm lashed across Fangrim, sent from the north. Out of season it wracked the mountains and felled many trees in the forest. This was no natural storm, but it was cast out of the far north by the fell sorcery of she who calls herself the Empress of the Frozen Empire.'

'Shareth,' Imorthesh muttered.

'The same,' Imgorthand said. 'Prior to this she had been sending great armies through the lands of the Barbarians on our western flank, Carorthane himself noted their passing. The Barbarians seemed to let these armies through and we assumed some new pact with the Heartstealer and readied our defences to the west. That attack never came, it seemed that those Iceguard armies ventured further south, into a land we thought sundered from our own. A land called Midnight.'

'Midnight?' Thigrand said. 'Beyond the Frozen Wastes?'

'It seems a passage beneath the everlasting ice was found,' Imgorthand replied. 'Those armies made that journey, not to attack us, but to bolster a conflict to the south. We have all heard the stories … A great Witchking of evil in those southern domains. It turned out to be true. That Witchking was none other than the father of Shareth, he who taught her evil crafts and placed her in Icemark.'

'The details are few,' Imgorthand continued. 'But it seems both the men of Midnight … they call themselves the Free … and the Fey of those lands rose up, combined their forces and assailed the might of the Witchking, overthrowing him and casting him down, his power broken.'

'But surely this is good news?' Thorthand said. 'With his power gone, Shareth is weakened, is she not? Is that why we are summoned, to deal with her too?'

'Good news?' Morildrane asked. 'Wait for the whole story, before you call it good.'

Imgorthand held up his hand. 'Patience. Shareth is indeed angered by the demise of her father, and she has sworn bloody vengeance on the one that slew him. A vengeance that may cost the people of Icemark dear.'

'How so?' Ingormiel asked.

'The pieces of the puzzle were slow to be found,' Ingormand said. 'Imorthorn received an emissary from Midnight, a young woman called Tarithel, herself Fey. She told us that Shareth intended to subdue both Icemark and Midnight and that the slayer of the Witchking, a Moonprince of Midnight known as Luxor would soon arrive.'

'This Luxor desires that all the peoples of Icemark rally against Shareth,' Imgorthand said. 'A stance that pitches the Fey on to a war footing. Thus far Imorthorn has agreed to this.'

Rumblings of discontent echoed around the hall.

'Can this Luxor rally the other races where none have succeeded before?' Thigrand asked. 'What if the Barbarians or the Dwarves play some game with us, pledging themselves to the cause but secretly siding with Shareth? Such treachery is in their nature, we all know this! We have seen it!'

'Imorthorn is doubtless aware of the risk,' Imgorthand said. 'And he summons us all in that regard.'

'And what of this emissary,' Thorthand asked. 'A woman from the Fey of Midnight you say? Can we assume there is assistance coming from them?'

Imgorthand looked across at Morildrane.

'... Or not?' Thorthand asked in dismay.

'With your permission?' Morildrane asked, looking back at Imgorthand. He nodded.

'This young woman,' Morildrane said. 'She was exceedingly fair, red-haired and green eyed. Imorthorn himself seemed quite taken with her. As you can imagine, she caused quite the stir in the city. By her account, she had travelled alone from Midnight to our lands – quite the trek, eluding the Barbarians along the way.

'What we did divine was that this Moonprince, this Luxor, brought with him only a token force. A thousand men at arms I believe I heard. There was no indication that any other support might be forthcoming.'

'And Imorthorn has based his decree on this?' Imgormiel asked. 'We know we can't trust the Barbarians or the Dwarves, but we would be well disposed to fellow Fey of another country ... but they do not come?'

'It seems not,' Morildrane replied.

'Then ... what prompted Imorthorn's decision?' Thigrand asked.

Morildrane looked uncomfortable. Imgorthand coughed.

'Morildrane has a theory,' he said. 'He is hesitant to voice it because it implies much that is disquieting. But I will utter it for him. This woman ... Tarithel, spent much time in Imorthorn's company, the pair of them alone. That alone might not arouse suspicion, but she also demonstrated what can only be described as powers of sorcery.'

'Sorcery?' Berormane echoed with a gulp.

'It might be all benign,' Imgorthand said. 'And all to the good of the Fey, yet following her meeting with him the decision to stand directly against Shareth was made forthwith and she departed in secret – heading north and I know not what she intends nor under what orders, if any, she was sent. None of the rest of the council of the Fey were consulted.

Imorthorn acted solely on his own judgement and committed us to this path.'

A muted rumble of conversation filled the room.

'I'm sure there is no true cause for concern,' Morildrane said. 'Imorthorn has always led us well …'

'But sorcery,' Berormane said. 'Could she have bewitched him perhaps? Turned his mind? If she was left with him alone …'

'In such things we cannot be certain,' Morildrane replied.

'Can we trust her story?' Tharand asked. 'Part or all of it. Have any met this Moonprince?'

'None,' Imgorthand replied. 'Imorthorn consults with him via a magic ring.'

'A magic ring!' Lorangriel said. 'This just gets better. We pledge our entire people to a war based on a story and some magic trinkets, who ask us to put our lives at risk yet won't send a force to aid us?'

'Imorthorn is no fool,' Ingormiel answered. 'He will have considered this carefully, surely?'

'We hope,' Lorangriel said. 'Regardless, a dangerous road lies ahead of us.'

'Such concerns as you have I share,' Imgorthand said. 'And I will represent them to Imorthorn when we arrive at his city. For now, we have our orders. Make ready, we depart upon the morrow. It is two days march to Imorthorn, we must not be tardy.'

There were nods from the assembled Fey, but expressions were downcast as they filed out in turn.

'Imorthorn will have to provide better answers for them,' Imgorthand said, rubbing his chin.

'Your concerns are warranted,' Morildrane replied. 'Let us assume this Moonprince and the young woman have been honest with us. Even so, to take a stand against Shareth without some surety that the other races will likewise do so …'

'Seems rash in the extreme,' Imgorthand said, finishing the sentence. 'I hear you, Morildrane. Whilst I fear the Heartstealer as much as any, having her as a distant evil on the edge of perception comforts me more than having her as an active foe.'

Morildrane went to say something, but then stopped.

'You can speak your mind with me,' Imgorthand said. 'I know that look.'

Morildrane nodded.

'I hesitate to speak against the will of my betters,' Morildrane said. 'But if Imorthorn has been … swayed by the words or actions of this woman of the south or by the magic ring of the Moonprince, there are few who can alter the path he has chosen. Carorthane and Carorthay will likely support him out of pure loyalty … my Liege …'

'It might fall to me to challenge him?'

Morildrane looked up. 'You command a great host of the southern and eastern Fey, you are a mighty warrior of renown and have always held the interests of the Fey uppermost. If there were to be a new leader of the Fey, our people would look to you, my Liege.'

'You speak wisdom as ever,' Imgorthand said. 'We go back to Imorthorn now. If the answers are not satisfactory … well then … we will see.'

'Very wise, my Liege,' Morildrane said. 'Very wise indeed.'

The City of Carorthay stood at the most eastern point of the realms of the Dwarves. It stood in the midst of a flat plain, which gave it visibility in all directions. To the east, a day's march away, was the barrier of the Frozen Wastes. To the south, a narrow valley led through the mountains towards the realm of the Fey. To the north, lay the border of the Frozen Empire, the lands of the Icelords.

Just visible on the horizon in that direction was another city. It belonged to Fangrorn, one of the six chief lieutenants of Shareth herself.

The lands hereabouts had seen many battles between the two races, but it had been many long moons since the last one.

Now smoke lingered on the northern horizon and the lights of many fires could be seen at night. Carorthay himself stood on the battlements, looking north, staring into the distance. He had seen many prior battles and he knew the signs well.

An army preparing for war.

Never trust an Icelord ... had only all our people heeded those words!

Hagudril's runners had arrived in the morning with missives of a potential attack, but their news was already old, Carorthay had already prepared his city for a battle he could see was marching towards him. Scouts had yet to report the size of the army that was assembling against him, but he knew the strength of the forces available to him, and they were few.

A messenger ran up to him.

'Sire, Hagudril and his army approaches.'

Carorthay nodded and made his way down from the city walls to the great gates that guarded the entrance. An army of Dwarves was marching towards the gate, and were being greeted with relieved cheers from the Dwarves who stood at the entrance.

Carorthay saw Hagudril himself at the lead, flanked by two other Dwarfs he recognised.

'Hagudril!' he called. 'It is good to see you in these dark times. Your runners reached us.'

'That is good,' Hagudril said. 'We have much to discuss.'

'Inside then, whilst ale and food remains,' Carorthay said. 'Imulorn and Imelorn, I would hear your tales too. What of Tarithel and her quest?'

'We will gladly tell them in exchange for food and drink!' Imelorn replied.

The Dwarves filed within the city and the gates were bolted closed.

Tarithel continued to follow the map. She was relieved to stumble into another cavern and find it undisturbed, with the compass rose on the floor showing a tunnel to the south as she had expected.

Just another league … then we can escape this fetid place!

She took a deep breath, rubbing the weariness from her eyes and continued onwards. The flames died behind her and the unremitting tunnel stretched before her.

The ground was rising again, promising that she might yet see the light of day before too long. She felt her spirits lift and some energy return to her body.

It cannot be far now.

It seemed only a short walk compared to those she had already taken until a final cavern came in sight. The familiar flames and compass rose stood before her, but there were no other passageways, just the rough-hewn flight of stairs leading upwards out of sight.

This must be it! I'm here at last!

She stepped forward.

The flames around her flickered and died down, guttering before extinguishing themselves, plunging her back into the gloom, lit only by the pale gleam of the rocks. She could only just make out the outlines of the cavern.

The air seemed cold, as if the very heat had been stolen away. She could see her breath floating upwards in thin traceries of mist.

The sound came again, its horrific keening much closer

now, emanating from the tunnel she had just left. She whirled around, peering into the inky blackness behind her, stumbling away from the tunnel entrance as Álainn whinnied in fear.

She stared in horror.

The darkness itself was contracting before her, twisting and stretching the very rock around her. A wind was rising about her, dust swirling around her, stinging her eyes. The voice was howling now, eerie, dark and filled with menace; a moaning wail that was growing in pitch and force.

Tarithel found herself trembling from head to foot, unable to move. She felt sweat trickle down her face and chest, her body shuddering, but she could not force herself to flee.

Light flickered in the tunnel, a ghastly, sickly, faded cyan glow, as if the rocks were being permeated by some evil spirit, all the while creeping closer to her, seeking her.

Whatever it was, it wanted her. She was prey, she knew it, she was caught in its lair. It had pursued her, sapping her strength until it was ready to strike.

And now it was here.

Some awful denizen of the deep, some foul creature she had disturbed by intruding into its domain down here in the bowels of the earth, possessed of fell and mysterious forces gathered from the dark world below the Icemark.

She screamed, but no noise came from her. Even that was stolen from her.

She sensed malevolence, older and darker than anything she had sensed before; something that bore her only malice and evil intent.

It was taking form before her, tendrils of foul, cyan light stretching out towards her body, encircling her in a sphere of ancient malicious power.

There were no words, the communication between her and the strange entity was far below that threshold of comprehension. She sensed hatred, anger and a hunger to steal the essence of whom she was and the power she herself held. Yet the creature, whatever it was, had been enslaved by a power she did recognise, caught and trapped into guarding these ancient underground passages.

Shareth!

Some vestige of consciousness remained to her, some part of her will that refused to succumb to the overwhelming force that swirled about her. The jewel still hanging around her neck pulsed as her mind wrenched itself back from the abyss.

No, you shall not have me!

The green light of summer fenced and flashed against the cyan of the gloom and depths, striking and wrestling back and forth. The light blazed around her features, outlining her form in shocking crashes of energy and power. For brief moments her clothes faded from view and even the bones in her body could be perceived as the unleashed energies writhed and twisted.

And then the light faded.

Defeated, the … whatever the creature was … retreated, howling and wailing its agonies and anger back into the cold, darkened depths of the passageway.

The light flickered and Tarithel was left alone.

She fell to her knees, panting and gasping for breath and shivering.

For a long moment she couldn't move, her body shuddering with shock and fear, her eyes wide and staring into the darkness that had almost taken her soul.

The jewel about her neck still cast a comforting green glow. She clasped it in her hand, feeling a strange warmth emanating from it.

You have defied Shareth's power once again, you have prevailed against the darkness that underpins the Icemark …

Tarithel blinked in surprise.

Fangrim?

She recognised the tones of the strange voice that had spoken to her, far in the south, mere days before, though it seemed like an endless stretch of time.

None before have faced the danger and survived the dank heart of the depths. We find you worthy, Tarithel, Lady of the Forest … Embrace your destiny …

Before her eyes, lights swirled in the air, glowing letters forming themselves into a flowing script. Words she couldn't read formed in her mind, burning their way into her consciousness. She tried to scramble away, but found she was mesmerised by the strange incantation. Words echoed in her thoughts, she had no idea what it meant.

Looking for the spell of Thigrorn …?

Then something broke in her.

'No!'

She screamed, a tormented howl of terror and dread. It rang back, echoing off the walls of the cavern.

'Leave me!' she screeched, pulling at her hair in torment. 'I want no part of this! No more darkness or sorcery! No more spells! No more magic! Be gone!'

Somehow her own words galvanised her into action. She was on her feet, grabbing Álainn's reins and dragging the horse bodily up the stairs.

A madness took her, she gave light heed to any sense of caution, climbing up higher and higher, not caring whether anyone heard or saw her coming. There was an overwhelming need to be free of the darkness and gloom of the catacombs below the Icemark.

She never did recall how she escaped from the tunnels, only that she stumbled out through a high and ornate stone walkway, shielding her eyes from the bright glare, before collapsing exhausted on the steps of a strange and silent palace.

Chapter Sixteen

Luxor the Moonprince stands in the Hills of Imirand looking North-east to the City of Carorthane.

The armies of the Barbarians had departed to the west, the dust from their passing had already settled. Luxor summoned his own men, the loyal riders of the Moonguard and they rode east, past the tower through low hills, between high mountains.

Their passage did not go unmarked. Within the hour Luxor's men spied riders heading towards them, the banners of the Fey held aloft at their fore. Luxor brought his men to a stop and waited for them to arrive.

'We are strangers in their land,' he said to himself. 'Let us hope they have heard the words of their leader, Imorthorn.'

The Fey were a few dozen in number, armed with spears and bows for the most part. One rode at their lead, dressed in a green and blue. They paused perhaps fifty feet away.

'Luxor the Moonprince,' the leader said. 'Welcome to the realm of the Fey of Icemark. Your presence is known to us. I am Carorthane, vassal of Imorthorn, leader of the Fey. I bid you welcome.'

'Your welcome is well received, 'Luxor replied. 'We have travelled far already and are sore weary.'

'My city is not far,' Carorthane said. 'Two leagues, no more. There will be food and rest aplenty. My Lord Imorthorn issued instructions to that effect.'

'We are much obliged,' Luxor said.

The Moonguard and the Fey formed up their ranks and rode alongside each other towards the city.

'It is good to ride amidst the Fey once more,' Luxor said. 'It reminds me of my home in Midnight. The Fey and the Free are staunch allies.'

'That is good to hear,' Carorthane said. 'In these lands men and Fey are estranged by long history and countless wars. You ride from the Barbarians do you not?'

'I do,' Luxor replied.

'And how did you find them?' Carorthane asked.

'Stubborn,' Luxor replied.

Carorthane laughed. 'I am not at all surprised. They are doughty in warfare, but not often given over to deep consideration from what I have seen.'

'They honoured their word,' Luxor said. 'For that much I can thank them. But they will not stand against the Heartstealer, neither will the Dwarves.'

'They are all scared,' Carorthane answered. 'For the Barbarians, I know that the Heartstealer sent forces through their lands to aid the Witchking even as he battled you before. The Dwarves position is precarious, caught between the other races. Even if they are not allied with her, they do not actively frustrate her efforts. Many others share that view alas … and so does the Heartstealer maintain her grip on all of us.'

Luxor caught the tone in his voice.

'Some amongst the Fey?' he asked, a frustrated expression creeping across his face.

Carorthane nodded. 'Imorthorn himself is truly set against the Heartstealer. Your emissary, the Lady Tarithel, galvanised many of us to action, but we would have been of that mind regardless … some counsel a path of appeasement though, and their voices are still heard by many.'

'Pander to this evil and it will slowly poison you into impotence,' Luxor said, with a heavy sigh. 'Why, the Fey of my realm would attest to that … they were lulled into co-existence with the Witchking … until he was ready to strike and wipe them from existence. That tide was turned, but only in the last hour.'

'Such battles still await the Fey of Icemark,' Carorthane replied.

'Imorthorn does not hold sway?'

'Oh he does …' Carorthane said, 'But there is much fear over angering the Heartstealer. Sides must be taken … and it will take much to win some of our folk over. Many would prefer a watchful peace rather than a declaration of war.'

'Longing for peace I understand,' Luxor said. 'But when implacable evil plots against you …'

'Imorthorn will welcome your voice,' Carorthane said. 'Your tales of the fight against the Witchking will win over hearts and minds. You see … Shareth has left us alone for many moons … sure she emboldens the Dwarves and Giants to test our borders, but we are strong enough to manage that without recourse to vast armies… to set ourselves against the Heartstealer is quite another matter.'

'Then I will lend my voice to that of Imorthorn's,' Luxor said. 'Let us hope we can win over faint hearts and confused conscience!'

As Rorthron approached the vast stone gates of the City of Carangrane, the guards blocked him. He held aloft the signed and sealed document Varangrim had given him and called out, his voice echoing around the mountainsides.

'I am sent by Varangrim, vassal of Carangrane and now leader of the Giants,' he called. 'I come to you with tidings and missives from him. I am Rorthron of the Wise. I am in great haste. Grant me access!'

One of the giants strode to him, took the parchment, unrolled it and studied the contents. With a brief nod, he gestured at the others. With a great rumbling the vast stone gates were pushed back. Another giant stomped out to meet him.

Rorthron bowed before him.

'I am Obigrorn of the northern giants,' he said. 'And you are truly one of the Wise?'

'Varangrim has vouched for me,' Rorthron replied.

'Aye he has,' Obigrorn replied, looking over the parchment Rorthron had brought with him. 'We have heard nothing from Varangrim for many days, we feared him perished in the Heartstealer's treachery. You come to us at a poor time, Rorthron of the Wise. Our people prepare to make their last stand and the Heartstealer has taken our northern lands and will soon lay siege to this city. Why are you here?'

'I am here to search your great archives,' Rorthron replied. 'I seek such weapons as might turn the tide of this war … and I bring news from the south. Luxor of Midnight, he who slew the father of the Heartstealer, offers an alliance to the Giants of Icemark.'

'Fair words,' Obigrorn replied. 'But words only. Alliances in the south can be of no use here, the enemy marches upon us. Tomorrow we will be besieged. Neither Varangrim or your Moonprince can aid us.'

'Alliances will hold,' Rorthron returned. 'And I am not without my own powers. As a pledge of good faith, and in the name of my Lord Luxor, I will stand with you against the foe and we shall make a battle of it that will be long remembered. This I have sworn to Varangrim. In return, if we have the victory, the Giants are pledged to my Lord, Luxor of Midnight.'

Obigrorn stepped back in surprise, but then bowed.

'Then you are most welcome, Rorthron of the Wise,' he replied. 'But when you see the forces arranged against us, your talk of victory will die upon your lips.'

Carorthay looked over his tankard of ale at the others gathered around the fire. Carorthay's city had little in the way of aesthetics; it had seen too much warfare in the many moons since it had been raised. Walls were patched, defences smashed down and rebuilt. The entire city was something of a ramshackle affair with little time left over for the niceties of grander dwellings. Such was life in the desolate east of the Icemark.

'So, we must trust to hope that Tarithel continued on her way,' he said.

'I sorely wish we could have accompanied her further,' Imulorn replied. 'If she survived the Temple, she will be far to the north by now.'

'And into the realm of the Heartstealer,' Imelorn added.

'Bizarre tales of sorcery and the Fey,' Hagudril said. 'Strange times indeed for the Dwarves.'

'Fell times,' Carorthay said with a nod. 'But more traditional problems await us now. War is before us. The Icelords are marching on our borders. Shareth flexes her muscles.'

The Dwarves had seen the fires of the Icelords growing in the darkness to the north. Armies were on the march and heading towards them.

'What strength we have is ready,' Hagudril replied. 'Some three thousand of our folk can bear arms against the foe.'

'The city is as ready as it can be,' Carorthay said.

'Do we know what size of force is marching against us?' Imelorn asked.

'Several thousands of both warriors and riders,' Carorthay said. 'Scouts report that Fangrorn himself rides at their head. Worse still, flags of the northern Dwarves have been seen in their ranks. Anvarorn marches with them.'

'Then this is no skirmish,' Hagudril muttered, spitting on the floor. 'This is the invasion we have long feared.'

Carorthay nodded.

'And my orders from Glormane are to hold this line as we have always done,' he said. 'That is what I intend to do. Let them come, they will have to fight hard and long to take this city.'

The other Dwarves nodded, their faces grim.

Preparations continued through the night. Carorthay's city was well provisioned for a siege. Axes were sharpened upon huge whetstones, arrows were stockpiled for the short bows the Dwarves preferred. The mechanisms that defended the walls were checked and adjusted. The engineering was intricate and ingenious; the Dwarves were masters of such things.

Dawn broke with a thick mist rolling across the plains to the north. Even then, shadows could be made out within it, dark and sinister. The light of dawn faded as day was revealed to be thick with low cloud and no sight of the sun, but an orange glow remained, the lights of fires and torches held aloft.

A deep rolling thrum echoed across the city, the sound of thousands of footsteps pounding in unison, softened by the distance. Dwarves stood facing the oncoming army as it emerged from the fog.

A line of infantry appeared first, flanked either side by row upon row of cavalry. The army drew up perhaps two hundred yards from the walls, out of bowshot. Flags were hoisted, chief amongst them the banner of Fangrorn himself. Alongside it were many banners of the northern Dwarves, the sight of them causing many of the Dwarves to yell out in anger and frustration.

The mist cleared, swept away by a strong wind out of the north.

Row upon row of warriors were revealed, stretching back

for hundreds and then thousands of yards. Amidst them, great machines of warfare could be seen, trebuchets and siege towers. The vast might of the Frozen Empire was displayed for all to see.

The sound of marching feet faded, only to be replaced by the crash of sword upon shield. The Dwarves yelled their defiance from atop the walls of the city.

The Icelord army advanced.

Dawn broke.

It was a relief to see the sun once more, but the air was chill with frost and a smattering of ersh blew around her. She led Álainn forwards. The horse whinnied in the sharp air, but seemed relieved to be out of the tunnels.

So cold! But a welcome change from that musty air, I should hope never to have to set foot in those dank tunnels again. Shareth … whatever power she sent … it almost stole my mind away!

She had no answers, but the fear and terror she had felt in the tunnels was seeping away in the dawn light. She was herself again; Tarithel the Fey, Lady of The Forest, on a mission to save her betrothed from the clutches of the Heartstealer.

There was no one she could ask, no one to offer counsel.

And then the voice of Fangrim again … and that word … Thigrorn … what does that mean?

She shivered, fearing to open her mind to any voices from beyond herself.

I did not ask for this, I don't want it! I will not be a sorceress … I just want Morkin back!

The jewel around her neck was dark, no longer imbued with the green glow she had come to expect. She felt a sense of relief.

When it glows it's as if a power overwhelms my will, turning me into its pawn as Luxor warned it might. It seems to work for good, but …

She pulled the necklace off, holding it outstretched in her hand, the jewel dangling from the end.

Does it work for me, or does it make me work for it?

She cast her mind back to the battles with the Dwarves, the words of Fangrim at the stones, and even further into her memory, when the power of the forest had come to her aid against the Doomguard of the Witchking.

She wavered, thinking to cast the jewel aside, but she could not unclench her hand.

I cannot leave it, what would happen if evil were to possess it? It was given to me, an heirloom of our people, but none have ever seen it act this way before.

She looked at it for long moments, but nothing changed, it seemed that the jewel's powers were dormant for now.

'I shall not use you,' she said, speaking out loud. 'I am Tarithel, betrothed of Morkin and daughter of the Lord of Dreams … and that is enough!'

She put the jewel and its necklace into a pocket, buttoning it closed and taking a deep breath. She felt better, now she could only go on.

Álainn was fed and watered once more. She, too, seemed relieved to have left the dark passageways behind.

Tarithel stepped forward through the ruined glory of the ancient palace, looking around her.

What was his name? Lorigriel? Something like that. Whoever he was, he matters little to me now. I hope Imulorn and Imelorn are all right …

She looked to her right, sunlight was streaming in, the pillars of the palace casting long shadows.

Dawn breaks! How many days have passed since I've seen the sun? Two, three, more perhaps?

She looked northwards, seeing nothing but an empty desolate expanse cloaked in writhing mist. To her left, westwards, mountains rose, sharp and austere. She stepped away from the palace and looked behind her. The mountains continued south and south-east to the limits of vision.

But they are behind me, I have truly passed the mountains of Anvulane at last! How many can claim that?

She felt a faint sense of exultation, but it was swamped by the knowledge of where she now stood. By passing the mountains she had left the kingdom of the Dwarves behind. She now stood in the Frozen Empire, homeland of the Icelords and …

The domain of the Heartstealer herself.

She shivered despite the clothing she wore, pulling her cloak tighter about herself. In her mind she recalled the guidance she had received from Carorthay. He had heard of the City of Imiriel, the vision of a place she had never been but had seen in the dreams sent by the spirit of the Forest of Fangrim. The city lay due north of where she stood, still a weary journey lay before her.

Yet I have travelled perhaps two thirds of the length of this realm thus far. Few would have given odds on me achieving that and yet here I am.

Between her and the City lay another forest. Carorthay had spoken of it in lowered tones, warning her that the Heartstealer's enchantments lay heavy upon it.

Farorn he called it. Dark and mighty, almost as immense as Fangrim so he said, but it may prove to be my salvation.

Travelling in the open across the Frozen Empire was far too dangerous. The rough map that she'd been given showed fortresses and cities spread out across the landscape she now stood on the edge of. The mist might give her some cover, but she already knew it to be fickle and subject to the whims of the Heartstealer. Riding a horse would make her even more visible to any passing patrol.

According to Carorthay the forest of Farorn reached almost to the uttermost north of Shareth's realm, jutting up against the Frozen Wastes that bordered the Icemark. It was there that Imiriel lay. With luck, if she could reach the forest, she might safely travel, both swiftly and with stealth, right to Imiriel with little chance of being seen.

And there I must go.

It was as good a plan as she could conceive. She shivered in the chill air, but determination rose in her once more. She ate a light helping of her rations, washing it down with a gulp of water from her hip flask.

The Forest of Farorn lay at least two days ride away. Her best chance was to ride along the foothills of the Mountains of Anvulane north-west and then strike northwards. The land away from the plains was sparsely populated and she would be unlikely to encounter anyone. Carorthay's map indicated that she would then arrive in a wide valley known as the Morormarg, perhaps two or three leagues across.

And it's there I must take a risk. Carorthay said the valley is well-travelled by the Icelords, with fortresses all along its length. Yet I must cross it if I am to gain the safety of the forest, if any safety is to be found.

There was nothing to be gained in waiting; the sun was rising, the shadows around her already shorter.

She mounted Álainn and spurred her around, directing them away from the palace and towards the mountains to the west.

Talorthane the Icelord watched as the warriors of Imgasharg prepared to depart from their fortress. They were heading onwards towards Kahudrun, two days long march down the valley of Morormarg. For several days Talorthane had been patrolling the southern reaches of the Forest of Farorn, following Lorelorn's orders.

There had been no sign of the Fey-girl, and no news of her had reached him.

Perhaps Shareth has already found and killed her? Thus emboldened we continue on our march to war ...

He spotted Imgasharg himself at the lead of the men; his banners held high about him by his escort. Talorthane hailed him.

Imgasharg turned to him.

'What news of the war?' Talorthane asked.

Imgasharg chuckled.

'The giants are weaker than we thought. Their domain all the way to the mountains of Anvormane lies under our control or in flames. My men cut down their leader, Carangrane! They have fallen back in disarray, we are poised to crush them. Even now we press our advantage, I have sent for reenforcements to press the assault. Half a moon, and the Giants will be nothing but a mention in the annuals of the Icemark.'

'And then?'

'I daresay the Dwarfs will be next,' Imgasharg said. 'The rumours say they have turned against the favour of our beloved Heartstealer. If so, they will rue that choice. Fangrorn will see to their extermination.'

'And the Fey?'

'Their time will come,' Imgasharg muttered. 'And I will take great delight in hacking them down.

Talorthane nodded.

'And you?' Imgasharg asked. 'Have you even drawn your sword yet in this fray?'

'My orders are to patrol the borders of the forest,' Talorthane replied. 'I have ridden south from Lorelorn and Kahangrorn, I complete my inspection of the southern realms of Farorn before turning back north once more.'

'For what purpose?'

'Because those are my orders,' Talorthane replied, seeing Imgasharg's eyes narrow. 'And I do not question the wisdom of those who command me.'

'Quite right,' Imgasharg replied, with a sneer. 'Perhaps they have the measure of what each of us is capable of and have assigned duties accordingly.'

His men laughed and Imgasharg stepped away before throwing a final comment over his shoulder.

'You may ride with us for a time,' he said. 'We real warriors head for Kahudrun and war, you may turn aside before things get too dangerous.'

Talorthane sighed and spurred his horse around, he and his men falling into line behind the legions of Imgasharg.

Tarithel had ridden to the northernmost reach of the mountains of Anvulane. A small forest bordered the land to the left and a series of hills led northwards away from the mountains. She could see the land opening out before her.

The valley of Morormarg. This is it.

She looked about her, her keen eyes scanning the terrain. The valley stretched north-east and south-west to the limits of vision. It was dreary and grey for the most part, she could see little was growing within its bounds. The reason was obvious, she could tell at a glance that the valley was a major route in regular usage, she was familiar enough with the destruction left behind to know she was looking at the aftermath of the passage of war. Many armies had come this way. Everything seemed quiet, nothing was moving.

She could see a large track that ran alongside a muddy river that sinuously wove its way across the floor, the valley before disappearing into the murky distance to the west.

Across from her, a line of thick and heavy trees could be seen on the opposite hills. They, too, looked grey and grim, with no hint of greenness visible at this distance.

That must be Farorn.

It was far enough away, more than two leagues across the open terrain of the valley.

She looked to her left around the edge of a small copse of trees and gasped, retreating. A fortress stood there, along the near edge of the valley, smoke rising from it. She pulled Álainn back, ensuring she was hidden from sight amidst the trees before crawling back to get a better look.

The fortress stood, grim and proud, dominating the valley. Tarithel could see banners flying from its towers and armies camped around its base. She looked across the valley, feeling her heart sink.

There's no way I can cross that without being seen. I'll have to wait for nightfall.

Travelling across unknown terrain in the dark didn't fill her with any enthusiasm either and there was a river to cross too. She looked around again; there was a bridge near the fortress, but no others that she could see. It was impossible to see how deep the river might be.

She sighed. She would have to wait until nightfall, there was no other choice. The sun was already westering; it wouldn't be long before she could set out. She walked back to Álainn and broke out some meagre provisions.

Her thoughts drifted to Morkin. What had happened to him in the weeks since she had set out? What would Shareth have done to him?

Kept him locked up for sure. Tortured him in vengeance for the death of her father at Luxor's hand? Or worse ...

She swallowed, remembering the vision of Morkin chained in a dank and gloomy dungeon and the images of him in a close embrace with Shareth.

Her lies! Morkin would never betray me so!

Yet she was getting closer, by her own estimation she had travelled more than two thirds of the length of the Icemark and, according to the Dwarves, if she could only head true north through the vast tracts of the forest of Farorn, she would come to the city of Imiriel.

And Morkin is there, I know he is.

She thought of Luxor. She knew he was far to the south, the faint warmth of the Moon Ring still flickered in her mind from time to time, but it was dim and distant now. Doubtless he was engaged in trying to rally the people of the Icemark in some fashion in order to defy Shareth.

More than enough of a challenge for him given what I've learnt of these people, they seem to prefer war to peace!

There was nothing Luxor could do for her now, she was on her own, with the hostile lands of the Frozen Empire between her and her goal.

And Shareth.

Tarithel had sensed little of the sorceress of late. Ever since leaving Fangrim and the heartlands of the Fey she had expected to sense her more and more. Here she stood at the edge of Shareth's realm and yet there was little feeling of anything. Just a bland greyness that stretched out before her. She kept her thoughts close, wondering if reaching out might reveal herself.

She knows I'm in the Icemark. She knows I will be coming for Morkin. Is she searching for me? Or does she not care, so sure in her enchantments and power? Yet Fangrim told me I was to challenge her …

There were no answers to be found, she could only continue on.

CHAPTER SIXTEEN

The Giants stood ready.

'The city is well provisioned,' Obigrorn said. 'We have salted meats and water aplenty, having anticipated the attack and had time to prepare. What we lack is warriors.'

Rorthron nodded. 'Then we must seek to frustrate the attack from Shareth's forces rather than trying to defeat them outright.'

Obigrorn nodded, but looked downcast. 'My runners tell me that one of Shareth's own warlords, Imgaril himself, rides with her host, granted powers beyond mere strength. Warriors we can contend with, fell powers not so.'

'I have faced her magic before,' Rorthron said. 'And yes, she is potent indeed. It seems now is the time for my own strength to be tested against hers. You are not without allies, Obigrorn of the Giants. I will contend with this Imgaril.'

'And I am grateful for aid unlooked for,' Obigrorn replied. 'The Wise of Icemark have not been heard from in all my years … even Carangrane himself scarce remembered them, so he told me.'

'My people abandoned their duties long ago,' Rorthron replied. 'I have made it my life's work to make recompense for that, if only in small part.'

Below they could see the armies of the Icelords forming into ranks on the plains at the foot of the mountains. The City was perhaps five hundred feet higher with the only access being via a winding pathway scarce three wagons width across that wove before the city on its way up the incline.

'They cannot use their larger siege weapons against us,' Obigrorn said. 'But ropes and ladders will serve their needs. For our part, the rocks will aid us!'

Already the Icelords were marching up the pathway. Rorthron could see them standing ten abreast as they marched onwards, shields held up. He looked about at the defences of the City. The walls were sheer and stark, huge and intimidating. It would cost the Icelords many lives even to reach the gates.

Behind him, vast piles of rocks and stones had been prepared. The Giants did not employ much in the way of machinery, their own strength suiting their needs. Even as he watched, Giants standing along the walls hoisted rocks by hand.

'Let's show these servants of the Hagspawn their folly in invading our lands,' Obigrorn roared. 'Pummel them!'

Rocks were thrown, launched high into the air by the mighty arms of the host of Giants. Their range was impressive, perhaps two hundred yards. The rocks soared through the air, cascading down amongst the Icelords with devastating effect. Shields and helms were no defence. Men were crushed on the road, or cast screaming into the abyss on either side. Dozens were killed within moments, but there were hundreds more to replace them.

Rorthron could see the discipline in the ranks, fallen comrades were ignored, the warriors stepped into line and continued marching along, despite the onslaught.

'They seem to care not for their own lives,' Obigrorn said.

'The Heartstealer has bewitched their hearts and minds,' Rorthron replied. 'They are little more than her tools when she has them cast in her thrall.'

The Iceguard made headway up the road. They soon learnt to angle their shields to give them the best possible defence against the hail of rocks. Yard by yard they gained ground.

Crossbow bolts, first sporadically, then with greater fervour, began to ping against the walls. Some of the giants were hit, crying out in rage and stumbling back. As each giant was cut down, the strength of the attack grew. The volley of stones and rocks fell away bit by bit.

The Iceguard advanced.

Dozens were still being crushed under the weight of rocks casts from the walls, but the arrows and bolts of the attackers found their targets, the marksmanship was impressive. The Icelords had the training and discipline they needed.

The Iceguard army reached the surrounds of the city, a flat expanse given over to markets in days of peace. There was little cover here, but it allowed the Icelords to expand outwards and widen their own field of fire. With a cry of exultation they surged forward.

'They will raise ladders next,' Obigrorn yelled. 'Stand by to repel!'

Ladders could indeed be seen in the midst of the troops below. The giants did their best to target them with rocks, but more of them fell to crossbow bolts and arrows the moment they appeared atop the walls.

The ladders were hoisted at some unspoken signal, within moments dozens of them were rising along the length of the walls. The Iceguard warriors were prepared well. Men were climbing the ladders the moment they came to rest.

Tens of them were slain as they began the climb, but the covering fire from below continued, striking down the Giants above.

'Hammers!' Obigrorn yelled, as the first of the Icelords reached the top of the walls.

The Giants were ready. The time for the stones and rocks was done. Their favoured weapons were akin to vast mallets, wrought of stone and huge timbers. They swung them with mighty strokes, casting two or three of the Icelords aside in a stroke, or crushing them to a bloody pulp on the stone walkways.

For their part, the Iceguard warriors relied on their ranged weapons, though increasing numbers bore halberds, which they struck at the flanks and loins of the Giants, immobilising them long enough for the archers to attack.

'Time for blood to be spilt,' Obigrorn said to Rorthron, hoisting his own hammer.

Talorthane and his men rode south-west down the valley of Morormarg. Not desiring any further irritation from the likes of Imgasharg, Talorthane had slowed his progress a little, leaving Imgasharg's men to gain a lead of perhaps a league or so ahead on the dusty road that led towards Kahangriel and Kahudrun.

They stayed on the southern side of the river, away from the borders of Farorn, as its sombre trees encroached down the sides of the valley making passage difficult on the northern sides. Around them the mists of the Icemark were rising, coiling sinuously out of the ground as they often did at the end of the day. A few leagues behind them stood the Tower of Berormium, its lower half already obscured. The top was still visible, seeming to hover above the ground, suspended above the fog.

Beyond lay the Fortress of Kahangriel, that marked their turning point back north, to approach the edges of the Forest and then turn back north-west along its borders. They would set camp in the valley and push onwards to the north in the morning, resuming their patrol as directed.

In the distance, he could see the faint glows of a camp being readied. It seemed Imgasharg and his men had already stopped and were preparing to stop for the night. The plains were quiet, even given the desolation of the area.

The mist was chill, already prompting grumblings from those around him. He signalled for a stop, directed some of his men to arrange a watch and rest to set about building their own camp.

CHAPTER SIXTEEN

Arrows turned the sky dark over the City of Carorthay. Volley after volley rained down upon the defenders on the walls. The Icelord attack was well conceived, their archers using mighty long bows with greater range than the Dwarves.

Under cover of the merciless torrent slicing down from above, the Icelords were bringing their siege towers to bear. Hauled forward by trolls that had somehow been forced in slavery for this very task, the huge towers were approaching the walls. No attempt yet had been made to storm the gate of the city, the massed ranks of cavalry and foot soldiers stood by, allowing the archers to continue their assault and escort the siege towers.

'Take cover!' Carorthay yelled. 'Unleash catapults!'

The Dwarves were by no means defenceless in such a fight.

Atop the walls, great mechanisms were turned to the battle. Dwarves were masters of such machinery, forged from rare ores wrestled from the ground and cast into intricate designs by their skill. Powerful springs had already been ratcheted back and great blocks of stone dropped into place. With the machinery primed Carorthay raised a flag and then, after a moment's evaluation of the battle field, he brought it down.

With a crash of rending noise the catapults unleashed their fury. Vast stone boulders were hurled into the sky with great precision. Some crashed down amongst the massed ranks of the enemy, others were more deftly targeted.

One of the nearby siege towers was struck head on by a massive weight of masonry. It disintegrated, exploding into shards, casting the men within to oblivion. The shattered remnants collapsed back in a wreckage of debris and twisted bodies.

A cheer arose from the dwarven ranks as the catapults were reloaded.

Carorthay was still gauging how close the siege towers were as they continued their slow approach. He squinted through the gloom, counting and measuring …

Then he signalled to the Dwarves below him. They were clustered around a series of huge spoked wheels half set in the ground. At his instruction they began hauling on them and thick metal chains were pulled into view, being coiled around a vast spool connected to the wheels by a complex mechanism of cogs. Nearby, at intervals within the walls, other groups of Dwarves were wrestling similar machinery into operation. The sound of metal clanking filled the air.

'More surprises for the scum?' Imelorn yelled.

Carorthay grinned. 'This old city has a few tricks left for them to enjoy!'

The wheels were being pulled back at an ever increasing speed. Then, there was a deep rumble that echoed through the ground beneath the city and out into the field of battle before its walls. Carorthay saw the Icelords look about themselves with trepidation. A faint swirl of dust rose around them and they felt the ground tremble beneath their feet.

The advance paused and a lull fell over the approaching army.

'Come on,' Carorthay muttered, looking down from the walls. 'Don't be shy …'

Horns blared from within the ranks of the Icelords and the march resumed. Now the warriors were pacing forward alongside the siege towers, and still the arrows sliced through the air in an endless barrage.

Even as they did so, the rumbling returned, this time not fading out after a moment, but growing in fury and intensity. Behind the line of siege towers the ground fell out beneath the feet of riders and warriors alike, casting both them and the horses into vast pits dug out of the ground and now opened by the warcraft of the Dwarves. A widening ring of collapsing ground spiralled inwards, marking out a huge moat-like chasm in the ground which increased in size, the ground falling away in quick succession towards the walls of the city. Vast plumes of dust rose above the chasms in the ground. Those within the perimeter were trapped, able only to stare in horror at the approaching collapse, until it consumed them too. One by one the siege towers toppled backwards and were shattered against the rubble below.

The dust began to settle. The battlefield was now a jumbled field of rocks and boulders, littered here and there with the weapons and men of the Icelords. A few had survived the carnage and were struggling back towards the vast armies that still stood further away.

'Round one to us I'll wager!' Carorthay called, shaking his fist at the Icelords. Raucous cheers greeted his yell all along the walls of the city.

Tarithel waited until the first stars appeared in the twilight. The moon, now in its last quarter, was yet to rise in the west. It would give her a little light for the later hours of the night. She would have to move quickly to reach the trees of Farorn.

She had watched the mist cover the valley. It was both a blessing and a curse. It would be easy enough to stay hidden, but the way would be obscured. It would be easy to get turned about and lost. She couldn't afford to be wandering around down there if dawn broke and the mist cleared.

She'd spent her time prior to nightfall wisely, memorising as many features of the valley as she could. Hopefully it would be enough to see her across without getting lost. Whilst she could still see, the stars would be her guide.

Climbing astride her, Tarithel spurred Álainn around and set off northwards.

The land sloped downwards, Álainn's hooves scrabbling for grip on loose shale. Progress was slow but steady. As she descended the valley sides, the mist rose up towards her, a pale white shadow across her path, writhing to and fro, despite there being no breeze.

It was unnerving. She recalled it from before, sensing there was more to it than just a simple fog in the air.

Shareth's doing no doubt!

There was no alternative though. Álainn continued on.

In a moment, Tarithel found herself cloaked in greyness. Above the stars faded from view, leaving her with no sense of direction at all. Visibility was limited to tens of feet. Álainn snorted, her breath drifting up in clouds of vapour around her muzzle. The mist swirled about Tarithel, leaching heat from her face and hands. She shivered.

But there was something else too. Not just the cold of the mist, somehow it felt as if it were seeping into her very being, seeking a way into her soul and her heart, trying to chill the love and hope that still remained, wanting to leave her with nothing but despair. She had to brace herself, resist it, whilst it swirled ever more intently about her.

I will not succumb to the will behind this. I am Tarithel, Lady of the Forest!

Álainn was picking up speed and confidence as the valley floor flattened out. The going became easier, the rubble giving way to smoother sand and dried cracked mud. Tarithel recognised the signs of land that must have once been flooded by water, long ago when the Icemark wasn't bound by ice and cold.

The river can't be far now.

She strained her ears, hoping to hear the sounds of running water and gauge the direction of the river. The mist was even thicker now, she could hardly see the ground before her.

In her mind she resisted the insipid malaise that tried to

subdue her mind and her will. She fought against it, seeking to keep the mist out of her mind and soul. As she did so, the jewel in her pocket began to shine, its green hue shining out through her clothes.

No …! It will give me away …

Álainn stumbled on the ground and Tarithel pulled on the reins to bring her to a halt, still listening hard. A faint noise reached her.

It wasn't water.

Too late she heard the sound of a bow being readied. Arrows cut through the mist about her, passing either side.

No …

Another arrow, this time from another direction. It struck Álainn in the flank. She whinnied in alarm, rearing up and fear and pain. Tarithel was flung back, tumbling down to the ground. The impact was hard, knocking the breath from her.

More arrows. Blood splattered across her.

Tarithel's vision was blurred, she could barely see, but she managed to roll over only to see Álainn's body collapse not far from her, half a dozen arrows embedded in her flank. Álainn was thrashing around, kicking her legs and tossing her head.

'No!'

Tarithel crawled across to her downed horse, pulling herself up to Álainn's head, stroking it, trying to calm her. A brief look at the arrows told her all she needed to know. Tears sprang into her eyes.

'No … please no …'

Even as she watched, Álainn's eyes began to glaze over. With a rattling gasp, the horse drew its last breath.

Shadows loomed out of the grey, thick, heavily cladded men.

'There!' a gruff deep voice called. Something swung in the mist …

Tarithel's vision swam and then everything faded into darkness.

Far to the south-east in the land of the Dwarves, the battle continued. The Icelords had not been prepared for such a stiff defence, but their strength had not been countered. Even as the dust from the first attack had settled, they could be seen working on the edge of the rubble field.

'What are they doing?' Imulorn asked.

'Miners,' Imelorn spat.

Carorthay nodded. 'They will drive a path to the front gate and attack with more traditional means. It will cost them dear, but they have the numbers.'

The day wore on and the Icelord activity became obvious, they were indeed clearing a path towards the city, perhaps a hundred yards wide. Through their work the catapults continued their barrage, but they were less effective against the troops below than they had been on the siege towers.

Archers had also crept forwards and had resumed the attack on the Dwarves on the walls, targeting those who operated the catapults. More than one Dwarf was slain at his post, the defenders on the walls grew fewer and the Dwarves were powerless to respond.

The Icelords used their shields to protect those working to clear the path. Inch by inch and foot by foot they closed in on the city.

Then flags were hoisted in the midst of the approaching army.

'Fangrorn!' Carorthay spat.

The banner of the dread Icelord of the Frozen Empire was easy to recognise, along with its own motif it bore the silver tiara emblem of Shareth herself. Silver on black, the sign of her wrath.

Riders could now be seen, breaking from the ranks of the warriors and charging towards the gate, flags streaming behind them as they galloped forward.

'What is he doing?' Imulorn asked. 'He rides towards the gates himself?'

Carorthay had already ordered his own archers to target the oncoming riders. Sporadic crossbow bolts and arrows from the sturdy short bows of the Dwarves began to find their mark amidst the riders, but they were already within a hundred yards of the greats.

'Take them down!' Carorthay yelled. 'All … mark your targets!'

They could see Fangrorn himself now, an armoured figure on horseback, holding a staff aloft even as he and his riders galloped forwards. Something glinted at the top of the staff, a gem perhaps, with a faint flicker of cyan light …

A blast of energy crashed out. Carorthay, Imulorn and Imelorn staggered back in shock and surprise, the glare blinding them. Before they could recover a blast of noise crashed into them, the ground fractured beneath their feet and hurled them to the floor. Debris crashed around them; splintered wood, shards of rock and twisted metal. Smoke and fumes assailed them, acrid and sharp, causing them to cough and splutter.

Their ears were ringing with the blast as they staggered to their knees.

Carorthay blinked, wiping at his eyes to clear them of the dust. He squinted, trying to see through the swirling miasma.

A breath of wind blew the smoke and dust away for a moment. He gasped in dismay.

The gate of his city was gone, shattered into oblivion. The vaulted archway that overlaid it was also missing, cast into ruin by the blast. About that, the walls were fractured, cracked and crumbling for yards in both directions away from where the gate had stood.

Now cheers were rising from the Icelord army and Carorthay could see them swarming towards the city like a black tide.

'To arms!' he yelled, managing to get back to his feet. 'Axes! Axes!'

'What do we have here then?' Imgasharg chuckled as his men dragged a hooded body up to him and flung it on its back.

'Some spy,' one warrior replied. 'Rode in on horseback, more fool them … some strange green enchantment about them …'

'Enchantment?' Imgasharg demanded with a laugh. 'You've been on the ale …'

'I know what I saw.'

Imgasharg growled, stepping over to the body to examine it. It was dressed in traveller's garb, grey, but with a finely tailored weave.

'This is Fey …'

He pulled the figure's hood back, revealing the face of a young woman with red hair.

'A filthy Fey spy!'

He looked up.

'Bind her,' he snapped. 'Best we find out what she's about this far north, the mistress will want to know.'

'And then?'

Imgasharg chuckled.

'I daresay she might afford a bit of sport before we gut her.'

The woman's supine body was hoisted up and dragged away.

The battle for the city of Carorthay raged through the streets of the city. With the walls breached, the Icelord army flooded in. Blood flew, axes hewed and chopped, blades flashed and sliced. Thousands soon lay dead or dying, but the Dwarves had neither the strength nor the numbers to resist the onslaught. Thousands more Icelord warriors lay outside the walls, now beginning to encircle the beleaguered city.

'The day is lost,' Imulorn cried. 'We have fought hard, but if we remain here we will all be slaughtered!'

Carorthay watched as one of the towers of the city burst into flame, the Icelords were burning and sacking as they went. He wiped blood from his face before nodding.

'Sound the retreat!' he yelled.

The remaining Dwarves fell back before the jeers and cries of the Icelord warriors. They still held the western gates and even as arrows cut them down the Dwarves ran towards them, dragging their wounded with them. The Icelord warriors chased them to the threshold pausing only to hurl abuse at them as they made their escape.

Ranks of riders drew up on their flanks to either side, as if preparing to charge and strike them down.

'They will end us …' Imulorn muttered, even as he continued to run.

But the riders didn't charge, they formed up in their ranks, allowing the Dwarves to retreat before closing up behind them, encircling the city. The Dwarves continued on, without pursuit.

A mile away the remains of the dwarven army staggered to a halt, unprovisioned and exhausted by their fight and flight. Fire and smoke rose from the city as it was consumed, the vastness of the Icelord army still about it, barely reduced in strength.

'My city burns,' Carorthay whispered, staring back at the ruin and the great plume of smoke that rose from it.

'We fought as well as any Dwarf could,' Imelorn said. 'Now we must see to the survival of our people and bring news to Glormane as best we can.'

'They didn't finish us,' Carorthay continued, his eyes narrowing, his voice still low and shocked.

'They want us to take news of their victory back,' Imulorn said. 'Not only do they fight by strength of arms, but they seek to demoralise us as well.'

'Yet,' Carorthay muttered. 'What can we truly do against such strength? The Dwarves that remain loyal do not have the power to turn away this hammer blow against us …'

'We must reach Glormane,' Imulorn said, grabbing Carorthay by the shoulder.

Carorthay nodded. He turned away from the smouldering ruins of his home, tears glistening in his eyes.

Tarithel's first sensation was of biting cold. Then there was pain in her wrists and ankles, her neck sore and stiff. She struggled for a moment before realising she was tied hand and foot to some sort of rough wooden stake. Her arms had been wrenched up above her. Judging by the painful ache in them, she'd been hanging by her wrists for quite some time. She staggered up, trying to relieve the pain.

Álainn!

Despair and sorrow flickered through her mind. Tears stung her eyes, brought on by feelings of pain. Her companion through all her journeys … gone … slain by … by whom?

'So you're awake, Fey,' a rough voice said from behind her.

She twisted, trying to look around, but the owner of the voice stepped around before her. She gasped in horror. The face, beneath a dark metal helm, was scarred and ugly, the nose broken and deformed.

An Icelord!

'You're in the wrong part of the world, Fey,' the man continued. 'Spying on our affairs, what were you doing here?'

'I am no spy,' Tarithel replied.

She saw his eyes narrow. He stepped back a pace and looked away as if in thought.

She didn't see the blow coming. It was fast and brutal, knocking her head back against the stake. A moment later his hand was at her throat, choking her.

'If I say you're a spy, Fey-girl, a spy you are,' he growled. He was so close she could smell his breath, foul and rank. 'I am Imgasharg, Icelord of this realm. You are my prisoner. I'll ask again.' His grip on her throat tightened further, 'What are you doing in my lands?'

'I will not tell you!' she managed to cry out. She could feel her face bruised and sore, the pain in her nose and cheek causing her to screw her eyes tight closed.

After a moment, he released his hold. She gasped, drawing air into her lungs, trying to get her breath back. She opened her eyes.

A flash of light …

Before she could react a knife was at her throat, she could feel the cold metal of the blade against her skin.

'I have killed many Fey in my time,' he said, his voice almost conversational. 'Some I have killed quickly in battle, hewing them down as they stood against me, others I have taken captive and let them bleed out, crying for mercy. It matters little to me how you meet your end Fey-girl, but an end you will meet by my hand. The question is … will you meet it quick, or will you meet it slow?'

He pushed the knife up her cheek, the point of it pinching at her skin, but not quite cutting it. He inched it closer and closer to her eye, until she could see its blurred outline. She struggled, but his grip was firm.

'We can start by taking away these pretty looks of yours,' Imgasharg laughed. 'Your people doubtless gaze upon your fairness and think you greatly blessed. I hope you won't talk straight away, there is much I can do to a woman to cause suffering ...'

Tarithel struggled again, rage building in her. A green glow grew about her. She knew what was coming.

'Let me go, or it will go ill for you.'

'Let you go?' Imgasharg chuckled. 'No woman tells me my business, least of all a Fey! You will know your place girl ...'

The knife slashed at her clothing, he grabbed at it too, ripping and tearing, his intentions clear.

'No ...'

Rage flared, burning hot. The jewel in her pocket was scalding her skin, her clothes began to smoke. Green light splashed out, casting bright beams and sharp dark shadows about her.

Imgasharg was flung backwards as eerie green fire consumed the Fey-girl. He fell backwards to the floor, watching dumbstruck as the flames ran up her body, burning away first her clothes, then the ropes that held her and then consuming the stake as well. She stepped forward, her face a mask of fury. An elemental sprite, filled with wrath.

Wind, summoned out of nowhere, was spiralling around her form, whipping up a blistering cloud of dust and dirt.

His men came up beside him.

'Kill her!' Imgasharg yelled.

Two of his warriors leapt forward, swords aloft, swinging at the girl. Green fire sprouted from her outstretched fingers, consuming them, immolating them in moment, leaving nothing but burnt husks before her. She stepped forward towards him again, reaching out to grab him.

Arrows flew from behind him; arrows that should have slain her on the spot. Their aim was true and good, targeted at her heart and throat. Yet the arrows kindled in mid-flight, evaporating in puffs of ash before they reached her.

Imgasharg heard his men panic and back away. He turned to see the girl upon him, her fingers at his throat now, lifting him up with unbelievable strength.

'I choose quick,' she said, her voice echoing around him in a terrifying cacophony of noise.

He felt her fingers tighten, then his world ended.

Talorthane looked up as the sounds of conversation reached him from the edge of the camp. He got to his feet.

'My Lord!' one of his men called, looming out of the mist alongside another.

'What is it?'

'Some disturbance in Imgasharg's camp, sire.'

'An attack?'

The confused look in his men's faces and their lack of response made Talorthane march forwards to a small rise in the land to the south of the camp and peer into the darkness.

Under the faint moonlight and starlight it was difficult to see much to the south, the mist was lying thick on the landscape, but the red fires of Imgasharg's camp could be made out, smoke rising about them.

Talorthane took a look and then turned to his men.

'I see nothing amiss?'

'There was a flash of green light … there!'

Talorthane looked again, this time seeing something. In the midst of the camp there was indeed a flicker of unearthly green light. It was bright enough to make the mist flare. Talorthane could even see it writhe away from the source, whatever it might be, the light casting flickering columns of light in the darkness.

'What is he doing? Conjuring something …?'

The brightness grew, the greenness flickering about the

camp. The mist seemed to recoil and Talorthane could see a funnel of air swirling about the area, centred on the eerie light.

'What devilry is this?'

The green light was extinguished. Talorthane and his men saw some kind of faint sphere expand from the point as they blinked their eyes, trying to see. The red fires of the camp were gone too, their smoke dissipating into the air. A moment later, a faint thump of noise echoed around them and the ground trembled.

'What was that?'

'We will find out,' Talorthane said to the two men. 'Saddle three horses and join me for a patrol. Be cautious!'

Tarithel staggered and collapsed to her knees as the power left her. Around her was nothing but smoke and ash.

No, I don't want this ... my life was not about death and destruction, however worthy of that fate these men were ...

Tears dripped down her cheeks and she clenched her hands, looking up into the dark sky.

'I do not want this!' she screamed. 'I do not want to be this sorceress you demand I be!'

Consciousness fled, leaving her lying prone upon the ground.

The Iceguard riders slowed at a gesture from Talorthane. Their horses' gallop slackened to a canter and then a walk.

Something loomed out of the mist. As they approached its form became clear, the body of a horse.

Talorthane looked. It had been slain; a number of arrows protruded from its flank. He dismounted to get a closer look.

'This is not one of ours,' he said. 'This bridle, the saddle … these are Fey.'

'A Fey horse?' one of his men answered. 'Here?'

'Imgasharg's camp lies yonder,' Talorthane said, walking forward into the mist, leading his own horse on.

The mist itself had thinned, it seemed almost to be avoiding the area of the camp. As they approached it cleared. Beside him, his horse snorted as if unnerved by the sight before it.

Of Imgasharg's camp, nothing remained. All about Talorthane was nothing but piles of ash, heaped here and there.

Talorthane looked about himself, drawing his sword and stepping forward, his two men beside him.

'Watch yourselves,' Talorthane said under his breath. 'Sorcery of some kind I fear …'

'Where are Imgasharg's men?' Another whispered.

As they stepped forward, amidst the ash they could see burnt shapes, crusted into contorted mounds upon the ground. Talormane stepped closer to one and prodded it with his sword. It crumbled away, appearing to be hollow. Talorthane frowned, peering closer. Within he could almost make out something …

Bones! Blackened twisted bones!

'I think we have found them,' Talorthane swallowed. 'They are all about us.'

'An entire detachment?' the other said. 'Wiped out? By whom, and how?'

Talorthane held a finger to his lips and gestured ahead. The three Iceguard warriors could make out a faint green glow before them.

Making as little sound as they could, they crept towards the light. There was a depression in the ground and as they approached they could make out it was circular. In a moment they stood upon the rim, looking down into it.

In the very centre lay the body of a naked woman. She was

unconscious, lying on her side, her arms wrapped around her chest and her legs curled up. Her hair was spread out all around her. Clenched in her hand lay the source of the green light, a jewel that sparkled on the end of a necklace.

They watched her for a long moment, but there was no movement. Talorthane sheaved his sword and the others did likewise. He scrambled down towards her and looked her over, his men standing beside him.

'A Fey,' Talorthane muttered.

Talorthane remembered the conversation he had with Lorelorn before setting out.

This has to be her ...

His hand went to the pommel of his sword. This could be none other than the red-haired girl Shareth's instructions had mentioned and Lorelorn had directed him to find. She was a vassal of the Moonprince who was causing so much unrest in the south, who dared to trespass into the realm of the Frozen Empire in defiance of Shareth's will. She was a sworn enemy, and, so it seemed, a sorceress too. Reason enough for Shareth to fear her.

Shareth wants her dead ... yet Lorelorn instructed me to bring her to him. What secrets might she be able to tell us?

Talorthane had no great love for the Fey, but when he had encountered them they had always fought in line with accepted rules of engagement. He had admired their discipline and prowess, even if they defied the will of his mistress.

And what will that mean for Lorelorn and I?

He looked down at the Fey-girl. Her face was pale and young looking, though age was not something you could ever gauge with the Fey. Her skin was fair, but bruised and marked with muddy stains.

What is your story ... why does Shareth want you dead?

'We will take her back to our camp,' Talorthane said. 'A cloak! Give me a cloak.'

'Sire … are you sure?' the first warrior replied, pulling a cloak from the saddle of his horse and handing it to Talorthane. 'She is a sorceress! If she does to us what she did here …'

'Knowing Imgasharg,' Talorthane said. 'I think I can surmise what happened. I will take a more subtle approach.'

'You know who she is, then?'

'I have a shrewd idea, yes.'

Talorthane wrapped the unconscious Fey-girl's body in the cloak.

'But have her bound and gagged,' he said. 'I want to find out what she's about.'

Chapter Seventeen

Tarithel the Fey stands on the Plains of Morormarg looking north-west to the Forest of Farorn.

The Moonguard of Luxor and the armies of Carorthane the Fey had made their way east and north through the vales of the forest. It was a land of rolling green hills and fair valleys, dusted with snow, but showing still the life of the land that slumbered beneath the ice. Here and there patches of green showed through, with the occasional wild flower by the wayside. Even had he not known he was in the lands of the Fey, Luxor would have recognised their mark straight away.

The armies paused atop a hill in the bright sunlight, looking across a forest that stretched out of sight to the north and the east. The trees were dark hued, but seemed welcoming in the high spring sunshine.

'There lies Fangrim,' Carorthane said. 'The greatest forest of the Icemark, and some say of all realms under the sun. Twelve leagues it runs to the north and more than forty to the east before it stops at the edge of the wastes. Long it has been our home.'

'It is greater than any of the forests of Midnight,' Luxor said, turning his horse alongside Carorthane. 'That I can say for sure. I dare say the Fey of my homeland would be jealous of such a territory.'

'We have lived here for long moons,' Carorthane said. 'And been sore put to it many times. The Fey control many lands hereabouts, particularly south of the forest, but it is the forest itself we call home. None have ever wrested it from us … to do so would mark the end of our people.'

'I hope such a thing will never occur,' Luxor replied.

'As do I,' Carorthane replied. 'Come. We must ride on swiftly if we are to reach Imorthorn ere nightfall. I will lead you on paths which you otherwise might not find and the forest will ease our passing.'

Giving orders to their men, both rode on down the hill and entered the boundaries of the forest. The paths within were wide and well made, smooth for their horses' hooves. They rode on through the eaves, continuing on their way.

'I look forward to meeting Lord Imorthorn,' Luxor said. 'Can you tell me much of him?'

Carorthane nodded. 'He is both wise and firm. He has the respect of those that matter and has long led us through difficult times in the Icemark. He is old, even as the Fey measure things, but his wit and wisdom have not failed. Some will always grumble of course …'

'And of what do they grumble?'

'Some accuse him of favouring the politics of the western ends of our realm over the east. You may hear rumbles from the Lords of the East. Imgorthand is chief amongst those. He will always counsel that we do not interfere with the politics of other races, especially if it involves the Heartstealer. Of course … hidden away in the east he does not have the Barbarians upon his flank like I do, nor the Dwarves causing mischief in the north!'

'Imorthorn has a great realm to hold together,' Luxor said with a nod. 'With many competing interests.'

'If Imorthorn has a fault,' Carorthane said. 'And I say this as both his friend and his vassal … it is that he will not always give time for our council to reach a conclusion. It was so with both you and your emissary, Tarithel.'

'How so?'

'She came to us unexpectedly, with the wildest of wild tales,' Carorthane said. 'If I was any judge of character, she was indeed true and honest. Imorthorn certainly thought so, but not everyone was convinced …'

'Imgorthand?' Luxor asked, with a raised eyebrow.

Carorthane smiled. 'How did you guess?' He chuckled. 'Well … she did come bearing tidings of war and conflict with the Heartstealer, not the most welcome of news to be sure! Imorthorn sent her on her way and pledged the loyalty of the Fey of Icemark to you Moonprince … on the strength of her conduct alone. Some might call that rash. Imorthorn decided … and the council was not involved directly in that decision.'

Luxor nodded, thinking it over. 'And what do you think, Lord Carorthane?'

'I think we have pandered to the whims of the Heartstealer for too many moons already,' he answered. 'We have seen her send armies between our realm and that of the Barbarians. She grows bolder all the time. She would keep us in what she thinks is our place … that irks me. I do not like the feeling we are hemmed in and she decides what our place is.'

'Such situations are not stable forever.'

'No indeed,' Carorthane said. 'But the Fey cannot tip that balance alone.'

'I hoped to have better tidings than those I do,' Luxor said. 'But the Fey are alone in their struggle against the Heartstealer this far. My efforts with the Barbarians may have come to naught, but there may be favourable news from the Giants. There is the chance of change, my Lord Carorthane … and with the support of the Fey, we might push things in the direction we all desire.'

'I would hear more of this,' Carorthane said.

'I must take tidings to Imorthorn first,' Luxor answered.

'Of course,' Carorthane said. 'Such things are right and proper. We make good time … see, the City lies just ahead.'

Carorthane was right. The eaves of the forest were thinning and a valley was opening up before them. Not far away one of the Towers of the Wise stood on the southern edge, its shadow reaching across fair and well-tended lands. Perhaps two leagues away, glowing in the setting sun, was a dramatic sight, the City of Imorthorn, rising up from the middle of the valley, surrounded by fields and a sinuous winding river.

'Imorthorn will be expecting us,' Carorthane said.

With the sun red behind them, the company descended into the valley and rode towards the city.

Tarithel woke again.

Pain thudded through her head, pulsing across her forehead. The greenness was gone, the rage had fled, she was herself once more …

Images flickered in her mind, herself, yet … not herself, raging with fury, obliterating the men that assailed her.

Not me … surely, not me!

She tried to sit up, but found she couldn't move. A few moments of struggle told her she was bound once more, her ankles and knees tied together with her arms held behind her back. She could feel rope around her wrists and a foul tasting gag in her mouth. A cloak covered her, tied around her neck. She was helpless and shivering with cold.

Before her, she could make out a campfire ringed with rocks. A simple cast iron pot was suspended above it. Beyond that a man sat, watching her.

He was dressed in dark, stained armour, with a black helm upon his face. The flames from the fire illuminated his eyes just enough for her to see them glinting in the darkness of his face.

Another Icelord!

She wriggled again, trying in vain to get free.

The man chuckled.

'I have captured you, little Fey,' he said. His voice was deep, but not rough. 'But one such as you may have the means to escape regardless. Either way, a Fey does not venture into the Frozen Empire unmarked. Your fate lies with me now. Can I trust you just to talk?'

She glared at him, watching as he got to his feet. She saw a knife appear in his hand as he came towards her. She recoiled, trying to twist away.

'I will hear what you have to say first if you are willing,' he said, drawing closer. 'Try to escape, summon your spells or scream for help and your end will be swift, do you understand?'

Tarithel stared up at him, but relented. She managed a nod.

The man slipped the knife inside the gag alongside her cheek. With a quick twist he cut the gag. She spat it out of her mouth as he let go. He turned his attention to the bonds around her wrists and ankles, untying them before sitting back and regarding her. The knife was still in his hand.

'Are you cold?' he asked.

Tarithel glared at him.

The man grabbed at a loose bundle of clothing and threw it towards her.

'It might not be the latest fashion, but it is all I have,' he said.

Tarithel pulled the cloak tighter about her, but it was not going to ward out the cold night air. She grabbed at the bundle and untied it, finding a rough hide tunic and leather breeches within. The man lowered his gaze, but she could see he kept his knife ready. She pulled the clothing on, throwing the cloak over the top. All the garments were coarse and musty, but they were warm.

Once she had finished she looked at him again, seeing him return her gaze. He was still sitting across from her, the knife in his hand.

'Your name, Fey.'

'I will not tell you my name!' Tarithel snapped.

'Your presence is known to us,' he said, tossing the knife in his hand. Tarithel saw how he caught it each time. 'It might be safest for me to kill you, though I'd sooner know of what you are about.'

'You will kill me anyway,' Tarithel replied. 'I know enough of you Icelords to know that.'

'You speak of Imgasharg,' the man said. 'You slew him and his men using sorcery so it would seem. I was not aware the Fey practiced such fell arts, I thought that to be the sole domain of my mistress.'

'I …' Tarithel decided not to answer the question. The man looked at her without saying anything.

'Why would I tell you anything?' she replied. 'We are enemies, you and I. If your orders are to kill me, then try it and reap the consequences!'

The man thought for a moment.

'I have no wish to die at your hand,' he replied. 'It would have been easy to slay you before you woke. Perhaps it would have been safer to do so given what I have seen you do.'

Tarithel didn't answer.

'However,' he continued. 'I think that I may have discovered the source of your arcane powers …'

He used his knife to unwrap a folded piece of fabric that lay on the ground nearby. Within the cloth lay the necklace with the green jewel she had carried. He hooked the necklace with the knife held it up, examining the jewel.

'Yes,' he said, watching her expression. 'This jewel was

clenched in your fist when we found you. I have not dared touch it, fearing it might spell my own demise. I daresay my mistress would be very pleased to receive such a Talisman …'

'No!' Tarithel said, lurching forward. 'It is mine, given to me! An heirloom of my house!'

'I think I will keep it safe for now,' the man said, returning the necklace to the fabric and wrapping it up again before secreting it away within his clothing.

Tarithel glared at him.

'I've been told you are an enemy of my people,' the man continued. 'And I see precisely how such as you can be quite so feared. I have not tried to slay you, not yet. I would hear what you have to say. So … what is it to be?'

Tarithel looked at him in surprise. The man had a faint grin upon his face.

'My name is Tarithel,' she replied.

The man nodded.

'Now,' he said, with a chuckle. 'That wasn't so bad, was it?'

'Who are you?' Tarithel demanded.

'My name is Talorthane,' the man replied. 'Of the Frozen Empire.'

'An Icelord,' Tarithel said. 'I will tell you nothing more. You are a servant of Shareth the Heartstealer, my sworn enemy.'

Talorthane nodded.

'What you say is true enough,' he replied. 'But not all of us are cut from the same cloth. We are doubtless painted as a despicable foe by your people, bereft of honour, thought and manners, blindly following the will of she who leads us.'

Tarithel swallowed.

'I see my words are not far from the mark,' Talorthane said, with a grin. 'You met Imgasharg and his men of course.'

'Those that … I slew,' Tarithel replied.

'Yes,' Talorthane replied. 'He was exactly as you've been led to believe, few will mourn his passing, least of all me. Many

Icelords are of a similar ilk, but not all are without some more enlightened thoughts.'

'What do you intend with me?' Tarithel asked, pulling her knees up close to her chest and wrapping her arms around them.

'Shareth has ordered your death,' Talorthane replied. 'Even by speaking to you I am breaking her command, it's treason probably, death for certain … if I am found to be disobeying her directives.'

'Then …'

'You have piqued my curiosity and that of my master,' Talorthane replied. 'Not all Icelords are mindless killers, bent on ravaging whatsoever comes our way. Some retain the wit to look at things beyond our immediate sight. We have heard of the Moonprince in the southern realms, we have seen the unease which that news has brought to those we serve. Change … is change. These are interesting times. Some of us would know what you intend.'

'And I will not tell you,' Tarithel replied.

'Ah yes,' Talorthane said, a grin splitting his face. 'Sworn enemies we are, and trust cannot be built. We are doomed to forever battle until one side lies dead upon the soil, blood spilt. Is this not so?'

Tarithel wasn't sure whether to nod or not.

'Or one side has to take something on trust, to believe there's another way, to take a risk …'

He leant forward, gesturing with his knife. In a moment he threw it aside, out of reach.

'There,' Talorthane said. 'You are free to cast your magic spells, to burn me and my men to death, or whatever it is that you do. Or … we can talk and determine whether this madness has another outcome.'

Tarithel didn't move for a long moment.

'Are you hungry?' he asked. 'Still cold? Warm yourself here.'

Tarithel cast a wary glance at him, but the warmth of the fire was too enticing and she shuffled across. Talorthane pulled meat from the spit and held a bone out towards her.

'Here.'

She looked at him for a long moment.

'Or you can starve,' he said. 'That will solve both our problems.'

She took it, biting down ravenously, she couldn't remember the last time she had eaten. The meat was good. She wiped juice from her chin.

'I cannot trust you,' she said. 'Even if I wanted to. Your mistress is my sworn enemy, that much is true enough and no secret.'

'She fears you, you know,' Talorthane said. 'She has her minions searching for you with orders to end your life. I think she cares little for you, it seems most likely to me that it is your jewel she seeks. Why should that be?'

He tapped his chest where Tarithel had seen him hide her necklace.

'She is the daughter of the Witchking,' Tarithel replied. 'She seeks to dominate all lands and wrest them to her will. Power is all she craves. The power to subjugate and destroy!'

'And this is not what you seek?' Talorthane asked. 'You come into our realm, bearing potent magic and despatching our people. Your purpose seems akin to hers. Just another woman's wrath?'

'I am nothing like her!' Tarithel cried. 'I came hither only to free my …'

Tarithel stopped and glared.

Talorthane smiled. 'Ah … a captive then. Someone close to you I surmise? Held at Shareth's pleasure.'

Tarithel pursed her lips.

'Very well then,' she said. 'She stole my betrothed from me … on my wedding day. She holds him locked away in some fetid dungeon. I will not leave him to that fate, I will die first!'

Talorthane looked at her, rubbing his chin. 'Then you have traipsed the length of the Icemark for the sake of love alone?'

'It is as you say,' Tarithel said.

Talorthane smiled. 'And yet you command your own sorcery … and this Moonprince of the southern realms has nothing to do with your quest?'

'The Moonprince has other reasons to defy your mistress,' Tarithel said. 'They are his own.'

'And your people were happy to let you ride north into our realm with no guard or escort?' Talorthane continued.

'Stealth is easier to achieve alone,' Tarithel replied.

Talorthane laughed.

'So it is,' he said. 'And I admire your fortitude and skill to have come thus far, but you must have known that your quest was in vain. None can travel through the Frozen Empire unless it be by the will of Shareth … or those who serve her.'

'I can tell you nothing more,' Tarithel said. 'You must kill me, or let me go.'

'I shall do neither,' Talorthane replied. 'Your fate will be decided by one greater than I. For myself I am not ranked highly in the ranks of our people. I am but a vassal of greater lords. My liege will listen to your story and make his decision on your fate.'

Tarithel didn't answer, but raised her head, ensuring she kept Talorthane gazed locked on her own.

'But beware, fair Fey-girl of the southern realms,' Talorthane said. 'I suspect what you have already told me is the truth, but if you do not give a fuller account of yourself and your intentions … your death awaits you within a short space of days.'

'Where are you taking me?' Tarithel demanded.

'I will be taking you to one of Shareth's closest servants,' Talorthane said. 'She has six trusted warlords and he is great amongst them. Your life will be held in his hands.'

Tarithel swallowed.

'I must ask one thing before we leave,' she said.

Talorthane narrowed his eyes.

'My horse was slain by Imgasharg and his men,' she said. 'You won't understand … but …'

Talorthane looked at her and nodded.

'A loyal creature,' he said. 'I do appreciate such things. We found your horse, not far from the camp. We raised a pyre as is our way.'

Tarithel clenched her eyes shut against the burning tears that gathered there.

'Then there is nothing more to be done,' she managed.

'We will depart immediately and ride north,' Talorthane said. 'Shareth's own armies and full strength are being deployed through this vale. If she finds us all our deaths will likely be painful and drawn out. His city is deep within the Forest of Farorn. Speak well in his presence … and I would urge you to tell the truth … to Lorelorn the Icelord.'

Barbarian armies stood on the Plains of Thenorn. Through the night they had made their way through the dark trees of the Forest of Firun, itself nestled in a narrow choke point between the twin mountain ranges of Anvulane and Anvormane. To the south lay their homelands, held by their people since time immemorial, to the north lay the country of the Giants.

And now, they stood upon the territory of the Giants, combative and ready for war.

Not far to the north lay the Fortress of Ganigrorn, the southernmost outpost of the Giants this far east. The fortress was well known to the Barbarians, it had been fought over many times in the past, but had never fallen from the Giants' control. It was the vital gatekeeper of their domain and they had always defended it well.

Imgorad brought his men to a halt and his captains saw to the organisation of the army. Alongside him stood much of the leadership of the Barbarians; Firak, Anvorthun, Thorthak, Lorangrorn, Thangrad and Thortheon. Kahudrak and Kahudrarg stood nearby too, conversing in low tones as they surveyed the lands ahead.

It seemed that the Giants had not been idle during the hours of night. The Fortress was always well guarded and smoke was rising from within its walls.

'They expect us,' Imgorad muttered.

'We have kept a watch for several days,' Thortheon replied. 'Armies have returned to re-inforce it, but we have the numbers to overwhelm them and there are no further reinforcements to come, the Heartstealer has seen to that. One of our scouts reported that several of their cities are aflame to the far north. They fight a battle on two flanks.'

Imgorad nodded. 'Never an easy thing to contend with. Then let us put them out of their misery once and for all.'

He gave a signal and rode forwards, the other Barbarians followed suit, riding from the protective cover of the forest on to the open plains. Banners were hoisted aloft, proudly displaying the grim devices of the Barbarians, knives, swords and halberds embroidered in blood red on black canvas.

'We will move to take the roads both north and south,' Imgorad said. 'Deploy our forces in that regard, but stay out of range of their defences for now.'

'You seek to negotiate?' Thortheon asked in surprise.

Imgorad laughed. 'Negotiate? Never. We will take by force what is to become ours, we must earn it. Besides, the Giants would never willingly give up their land to us. Once we're in position …'

Thortheon grinned in response.

'They will make a good fight of it,' he replied. 'They always do.'

'I expect nothing less,' Imgorad replied and spurred his horse forward.

It took several hours for the Barbarian armies to encircle the Fortress. Following their instructions they had left a gap of more than a hundred yards around the perimeter, keeping out of range of any potential rocks being hurled at them. As dawn gave way to morning, the sound of hammers filled the air. The engineers they had brought with them began working on assembling the devices and weaponry required to mount an assault on the fortress. Imgorad surveyed the progress with a watchful eye.

'What do you make of their defences?' he called to Thortheon.

'Unchanged,' Thortheon replied, squinting at the fortress and giving it a further look over. 'The walls are thick, thicker than our own, we have no way to breach the rock and stone. Either we go through the gate, or we scale the walls.'

'The gate will cost us many lives,' Imgorad mused. 'We will stick to our usual tactics I think, reaching the walls with ladders and towers will serve us best. A combined attack from all points of the compass should overwhelm the defenders on the walls. With those gained, our superior numbers will win the day.'

Thortheon nodded. 'So shall it be.'

'We will attack at the second hour,' Imgorad said. 'Be sure all is ready.'

Glormane looked up as messengers stomped into his hall, they bowed low before him.

'What news?' Glormane said, fearing the worst from the

downcast expressions on their faces. 'Have there been tidings of Imulorn and Imelorn?'

'None have heard from them, my Liege,' the first said. 'We bring news from the east. The Icelords have moved against our eastern defences in great force.'

'Carorthay?' Glormane asked.

'His city has fallen to the enemy,' the messenger replied. 'Carorthay and what remains of his army retreat towards us.'

'He lives?'

'He did when I departed at his instruction to bring you news.'

Glormane staggered back, shaking his head. 'The Icelords have invaded our realm?'

The messenger nodded. 'I set out but a day ago, my Liege. The Icelord army was vast beyond count, tens of thousands of warriors march upon us out of the north and east. None could defy them … but there is worse news …'

'Worse?' Glormane echoed.

'They knew of our tactics and defences,' the messenger said. 'Dwarves march in their ranks …'

'Imgorarg's legacy,' Glormane spat.

'Banners of the northern Dwarves were seen amongst those of the Icelord Fangrorn,' the messenger said.

'Treachery then,' Glormane said. 'Doubtless there are still those who believe the false promises by the Heartstealer. Where is Carorthay now?'

'He had retreated to the Fortress of Hagudril,' the messenger answered. 'Falling back from the Icelord advance.'

Glormane shook his head.

'If some of our folk march with the Icelords that will go ill for Carorthay,' he said. 'Mark my words and send fresh messengers out. All forces loyal to my banner are to retreat here, to my city as fast as they may come, including Carorthay.

Our strength must be concentrated if we are not to lose our homeland. Be swift!'

The land was black with them. The might of the Icelords marched south unopposed. Their banners were black with fierce emblems emblazoned on them, devices of claws, teeth, fangs and horned tails. Such a host had rarely been seen in the Icemark. Tens of thousands of Iceguard warriors marched and rode in tight precision.

They had begun to muster at the City of Zarashand and a mighty host had set forth once provisions and weaponry were made ready. Their march took them first south through their own lands, rendezvousing with yet more armies along the way. They had turned to the west, entering the Vale of Morormarg, south of the great Forest of Farorn. As they had made their camp, more might arrived, with the armies of Glormarg, having assembled their strength and marched up from the south-eastern end of Shareth's territory.

Now Zarashand and Glormarg rode at the forefront of the mightiest army upon the face of the Icemark. Tens of thousands of warriors and riders were at their command.

But they were not alone.

Bearing a crown that sparkled with some light not of this world, a woman led them all. Zarashand and Glormarg rode either side of her, submissive and attentive to her direction. She was cloaked in a deep magenta gown, girded with a sword. She held a staff aloft, her dark hair braided with metal charms, themselves decorated in ancient rune work. Her eyes blazed with fierce intent and none could hold her gaze.

She raised the staff and the armies about her came to a halt on the borders of her realm, alongside the Fortress of Kahudrun.

'Here of old and of late is the boundary of the lands I call my own,' she said, her voice carrying over the air in a manner none could explain. All heard her words as if she was standing nearby, yet she never raised her voice to a shout. 'Within the realm of the Frozen Empire I have bided my time, content to wait for my inheritance to be given to me … but now I have been usurped and challenged. The pathetic Moonprince of the realm of Midnight has slain my wastrel father and sets himself up in my place.

'But no longer,' she continued. 'The Icemark is mine as are the lands beyond it. Icemark will be subdued and those who will not turn their loyalties to me alone are to be eradicated from the lands be they Giant, Dwarf, Barbarian or Fey. I will spare them not! All these lands I claim and so shall it be. I, Shareth, am Empress, not just of the Frozen Empire, but of all Icemark!'

Cheers greeted her words, a rousing chant rose and fell to the rhythm of her utterances.

'And when Icemark finally belongs to me in its entirety,' she called out. 'Then other realms will know me too, starting with the realm of Midnight. He who slew my father will feel my wrath! I will flay the flesh from his bones and hoist his carcass aloft as a warning to all who defy me. I will be Empress, not just of Icemark, not just of Midnight … I will be Empress of all!'

She raised her staff higher and a strange blackness grew from it, writhing and twisting, lit here and there with a cyan fire, cold and evil, crackling and flickering around her.

She thrust her staff down upon the ground. A shock of noise and a great tremor went out from it, making the Iceguard warriors stumble and their horses whinny in fear. Beyond them the tremor grew stronger, shocking through rivers, raising spray and waves, rumbling through both the hills and the mountains, bringing down rocks from great heights. Across the Icemark it rumbled. The Giants felt it and turned aside from their work, looking east and wondering at the darkness gathering in the sky. To the east the Dwarves felt the foundations of their cities tremble and they cried out in consternation. Even the Barbarians paused in their war to gaze at each other. Even as far as the forests of the Fey, the trees swayed above the bewildered people, moving against the wind.

'Be it known!' Shareth said, raising her voice to a cry. 'Shareth is upon you now! Let all the Icemark tremble before my might! My wrath is unleashed and will fall upon all who will not bow to me. Woe to all, fear will be your constant companion from this moment forth!'

Lightning crackled about her, scattering down to the ground and flickering around the forest edge and the mountains to the south.

She rode on.

The vast army entered the lands of the Giants, turning south between the mountains of Anvormane and Anvulane. Their thumping footsteps echoed for leagues around, but they had no need of stealth.

The great war of the Icemark had begun.

Messengers had returned to Glormane by sunset of the day after he'd sent his missives. The remaining armies of the Dwarven realm loyal to him were already marching, from the west and the south where their strength was greatest. To the east Carorthay had been making a strategic withdrawal ahead of the Icelord advance and was marching back towards the City of Glormane in as swift a manner as he could. Nothing had come from the north, the forces that had been loyal to Imgorarg were now pledged to the Heartstealer.

As dawn broke across the hills to the north of the City, Glormane could see the banners approaching.

'Torelorn, Thatruk, Thudrun and Lorangrarg,' he noted with a grim smile. 'Five thousand of our best will be here by nightfall. It's a start. Thigrak has sent his army, along with those of Imulorn and Imelorn ...'

Glormane's thoughts turned to the two brothers.

What has transpired there? Has Tarithel made her way safely into the north ... Imulorn and Imelorn have yet to return ... there has been no news and I can spare no one to search for them.

Glormane spied more banners in the hills to the east. He squinted into the early morning glare.

'Carorthay!' he whispered and then called out. 'Carorthay is here!'

The gates of the city were flung wide at his command as the army approached. Glormane could see the army was far smaller than he had hoped, scarce a thousand Dwarves by a quick count. Glormane hurried down through the city and walked out to meet them as they approached.

Carorthay walked at the fore, and Glormane could see that he was battle-weary, his face streaked with blood and grim.

'Carorthay ...'

'We fought hard, my Liege, but their numbers are like a plague of insects issuing out of the north. Fifteen, perhaps twenty thousand, of their foul warriors march against us. They are less than a day behind us so my scouts report, mounted on horseback ... they will be here before sundown ... and those traitorous northern Dwarves stand within their ranks!'

'I have so heard,' Glormane answered. 'We can do little about that but stand and defend what is rightfully ours. Armies have been summoned and we have done all we can to hasten their arrival.'

'It will be our sternest test,' Carorthay answered. 'Shareth's reach grows long and greedy.'

'We will defy her,' Glormane said. 'We are Dwarves!'

'Yet I have one piece of good news for you,' Carorthay said.

'Good news?' Glormane replied. 'Glad tidings are always welcome, but what can this be in this time of war?'

Carorthay smiled.

'Two waifs and strays found wandering in the wilderness,' Carorthay said with a chuckle and then stepped aside. Glormane saw two Dwarves standing in the shadows behind him.

'Imulorn, Imelorn!' he cried. 'I feared you dead!'

'We very nearly were a number of times,' Imulorn replied. 'Hagudril rescued us ...'

'A tale that needs to be told,' Glormane said. 'But perhaps when there is more time. What of Tarithel?'

'We saw her safely to the Temple,' Imulorn answered. 'We ventured inside. What became of her after that ... we do not know.'

'The Temple was cursed,' Imulorn said. 'Some dark magic that stole away our strength and we were captured by traitorous northern Dwarves ...'

Glormane sighed. 'Then she is beyond our help. We have done our part as best we can.'

The Fortress of Ganigrorn was besieged. All about it lay the forces of the Barbarians, in numbers that the Giants could not hope to assail. They huddled down within their thick walls of stone as the final preparations for battle were made beyond. Rain and sleet slashed through the air, but fires below were kindled nonetheless. Within moments great flaming missiles were launched into the air by the arts of the

Barbarians, crashing down within the city and setting the buildings within ablaze.

The Giants could do little but withstand the attack as best they could. They did not employ the ranged weapons of their foes, long trusting to the strength of their defences. Giants were fierce enemies at closer range, but they had not the cunning and inventiveness of their foes to the south.

Yet the fires caused little overall damage to the Giants' halls of stone, and their warriors shrugged off the flames, taunting the Barbarians from the battlements and throwing heavy rocks at those who ventured too close to the walls.

The respite did not last long.

Heavy devices in the form of ballistae, great crossbow-like siege weapons, were unleashed against the walls, some throwing bolts and stones, others sharp pikes attached to ropes that fixed themselves into the stonework. Where they secured themselves, the ropes were pulled tight and the ladders were winched into position.

The Barbarians were well versed in the arts of war, the ladders being raised in quick succession, slamming down upon the walls and securing themselves in place with great claws of iron. Armed with swords and axes, supported from below by more soldiers with crossbows and bows, the Barbarians stormed the walls of the City.

For their part, the Giants responded in their own fashion. Rocks were hurled, pulverising men at close range, for the Giants could heft and swing rocks that required two men to even move. Barbarians were flung from the walls by blows or crushed to pulp beneath hard stone. On equal terms, none could withstand the fury of an angered Giant, but the Barbarians were wise to this, relying on ranged weapons, nets and cunning to defeat their opponents … and sheer numbers began to dictate the course of the battle.

Imgorad and Thorthorn looked on as a flag bearing the

device of Ganigrorn mounted on one of the four turrets of the Fortress fell. Moments later a banner of the Barbarians was raised in its place.

'The battle goes well,' Thortheon nodded.

'Press the attack on the gate,' Imgorad instructed. 'Let us ride now and take the Fortress!'

Horns summoned the ranks of Barbarians to attention about their leaders. Several of the ballistae were targeted now on the great gates of the city. They were sturdy, made of oak long aged and strengthened by the lore of the Giants, but they remained the weakest point of the fortress. Missiles and bolts crashed against them and flames rose. Under the onslaught the great hinges spat their rivets, buckled and failed.

Another round of battering from the weapons of the Barbarians splintered it into ruin. The Barbarians gave a great cry, and with Imgorad and Thortheon at their head they charged the ranks of the Giants who attempted to swarm out and stop the entrance.

Thousands were already dead or dying, the walls running with blood and streaked with the black marks of flame.

The Giants must have known that their defeat was at hand but they gave no quarter, each of them defending the fortress with their lives. Thortheon found himself unhorsed, his steed killed by a Giant in a murderous rage who was only felled by the quick actions of archers behind him. The gateway to the fortress was plugged by the bodies of Barbarians, Giants and the horses of the cavalry, the losses mounting as the day wore on and still the gates were not taken.

Imgorad downed several of the Giants that came against him, only to find his own horse was slain, but still upright due to the ghastly press of battle. He clambered up and away, wielding his broadsword to the dismay of his opponents. The Barbarians reached the threshold of the gate, standing there streaked in blood and gore, ready to flood into the fortress beyond when …

Horns sounded to the north, deep and sonorous.

They were not those of the Giants, nor were they those of the Barbarians.

Banners were hoisted, with black fabrics and garish fierce devices emblazoned on them. Imgorad turned in confusion as he recognised them.

'Zarashand! Glormarg!' he muttered, before his voice turned to a yell. 'Icelords!'

A vast army could be seen approaching from either side of the great stones that rose amidst the plain, looking like a black swarm spreading towards them.

'Form ranks!' Imgorad shouted amidst the confusion.

Even as he did so, another banner was hoisted from the approaching army. Even Imgorad felt cold seep into his heart and his courage falter. That banner was also black, but with a silver crown emblazoned on it. A banner that had never fallen in battle and the army that bore it had never been defeated.

'Our scouts reported nothing …' Thortheon muttered. 'How can the Icelords be here? They are engaged far to the north with the Giants, so we understood! What business do they … ?' He caught sight of the third banner. 'Is she…!'

Imgorad nodded.

''The Heartstealer cometh.'

The Icelord army marched forward and then came to a halt. The battle for the fortress ebbed and an uneasy peace settled amongst the protagonists.

Then, to the right flank of the Barbarians, two banners were hoisted anew and riders could be seen galloping northwards.

Imgorad stared in disbelief.

'What are they doing?' he demanded. 'Send the signal to stand their ground!'

Horns blew out from their ranks, but the Barbarian armies to the right did not heed the call.

They were not riding to the attack. Instead, the Barbarians in the fortress watched as the army turned ahead of the Icelords, taking up a position alongside them.

'Kahudrak and Kahudrarg have betrayed us,' Thortheon whispered.

Imgorad yelled out in anger, slamming his fists down on the crenelated walls of the fortress hard enough to crack the mortar.

His face was fierce with rage, his body trembling from head to foot. Those about him backed away.

'So … treachery is the order of the day, as the Moonprince foretold,' he rumbled. 'I have been blind to the Heartstealer's strategy. We have weakened ourselves by battering our forces against the stones of the Giants, robbing both them and us of strength. Now she will defeat us both. Curse the traitors! I will rend them to meal if I get a chance.'

As if they had heard him, more horns sounded from the Icelord army and it began to advance. Thousands upon thousands of warriors and riders could be seen approaching.

'We cannot hope to stand against such numbers,' Thortheon muttered.

'No indeed,' Imgorad said. 'And nor can the Giants, for we have done the Iceguard's work for them. Signal for an orderly retreat! Make haste! We make for your fortress, Thortheon, there to consider our options. If any there be.'

Chapter Eighteen

Talorthane the Icelord stands at the City of Lorelorn looking south into the mist.

Talorthane escorted Tarithel deep within the walls of the city. It was lit by many torches, the darkness of the Forest of Farorn close about it, cutting off the light of the sky. Under the watchful eyes of the guards she was led into the great halls within the city, until she stood before a dais flanked by a long table.

Behind the table a man sat upon an ancient carved wooden chair, looking down at her. He was old, but his grey beard was worn well and neatly trimmed. The hair upon his head was a matching shade of grey, but his eyes sparkled like black coals in the dim light. He was dressed in leather armour, a thick cloak of fur wrapped around him, his hands covered in thick, black gloves. Around his neck hung a golden chain and from that a black gem. Tarithel had seen its like before; it was identical to the one that Imgorarg had worn.

Lorelorn the Icelord!

Tarithel shivered, but returned his gaze.

The guards were dismissed and the doors to the hall were closed behind her, leaving her alone with Lorelorn and Talorthane.

'So,' Lorelorn said after a moment's consideration. 'This is the Fey-girl that has left Shareth in paroxysms of rage.'

Talorthane nodded.

'I found her on the edges of Farorn to the south,' he said. 'She had vanquished Lord Imgasharg and his men.'

'By what means?' Lorelorn asked, frowning at Talorthane.

'Sorcery,' Talorthane replied. 'She bore this. It would seem to be a most potent Talisman.'

Talorthane withdrew the fabric pouch from with his cloak and placed it upon the table, unwrapping it to reveal Tarithel's necklace and the jewel held in its clasp. The jewel's light was faint, but slowly pulsing.

Lorelorn peered at the jewel, but made no move to touch it.

'And what is this?' he asked.

'It belongs to me,' Tarithel answered. 'It was given to me, an heirloom of my family many moons ago. I bear it as my mother bore it before me. Fey craftsmanship that captured the light of the long summer many moons ago.'

'And you saw it destroy Imgasharg?' Lorelorn asked, looking over to Talorthane.

'Indeed my Liege,' Talorthane replied. 'Burnt up by green fire.'

Lorelorn looked at Tarithel. 'You have tasked my mistress sorely. She has vowed much against you.'

Tarithel swallowed, but did not look away.

'I bear her just as strong a rage,' Tarithel answered. 'She has taken much from me and caused immense suffering to others. That is a debt that must be paid.'

'You realise your life is in my hands,' Lorelorn queried, pulling his gloves from his hands.

'I do,' Tarithel said. 'But I have overcome more obstacles than I can count, found my way through dark and dangerous paths that many have foretold would be the end of me … and yet here I stand before you, whole and unhurt, in the very heart of the Frozen Empire.'

Lorelorn smiled.

'I have been told you are both brave and have a great measure of assuredness that belies your age and stature,' he said. 'I am gratified to find that it is so. Such deportment is rare in one so young.'

'Then you will be swift on your judgement of me,' Tarithel asked. 'For I am ready for death, and if that is not to be, I must continue on with all haste.'

'Then let me be plain. My orders are to have you killed,' Lorelorn said. 'As were Talorthane's.' He cast a withering look at Talorthane. 'He is already guilty of treason and has put his life and yours into my hands. Mercy is not a word that Shareth knows. Should I spare you, my own life is forfeit. If I let you go and you are found and tortured into confession, my own life is also forfeit. If I disobey my orders … my life is once again, forfeit. So … if I give you your life, what will you do with it?'

'My destiny has been revealed to me,' Tarithel answered. 'Through whatever means I have, whatever powers reside in me, I seek the end of this foul Heartstealer and the safe return of my betrothed from her wicked clutches.'

Lorelorn nodded.

'And you have made your way here to the very heart of the Frozen Empire undetected until now,' Lorelorn added. 'Aided by this jewel? Which imbues you with the powers of a sorceress?'

'I would not describe it so,' Tarithel replied. 'What I will say is that on the day I received this jewel from my father, I was given the title of Lady of the Forest. My people and I believed it to be merely an honorary deed, symbolic of my people's long association with the trees of our realm. I have discovered it to be something more. The trees talk and I listen. Sometimes they are mine to command …'

'It gives you a mastery of the Forests?' Lorelorn whispered in response. 'I know much of the lore of this realm, but I have never heard of the forest being mastered by any. Farorn has long been a silent, darkened place, bereft of joy and colour, held fast in great enchantment from long ago. A malevolence resides here, far older than my mistress, older perhaps than her father, the Witchking. We are careful not to disturb it.'

Tarithel didn't answer. Lorelorn tapped his fingernails on the wooden arms of his chair.

'So,' he said. 'Who are you to command such obedience from such an ancient power?'

Tarithel sighed.

'In truth?' she replied. 'I do not know. There are greater powers than I understand at work both in my homeland of Midnight and here in your realm of Icemark. Nothing has been the same since the winter solstice, powers have risen all about us which none can fathom. All I know is that those forces which have aided me on my quest oppose the will of your mistress, Shareth the Heartstealer. I have tried and failed to defy the will of this power, now I know with great surety what I must do.'

'The End of Shareth herself,' Lorelorn mused. 'This is no small thing. What makes you so sure you can accomplish such a task?'

'Through me this jewel can wield a power,' Tarithel said. 'I do not know whether it is strong enough to defeat her, all I can say is that I will try to my utmost.'

'And then?' Lorelorn said. 'Will you take her place, would we replace one sorceress with another of similar kind?'

'I am not like her!' Tarithel cried.

Lorelorn shrugged. 'You are very much alike to me,' he said. 'Both fair, young women in appearance, imbued with magical powers far beyond any others I know, perhaps equal to the Wise themselves, should they ever emerge from their towers ever again.'

'I do not seek to dominate or control,' Tarithel snapped. 'I would see all people free to find their own destinies, not rule over them. I am no Empress, nor would I seek to be. All that matters to me lies locked in a dungeon in your mistress's City of Imiriel.'

'Ah yes,' Lorelorn said. 'Shareth's great treasure.'

'Treasure?' Tarithel asked. 'What do you mean?'

'That is how Shareth refers to her captive,' Lorelorn said. 'She guards him jealously.'

'He is my betrothed,' Tarithel said. 'He will be freed and returned to me. I swear it!'

'And your Moonprince,' Lorelorn asked. 'He who slew my mistress's own father and set these events in motion. What of him?'

'He is my liege,' Tarithel answered. 'He seeks the return of my betrothed too, and he would resist Shareth's pledge to subjugate my homelands by fighting her here.'

'So he kindles war in the Icemark,' Lorelorn said.

'War was already kindled,' Tarithel replied. 'Shareth vowed to attack Midnight long before we set foot in this realm.'

Lorelorn smiled.

'You are correct,' he said. 'Shareth swore revenge for the death of her father. Her will is bent to that objective. Even now she begins her assault on the Icemark in earnest. She will extinguish them all this time. The Giants, The Barbarians … the Dwarves …'

Tarithel swallowed. 'It mustn't be allowed!' she cried.

'You have friends amongst them?' Lorelorn asked, with a raised eyebrow. 'I thought the Fey and the Dwarves rather estranged. Is this not so?'

'The Dwarves are a good people, they do not deserve such a fate,' Tarithel said. 'Surely you can see that? This endless war will lead to death on all sides. Icemark is already ablaze from north to south. Midnight has just extinguished those very same fires … would you reignite them? The hatred, the bitterness, the envy and the greed … it all stems from the very same evil … the Witchking first … and now his daughter! She cares nothing for you, only that you do her will … follow her no longer! Turn aside like others have done. Resist her! Join the fight to free our lands from this tyranny!'

Tarithel ran out of breath, gasping for a moment.

Lorelorn turned to Talorthane.

'I see what you mean,' he said. 'She is quite the orator.'

'She has a habit of speaking her mind,' Talorthane replied.

'A trait that I'm surprised has not led to your demise already,' Lorelorn said, turning back to Tarithel. 'I'd have been tempted to end you merely on account of your loquacity. Yet, as you say, here you are. I sense that much hangs on my decision regarding your fate.'

He sat back, regarding her for long moments. Tarithel glared back, refusing to break eye contact with him.

Lorelorn sat forward again.

'You already know I have no intention of killing you,' he said.

'Then what will do you?' Tarithel countered.

Lorelorn smiled.

'What would you ask of us, Tarithel of the Fey?' Lorelorn said. 'To what purpose would you put two Lords of the Frozen Empire, prepared to betray their mistress?'

Talorthane gasped at the words, but said nothing.

'Pledge,' Tarithel said. 'Pledge your allegiance to my own liege, Luxor, Moonprince of Midnight! For he bears a Moon Ring of my realm and through it he can perceive what you perceive, give you direction and thus such protection as is his to bestow.'

'A Moon Ring?' Lorelorn asked.

'Yes,' Tarithel said. 'It is how he guides all who seek an end to tyranny and oppression. Through it he summoned all who were prepared to stand against the Witchking in Midnight and he seeks the same here in Midnight.'

'I see,' Lorelorn answered. 'I know of such pledges. Shareth uses something similar herself.'

He looked over at Talorthane.

'Time for a decision then,' he said.

Lorelorn took a deep breath and then got to his feet, striding towards Tarithel. As he did so, he drew his sword, the long blade sighing out from its scabbard with a faint metallic ring. He swung it before him, point foremost before drawing it back, ready to strike.

The Barbarian army under the command of Imgorad had beaten a hasty retreat from the Fortress of Ganigrorn. To his surprise, the forces of the Heartstealer had not pressed an attack on his army, but had taken the Fortress once his armies had departed from its walls. The remaining armies of the Giants had also fled, much reduced in number.

Both antagonists now stood in the forests to the south, in the borderlands between the realms of the Giants and the Barbarians.

'Sire!' One of the Barbarians beside him called.

Imgorad looked up.

A Giant approached, bearing a white flag of truce.

'Ganigrorn,' Imgorad whispered.

'Barbarian!' Ganigrorn cried, as he approached. 'Stand before me and answer for your perfidy!'

Imgorad straightened and walked towards him, glaring up at the huge Giant, who stared back down with fierce intent.

'If I had not my people to protect I would smite you here and now,' Ganigrorn roared. 'Your wanton and brazen attack on my fortress … look what you have done! My lands now lie in the hands of the Heartstealer and you have achieved nothing but death and destruction. Contemptible fool!'

Around him, Imgorad's men drew their swords, ready to fall upon the Giant.

But Imgorad did not respond.

Instead, he took the helm from his head, and bowed the knee.

'I have been a fool,' he said. 'I was warned of the Heartstealer's treachery and in my greed I sought to take advantage of it, thinking I had the upper hand. It seems I have been a pawn in her stratagems.'

The Barbarians muttered amongst themselves. Thortheon came up alongside him.

'My Liege …'

'No,' Imgorad said. 'Ganigrorn speaks truth. The Heartstealer has shown her true intent and it is not goodwill to us or our erstwhile foes …' He got to his feet. 'Ganigrorn of the Giants. I cannot undo the deeds wrought today, nor do I expect forgiveness for them, but it seems we are poised on the edge of a battle against a greater foe. If we do not come to terms, we will likely perish. I will offer you safe passage and aid for your folk. Will you treat with me?'

A frown crossed Ganigrorn's face.

'Speak your terms.'

'I will end the conflict with your people,' Imgorad said. 'We will travel swiftly to the Fortress of Thortheon, nigh to the south. Provisions we will share and we will tend to your wounded as if they were our own.'

'How can I trust your words?' Ganigrorn rumbled. 'And why should I?'

Imgorad looked up at him.

'Because I will this day pledge allegiance to another power, as I should have done before. You have heard of the Moonprince of the southern realm of Midnight no doubt, he seeks to combat this wretched Heartstealer. I will pledge my people to his command. His will … to unite the people of the

Icemark against her foul ambition … whatever I can do to thwart her, I will see done before my time is ended.'

Imgorad held out a gloved hand.

'Will you join me, Ganigrorn of the Giants?'

Ganigrorn recoiled for a moment, considering the matter.

'There will be reckoning after all this is done, Imgorad of the Barbarians,' Ganigrorn replied. 'But for now … I accept your terms.'

The pair of warriors shook each other's hands.

Tarithel flinched backwards, struggling to hold her ground. She heard the sword swing through the air with sharp whistle of air and she braced herself for oblivion, still refusing to yield.

If I am to die I will die on my feet, proud until the end!

There was a sharp clang.

Lorelorn stood before her, the sword point downwards, touching the flagstones of the hall. Lorelorn rested on the cross bar, his hands around the pommel. He was bent forward, looking into her eyes. Tarithel swallowed, trying to repress the trembles in her body.

'I will not slay you,' he said, stepping back from her.

Tarithel gasped, her breathing short and sharp, gasping for breath.

'I see no lie in your eyes,' Lorelorn continued. 'But, in truth, that matters little to me. Rather, it is because I will not be party to the extermination of the other races. I have reason enough to hate the Giants, Barbarians, Dwarves, and the Fey for that matter, but to eradicate them entirely, their crimes do not merit such harshness, that can only come from vindictiveness or madness, neither of which are qualities I can support. Shareth has always been swayed by her emotions, but she has never let them take control of her wits before. The path she follows leads to death for too many, perhaps even our people too. I would see that avoided.'

'Well said,' Talorthane called from the side.

'Think so, do you?' Lorelorn called, casting a wary glance at him. 'I may have signed our death warrants. Shareth is commendably thorough in such matters. Treachery is always punished by death … and we have just become traitors.'

He straightened and looked at Tarithel. From around his neck he took off the golden chain and laid on it on the table alongside her own jewel. She watched as he drew his sword from its scabbard, hoisted it, and brought the pommel down upon the black gem.

It shattered with a sharp crack, tiny pieces scattering across the table.

'Thus I pledge my loyalty to your liege, Luxor, Moonprince of Midnight,' he said in a loud voice.

'As do I,' Talorthane said, stepping forward alongside him.

Tarithel felt the sudden warmth of the Moon Ring filter into her mind. It was faint at such distance, but she perceived a rather astonished Luxor gazing across a valley dotted by trees.

Tarithel? What is this?

Allies, dear Luxor! Allies unlooked for here in the far north of the frozen empire!

You have convinced Shareth's own servants to join us?

Two of them, but there is much they can advise you of, and much you must know of what faces you!

Such things are more timely than you can imagine, Tarithel. But what of you, are you safe and well? It is hard to see you so far away …

I ride on to seek Morkin's freedom! Nothing will stop me, no ice, no storm, no sword or shaft has kept me from my quest. Shareth's twisted nightmares have not prevailed. I ride on and I will find him!

All blessing that I can convey are yours … success to you, Tarithel!

Tarithel heard Luxor begin a conversation with both Talorthane and Lorelorn, but she couldn't concentrate on the words. For long moments she rested in the warmth of the Moon Ring's embrace, enjoying the sensation, allowing it to sooth her troubled soul.

Lorelorn's voice brought her back to her senses.

'It's actually quite liberating,' he said, a grin passing over his features. 'Have you nothing to say, Fey-girl? Have you no words for such a momentous occasion?'

'I …' Tarithel stammered. 'Your mercy is great … Lord Lorelorn. I thank you for it. My Liege, Luxor, will not let you down.'

'You have manners too,' Lorelorn said. 'Such things are to be applauded, but you may regret your thanks. I would have granted you a swift death this day, an execution that befits your rank, station and deportment. Since I have spared you, your death is now delayed, it will not be by my hand that you shall meet your end. If you are found by Shareth's more loyal servants, your end will be long, drawn out and painful, that I can promise you.'

Tarithel swallowed.

'I'm not afraid,' she replied.

'Then you're a fool,' Lorelorn replied. 'Or you are naïve. Both are dangerous.'

Tarithel glared at him. 'All right then, I am afraid! Terrified even! Does that satisfy you? Anything else you require me to say to sate your appetite for crushing my resolve?'

Lorelorn smiled.

'Stop with that infuriating grin,' she snapped. 'Or …'

'Peace,' Lorelorn replied, holding out a hand. 'I have chosen well … or I have chosen rightly. Either will do. Now that the die is cast, we must decide what we might do to aid you and the Moonprince, and how to best accomplish it.'

Luxor concentrated hard, the Moon Ring pulsing on his finger, hot and burning. The ring seemed to be struggling to spread its strange influence at such a distance.

Your servant Tarithel has much to commend her, Moonprince of Midnight. I am Lorelorn, formally a loyal servant of the Heartstealer.

Luxor perceived the two Icelords in his mind. To his surprise they seemed less intimidating than he had supposed. He'd expected some fell magic about them, but they were men, hard men and cruel perhaps, but men akin to himself.

'I am surprised, yet humbled by your pledge to me,' Luxor replied. 'Tarithel and her quest are my greatest concern ...'

We will speed her on her way with everything at our disposal, Moonprince. But you must know of the strategy of the Heartstealer herself. She comes for you and her wrath is greatly fanned ...

'Tell me!' Luxor answered.

Long has Shareth planned the subjugation of the Icemark, but your arrival has pushed her into precipitate action. She has all but crushed the strength of the Giants and now she moves against the Dwarves in great strength, hoping to eviscerate them as well. She has the Barbarians tantalised with the promise of taking territory from the Giants ... but she will turn on them too. With that accomplished she will fall upon the Fey and eradicate them once and for all. Then your homeland in Midnight will be the next target. She is aided by Crowns of Power. Two she already has and more she seeks. Both her magic and her armies must be countered if the Icemark is to be saved.

'I hear your words,' Luxor replied. 'And I am grateful for them. Such strength ... can it truly be countered?'

I know not the disposition of the forces loyal to you ... and it is likely better you do not tell me. But you must consolidate them in order to face her, otherwise pockets of resistance will be swept aside.

'We cannot reach the Dwarves in time,' Luxor replied. 'If an attack on them is imminent.'

I can frustrate that to a degree, but the Dwarves must be warned.

Luxor nodded. 'Then do what you can, I will do what I can for the Dwarves. Safeguard Tarithel as best you can and I will rally all the strength of Icemark against the Heartstealer. Well met, Lorelorn of the Iceguard. I hope we will meet in person.'

Well met indeed, Moonprince of Midnight. Victory or death awaits. There will be no middle ground …

The baleful influence of the Moon Ring faded away.

'My Lord?' Carorthane frowned as Luxor shook his head as if to clear it. 'News?'

'News indeed,' Luxor replied, 'Of a wholesome type for once, but it must be related to Imorthorn first of all.'

Carorthane nodded.

They rode up to the City of Imorthorn. Luxor could see armies camped around it, perhaps numbering six or seven thousand in number, but not as many as he expected to see. He mentioned it to Carorthane. He nodded.

'I see perhaps half our total strength before us,' Carorthane acknowledged. 'Some will doubtless still be en route. Much lies under the command of Imgorthand and it will have been a long road to summon them all. They will come, do not fear. For now, Imorthorn and my brother, Carorthand, will wish to see you.'

Luxor nodded, but he was troubled by the mention of Imgorthand.

Satisfied that the needs of his men would be catered for, Luxor followed Carorthane within the walls of the City. Imorthorn and Carorthand were waiting and walked across the moment they saw the new arrivals.

Luxor appraised Imorthorn, seeing a Fey as old as he could remember one being. That spoke of very many moons, perhaps rivalling even Rorthron's time in the world.

'My Lord Imorthorn,' Luxor said bowing low before him.

'Luxor, Moonprince of Midnight,' Imorthorn said, bowing himself. 'I welcome you to my court. Long it has been indeed since the Free of Midnight have come before me, but I am glad to see you. We have much need of tidings from beyond our borders.'

'Such news as I have I will gladly share,' Luxor said. 'Even if it is not all good.'

'Come within,' Imorthorn said.

Before long Imorthorn, Carorthane, Carorthand and Luxor were seated in Imorthorn's great halls overlooking the city.

'First,' Luxor said. 'I must thank you for sending Tarithel safely on her way.'

'I only wish we could have done more,' Imorthorn said. 'Have you news of her?'

'It is with her I will start,' Luxor said. 'She made her way to the Dwarves as you directed, there she found herself deep in their problems. A civil war so she reported, but she was able to aid the victory, a Dwarf known as Glormane. Perhaps you know him?'

'This is news of a wholesome type,' Imorthorn said. 'Glormane is known to us, and though we have had our differences, there is a respect between his people and ours. We feared that his authority was crumbling.'

'Indeed it was,' Luxor replied. 'Tarithel told me that the northern Dwarves were set against him, a fellow called Imgorarg attacked the city. Tarithel helped frustrate the attack … and she slew Imgorarg himself.'

Carorthand's mouth fell open.

'She killed him?' he asked. 'The Fey-girl?'

'Clearly not to be underestimated,' Carorthane said with a wry chuckle, looking over to Imorthorn. 'As you foresaw.'

'I saw she was full of spirit,' Imorthorn said. 'But to slay a Dwarf-lord? That is worthy of a song or two!'

'She has given me allies amongst their people,' Luxor said. 'Even now they await news as to how they might assist us. They sped Tarithel along her way, she has passed into the realm of the Heartstealer now.'

'Then she has done what no other Fey has ever achieved,' Imorthorn said. 'But what of the Barbarians?'

Luxor's face fell.

'With them I did not succeed,' he said. 'Careneon and Torinarg spoke in my favour to Imgorad, but his view was poisoned by two brothers, Kahudrak and Kahudrarg. I have been banished from their lands.'

'We have found them ever so,' Imorthorn said. 'Stubborn and unwilling to change their course. Careneon trusts us not, but he has never been given to rash acts. Kahudrak and Kahudrarg are infamous though … they have killed many fair Fey in their time, oft with no good reason. We do not need allies like them.'

'News came of the Giants whilst I resided with them,' Luxor said. 'And Imgorad was quick to see it as an advantage he could take. From my other companion, Rorthron the Wise, I hear that the Giants are sore oppressed in the north by the Heartstealer's own forces. The Barbarians seem fit to make that trouble worse by attacking them from the south. Taking advantage of others when they already fight a war on their borders, this is not honourable warfare to my way of thinking.'

'But it is the way of the Barbarians,' Imorthorn said. 'We have seen it many times. And … from others besides … and amongst our own people too. Such is the way of the Icemark. Trust seldom lingers long and past insults are easy to recall.'

'And Shareth?' Carorthand asked. 'What is she doing? We have heard little of her, only rumours upon rumours, little of any substance.'

'I have such news,' Luxor said. 'We can thank Tarithel for it once again, for having left the Dwarves she took a dark road into the Heartstealer's realm, to be caught by the Icelords.'

'Caught?' Imorthorn echoed. 'Yet … she lives?'

Luxor nodded. 'She not only lives, but she has turned two of them from their loyalty to the Heartstealer.'

The three Fey stared at him.

'Then she truly is a sorceress!' Imorthorn said. 'Icelords, betraying Shareth? Such a thing … I have not heard of. This is unprecedented … who are they?'

'Tarithel tells me their names are Lorelorn and Talorthane.'

The Fey looked amongst themselves, muttering in surprise.

'Lorelorn we know,' Imorthorn said. 'He is great amongst the Icelords, one of six fell servants of Shareth herself. If he has pledged service to you …'

'Via the Moon Ring I can speak to him,' Luxor said. 'He has revealed much. I know what Shareth intends.'

'And?' the three Fey said as one.

'Shareth seeks the Talismans of the Icemark,' Luxor said. 'Two she already has in her possession, these she calls upon to give her magic the potency it has. She seeks more, and it would seem they may still be at large in the Icemark. They are akin to the Ice Crown which was the bane of my existence not long ago. The same power is behind her sorcery. If she does locate another she will become impossible to stop.

'She has fomented the civil war of the Dwarves, hoping to depose Glormane. In that Tarithel has frustrated her, to no little anger. She has moved on the Giants already, crushing much of their strength. An attack on the Dwarves from the east will come soon. Lorelorn believes that she will wait until the wars between the Giants and the Barbarians have run their course, then she will sweep them both aside.'

'If the Dwarves fall and so do the Barbarians and the Giants.' Carorthane said. 'Then …'

'The Heartstealer will ride into the south unopposed until she reaches our lands,' Imorthorn said. 'Her strategy is clear. She has weakened the other races until she was strong enough to overpower them. The Fey will matter little to her as she will be able to crush us if we stand alone.'

'Rorthron yet talks to the Giants,' Luxor said. 'But they are beset with their own woes and even then are on the wrong side of the map. The forces of the Heartstealer and the Barbarians lie between us and them even if they do decide to pledge their loyalty to my cause.'

'If only the Barbarians had seen sense,' Imorthorn said.

'What news of the Fey?' Luxor asked.

'Half our strength is here,' Imorthorn replied. 'Half is en route from the east, they will be here within two days.'

'We must be ready to set out as soon as possible,' Luxor said. 'If we cannot help the Dwarves and the giants somehow, we will all be annihilated one by one.'

As he spoke they felt the ground tremble beneath their feet. Cries of consternation rang out through the city. Imorthorn led them out of the hall to stand on the promenade beyond, which looked out across the city towards the west.

Dark clouds were gathering in the sky to the north. A flicker of lightning crackled from them.

'Somehow I think that day of reckoning may not be far off,' Imorthorn said. 'The Heartstealer is making her move for the Icemark. Our doom is at hand.'

'Then it is time,' Luxor said. 'I will summon all the forces that have pledged themselves to me. We must confront her … and confront her we will!'

Lorelorn strode to a cabinet against the wall, opened the doors and pulled out a scroll. He untied the binding and unrolled it upon a trestle table nearby, weighing it down with two heavy weights at either end.

Tarithel and Talorthane stepped alongside, peering down. Tarithel saw a detailed map.

'You were heading to Imiriel as I recall,' Lorelorn said.

Tarithel nodded.

Lorelorn pointed at the map.

'It lies here, in the uttermost north of our realm not far as the crows flies,' he said. 'But you would never have reached it. It lies in a valley of ice, ringed by the Frozen Wastes themselves, there is no way through from here.'

'No way through?' Tarithel echoed in dismay. 'But there must be? How can there be a city sealed off in such a manner? I saw it!'

'Doubtless Shareth has witchcraft that grants her access,' Lorelorn replied. 'But before you ask, I know not of it, nor how it might be used. Such secrets are hers alone.'

'Then what am I to do?' Tarithel demanded. 'I will not turn back, I will take my chances in the Frozen Wastes, they cannot be impenetrable!'

'They are exactly that,' Lorelorn replied. 'You would be dead from chill before you had taken a hundred steps within. None venture into the Frozen Wastes and live.'

Tarithel shook her head. 'I know you speak the truth … but, there has to be a way to reach the city, there has to be!'

'There is none,' Lorelorn replied. 'Save the magic of Shareth known only to Anvireon …'

'I have not come this far to turn back now,' she said. 'You say the way is closed, I will find a way to open it. I did so long ago when I forged a path from Midnight to the Icemark … I can do so again.'

'How did you manage such a feat before?' Talorthane asked.

'I was guided …' Tarithel said, casting her mind back to her strange journey when she had rushed from her home and ridden out into the snow. 'I was given instructions by … the spirit of the Forest. I first rode to a Lith near my home, the only one in Midnight placed within the forest so it is said. There I was spoken to …'

'There are Liths hereabouts,' Lorelorn said. 'Mere stones so far as I know, but they lie within the forest bounds. The nearest is two or three leagues to the north-west, an easy ride …' He paused, remembering. 'I … have not spoken of this to anyone before … I hesitate to mention it now, it may be a false hope … I thought it just a dream.'

'Mention what?' Tarithel demanded.

'I rode out into the forest not long ago,' Lorelorn said. 'There I saw a man … a strange fellow, dressed as a lord … garments favoured in the southern realms I assumed. About him was a glade I have never seen before. Dreamlike and yet solid and real.'

Tarithel gasped. On the table, the jewel flickered with a faint green light.

'His name,' she said. 'Was it Midwinter?'

Lorelorn looked at her with a frown. 'Yes … that is what he called himself. I took him for some sage … perhaps a member of the Wise still walking the lands.'

'I don't know who he is,' Tarithel said. 'But I encountered him in much the same way, moons ago, in Midnight. It was he who encouraged me to rouse my people against the Witchking.'

'He showed me an image of you,' Lorelorn said. 'Carefree and running through a meadow. Perhaps he knew we would meet.'

'Yet he told me I would never see him again,' Tarithel said. 'But if he is hereabouts … perhaps the Lith might tell me …'

'I sought solace in the forest,' Lorelorn said. 'Perhaps that is what you should seek?'

Tarithel nodded.

'Then I must ride,' she said, already gathering her things.

'Yes, you must,' Lorelorn said. 'Take your jewel and wear it well. It may be the only way you can find your answers.'

Tarithel picked up the jewel by its necklace and held it up. It sparkled in the dimness of Lorelorn's hall, a glitter of bright green light. She took a deep breath and then placed it around her neck.

'But know this,' Lorelorn said. 'Shareth has divined your intent, she likely planned it. She knows you are coming and she has instructed Anvireon in this regard. Your destination is therefore a trap. I know not what foul arts she will have used, but used them she has. If you go that way, beware.'

Tarithel nodded. 'I hear your warning, but it will not change my plans.'

Lorelorn nodded. 'Beware Anvireon, he who guards the City of Imiriel. He is a treacherous coward, but he is cunning with it. Shareth and he have discussed much in secret. I do not believe Shareth knows you are here, but she does not need to if she knows where you are going.'

Tarithel nodded.

'I did not expect allies amongst Shareth's servants,' she said. 'But I thank you for your mercy and your guidance.'

'Talorthane and I have orders to go guard the Icemark as directed by Shareth,' Lorelorn said. 'But instead we will go to the Dwarves to see if we can hinder Fangrorn's attack.'

Tarithel nodded. 'When you see them, ask for Glormane and Carorthay,' she said. 'Tell them … the sorceress of Fangrim sends her regards.'

Lorelorn nodded.

'If a peace is to be had in Icemark,' he replied. 'You will be one of its architects. Now depart, with great haste. May good fortune follow you wherever you go!'

The Fortress of Thortheon now played host to armies that just the day before had been bitter enemies. Imgorad had stayed true to his word, injured warriors and folk from all sides had been cared for, fed and watered as needs dictated.

Imgorad had left the organisation of the Fortress to its owner, Thortheon, whilst he retreated within. He made his way into one of the halls of the Fortress, locking the doors behind him and seating himself in a great, carved, oaken chair before a roaring fire.

A fool I have been, but perhaps, I can still make amends …

'Luxor!' he cried out. 'Moonprince of Midnight! I pledge my allegiance to your banner, you called upon me once before and in my ignorance I availed you not. Now I recant my refusal and offer you my pledge without let or hindrance. Speak to me Moonprince and let me know your will!'

A strange sense of potency swirled about him. A moment later the face of the Moonprince from the southern realm of Midnight appeared in his mind.

Imgorad?

'Aye, Moonprince, it is I.'

You have pledged your loyalty to me? So the Moon Ring tells me …

'I have, Moonprince. Shareth betrayed me as you said she would and I have caused much death and consternation due to her deceit. You were right and I was wrong. My service and my people, if you will have them, are yours to command.'

Great Imgorad, it gives me no pleasure to hear more of the Heartstealer's perfidy, knowing it would come. Time is short, but we can still turn the tide. Where are you?

'I stand at the Fortress of Thortheon, do you know it?' Imgorad replied.

I have a map given to me by the Fey … I see it lies between the mountains and the pass into the lands of the Dwarves.

'Aye,' Imgorad replied. 'It is a natural choke point between

Anvulane and Anvormane. None can pass through unless we permit it, or have overwhelming strength to force a passage.'

Overwhelming strength will soon be upon us no doubt, but such a strategic location promises to be a chance to hold the forces of the Heartstealer at bay.

'What would you have me do?' Imgorad asked.

Summon all your strength to defend the fortress. Summon every warrior you can muster. I am doing the same with the Fey. All will converge upon that fortress ... and there we will make our stand. Will you do this?

Imgorad nodded. 'I have been deceived by the Heartstealer once, I will not be deceived again. We will hold this place until you arrive, Moonprince, or we will die in the attempt. Be swift and we will draw swords together!'

In the City of Glormane, the capital of the Dwarven realm, all was in disarray.

'We must focus our attention on defending what remains of our land from the Heartstealer's grasp!' Glormane cried out.

Imulorn and Imelorn made to speak, but hesitated. Carorthay pushed to the fore.

'No, my Liege,' he said, his voice thick and stern.

'No?' Glormane asked, his eyes narrowing.

'The time for that has come and gone,' Carorthay said.

'What are you saying?' Glormane demanded.

'We cannot save our homeland ...' Carorthay began.

'We have thousands here,' Glormane said. 'This city is strong, we have won a battle recently, we can win more.'

Glormane looked at Imulorn and Imelorn for support, but they were mute before him.

'The Heartstealer's forces are far more numerous,' Carorthay said. 'My city is lost, Hagudril's too. They sweep in with overwhelming force …'

'You live!' Glormane retorted. 'You will fight another day!'

'If we make a stand here it will be our last,' Carorthay said. 'The Dwarves will come to their end under your rule.'

'Then what would you have me do?' Glormane demanded. 'Lie down and die?'

Carorthay shook his head. 'Call it impertinence, for I should have spoken sooner, for that young Fey-girl spoke wisdom we all should have heeded long days ago. Our salvation lies in the hands of others. A single race cannot combat this evil. We need allies, we need help … or we will be exterminated.'

Glormane grimaced.

'A Dwarf does not cry for help …'

'You accused Imgorarg of hidebound thinking,' Imulorn said. 'Carorthay is right, we have fought and lost, to stand further is suicide against such might. Tarithel told us that her Moonprince sought to recruit the people of Icemark to make a stand against the Heartstealer. If we join them, perhaps we might yet prevail.'

'And abandon my own city? Our capital?' Glormane cried. 'Is that what you tell me I must do?'

'Yes,' Carorthay said. 'Or we perish here tonight, or tomorrow on the dawn.'

Glormane turned away, walking to the great stump that served as the centre point of his hall. There, still embedded within it was the axe that was said to have felled the tree that formed the stump. He grabbed at it, wresting it free and then turned, holding its blade aloft.

The other Dwarves awaited his decision.

'If it be a choice between preserving tradition and preserving the lives of our people,' Glormane began, looking around at the hall about him. 'Then it is the people, what else are we if we are not a people?'

Carorthay nodded.

'Make the pledge to this Moonprince,' he said. 'And let us hope it is not too late.'

Glormane stood, holding the axe higher in the air.

'Luxor, Moonprince of Midnight and liege of Tarithel, Lady of the Forest and of the Fey. I hereby pledge the Dwarves to your purpose. Speak to me Luxor!'

Glormane heard voices in his mind.

Glormane! Leader of the Dwarves?

He blinked in surprise, feeling the strange magic of the war ring of the Moonprince.

'Lord Luxor!' he answered.

Glormane, time is short and I have much to tell you. The Heartstealer marches on your realm in great force ...

'This we know. We have been invaded to the east by the army under the command of Fangrorn. We are prepared to make a stand to defend our lands ...'

No Glormane, you must retreat ... and you must retreat now! The forces arranged against you are overwhelming. Tarithel, she who you helped to reach the Frozen Empire, has persuaded Lorelorn the Icelord to pledge his loyalty to me and he has vouchsafed much of Shareth's plan. She intends to strike the Dwarves down here and now before any help can reach you. The Icelord army has orders to exterminate your people utterly. If you remain in your city, she will succeed in her aims! Retreat now!

'Tarithel? Lorelorn?' Glormane exclaimed. 'An Icelord sworn loyalty to you? This is unheard of!'

Perhaps, but the army that invades is real enough. You have time enough for an orderly retreat. I have the pledges of the Fey and Barbarians to my banner, we muster forces even now. We all make for the Fortress of Thortheon, do you know it?

'Yes,' Glormane replied. 'I do. It lies two days march from here, directly west through the Pass of Carormarg ...'

We will consolidate all our strength and defy Shareth there. Together we are stronger … the time for standing alone is past. United we can prevail, apart we will be destroyed one by one. Glormane, heed my words!

'But my home …'

Glormane looked out across the walls of his city, the sun was rising, blood red, before him.

You trusted Tarithel, this I know. She spoke most highly of you. Trust me now! Make haste for Thortheon, Glormane!

Glormane swung the axe back down, embedding it back into the ancient stump.

'Agreed,' Glormane said. 'Thortheon it is, and a battle to decide all battles!'

The link with Luxor was severed as the cheers of his comrades erupted all about him.

Deep within the Forest of Fangrim, trumpets sounded from the pinnacles of the City of Imorthorn. To the east, the faint snatches of answering horns could be made out in the early morning air.

The armies of the Fey of the east had arrived, their banners held high.

Luxor, standing next to Imorthorn, assessed their strength with an appraising gaze. Fresh from the news of Glormane's pledge, Luxor's mood was upbeat.

'A good number,' he said. 'The Fey of Icemark are a force to be reckoned with! Alongside the armies of the Barbarians and the Dwarves … perhaps we have a chance!'

'We Fey can muster perhaps fifteen thousand warriors to this task,' Imorthorn said. 'Strong for sure, but not overwhelming unless we can reach this fortress of the Barbarians in time. Come, let us go welcome Imgorthand and his vassals. Alas, a brief rest is all they can hope for, we must march onwards before the day is out.'

Luxor and Imorthorn made for the east entrance, riding out with a small vanguard of warriors to meet the arriving armies, which had set themselves in order perhaps half a league from the city.

'There stands Imgorthand, with the mighty lords of the eastern and southern Fey about him,' Imorthorn said, as they rode side by side. 'Berormane, Lorangrim, Tharand and Imorthesh from the south. Lorangriel, Thorthand, Ingormiel and Thigrand from the east. Ah … and Morildrane too, I see.'

Luxor caught the change of tone in Imorthorn's voice.

'This Morildrane, he concerns you?'

Imorthorn grimaced. 'Ever he is seen to be loyal. I have found no evidence of any wrongdoing on his part …'

'And yet?'

Imorthorn looked across. 'Wherever there is strife or tension, Morildrane always manages to find himself nearby.'

Luxor nodded.

The pair rode up to the army, Imorthorn in the lead. They dismounted and the Fey before them did the same.

'My lords,' Imorthorn said. 'It is indeed good to see you once again and your skill and speed at rousing our armies at our call is a great credit to you and your households. Well met.'

The Fey Lords bowed before him.

'We have come as swiftly as we might,' Imgorthand said. 'But we would know what we were about.'

'That can wait until we're within the walls,' Imorthorn said. 'Come now, your folk will need rest after their journey.'

The Fey lords before Imorthorn and Luxor did not move.

'Forgive me, Lord Imorthorn,' Imgorthand replied, his voice low. 'But the Fey of the east and south would hear those words ere we come within your walls.'

Imorthorn frowned. 'Were not my orders clear, Imgorthand? Rally the Fey of the East and the South in readiness for war upon the Heartstealer.'

'We have rallied as you commanded,' Imgorthand answered. 'And we are prepared for battle. Yet we consider an attack against the Heartstealer to be rash and foolhardy, not in the interest of the Fey of Fangrim, such a stance risks the destruction of our homes, our people and our lives … and for what?' Imgorthand looked over to Luxor. 'The wars and troubles of a foreigner who knows nothing of our realm?'

'My lord Imgorthand,' Luxor said, holding up a hand. 'I have no wish to see a quarrel between kindred folk on my part, such things can be undone with words of wisdom and a good ale. Come, let us talk this through further, but not out here on the field …'

Imgorthand turned his gaze away from Luxor. He looked back at Imorthorn. 'Or the tender affections of a Fey maiden steeped in magic?'

Luxor frowned, his hand slipped toward the hilt of his sword.

'I am your liege, your fealty is required.' Imorthorn said after a moment, his voice low. 'Or do you consider another to be leader of the Fey now? State your intentions, Imgorthand.'

'I am your vassal, sworn and written,' Imgorthand replied. 'And if you will turn from this rash course of action, sue for peace with the Heartstealer rather provoking her to wrath and ruin, then all will be well.'

Imorthorn laughed. 'So you will follow me and honour your pledge if I will but take decisions you find acceptable? No Imgorthand, I require you and your own vassals to follow me into battle. My decision is made, will you obey it or not?'

Imgorthand did not respond, but his hand closed around the amulet hung around his neck, his fingertips touch the black gem embedded there. Luxor frowned.

An amulet … with a black gem as Tarithel told me!

The Fey lords he had ridden with stepped up beside him.

Luxor saw Morildrane standing just behind them, a faint smile of satisfaction on his face.

'Treason then,' Imorthorn muttered.

'Seize them,' Imgorthand said. 'The Fey will not take up arms against the Heartstealer!'

Before the Fey could move, Luxor leant forward, seized the amulet about Imgorthand's neck and wrenched it free with one hand whilst drawing his sword with the other. Even as the other Fey Lords ran to stop him he grabbed the gem and threw it upon the ground, smashing down upon it with the pommel of his sword. The gem cracked on the first impact and then shattered on the second.

The Fey grabbed him, pulling him back. A moment later a ring of steel swords was at his neck.

'You dare assail Lord Imgorthand!'

'Hold!'

The Fey about Luxor paused.

It had been Imgorthand's voice.

'Release him, release them both!' Imgorthand cried, in a loud voice. 'Lower your swords! This madness is at an end.'

Imorthorn and Luxor were allowed to get back to their feet. The Fey backed away.

Imgorthand strode forwards and then fell on his knees before Imorthorn.

'My Lord,' he said. 'I have betrayed you in word and deed. I have no excuse for my actions or my words. My life is forfeit and I give it to your mercy.'

Luxor held up the shattered gem.

Imorthorn looked at him.

'I believe this is a valid excuse,' Luxor said. 'The art of the Heartstealer herself. A black gem, doubtless laced with her foul sorcery. Yet its baleful influence over you is ended now.'

Imgorthand raised his head. Imorthorn held out a hand.

'Rise Imgorthand,' Imorthorn said.

Imgorthand staggered to his feet, looking at the gem in bewilderment.

'I remember …' he said, frowning. 'Words distorted as if angry and confused … your words poisoned and ill-heard …'

'This is not the work of the Fey,' Imorthorn said, looking at the gem. 'Who gave you this?'

'Why … it was a gift,' Imgorthand said. 'And a fair one, given in great honour my by vassal Morildrane … Morildrane?'

Imgorthand turned around, scanning the Fey behind him.

'Where is he?' Imorthorn demanded.

There was no sign of Morildrane.

'Find him!' Luxor called. 'For he is doubtless in the service of Shareth! Casting her evil spells over your people by means of his perfidy! Find him!'

Some of the Fey turned and ran off and orders were barked for a search.

'As for you, Imgorthand of the Eastern and Southern Fey,' Imorthorn said. 'I will not hold you to blame for the influence of Shareth's fell magic. Yet, I require your service and I would hear you and yours swear loyalty to me once again. I ask you, will you serve the Fey and ride to battle at my behest, forsaking any other call … for against the Heartstealer, I determine that the Fey are set to ends bitter or sweet. Will you swear to follow?'

Imgorthand straightened.

'For my part in this I deserve no mercy,' he replied. 'Yet, you are Lord and Master of the Fey of Fangrim. To your banner I pledge my allegiance once again. I will take up metal against the Heartstealer, ride with you in hopes of vanquishing her evil once and for all!'

Imorthorn raised his voice.

'And the rest of this company!' he called. 'Do you so swear?'

'We will follow you Lord Imorthorn!' the rousing cry came back.

'Then I command you now,' Imorthorn said. 'Make provision and readiness to ride upon the day break. Time is short and we have weary leagues ahead of us. We ride into the realm of our former foes, there to stand alongside them in a battle which will settle the fate of all the Icemark. Let us make sure the Fey are well represented in this present chapter of the age!'

Trumpets blew from the assembled armies. Imorthorn turned to Imgorthand.

'And find Morildrane ere we leave,' he rumbled. 'I want him brought before me.'

Lorelorn had already sent messengers out with instructions to assemble those armies loyal to him in the southern realm of the Frozen Empire nigh to the mountains of Anvulane. He and Talorthane had ridden south and east from his city. Within two days they had covered many leagues, the forests and the hills falling behind them as they rode on.

The armies had marched ahead on receipt of Lorelorn's missives and they were already camped within the forest that surrounded Fangrorn's great city at the eastern end of the mountain range. The city marked the border with the Dwarves, not far to the south lay the dwarven city of Carorthay itself, a great stronghold in their domain.

Yet Fangrorn's army was not there.

Lorelorn and Talorthane rode into his city and signalled for the courtiers to approach.

'News of Fangrorn?' Lorelorn demanded.

'He has already begun his campaign against the Dwarves,'

the courtier replied. 'The City of Carorthay has been defeated and the Dwarves retreat to the east. My Lord Fangrorn has besieged the fortress of Hagudril and plans to march on Glormane before the moon is out. He bids you join him there if you wish.'

'He didn't wait for us?' Talorthane asked in surprise.

'It would seem he felt he did not need additional support,' Lorelorn replied. 'Or the Dwarves are weaker than we supposed.'

The courtier bowed. 'My Lord Fangrorn believes the Dwarves are exposed after their own foolish internal squabbling. He has orders to exterminate them once and for all.'

'Then we will ride on today,' Lorelorn said, dismissing the courtier. 'And see for ourselves the great work of Lord Fangrorn.'

Lorelorn cast a look to Talorthane and spoke under his breath.

'It seems Tarithel's warning was correct in all respects,' he said. 'Our choice will soon be known to all, my friend. Are you prepared for treachery? Fangrorn is mighty, with a host stronger than ours combined. Even if we side with the combined armies of Luxor, victory is by no means assured.'

'My heart is decided,' Talorthane replied. 'I would prevent this wilful destruction if I can.'

'Then let us ride on,' Lorelorn replied. 'Their doom lies before them and Fangrorn will spare none. If he is a sound strategist, Luxor consolidates what forces he has. There can be only one place they can hope to make a stand. Beyond the Carormarg! Thortheon's fortress seems the most likely place in my mind. We must be swift to join the battle.'

Lorelorn spurred his horse and galloped south.

Chapter Nineteen

Obigrorn the Giant stands in the City of Carangrane, looking west to the Forest of Thenarg.

Great reeks and fumes leapt into the sky over the City of Carangrane. The hordes of the Heartstealer flung themselves into the fray with utter abandon. Thousands had died forcing their way up the narrow and winding road to the city, but still more had been ready to replace them. Ladders now festooned the walls and fighting along the battlements was fierce.

Yet the Giants held their own, knowing that to lose was to be vanquished utterly and that no mercy awaited those within that they sought to protect. For every Iceguard warrior that gained the walls, another was cast down from them.

'A stalemate,' Obigrorn said, with a grim nod. 'They cannot assail us further by strength of arms, nor can they bring their machines to bear upon the City.'

Rorthron observed the battle from alongside him. 'Perhaps, but the day will soon fail and night will be upon us. The enemy has the numbers to drive us to exhaustion.'

'We Giants have strength enough,' Obigrorn countered. 'We will last the night and the following day … and into the night once more if we must!'

'This battle will be decided long before then,' Rorthron said.

Already it was getting hard to see the more distant parts of the army. The sun had dropped below the distant hills across the valley and only the tips of the mountains behind them were lit by its glow. Twilight was upon them, and the fires of torches were already visible below as the battle continued. The fight atop the walls ebbed and flowed, but neither defenders nor attackers made any appreciable headway.

'What is that?' Obigrorn said, pointing out towards the city approach.

Amidst the dim and indistinct shapes of the Iceguard warriors, a strange flicker of light could be made out. It was akin to lightning, flashing for a brief moment before disappearing again. Whatever it might be, it was moving towards the city.

'Sorcery,' Rorthron said. 'And how Shareth hopes to decide the battle. Be ready, this is a power you are ill equipped to counter. I will do what I can!'

A figure could now be made out, riding through the ranks of the warriors on horseback, the source of the light held aloft in one hand. As the rider came close they could make out that the light was fixed upon a staff, crackling this way and that with an eerie cyan glow.

The Iceguard warriors were making way for the rider now. As they drew closer Rorthron and Obigrorn could make out that they were surrounded by a vanguard of other riders armed with lances and spears. They stopped out of reach of the Giants on the walls.

Then, at some unspoken signal, the warriors upon the walls retreated, the ladders abandoned with the Giants wrenching them from the walls and casting them down. The Iceguard warriors retreated out of range, formed ranks and waited.

'What are they doing?' Obigrorn demanded, peering into the gloom. 'That is Imgaril's banner … Imgaril himself expects us to parley?'

Rorthron shook his head.

The cyan light crackled and spat, growing in intensity. Then with a sharp thump of concussion the staff emitted a blinding shaft of light that lanced across the walls of the city. Where it struck, the stone work of the wall was rendered into fine powder, exploding outwards in choking clouds of smoke and dust. The Giants along the wall stumbled back, seeking shelter from the blast.

The beam of light arced upwards, striking one of the towers. It detonated with a cataclysmic explosion, showering debris and bodies in all directions amidst a rising conflagration.

The armies of the Iceguard roared and jeered in approval.

'If that strikes the gate, we are lost!' Obigrorn yelled.

Rorthron was already running along the wall where it overhung the gate. He gestured for the Giants there to step aside and then stood, his own staff poised above the entrance.

It was not a moment too soon.

The cyan beam lanced out, striking towards the great oaken doors of the city. Rorthron raised his own staff in defence.

The beam was arrested, crashing against an invisible curved barrier with Rorthron's staff at its focal point. The cyan glow writhed and twisted, clawing and shocking its way outwards, as if trying to find a way through. Sparks and flashes struck the ground, cracking stones and shattering the rocky pathway into gravel. Dust swirled into the air, whipped into a furious maelstrom by the raging energy of the attack.

The light faded with a booming echo of sound which reverberated around the walls and mountainsides before fading away.

Silence fell as the dust settled. The glaring torches of the Iceguard warriors and those arranged along the city walls shone out once more.

Below the walls of the city, Obigrorn and Rorthron could just see Imgaril himself on horseback. He was positioned just in front of his men, his own staff outstretched. The flickering light now subdued, fizzing and hissing around the tip.

'They did not expect to encounter you, I think,' Obigrorn said with a grin, clapping Rorthron on the back.

'No indeed,' Rorthron replied. 'But I only just defied that attack. This is Shareth's magic and it is potent, but Imgaril commands only a fraction of it.'

'Can you strike back?' Obigrorn asked.

Rorthron shook his head.

'Such is not my power,' Rorthron said and Obigrorn looked downcast. 'The Wise never sought to destroy things in such a manner.'

'Then we remain in a stalemate until they relent or we are starved out …'

Rorthron shook his head. 'This is magic that has been twisted and tortured against the natural order of such things … but … we might use that against our foe in ways they cannot counter.'

'How so?'

'I have an idea,' Rorthron said. 'But we must entice them into another attack on the gate.'

'That we can do,' Obigrorn said with a wry grin, signalling to the Giants nearby. 'Stone them!'

The Giants wrestled up great chucks of rock and stone from the cracked and damaged walls about, hoisted them and then flung the huge chunks towards the Iceguard far below. Some were caught in the barrage and dashed to the ground.

The glow above Imgaril's staff grew brighter once again.

Rorthron raised his own staff as the tumult of spiralling rocks hurled by the Giants continued to crash down upon the forces of the Iceguard.

Imgaril's staff blazed in the darkness, casting its eerie cyan glow across the battlefield, sharp shadows flickering this way and that. Then, with a screech of noise, the blazing beam struck forth once more.

Again it was frustrated by Rorthron's own powers. It spat

and crackled furiously, writhing and twisting trying to find a way around the ephemeral barrier that Rorthron's own power had thrown in its path.

Rorthron was mouthing strange words, arcane mutterings that spoke of powers long forgotten to mortals.

He twisted his staff in his grip, as if fighting an attacker and warding off a blow, sweeping the staff around in a savage arc.

The invisible shield rippled in the air, shrinking and coalescing as it did so, into a bright flurry of scintillating light. For a moment it held, vying with the writhing cyan of its foe, clashing in the sky like a miniature sun, casting a harsh light over the hordes of attackers below.

Rorthron swung his staff again.

His own light faded, but the beam of cyan was diverted, blasted at right angles in a spiralling dazzle of energy up and away from the city walls. All eyes turned to follow it as it blistered through the air in a shining arc …

… and then crashed upon the mountainside.

With a great cry, Rorthron twisted his staff around once more.

The light faded, and only a faint rumble echoed back from high above, fading into the gathering darkness.

Course laughter could be heard from the ranks of Iceguard below the walls. The light atop Imgaril's staff flickered back and grew in strength.

'Should we attack once more?' Obigrorn muttered.

'Hold …' Rorthron called.

A faint cracking sound echoed around them, magnified by the mountain peaks all about. A moment later a tremor was felt underfoot.

Then an immense roar of noise crescendoed about them, the ground shuddering, masonry and debris cascading down from the damaged walls of the city.

The giants looked at each other in fear, bracing themselves as the tremors grew.

'Hold!' Rorthron called aloud.

Then, great boulders could be seen careening down the mountainside, appearing out of the gloom as they caught the flickering firelight. With a deafening roar they crashed amongst the armies encamped before the gates. Others smashed into the walls and broke upon them.

'Back away from the walls, to the north!' Rorthron yelled.

The giants began to flee as the tumult of rocks and debris crashed upon them. The roar continued, growing in intensity until the very ground cracked and tore beneath their feet. The mighty walls of the city cracked and broke. Dust smote across them, blinding them.

Below, rocks, gravel and more boulders flew alongside the tortured walls, covering the plain before the city. Cries of fear and dismay from their foes were scarce heard above the terrifying rumble of the avalanche of rock … and swiftly silenced.

Dirt, thick and cloying, settled upon them as the noise subsided. Dust wafted past, circling in the air and clearing aside in a gentle breeze.

The city limits came into view first. The southernmost bulwark of the walls had been crushed and overcome by the tumult of rock that had broken free from far above and smashed down with irresistible force.

Then the dust swept clear.

The plain before the city was full of rubble. Here and there small fires glistened amidst the rock and debris. Of the Iceguard army before the gates, none could be seen alive. The landslide had covered the entire approach to the city and further half a mile down the narrow access road that led to it. Save for some stragglers at the back, the Iceguard warriors had been crushed, or swept off the road to their doom.

Obigrorn wiped his eyes clear of the dirt that caked him.

'A victory unlooked for,' he managed to say. 'Victory goes to you, Rorthron the Wise!'

Tarithel walked north, but the way was difficult and progress slow. A narrow path ran from Lorelorn's city through the dank gloom of the Forest of Farorn. It was a dispiriting place, the trees about her seemed indifferent and cold, their bark almost black, sucking away life and light. Underfoot was nothing but the mulch of seasons long ago, hardly any snow reached the forest floor and the way was muddy. Only far above, could any daylight be seen, even the leaves seemed black, there was no colour at all.

She reached the Lith around midday based on her own reckoning, walking into a tangled, overgrown clearing full of brambles and weeds. At the centre she could see the Lith itself, its sides covered in algae and mould. There seemed little life about, there were no birds, no animals, it felt more like a tomb than anything else.

She pushed her way through, trying her best to avoid the thorns and tangled creepers about her. It took her a while, the vegetation was thick and unyielding and she had to resort to using a knife on the most stubborn brambles.

Climbing the stone, she placing her hands upon it.

It was cold.

She looked about her in dismay. Still nothing moved.

Where the Lith in her homeland had always felt warm to the touch, as if heated by some strange power deep within the earth, here there was nothing. She felt nothing, no presence, no sense that anything had ever resided here.

The sense of purpose that had spurred her onwards faded. A blast of freezing air whistled past, chilling her.

'There must be something ...' she called out, getting to her feet and pacing around the rocks. Yet everywhere she touched, the stone was still the same, cold and lifeless, with no hint of any presence she could detect.

Long minutes passed.

'Where are you?' she called into the gloom. 'I have come all this way in your service! I have defied the Heartstealer as you directed me … I wish only to find my betrothed and set him free. You have led me to this point and I have followed … what now do you ask of me?'

There was no answer, the words were swallowed up by the forest and lost. There was nothing, desolation was all about her. She could sense nothing but the dank smell of rotten leaves and dying plants.

Despair caught her. Tears came to her eyes and the stresses and strains of her long days of travail overwhelmed her. She sobbed, crying into her hands.

She turned to look north, seeing the faint glimmer of ice upon the horizon. She knew it to be the impassable barrier of the Frozen Wastes.

I have failed … I know where my beloved Morkin lies, but I cannot reach him and I cannot help him … I have lost Álainn, I am alone, lost in a wilderness far beyond help. The lands about me are beset with war and vast armies stand between me and my home …

The tears were hot on her cheeks.

'Luxor!' she cried. 'Can you hear me? I have failed! I am so sorry … but I have not found a way to free your son! He is lost … and I am lost …'

She waited, still crying, unable to stop her grief.

There was no answer. She could not sense the Moon Ring at all. Was Luxor beyond its range, or had some other fate befallen him?

Perhaps he has been slain and the Heartstealer already rules all the Icemark. Perhaps I am already too late …

She looked around herself, desperately trying to think of what she could do, each option more outlandish than the last, all futile, all folly.

Do I give up? Try to return home.

Her tears dripped further down her cheeks, but anger boiled within her, determination flaring once again.

Return? How can I return in failure, knowing that Morkin will spend the rest of his days imprisoned as a toy of that hateful woman? I will not stop ... the Frozen Wastes may be an impassable barrier ... they may freeze my body the instant I set foot within their boundaries ... if so ... so be it! I will not stop searching for a way until my death! I will not!

She screamed into the forest. 'Do you hear, Shareth? Cursed Heartstealer of Icemark? I will not stop. I will never give him up! And if death is not the end, even then I will search beyond. My shade will haunt the Icemark until the end of time. Even with my death you will know no peace!'

Tears fell from her, splashing on the stone of the Lith.

Something touched her hand. She looked down in surprise.

Where her tears had touched the stone they had dripped down to the soil below. Now a thin shoot of green had risen up from the same soil, coiling back and forth, caressing the skin of her hand.

As she watched, entranced, she heard words in her mind.

Tarithel ...

'Who are you?' she whispered. 'Fangrim?'

The voice seemed amused.

Not Fangrim ... older, deeper am I ... Farorn!

'Farorn ...'

Yes ... what is it that ails you, Tarithel the Fey?

Tarithel gasped.

'Know you not?' she asked. 'I seek a way to save my beloved Morkin, held hostage at the City of Imiriel ... but there is no way that I can reach him ...'

If there was a way, what would you do in return for such knowledge?

Tarithel blinked in surprise.

'To save Morkin? I would give anything!'

Then I ask another question … Look around, Tarithel, Lady of the Forest … what do you see?

Tarithel blinked and rubbed at her eyes, wiping the tears from her cheeks.

'I see a Forest, dark and gloomy …'

It was not always this way …

For a brief moment Tarithel felt warmth upon her face, the sweet smell of blossom and pollen reached her, the scents of spring. About her the forest was transformed to a lush green, with wild flowers, ferns and broad-leaved trees growing strong. A canopy of leaves above her rustled in a gentle breeze. The Lith was free from moss and mould, clean and placed within a neatly tended clearing. Tarithel gasped in delight.

She blinked … and the vision was gone. The gloom seemed heavier, darker and more malevolent than before. The shock of transition brought fresh tears to her eyes.

Once things were thus, perhaps they can be again.

'But how?'

The forests of Icemark suffer … you know by whom the curse is wrought. The Sorceress.

'Shareth!'

Yes … life cannot bloom once more until she is gone.

'She may yet perish by the sword! Luxor …'

Luxor, Rorthron and all the forces of men, Dwarves, giants and Fey cannot cast her down.

'But I have not the power to end her,' Tarithel said. 'She will smite me!'

If you do not, the forests will succumb. And with them all things will end. Icemark itself will perish in war and devastation. The future is set before you. You have seen the fire and smoke.

'Then what do you ask of me?'

You wish to save your beloved. We wish to save the forests and thus the Icemark itself. In exchange for his life will you swear a vow to end the Heartstealer, destroy her utterly, even at the cost of yourself?

Tarithel's face was free from tears now. She looked up determined and resolute once more.

'Then you set my life against his and the people of the Icemark,' Tarithel said. 'Such a choice is no choice. To set Morkin free alone I would gladly give my life … I will do as you say … I promise to end the Heartstealer if it be within my powers, I swear this upon the Citadel of my father, and the forest of my home. Either she perishes, or I do.'

Very well … first seek your betrothed … then, once you have rescued him … the Heartstealer you will face!

Before Tarithel's eyes the brambles nearby coiled tight. A faint green light flickered within the thorns … they writhed up in front of her. The lights flashed before her eyes, revealing words she could somehow read, hanging in the air before her.

When evil grips the world so tight, in coldest days and deepest night,

When darkness rules by means of might, and hides the truth from all your sight.

When the moon is new and sounds the knell, the hour is come for deeds most fell,

In another place would you choose to dwell? So weave the words of Thigrorn's spell!

Light flashed and colours sparkled in her mind and vision.

'Thigrorn …'

I have heard this name before …

Memories of darkness and a passageway far below the ground, a shivering madness that had threatened to consume her mind and sanity. She shook her head, trying to clear it.

Here in the Forest of Farorn stands Tarithel the Fey. She is good, forceful, generous, stubborn, brave, swift, loyal and only a little reckless ...

Her mind was awhirl with light and sound, she tried to think again ...

Who do you seek, Tarithel the Fey, Lady of the Forest?

Her answer was clear.

'I seek Morkin the Free, son of Luxor, Moonprince of Midnight!'

It is dawn. Here in the Forest of Farorn Tarithel has found the Spell of Thigrorn!

The light blazed in her eyes, blinding her. She cried out in confusion as she felt herself falling, the air roaring in her ears.

Thigrorn!

Arms flailing, she spun. Opening her eyes she could see only a swirling brightness about her, as if she had been caught in a blizzard and was somehow falling through clouds swept with ice and snow.

Thigrorn!

With a thump, she landed. The breath was knocked from her and it was long moments before she could do anything but gasp for air. She managed to raise her head.

A voice whispered in her mind, swiftly receding.

Thigrorn ...

It faded into the distance.

She was lying in a snow drift. It had cushioned her fall from wherever she had come. She looked about her in surprise and astonishment. Snow stretched out in all directions as far as she could see, powdery and deep. She managed to crawl to her knees.

Her mouth dropped open in surprise at the sight that greeted her.

A sparkling city, its buildings glistening in the warm glow of sunrise. She knew it at once, she had seen it many times in dreams and vision.

Imiriel! The City of Imiriel!

She gasped, her heart quickening and beating hard in her chest.

Morkin!

The Fey had ridden hard from the City of Imorthorn, heading west through the eaves of the Forest of Fangrim. Their progress was swift in their own realm, but it wasn't long before the Forest fell behind them and they rode out on to the plains of the Barbarians.

'A long ride remains through territory which is hostile to us,' Imorthorn said, riding alongside Luxor.

'We will not be harried here,' Luxor replied. 'Much has transpired whilst we gathered strength in the Forest. Shareth's forces have struck Giant, Dwarf and Barbarian alike. The news from most is ill. On my instruction, the Dwarves have abandoned their own capital and fall back towards us as swiftly as they can. The Barbarians war with the Giants is at an end now that Shareth has betrayed them both. Their forces both retreat southwards with the Iceguard at their heels.'

'Is there any news which does bode well?' Imorthorn asked.

'There is hope in the north,' Luxor replied. 'My friend, Rorthron of the Wise has aided the Giants. There they fight a battle against one Imgaril of the Frozen Empire.'

'Imgaril,' Imorthorn replied. 'This name I do know. One of Shareth's close and trusted warlords.'

'So Rorthron tells me,' Luxor replied. 'Rorthron is mighty himself in magic and such sorcery. If victorious, I have instructed them to march to us, in the hope we can join our forces against the Heartstealer before she cuts us off from each other.'

'That would be welcome tidings,' Imorthorn said. 'What of the Icelords that swore their loyalty?'

'They ride also in great haste,' Luxor replied. 'All make for the Fortress of Thortheon, that is where we will make our stand, if fate allows our would-be allies to reach it in time.'

'Then our strategy is one of concentration of strength,' Imorthorn said. 'What remains of the Giants, Barbarians, Dwarves, Fey, even the Icelords standing as one. I will give you this, Luxor Moonprince of Midnight, such a thing has never been achieved before. Even if the end is ill, it will have been a worthy attempt.'

'Let us hope the ill end does not lie in wait for us!' Luxor said.

Another Fey rode up alongside them.

'My Lord Imorthorn.'

'Speak,' Imorthorn replied.

'Lord Imgorthand sends word,' the rider said. 'He has apprehended Morildrane and holds him captive. They ride to rendezvous with us.'

'Good news,' Imorthorn said, looking at Luxor. 'A snake in the grass that I should have dealt with sooner.'

'Shareth's deceptions stem from misdirection and stealth,' Luxor replied. 'Do not be hard on yourself that you did not see it for what it was straight away. She is cunning and sly.'

'Perhaps,' Imorthorn replied. 'But I am accountable for such things regardless.'

Both dismounted as Imgorthand arrived. With him were two other Fey warriors and between them they held Morildrane.

'Am I to be tried here, without due process?' Morildrane called out. 'See the failed leadership of the Fey in all its shabbiness! Your leaders are indecisive and vindictive … they lead you onwards towards ruin and death … mark my words. The Fey will fall under your leadership, Imorthorn!'

'Silence in the presence of your betters,' Imorthorn snapped back. 'I did not bring you here to listen to your poisoned tongue, Morildrane, but to dispense summary justice for your crimes. You're a spy in service to the Heartstealer and your life is in my hands. Release him.'

The two Fey warriors either side of Morildrane stepped away and Imorthorn stepped close to Morildrane until they were face to face.

'Why?' Imorthorn demanded. 'Why betray your people to the Heartstealer?'

'The Fey need a real leader,' Morildrane answered. 'You ride here with our armies thinking you can challenge her, you fools! You have already lost, you just don't yet know it. There is no defying the Heartstealer. The Fey would have been left alone, content with our lot, subservient to the Heartstealer had we not taken up arms against her. That was her promise to us … but you would not listen …'

'The Heartstealer tells nothing but lies,' Imorthorn replied. 'Those who believe her, she turns upon. I see you are beyond redemption, Morildrane, and I must sentence you. No Fey will willingly take the life of another Fey, that is not our way. Thus your goods and home are forfeit and you are banished from our lands from this moment forth. Go to your precious Heartstealer if you will. I doubt she will have much use for you now.'

Morildrane spat at him.

Imorthorn was unmoved and wiped the spittle away without taking his gaze away from Morildrane's.

'Be gone, lackey of the Heartstealer.'

Morildrane reared back, crying out with fury and then swung at Imorthorn.

A sword flashed, its cutting stroke swift and precise.

Morildrane fell without a sound, cut down.

Luxor held his sword aloft, gesturing at Morildrane's right hand.

'A Fey will not strike down another Fey, eh?' Luxor said. Imorthorn could see that a dagger was clasped in Morildrane's fist. The intention was clear.

Imorthorn looked up. 'I thank you, Lord Luxor,' he said. 'A stroke I should have delivered long ago.'

'And I,' Imgorthand said. 'Yet, we were all deceived.'

Imorthorn pursed his lips.

'Onwards,' he called. 'Let us waste no more time here. The real foe awaits us still!'

They mounted their horses and Imorthorn let out a blast on his horn. He led them away at a gallop.

The Mountains of Imorthay were rising on their right hand flank. Imorthorn blew his horn and the Fey resumed their ride, heading north-west across the plains of the Barbarians.

The flaming ruin of the Fortress of Ganigrorn lay a league behind them. All about the plain the vast army of the Iceguard was arrayed; foot soldiers, riders and the dark machinery of warfare. The army was vast, spreading to the east, west and north as far as the eye could see. Smoke and fumes hung low overhead, and all about, flames and destruction had spread to the limits of the valley.

The forest was burning and everything between the austere arms of the twin mountain ranges of Anvulane and Anvormane was a blasted ruin.

The army of Shareth the Heartstealer had almost reached its zenith, poised to crush the south lands into submission.

Yet doubt had weaved its way into her cold and icy heart.

Imgaril has failed to subdue the giants. Incompetent fool! That frail lackey of the Moonprince, Rorthron of the Wise, has somehow defeated him ... If he finds the Crown now ... such powers will be used against me!

She screamed in rage and fury, but spoke no words.

My strength is sufficient to destroy those who stand against me. This is but a setback. The Giants reel from my attack, they will not be able to respond in time. I will deal with what remains of their people later. For now, I must press onwards!

She gathered herself, summoning her warlords to her.

'All to the north we have held for long moons,' she instructed them. 'To the east the Dwarves are being beaten back as we speak, soon our forces there will join us and our overwhelming strength will be unleashed upon the south. This day we have vanquished much of the remaining strength of the Giants and the Barbarians. Our strength will soon be assembled and we will ride to vanquish all before us.'

The Icelords bowed before her.

'My spies tell me that the Fey are on the move and the Moonprince rides with them,' she said. 'They have been delayed long enough for their arrival to be in vain. Thus we will strike onwards whilst we may. The Fey will ride to the battlefield and find that the allies they hoped to join with are already slain and dashed to the winds and that their fate is to die alone as the others will have done. Make ready! Today will be the last day for the Dwarves, tomorrow for the Barbarians and then everlasting night will fall for the Fey ere the next moon begins! There will no longer be an Icemark, the boundaries of the Frozen Empire will extend everywhere and I will be Empress of all. Sound the advance!'

Horns blared across the valley and the armies of the Heartstealer made ready to move south.

Dawn had broken, cold and frosty, over the City of Carangrane, capital of the Giants. At its southernmost end the walls were submerged in the landslide of rock that had cascaded down the mountainside. In the early light, the scale of the destruction could be seen. A vast bowl-like depression had been scooped out of the mountain that stood over the city and that mighty mass of rock and rubble had smashed its way down towards the city, burying everything in its path.

Of the Iceguard army, Imgaril himself and all that had stood before the gates, little trace was found. A few bodies were hauled from beneath the rubble, but most seemed to have been swept over the precipices that dropped away from the City and the access road that led to it, never to be seen again.

A few stragglers who had escaped the fall had fled from the scene, but had been rounded up, caught, killed or captured.

The Iceguard invasion of the realm of the Giants was at an end.

Obigrorn and Rorthron looked out at the wreckage.

'We giants can work with rock and stone,' Obigrorn said. 'It seems fitting that they should come to our aid in time of need.'

'The power of the land itself should never be underestimated,' Rorthron replied.

'But it was at your command they came,' Obigrorn replied. 'We are in your debt, Rorthron of the Wise. You have delivered us beyond our most desperate hope and slain our foes. If it be within my power, I will grant you any wish you desire.'

Rorthron nodded, turned and smiled.

'I came here upon my own desperate quest,' he replied. 'Shareth's evil might have been foiled here, but her strength is still great and she stretches out her hand against others. More battles lie ahead for all of us until such evil is defeated, if indeed it is possible so to do.'

'And what do you seek?' Obigrorn asked.

'Varangrim told tale of artefacts buried deep in the vaults

and catacombs deep within this City,' Rorthron said. 'Likely the reason Shareth sent Imgaril here to take it. Such things may hold the secret to defeating her.'

'I know little of such things,' Obigrorn said. 'But, you are most welcome to search where you may, Carangrane himself would wish it, were he here.'

Rorthron nodded.

'Then I must also make another request,' he said. 'We have frustrated Shareth's plans here in the realm of the Giants, but she moves against your southern brethren even as we speak. They cannot resist her alone. My Liege, Luxor the Moonprince, seeks to unite both Fey, Dwarf and Barbarian against her. Such aid as you can give in battle is what I must ask you for.'

Obigrorn looked at him.

'You ask much,' Obigrorn said. 'But you have proven yourself to me, Rorthron of the Wise. We will not defy that request or the orders of Varangrim himself. Doubtless you need us to march as soon as we are able?'

'Very much so,' Rorthron said. 'And I will travel with you on the road.'

Obigrorn nodded.

'So shall it be, with one proviso. I cannot in good conscience leave my homeland undefended. I will summon what strength I can here and more will join us as we march.'

Rorthron rubbed his chin.

'We have to muster what strength we can. Shareth will not wait.'

'It is a long road to the south,' Obigrorn said, 'We must march northwards first, through the gap of Thudrane before turning to the south. There is no path through the mountains for an army.'

'Then summon what strength you have and make ready to depart without delay,' Rorthron replied. 'With your leave I will search the vaults of the city.'

Obigrorn bowed. 'I will show you to the vaults.

Rorthron followed Obigrorn as they walked down from the walls and paced amongst the ranks of wounded Giants being tended in camps within. Before them the straight and vast walls of the buildings of the city rose above him. The Giants used no curves in their architecture, preferring straight lines at all times, with thick and heavy construction. Everything was squared off and wrought without decoration.

Venturing within, the interior was plain, the Giants finding little use for anything much beyond vast stone tables, chairs and wrought iron braziers for light and heat. Doorways were bereft of actual doors, the Giants preferring airier accommodation.

Together they strode onwards. Obigrorn lit a torch and led the way. Great steps led downwards within. Rorthron was forced to negotiate them one at a time due to their immense size.

A thick, iron portcullis guarded a doorway. Obigrorn signalled to two guards stationed either side for it to be raised, and it was pulled up and out of the way with a rumble of heavy and seldom used machinery. A doorway beyond led to a junction where a corridor ran out in both directions.

'These are the vaults,' Obigrorn said. 'I know not what they contain, if they contain anything at all. Only Carangrane himself ventured down here at his leisure. Unlike other races, we do not put much stock in gold or jewels. Clean air and clean rock to be shaped to our service is our currency.'

They walked up the corridor, peering into darkened but empty rooms, each one barred by a similar portcullis arrangement.

'What were these rooms used for in the past?' Rorthron asked.

'It is said they were used to hold prisoners,' Obigrorn said.

'We giants have not always been at peace amongst ourselves … sometimes it was necessary to imprison our own.'

Rorthron nodded.

All the rooms thus far had been empty, but the next one contained a series of dusty boxes. Obigrorn raised the portcullis and Rorthron walked inside. Within each box were mouldering records, long scrolls and parchments, with maps and other information.

'From a time long ago I would say,' he commented.

'Carangrane had lived long and acquired much knowledge,' Obigrorn added.

Rorthron stepped back for a moment and then tapped his staff on the ground. A flicker of light etched across the ground, sweeping around the room, outlining the interior.

One of the boxes glowed in the dark, and a faint hum could be heard.

'What is that?' Obigrorn demanded.

Rorthron, taking great care, opened the box, finding the inside filled with sawdust. Within was a dark, metal object, tarnished with age.

Before he could touch it, light sparkled before him, forming words in the air.

Seeking far and seeking long,
Aid you have found, oh Wise forlorn.
For many troubles have you borne,
Learn now well the runes of Finorn.

The light spun about Rorthron and he staggered back, his face lit from within by youth and vigour.

Service you have given, alone of all the Wise,
Furthered aims we set, ere our fell demise.
Across the lands you've stridden, these realms you have long roamed,
And further journeys call you, to places yet unknown.

Obigrorn backed away, but Rorthron gestured for him to stop.

'Do not be afraid,' he said. 'The Wise of old left this here in case one of their own came looking ...'

Evil will assail you, intent on devastation all about,
Armies must be succoured, or face defeat in rout.
Strength I give you, in your struggle against the foe,
I, Finorn, last of the first, do thus deem it so!

The glowing words faded. Rorthron took a deep breath.

'The last of my kindred,' he whispered. 'From long before the evil and the Ice, when the Wise were still abroad in these lands. A message and ...'

He grasped his staff tighter.

'... And renewed strength!'

He reached down to the object in the box, lifting it out.

It was shaped in the manner of a crown, with eight spires wrought around its band.

'This is what you have come to seek?' Obigrorn asked. 'Some old trinket? It looks like dwarven make to me.'

Rorthron held it aloft.

'Not dwarven,' he said. 'Much older than that. Let's see if it remembers the words of the Wise after all this time ...'

He muttered strange sounds under his breath, turning the crown around in his fingers.

Obigrorn watched as he did so, stepping back in surprise as, with a faint ring of metal, the tarnish began to dissolve from the crown, leaving a bright silver in its place. Gems, hidden by dirt and age were revealed, blazing out with dazzling colour.

'What is this?' Obigrorn whispered.

Rorthron listened for a moment.

'It calls itself the Crown of Varenand.'

Rorthron concentrated hard.

'Luxor!' he called. 'I have with me the Crown of Varenand. We have defied the Heartstealer here in the realm of the Giants and won a victory over her servant, Imgaril. Now I make my way back to you with what strength the Giants can muster …'

Rorthron! It is most joyous to hear from you! We have the pledges of the Barbarians and the Dwarves! We assemble all our strength at the Fortress of Thortheon at the northernmost tip of the Barbarian's domain. Meet us there with all possible haste, time is short.

Rorthron looked at Obigrorn.

'I hold you to your pledge, Obigrorn of the Giants. We must depart for the south immediately!'

Tarithel trudged on through the thick snow. The City grew closer. There seemed to be no one about at all, the snow was pristine and unmarked. Some distance behind her she could see an ornate and impressive colonnaded building, it was similar to the palace she had escaped the tunnels from as she'd left the Dwarfs. A little to the left she could see a Lith poking up from the snow and beyond that a fortress. She kept a wary eye on it, but saw no movement.

As she drew close to the city, the snow thinned out beneath her feet until it was a fine layer of powder. The city seemed made of glass or crystal, its minarets towering above her and reflecting a kaleidoscope of colours into the air and across the snow. Red, blues, cyans, magentas and greens flickered all about. It was starkly beautiful.

This is where I was bound. Through forests and tunnels, across mountains, rivers and lakes, defying mist and fog and many dangers … here at last I am. Imiriel where Morkin is held prisoner in the clutches of the Heartstealer … so … where is he?

She stepped into the streets of the city. It was unlike any place she had ever been before. There were no houses, no shops, no courtyards or even defence walls. The city was composed of lofty towers which seemed to have no entrances that she could see. There was a single street which ran its length and at the far end the greatest tower rose before her.

Set before her in that tower was a pair of gates, also somehow wrought of crystal, she saw no metal, wood or other material at all. That the city stood seemed somehow magical, how it had been made she could not fathom, certainly not by any craft of Free or Fey.

She stepped through the doors, finding herself in a hall. Before her rose a crystal staircase, inviting her to ascend. Arches divided the hall into anterooms, but there was nothing in any them that she could see, no chairs, no tables, no decorations of any kind at all.

Trying not to make any sound, she stepped on to the staircase and walked up. It split halfway, curving around to a mezzanine floor which looked down on the hallway below. She turned around to see where she was going, climbing the final few stairs to the top.

Ahead of her, more alcoves decorated a glistening balustrade, overlooking the city street she had walked up.

In the middle of one alcove, a figure stood.

Tarithel gasped. The figure was obscured, thrown into silhouette by the light of the rising sun. She squinted into the glare, her voice catching in her throat.

'Morkin!'

Gasping, tears filling her eyes and clouding her vision she stumbled towards him, arms outstretched, until she stood a few feet from him. She remembered his stance, his hair, the line and curve of his shoulders.

It is him!

He turned to her, his face coming into view, the familiar features so long missed. She reached forward to touch him …

His outstretched hand caught her wrist, twisting it around, straining her arm.

'You …' he said. His voice was cold, his expression filled with anger and hatred.

'Yes … Morkin! It is I, Tarithel! I have travelled a long and weary way to find you …'

He twisted her arm further, causing her to yell out in pain. With a jerk he spun her around, throwing her to the floor. She heard the sound of a metal scraping. By the time she looked up a sword was poised at her throat.

'Morkin …'

'I have waited a long time for you to arrive,' Morkin said, his voice was grating, raspy and cruel. 'She said you might come, to weave further sorcery over me and addle my mind still further … but I am prepared. Foolish Fey-girl … I will be bewitched by you no more!'

'It is she who has bewitched you!' Tarithel cried. 'Do you not remember our love? We are betrothed, Morkin! Betrothed! We pledged our futures together!'

'Lies!' Morkin shouted at her. 'Speak no more of your foul enchantments, sorceress!'

Tarithel backed up, but he moved forward to keep pace with her, a grimace etched upon his face. The sword followed her, never more than a few inches from her skin.

'It's not a lie …'

Tarithel struggled back to her feet, sobbing. She turned and found her way blocked by a dark, cloaked figure. In a moment she was in his grip, arms pinned by her side and held fast.

'Well done, Anvireon,' Morkin said, with a laugh. 'Together we have caught this witch in our snare.' He raised the sword, scrapping its edge along Tarithel's cheek until the blade rested against her neck.

'Then end her,' Anvireon said. 'Do the bidding of our mistress and all will be well.'

Tarithel cried out in grief. 'Remember me, Morkin! Remember the glade in which we met, the greenness of the forest, the laughter and the love we shared ... Morkin, please! It is I who love you, not Shareth! She is the one who has bewitched your mind!'

Thortheon's scouts had told him of the impending arrival of armies long before they came into sight. His Fortress was the northernmost of those held by the Barbarians in modern times, standing as it did on the border with the Giants and at the western end of the Pass of Carormarg through the Mountains of Anvulane to the east. None could pass north or south, nor east or west, without coming into sight of his Fortress and so it had long been one of the most strategic locations in all of the Icemark.

'Dwarves,' the scout told him. 'A few thousands at most.'

Thortheon looked at Imgorad. The elder Barbarian nodded in response.

'As the Moonprince said it would be,' he said. 'But not in enough strength to resist the Heartstealer.'

Thortheon had already made a count of all the warriors within the Fortress. Giants and Barbarians held an uneasy truce after the disastrous battle for Ganigrorn and the ignominious flight south. Of the Barbarians, just short of ten thousand warriors remained, of the Giants, less than three.

'And yet the Heartstealer has yet to press her advantage,' Thortheon replied.

'It will not be long delayed,' Imgorad said. 'My folly has led us to this end. The Moonprince was right, Shareth has played us all and played us well. The Dwarves retreat, the Giants retreat and we retreated too, all given bloody noses at the hands of the Iceguard. An alliance is forced upon us now, but we should have all joined forces before. Now our reduced strength is not enough.'

'The Moonprince and the Fey ride swiftly from the south,' Thortheon countered.

'It is many leagues from the Forest of Fangrim,' Imgorad replied. 'They are three days away, perhaps more. If Shareth strikes soon, and her scouts will soon tell her it is safe so to do, then Luxor and the Fey will find Shareth's army south of here and no trace of us but a burning pyre.'

'Then we should retreat, take a stand further south?' Thortheon said.

'And where would that be?' Imgorad asked. 'We have not the strength to hold our lands against such overwhelming force. The nearest defensible fortress is that of Thangrad, but that is two days march. We would be overtaken on route and would fare even worse. No, this remains our best chance, if only a slight one. We have stout walls and nowhere to flee to!'

By the eve of the day, the armies of the Dwarves had arrived, some eight thousand doughty looking warriors bearing axes. They were tired though and stories of their rout by the forces of Fangrorn far to the east soon made the rounds.

Imgorad and Thortheon ventured down to the gates to meet the new arrivals. Four gruff looking Dwarves, dressed in the array of leaders stood before him.

'You know me,' he said. 'Imgorad, leader of the Barbarians. I bid you welcome in these strange and difficult times.'

One of the Dwarves stepped forward.

'I am Glormane, chief of the Dwarves of my realm,' the Dwarf answered, with a bow. 'These are my loyal countrymen, Imulorn and Imelorn. We stand before you as exiles from our homelands, evicted by the might of the Heartstealer and her Icelords.'

Imgorad nodded. 'We too have suffered at her hand …'

Horns blew on the towers of the fortress. Imgorad and

Glormane and the other Dwarves turned and looked out towards the east.

'More armies?' Imgorad said, squinting into the distance. 'Wait … those are Iceguard banners! Are we under siege already?'

Glormane held up a hand.

'Believe it or not, these are friends, not foes,' he said. 'Luxor told me of their approach. Tarithel, the Fey-girl who came to us not long ago has turned their loyalty to our cause.'

Imgorad looked unconvinced, but it was soon clear that perhaps two thousand Iceguard warriors were riding towards the Fortress of Thortheon. They kept a neat and tidy formation as they approached, stopping a hundred yards short of the gate of the fortress, two Icelords in the lead.

Imgorad and Glormane met them there.

'No Icelord has stood within these realms and remained alive for long,' Imgorad rumbled. 'Yet, strange times mean strange bedfellows, and the word and loyalty of the Moonprince has been revealed to be a stronger bond than I first thought.'

The Icelords bowed and dismounted.

'I am Lorelorn,' the first said. 'And this is my vassal Talorthane.'

'Imgorad,' Imgorad said.

'And I am Glormane of the Dwarves,' Glormane added.

'We come here on the instruction of Lord Luxor,' Lorelorn said. 'We have pledged to him.'

'And how easily is the loyalty of the Icelords swayed?' Imgorad said, his voice lower.

Glormane stepped forward.

'Trust is something none of us can expect from each other,' he said. 'But a pledge to the Moonprince is something we do all share in common. Let us hold fast to that, if we can do nothing else.'

Imgorad nodded.

'Your fears are justified,' Lorelorn answered. 'To throw off loyalty to the Heartstealer is no idle thought. Yet should I, along with you, fail to stop her, your fate will be to die upon the sword in battle. She will see that a far worse punishment awaits me and my folk for our betrayal. We have no hope unless it with lies in victory with the forces loyal now to the Moonprince.'

'Yet, you haven't even met Luxor,' Imgorad said.

'No,' Lorelorn replied. 'A meeting I greatly anticipate. Yet we were approached by his vassal, one Tarithel of the Fey, sorceress and foe of the Heartstealer. She made a compelling case and thus secured our pledge to destroy Shareth.'

'And Tarithel came to us too,' Glormane added. 'She is mighty in her own sorcery and loyal to the Moonprince.'

'She bid me to send fond greetings to you, Glormane,' Lorelorn added. 'From Tarithel, sorceress of the Fey.'

Glormane smiled.

'Yet she is not here,' Imgorad said. 'But your strength at arms is sorely needed in defence of this place. Shareth has a force camped but a day's march from here at the ruins of the Fortress of Ganigrorn. She has yet to assemble her full strength, but it will not be long delayed. Luxor and the Fey are en route, but two days remain before they will arrive. See to your people, see to your weapons. It is likely that battle awaits us on the morrow.'

'We managed to outpace the forces of Fangrorn,' Lorelorn said, 'They have stopped at your city, Glormane …

Glormane scowled.

'But their arrival will not be long delayed,' Lorelorn said. 'Shareth's strength is coming together as if it were a pair of great crushing claws …'

The armies of the Fey surged northwards at a charge, their steeds galloping hard across the plains of the Barbarians. Through the Forest of Carelorn they had ridden at speed, their travel aided by their skill and art at finding paths through the trees that none but the Fey could spy.

Now the landscape had opened before them. Imorthorn had led them well, by noon they had arrived at a fountain that stood amidst the plains. There, both rider and horse found new strength in the fresh waters, provisions were broken out and a brief rest given to all.

'We have made good time,' Imorthorn said, looking about him. 'By my reckoning the Fortress of Thortheon is some fifteen leagues north of here. We should reach it by tomorrow eve if nothing stands between us.'

'We must retain enough strength to fight once we arrive,' Luxor replied. 'Imgorad reports they are yet to be besieged by the Heartstealer, but if she knows we are coming, she will likely move to surround the Fortress before we can arrive. Our chances of victory are reduced should we need to break such a siege.'

Imorthorn nodded. 'What news of our great alliance?' he asked with a chuckle.

'Dwarves have arrived, in fewer numbers than hoped,' he replied. 'Two Icelords stand with us, which will doubtless fan Shareth's wrath when she finds out! Rorthron rides from the north and I have high hopes the Giant's will finally all declare for us … and the Barbarians hold the fortress. All are accounted for.'

'And will this strength be enough I wonder,' Imorthorn said. 'We all ride to our doom now, so it seems. A chapter in the history of the Icemark draws to a close, Moonprince. You are its author. I hope we will still be around to play further roles!'

'That is my fond wish,' Luxor replied, with a laugh. 'I'd

rather not be remembered as he who brought us all to a dismal end!'

The armies were mustered once more, their direction set northwards. Trumpets blared once again and the might of the Fey thundered across the plains. Night fall saw them weary, but satisfied with their ride having negotiated their way through a dreary range of hills.

Their camp was set under darkening skies.

'There are no stars tonight,' Imorthorn said as the captains of the Fey stood with him alongside Luxor.

To the north, towering clouds could just be seen gathering in the gloom. Faint flashes of cyan hued light outlined their shape and form.

'The Heartstealer is almost ready,' Luxor said. 'Tomorrow will see all fates decided.'

'There!' Thortheon yelled. 'There!'

To the north of the Fortress lay the Forest of Firun, dark and sinister in the depth of night. Now the watchers upon the walls could see torchlight illuminating its southern edges and just make the forms of men marching through.

'Fangrorn's army has arrived,' Lorelorn said. 'Now Shareth has her full strength. Ahead of us lies the might of Fangrorn, Zarashand and Glormarg.'

The night wore on and the torches faded from sight.

Hours passed as the sentries on the walls paced back and forth.

Then there was movement once more.

First there were a few, but with minutes the length of the forest wall to the north was illuminated by torch light. Armies were marching. Moments later, chant and heavy drum beats reached their ears. Soon the entire northern horizon was lit with the faint spark of torches held aloft.

'They will be upon us ere day break,' Thorthorn said, watching their progress. 'And their numbers are beyond my ability to gauge.'

Beside him, Glormane, Imulorn and Imelorn, Carorthay, Ganigrorn, Lorelorn and Talorthane watched the approach.

For long minutes only the thump of booted feet and the roll of drums could be heard, growing in volume.

Then, with a flicker of cyan light a blazing torrent exploded upwards from the ground, a vast column of energy, writhing and crackling. At its base they could just make out a figure, standing arms outstretched, the source of the display. An echoing boom shook the fortress to its foundations, causing everyone to stagger. The very air buzzed and crackled with static. Lightning crackled above, thunder crashed and reverberated around them. The eerie light flickered around the stone of the Fortress, casting long deep shadows.

'Shareth,' Lorelorn said.

'We cannot defend against her sorcery,' Imgorad said.

'You will not need to,' Lorelorn replied. 'Not until the battle is done. Shareth enjoys the death and destruction of battle and the lives of her servants matter little to her. She will throw a mighty force at these walls and conduct the battle in traditional ways … until such time as she feels our strength ebb. Then she will play with us as a cat plays with a mouse. That is when you must fear her sorcery.'

'If those words are to give us comfort,' Glormane replied. 'I dare say they are not well chosen.'

'Such is the foe you face,' Lorelorn said. 'Shareth is both powerful and cruel. She has strange lusts and a craving to satisfy them. I have seen it often first hand.'

Glormane shuddered at the thought.

'If she wants a traditional fight to begin with,' Ganigrorn said. 'So much the better.'

CHAPTER NINETEEN

Obigrorn and the army of giants strode the long road from the north. Now at last, having left the shadow of the mountains they could turn south.

Night had fallen as they approached their destination, the great City of Imgenarg from which Rorthron had set out scant days before.

Their approach had been seen by the giants that held the city and it wasn't long before Rorthron was reunited with Varangrim, Imgenarg and Thorarg.

'I can scarce believe you were victorious,' Varangrim cried. 'Yet, you have saved our homelands from the hand of the Heartstealer, all Giants are in your debt, Rorthron of the Wise.'

'A debt I must call in immediately,' Rorthron replied. 'Time is pressing. Tell me, what do your scouts know of the movements of Shareth's armies?'

Imgenarg stepped forward.

'We have seen great strength moving south along the flanks of Anvulane,' he replied. 'Iceguard warriors beyond count. It is said that Shareth herself stands amongst their ranks.'

Rorthron nodded.

'Then we must leave immediately. Luxor concentrates all the forces that might counter her at the Fortress of Thortheon in the realm of the Barbarians. We must reach it before it is wholly besieged. Will you give your pledge, as promised?'

Varangrim stood tall.

'Our forces are all assembled,' he said. 'And my pledge will be given as agreed. But those who marched from the north … they can go no further today. It has been a long and weary march through day and night to get here …'

'We must be swifter still,' Rorthron said. 'Even now, Shareth makes her move against our comrades and if we are not there to fight soon, there will be none left for us to fight alongside.'

'If we stride on to the point of exhaustion we will be slaughtered where we stand,' Obigrorn replied.

'One more spell I can spare,' Rorthron said. 'What remains of my strength I must too reserve for the coming battle … and yet …'

Rorthron raised his staff. Its tip blazed out in the evening gloom above the city. The giants paused as the old man began uttering strange words. A redness gathered about the staff and the light of the sky changed.

'Behold the Flames of Dawn!' Rorthron called out in a loud voice.

Fire burst from his staff. To the west the sun was already setting behind the mountains, yet, as they watched bewildered, the Giants saw it rise back above the peaks. Clouds flickered across the sky as if driven by some immense but soundless wind. The colours of sunset faded to be replaced by bright azure.

Startled, all watched as the sun retraced its path across the sky and then sank into the east, its light catching on forests and hills as it did so. Shadows lengthened again and then the sun stood still, low in the sky.

'It is … dawn!' Varangrim said, staring out in awe.

'Dawn breaks,' Rorthron replied. 'And the weariness of the day is also past. We can use this but once, I do not have the means to do so again, but it gives us time. Time enough, with hope and chance, to make a difference.'

Varangrim's face was split by a huge grin.

'We will give this hagspawn such a fight!' he cried. 'Moonprince! I hereby pledge the Giants to your cause and her destruction! Obigrorn! Thorarg! Imgenarg! Sound the horns for the march. We will not stop until we reach Thortheon. Our doom awaits. The Giants will arrive in time, Rorthron, have no doubt!'

CHAPTER NINETEEN

The jewel about Tarithel's neck flickered for a moment. She saw the light reflected in Morkin's eyes. For a moment his expression softened. He looked dazzled and confused.

'No …' he uttered. 'I will not be swayed.'

He backed away, lowering the sword, gesturing to Anvireon.

Tarithel found herself forced down upon her knees.

'I will be merciful,' Morkin said. 'Your end will be quick, more I cannot offer you.'

Tarithel clenched her eyes shut, tremors shaking through her body. She took several deep shuddering breaths before looking up.

'Then if you are to end me,' she said. 'Grant me one last thing, for I will never stop loving you and you will always know it …'

Morkin looked down upon her, but said nothing.

'I am your betrothed, your true love,' Tarithel whispered.

'What do you want?' Morkin asked.

'A kiss,' Tarithel replied.

Morkin laughed and Tarithel heard Anvireon chuckle from behind her. The sword was sheathed and Morkin stepped forward, grabbing her around the throat and hoisting her aloft.

'A taste of your lips is no great cost to me,' Morkin sneered, wrestling her close until they were face to face.

Tarithel stared into Morkin's eyes.

If there is any memory of me left in your mind … let it be released.

She closed her eyes.

She felt Morkin's lips push hard against hers, brutal and careless. His hand pushed on the back of her neck. She didn't resist, but filled her mind with thoughts of happy memories of the past, dancing in the glades of her homeland, his hand in hers, the warm glow of the sun on the fresh, new spring mornings of Midnight. Her imagination furnished pictures of the wedding she had hoped to see, Morkin standing there in the finery of the Lords of Midnight, smiling with pride as she walked towards him …

If it cannot be, then this truly is the end.

The pressure on her lips faded, the grip on her neck lessened.

The kiss became tender …

She opened her eyes and found herself staring into Morkin's dazed expression. She saw him blink, once … twice. Then his gaze darted away for a moment.

She blinked.

Morkin threw her aside, pulling his sword out in a smooth motion. Tarithel found herself cast upon the floor, rolling to keep him in her vision.

Morkin had struck at Anvireon.

But the Icelord was no fool. He had stepped back himself, giving him time to draw his own sword. He brought it up to fend off Morkin's downwards blow.

'Traitor!' Anvireon yelled.

Metal clashed as the two fought. Tarithel scrambled away, out of range.

Morkin's blows were strong, but Tarithel could see that Anvireon was the greater swordsman, stronger and more skilled with his blade. The pair circled, striking and parrying. Tarithel could see Morkin was tiring.

She scrambled up, pulling a blade from her belt as she did so, aiming at strike at Anvireon's unprotected neck.

He saw her coming, and with reflexes that surprised her, kicked out and sent her spinning back to the floor. Tarithel saw the sword blade sweep towards her. There was nothing she could do to stop it …

She flinched as a crash of metal echoed around her.

Morkin's sword had blocked the blow that would have ended her, but his sword had been ripped from his grasp. As she watched Anvireon kicked it away, his sword twisting and thrusting.

Morkin yelled and fell down beside her.

'Morkin!'

Morkin struggled to get up. Tarithel could see blood pouring from a wound in his side where Anvireon's sword had pierced him.

The Icelord stood over them, his sword raised.

'She foresaw this ending you know,' Anvireon said with a grim chuckle. 'And left instructions for it. Your quest is at an end Fey-girl, and as for you boy … think on this in your last moments … you have been a pawn throughout and led your betrothed to share your death.'

Tarithel and Morkin exchanged a final look as Anvireon's bloodstained sword was poised above them.

The vast scale of Shareth's army could be made out by the fires below. Companies of Icelord warriors had marched within two hundred yards of the gates of the fortress, further legions were marching about the walls, for now staying a respectful distance away, but encircling them.

'She means to cut us off from any support,' Ganigrorn said.

'She is no fool,' Talorthane replied. 'She might appear as a beautiful young woman, but she is ancient and has much experience. She takes nothing for granted and knows the arts of war well.'

'I count perhaps some twenty thousand,' Glormane swallowed. 'Within the hour, they will have us surrounded. None will be able to break the siege even with great strength!'

The thump of drums and footfalls ceased in a moment as

if commanded by some invisible voice. Silence fell across the fortress, a faint mist blotted out the stars above, and the waning crescent moon was visible as only a faint shape in the sky.

'Hold firm,' Lorelorn whispered.

Thin tendrils of mist writhed their way out of the ground, forming strange distorted shapes amidst the folk of the fortress. They looked almost like wraiths, twisted demented spirits, sometimes almost formless, but leaving the faint impression of grasping hands or the outline of a skull before the mist evaporated into the air. A cold clamminess descended about them and the torches along the walls flickered and grew dim.

A voice, thin and hard to hear, but laced with ill intent and a cruel mirth, sounded in their ears, inaudible, but distinct and sepulchral.

TORMENT YOU SHALL ALL ENDURE FOR YOUR DEFIANCE … AND PAIN THAT WILL TRANSCEND YOUR DEATHS.

Cyan light flickered in the darkness. Torches were raised high and more fire glowed amidst the ranks of the attackers.

'Hoist our colours,' Lorelorn called. 'Now is the time to declare against the Heartstealer!'

Along the wall of the fortress, the banners of the armies camped within were set. The great banners of the mighty warlords of the Icemark caught the wind, their colours bright in the torch light

For the Barbarians: Imgorad, Careneon, Torinarg, Thortheon, Firak, Anvorthun, Thorthak, Lorangrorn and Thangrad.

For the Dwarves: Glormane, Carorthay, Imulorn and Imelorn with the banner of Thigrak alongside, Hagudril, Torelorn, Thatruk, Thudrun and Lorangrarg.

For the Giants: Ganigrorn and Torelak.

And finally, the colours of the Icelords fluttered out in the breeze: Lorelorn and Talorthane.

Shareth saw the banners unfurl from the fortress. She counted them one by one, knowing to which warrior they belonged. She gestured with scornful laughter until the last two were unfurled.

Muttering went up amongst the ranks of the Icelords.

Her laughter died on her lips.

She stared, unable to believe her eyes.

What is this? Treachery from my own? How can this be? Lorelorn … and Talorthane!

'Lorelorn and Talorthane have declared for the Moonprince!' Zarashand said, his voice stiff and shocked. Likewise Fangrorn and Glormarg were staring at the fortress in mute surprise.

Shareth's scream of rage echoed across the plains.

'Destroy them utterly,' she screeched. 'And bring me their carcasses! They shall know endless torment and pain for this perfidy! Attack, now! Attack!'

'Trebuchets!' Imgorad called.

Fire erupted from the ranks gathered below, great flaming spheres trailing sparks as they arced through the air to crash upon and within the walls of the Fortress. Arrows flew out of the darkness, smiting down many upon the walls. Within, the warriors worked with sand and water in an attempt to extinguish the flames before they spread.

Behind the parapets and crenellations Barbarians, Giants, Dwarves and, here and there Icelord resplendent in dark-hued armour, stood together as the foe advanced about the walls. Scarlet and cyan lights flashed in the darkness as jeers and screams filled the air.

Then, an answering call of trumpets and horns sounded out of the darkness. From the west, a flash of lightning illuminated a mass of huge bodies running towards the battle, somehow summoned out of the very mountains. Great creatures they were, strong of body, running forward at a vast speed, striking all in their path. At their head was an old man upon a horse, his beard flowing in the wind, a staff raised in his hand.

More banners flew proudly in the air.

Even as they watched, a great arcing blast of fire issued forth from the old man's staff, splashing amongst the Icelord's front ranks. They fell back from the onslaught.

'Giants!' Glormane said, in disbelief.

'My kindred out of the north!' Ganigrorn said. 'They have come! See there, it is my Liege Varangrim, Obigrorn, Imgenarg and Thorarg! The Giants will see this done!'

Even as the Giants fought their way towards the fortress, from the south came the rumbling thud of horses' hooves and the cries and yells of voices higher and more fair than the dark warriors of the Icemark.

'It is the Fey!' Imgorad yelled. 'And the Moonprince with them. All have reached us, against the odds!'

The banners of the Fey were thus unfurled as they rode in towards the fortress. Imorthorn, Carorthane, Carorthand, Imgormand and Thormand. Then came Berormane, Lorangrim, Tharand and Imorthesh. And finally Lorangriel, Thorthand, Ingormiel and Thigrand.

A wave of warmth spread about the defenders, a strange mental embrace that smothered them. Luxor's Moon Ring blazed forth.

FEAR NO EVIL! THE MOONPRINCE RIDES! TO ME, FOES OF THE HEARTSTEALER, TO ME!

Yet, even as the words and warmth surged through the hearts of the beleaguered defenders the forces of the Heartstealer turned about. Reforming their lines they marched away from the attack leaving the approaching armies a clear path to the fortress.

The mists thickened in the air and the wraith-like forms curled up out of the ground as before.

Words, woven with menace and hatred crashed into their minds, battling with the warmth that tried to reassure them.

IT IS BUT A BRIEFEST OF RESPITE, FOOLS! JOIN YOUR FRIENDS, FORM YOUR POINTLESS ALLIANCES. ALL YOU THINK YOU HAVE WILL COME TO NAUGHT UPON THE MORROW. I, SHARETH, SHALL VANQUISH YOU UTTERLY AND PUNISH YOU FOR YOUR TREACHERY!

The warmth of the Moon Ring battled back, an ephemeral struggle unseen, but with the people of the Icemark as its pawns.

The Giants and the Fey joined as one and made their way to the gates of the Fortress of Thortheon as Shareth's army backed away. The onlookers above cheered.

Luxor stood at the forefront of the armies, with Rorthron at his side. Luxor had his sword raised and Rorthron his staff. The defenders within the fortress crowded the walls to see.

'I defy you, Shareth Heartstealer!' Luxor called out. 'Long you have coveted the rule of all the Icemark, but here the people of the Icemark refuse your rule. We stand against you, hagspawn of the Witchking Doomdark! He is slain and his realm gone, you shall find the same doom at our hands, this I swear as Moonprince!'

There was no answer from the Icelord army. The slow retreat continued, the torches flickering and then being extinguished.

Only faint laughter echoed in their minds.

Chapter Twenty

Luxor the Moonprince stands at the Fortress of Thortheon, looking north to the Forest of Firun.

The representatives of all the races sat in the central hall of the Fortress of Thortheon. It was not the grandest room imaginable; the fortress was no city and had functioned for most of its time as a remote and far flung border outpost facing off against the territory of the giants. Now it paid host to a gathering far above its humble station.

Here at the Fortress of Thortheon stood Luxor, Moonprince of Midnight. Alongside him was Rorthron of the Wise, Lord Imorthorn for the Fey, Imgorad for the Barbarians, Glormane for the Dwarves, Varangrim for the Giants and Lorelorn for the Icelords. They made for a strange tableau, yet all the races of the Icemark were present.

'My lords,' Luxor began. 'This meeting calls to mind another not so many moons ago, where I stood before an assemblage of mighty warriors alike unto yourselves, urging them to battle against a foe of seemingly overwhelming might. Yet, we had the victory then and it can be ours again, if we can agree an alliance of interests. Shareth, this fell Heartstealer, has retreated beyond the forest dismayed by our strength now fully declared, but no more allies are left to us. Are we resolved now to fight her and stand side by side to whatever end that takes us?'

Imorthorn leant forward.

'The Fey are sworn to your side, Moonprince,' he said, before leaning back and looking around at the others assembled.

'I thank you for your pledge,' Luxor said. 'And for helping Tarithel upon her way.'

'The Giants will follow you, Moonprince,' Varangrim said. 'Rorthron himself has already saved our lands from the ravages of the Heartstealer based on the testimony of Obigrorn. The Giants thus owe you a great debt of gratitude.'

Luxor nodded. 'Rorthron has always been a powerful ally, we owe him thanks again. Your aid is much appreciated.'

Rorthron bowed.

'As for we Dwarves,' Glormane said. 'We have another to thank, the lady Tarithel made good account herself and helped us against our foes making the case for this alliance. I wish she was here, as she would doubtless have something forthright to say about it. She would have us contest the will of Shareth … and so we shall. My pledge was long delayed, but you have our loyalty, Moonprince of Midnight.'

Attention turned to Imgorad of the Barbarians.

'You spoke eloquently at our first encounter,' Imgorad said. 'And my foolishness cost both my people and those of the Giants dear when I thought to ignore your brokering of a possible peace. We have many disagreements with those around us …' There was a rumble from both Glormane and Varangrim. '… but there are greater woes which face us. Shareth has betrayed me, and caused much division within my people. This I see is her strategy throughout between us all. Perhaps there are friends which I have missed, thinking I was guarding my own. Nevertheless, the Barbarians will try to right this wrong. We stand with you, Moonprince of the South.'

'I thank you for your words, Imgorad,' Luxor said and turned to the Icelord Lorelorn.

'My presence here may disturb you or those who serve you,' Lorelorn said, his voice grave. 'This charge I understand. My decision to join you was not made easily. Not so many moons ago I considered Shareth's approach, brutal though it might be at times, to be the correct one. I would see Icemark unified and no longer at war. Yet she would see that done at the expense of contrary opinion, race, creed or outlook with herself as Empress of all, everyone in slavery to her whim. The power she has acquired has corrupted whatever sensibilities she once had. I have stood by as she sanctioned atrocities before. I will not do so again. I mean to stop her. This, I deem, is your intent, thus I swear my loyalty to you, Luxor, Moonprince and foe of Shareth.'

'You were an ally unlooked for,' Luxor said. 'I did not expect to find any allies in your people.'

'Shareth's yoke lies heavy upon us,' Lorelorn said. 'Too heavy for many to be redeemed I would say, but there is always hope.'

'Yet,' Luxor said. 'I cannot speak for all assembled here. You have done no wrong to me, but others may not share that view.'

The other members around the group looked at each other for a long moment.

It was Glormane who spoke.

'The Dwarves, perhaps by virtue of where we live have had reason enough not to care for Fey, Barbarian, Giant and Icelord,' he said. 'I have counted you all as foes at one time or another. As Imgorad said, this has been Shareth's strategy all along. If I am not to accept an Icelord with a warming heart, than I can accept none based on past wrongs. If that be the case, this alliance is doomed from the off. Thus, there is, to my way of thinking, only one route forward.'

Glormane stood up and held out his hand to Lorelorn.

'I will venture trust,' he said.

Lorelorn's eyes narrowed, but he, too, stood up and reached out, taking Glormane's hand and shaking it.

Luxor stretched forward and placed his hand on top of the others.

'Then this alliance has a start,' he said and then looked up. 'Who else will see this done?'

Imorthorn copied his act.

'The past cannot be changed,' he said. 'But the future is ours to decide. The Fey will be part of this alliance.'

Varangrim and Imgorad looked at each other.

'We have had many quarrels,' Varangrim said. 'Many are the feuds we have kept and held, but they have not brought us peace or profit. There will be much to make amends for after a victory has been won.'

The giant placed his huge hand on top of the others.

Imgorad had his arms folded.

'I cannot say that we can forgive past wrongs on the basis of some pretty speeches,' he rumbled. 'And the Barbarians have much to atone for. But an accord does serve all our purposes. If this alliance sees the end of the Heartstealer I will deem it worthy, and we will talk about what can be done about the sins of the past. For now, this alliance will have the Barbarians as a part of it.'

He placed his hand on top of Varangrim's.

'Then this alliance is sealed,' Luxor said. 'An attack on one is an attack on all, we will live and die in the defence of each other, united against a common foe. Our purpose then, to see the end of Shareth the Heartstealer if we may. Lords of the Icemark you are, swear your oaths before me!'

All five of the leaders looked up.

'We so swear, Moonprince!'

Luxor and Rorthron strode the walls of the Fortress as preparations continued. Luxor spied Careneon and Torinarg amidst the Barbarians making ready.

'My Lord Luxor!' Careneon called out.

Luxor walked across and clasped Careneon's outstretched arm in friendship.

'When we parted we were enemies,' Careneon said, 'Though not by my choice. I am heartened that we will soon draw swords together as friends and allies.'

'I wish we did not have to draw swords at all,' Luxor replied. 'But to stand to together side by side to face the foe is no mean thing. We will make a fight of it to be remembered.'

Careneon nodded. 'We will at that, success to us all!'

Luxor and Rorthron resumed their tour of the walls.

'Shareth must have had some doubt,' Luxor said. 'Otherwise she would have pressed the attack last night.'

Rorthron nodded. 'She is cautious and circumspect. She only engages when confident of victory. Our arrival was faster than she anticipated and our strength greater. She knows doubt and fear. Once she has the measure of us, she will attack again.'

'What strength we have now is consolidated,' Luxor replied. 'She would have been better to overwhelm us before we managed that.'

'If she wins victory,' Rorthron said. 'It will be all the sweeter for her.'

'Perhaps,' Luxor muttered.

'You did well forming the alliance,' Rorthron said. 'Quite the diplomat you've become.'

'I wonder if you do not merely find me amusing,' Luxor replied. 'As a parent does with a child who accomplishes some mean feat.'

'I think very highly of you Moonprince,' Rorthron replied. 'You have accomplished much and deserve the accolades you receive.'

'Yet you feel it your duty to keep me humble,' Luxor said with a grin.

'A responsibility I take most seriously.'

Luxor chuckled.

'And I have something for you,' Rorthron said.

From beneath his cloak he pulled a leather bundle and unwrapped it. Luxor watched as a crown was revealed.

'Is this the Talisman you spoke of?' Luxor asked. 'A Crown of the Icemark?'

Rorthron nodded. 'Found in vaults of the Giants to the north and given freely to you. Carangrane, their previous leader knew something of it, but that lore is lost to us. What we do know is that it is alike to the Moon Ring, imbued with the power of the Wise from long ago. Shareth herself has keenly pursued it and is doubtless frustrated she has not acquired it.'

Rorthron handed it to Luxor and he turned it around, inspecting it.

'It is the Crown of Varenand,' Rorthron said.

'As the legends of the Giants and the Barbarians told,' Luxor whispered.

'So indeed.'

'And what is its potency?' Luxor demanded. 'What does it do?'

'Of that I am not sure,' Rorthron said. 'I have probed it as best I can, but it is finely crafted and possessed of power intricately woven in its very form and function. That it is of the Wise there can be no doubt, but as to what they intended it for, I cannot be sure.'

'Then I must trust to luck?'

Rorthron sighed.

'All I can tell you is that Shareth has two of these, doubtless she carries them with her even now. If she deems them of assistance, then we must try the same, if we are to counter her.'

'That seems wise enough,' Luxor said. 'Yet, the Moon Ring itself casts enough of a pall across my very being, the thought of another of your magical Talismans upon me does not fill me with great anticipation!'

'Use it in only the most dire of needs then,' Rorthron said. 'I fear such a moment will not be long delayed.'

As dawn neared, smoke could be seen issuing from the forest to the north of the fortress. Luxor and the alliance of Lords of the Icemark gazed out upon it, hearing the distant rumbling of approaching armies.

'Our scouts report Shareth's armies have been busy arranging themselves overnight,' Thortheon reported. 'Everything that can be done here is done. All our strength is within these walls. We are still outnumbered, I deem, but perhaps not by as much as Shareth would hope!'

Luxor nodded and took a deep breath.

'I have stood upon the threshold of many such battles,' he said. 'As I know all of you have too. Battles that seem against impossible odds can yet be won with stout hearts and firm wills. We all know well the evil that will soon throw its wrath against us. But take heart! Such evil is not invincible, it can be defeated. Shareth's own father was thrown down by valour, bravery and desperate chances. What has happened once can happen again. We can defeat this hagspawn Shareth and end her reign of tyranny forever.'

The assembled lords bowed in agreement.

'Should we prevail, a great peace shall there be between the people of the Icemark and of Midnight,' Luxor continued. 'We will all prosper and be merry. Fight for freedom, fight for your families and a future worth having. Dawn breaks!'

As he uttered the words, sunlight streamed across the walls

of the fortress, bathing them all in crimson light. The fortress glowed red, as if summoning its own anger and defiance from the flames of dawn.

Far below, the massed ranks of the Iceguard could be seen marching towards them. A scattering of Dwarven and Barbarian banners could be seen in their midst. Their strategy seemed to be as before, first to encircle prior to attacking. Even as the approaching army surrounded the walls, still more were marching from the north.

'Such a force,' Glormane said.

'Shareth's entire strength,' Lorelorn said. 'She means to subdue opposition utterly.'

Once more fires were lit in the ranks of the Iceguard and the defenders braced themselves for attack. Within minutes the flaming bolts were launched, crashing down upon the fortress walls and streets in sheets of fire.

The defenders also knew their crafts though. The streets were well prepared and the fires were doused with sand and water.

Next came huge rocks, debris from the sacking of Ganigrorn's fortress, hurled through the air by trebuchets assembled at the rear of the first rank of the Iceguard force. They crashed upon turrets and minarets, and some were cast down in ruin, but even as the dust from the impacts blew away in the early morning breeze, the fortress still stood indomitable.

Then deep horns blew through the legions of the Iceguard, echoing around them again and again. As one they began marching towards the fortress, swords glinting in their hands.

'Here it comes,' Luxor muttered. 'Defend the walls and repel the ladders!'

Archers on the walls began exchanging arrows with those down below. The Iceguard took the brunt of the attack, but their numbers were now vast beyond counting and despite the rain of arrows that descended upon them they reached the walls in minutes. They were co-ordinated and no part of the fortress was free from their advance.

Further horns blew and at that signal, ladders were hoisted in rapid succession. The Icelords knew the craft of war well.

The ladders crashed down upon the crenellations of the fortress, locking in place with great claws of metal, making it impossible for the defenders to remove them. Within moments, Iceguard warriors were climbing them hand over hand. Dozens were slain as they climbed, falling back in the dense crush of warriors below, but others were always ready to take their place.

Those that reached the top were hewn at by the defenders. At first, few managed to scale the walls, being stabbed, rent and hacked at before being thrown down. Yet, little by little, their numbers increased, and as each new arrival forced their way atop the walls, more swarmed in from behind.

Giants strode amongst them, swinging huge stone clubs, each blow crushing two Iceguard warriors. Dwarves hewed and swung with their great two-handed axes of metal, the Fey used their bows at range and then swept in with deadly precision using sharp ice-bright knives. The Barbarians preferred short swords and maces.

The Iceguard and the remaining Moonguard that had followed Luxor from Midnight engaged with similar weapons, long swords and daggers for when the melee grew too confined.

The morning wore on as the battle for the walls continued. Hundreds were slain upon both sides and little progress was made. More rocks were hurled and flaming brands crashed down upon the Fortress, yet the Iceguard made no further advance.

'We hold them!' Imorthorn yelled above the cries and screams, finding himself alongside Luxor in the press of bodies. 'They cannot breach our concentrated strength!'

Even as he uttered the words, shouts arose from the gatehouse. Luxor and Imorthorn looked up to see the armies of the Iceguard separating before the gate, making a clear pathway. They followed the opening ranks to see a vanguard of Iceguard troops marching towards them, surrounding a figure with outstretched arms. Even as they watched, cyan light crackled and flashed.

'Shareth!' Luxor called. 'Shareth is here!'

The ghastly light coalesced, shocking into a writhing torrent that spun and crashed against the walls. Where it touched, the rock exploded into fragments, hurling attackers and defenders alike into the air. Luxor ducked as spiralling debris and dust cascaded down around him.

'She makes for the gates! Fortify the gates!'

Another blast, and the air was filled with murk. It was impossible to see what was happening. Luxor struggled forward with his men around him, forcing their way to the wall that overlooked the gates. It was still held by the defenders, but as the dust was swept away, they could see Shareth was not far away. She had approached within a hundred yards, her arms outstretched, dressed in a dark cloak, a bright crown upon her head. Cyan light crackled around her figure, and at a sharp gesture, it flashed against the walls again.

Luxor saw Barbarians, Giants, Fey and Dwarves ripped asunder as the very foundations of the walls shattered and broke. Rock and stone smashed and disintegrated under the assault. A blast of hot air knocked him and his men off their feet; they struggled to rise in the tumult.

Luxor blinked, his head ringing from the concussion.

Before him stood Rorthron, his own staff raised in defence, his voice crying out words that reverberated around him, echoing in some unearthly fashion.

Another blast of light issued from Shareth's fingertips, spiralling towards the beleaguered walls in a frenzy, yet this time it struck an obstacle, some invisible defence that Rorthron had conjured in the very air.

Luxor saw him stagger back with the onslaught, but the writhing lightning at Shareth's command was frustrated in its intent, striking down at the road and amidst the Iceguard warriors rather than crashing against the walls or the gate.

Luxor wrestled himself back to his feet, yelling at the archers below.

'Loose! Loose!'

The whistling thump of arrows filled the air. The Iceguard fell from the walls. Horns blew out from the ranks of the attackers. The alliance forces rallied and pushed back, regaining the walls.

'She will not have it all her way!' Luxor cried.

Anvireon stepped towards them, the sword raised. Tarithel saw the icy light of snow reflecting in the blade. They were cornered, there was nowhere to run.

'Flee my love,' Morkin gasped, trying to undo her grip on him. 'There's no sense in us both dying.'

'I came here to free you,' Tarithel answered, tears streaming down her face. 'I will not leave you now, not ever!'

Morkin smiled at her, despite the pain in his shoulder. 'But you have freed me, dear heart,' he said. 'Since being captured by that hagspawn I have been in a grey half-life, not myself, traitor to all I held dear and fair. You have released me from that living death. I am Morkin once more, Morkin the Free.'

'Then we will die as we would have lived,' Tarithel whispered. 'Together. I do not fear the next life if we enter it together.'

Morkin slumped in her arms. She, too, was utterly exhausted, her arms and legs trembling. She could not rise as

Anvireon stalked towards them, the sword high in the air. One swing of the heavy weapon was all that it would take.

'Victory goes to Shareth then,' Anvireon said, laughing. 'And I will ensure your bodies are kept for her sport when she returns from her conquests. Your skins and bones will decorate her abode for all the moons of her life. A lesson for all those who would dare defy her.'

Tarithel glared up at Anvireon, defiant. She uttered no words, but waited, resolute, for the end. Anvireon drew back the sword.

She grasped at the gem, but it was dark. The green light that had suffused it was absent. Weariness stole over her. Even her rage and anger was spent.

We are lost, this is the end!

Tarithel closed her eyes.

The hosts of Shareth raged on against the Fortress of Thortheon. At intervals Shareth would approach and cast her sorcery against the walls. Time and again Rorthron would pace the walkways and shield the defenders from the attack.

The day wore on with neither side making headway. The sun reached its zenith and began to sink into the west. A chill wind blew from the north.

'It is a battle of attrition,' Imgorad said, surveying the battle from a walkway overlooking the gate.

'And our numbers reduce at an even pace,' Glormane replied. 'Yet, that favours Shareth and not us. Soon we will not be able to hold all the length of the walls.'

'A stalemate that we must find a way to break or turn,' Luxor said.

The noise of the battle ebbed about them. Horns sounded from the attackers below the walls.

'They're retreating!' Imorthorn called. 'They're calling off their attack.'

The Lords of the alliance watched in surprise. Imorthorn's words were true. The ladders were being abandoned, the defenders on the walls hacking at them and casting them down. The Iceguard warriors were retreating out of bowshot.

'Shareth has something else in mind,' Luxor rumbled. 'Perhaps she does not wish to fight at night?'

'Perhaps she has seen the strength of our defence,' Varangrim answered. 'And she now plans to starve us out.'

'A strategy she might well adopt,' Rorthron added. 'We have not the provisions to endure a protracted siege, barely a day's worth for the might we have here. Perhaps she knows, or at least suspects that.'

Luxor looked at Rorthron.

'It seems the time you spoke of is at hand,' he said.

'It would seem so, Moonprince,' Rorthron answered.

'What is this you speak of?' Imorthorn demanded.

'Out of legend,' Luxor said. 'Rorthron has found a Talisman of the Icemark, a Crown, much like the one that Shareth bears upon her brow. It is named in many of your legends, Imgorad – the Crown of Varenand. Long it lay in the hands of the Giants, forgotten. Now it is here.'

'Tales out of the dim and distant past,' Imgorad said. 'But what power does it have?'

'None know,' Varangrim replied. 'It served no purpose according to my late Lord Carangrane. He hoped it would bring good fortune to our people, it did not.'

'You speak the truth as far as you know it,' Rorthron said. 'But this, the Crown of Varenand, was made by the Wise long ago and imbued with some great part of their power as it was. Luxor is a Moonprince and is thus entitled to wield it, whatever that power will be.'

'And if it gives us something to contend with Shareth,' Luxor said. 'I will welcome it, though I dislike magic!'

At an instruction, the Crown was borne to Luxor. He took it from the leather wrapping and held it up, it sparkled in the evening light.

'May this bring us fortune in our fight,' he said.

He placed it upon his head.

As he did so, the sun slipped behind the mountains to the west and the Moonstar flickered bright in the sky.

There was gasp of sound. Then a roaring grew in her ears. She opened her eyes in surprise. Anvireon and his sword were gone, around her she could perceive the frozen expanse of the Icemark all about her, lit by some strange golden glow. It seemed she was flying, poised above the landscape in such a manner that she could see far beyond the limits of her eyes.

There were the Frozen Wastes far below, and the vast stretch of the dank Forest of Farorn. She felt a strange lurch in her soul and found herself being pulled inexorable southwards, hills, forests and mountains unrolling beneath her vision.

Morkin was still with her, still clutched in her grasp.

'Morkin! Look!'

Her cry was faint against the great noise that hammered around them, but she saw him open his eyes and stare about him in wonder.

'Tarithel?' he gasped.

'You see it too?' she asked.

Now a vast mountain range loomed in their vision. Tarithel remembered it well, the backbone of the Icemark, the cruel and sharp Mountains of Anvulane. More mountains rose up to their right and they found themselves pulled at a terrifying speed into a steep sided valley marked with the burning ruins of razed fortresses.

Battles have been fought here! Many have died!

The valley reached its narrowest point and Tarithel beheld a fortress, besieged, surrounded by armies of the Icelords, their black pennants clear to see. Within the fortress and along its walls were other armies, she recognised the banners of the Fey amidst them, and then she spied one bright banner, fluttering over the gate.

The banner was bold and colourful. A cyan moon and a yellow star on a bright magenta background.

It is Luxor! Luxor!

'Morkin …'

'It can't be …'

Whatever strange power was transporting them began to ebb. They were drawn ever closer to the ground …

And then there they were, crouched amidst the men of the Free and the warriors of the Fey. Before them stood Luxor and beside him Lord Imorthorn and Rorthron the Wise. Luxor wore a bright golden crown upon his head.

For a moment no one spoke, shock and surprise evident on all the faces before them.

Luxor got to his feet.

'Morkin? Tarithel?'

Tarithel struggled up.

'Morkin is hurt, he needs aid!'

Luxor ran to them, gesturing for his men to help.

'Send for the healers!' he yelled.

Between him and Tarithel they lowered Morkin to lie upon the ground.

'What happened?' Luxor asked.

'Anvireon the Icelord stabbed him,' Tarithel cried, brushing tears from her cheeks. 'I tried to stop him, truly I did, but …'

Two more men arrived. Tarithel recognised them as healers.

They carried packs with them. Both looked over Morkin, conferring in quick sharp tones as they examined his wounds.

'He must be tended to,' the first said. 'And quickly. But his wounds are not fatal. We will see to him. Stretcher!'

Luxor helped Tarithel to her feet as Morkin was moved on to the stretcher. She reached out to him as the healers bore him away, fresh tears in her eyes.

Only then did she look up into Luxor's face.

'I don't understand,' she said, blinking in confusion. 'How came we to be here? Anvireon was poised to kill us, are we indeed dead and this is the next life?'

'I think not,' Luxor said, with a smile. 'I have not yet come to the end of my time, though that may not be long delayed. Rorthron?'

Tarithel looked across as Rorthron the Wise joined them. She smiled in greeting, bowing her head.

'Lady Tarithel,' he said. 'It is good to see you once more.'

'This Crown,' Luxor said. 'I am pleased beyond measure to have my son and his betrothed returned to me in such an unexpected fashion, but … tell me … is this all we can expect? No further aid in our battle against the Heartstealer? If so, this reunion will be short lived.'

'She is here?' Tarithel asked, her face going pale.

'We are besieged,' Luxor said. 'The Heartstealer is here in force. We stand with what remains of the free might of Icemark, worthy Barbarians, Dwarves, Giants and Fey standing shoulder to shoulder. There are even two Icelords of your acquaintance. Despite that, the tide of battle turns against us all.'

'The Crown promised the means to defeat the Heartstealer,' Rorthron said, leaning on his staff. 'But alas, despite the joy of this homecoming, perhaps I was wrong.'

Tarithel felt faint, staggering in Luxor's grip.

'My Lady, you are exhausted. I will see you to the healers myself.'

'No wait,' Tarithel murmured. 'I must …'

But words forsook her and she slumped in his arms.

Luxor paced the great hall of Thortheon's fortress alongside the table that ran its length. About him the great leaders of the alliance of the Icemark stood in attendance. Imorthorn for the Fey, Varangrim for the Giants, Imgorad for the Barbarians, Glormane for the Dwarves and Lorelorn representing the scant armies of the Icelords loyal to the Moonprince.

'Here then is our situation,' he said. 'Our supplies run low. Our food will be exhausted in a day. A siege will force us out, weakened and weary within a week. No further force can come to our aid and, it seems, the hoped for magic of the realm is found wanting.'

Luxor looked over at Rorthron and then flung the Crown he had been wearing on to the table. It landed with a heavy thud and sat there, impotent, before them.

'I have ever been suspicious of magic,' Varangrim said, straightening to his full height and standing over them all. 'We will have to rely on what we have always relied on in adversity, stout courage and strength of arms.'

'Of that we have much,' Imgorad agreed. 'What we lack are enough warriors. If we give up the safety of the fortress and fight in the open, we will be outnumbered two to one, if not more.'

'Or we can sit here and starve,' Glormane replied. 'I daresay we can hew a few more necks before our passing.'

'Shareth will not relent either way,' Lorelorn said. 'Once she is determined upon an outcome she will see it through to the bitter end.'

'Can you tell us how she will react if we come out in force?' Luxor asked.

'She will match us, blow for blow,' Lorelorn said. 'She has no fear of our strength of arms. Those loyal to her will hurl themselves at us with great abandon, such is the hold she has over them. Better to die in battle than risk her wrath.'

'She has never been a fool,' Varangrim said. 'She always strikes from a position of strength.'

'I do not wish to die cooped up in a hole,' Imgorad rumbled. 'Even if it is one of my own making. Let us ride out and finish this.'

Luxor nodded.

'I have led you to this point,' he said. 'Confident, based on how we beat down and slew Shareth's father in the battle for Midnight. That was a battle that seemed desperate and might not have been won save for the intervention of my own son, who destroyed the Witchking's power at its zenith.'

He shook his head.

'But Shareth has no such Talisman. She needs no Talisman. There is no way to break her and what magic we thought we could bring to bear has not availed us of even an advantage, let alone a chance of victory.'

'You still have the Moon Ring,' Imorthorn said.

'Aye,' Luxor said. 'And it will aid us should Shareth try to poison our minds and steal away our courage, but it cannot summon armies out of the snow, nor turn aside her own magical prowess. Such crafts as she has we cannot counter.'

'I will counter what I may,' Rorthron said. 'Whilst her power exceeds mine, what I have will always be in your service, Moonprince.'

'And what of the Lady Tarithel?' Glormane asked. 'She stood with us when my own city was under siege. She slew Imgorarg my foe and she has sorcery of her own. Can she not also fight against the Heartstealer?'

'Tarithel is utterly tired,' Luxor said. 'She cannot continue. She is ill and near death after her travails to find my son. She lies in the healer halls now, being tended. We must defend her, she has done her part in these battles and can do no more.'

Glormane nodded.

Luxor straightened and looked around the hall.

'Then it seems there is only one route laid before us,' he said, with a solemn nod. 'We fight against her and hope to prevail. Right is on our side, the defence of our homes and realms lies in our hands. If we do not stop her, she will destroy all that we hold dear.'

He straightened and looked at each one in turn.

'We have all faced this evil before. We know it for what it is. Strong and irresistible it may seem, but this evil has been broken in the past, with our combined valour we may yet see it broken again. She is not invincible, no matter what fell crafts she summons to her side. We have already achieved that which she said could never happen. We have cast off our differences and worked together for a common good. Such things make us great and powerful, warlords to be feared, legends in the making. Regardless of the battle ahead, you can be proud of that.'

Luxor took hold of the pommel of his sword and drew the blade, holding it aloft.

'If an end is to be made, we will make it one worthy of the annals of the Icemark. Let today see the end of this hagspawn Heartstealer! Ride out with me!'

'To her end!' Varangrim cried aloud and others joined in the chant. Axes, halberds and swords glittered in the gloved hands of the warriors of Icemark.

The last council of the alliance of the Icemark was complete.

Chapter Twenty One

Shareth the Heartstealer stands in the Forest of Firun, looking South to the Fortress of Thortheon.

Tarithel was roused to consciousness by the terrifying rumble. She sat bolt upright in her bed to the alarm and consternation of the healers. She looked about her in shock and fear, her eyes wide. Morkin was lying in the bower next to her, his wounds dressed. He was asleep, so it seemed, his skin pale but less white than she remembered.

'My Lady,' one of the healers said. 'You must rest, please lie down!'

'What was that?' Tarithel demanded, ignoring the request.

'The tides of battle, nothing more,' the healer said. Tarithel frowned at the waver in his voice.

'The battle does not go well, does it?' she asked.

'My Lady, you should not concern yourself …'

'Tell me!'

The healer knelt beside her, whispering.

'The armies fall back against the walls,' he said, his voice low. 'The end cannot be long delayed. It will be as well to prepare yourself for it. The Iceguard never show mercy to those they defeat in battle.'

'Help me up,' Tarithel said. 'Take me to the walls.'

'You are sick, my Lady,' the healer admonished. 'You can hardly walk, let alone stand before the hordes of the …'

'Take me to them!'

The jewel around her neck pulsed with fierce green fire, splashing around the room, casting sharp dark shadows. Tarithel's own eyes were lit from within as if by the same eerie light. The healer stumbled back in fear.

'Now!' Tarithel shouted. 'Take me to the walls!'

The darkness fell deeper about the besieged Fortress of Thortheon, lit only by the red flames of the Icelord armies and Shareth's own blazing cyan sorcery. The fell light would flicker unnaturally about the walls and across the armies of the allies. Wherever its light touched, the defenders would fall back, clasping their heads in pain and succumbing to the renewed attack.

Flaming missiles flew through the air, slamming down to cast the defenders into ruin, each strike causing more consternation and confusion amidst their ranks. The Iceguard warriors continued to advance, striking down those afflicted by the sorcery of Shareth with no mercy.

The Lords of the alliance, Luxor, Imgorad, Imorthorn, Glormane, Varangrim and Lorelorn had ridden out in force to engage the enemy, but were now being pushed back towards the walls of the Fortress, and those walls were already much aflame and broken down by the irresistible strength of the Heartstealer's approach.

Were it not for the valour of their leaders, the alliance army would have already been routed.

And yet, such was the pitch of the battle, such an hour could not be long delayed.

Tarithel gasped at the horror that greeted her. Below the walls of the fortress the beleaguered armies of the Icemark loyal to Luxor were pressed back by the hordes of the Iceguard that were easily twice the size. Tarithel saw the defenders assailed on all sides, pushed backwards towards the walls.

And then she saw her.

Astride a black horse, standing upon a raised hillock in the field, a crown upon her head, a staff held aloft, around which a dark smoke was whirling. Lightning flickered from it as she turned and rode against the armies of the Moonprince.

Wherever she appeared, their lines fell back. She saw men and Dwarves hurled aside by the mighty blows of the staff, even Barbarians and Giants were slain with apparent ease. Shareth's might could not be countered by mere valour. She was possessed of greater strength, a fell power that none could withstand.

She rode on, smiting those before her and to the right and left, driving towards where Luxor stood under the banner of the moon. In horror Tarithel saw Rorthron bring his own horse about and ride towards her, his own staff aloft.

Light, like a blazing comet from the skies above, formed around the tip of Rorthron's staff and a harsh blasting stream of dazzling white burst forth from it, blistering across the closing gap between the two antagonists. Shareth brought her own staff up to counter the blow. The dark mist grew, smothering the light and extinguishing it before it could cause her any harm. The mist grew about Shareth, like the outstretched legs of some horrendous giant spider, stretching further and further. Where it came into contact with living men they gasped, turned pallid and fell upon the ground, dead.

Shareth's voice echoed across the battlefield, both out loud and in her mind.

YOU CANNOT DEFY ME, RORTHRON OF THE WISE! YOUR WISDOM HAS COME TO FOLLY. NOW PAY THE PRICE FOR YOUR LACK OF DEEDS!

Shareth gestured with her staff and the darkness coalesced, striking towards the old man upon his horse like a smoky writhing snake. Rorthron countered the attack with his own staff, light continuing to blaze from its tip, his own voice magnified in response.

All the peoples of Icemark and Midnight stand against you, Shareth! You shall not prevail!

Shareth snarled in response and the darkness grew further, counterpointed only by a glowing cyan aura about her body, which flickered and flashed as if drawing strength from some unseen source of power.

Tarithel recognised it.

That strange evil I encountered in the tunnels! Shareth draws upon the very substance of the Icemark, magic that underpins the world itself … Rorthron cannot stand alone with only the power of the Wise, this is an elemental force which …

As she watched the fierce light of Rorthron's staff flickered and failed. She saw, in dismay, Rorthron thrown from the saddle of his horse, his staff broken in twain.

No!

Tarithel ran from the battlements.

Luxor saw Rorthron thrown from his horse. He knew not whether he had survived the altercation with Shareth. Now it hardly mattered.

Our end is at hand.

'With me!' he called, turning his horse about. Those alongside him formed up. He saw Fey, Barbarians, Giants and Dwarves still amongst their number, some sorely wounded, but still afoot and continuing the fight.

'Slay the Hagspawn!' he cried. 'Slay the Heartstealer!'

He spurred his horse and then kicked it in the flanks, ready to charge upon the hated enemy before him, the wrath of battle in his heart and mind.

But his horse whinnied and turned aside. About him cries of surprise and consternation arose. He blinked, peering through the smoke, mist and ruin all about.

A figure stood there, between him and Shareth, standing over the fallen form of Rorthron. The figure was slight, hair waving in the wind, red and long. It bore no weapon, no armour, not even any shoes. Shareth had seen her and had climbed down from her own steed and was walking forwards, staff outstretched, the black mist lit from within by an unwholesome cyan glow growing around her.

Luxor's heart thumped within him.

'No ...'

What is she doing?

He yelled out. 'Tarithel!'

Tarithel could sense the darkness growing about her. Feel its potent touch upon her skin. She closed her eyes, knowing what she had to do.

Some wisdom, more ancient than her, more ancient even than the Fey itself had prompted her. The jewel about her neck pulsed with power, a green light, fresh from the summer of a long, lost world blazed out. Wherever that light fell the dark mist evaporated, hissing back out of range of her.

Tarithel opened her eyes. They had always been green, now they glowed with the potency of the power she had surrendered herself to.

Shareth stood perhaps twenty yards away, her own features outlined by another glow, cyan, and laced with menace.

WHO ARE YOU TO STAND BEFORE ME?

The voice crushed against Tarithel's mind. She swayed under the mental barrage, but did not break.

You know me. I am Tarithel, Lady of the Forests of Midnight and of Icemark. It is I who have foiled your plans at every stage and I who stand against you now!

Before her, Shareth cried out in twisted rage. The black mist shrank about her before striking out at Tarithel. Tarithel held up a hand as the attack pummelled her. Cyan lightning crackled about her, burning her skin. Tarithel screamed in pain and fell to her knees.

But the green light of the jewel grew all the stronger. A sphere of light formed about her. Tarithel regained her footing and stretched out her hand. The sphere abruptly expanded outwards, the mist fizzing and hissing into nothingness. Shareth flinched back in shock and surprise.

WHAT POWER IS THIS?

Tarithel stood, trying to maintain her balance. The jewel about her neck glared bright, its radiance flooding through her. For a brief moment her clothes, skin and bones flickered in scintillating silhouette.

I am the voice of the oppressed realms you and your father have sullied over countless moons. I am the voice of Dreams, of Dregrim, of Thrall and Whispers. I am the siren song of Farorn and Fenun … and I am the wrath of Fangrim!

The green fire sparked and twisted about Tarithel's form. From the ground, roots exploded upwards with a rumble of dislodged earth and swarmed towards Shareth, coiling and growing at a frenzied speed.

The roots swirled around the Heartstealer, snapping around her arms and legs, still more moved to spin around her neck. Cyan light blazed out and then red fire blazed in the dark smoke. The roots fell, burnt to cinders and ash upon the ground.

YOU DARE ASSAIL ME?

Smoke roared into the air, swirling high above them both. Tarithel saw a whirlwind of darkness, lit by flashes of cyan lightning rotating over her head. She looked up in terror as huge funnels of whirling darkness were wrenched down out of the sky towards her. She was hoist aloft by a ferocious gale, her hair whipped about her face.

Yet, before she had risen a yard, trees exploded from the ground about her, growing in seconds as if a thousand moons had passed. She caught the outstretched branches to steady herself. Leaves grew, shielding her from the gale. The trees swayed in the storm, but were unmoved. The spiralling winds tried to wrench her from their grasp, but were defeated.

In a moment they abated. Shareth stood still before her, arms folded.

YOU HAVE LEARNT MUCH THEN, LITTLE FEY-GIRL.

Tarithel lowered herself down from the tree. A strange peace had descended all around her. She looked to her left and right, seeing the embattled warriors frozen in time, some poised in the acts of striking each other, others suspended as they fell. Here and there, plumes of blood and gore hung in the air. Tarithel could almost hear the silent screams of the dying, yet there was no movement at all.

Unneeded, the trees shrank back into the earth once more. Tarithel stood before Shareth.

'I have learnt enough,' Tarithel replied. 'Why do you do this? Why do you hurt and kill and maim? How can you find satisfaction in such things?'

Shareth tilted her head to one side.

'You are young,' Shareth said. 'What are you? Not even three hundred moons have you seen. You cannot comprehend an eternity of time.'

'I do not need an eternity to recognise evil and cruelty,' Tarithel replied. 'It is plain enough.'

'You think that is what this is?' Shareth answered. 'All of

this? Just some game for my amusement? You think I wage war because it pleases me to do so?'

'Why else?'

Shareth laughed. 'I have loved, little Fey-girl! I have had a thousand lovers. Each warm and youthful and full of vigour! I have watched them grew old and die, each in their turn. I shed tears for the early ones, until I realised such was the inevitability of my existence. I have supported kings and queens, fanning their wisdom through many moons, only to find their descendants throw away the gains and achievements on petty squabbles with their neighbours. Nothing is permanent; nothing is forever, save me …'

'Then you have already lived beyond your time,' Tarithel shouted back.

'You think so?' Shareth replied. 'What do you know of time? My plans have been shaped over longer times than the lives of men or Fey. Their petty squabbles are merely tools I can use to move things in the directions I desire. Such has been the way of things for many moons before you were even born.'

Shareth walked towards her.

'And it is my destiny to rule this world. My father started that work, but he was consumed by his own creation, pouring too much of his very essence into the Talisman that bore his will. Ah yes, you remember the Ice Crown do you not? It was his great achievement, his mightiest power and … his undoing. I have made no such mistake. My power is mine and mine alone. I have no weakness you can seek to exploit.'

'I will still do all I can to stop you,' Tarithel answered.

'Stop me?' Shareth chuckled. 'You have already tried and failed in that, little Fey-girl. I have spared your life to offer something to you.'

'I want nothing from you!'

'Is that so?'

Shareth gestured and an image formed before Tarithel's eyes.

'Then see your fate, little Fey-girl!'

Tarithel saw an image of herself, her hair longer, her eyes sore and puffy from tears shed. She was standing before a man, dressed in a long flowing cape. In his arms was another woman, dark haired, young and pretty, held in a close embrace. The man was blonde of hair, tall and fair in the manner of the free.

'Men are fickle,' Shareth said. 'He will grow weary of you and cast you aside for another.'

'Morkin would never do such a thing,' Tarithel cried. 'He loves me now, he loves me forever!'

Shareth laughed.

'You are naïve,' she said. 'You will learn in time that men are fickle and easily led. Your betrothed is no different, he is not special. He is a plaything …'

'You …'

'Yes little Fey-girl,' Shareth cried. 'I took your precious princeling in every way a woman can. He was mine, body and soul. You do not believe me? Shall I conjure an image of our lovemaking? He was quite … robust. His strength and vigour …' Shareth bit her lip. 'So satisfying.'

'You seduced him with magic,' Tarithel cried. 'You might have taken his body and mind, but you could never have taken his heart from me! I have freed him from your clutches …'

'And you have wrestled him back using your own magic?' Shareth argued. 'Are we not then two powerful women fighting over a toy?'

'No …'

'You can be so much more than what you are, Tarithel of the Fey,' Shareth said, taking a step closer. 'Through the power you wield you can have a longer life than even the Fey can count, you could span generations of your people. Forget the boy! Forget men! You are marked for greater things than to be the wife of some pathetic Lord of the Free. How long will he live? Hundreds of moons at most?'

'I will love him for all his life,' Tarithel answered. 'Such is the vow I have already sworn.'

'And when he is gone? For gone he will be when those moons have swiftly passed. What then? Will you be a widow for the span of all your moons? Trust me, you will tire of the company of men in time, I know your destiny. We are alike, creatures of endurance, placed here to navigate the long years of this world, bringing order in the wake of chaos, imposing will on the witless and bringing peace to all lands. Give up the childhood desires of the flesh and embrace all you can be. Use your powers to serve all the lands. We are sorceresses both, the power belongs to us … together.'

Shareth was beside her now, hand outstretched.

The two women stood, facing each other, Shareth with her raven dark hair, Tarithel with hers a flaming red.

'Join me,' Shareth whispered. 'We can end this bloodshed here and now. All must swear allegiance to either you or I. We will lead them, not these warmongering men, Fey, Dwarves and giants. Us … Shareth and Tarithel, sorceresses of Icemark and Midnight! See what we might achieve!'

Another vision spun about Tarithel. She looked and saw the armies of the Icemark disbanding, people returning to their homes. Cities were rebuilt, families reunited. Her gaze roved across the Icemark, and then was turned south. She recognised the familiar mountains and forests of Midnight. There she saw more people, the proud flags of their Citadels …

She frowned.

The flags were not those she remembered. Instead of the heraldry of Midnight they bore a different device, a pair of crowns, cyan and green, interwoven together.

The sky was grey and overcast, her vision was wrenched back to the north, streaming across the landscape so quickly she reeled from the dizzying speed. There, at the gates of a darkened Fortress Shareth stood, cloaked in black, standing before thousands of supplicant minions, all bowed before her …

And at her side …

Tarithel beheld a vision of herself. She was dressed in a dark green gown, with silvered belt and sash, upon her head was a crystal crown, her left hand holding a staff.

'Yours to command,' Shareth whispered in her ear. 'Yours to use as you see fit …'

Power thrilled through Tarithel. She could take her place above others. Had she not proved she was capable of it? Where Fey and Free, Men, Giants, Dwarves and Barbarians had faltered, she had continued, against all odds. Was it not she who had roused the Fey of Midnight and turned the hearts and minds of many in the Icemark? She had proved her merit, was she not worthy of reward far beyond mere thanks and praise? She had earnt it!

I could mend the hurt, fix what is broken, stop the conflict here and now. All these peoples, all these leaders … they have never known peace, they need benevolence and authority, someone who could rule fairly but firmly … that could be us …

The vision flickered for a moment. Tarithel saw her own face, aged by some years, looking down upon those who bowed before her.

She gasped.

Disdain and indifference were written across her pale face, her eyes narrowed in distaste. Her mouth set in a cruel hard line, her lips pale. As she watched, what could only be a sneer grew on her features.

This is not me … but it is what I would become!

Tarithel screamed and pushed Shareth away.

'I will not become your lackey!' she cried. 'I will not be a sorceress! I will not allow any power I have to be abused in this way. People should be free to choose their own destinies, not forced to the whim of any other! I would rather die than see this vision of yours come to pass!'

'You will join me,' Shareth hissed. 'You will use your powers to …'

'I will never use these powers again!'

Shareth's face twisted in sudden rage.

'I thought you would prove to be weak and craven,' she snarled. 'Then die you will, little Fey-girl! Your choice is made!'

Morkin woke. Pain smote across his chest from the wound he had received. He blinked. The roar of fire and a yell of men at arms reached his ears. The stone walls about him shook and rang with some deadly impact.

Tarithel?

She had been with him. Where was she?

He stumbled to his feet, looking around in a daze. Pain rose about him like a wall, but he pushed through it.

'My Lord … you can't …'

Morkin pushed passed a woman who tried to stop him, staggering towards the arched doorway.

Tarithel!

Shareth stretched out her hands and the twisting baleful cyan glare of her magic cascaded out from her fingertips, wrapping around Tarithel. She felt as if she was on fire, the tendrils of light crushing down around her, forcing her to her knees. Wind whipped about her, a whirling maelstrom of dust and darkness.

'I will take what potency you have,' Shareth yelled above the torment. 'You had your chance at greatness and you cast it aside. Now, only as you die, will you realise your foolishness.'

Tarithel cried out, helpless and in agony. The burning flashed up her limbs, excruciating. She choked, struggling to draw breath, collapsing on the ground as Shareth's magic began to consume her.

I will not use the magic … no more … I will go to my death willingly to stop her gaining any more power …

Her conscious thoughts cascaded inwards. Her vision faded into blackness. The pain began to ebb away.

What will become of my friend, my family, my home? Shareth's evil will spread unchecked …

No, Tarithel. It will not.

The voice resonated in her head and a thin slither of recognition flickered in her mind. She knew that voice. It had spoken to her before.

You have shown yourself to be worthy of the trust placed in you …

Tarithel had momentary clarity of thought, a peace fell about her, the pain was washed away as if by a sudden, cool, spring rainfall.

That which you have willingly given up will prove to be the deliverance of all …

She gasped and found herself on her feet, the crackles of Shareth's power sparking all around her, but thwarted and powerless to touch her. Her gaze met Shareth's.

'How can this be?' Shareth cried. 'Your power is no match for mine!'

Tarithel took a step forward, her own arms outstretched.

'Because … this power is not mine,' Tarithel replied. 'But it will work through me!'

The jewel about her neck blazed with green fire, sparkling

about her form and casting sharp shadows all about her. From her fingers swirling patterns of bright green light, as sharp as a summer's day, deftly wrapped themselves about the sharp cyan tendrils, smothering them and extinguishing their brilliance.

Shareth backed away in horror.

'No …!'

The green radiance sought her out, cascading around her in an elegant tangle of glowing fronds. The cyan light was forced back, crackling angrily in its confinement. Shareth's howl of impotence was cut off as the green glow suffused her form.

The brightness grew. Tarithel had to back away, shielding her eyes. She squinted, trying to see.

Shareth's body writhed in the midst of the glow, her scream of rage rising to a fever pitch.

The light exploded outwards.

Tarithel was cast upon the ground, then the blackness took her.

Light flared in Morkin's vision. Limping and struggling he made his way to the battlements. About him, all was confusion. The air was rent with fumes and smoke. Warriors lay all about, some slain, some cast insensible. Around him Fey, Giants, Dwarves, Barbarians and Icelords fought as if in a languid slow motion, dreamlike and turgid. He tottered through the gates, trying to peer through the gloom. The ground was churned to mud beneath his feet. He could hear the cries of battle all about, but they were somehow muted, slow and strange to his ears.

Then he could see something. A woman … no … two women, both with arms raised, one framed with a sharp cyan light, the other wreathed in a softer green. He knew them both. One he despised, one he loved …

'Tarithel!'

A hot blast of air shocked him off his feet to lie stunned and breathless on the battlefield. He blinked, his ears ringing with a high pitched whine as he tried to get his body to respond. For long moments he lay immobile, struggling to move.

The light faded and Morkin could see little other than smoke and ash all about him. The cries of the wounded reached his ears, but the sounds of battle were gone.

He pushed himself up to a crouch, shaking his head to clear it, peering around.

Before him was a crater, blasted out of the mud. Beyond it, the legions of the Iceguard stood, their swords slack in their hands, their shields cast down. He looked over his shoulder and saw the ranks of Fey, Giants, Barbarians and Dwarves standing in a ragged line, their faces showing the same shock and awe.

Shareth was gone, consumed in a blast of light.

Tarithel? Tarithel!

Morkin stumbled to his feet and ran, limping, forwards, falling down into the mud and scrambling to the lip of the crater.

He pulled himself over the edge.

Within the pit, Tarithel's lifeless body lay, her clothes and hair singed, smoke rising from her body.

'No …' Morkin managed to get to his feet and struggled down to her. 'Tarithel!'

He turned her body over, seeing mud and grime smeared across her face. Her skin was reddened and burnt in places, her eyes closed.

'Tarithel!'

He had seen her defy the Heartstealer, stand amidst the

carnage and face the cursed Witchking's offspring. Morkin cast about him, but there was no sign of Shareth at all.

Has she vanquished the hagspawn? My Tarithel!

He gathered the girl's limp form in his arms and somehow managed to get to his feet.

'Morkin!'

Morkin recognised his father's voice and saw Luxor striding towards him, Rorthron limping at his side, his own robes torn and tattered.

'It's Tarithel …' Morkin managed. 'She's gone …'

'She slew the Heartstealer,' Luxor managed to croak. 'Rorthron?'

Luxor grasped Morkin by the shoulder as Rorthron knelt beside him, muttering strange words that Morkin could not understand.

'Stay with her,' Luxor said, stepping beyond him and climbing the crater to the other side, facing the silent Iceguard.

Morkin heard Luxor cry out in a loud voice.

'Your mistress is slain!' he said. 'Throw down your weapons and you will be treated with mercy!'

Morkin could hear nothing for long moments, before the sound of metal crashing to the ground reached his ears above Rorthron's faint chanting.

We've won … but at such a cost. After all this, my dearest Tarithel has given her life to end all this hatred! The Icemark might be freed from tyranny, but I have lost everything I ever cared for …

Tears burnt at the edges of his eyes and then became a flood as sobs wracked his body. He pulled Tarithel's limp form close to him, shuddering into grief.

Spring.

Sunlight on dappled leaves; their shadows dancing upon the forest floor.

She felt the warmth of it on her face.

She stood in a glade on the edge of a forest. Greenness suffused her. She smelled the scent of pollen on the air. Insects buzzed and birds called.

Your task is done, Tarithel, Lady of the Forest.

She looked about her for the source of the voice, but it was nowhere to be seen. There was only the forest and the glade.

'Shareth is defeated?'

Slain.

Tarithel frowned.

'Then … where am I? The battle … Am I dead?'

She sensed only a faint amusement as the wind rustled the leaves around her.

That is a choice of sorts. You can continue on, or you can return.

Tarithel looked around her.

'On?'

Many paths await you; there is much that still needs to be done …

She could feel it, a sense of exhilaration at possibilities unguessed, places unknown and experiences unimagined … and yet.

Return? Morkin!

Those you would leave behind …

'I cannot leave those I love!'

Then your choice is made, Tarithel, Lady of the Forest. We send you back …

The sunlight brightened. She winced in the glare, shielding her eyes, and then …

Tarithel stirred, her body contorting in Morkin's grasp.

She coughed and choked before opening her eyes. Morkin stared at her in disbelief.

'Morkin?' Her voice was little more than a rasp.

'My love!' he cried. 'Tarithel. I thought you surely slain!'

She managed a smile. 'I was … they … they sent me …'

Her hand went to her throat, fumbling for the necklace that she wore. Morkin could see the burnt imprint of the chain on the skin of her neck, as if the necklace itself had burnt her. Tarithel pulled on the chain, raising the jewel to her eyes.

But the jewel was smashed and cracked, its green hue was gone, replaced by a featureless grey.

'Then it is done,' Tarithel managed. 'No more magic, no more powers … I am become myself once more.'

She sobbed, then raised her arms to Morkin as he bent lower to pull her into an embrace.

Epilogue

Morkin the Free stands on the Plains of Anviniel looking south to the Gate of Varenorn.

The surviving armies of the alliance had fallen back to the Great Barbarian city of Imgorad, the Barbarians in the lead, with the Giants, the Dwarves, the Fey and finally Rorthron, Tarithel, Morkin and Luxor with his remaining men of the Free. Alongside them rode the Icelords, Talorthane and Lorelorn, who had taken charge of the remaining Icelord warriors. Across all the races many thousands of lives had been lost, not least in Shareth's final show of spite and vengeance. Across the Icemark, fortresses and cities lay in ruin or flame, the task of rebuilding would be long and heavy work.

Yet spirits were higher and grew higher still as the news spread, taken by messengers far and wide. Shareth was slain, and the oppression of the Icemark was at an end. Those same spirits rose still further as mead, wine and all manner of food was provided at Imgorad's table.

'It is a strange tale to recount,' Imgorad said, banging on the top table in his hall for attention. 'How a man from the southern lands came to us with the ridiculous notion of toppling the Heartstealer from her dark pedestal. But we all stand here today, freed from her tyranny by efforts combined in a plan of his devising. I give you, Luxor! Moonprince of Midnight!'

Luxor raised his arm as great cheers swamped the room.

He waited for the noise to subside so that he could make his voice heard.

'I thank you for your kind words Imgorad of the Barbarians,' he said. 'But truth be told, I did not came here with such a plan. I came in hope of rescuing my son. I was persuaded through both the wisdom of Rorthron the Wise, and the valour I perceived in the disparate peoples of the Icemark. Yet … it would have come to nought had not the pledges of honour from all of those now present here been given to this cause. Barbarians, Giants, Dwarves and Fey. Icemark now stands free as a result of your combined actions, your resolute will and your loyalty to each other. Let us never forget that together we are stronger than we ever can be apart. To the Barbarians! To the Giants! To the Dwarves! To the Fey! And to the loyal Icelords of Icemark!'

There were more cheers, some more raucous than before. The mead continued to flow.

'But even then,' Luxor continued. 'It was not by force of arms that Icemark was saved. We fought as good a fight as any battle I have ever seen, but Shareth was beyond our means, beyond the combined power of our warriors and even beyond that of the Wise. I thank Rorthron for his unfailing work in seeking a way to bring down the foul Heartstealer, but there is another we must thank for that final task.'

The cheers began to fade, everyone now concentrating hard on Luxor's words.

'For we have learnt that there is a power greater than vengeance, greater than war, greater than hatred and destruction. What is that power, I hear you ask? I will answer you my friends. That power is love! Pure, untainted, unfailing love. Against all warnings, all obstacles, all powers sent to frustrate the quest, love has found a way. As the epitome of that love, I give you the slayer of Shareth the Heartstealer … Tarithel, Lady of the Forest.'

Tarithel was staring at him, with a stunned expression on her face. Morkin nudged her and she jumped to her feet in shock and surprise.

'The lives of all of us assembled here,' Luxor continued, 'are at your disposal, fair Lady of the Fey. We bow to you.'

Tarithel watched, bemused as Luxor took the knee before her. Imgorad was on his knees too a moment later. She looked around in wonder as Rorthron did likewise. She looked across the hall to see the other great leaders of the Icemark follow suit. Varangrim of the Giants, Glormane and Carorthay of the Dwarves, Imorthorn of the Fey, even Talorthane and Lorelorn were prostrate before her.

She swallowed, her throat dry, trying to think of words she could say in response.

She looked across at Morkin. He smiled up at her.

'My lords,' she said, summoning the courage to speak. 'Such words touch me to my very heart. I set out on my quest not to free Icemark from the clutches of evil, but only to seek the safe return of my beloved Morkin, who now stands before me, whole once more.'

She reached out and Morkin took her hand.

'We have all played our parts,' she said, words forming in her mind. 'All of you have helped me, some more directly than others. Such things as I have seen and done are thanks to companionship and loyalty, and a choice to look beyond animosity and fear, to embrace friendship and trust. Yes, I slew Shareth, but only because you all stood behind me, all together. That, with the powers hidden and yet imbued in this realm of ours, is what gave us victory. Vow now to always stand alongside each other, vow to honour generosity above greed, bravery instead of cowardice, strength instead of weakness. Seek understanding, not territory, search out trust and friendship instead of gold. Will you vow that to me?'

Luxor was on his feet.

'Such a vow, I make this day,' he called out.

'And I!' Imgorad called.

One by one, every Lord in the room made the vow.

'To Tarithel!' Luxor roared and the cry was taken up by all. 'To Tarithel! Lady of the Forest!'

The Lords of the Icemark stayed in the City of Imgorad for a week before they began to make preparations for the returns to their own lands. The Giants went first, Varangrim towering above both Luxor and Rorthron.

'I think it fair to say you saved my people from extinction,' Varangrim said to Rorthron. 'Without your counsel, this war might have ended us.'

'Your people are strong, stronger than any other in Icemark or Midnight,' Rorthron replied. 'Use your strength wisely. Your old master, Carangrane, would be proud of your leadership. Go now and honour his memory.'

Varangrim nodded. 'You know me well enough, Rorthron of the Wise. I hope we shall meet again someday. Your name will be honoured in the realm of the Giants.'

Rorthron bowed and Varangrim turned to leave.

Luxor was watching Tarithel say goodbye to Glormane, Carorthay, Imulorn and Imelorn. He could see the Dwarf leader rubbing at his eyes. He walked over to catch the end of the conversation.

'… and it seems a long, long time since you were dragged ungraciously into my hall,' Glormane said. 'I shall miss you, Tarithel sweet Lady of the Fey.'

Tarithel curtseyed before him. 'The Fey of Icemark I thought would be my friends,' she said. 'But I had not expected such kindness of spirit from the Dwarves. You saved my life, all of you, when otherwise I would have been killed. I can never repay that debt.'

'There is no debt, my Lady,' Carorthay answered. 'And believe me, we Dwarves keep good accounts.'

Tarithel smiled and then turned to Glormane.

'I will miss you too, great leader of the Dwarves.'

She leant forward and kissed him on the forehead.

'Let that be a sign of everlasting friendship between Dwarf and Fey,' she said.

Glormane bowed. 'In your name,' he said. 'That friendship will be honoured by me all the days of my life.'

She pulled Imulorn and Imelorn into a hug. She needed no words for them.

Imorthorn came up alongside Tarithel as she released the pair of Dwarves.

'And for my part I will see that honoured by my people,' he said. 'Too long have suspicions kept us all apart. Now we can build a better future.'

Tarithel smiled at him. Glormane held out a hand to Imorthorn and they exchanged a firm shake.

Both then turned to go, bowing and walking out of the hallway together.

'You will have to be giving us all lessons in diplomacy,' Rorthron observed with a smile. 'And I would hear more of your story regarding the strange spirits of the Icemark.'

'In truth I'm not sure what I can tell you,' Tarithel said. 'Sometimes I do not believe my actions were my own. There are great powers here, Fangrim itself for certain, perhaps all of the forests besides.'

'For my part,' Luxor said. 'I have once again had my fill of magical Talismans, sorcery and witchcraft. I feel the comfortable familiarity of the halls of the Free back in Midnight are calling me. We have been away too long. What say you, my son?'

Morkin smiled, his expression still gaunt.

'If I have Tarithel beside me, I care not where I go,' he said.

Tarithel pulled him close.

'There is one more goodbye I must make,' she said. Luxor, Morkin and Rorthron watched her go as she approached the two Icelords, who were standing on their own, waiting for her.

'She turned Shareth's own against her,' Luxor muttered.

'Indeed,' Rorthron acknowledged. 'She is a force to be reckoned with.'

'You are a lucky young man, my son,' Luxor observed with a grin. 'I wish you the very best of luck. I think you're going to need it.'

Rorthron chuckled.

Tarithel had made her way to Talorthane and Lorelorn, curtseying before them. They both bowed.

'My Lords,' she said. 'I fear there will be difficult times ahead for you. Of all the peoples of the Icemark, rebuilding will be hardest for your people. I wish you every success.'

'I observed before,' Lorelorn answered. 'That you have an assuredness and insight quite at odds with your youth. It's most disconcerting. But I will heed your words, my Lady.'

Tarithel smiled and turned to Talorthane.

'And to you,' she said. 'You were prepared to trust me when I did not deserve it. I did not have the faith that your people had grace and mercy in their hearts. You showed me I was wrong and I am sore sorry for how I treated you.'

Talorthane bowed low. 'You had many bad examples from our people before we even met,' he said. 'I do not blame you for such assumptions.'

'You saved me,' Tarithel said. 'And thus I stand here today. You didn't let the past taint what the future could be. A lesson all can learn from you.'

'I hope we will do justice to the freedom you have gained

for us,' Talorthane replied. 'Safe travels, my Lady. And come back to visit us when you may.'

'I will,' Tarithel replied. 'Be sure of it!'

On the far side of the hall, Luxor looked across at Rorthron and noticed he was watching the Fey-girl from underneath bushy eyebrows. A faint frown creased his features.

'I know that look, Rorthron of the Wise.' Luxor said, under his breath.

'It seems my ability to keep my secrets from you is diminishing,' Rorthron said with a chuckle. 'You are not wrong, Moonprince.'

Luxor looked over to Tarithel.

'She achieved remarkable things,' he said, under his breath so no others could hear. 'Remarkable things indeed. Without her … we would have been lost. That jewel she carried, the magic she commanded …'

'Magic of a potency I have never seen before in all my moons,' Rorthron said. 'But it was not hers I think, rather it worked through her via the jewel she bore; that ancient heirloom of the Fey.'

'Truly one of the Talismans you spoke of?' Luxor asked.

Rorthron nodded.

'I think it is as well that it has been broken and its power gone,' Rorthron said. 'Tarithel will be safer without it. Already she seems much more Fey than sorceress to my eyes. This is for the better; she and Morkin deserve a chance at happiness now.'

'As usual, your words leave me feeling uneasy,' Luxor replied.

'I have no answers Moonprince,' Rorthron said. 'The power that Tarithel manifested and her account of the Forests of Icemark empowering her, the potency of the Talismans we do know of, Gryfallon and Shareth's quest to unite them all, even your description of how the Moon Ring affects you, that the Eye was lost by Rarnor … all these things speak of a higher purpose than I can yet perceive.'

Luxor looked down at his hand, seeing the Moon Ring still upon his finger.

'It has cooled like it did before,' Luxor said. 'Its power gone, as if its task were complete.'

Rorthron nodded. 'But where there are tasks, surely there is a task master? It is as if something is bending events to its will and thus controlling our lives. It sought the demise of the Witchking and achieved that aim through you. Now, here in the Icemark, Shareth has been defeated by a force working its will through Tarithel.'

'What force, to what purpose … and to what end?' Luxor asked, his voice a whisper.

'And who will it choose next?'

Luxor shot Rorthron a look.

'I do not know, Moonprince,' Rorthron said in answer. 'But I fear we are doomed to find out. Once we return to Midnight I will resume my quest for knowledge of this power … this First Power … that lies behind the Talismans and the great events we have seen. There is much I need to scrutinize and understand.'

Luxor nodded, his face set in a grimace.

Dawn broke on the following day. The lords and leaders of the Icemark began to file out of the halls, walking down through the city streets to meet once more with their armies. From there, they gave orders to begin the long marches back to hearth and home.

Luxor, Morkin, Rorthron and Tarithel climbed to the highest point of Imgorad's city, watching the armies march away. The Giants and the Icelords marched straight north, the Dwarves to the north-east with the Fey taking a road to the east. The sun sank into the west and the day was done.

'Our road lies to the south,' Luxor observed.

'It is time to go home,' Morkin said, with a smile.

'At last,' Tarithel said, hugging him close.

Torinarg's fortress was not far from the Gate of Varenorn and Imgorad had taken his leave of them, with instructions for Torinarg to see the people of Midnight to the Gate. Careneon had come with them too.

Two days travel had seen them ride south with ease, before turning south-east across a low range of hills.

Then, the gate was before them.

'It is time now to say farewell,' Careneon observed. 'It is many score days since we first met, Moonprince of Midnight … but I am glad to have done so. I thought not to see such change in my lifetime, let alone within scant moons of meeting you … yet, here we are.'

Luxor smiled. 'I hope our remaining days will now be peaceful and free from war.'

Careneon shrugged. 'A little battle now and then is good for a warrior.'

Luxor grinned. 'Safe travels then, my friend.'

Careneon nodded, signalled to Torinarg and his men and then rode away to the east, their torches flickering in the gloom.

At last, they who had journeyed into Icemark moons before were alone once more. Few of the men of Luxor's garrison remained and they were weary of battle, but somewhat invigorated by the thought of returning to Midnight.

'It is four score and ten days since the Moonprince rode forth in the Icemark,' Rorthron intoned. 'Dawn breaks.'

The sun was rising above the forests to the east, the sunlight stronger than before, illuminating the plains before the gate with a ruddy hue. Here and there they could already see the ice was retreating across the landscape, the ancient curse of winter being lifted as Shareth's taint drained away.

'And I would be back in Midnight all the sooner,' Luxor replied. 'Let us reach the gate this day, there we will rest and take the tunnel on the morrow.'

The four turned their horses to the south. The ride was not taxing and soon the great Gate of Varenorn stood before them, the rising sun casting its pillars and arches into sharp relief. Shadows stretched across the plane, stark and long.

Luxor got down from his horse and the others dismounted alongside. He walked up the stone steps leading to the gate, drawing his sword as he did so.

'Father?' Morkin asked. 'What is it?'

Luxor continued up the stairs, his gaze roving from one side to the other, as if he were searching in vain for something … yet he knew not what it was.

'Morkin is here,' he muttered. 'Tarithel is here, Rorthron is here …'

'And Luxor is here,' Rorthron said, his voice amplified, perhaps by the stonework about them. 'Shareth is dead. The warriors of Midnight have returned to the Frozen Gate.'

Morkin stepped forward, as if possessed by some will that was not quite his own.

'The Victory of the Moonprince is overwhelming!' His voice sounded around them, even louder than Rorthron's, the echo of it reverberating back and forth.

There was a sharp cry from behind them. They turned to see Tarithel, her arms outstretched, her face lifted to the heavens, her expression one of utter joy.

When she spoke, her voice was as clear as crystal, as pure as a mountain lake and as melodious as the first call of the lark in spring.

'The Watchwords of Midnight are revealed!' she sang out.

Sunlight blazed about her, the warmth startling in the cold ice-bound world about them. Her red hair gusted in the wind and it seemed as if everything in the world focussed its gaze upon her for a fleeting moment of time.

'The brave and the Free fear no foe!' she called, tears streaming down her face. 'Forth, mighty hosts of Midnight! Unto death or victory we go!'

Imorthorn lowered himself into his favourite oaken chair and gave a long sigh. His body ached and his muscles felt tired and stretched. The ride back from the City of Imgorad had been without incident, but both he and his people were still weary from the battle. A moon had already passed since Shareth's death, yet much was left to be done in the ordering of both the Fey and the other races. Politics never slept.

But that can wait until dawn breaks on another day.

He closed his eyes for a brief moment, a faint smile on his lips.

Peace? Peace at last? Can it be so?

He heard a rap at the door.

It seems not …

He opened his eyes and chuckled to himself. Whatever it was, it could not match the horrors and tribulations involved in the demise of the Heartstealer.

'Come!' he called.

A steward walked in.

'My apologies for disturbing you sire …'

'Think nothing of it,' Imorthorn replied, sitting forward and then getting to his feet. 'What has transpired?'

'A small bit of news,' the steward said. 'I did not wish to trouble you with it, yet …'

'Out with it!' Imorthorn cried.

'Our scouts patrolling in the north have come across a group of four women alike as to the Free,' the steward said. 'They were starving and lost amidst the trees of Fangrim.'

'Starving? Have they been tended?'

'Yes, sire. Healers have seen to them and they reside now within the city and are safe, if grievously undernourished.'

'From whence did they come?' Imorthorn asked, with a frown.

'It seems they were slaves,' the steward replied. 'Incarcerated in the Fortress of Kahangrorn as unwilling handmaidens by their own account. After the defeat of the Heartstealer the walls of the fortress cracked and fell. They managed to escape and fled south through many trials, but hoping to find safety and shelter.'

'Then we shall care for them,' Imorthorn said. 'To have been a slave of the Heartstealer must have been torture indeed. We shall see that damage made good. Too many lives have been ruined by that hagspawn, here at least is a chance to undo some of that.'

'Very good, sire,' the steward replied. 'There is one more detail ...'

'Yes?'

'One is very young, a girl I suppose as the Free would reckon these things,' the steward said. 'She is with child.'

'And she has walked all the way from Kahangrorn?' Imorthorn said in surprise. 'Such a girl must be hardy indeed.'

'Yes sire, the healers say the baby is due within the moon.'

'A strange tale to be sure,' Imorthorn said, pacing around for a moment. 'I will go to them all and reassure them that they have indeed found safety and shelter. Ensure the girl is tended at all times, I fear for her health after such an arduous journey. Come, I will meet them now and give them welcome as the Lord of this City.'

The steward bowed and stood aside as Imorthorn marched to the doorway.

At the threshold Imorthorn turned, a thought occurring to him.

'This girl,' he said. 'Has she given her name?'

The steward nodded.

'She called herself Cirithel, sire.'

The End

The Chronicles of Midnight continue in book 3,
'The Citadel.'

Imiriel
Fororn
The Frozen Empire
Imgaril
Kahangrorn
Lorelorn
Kingdom of the Giants
Varangrim
Zarashand
Thudrane
Obigrorn
Morormarg
Glormarg
Lorigriel
Kahudrun
Carangrane
Ulformane
Theleon
Fangrorn
Imgenarg
Imgorarg
Anvildrak
Ganigrorn
Carorthay
Carormarg
Glormane
Kingdom of the Dwarves
Thortheon
Outlands of the Barbarians
Thormand
Sirium
Imgorad
Imorthorn
Morildrane
Kingdom of the Fey
Zarorthane
Carorthane
Careneon
Lorangriel
Varenorn
Torinarg
ICEMARK

Also by Drew Wagar

The Lords of Midnight

* * *

Elite: Reclamation
Elite: Premonition

* * *

Shadeward: Emanation
Shadeward: Exoneration
Shadeward: Enervation
Shadeward: Expiation

* * *

Torn

* * *

Hegira Series – Coming soon!

About the Author

Drew Wagar is a science fiction and fantasy author. He lives in Kent with his wife, two sons, a dog and a cat. His favourite colour is dark green. He drives a small convertible car which occasionally works. He doesn't require a conservatory or any double glazing.

You can reach Drew as follows:

Drew's Website: http://www.drewwagar.com
Facebook: http://www.facebook.com/drewwagarwriter
Twitter: http://www.twitter.com/drewwagar

Printed in Great Britain
by Amazon

73814391R00353